THE
GIFTS
OF HAPPINESS

Oliver Smuhar

Published by Mountain Blue Publishing 2020
Copyright © 2020 Oliver Smuhar

www.oliversmuhar.com

All rights reserved. No part of this publication may be reproduced, stored in a retrieval system, or transmitted in any form or by any means, electronic, mechanical, photocopying, recording or otherwise, without the prior written permission from the publisher.

Disclaimer

Every effort has been made to ensure that this book is free from error or omissions. Information provided is of general nature only and should not be considered legal or financial advice. The intent is to offer a variety of information to the reader. However, the author, publisher, editor or their agents or representatives shall not accept responsibility for any loss or inconvenience caused to a person or organisation relying on this information.

Cover Design: Jessica Bell

Typesetting: Book Covers Australia.com

ISBN:

978-0-6483320-2-2 (pbk)

978-0-6483320-3-9 (e-bk)

Once Again, Thank You!

Dear Reader,

First of all, I would like to thank you again for your ongoing support! I am glad you've decided to continue the series I started writing when I was sixteen. And although I am now twenty at the time of this release, I have spent the last two years creating the most perfect product I can offer. It gives me great pleasure to present to you the second book within the Colours of Humanity, **The Gifts of Happiness**.

As I said in the previous book, with the release of The Gifts of Happiness, I plan to continue this series and grow, develop, learn and eventually become an adult, a parent, and maybe one day, a full-time writer. As I grow, I invite you to watch these characters in this story grow with me. As I age from 16 to 20 to 22, they too will grow. My main characters, Perry and Faith, will always reflect my age at the time of writing. And regardless of what edition you buy, these stories will be staples of the time period I have lived in and my growth as a storyteller.

If you would like to help me on this journey, please rate and/or review this book online, follow us on social media, or tell a friend about the journey. I salute you and wish you a fantastic time in the world of Euphoria. See you next time!

All the best,

Oliver Smuhar

*If you would like to support me please visit

http://www.oliversmuhar.com/

To my two sisters
Mariah and Temika
Thanks for everything!

Contents

	Character Crests	vii
	Prologue	xi
1.	Papered Rooftops	1
2.	Troll Hunters	7
3.	A Town in a Nutshell	13
4.	Never Easy	22
5.	Oddities Beyond our Control	30
6.	Master Prophet	39
7.	The Melting Boy	45
8.	Train Trips	53
9.	Welcome to Central City	67
10.	The Sporangia Sector	79
11.	The Drowning Girl	87
12.	Mr Bear's Reunions	98
13.	Omahwei	104
14.	Once Eight, Now Seven	112
15.	Paper Thin Consequences	123
16.	Gravity is Weird	135
17.	Odd Explains	143
18.	The Banana Cabana	150
19.	Boys will be Boys	162
20.	Serenity	177
21.	Home Away From Home	183
22.	One Last Day	190
23.	Another Reality	197
24.	The Sudden Express	205
25.	The Man on The Boat Waits	214
26.	Kattagow On Fire	224
27.	The Day That Followed	239

28.	Milky Complications & A Lack of Fur	247
29.	The WoodWood House	259
30.	The Oogali Swamp	271
31.	The Sixth Day	282
32.	The Place Where the Water Splits	295
33.	Above and Below the Full Sea	308
34.	The Third Way to Drewmora	317
35.	What We Know	329
36.	Visiting The Militia	335
37.	The Secret Beneath WonderWorks	344
38.	The Blue Beacon	356
39.	Pulling Strings	368
40.	A Prideful Spy	375
41.	Promises	383
42.	Uninvited Interruptions	393
43.	Insanity Begins	399
44.	A Poet's Duel	410
45.	Open The Gate	423
46.	Escape Plan	432
47.	Closing Eyes	441
48.	How Did We Get Here?	454
49.	The Fourth Way	463
50.	Paper Snow	472
51.	Spreading Gifts	483
	Glossary	498
	Ever Slang	506
	Giea Translation	508
	The Art in The Gifts of Happiness	509

Character Crests

Perry Caduca

Faith Brooks

Bailey Giggles

Zia Kelton

Teala Caduca

Odd

Dalton Lee

Titan Kelton

Assonance Milk

Kyle Matthews

Felicia Moore

Papercut

Harry Doubtson

Olivia Caduca

Generalissimo Hartway

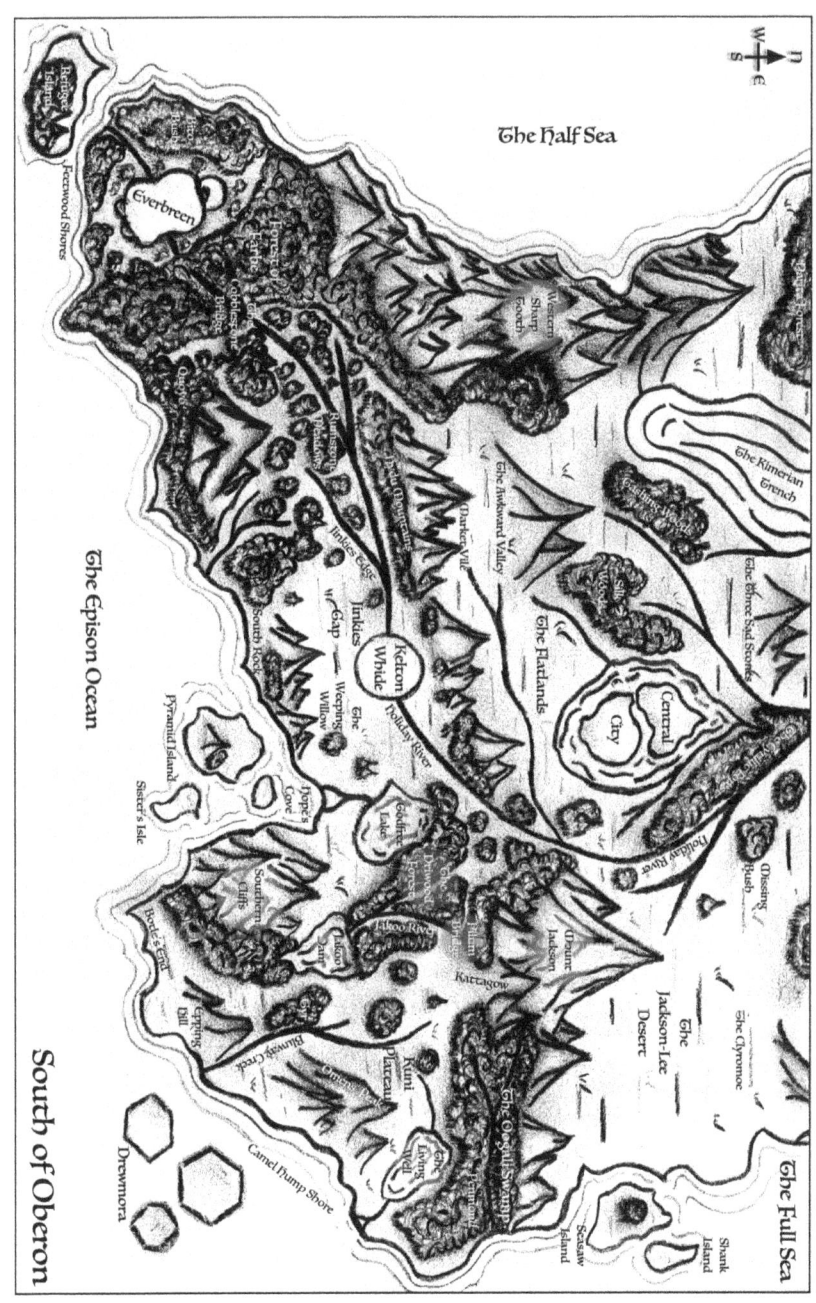

Prologue
Odd

"Does the sea make you happy?" Teala asked.

Admittedly, the Full Sea was ahead, its hefty scent of salt and seaweed fresh and wild. I grinned, rejoiced by the query. In comparison to Perry, Teala always thought before she spoke—she had meaning behind *most* of her words. "I suppose the sight of the waves is refreshing. But then again, the sight of a wild forest filled with overgrown canopies is also a blessing. Or even the purity of a sand dune in the middle of a desert. Even a mountainous view overlooking Central City is soothing to someone."

The little Kelt rolled her eyes and trampled in front of me. "Yes, yes, but does it make you happy? Stop trying to ignore the question."

Before I could answer, another all too familiar cry wept behind us. "I'm so hungry, I might die ... Or is this hell?" Titan admired his surroundings. Epping Hill was to our left, its wavy grass aplenty. He rubbed his belly and scoffed, "If it is, it's a little anticlimactic. So much for the hype."

I turned to him as he staggered behind Teala and me. "If your hunger is such a pest, we can go fishing."

"Fishing?" Titan stopped and raised a brow. "You mean like chucking a string into the water and waiting. I'll pass."

My grin remained firm. "Yes, but what if the reward for that waiting is a fish at the end of that string. We could have a fire, cook it up and feast like how you would in the Castle of Glass."

Titan rubbed his chin. "Hmm, tempting, but — "

A crash of waves disturbed his thought. Teala shook as we investigated the sound. I towered over the grassy plateau, sand mixed through the soil, and the wind began to howl. There was something quite unnerving at the edge of the world. "The waves are angry," I told them. "Something bad is about to happen. A ploy is underway. We must make haste and find the others—*before it's too late!*"

Teala folded her arms. "Like you haven't known that since we left Everbreen." She took a step closer and admired my eyes. "Since the Pilum Bridge, we've cared for a cat, been attacked by two paper swords and met another Good Spirit! Not to mention that Titan's been whinging about food the whole time. So what are you hiding, Odd?"

I glanced at the cloudy skies ahead. For a thirteen-year-old, Teala knew precisely how to read people—even demigods like myself. I sighed, "Truth be told, I'm trying to hide you." It was hard to admit, but like her brother, Teala's curiosity was more a nuisance than anything. Behind her crossed arms, someone caught my eye.

Upon the sky, he rode his flying carpet as fast as lightning. His long grey beard shrivelled in the wind with drops of blood smeared through it. Descending down, Master Othello took voyage on the plateau. His carpet stayed dormant as the old man's feet crushed the grass beneath him. As his figure rose, I noticed a peculiarity. His right eye had been gauged as if a bird's beak or a knife had torn through it, making it tender and bloody. Teala stumbled back, repulsed by the prophet's stench. He reeked of mould, wet cotton and death.

Standing in his green gown, Othello adjusted his collar and patted the dust from his legs. I was surprised he could still lean so low. Staring at me with only his left eye, I caught him off guard and laughed. "I see you've met the bird girl. I was always fond of her. Now I know why … What brings you here, Master?"

Othello rubbed his bloodied eye. "I am losing my hold, Odd. Drewmora is in grieve danger. With Hebi in Fæh at odds with one another, I believe there's not much time." I knew what he meant. He was weary of Teala—of her dream.

"You're still looking for her, aren't you?" I asked.

He nodded, blood now covering his palms. "Yes, and it may take some time before I find answers. Tell me Odd … Is she really worth all this trouble?"

I paused for a moment and smelt the salty air. "No. Because she is also searching for answers. She'll surface before too long. As you said, it'll just take time!"

Othello laughed, blood staining his teeth. "Time. Now that's a miserable concept, isn't it? Hebi has gone too far... The dreamcatchers are ready."

"Are they the same from the train? As mine?" Teala cried, protecting Titan. Othello had a grim frown. "Yes. And they'll infect everyone in the Lower Hexadomes." He looked at me. "I have a message from Fæh Jiwa. He has plans for the wolf and the possum. Let them fight. They will have need of each other when Araidian is found. Keep Charles close, keep Daegon's alchemy with you, and let their anger settle. What happens in the blue city is meant to happen. Those are the rules. The path has already been laid out." His eyes lingered on Teala. "How fortunate that you've managed to be caring for Leila's offspring." Leaning down to Teala, the prophet pointed at her wolf crest, its white light covering his left eye. "Ask yourself this, curious one. Is this just another dream waiting for you to unlock its finale? What happens when you reach the end?" Teala stumbled back, gulping. Othello stood, nodded to me and took refuge on his flying carpet. Floating higher and higher into the air, he smiled. "I'll be seeing you. Watch out for the water. I hear there are masked ones hiding inside."

Flying towards Fleddington, the wise old prophet left us. The crashing sounds of the waves returned as Teala stared at the sky. Her hand was gripped tightly as Titan scratched his scalp, "What was that all about?"

"Simple," I said. "Someone's crest has been tampered with. They are hiding in plain sight. As if they're wearing a —"

"Mask," Teala uttered. "If there are dreamcatchers in Drewmora, we should hurry and find the others. Perry, Faith, Bailey, they're all in danger!"

"What about fishing?" Titan asked.

"Maybe another time, Tye. We have a mine to venture through, a train station to visit and a king to find. And I still have paperwork for WonderWorks. So much for being happy."

"So the sea does make you happy?" Teala asked.

xiii

We marched up Epping Hill, the blue beacon shining amid the ocean. I shook my head. "No, Tea. Unfortunately, the sea can only do so much. Understanding the world makes me happy. Being able to do what I please makes me happy. And right now, I'm in no mood to save another city. Alas, when this is all set and done, I'll be able to sleep." I winked at her. "And sleeping, *dreaming*, now that's what makes me the happiest person in the world."

"Why?"

"Because no matter where I am, who I'm with or what I've done, when I dream, I can be with the ones I love."

Titan chuckled. "Yeah, yeah, and I can dream about food. We all have our fetishes. Onwards, team Titan! To Drewmora!"

And so, we travelled to the mine atop Epping Hill. I realised that our story was just beginning. The end was far, and I knew through Othello's words, that I would not be here to see its end. But that would take time—and time is a weird, funny and odd concept.

So long, good luck and watch out for your dreams. You never know what you might find!

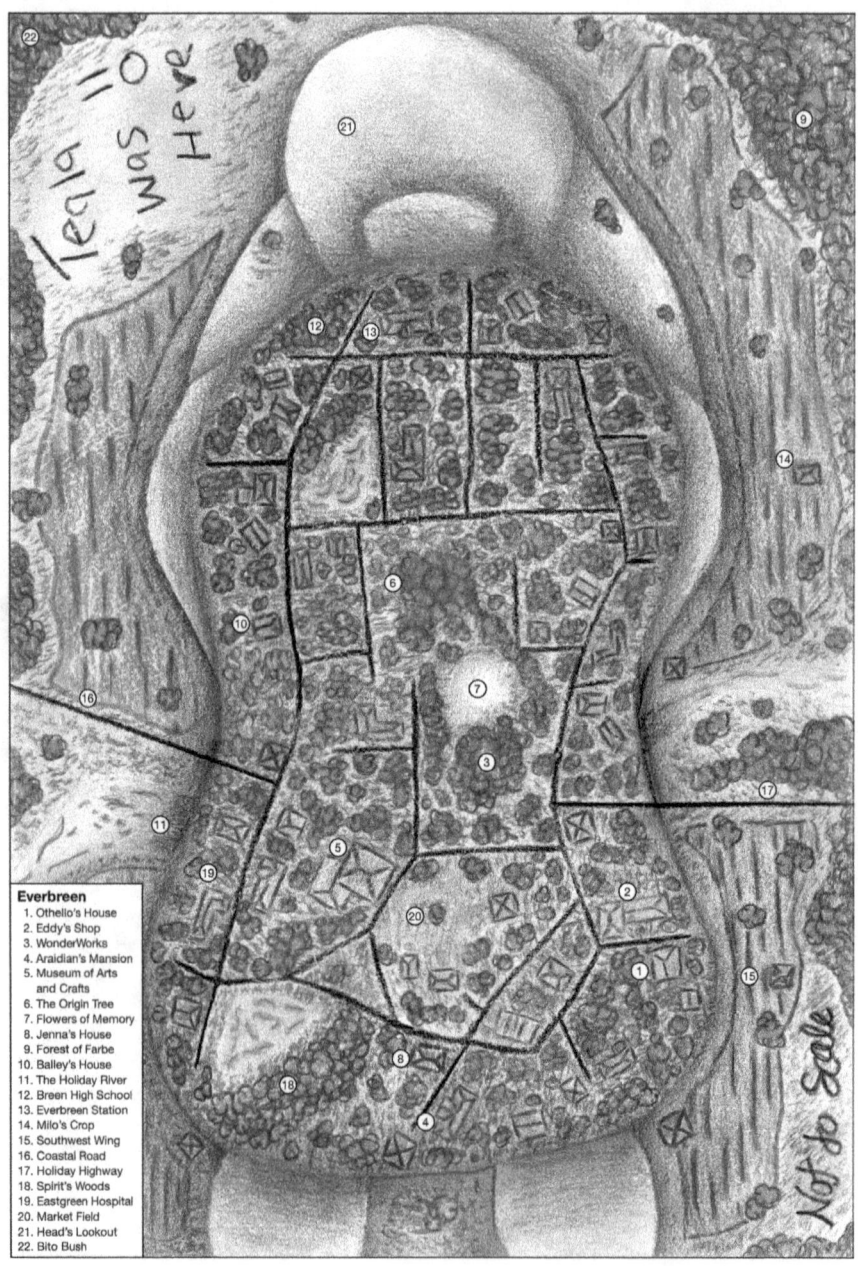

Chapter 1

Papered Rooftops

Perry

Tap, tap, tap. Jeez, that's a loud clock! I couldn't even hear myself think. My heart was pounding at these stupid filed papers—*I've flicked through so many*. Odd said it was here, but ... well, I can't seem to find the right one. I rubbed my fingertips along so many files, analysing each title until my eyes started to water. I inhaled deeply, hoping the words *Everbreen Tower Incident, 4/11/2117*, was in this damn cabinet. I had checked the whole office and there was nothing.

And did I mention that it was pitch-black, and Zia was screaming into my earphone?

"Have you found it yet?" she demanded.

I whispered aggressively, "If I had found it, I wouldn't be silent, now would I? Give me a few seconds Zi. It's hard enough with the guards being outside, so can the nagging lighten a little?"

Zia went on about how she doesn't nag, about how she only talks a lot because, for her, talking was like a reflex. She wondered aloud, "Are you looking in the right cabinet?"

"Yes, Zi! This is the only cabinet labelled *two-one-one-seven*. It even says *Light Age Era* on it. Now Shh!"

As I fingered more papers—thick with diagrams, bundled with unorganised staples and covered in doctor's handwriting—I finally discovered the file Odd wanted. As my face lingered on its beautiful title, something erupted behind me. With a rattily bang, Dally yelped, "Argh! By the frickin' ... Stupid bin!" I turned to him and waved my arms, silently asking him *why*. He whispered *sorry* and held his foot as though his hand were a band-aid. Opening the file, I wanted to see if it was the real deal. As I scanned through it, mumbling drifted from the other side of the office door. Dally stared at me with his mask and placed an ear against the wall closest to the noise. Apparently, they were discussing their new operation to begin mining in Tinkette Valley. I closed the folder and whispered, "Got it!"

Before anyone could think, Dally took charge. "Ah, shoot! We gotta head. Now!"

Dally extended his right arm towards the office window and raised it upward. The window—by itself—opened, sliding up to the motion of his arm. I held the file and ran behind him as we launched ourselves out onto the rooftop. As soon as my feet touched the windowsill, I could smell the freshness of the Everbreen air. Although I know I looked pretty dope with my white hood and the staff resting in its hold along my back, the moment kind of got lost. As Dally jumped over to a neighbouring apartment block that was the shape of a giant oak stump, the lights in the office flicked on. I slumped forward, noticing my dark shadow was surrounded by a yellow light. and glanced back to see a middle-aged lady, cross-eyed and confused.

She crept into her office with suspicion as I gasped, ducking down. Fortunately for me, she didn't notice anything. No awkward young adult hanging out of her window tonight; no two idiots scavenging through her filing cabinets. Just a normal-looking office for the new CEO of Everbreen's WonderWorks. But I could still get a kick out of these little nightly ventures. So, as I stared at her, and she examined her mildly vandalised workplace, I climbed out, closing the window. *It's funny sometimes when I'm invisible.* I'm sure she'll tell all her colleagues about how scary it was when a ghost haunted her office at three in the morning—*Jeez, by the Light of Hope, it's three in the morning!*

I jumped and vanished. As I reappeared with my hoody, white ash fell onto the oak roof. Dally leaned against a pillar with Odd's mask wrapped around his face. It was black on the right side and white on the left. Some say it's the mask of the first demon's daughter, Hebi. Shaking his head, he smiled. "You have to stop messing with people when you're invisible. Odd's gonna hear about it and I'm going to have to deal with 'im!"

I laughed, "And you say that like you don't love arguing with him. Come on, Dally. It's just a little fun and I'm not the idiot wearing the mask ... What's the worst that could happen." *I wish I had never said that.*

The lady from her office window screamed, "Hey, you! You have ... You have my—Get back here! I'm calling security!"

Before I had time to apologise, the sound of footsteps rushed over the roof slats and the fallen leaves that covered Everbreen like snow.

Dally and I stormed across building after building—an apartment, a restaurant, a shopping complex, a three-storey house, a tree branch large enough for us to run across and a bloody warehouse. Unable to jump as far as Dally, I ended up at the foot of the warehouse. I ran through one of the walls, dodging late-night workers and storage boxes filled with who-knows-what; I dashed through aisle after aisle of products and then I ran through a forklift, up some stairs and finally fazed through another wall on the opposite side of the building. Once through, I couldn't help but laugh, thankfully in one piece.

The inside of my chest was aching. Once the coast was clear, and the obnoxious screams of sirens had faded, I stopped to recover on the rooftop of an ancient building carved within a gigantic boulder. I stood on the leaf-covered roof, breathing heavily and staring at the stars.

Zia was screaming in my earphone.

"Yeah! I ran through a warehouse. It was quite crowded for the early morning ... Zia, please stop yelling! It's hurting my brain ... Yeah, I do have a brain, and no ... it is bigger than you'd think."

"Is Dally with you?" Zia sighed.

I searched the streets below. "No, I lost him. I'm sure he'll make it soon. He can't walk through walls, so he probably had to walk around the warehouse. Or over it or —"

Before I could finish, Odd muttered, "Or beneath the warehouse. Is that right?"

I propped my hands on my hips. "Odd? Since when were you home? I thought you were preparing for tomorrow."

Odd's voice was rather unamused. "Perry, it's three in the morning. Why would I be preparing for something at this time of day? I've already installed the tracker signals on my laptop!"

"Argh, well—because you're weird like that. I don't know."

In the background, I heard Zia agree. "It is something you would do ... Oh, actually, Perry said there were workers in a warehouse he ran through. Do you know why?"

Odd mumbled to himself, before asking, "Perry, do you know what kind of warehouse it was?"

I shook my head. "Nope. I was kind of running for my life at the time. But if I wasn't, I'm sure I could have gotten a nicer look for you. It's not like I had other things on my plate."

Odd was moody tonight. "Perry, shut it! My guess is that they're unloading imports from Central City. The Birth of the Trees is the day after tomorrow. The mayor and senator must be having them work overtime. On the other hand ..."

While Odd rambled, I heard something screech below me. I climbed the stone bannister and stuck my head out to witness a van pull into an alleyway. Its headlights were almost blinding as its brakes yielded. Armoured men scurried from its back door. They were in some heavy stuff, like what Araidian used to put his men into. *But these weren't his men.* Their guns, their movements, their procedures were too military. As the six soldiers in dark blue left the van, someone unexplainable—wearing a white cloak similar to my hood—followed them as if he were in charge. His face was covered. His demeanour was calm, yet alert, as though he had studied that art of ninjutsu; upon closer inspection, I noticed that his cloak was made from paper maché.

His whole form was origami—his hair and forehead were covered by a hood, his nose and chin by a thick bandana. Strapped tightly to his back were two sharp katanas, crossing each other like a crossbones. Without a word, he ordered his men by pointing forward. The six men barged into a small house and gunfire lit up the master bedroom. I clenched at the bannister. I couldn't do anything—*there were too many.* By the Light, they rampaged through the house in seconds, and dragged out a young unconscious Ever, an ape they had handcuffed. Zia and Odd asked what was going on. They were so loud, yet their voices were simply echoes. I wanted to stop it, to save the Ever, but I couldn't—*I just couldn't!* The men retreated into their van, and I swear on Hope herself that the man in white paper stared right at me, as though he wanted me to see this injustice.

CHAPTER 1: PAPERED ROOFTOPS

The van vanished into the distance. Dally's voice shocked my ears.

"Hey!" I turned, slapping his arm away. *How long had he been tapping me? Had he seen what I saw?*

"Okay, calm down. I'm sorry I didn't make it earlier—some of us can't walk through tree stumps ... What's wrong?" he asked.

I pulled my staff from its hold. "I'm sorry. I just ... They took the ..."

"Perry, what happened? You look freaked!"

I nodded. "I am! You didn't see it? We have to do one last thing before we go back. Are you with me?"

My hands were shaking as I attempted to open the front door. The house still smelt of burnt gunpowder. Dally whispered that there was a ghostly coldness inside. My breath made wisps of fog as the two of us searched the lounge room and dining area.

"Hello?" I urged.

There was no response.

"What the hell happened in here?" Dally asked, pushing his mask off his face and onto his scalp.

I grasped at my gloves. "Nothing good. There were men and ... Huh, let's just see if anyone needs help and get out of here."

His eyes became wide and he nodded. The stench of blood was fresh. Something dripped in the distance. We split up. I searched the left side where the master bedroom was, and Dally searched the kitchen. A red coating soaked the bedroom's walls and sheets. Above the mattress was a woman with a green crest, eyes open and lifeless. My shaking fingers pushed her eyes closed. *No one deserves this!* But as her blood stained my gloves, Dally called my name. "You better look at this, Pear!"

I marched to the kitchen and my throat tightened. In the middle of the island bench, there was a note pricked under the soft blade of a bread knife. Dally forced its hold off the piece of paper. You could hear the marble crumble as he handed me the note. I read its dark black calligraphy. *Your move, White Wolf.*

Dally sighed, "Whoever these people were, they saw you!"

Odd and Zia weren't as speechless as I was.

"Who saw you, Perry? What'd you see?" Odd demanded.

I looked Dally dead in the eye. "Let's get out of here! Zia call the authorities. Tell them there's been a shooting at the end of Sycamore Close, near the Museum of Arts and Crafts. Now Zi! *Please*. I'll explain everything when we're in the clear. Come on, Dally."

I led the way, teleporting Dally and me over the museum and down McNeill Avenue. I could hear in his voice that he was worried. So when he spoke, I couldn't help but smile.

"You know, for a guy who can literally turn invisible, you sure get seen a lot!" he said.

I laughed, "Yeah, well ... at least I get seen with style. I wouldn't be caught dead in that mask!"

"You're just jealous you didn't think about wearing it before I did. Hey, last one to Odd's has to spar with Titan for the next week!" Dally snorted.

I groaned, "You're on! I'm not getting my arms sliced up aga———"

"Uh, uh! I'm not finished. *Without* using their powers."

I could picture Zia rolling her eyes. She sighed, "Uh, this is going to take a while. I'm going to bed. And Titan's not that bad to spar with. He's still learning ... kind of."

I huffed and hurdled over Odd's gate. "Zia, it's fine. We're already here. *Hooo!* I am so light-headed right now ... Damn it, I'll get you next time Dally."

Dally skipped past the van. "I don't think so. Come on, Zi. No time for sleep. Meet at the back. It's time to return to our Town of Tents."

Chapter 2

Troll Hunters

Faith

"Gabe, hold its arm!" I instructed. Gabe flew into the air like a ballerina and intercepted the troll's arm. *Oh my*, this beast was a pain before, but I was positive it was now stronger. With its right hand missing and surrounded by layers upon layers of crisscrossing vines, the troll used its cobblestone body to crush the nearby bush and the piled leaves that had fallen last Windy Season. Gabe heaved back its left arm as though he were performing an aerial dance with invisible silk ribbons hanging from the canopies. As the clouds drifted, blocking the sun's rays, Gabe screamed, "By the salts on my own darned chin, can someone do something! Anything. I'm … I'm … slipping!" I jogged to his aid, and …

Titan? … *Wait, huh? Titan! What's he doing here? As if he … mmm!* He huddled beside Connor. The two were exasperated yet cautious. Whispering something, Conner itched the small line of hair he had kept in the centre of his scalp.

Titan handed him a box of matches. "I'll try, but this thing's huge!"

Connor lit a match along his smooth forehead. As he did this, Titan threw several glass shards at the troll's legs and waist. They struck through the creases of the troll's cobblestone skin. Upon the end of each shard, a small pink rose had been pierced; the roses were now pinned over the troll's mangled body. It glared at Titan.

"FRI!" it growled, throwing Gabe from his hold. The Drewan's body leapt over the dark grass. I staggered to my feet and ran towards the two buffoons. Connor readied the match, holding another pink rose in his hand. He stood beside Titan and smiled.

"*End*, right?" Connor mocked. "That's all you've been saying this whole fight—End and Fri."

The troll stopped in its tracks as everyone admired the ex-Araidian Warrior.

Connor licked his lips, "Well, I got a new one for ya. *Boom*!" He lit the rose's petals alight. As it shrivelled from the heat, each of the roses at the end of Titan's shards exploded. All eight, one after the other, like fireworks.

Before I could do anything, Titan threw another rose-pierced shard at the troll's forehead. I begged for him to stop and dropped to my knees. We didn't want to kill the troll. Gabe sat up, bewildered by the smell of burnt pollen. He stared at me with the same awe-inspired eyes as the other few who have seen my gift. Like the kind soul he is, Titan listened and relaxed, while Connor clasped at the burning pink flower and snickered at me. I was half surprised myself. As I dropped to the yellow leaves, I clasped myself against the stump of an old pine tree. All my emotions stopped—I could hear the world as though it were speaking to me. It sang and danced, answering my call. The branches from each of the oaks surrounding the troll grew larger and larger, catching the troll before it could fall face-first into the ground. The wind took hold of the many fallen leaves; each stuck to the troll's torn legs. Vines crawled from above and wrapped themselves around the troll's arms as though placing it in an armlock. Pinecones piled over the troll's feet. As it swayed down towards me, the forest clasped its body, and it fell gently as though laying down in a hammock.

The troll took a long, slow breath, shivering as I stood. Connor put out the rose and sighed. A few Evers growled and roared—one was a golden fox named Jaimie, who snarled at the troll's caged side, and another was an olive snake named Kate, who slithered onto Gabe's shoulder.

"That sure handled it! Didn't know you could do that, Faith," Kate said.

"Neither did I," Gabe muttered.

Connor rolled his eyes. "Well, I don't like wasting roses like that. Maybe let us know before you go do something like that, huh Faith?

An' ain't this thing a marraboo? It's meant to be part of the land, ain't it?"

Jaimie loosened his grip. "We don't all have time to go as eco-friendly as you, Connor. But if I had de time to make a ... *what was it?*—Jar of Sincerity—I'd dig de roses too ..."

"Jaimie, the Jar of Sincerity was a birthday gift for my sister. I was making an ecosystem inside a jar. And she loved it!"

Jaimie raised his paws. "Oi, no one's stoppin' ya."

"Except Faith!" Titan burst out.

"Oh shut it, Titan! How'd you even get here?" Gabe scoffed.

I sighed, "I'm sorry, Tye. Zi told me you weren't allowed to come. If I knew you'd be this sensitive about it afterwards, I would have ——"

"Sensitive? I'm not sensitive, Faith!" The little prince of Kelton Whide was in a crummy mood. "I'm just sayin', you kind of ruined Conner's and *my* plan." Titan turned towards the caged-up, legless troll and patted one of the branches that clasped it inside its hold. "That's okay. I think your idea was better ... Oh, and as a matter of fact, you *Drewan*, I followed you ... *and asked Bailey*. I might have told him that Zia said it was okay, so it's no one's fault really!"

I rubbed my head as Gabe and Titan argued over Gabe's lineage in Drewmora.

As everyone celebrated our minor victory, my eyes drifted onto the worried and broken face of the troll. The troll said, "Doll!"

When I looked closer, I realised I could see a human face behind all that cobblestone. Under the layers of stone, vine and what seemed to be skin, there was a boy's face. I pushed through to get closer and, through the ash, I saw something familiar. Everyone gathered as I rubbed away the stone. Beneath it, the boy's brown eyes glanced at me with tears. He searched me with a dryness to his tender voice. As I looked back, feeling the softness to his skin, the boy croaked one word.

"Fri ... End. Fri-fri-friend?"

My eyes shot open and I gasped at Titan. "He's from Kelton Whide. Titan, this is ... this is ... It's Kyle. *It's Kyle!* I know him!"

"Kyle? Never heard of a Kyle," Titan said, furrowing his brow.

I shook my head. "He used to go to my school. He's a friend. He's my friend—and Perry's and Dally's and Zia's too. Everyone, he's not here to hurt us, he's … he's—well, I don't know why he's here."

Connor waved his hands in the air. "Whoa, whoa, whoa! So you're, *what?* Implying that this troll, which took the six of us three weeks to hunt and then take down is really some kid from Kelton Whide? I thought it was a marraboo—whatever that means."

I nodded. "He *is* a marraboo, although he's also Kyle. I don't know how it works—you have to trust me!"

Everyone continued to argue about what marraboo were and how Kyle had ended up inside the troll, but between our words, the sound of water began to trickle.

"Marraboo are conjured spirits who have passed, yet have not entered the afterlife. If what Faith says is true, this Kyle is … dead!" Kate gasped.

My heart burnt. "No, Kate, don't say that. It can't be, he can't be dead. He's right there, you can see him, can't you? He can't be a spirit, maybe ——"

Titan raised his foot off the ground in disgust. "Ew, what the heck? Where'd all the water come from?"

We all searched the dirt and between the leaves, gushing water seeped through, making the solid ground into a muddy wetland. A moment later, my foot was enveloped by the seeping water as if the forest were flooding. Gabe placed his hand into the water and tasted his moistened fingers. It was as though we had entered a shallow spring.

"This can't be right! We're in the middle of the Forest of Farbe. There shouldn't be enough freshwater in the small lakes and rivers to do this, and it hasn't rained in days," Gabe said.

Jaimie lifted his paw from the clear water. "You have a fair point, but where's the water coming from?" I felt the water rise to my knees. No one could have prepared us for this.

More water bled from the ground, soaking our cloaks, and the troll was soon completely saturated in the magical clear liquid. Eventually, I had to hold onto Titan as the water swept us off our feet and splashed against my chest and face. We had become marooned in a forest, consumed by an ocean in seconds. As we bobbed in the growing rapids, Gabe clasped Kate up high. She was so frightened—she couldn't swim! When the water reached its peak, surrounding all of Jaimie, except his eyes and snout, its waves began to whirl and whimper.

Something had answered our prayers. The water stopped and had begun to sway the opposite way from where it had seeped. It was like the dirt below—or, rightly so, the mud below—had become a drain, sucking up the freshwater. We were all safe on the dry ground again, steam sizzling into the air around us. Yet, as the freshwater disappeared and evaporated—as though the forest had never become a swamp—so did the troll! Everyone regrouped on the warm earth. Laying in the many piles of leaves was a boy. Kyle was unconscious and naked ... *Oh, gosh!* He really was naked, rolled up in a ball beneath the trees and vines that had previously caged the troll. I was still clinging onto Titan, who was recovering from his own jelly legs. Jaimie shook his hair about, drying off before he approached Kyle, water still dripping from his fur.

We joined them while Gabe checked Kyle's pulse. He stared at Connor and me, "He's alive. What do we do with him?"

Connor shrugged, expecting me to have an answer.

I clasped Titan, who had begun to shake under my arm, and thought about the one person who would know what to do. "Let's take him back to camp. I'll have to ask Odd what we should do after that."

Connor eyed Jaimie. "You heard the girl, Jaimie. Quick. Go to the alert point and tell Assonance. Get her to warn Bailey, I'm sure he can think of something."

"And ask her to gather some supplies. A blanket, clothes ... Go as fast as you can Jaimie. Please," I pleaded.

Jaime nodded and before he scurried into the distance, he smiled, "I'll go as fast as my legs can take me. Safe journey home, okay?"

As he disappeared, Gabe leant back into the ground. "Argh, what a day! I guess we can call ourselves troll hunters now, huh?"

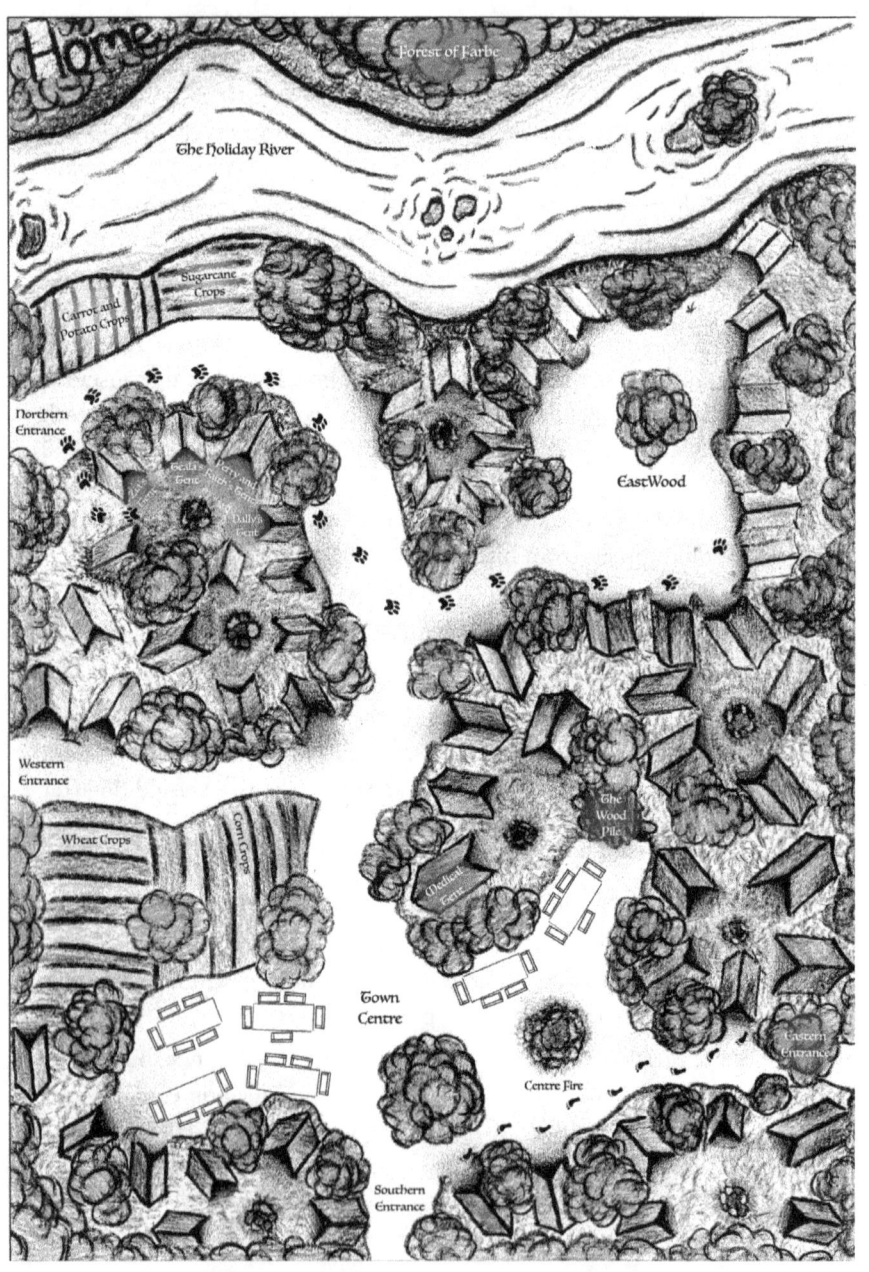

Chapter 3

A Town in a Nutshell
Bailey

Assonance flew down an' greeted me today. It was whack, right after my mornin' meditation. My gut gurgled as she asked me so many things. *I thought I was goin' to faint!* But as she warned me of Kyle—a familiar name from my time in Kelton Whide—I bombarded her with a blanket an' some pants I almost tore yankin' 'em free with my teeth. As soon as she got 'em, she patted my noggin, told me not to worry an' wandered off, placin' the pair of pants an' blanket into her mouth. From a girl 'bout a year younger than myself, she, with her long honey-brown hair an' pale Centrillian skin transformed from a young woman with a button nose, freckled cheeks an' smooth palms into a small, brown an' orange raven. The raven took flight into the low hangin' canopies an' over the many tent-lets.

I hope she reached Jaimie an' the others with everything. Between the chaotic news an' Xanda's request to buzz off with the hunting gatho so he could learn how to chase marraboo—*he had gotten the blues from pickin' berries with Jeremy an' the other Ever cubs*—a familiar face yawned beside my snout.

Out from her tent-let, Teala scratched her eye at the mid-morning brightness under the few real birds that chirped above us. The subtle murmurs from the river echoed behind her yawn. I could smell she hadn't brushed her teeth yet.

"Morning!" she cheered, stretchin' an' playing with her blond hair. It dangled wild-like over her shoulders. Some clung onto my fur as I could feel her warm arms tug at my side. An' as she hugged me, she sighed.

"Was ye dream nutty yesternight?" I asked.

Within my fur, I could feel her shakin' her noggin. "No Bailey. My dreams a little boring at the moment. And you shouldn't worry about it anyway."

I chuckled, "If it's borin' at de moment, I'm sure it'll steam up soon." I paused as she continued to hug me. "Teala why are ya clammed up?"

She sighed. I liked sittin' on my bottom with my arms an' hands—or front paws—free from the grass an' dirt. It also made me look wiser, accordin' to the princess, so I wasn't complainin'!

As Teala slumped, kickin' at the charcoal, she grimaced, "I don't know Bailey." Her voice had matured since we lived in Odd's house. It wasn't all lady-like, similar to Faith's or Kate's or even the princess', but it wasn't as—for lack of a better word—*cute*. She continued, "I just feel weird, like I can't explain it. I feel like things are changing too quickly and I miss the old days. But … But, no! I like how things are now, and … and everyone's happy, but I just feel strange, okay?"

I waved my paws. "Ease up, Tea. I'm gonna be real frank right now, but if dis is about ya body changin' or blood in whack places, I'm a simp when it comes to talking 'bout those particular things."

Teala stopped slouchin' an' gandered at my eye. "What? No, Bailey, I'm not … No, don't be silly. It's just, I'm worried about my birthday. I turn thirteen in five days, and I'm pretty sure no one cares."

I fell back after my paws had stopped their wave. "I care, Tea! Heaps of fellas care. It's ya birthday! I reckon Perry has somethin' planned, an' if not, Faith will remind 'im … Are ya worried?"

She dropped, sittin' on the log beside me, between all her plants she had collected over the last three years. With her noggin resting in both her palms, Teala sighed, "I don't know. Well, I don't think so … No, I'm not worried."

I leaned forward, closer to her mopey eyes. "It's swell, Tea. We're all gettin' older. If you're turning thirteen, dat means Perry's not far off twenty an' *I jus' had my nineteenth*. Don't worry 'bout gettin' older, I'll make sure everyone chips in an' makes ya birthday dandy." Her face slumped towards the ants crawling. I showed her my grizzly teeth.

"Do ye wanna hear 'bout what happened with de troll dis mornin'? I just got word an' might need ya help."

Teala glanced at me with a curious grin. "Yes, please. Did they finally catch it?"

I explained to her what Assonance had told me, an' after, her shook mood faded as the two of us prepared a tent-let for the wounded. The whole town helped grabbin' supplies from Everbreen, setting several sacks for sleep an' maintaining the small number of crops we managed to grow in the thick soil of Farbe. Amid the Evers, Fleddings an' other kinds of coloured crests, the town had become, for the first time ever, *a nutshell*. There was no arguing, an' the cubs an' young'uns did what they were told. Teala helped braid some of the little ones' hair. Liam had become the star of darts, so after he an' a few others had finished their mornin' chores, they ventured to the eastern tent-lets to see if he was still the reignin' champion. In that moment, things were schmick—that was 'til the cavalry arrived from their hunt.

Flyin' from the sky, Assonance turned back into a girl right beside me, sitting with a proud smile on her face. She had a braid down the left side of her hair an' a windbreaker with an orange line wrapped 'round it. She balanced herself on the grass an' said, "That was a long flight. I almost dropped the blanket you gave me!"

I moved to see her slumped over a stump, pickin' at a bundle of leaves entangled within her hair. Her orange raven crest lost its sparkle; peach lingered from her aroma. "I told ya you weren't bonkers enough. I'm guessin' their comin' in now?" I asked.

She nodded. "Well, I can only turn into a small raven— it's hardly my fault, big guy. But yes, you're correct. Gabe was flying behind me; if it wasn't for him, that blanket you gave me would have been lost in the centre of Farbe. Is everything ready?"

I raised my black splotches that surrounded my cat-like eyes. "Do I look like a crackpot? I'm not just sittin' on my bum for nothing. Everything's in check: chores are done, de garlic in the western garden has been gathered, de hunters have been told to wait 'til de others have returned, Liam's winning darts again an' Max came by with a delivery from Eddy. We've emptied it, rationed de food between de tent-lets—I even helped Teala out with one of her moods."

Assonance glared at me. "She is a little moody, isn't she?"

"Eh, dat's just Teala. She'll grow outta it."

Gabe flew down an' joined us from the clouds. His feet were graceful as they touched the rich grass; however, he was still learnin'. As graceful as it was, I heard a slight stumble an' off he went, layin' with his hands holding up his noggin from the charcoal of the fireplace. He huffed ash away, pushin' himself to his boots. "Geez. You two didn't see that, right?"

I nodded. "I've never seen ye fall, ever." I winked. "It looked pretty dilly though."

"Yeah," Assonance smiled. "Maybe you just need to work on your balance a little more. You were doing great."

I pointed at her. "An' that's coming from a spunk who can also fly!"

Gabe wiped the black smears from his burgundy pants. His blue dugong crest lost its light. "Thanks for the heads up." He mumbled to himself, "Balance, balance, balance." He paused awhile. "By the salts, that was a weird hunt!"

"Oh, I bet. How'd it go?" I asked.

Gabe motioned for us to follow. "It's better for you to see. The others were right behind me." He led the way through the northern tent-lets where the river skedaddled an' our makeshift canoes made from oak an' branches had been resting; half-completed an' not at all ready for the water. The gatho marched home with Kyle snug atop Connor's arms under my blanket.

I pushed myself towards 'em with Gabe at my heels. They all seemed buggered—dark bags under their eyes, bruises on their skin an' scales, some cuts through fur an' hair, an' muck under their nails an' claws. I told Connor where we had made Kyle's tent-let an' he took him there right away with Jaimie by his side. Faith smelt like a wet dog—unless that was Jaimie—but either way, she was damp for some reason. She looked me in the eye, "He was it! He was the troll from the bridge, Bailey. It was Kyle the whole time."

I put my face close to her noggin. "An' ye saved 'im, from whatever it was that made 'im into that *beast*!" I stared at their grubby faces. "What's wrong?"

Faith let Titan wander off towards Teala, who stood outside a nearby tent-let. "But I hurt him." Faith sighed. "I ... He's still missing his hand, the one I forced off."

I bit at my gums. "We didn't know, Faith! It's gonna be fine. Odd will figure it out, I'm sure."

"There's no reason for you to be so glum, Faith," joined Kate. "We won. And even though he was the troll, he wasn't in control if he was once your friend. I'll go sit with him until you decide what to do next. You did what any of us would have." Kate smiled and wandered towards the others.

But even with Kate's words, Faith's eyes continued to ask for forgiveness.

"Is Perry back?"

I sniffed. "He was in the early morning; ye just missed 'im when ya left. Dally said de two wouldn't be much longer—they ate an' left again. Something to do with a letter. De princess is sleepin'."

Faith placed her forehead down an' I pushed mine against hers. "Thank you," she whispered, saunterin' towards Teala an' Titan.

I joined 'em as Titan jumped in awe at his own story.

"And then the water took us and covered all the ground for kilometres," he said. "The whole forest was covered, I swear. And then when we thought the Forest of Farbe was going to become a swamp, it all just vanished. And it got really hot, and steam erupted from the ground, and then the troll was gone! It was crazy, Tea ... You don't believe me, do you? Faith, tell her that it happened! It really did—I swear it on Hope's Light, it did!"

Teala raised a brow while Faith untied her hair from its two plaits an' settled the facts. "It's true, Tea. There was a lot of water, almost too much. And we got wet. Very, very wet. When it all evaporated, the troll was gone and laying in its place was Kyle. Do you remember Kyle? He was friends with Perry and me in Kelton Whide."

Teala shrugged. "Was he the small geeky-looking one? I don't really remember half my own friends from school, let alone Perry's."

"You guessed right! So maybe Kelton's got a special place in that memory of yours," Faith cheered.

Teala laughed, brushin' her hand against my fur as she wandered outside the tent. "Of course Kelton has a special place in my head. *It was our home* ... Come on, Tye, I heard lunch was getting prepared. Bailey will get grumpy if we don't go. It's our turn to help."

I was gonna argue back—'cause I wouldn't have gotten angry if they didn't help the others. *Really!* I would have just told 'em the rules for sprucing off an' warned 'em to do it tomorra' ... *Wait, is that angry?*

As I stuttered, Titan turned red. He drifted further into the back section of the tent-let. "Uh ... Um, don't worry Teala. I'll join you later. I'll go help Bailey; it's just I need to get changed first! And ... and wash myself off. I did help take down a troll after all."

Teala smirked, skippin' outside. "Okay, suit yourself!" She raised her brows at me, "*See*! I'm going to help with lunch, *Bailey*!"

As she laughed, a fierce, commandin' voice screamed at the top of her lungs. "*Titan*! Where the—huh! Teala, have you seen Titan, that little ... Gosh, by the light! TITAN! If he went on that hunt this morning, I'm going to ——"

"What, the troll hunt? He just got back with Faith. They're in there!"

The princess stormed into the tent-let, analysing every little detail. Faith an' I both moved out of the way, not wantin' any trouble with a sleep-deprived Zia. The two siblings quarrelled for what felt like thirty minutes. After Zia rehashed her first point 'bout how dangerous the hunts were an' how worried it had made her, Titan apologised for the sixth time an' the two relaxed.

Zia opened the tent-let, while Faith, Assonance an' I watched her lead the prince out under her arm. She pushed him forward. "Now go get changed. Teala and the others are going to need help with lunch." However, before he left, she held his shoulder. "Promise you won't do it again. Tye?"

Titan nodded. "After that argument. *Never*!"

He ran off as Zia let out an exhausted sigh. She joined us on the side where the grass was a hint greener. "That boy is going to kill me one day! Like honestly, he's just too much and ——"

"Zia!" Faith urged. "A rant's coming on. *A little rant.* You sure you don't want to write it down?"

Chapter 3: A Town in a Nutshell

Zia nodded, grabbin' her journal from a little satchel she wore 'round her neck, danglin' by her waist. She mumbled, writing furiously. When it seemed she had finished, Faith asked, "How was last night? Did Perry ——"

Zia stopped her pen instantly, glancin' away from her journal. She gandered at me, then Faith, an' raised her right brow. She stared back at her writing book. "Perry's good. No one's gotten hurt and Odd's still alive, so that's a plus. Dally hasn't lost it either, so the two are doing well. Are they not back yet?"

Faith shook her noggin. "No, they're not … Gosh, why didn't Odd ask me to help? I could have ——"

"Ye could have taken down a troll," I cheered. "Which is what ya did. Odd's got his reasons, he always does. At least he doesn't hide behind some rinky-dink book of rules anymore. If he needed ya, he would have asked."

As Faith's voice began to wear, Assonance politely mumbled, "I'm sorry to interject guys. But I'm not too familiar with Odd; he does seem rather wise, but why does he randomly need Dally and Perry's help? I haven't seen either of them for days now. Oh, I … you don't have to answer, I was just curious."

We all smiled at her. She was too swell for this world. Zia placed her journal away, an' Faith said, "Oh, Assonance. It's okay, really. We don't mind. There are no secrets here."

"Except with Odd!" Zia snorted.

"Yes …" Faith said. "*Except with Odd*. He's like family. If it wasn't for him, we wouldn't be here right now. Bailey, Tea, Zia, Perry—we all owe him for something. To be quite honest, I don't know what the two goofs are doing with him. He doesn't even like Dally. Something to do with a note, right Bailey?"

I nodded. "Dat's what I heard."

Zia sparked up. "*A note?* You mean the one they found last night … Oh, someone kidnapped an Ever last night." She paused an' rolled her eyes at us. "Okay, okay … All I know is that Odd needs help to clear some information about the WonderWorks we busted up. He didn't really tell me much, just ordered me to keep an eye on Perry and Dally. That's all I know." Her eyes drifted off. "Speaking of

19

the little devils." Faith an' I turned 'round, an' entering the western entrance was Dally an' Perry, unhooded an' unmasked.

The two had massive bags under their eyes, an oiliness to their hair an' new smudges an' stains of who-knows-what on their jackets. Dally yawned, crackin' his back. "Boy! Is it good to be back!"

Perry smiled. "Yeah, I missed this place." He sniffed at the fresh air, strollin' towards us as if he had woken inside his tent-let. "Hmm. Smells like lunch is getting made. What do you think it'll be?"

Dally chewed at his gums, glarin' at the sky. "I'm thinking some sort of salad ... maybe carrots and—*hmm*. Chicken?"

Perry shrugged. "Let's just pray that whatever it is, it isn't Ever. I do smell chicken though, or is it bacon?"

Dally smelt the air. "Yep, bacon ... I don't know why you worry—we've never killed an Ever by accident and we never will. We've got protocol."

Perry stuttered, "I know, it's just ... I trust the gang ... *What?*"

He an' Dally were standin' in front of us, half slouched over an' greasy. I could smell their rank body odour—as if they hadn't showered in days.

Faith pouted. "Really? *What* ... Where have you two been? You've been missing for days."

Perry's face went white. "Uh ... at Odd's place. Was that right? Odd's place?"

"Yep, that's where we've been. Unless ... No, that's it really!" agreed Dally.

"Just Odd's, huh? I don't ..." Faith was face to face with Perry. "You could have said something, wrote a letter or stayed back for five minutes! I was worried."

Perry rubbed at his cheek. "Faith, I'm sorry. I didn't mean to make you upset. It's just—you know Odd and how he can be. Dally and I had to help. We didn't know we'd be gone for so long. I didn't think you'd care."

Faith's eyebrows rose, then sank into a deep frown. "Didn't care? I ..." She sighed, pushed past his shoulder and stormed off towards her tent-let.

Perry's face dropped. "What the heck did I do?" he asked Dally an' I.

Dally shrugged an' I could only fetch my best advice. "Ye should go chat with her. She's had a hard day."

Dally's eyes widened. *"The troll!"*

"More like—what was it—*Kyle?*" Assonance mumbled.

I nodded with a smile, but Zia, Dally an' Perry all stared at me as though I had just been thrown in a hoosegow.

"*KYLE?*" they demanded in unison. I was all balled up, but the three were able to figure a little while I stuttered applesauce.

"Kyle from Kelton? What, like school, geeky, always ate rice cakes Kyle?" Dally guessed.

"Was he the short stubby one?" Zia asked.

"Who describes people like that?" Dally said. Beside 'em, Perry was hard-pressed. He put his hands in the air, "Can we figure it out later?" He lowered his arm. "I need to talk to Faith first. She'll know what happened." He sighed. "I'll uhh—see you all at lunch."

"Good luck," Zia cheered. Perry marched to his tent-let.

Dally moved beside Assonance an' I, pulling his mask from his scalp. "Wow, the troll made it this close to the town in a few weeks. I thought Perry and I would have been finished with Odd to help with the hunt. But it looks like you, Bailey, have this town wrapped around your finger. Look at this place!"

"It's a nutshell!" exclaimed Zia.

Assonance sighed in frustration. "It's not that bad."

I smiled. "No, it's dandy, Assonance. It's just de way it should be!"

Chapter 4
NEVER EASY
Perry

Argh! What the heck did I do this time? It's not my fault Faith wasn't here when I got back to the town. *You know what? I blame Odd!* Every time he gets a stupid idea, Faith gets angry at me. Well, I think she's angry ... Something's very off! She would have complained or proven me wrong or something. But instead, she just took off without making a single point. Man, Kyle and the troll? What the heck's going on and why the heck is everyone so busy all of a sudden? *Like seriously—what the heck?*

I lifted the tent-let's flap. It was hard to unbundle—the damn thing was stuck under some tree roots. Weird, they weren't here before. *Right* ... I'm sure it's just someone's gift to grow the tree roots from the oaks nearby. No biggie. I entered our blue carpeted tent-let that had been covered in weird markings from the Evers and spirits. I could tell by Faith's empty gaze that this was a place of silence. Faith sat on our bed, her hands pinching at the handmade leaf-sown sheets. The smell of coconut mixed with strawberries increased the further I crept. I began undoing my gloves, revealing my white wolf crest burning beneath.

"I heard a rumour. Something to do with a troll hunt," I murmured. "Do you want to ——"

Faith stared at the ground and sighed. "Not really ... Why is it never easy?"

I leaned down, so we were eye to eye. "What do you mean? We're alive, the town's as productive as it's ever been and everyone's safe and happy."

Chapter 4: Never Easy

Faith's grip tightened; her eyes pierced my heart. "Not everyone, Perry. You remember the troll, the one under the Cobblestone Bridge."

"Where we met Eddy. When you and I were ... struggling to *talk*. Everything seemed hard then, but look how far we've come," I said.

She grinned for a second. "You listened to me that day." But her smile went stale. "And I ... I took the troll's hand clean off."

I sat next to her, holding her hand. "Because that beast was trying to hurt us. And when Jaimie found it scouting just east of town, we had to get rid of it or lure it away. And I remember what we decided. You managed everyone well. You did well."

I noticed how she grabbed my arm. Her grip looked firm. "Yes, we did. But now Kyle doesn't have a hand. It's missing ... Kyle, from Kelton Whide, was that beast. I don't know how, or why, or who, but he's the troll."

I covered her shaking hand with both of mine. *Hopefully, they're warm!* "I understand! And it's not your fault. It's not mine, or Kyle's, or Eddy's. We can fix this; we can help him and make him better."

"How?"

"You know the answer. He'll know what to do." I stared towards town. "And if he doesn't, I'm sure we can look it up at the library in Everbreen."

Faith leaned her forehead into my shoulder and laughed. "Now that sounds easy ... I missed you."

I couldn't help but feel a rush inside. I leaned my head onto hers. "I missed you too. Odd's gone goofy. He has a master plan or something like that. But Everbreen isn't safe at the moment. Only a few of us should go and visit."

Faith nodded. "What happened to you?"

I straightened and inhaled. "Lots. Come, let's get lunch. I'll explain on the way and we can check on Kyle."

"Gosh, you met a ninja that wore a cloak ———"

"Ninja clothes. Hood, uh ... I don't know what you call it. And I didn't meet him, I just saw him," I blurted.

"So you *saw* a ninja wearing *ninja clothes* made from paper," Faith clarified.

"I think it was paper. And he had two swords! And an army of men, kind of like Araidian's Warriors." Faith and I entered the centre of town, where everyone had gathered to eat lunch. It was the best time because we all ate together. Evers of all kinds—horses, cats, goats, anteaters—the list goes on—scrambled by and gathered their bowls. Children still played while the ones preparing today's meal called for them and our usual team sat together, discussing stupid things loudly.

"PERRY!" Teala screamed. I knew in an instant it was her and that she'd jump at my chest for a hug. And when my arms gave way to her childish weight, Teala wrapped herself around me. "Did you get any mementoes in Everbreen?"

I dropped her onto the grass and checked my pockets. "Uh ... I don't—hmm. Don't you think we have enough from Everbreen?"

Teala's face went stale. "Not even something silly?"

I glanced away from her, noticing Dally, Zia and Bailey arguing at their wooden lunch table. Bailey's mouth was covered in the cream they had made for the salad; on the table, Dally's mask rested like a display. "You know what? Dally might have picked something up. I'm sure if you ask nicely, he might give it to you for the collection."

Teala smirked, "Nicely? Maybe you're right. I have enough things from Everbreen. Maybe I should stop."

"I didn't say that, Tea."

"It's okay. I'm glad you're back in one piece. The town wasn't the same without you. I have to help with lunch. Gotta wrap the leftovers. Talk soon."

She wandered off and I could hear Dally cheer, "What's up little dude," when she reached his table. "What's up with her?" I asked Faith.

Faith shrugged, "I'm certain it's nothing. Her birthday's soon, so ... Maybe she's worried you forgot."

I raised my eyebrows. "Her birthday! Argh, I knew something was coming up. When is it exactly? I just don't want it to end up like her other birthdays. Like when we had to leave Kelton Whide!"

"It's five days away. She's told Bailey she's worried about it."

"Of course she did ... We'll figure something out."

An eerie breeze echoed past us, causing Faith to hug herself. As it poured through the town, Connor stumbled into the town's centre with Kate wrapped around his arm and crisscrossing down his shoulders and neck. Her small green head dangled next to his neck, hissing, "There you two are. He's awake. The boy!"

Faith turned to them. "Kyle. How is he?"

Connor's eyes were grim, his teeth bit at his gums, and he slouched towards us. "It's not good, Faith. He's got a fever; he's shivering and he's barely sleeping. He's sweating a lot. We've already gone through three blankets."

"He's talking!" Kate cheered.

Connor shook his head. "Mumbling, more like it. He's completely deranged. I think we'll be needing that help from Odd soon. 'Cause if he doesn't get help, I don't think he has ——"

"Enough!" Faith insisted. "Are you sure there aren't any doctors here in the town? Nurses, chemists—even someone who might have worked at the counter in a pharmacy?"

I could see the two had seen and thought of every way to help Kyle. Connor's words just proved it. "We've asked and the people who have had experience with medicines, doctors, drugs, they're not ... I don't know."

Kate sighed. "The fever is getting worse. According to Hannah, he only has a few days at most. That's if the fever continues at the rate it is."

I finally opened my mouth. "Hannah! The Ever?"

Connor nodded. "Yeah, the uh ... She's a deer, I think."

"A muntjac!"

"I trust her!" I admitted. "She's smart ... Whatever she told you it's most likely true. But ——"

"But what?" Connor argued.

I calmed my voice. "But ... Everbreen isn't safe for the time being. I want to see him. If he's talking, maybe we can get something out of him, or he can offer some advice."

Faith smiled. "And once we know a little more, a small group of us can visit Odd and ask him if he knows anything."

Connor beckoned for us to follow and I waited behind, telling Faith I was going to get Bailey. He wasn't a doctor, no, but I know he could vouch for the best decision. Especially in harsher times!

By the time Bailey and I had found Kyle's tent-let, the others were already gathered inside. Gabe was the first face I saw, discussing with Hannah the possible sicknesses Kyle could have. Words like *heat stroke, overexposure, pneumonia* and, ironically—from the stories I've heard—*dehydration* echoed inside the tent. I didn't think Gabe knew what half of it meant, but he agreed with Hannah and offered her a hand.

Passing Connor and Kate, Bailey and I trudged through the high-hanging cover of the beige tent-let to see Faith kneeling next to a black-haired, sweaty idiot. *Nuts, it really was Kyle!* His brown eyes were still the same, his teeth were still small, and I could smell something like manure, as though he had freshly cut several weeds and vines. His eyelids were heavy, flicking open and shut. However, as I approached him, they widened.

Bailey's grotesque, bear-like teeth gleamed next to me as Kyle laughed his famous croaky laugh with a long wheeze at its end. "Now that's a sore face," he murmured. His forehead was red. He looked like he was boiling on the inside, his lips chapped, and cobblestone scattered across the sweat-soaked sheets that surrounded him. Around the brown of his iris, his eyes were stained red; his tense fingertips were bloodied and bruised.

I smiled at him. "Speak for yourself! It's good seeing you. Just take it easy. We got you."

He nodded his head vaguely and closed his eyes, releasing a sound of exhaustion. I'd barely noticed how his body shook the mattress he laid on. As Faith took her hand away from his forehead, Bailey whispered in my ear.

"He smells exactly like de troll from de bridge. An' his eyes ——"

I whispered back. "You think we should see Odd?"

"A hundred per cent," Bailey said. "It'd be swell if we saw 'im today."

I stared at Kyle. "It'd be risky going up with him. We'd have to take more people."

"Strap 'im to my back. I'll get Dally to prepare things. Ye try an' find whatever ye can ... If my nose isn't applesauce, he really was dat troll. An' whatever made 'im a marraboo might still be out dere. Odd needs to know, mate."

I sighed. "You're right! Get Gabe to help. I'll meet you and the others when Hannah believes he's strong enough to be moved. I'll send Jaimie out with the message."

As Bailey started to leave with Gabe, I called him back, "Bailey! Just get Zia and Dally ... Actually, the bird girl too. Assonance. Got it?"

Bailey smirked. "Righto!"

As Jaimie closed the tent-let's flaps with his teeth, I stood next to Faith. Kate had slithered down onto Kyle's side table. "Has he been like this since you found him?" I asked.

Faith continued to look at Kyle's red skin. "He wasn't red when he transformed back into a person. He was just unconscious."

"He was freezing to touch," Connor mused. "I thought my fingers were going to fall off when I was carryin' him. But once we put him in 'ere, he burned up like the sun."

"More like a beacon!" Jaimie argued. "His crest lit up when we walked inside. Got any ideas, Hannah?"

Hannah shook her head, admitting that it could have something to do with his gifts. I leaned down next to Kyle and Faith. His family's gift was as old as the Keltons. Something to do with manipulating rock, if my memories of the past Ascension Ceremonies were right. *Ah, nuts!* His brothers and sisters. He had nine ... If he had to escape Kelton Whide like us, they might have—*No! I can't think like that* ...

Kyle's eyes fluttered open again. I whispered gently, "Hey. Can you hear me?"

He nodded.

Faith's voice was almost silent. "Kyle, it's Faith ... from school. Can you remember Kelton Whide? Where we lived?"

Kyle started to breathe at a steadier pace. He stared at us from the lower corner of his eyes and nodded. "Kelton? It was attacked! There were explosions, screaming ... M-my family split up. I-I ..."

His voice shivered. "Maggie. I escaped through the ... The floral was turned off and I had Maggie. Her doll ... HER DOLL! Sh-she ... disappeared."

Tears emerged but never fell from his eyelids. He stopped what he was saying and rolled around, holding back whatever rested inside his fragile mind. I made my voice a little more demanding. "Kyle! How did you become a troll? Who did this to you?"

Instead of answering, he stuttered and started to cry. "Friend. Friend. Fri ... end." The cries became shouts, and those shouts, painful screams. After what felt like an hour, he soon screamed himself into a bizarre state of sleep.

After discussing what Bailey and I had planned, Jaimie ran out of the tent-let like a bullet. Hannah didn't want us to leave but knew there was nothing any of us could do for him. She wanted to watch Dally strap Kyle to Bailey's back and Faith agreed the extra help would be welcomed. Connor tapped my shoulder and said he'd take Kyle when it was time. Faith and I left Kyle in their hands.

The town had lost its hustle; a silence emerged. The wind, the river and the town's talk dissipated. Faith walked with me with her arm wrapped 'round mine. "Do you think Odd will know what happened to him?"

"Probably. He knows everything." I smirked at her with mixed thoughts. "You were right. Things are never easy. It's either we help him now or he dies. But if we go to Everbreen with Bailey, *we* could die. I'm telling you, it's not safe."

Faith placed her finger on my mouth. *I wonder what it feels like. Warm? Cold?* Nevertheless, she titled her head to the left. "Whatever you say will not convince me to stay. Gabe, Kate, Jaimie—they can care after the townsfolk without Bailey. They'll be okay without us. And I'm more powerful than you. You and Dally and Zia need me more than anyone ... I *did* take down a troll, remember?"

I raised my eyes with a grin. "Well, I took down Araidian. And Connor once, and the guy in that van that one time. I forgot his name, but he went down."

Faith's face grew confused. "Wasn't that an accident?"

"I still jumped onto the van. It wasn't easy. Nuts, I wasn't saying

Chapter 4: Never Easy

that you shouldn't come. I was just saying … you were right. Things are never easy, but no matter the danger, I'm happy that you are with me."

Faith leaned forward until we were nose to nose. "Now, what did you do with Perry? He would never let me go somewhere dangerous."

I kissed her and, afterwards, both of us were caught smiling. I laughed, "It's the troll story. I think it made you hotter!"

"Perry!" She slapped my shoulder. "I'm flattered, yet—I don't know. I'm never going to take down anything ever again."

I examined my nails. "Not even a cute blond girl with no crest?"

She slapped me again. Her hand was red when it left my arm. "Don't bring up Alice. You know that's a sensitive topic. Gosh! When we get to Odd's, I'm doing the talking. He's just going to bully you."

"Bully me?"

She led me towards the others. "Well, if you mention Alice like that! We don't have much time. We'll continue this little dance later!"

Chapter 5
Oddities Beyond our Control
Faith

"Okay, I think he's ready to go!" Dally cheered. He placed his hands onto his hips, sniffing the grassy breeze that echoed past. Connor pulled the last straw of rope, patting Bailey's shoulder. "How'd he fit, big one?"

Bailey, sitting like an excited puppy, stood, shaking his black and white fur. "Er, a tic tight ... But I'll manage. Ye didn't have to tie so much rope 'round me though." He crawled past the two, facing them. "How do I look?"

Dally put his thumb up and Connor cheered him on. Gosh, they're both so kind, making Bailey smile.

Holding another line of rope, Gabe followed the panda as if they were holding hands in a crowded shopping mall. "Ei, wait a second there, Bailey. I'm trying to cut this." He gnawed at it with his teeth.

Bailey's eyes lit up, and he sat down like a cat, propped tall and mighty. As soon as the ends of the scissors crossed paths, Bailey shook his fur more furiously. Hannah raised her voice. "Gosh, Bailey. Don't shake too much, you might make his fever worse! Oh, I'm not sure about this. Everbreen is a while away and he's so pale. He'll need to be hydrated and fed, and someone has to keep a sharp eye on him."

Perry and I wandered into the meet-up as a small raven flew above our heads. "I'm on it, Hannah. I'll keep an eye on him. I'm your eyes in the sky!" The raven laughed, morphing larger into Assonance, who dropped to the ground beside me.

CHAPTER 5: ODDITIES BEYOND OUR CONTROL

Instead of being gobsmacked by her transformation, they were fascinated by Perry and me. "'Bout time you two rocked up!" Dally uttered.

I smiled, "Oh, sorry for ——"

Perry slapped Dally's back. "Better late than never, huh! *What?*"

I glared at him. "As I was saying, you've all done a great job. You look wonderful, Bailey!"

"Cheers," Bailey said. "We should start movin'—it's a long trek to Everbreen. We should get dere by de start of sunset if we head now. Wait a minute, where's de princess?"

We all glanced around, searching the small section of tent-lets huddled nearby.

After a quiet moment, Zia's sigh echoed nearby.

"Oh, don't mind me. Just grabbing everyone supplies, because apparently we adventurers can't remember to pack some bags with water and blankets in case we get lost or—I don't know—*attacked*. It's a crazy world out in the Forest of Farbe; could be evil spirits lurking about. Trolls, I heard?" She carried several backpacks with Jaimie giggling, two resting above his arched back. He trotted past Bailey, "Nice hat, Bailey. Suits ya noggin." He offered Dally a bag with his fox teeth. I took some weight off Zia, tossing my own bag over my shoulder. "You're a genius, Zia! Hannah, did you find any medication that could help Kyle's illness?"

Hannah shook her head. "The best I could do was find some herbs that may cool his temperature. Kate and a few others went out looking. When you leave, Liam should have them for you."

I rubbed her small antlers. "Thank you."

While us girls discussed the importance of finding Kyle help, Perry examined something a little more fruitful. He stared at Bailey, round eyes and a curious smile. "Since when do you wear hats?"

Bailey shrugged. "I find 'em *cap*-tivating. Haha, get it?"

Gabe and Dally laughed, yet Perry remained confused. "No, seriously. I don't think I've seen you wear one since … gah, the Hemlocks! You could have asked me to buy you one when I was in Everbreen, y'know?"

Bailey plucked his lips. "But Miss Fishburne sewed dis one for my big noggin. It's hard to pinch a hat with earholes my size." Bailey's ears twitched. "Ye hear dat?"

We all turned to see Titan and Teala running up to us with several younger Evers—rabbits, donkeys and the two panda cubs, Jeremy and Xander. With their bags on, Teala said, "You can't forget about us! If you're all going to see Odd, so are we!"

Bailey almost leapt on top of his brothers, forcing them to stop while the other Evers crowded around. Before we knew it, the whole town was here to bid us farewell. We had to explain to the little ones why it was dangerous; Bailey told them that they were important for the town—*the Town of Tents needed them!* Most were convinced, except Teala and Titan.

"No, we're going!" Titan argued.

Zia complained and Perry seemed somewhat relaxed. He played with his nails. "Eh, Teala's seen worse. Titan, if you make one annoying remark, I'm going to make sure you return to the town by throwing you in the river. Deal?" The boys laughed.

I relaxed Zia as she began to scold Perry. Titan explained what his best behaviour was, and we finally set off. All of our friends followed us until we reached the western entrance, where Liam was on guard. He handed me a small bag of herbs and his hands danced a few symbols I somewhat understood. Gabe had taught me a little sign language throughout the years. With four hand gestures, Liam emoted through sign language, *"For his nightmares and scream."*

Everyone wished us good luck and lots of cheers and laughter echoed as the Town of Tents was soon swallowed by evergreen forest, as thick as curdled milk. Gabe, Liam, Connor, Kate, Hannah and all the rest waved goodbye as if we were going to see them when morning comes, healthy and smiling with a new member to introduce to the family. But that morning came and went because, to our surprise, it was going to be a long time before we returned to our beloved home, the Town of Tents.

The sound of drizzling water against the hard surface of rock vibrated the ginormous branch we walked across. The scent of moss and pollen filled my nose, while Dally led the group down towards

Chapter 5: Oddities Beyond our Control

an old battleground. I could feel the light mist from the waterfall sprinkle across my face. An old half-inflated tent-let slouched beside a log where chunks of grass were scattered across an ocean of mud. Assonance flew down, following the rest of us on foot. We retreated behind a water into the Heart of the Forest.

As Assonance's head dampened from several hard droplets, she paused in awe behind me. "Wow ... This is—this is it! The Heart of the Forest. Is this where the giant turtle lives?"

I smiled at her and Teala's jaw dropped. "You're joking—you haven't seen Ted? No, he doesn't sleep in here, just the spirits. He's about—what, two days walk east from the town?" she guessed.

I unbraided my hair, still strained from the morning brawl. "Ted? About a day's walk. I'm surprised you haven't seen him, Assonance. You could get to him twice as quick as anyone. I suppose he would be a little difficult to see through the thick canopies."

Assonance shrugged. "I had no idea. I try not to fly too much. It hurts, turning into a bird."

"Hurts! How?" Teala asked.

Assonance stared at her hands. "I'm not sure how I could explain it. It burns, as though I can feel every bone in my body crack under the pressure when it changes." She paused, admiring the walls with furious eyes. "Oh, I wish there was someone else who knew how to do it! They'd know how to explain it."

Dally, under the thick oakwood that surrounded the walls of the cave, laughed, "You definitely are a unique one, Assonance. I say we take five."

"Good idea. I'll try and give Kyle some water. Stay steady, Bailey," Perry said.

"Bett! But try not to play with my tail. Ye know it's ticklish when ya rub ya jacket against it." The two goofs cared for Kyle, whose temperature was now *quite cool,* according to Dally.

Zia wondered aloud, "Are you sure we don't have any other Centrillians in the town? I could have sworn we had one or two more of you from Irene's family."

"We do!" Titan cheered. "Lawrence's got an orange crest, but he can't turn into a bird like Assonance."

I pushed myself in front of everyone. "Hey, let's relax. I'm sure Assonance doesn't want to talk about her time with Irene."

"Central City is on the bucket list. I'm sure we'll find someone like you!" Teala said.

Assonance blushed, "Oh, no, it's okay." She paused, staring harshly at the ground. "I know I'm not the only one who can turn themselves into an animal."

Bailey mumbled, "*Milky*," before standing tall and shaking Perry off his tail. He laughed, "I told ya not to get too close!"

A loud bang roared. "Ow! Bailey, I was keeping Kyle's head straight. Warn me next time you move." Dally picked himself up.

"Well, let's get to it, gang. To Odd's!" Perry declared, pointing at the cave's stone ceiling. "Wait, you guys haven't seen the renovations," Perry mumbled. "Bailey, I think you'll be able to fit inside now, and there are more bedrooms. Just don't mention it to Odd. He's a little stuck up about it, being so considerate and all. Oh, and Assonance, I'll make sure Central City is on the top of our list. We still want to visit Drewmora and Fleddington. Who knows—maybe Tinkette Valley one day—I heard there's a nice market stand near the Ptak Isles ..." On and on he went.

The Heart of the Forest was still as healthy as ever. Its waters guided us to the outside, where the walls of Everbreen waited. The giant, Aeithalis, who held the city above his back, was still in a deep slumber. You could practically taste the corn and rice from the many farms that surrounded his kingdom. Dally and Perry searched ahead before any of us continued. They were anxious; you could sense it. I hadn't seen either of them like this since Araidian!

We scurried into the secret entrance, one by one, as Zia opened its blood-sealed door. Titan argued that he should do it for once. The princess argued that slicing your own hand and enduring immense pain to merely open a wall of rock was too much for the little prince. *He was only thirteen.* Leading us forward with a torch and flame, Perry was hooded and ready. I stayed behind with Zia, making sure the coast was clear as she closed the door. Then darkness.

Journeying through, I could already hear Odd's outlandish comments about how ridiculous we all were. But when the light of

CHAPTER 5: ODDITIES BEYOND OUR CONTROL

sunset dripped down from the staircase and Perry helped me into his arms and onto Odd's lawn, something felt peculiar. We closed the grass lid and gathered ourselves after several hours of walking. Zia kneeled. "We should have placed the darn town closer to this bloody house. I am so fed up with walking here every third day; I'm gonna lose it soon."

Teala scratched her head, "I thought it was a really nice walk."

I wandered past them, smelling the linger of incense waft from the back door. "Dally, could you untie Kyle. I think it's time we said *hello*," I said.

Odd still had the same jade-coloured door and red curtains around his windows. Bailey reminisced about all the times he had slept inside the barn, stretching his back when Dally lifted Kyle into his arms. Titan took the rope, opening the new sliding glass door for Bailey and entered the lounge room. When Perry and I entered, it was hard to spot the differences. Besides the walls being taller and the ceiling feeling lighter, the kitchen remained next to the back entrance, many types of pans hanging above the marble island bench. The subtle pluck of strings echoed as a wheeze of laughter sprung from behind the closed timber of the lounge room's doors. Perry's brows dropped as he opened the sliding doors.

Odd had his eyes closed. He was bent over a stool, strumming this magnificently carved walnut harp. It almost reached the ceiling, resting beside the main orb where we used to keep up to date with the news and watch movies every half-week. Odd's eyes bolted open. "*What!* I bought a harp ... Can I not treat myself?" He stood from his stool, pointing at Dally. "Don't even say it, Dalton. I swear to the bloody Light if there is any Hope out there you better not even murmur what you're thinking." His hand gestures became wild. "I've decided to introduce a hobby into my mundane life, seeing how it's gotten a lot *quieter* since Araidian was plopped into Golden Time Jail." He paused, nose flaring, eyes squinting as his head danced from person to person. "What's happened now? Don't tell me, you found this kid in your little town eating too many marraboo berries, and now he's out cold. Look, I warned you years ago—hallucinogens are pretty messy. Oh. He's missing a hand. How ravishing!"

He lectured us about caring for the town and how we were all so terrible at it, passing Zia, who was scribbling in her journal. He pinched the booklet, causing the princess to revolt, red-faced, with an agonized voice. "I love that you've lost your thoughts," he told her. "Your journal is such a great record of your outrageous, yet benign adventures." His eyes widened as he handed back Zia's journal. "Oh, that can't be right."

Zia snatched the booklet. "Well I can't really lie, can I? We need to talk!"

Dally walked into the main hallway. "And yes, Odd. It is about the guy in my arms. Imma put him to bed!"

When his footsteps faded, I stepped forward. "He's a friend, Odd. He's from Kelton ——"

"And he's dying!" Perry affirmed.

Odd's face dropped. "He's sick! Maybe it's a fever; he's not dying. Don't be so dramatic, Perry. One of you could have just explained what was wrong with him and I could have brought you some medication based on his symptoms. Why bring …" He counted us. "Seven more than necessary."

"It is necessary! Why else would we all be here?" Teala argued.

Odd turned to her, facing Assonance. "What's up, Tea? Don't tell me. This was in your dream …" He trailed off, laying eyes on Assonance. "I'm sorry, I don't believe we've met! I'm Odd."

Assonance waved. "I've heard plenty about you. Your house is lovely."

Odd smiled. "Thank you. Wow, a Centrillian! Welcome to the family—we're just full of lawful debate this time of sunset."

"Odd, stop messing about. This is serious!"

Odd rolled his eyes and leant back, like a child having a tantrum. "Oh, fine Perry. Gosh, if you really want my opinion, he's a rare albino who happens to have a little too much Ever blood in him. So, fortunately, he's turned back into a human. That's all I got!"

I rubbed my forehead. "And how did you figure that out?"

Odd pointed to the spare bedroom. "I read Zia's messy journal … That is Jaimie, right?"

We all sighed.

Chapter 5: Oddities Beyond our Control

"Wait! Evers can turn back into their human form?" Bailey roared.

Odd's face went pale. "Uh ... Don't quote me on it, Bailey. You know that if I knew I would tell you the minute I found out. I'd even run to the town for it. I'm just saying, it could have been luck—what morphed him back."

Zia slapped the back of Odd's head with her book. "That's not Jaimie, you arrogant piece of ———"

"Well write better entries in that book of yours," Odd fumed. "I am the one who gave it to you, am I not? Who the hell is the kid then?"

Perry sat on the green cotton couch. "His name is Kyle. He went to our school in Kelton Whide and I've known him as long as I've known Faith, Zia and Dally. He needs your help—*our* help!"

Odd nodded, moving his eyes towards me. My head dropped as soon as our eyes met. "Odd, we don't know how to help him. Please! Help us. It's my fault. He wouldn't be like this if it wasn't for me!" I said.

Odd rolled up his sleeves. "Fine. I'll help, but you all have some explaining to do. Give it to me."

We all began to talk at once.

"One at a time! Please, for the love of the spirits!" Odd said wearily.

First, Perry explained about the time we crossed the Cobblestone Bridge. For both of us, that day seemed to be a little hazy. Bailey finished, saying that I turned the troll's right hand into sand and we escaped. I continued with the tale of this morning's hunt with an overexcited Titan adding comments. After the others talked, Odd sat, his face scrunched, and his eyes focused on the table between him and Perry. We had all calmed, sitting on stools, couch armrests and poofs, waiting for his mouth to move.

"So, do you know why he was a troll?" Perry asked.

Odd shook his head. "No, he wasn't a troll. No, no, no—not if he was what you described. Maybe a marraboo, but the description, it's ... off." He paused and searched Titan's smug face. "You said there was water, lots of water when he changed. Where'd it come from?"

Titan shrugged. "The ground? I don't know."

I raised my voice. "Yes, the ground. It seeped through the dirt and the leaves that had fallen after the Windy Season. Before we knew it, the whole forest was covered in water. What could do something like that? As soon as I saw his face, the water appeared."

Odd played with his chin, breathing in the flower-like incense that Assonance had burnt. As he rubbed his forehead, Dally laughed, "Holy crap! Don't tell me you don't know, Odd! Well, this was a waste of time."

Odd rolled his eyes. "If you speak less, Dalton, I'm more than capable of figuring things out, even if these oddities are beyond our control." He searched the rosemary carpet, each incline, and then Teala and Bailey, biting his lip. His gaze stopped between Perry and me. "You could ... No, you're right! I'll admit, I don't know."

Perry argued first. "What? You have to know! You know everything—you always know everything, it's why you always do the things you do. You just—you can't ... I don't believe you."

Bailey crawled closer. "Come on, Odd. You can figure it out. What if it has something to do with Evers? You could help a lot of people."

I stared at his reflective eyes. "You really don't know for once."

Odd stuttered. "I've never heard or even seen something like this. But if it's something that I can't put my finger on, it must be from before my time. I do know some things you may not, especially concerning ancient culture like this. First of all ..."

Suddenly, the mumbles of bells echoed behind my ears. It was as though they were ringing from behind the front door. As soon as they echoed, Odd's eyes lit up. He leapt to his feet. "Argh, not now. My, my, my, he's early." With half a gesture, he instructed, "Stay here! I have matters to attend to."

Perry gave me a weary grin. "You think that has something to do with us? We really scrambled his brain, huh?"

"Didn't you hear the bells? I think that's what he was walking towards—the ringing."

"Bells? What bells?" Perry picked himself up, charging after Odd. I joined Zia as everyone retreated outside into the cooling breeze, the last rays of the sun and the rising aroma of chimney fires settling over us.

Chapter 6
Master Prophet
Bailey

Outside, the rough concrete beneath my paws was real chilly— that's 'til Titan leapt on my back. He tugged back an' forth, pinchin' at my hairs. "Oi, ye mind?" I yelped.

"I can't see anything. I'm not that heavy, am I?" he said.

I sniffled. "No, it's dandy. Just a little warnin' next time, righto?"

We crowded the front yard; across the road, Eddy's face had turned white. He scurried inside his house as I tiptoed just barely past the front door.

Odd stared at the sky with an unimpressed gaze. Perry blocked the sunset's rays with his hands as Assonance scratched her noggin. What was coming? What was Odd lookin' for? And would Titan stop pinchin' my —

The wind began to rush against the purple-pink sunset as a man rode in on a flying carpet. His skin appeared brittle in its old age, and his snow-white beard fluttered behind him, entangling itself in his black an' green gown. The carpet—woven in shades of pink, yellow an' blue—was sewn by Tinkets in patterns unimaginable to anyone but the natives. As he drifted onto the front lawn, Odd sighed. The carpet flattened an' the old fella disembarked with his walkin' stick.

By the spirits, I knew his face from somewhere. At first, I thought the stick was to help him walk, but once he stretched an' his spine cracked, he threw it aside, cheerin' croakily, "Oddington, my boy! How are we?"

Odd scrunched his face. "Master Othello! What a coincidence. I was just thinking about you."

Othello raised his eyebrows. "Is that so?" He searched everyone, smiling at me. Not the princess, not Perry or Dally. *Me!*

Perry stepped forward. "Othello the Wise. You're the Master Prophet of Everbreen. My mother used to tell stories about you."

Othello shook Perry's hand. "Yes, and Leila is a sagacious woman herself. I'm surprised she'd even want to tell a story about me, knowing all that she knows. It's wild, isn't it?" He pushed his way towards the circle door. "Come, come, please, come in. I'm rather intrigued by this small group of misfits that seem to be crowding my front door." He pointed at me, "Especially you, panda."

Odd raised his hand. "Uh, Master, I don't think ..." But it was too late. We had already begun to follow the old man inside.

It felt as though the whole room had lost its colour. But Othello never lost his footin', always skippin' along as though he were dancing. He rubbed his hands against each wall of the entrances' corridor. Behind me, I could hear Teala gasp to Zia, "He's from my dream, Zi. But this doesn't make any sense."

"Your dream never makes sense, Tea. I'm sure things will unravel just fine. It's not like one of us is just going to fall over and die."

Faith sighed, "Keep it down, Zia. The prophet might hear you."

Zia folded her arms. "Oh, who cares if he hears me? And since when was this his house anyway? Isn't it Odd's?"

Othello took off his sunglasses. "No, no, no! Dearie me, Royal Majesty Glassion Kelton. For a princess, you have a rapid and honest tongue. Oddington's house, how daft? This is *my* house—it has always been my house; for multiple eras, I've eaten here ... Well, at least it is somewhat my house. I believe many obvious changes have occurred. Nothing to do with any of you, I'm sure." We all nodded.

As Othello rambled, he waited for us at the end of the living room beside the harp. He plucked one of its thinner cords. A high-pitched screech echoed as I sat on the carpet.

Titan's fingers loosened their grip. He crossed his arms beside me, eyeing the prophet. Othello continued. "And an eager-eyed prince— what an unique arrangement of crests." He pointed at Perry an'

Teala, "Two wolves," before turning to Titan an' the princess, "Two koalas." Pointing at Odd, he said, "My favourite, the rabbit," then to Assonance, "A raven." His fingers lingered over Dally an' I, "A tiger and a panda." Finally, his gaze stopped on Faith. My hairs tingled an' I bit at my snout. I could feel his curiosity on the tip of my wet nose. "And, how particular. A dragon ... What a unique combination indeed!" Suddenly, he took a large gasp. "Is anyone going to explain why my house has a glass sliding door? I don't remember a time when beasts the size of you, panda, could walk inside on all fours! Or am I just delusional in my old age? Oddington?"

Ye could hear the spit ripple down Odd's throat as he stepped forward. "Well, that's a great question, Master. It's rather simple, actually. WonderWorks gave us an upgrade. All the hours I put in and then the boss' kid going missing and that whole conundrum. We got a raise, and they came in, did some renovations—no big deal!"

Othello examined the room, sniffin' from corner to corner and eventually reachin' a colourful display of seven strings—*The Strings of Reality*. "Ah, yes. So the strings survived another blast. Was the demolition that bad, Odd?"

Odd licked his lips. "Demolition? I ... I don't know what you're talking about." He searched us, slappin' Dally on the arm. "Isn't that right, kids? You hear about some sort of demolition, here, on Wedes Close?"

We all shrugged an' carried on as if all the memories we had made here never existed.

Between Othello's twitchy half-raised brow an' Odd's prideful ignorance, gushin' screams arose behind us.

Othello jolted, "Good hummers! By the Spirits, what is that ghastly noise?"

Faith an' Dally rushed inside the spare bedroom, while Odd stepped towards his harp. "The reason why I was thinking about you. The reason why you're here." Odd began to head towards the sound before turnin' back to his master briefly, "So are you going to help or not? We both know that those screams mean we don't have much time."

Othello sauntered after Odd, his arms behind his back. "Yes, yes." He stared at me again and I felt a little swirl in my gut. "What a strange group indeed. A troll an' a sheep each within its own. One for two, two for one. Come join us, panda. I'll need your masterful skills of obedience—not all have the ear of a slave!"

The sound of crying an' ghastly screamin' echoed like a constant ringin' in my ears hours after they had stopped. Odd opened the door for me. Curtains covered the windows as candlelight bounced, dancin' yellow off the walls, an' a fresh smoulderin' simmered. Warm, smoky air drifted gently inside from the fireplace.

Perry stood the second I stumbled in. Everyone went silent, even Dally.

Thankfully, Teala spoke up. "Bailey … What happened in there? Dally said he was doing magic, but that … that shouldn't exist."

"Was it magic?" Assonance implored.

I shook my noggin. "I don't know. It didn't look like magic. Dere was no flashin' colours, no wands or sparkly lights; he just wrote strange symbols, pulled my hair, placed his hands in so many strange places." Visions from the procedure ricocheted in my noggin as I struggled to continue.

"It's all right, Bailey. Take your time," Perry said.

I grinned. "No, no, it's dandy. I saw symbols, strange symbols."

"Like the ones on Othello's dressing-gown?" Titan guessed.

"It's not a dressing-gown, Tye," Zia snapped.

Titan rolled his eyes. "Well, it's still a gown, butthead."

"What'd you just call me?"

Faith spoke up. "Hey! Let Bailey speak, please. It's been a long day, let's try and not make it any longer."

Dally nodded. "Agreed. Go on, Bailey."

"What did the symbols look like?" Teala asked.

I described 'em as well as I could. One was a circle with two triangles inside, pointin' towards each other; another was an elongated trapeze with two lines scratched horizontally through it. There were some that were simply scribbles, others that looked like ancient writing from the Spirits; after all that I described, Teala had a clear picture in her noggin. She drew a few she knew by heart, questionin' me on their colours as she went.

"Colours? What's the colour got to do with some whacky symbols?" Perry asked.

"Everything! Do you remember Bailey?" Teala demanded.

I nodded. "Okay, let's ease up. Most were blue, some red—a final few were de colours of de eight major cities."

Teala painted the first one I described in Zia's journal. "Like this?" she smiled.

Before I said yes, Odd cheered, "Close enough. You've a finger for ancient Drewan. The language of Euphoria's heart."

"The planet's core?" Faith asked.

Odd nodded. "Indeed. The Drewans were mining people, supposedly born with gills and cold blood. And as we built our home on land, they built theirs in the ocean. Their language was found when a woman named Happiness dug too close to the core of the planet. Apparently, her eyes were such a magnificent blue, from that day onwards, men would go mad from staring into them for too long. You could hear the water just by looking at her, and when she got mad, salt would fall from her chin. Othello was writing the symbols she scribed the day after she emerged from the mines. It's still taught, but not by many. An almost-lost language."

Dally rolled his eyes. "Thanks for the history lesson. You want to tell us what's up with the magic?"

"Yeah, Odd! Why's the bald guy doing voodoo?" Titan urged.

"Magic? Voodoo?" Odd sniggered. "Cute … You *do* know why they call him Othello the Wise, no?"

"Because he knew who would be declared king in Fleddington, five days before the Ritual of Lava," Zia guessed.

I sighed. "Nah, it's 'cause he planted de largest tree on top of Aeithalis' back, an' through reincarnation, knows all de knowledge de tree does … It's millions of rotations old."

Odd shook his noggin. "Nope. And the tree's not that old, Bailey. Sorry to break it to you."

Assonance guessed it was because he had lived in solitude for many weeks inside the vast cave system under the Jackson-Lee desert, the Clyromoe.

Odd continued to shake his noggin, 'til Faith said, "Alchemy! He mastered alchemy and no one has been able to bond objects together like him for eras."

Perry's eyes narrowed. "How'd you know that?"

Faith giggled. "I read, doofus."

Odd joined the laughter. "Well, she's right. He cracked the bloody light of alchemy inside these walls—actually, the older ones that were here before—but … he's old, forgetful and arrogant." Odd brushed past me and stared at the fire. "He couldn't fix whatever was broken or … cursed. However, there is someone who can. Two of you have already met him."

Odd stared at Titan an' the princess. "That mechanical stomach of yours, Titan; it's not just gears and oils moving about. It's alchemy."

Titan clenched his hand into a fierce fist, gulpin'. "The Doctor? Why would we want to visit him!"

Zia went to calm him. Odd sighed. "Because of all the people that understand Othello's teachings, he is the smartest and most advanced."

Perry rubbed his hands together, "But how's alchemy going to help? Kyle has a fever; Titan's stomach dissolved. They're a little different, don't you think?"

"And that man's no good for anyone. We shouldn't go near him!" Zia added.

Odd rubbed his eyes with his dirty fingers. "Well if we don't, Kyle will melt and die in such a painful and slow way, I don't even have the words to describe it. There's a reason he keeps cooling and heating up. His body's slowly realising that he isn't a troll anymore; without those cobblestones holding his skin together, he's …" Odd searched us all. "He's going to melt to death within the next week."

Chapter 7
The Melting Boy
Bailey

"Melt?" Teala gasped.

"The hell does *melt* mean, Odd?" Dally demanded. "What? Is his skin just going to fall off?"

Perry argued an' Zia pleaded for another way to help Kyle, but as Odd tried to answer everyone, I crawled to Faith. She was white in the face, a sort a' steady breathing that's found when ya realise you've been caught doin' something nutty. Her eyes were wide enough to catch a small ball, her lips dry an' her hands so tense she almost ripped the stuffin' from the couch. The yellow danced on her face as I nudged her elbow with my snout. "Ya right?"

For a long moment, she was clammed up. Her voice was raspy as she mumbled, "I did this, Bailey! It's my fault, I shouldn't have …" Her tongue twisted and her eyes lowered, the flames of the fire becoming an orchestra in her emerald irises. I rested my noggin on her lap.

"I don't know," I admitted. "Ye blame yourself for a lot of things, Faith. I gotta be frank, 'cause I don't know how to process dis either."

She rubbed my noggin and I could sense her eyes above me.

"I want to tell ya that it's not ya fault, 'cause it most likely isn't," I whispered. "But please, for me. Before we have to explain to everyone why you're so pale in de face, can we just figure things out first an' then point fingers?"

Faith sniffled. I could feel her body shake as she began fiddling with my ears. "You're right. The world's a strange place, isn't it?"

"It is, but you're not de one to blame for all de weird things ... Do ya need some water?"

I went to fetch her a glass from the kitchen. As I returned, Perry leaned over the couch, nose perched an' lips pursed. "Faith, are you okay? You look a little ———"

Faith rubbed her eyes. "Right as rain! Bailey and I were just discussing what exactly Odd meant by *melting*."

Perry's eyes darted between Faith an' I. "Well, uh ..." He paused. "It's what it sounds like. Odd said, in theory, Kyle's insides are going to dissolve as though his whole body—his lungs, kidneys and his heart are covered by an invisible acid. Then the rest of him will melt. So let's hope this alchemy thing works."

"Sounds pretty rank." I groaned.

Eventually, Odd finished his mumbling. "Then it's official," he said. "We're going to Central City tomorrow!"

"Tomorrow?" Zia spat. "How the fu———"

Perry exploded. "You want to go to Central City? *Tomorrow?* What about the town?"

"Odd, they need us!" Teala added.

Odd raised his hands. "Well, then Clyde can melt! If we don't get on a train tomorrow, it'll be too late!"

"It's Kyle!" Dally demanded. He rubbed his eyes. "Gah, we can't just let him die, guys."

"We never said we were!" Faith argued. "If we have to leave, we leave! But we come right back as soon as he's healed."

Everyone nodded. A white light covered Perry. He vanished.

He reappeared beside Assonance, white ash burnin' the carpet 'round 'em both. "Assonance, how fast can you fly to town?" he asked.

"From here? It depends on the wind," Assonance said.

"Can you make it there in two hours?"

Dally joined them. "Good idea, Pear. We're going to need to let everyone know that we're going."

Assonance's face dropped. "Going to Central City?"

Chapter 7: The Melting Boy

He smiled. "When you get there, have a break, drink as much water as you can, and come right back."

She pointed at herself. "Me? Back? *Why?* You want me to come?"

Zia laughed. "Well, of course we do. You're our Central City expert!"

I waddled over hearin' the shock in Assonance's voice. "We've already got a panda. Might as well have a raven too."

She still didn't believe it, even after Faith grabbed her hands an' led her outside. She said her goodbyes an' flew off, faster than the sound of the wind. When she was a shadow, Dally sat at the glass slidin' door, waiting for her. Zia mentioned the new laws in each of the major cities after the *Great Transformation of the Light Age*. I was freaked. She told me that transformed or manipulated Evers were prohibited from inside Drewmora. Apparently, Tinkette Valley didn't allow 'em in either, though no one knew for sure; the city lost contact with the other major cities after the beacons were turned on by Araidian.

Odd explained everything; told us that Central City was safer than most when it came to the new regulations about transformed Evers. Teala spoke up 'bout visitin' her sister once we arrived. Olivia would be able to shelter us while Kyle healed from his alchemic surgery.

Perry pouted. "Whoa, you're right, Tea. Liv should be there unless she went home to look after Mum. We could always give it a go! Do you know anything Odd? Wait a minute—Othello! He'll know. She was under his regiment in the labour party when we were looking for her!"

"Would he remember? That was almost three years ago!" Faith asked.

"Remember? He could recite every day to you for the last decade. He'll know; I just don't think he'll wanna tell you!" Odd laughed.

Teala crossed her arms. "Why wouldn't he want to tell us? Did Perry offend him already?"

Perry's hands flew into the air. "*What?* Me? Why—How could I have already offended him? I've barely said a sentence to him."

Odd grinned. "Well, a sentence from you is enough to cause people to go mad. I wouldn't say it's so far-fetched."

A door slammed closed. Othello, perfectly tall, hands gently behind his back had a calmness in his demeanour as he traipsed towards us. "Unique indeed, this group of people I find myself talking to." He examined our faces, one by one. "Your friend's very ill. The lighting of Kelton Whide's beacon has caused him much pain. It has caused you all a fair amount of pain."

"Why haven't they been turned off yet?" Perry asked.

Othello smiled. "It's a passing time now. It's too late to undo what has been done. Evers have become animals, Albinos have lost their homes—not to mention the travesty in Bellow's Curve."

"But the yellow beacon's on!" Zia mused.

Othello nodded. "All eight beacons are on. Central City even decided to voluntarily turn theirs on after brooding threats from Araidian Leap—a familiar name, I'm sure."

Titan spoke up. "What about Father? Certainly, he wouldn't allow this; he's too passionate about tradition—he'd wage a war just to turn off the one in Kelton Whide, I just know he would!"

Othello closed his eyes. "Tsk, tsk, tsk. Poor little prince. You haven't heard—Lord Kelton's been missing for almost three years. Kelton Whide is ruled according to an agreement between the parliament in Central City and the government leading Drewmora. Most contributors are bankers from Fleddington—they're what's keeping tides from turning. Well, them and your mother, Lady Kelton. She rules from her Castle of Glass, day and night, alone with only her people and her Hand to keep her company."

"And what about Father?" Zia demanded.

"Rumours say he was last seen near the Ptak Isles. Somewhere in the Jackson-Lee Desert. I was part of the search party. Nobody. No evidence, nothing ... That was last year!"

The prince an' princess mourned, a coldness settling in the air.

Othello told us many things. We were all able to ask him questions, Dally too. His voice was rough, old from many experiences, yet he never seemed surprised, just merely amused. He told us that Olivia was indeed part of his party when he was advocating for the integration of dissolvable plastics in Everbreen—a policy he knew would triumph. However, their progress was cut short once the sixth

Chapter 7: The Melting Boy

beacon in Tinkette Valley was turned on. Everbreen was becomin' more dangerous, overruled by outlaws, an' seein' that his influence couldn't help the people here, he went to research the beacon's lights.

He told Odd that they were fascinating, absolutely—an' I quote—*ludicrously unrealistically logically based on neither law of spirituality, worship or even the gods*. Inside each light beam, as they pulsed upwards, he said he could cypher codes in their rhythms. Not only were they a heartbeat, they were talkin' to something. An' that's why he returned to Everbreen. Hearin' that Araidian was behind bars, an' finishing his research at the University in the Ptak Isles, he rode his carpet, Greg, as fast as he could. Ye could hear the excitement in his voice, as though he was a young'un who had scored the winning goal.

Odd wasn't convinced. "Then why come here?" He raised an eyebrow, "Is it because Everbreen's kaiju is the eldest? Aeithalis maybe more ——"

The old fella's face brightened. "Maybe *easier* to analyse. He's also the kaiju I've had to most time with. Like how Leila's has had more time with Teleios."

"So Teleios is the name of Hope's body, tied down beneath Whide's Cathedral, right?" Faith said.

Othello an' Odd laughed at each other. "No dearie. Teleios is in de wind," Othello explained. He yawned an' stretched. "Well, Oddington. I believe you need some time to make calls. You can use the office. Good night and sweet dreams, especially young Teala here."

We all said goodnight. When the old geezer had finally stumbled upstairs, a loud clunk rattled the glass wall. Dally opened the slidin' door, laughin'. "Give us a hand. Assonance hit her head on the way in."

Zia ran to get an ice pack, while the rest of us retreated outside. Assonance had sweat coverin' her noggin, black smudges 'round her eyes, branches throughout her clothes an' leaves in her hair. Some fell as she rubbed her forehead, revealing a large blistered lump. Dally offered her his hand an' she smiled. "Good! You didn't knock yourself out!" Dally lifted her up. Zia made sure she used the icepack properly an' we helped her inside.

"I recommend that all of you get some sleep," said Odd. "We'll be leaving before sunrise to catch the first express train to Central City. I'll see you in the morning."

No one said anythin', except Assonance. "Thank you, Odd." He smiled at her an' continued into the office to make the arrangements for tomorrow.

Teala grabbed Assonance's hands. "So, what'd they say?"

"The town's okay," Assonance smiled. "They said they'll keep our tent-lets up and clean, waiting for our return. I told them we shouldn't be too long, but if anything were to happen, they should use the space for more practical things. Gabe insisted that he'd make sure everyone was doing their chores. It felt like the only person they didn't want to leave was you, Bailey!"

Dally folded his arms. "Hey, Bailey, you don't have to come to Central City, just for Kyle—you barely knew the guy. If you want, I'm sure you can make it back to town by yourself."

I laughed away his comment. "Nah, don't be ridiculous fellas!"

Perry stood up. "It's all right, Bailey. It's up to you. We don't make the decisions for you anymore. Go back if you really want."

I shook my noggin.

"What else did they say, Assonance?" Faith said, changing the subject.

"I think they'll be just fine. Most of the grownups will look after the children, and if I know anything about the Town of Tents, it'll stay strong no matter how many people leave."

Titan yawned.

"Agreed," Zia mumbled. "It's getting late. Where are we all sleeping?"

Dally an' I volunteered for the living room. When the fire sizzled, the room emptied an' the lights went out, the two of us talked awhile.

"I wish more people were like you, Bailey," he said. "It's getting hard, y'know. All this fighting, sneaking, running—all for what? Odd? His delusions, his insistent nagging. His dumb name."

"An' who would name their kid Odd in de first place?" I mused.

It was soothin' to hear laughter for once.

Dally continued. "You're right. I mean it though. You should stay in the town. Who knows what's going to happen in Central City? What if we die?"

I rested my noggin on the tops of my paws. "We die together. Perry was de first fella to see me like dis—as a panda. An' yeah, at first he was confused, though he was high, de whole nine yards, but he stayed by my side for de night. Convinced me to not hide an' to face Faith an' Tea. I haven't been called a slave in many rotations an' I haven't felt like one for much longer. I'd like to stay; I feel at peace an' like I belong in de town, but if ye fellas are risking your lives in another city that isn't Kelton Whide or Everbreen, then I'm comin'. Whether we die or not, I'll be dere."

Dally laughed to himself. "You've nailed Perry in a few sentences." He went quiet, bitin' his tongue. "Before this, back when I was with Ada, I watched someone—an Ever. I watched her bones break, heard them snap and crack; I heard her screams, watched her cry as her whole body changed. In a minute she had become a bat ... And right after, in the middle of her screams, a hunter shot her down. He was so confused when Ada started yelling at him, but no one knew what was going on back then. I suppose what I mean," he gandered at my eyes, "is that things have changed. Have you ever tried changing back into—you know?"

I raised my noggin. "My human form? Every leap of the moon." I shook my snout. "Don't think it's worked jus' yet."

Dally hugged his pillow, turnin' over onto his side. "Give it a go tomorrow. You never know what's gonna happen!"

In that blurry mornin' haze, I saw Othello's flyin' carpet walk past the living room doors. It acted like a human, strolling into the kitchen. I could hear it slammin' cutlery an' a chopping board onto the bench. Lots of thuds an' then an elderly voice, "Why thank you, Gregory. What was that? The panda's up? You saw, he's—why he's ..." I missed the last few words, but after he finished, Master Othello's noggin dripped over from behind the wall, starin' at me like I were a critter. His eyes barely shined his green irises. They were just white. Before I knew it, he was pluckin' my hairs, examinin' my paws an' listenin' to my chest. He did so many things a man shouldn't, I felt I should bite him. As I began to bare my teeth, the wise prophet stood in front of his carpet with a smile.

"Whoa, whoa, whoa, don't mind me, Bailey. I'm merely interested in how you work."

"How I work?" I stood, holdin' my empty belly.

Dally spun in his sleep. "Enough growling, Bai, it's too early for that," he yawned, mumblin' the rest.

Othello's smiled blossomed as he rubbed my side. "Yes! How you work. You are like everything and yet nothing I have ever seen before. I'm still attempting to figure out how exactly you Evers work. You're the first I've ever had the chance to be in the same building with. Even Gregory was curious."

"An' why exactly do ya wanna figure out us *Evers?*"

He flicked my snout. I could see some water moisten his wrinkly fingertip. "Because I am one of the only people who can manifest some sort of cure. You do want to be Bailey again, don't you?"

I pulled away. "I am Bailey. It doesn't matter what I look like … How exactly would ya be able to find a cure?"

He winked at me. "Simple really. I need to kill ———"

Perry barged in. "UPPEDY UP—ooh, bad timing?" he asked, spotting Othello and me. The bells at the corners of Gregory rang back and forth.

Othello turned to him, his eyes returning to their normal shade—dark green irises fillin' their centre. "Caduca. How curious."

Perry picked his nose. "And why's that?"

Before the master prophet answered, Odd screamed, "Othello! There you are. Quick. I need your assistance with Martin. He's become nosey again!"

Othello agreed, wandering off an' fiddlin' with his hands. Odd told us to get everyone up an' meet him an' Othello outside the station in thirty minutes.

As everyone got ready, I couldn't help but tense my front paws. *Kill what? What did the old prophet mean?*

Chapter 8

Train Trips

Perry

"Oh, it's far too early for this bullshi——"

Together the gang told Zia to shut up.

Bailey asked, "Are we almost dere?"

I smiled at him. "I think we're almost there. Yo, this is the right way, right?"

Thankfully Faith's voice was not far. "Should be. Just down Walding Drive, up ahead and down the left."

We emerged from the road to discover a tall sandstone building with green stained-glass windows, which reflected several images of the many spirits that had once lived in Everbreen. Maple and elm trees sprouted from the station's red roof shingles. We left the pebbles of the main road and climbed the lacquered timber staircase towards the entrance. Marble statues loomed, mighty, tall and ghostly. Below them were metal scriptures in an unfamiliar language. Zia announced each one she passed. Dally ignored them, while Assonance asked about the statues' design. Bailey led the way and Faith's eyes lingered on the furthest one that towered next to the station's sizeable two-door entrance.

"What exactly are these spirits, Bailey?" Teala asked.

"And what's with the weird words under them?" I added.

Bailey halted next to Tea and me, smiling. "It's de tongue of Mother Nature herself. Not as common today as when dis station was built."

Assonance skipped up the stairs. "During the formation of the regiment, right?"

"'Dat's right." Bailey took a deep breath. "Dis was de first buildin' to ever be constructed through de labour of de many. I think de Regime forced the spirits in Everbreen to build it as a necessity for … what's de word?"

"Globalisation?" Faith suggested.

Titan crossed his arms. "Hey, can we dumb it down? The heck's globalisation?"

Bailey sighed. "What I was told is that de spirits had to build this so they could trade with other major cities. Trains back then were de fastest mode of transport, and although it doesn't exactly scream *Everbreen* in its design, it's kinda dandy. Still being used after all these moons."

"And the words?" I pointed at this metallic clam-looking spirit that was on its side like a Venus flytrap. Bailey examined each statue. "I'm not dat familiar with de old ways. That's Hurah, de Spirit of Entanglement. Next to 'im is Oonbak, de Spirit of Nurture. She's got some swell stories. Her mother, Serenity, was a Good Spirit. Beside her is ——"

"Hebi!" Faith mused. "The Spirit of Darkness."

Dally climbed to the top. "Now, why would a town place a statue for her? Wasn't she ——"

Othello appeared behind him. "Don't be so rude." He sounded almost nostalgic for the demon. "Hebi had a fractured heart. Doesn't mean she didn't have goodness inside of it."

Dally jumped. "Master prophet! Where'd you come from?"

He grinned. "Simple. Before, I was somewhere where I am not now, and now I am here to be somewhere else later. I'm moving forward, not back like you, my child."

Dally raised a brow. "Sure thing," he mumbled.

We entered the station—eight train tracks in total. However, by the magic orbs floating in the air—glowing green, like all the rest we'd come across—there seemed to be at least twenty-five platforms.

"Do you think they're underground?" I asked Faith.

"Oh my. No, they couldn't be. We're standing on a giant, remember?" she said.

"True. But what if they carved into him?"

"Perry, that's inhumane. Surely they're somewhere, possibly in the trees?"

I stared at her. "Trees! Now that's even more farfetched. How would a train be able to rest its weight on a tree branch?"

Faith bit her lip. "Gosh, they have to get trains into Everbreen somehow. And if they're heading east, the Forest of Farbe is in the way. That place would likely have branches that tracks could go on."

She was right! This was going to be one heck of a train trip. "This might end up being a rollercoaster, rather than a detour to Central City."

In the distance, we could hear Odd bargaining. "Come on Martin. It's one time and what do you even use those carriages for? Look, I'll hook it up onto the back of the express train. All I need you to do is move it a little so there's enough space."

"I'm not doing it, Odd. Not after last time!"

As Odd tried to reason with the station clerk, I could almost taste walnut. "Walnuts?"

"I smell it too. Bailey, explain." Teala asked.

Bailey rolled his eyes. "I didn't know I was runnin' a tour."

"Well, you are the native," Zia laughed.

"Look up, ya simps. Walnut trees. De soil 'ere is rich an' dense—it's one of de only joints dey grow. I reckon there's a farm next door, isn't dat right Othello?"

Othello nodded. "Indeed, young panda. The best walnuts money can buy. A luxury for most in Everbreen. Have any of you caught a train before? Most stations are like this one. Though there are minor deviations."

"Perry and I did when we visited our Auntie in MarketVilé," Teala said.

Faith watched the walnuts. "I have too; my parents and I would visit family down in South Rock."

"South Rock, you say?" Othello pondered. "A lot of old traditions rest in South Rock. Not many Albinos last time I visited—did you live there long?"

"How'd you …"

"I'm a prophet, young dragon."

Faith smiled. "I moved to Kelton Whide when I was four. But my crest has always been white. I was born under the Floral."

I tipped my head. "Not many people in Kelton are simpletons. I think only Ada was, from what I remember."

Faith laughed to herself.

Dally jumped between us. "Ada?" He asked. "I haven't heard someone say that name in a long time. Geez, she was a simpleton, huh?"

Bailey interrupted, "What's a simpleton? Do ya mean a brownie?"

"I believe they do, panda. So this … *Ada* … her crest changed colour?" Othello asked.

Dally rambled about how amazing she was, Faith and I debated about whether or not her crest had changed colour, and Teala crept behind Odd. Othello reiterated, "That's all well and good, but did this girl have a brown crest when she moved to Kelton Whide? Do any of you remember?"

"She did," Dally lost his smile. "Why? You look like something's caught your tongue!"

Heck, something had caught his tongue. Othello, white in the face, licked his lips and frowned. "I apologise. I have made arrangements for Gregory and I. Something has come up. I hope to see you all in Central City. I'll make it a priority to be there when you all migrate safely. Tell Oddington *flashlights*—he'll understand."

And, like that, the man turned and left the way we entered.

"Hey, Odd! What time is the train coming?" Teala asked, scratching her head. Odd turned away from the station clerk, grabbing hold of a suitcase. The clerk was balding, retaining only some fair blond hair around his ears. He had hazel eyes with soft yellow and a thin moustache that twirled at each side. His teeth were uneven and his tongue almost purple with pasty skin, fresh with several moles.

Chapter 8: Train Trips

"Hmm? The train ... well, I don't think we'll be able to go," Odd said.

Teala eyed him down as he smirked at the station clerk. Odd frowned. "See, this man right here—this big ol' fool—he won't let us board with an Ever the size of Bailey. I tried to convince him, but the man, he's being *very* mean."

Teala's eyes narrowed. "Why are you speaking to me like I'm nine?"

Odd hit his head with his palm. I heard the soft impact as I approached them. "Tea. I'm not ... *Look*, this guy's discriminating against Bailey." He leaned to her ear and mumbled something that made her giggle. She wandered towards Zia and told her something that made her face all red.

I stared at Odd. "What are you up to?"

He smiled. "I'm organising things. We're very fortunate that there are a lot of loudmouths in this group."

Zia was furious; her mouth was twitching, ready to explode. She turned to the station clerk. "How dare you hold down a fragile little Ever! He may be a panda, but he has the same rights as you. Do you even have a green crest?" She judged his uniform like the old Zia from Kelton Whide would have at a party. "Gah, and to hold such a vulgar attitude—disgraceful. You're lucky you didn't have to go through what that Ever did. He was out there, alone, in the wild, all changed and confused. And here you sit, with your shoulders all mighty and your crappy insignificant uniform." Her finger was firm, pointing at the clerk's heart. "Here you are, thinking about how much power you have, when really, what are you without that crappy little uniform? You work at a train station, hun! Which means, by the law of both the new Regime and the Council of Spirits, you have a responsibility to provide public transport to all citizens, including simpletons, Kelts, Drewans, Tinkets and so on. This includes the people who are part of the land. This panda is one of the kindest, humblest and sweetest Evers I have ever had the good fortune of knowing, and you're telling me that I'm misinformed? That *I'm* wrong? That you can't find a way to get him onto the next train to Central City? *Really?*"

Martin tried to speak, but Zia was on a roll. "This is disgraceful; I'm appalled by your behaviour. I want to speak to your manager!"

Martin froze, his mouth wide open and his eyes stuck on Zia. He stared at her, then at Bailey and then back to Odd, closing his mouth. He turned around to the wall behind him and the sound of metal against metal rustled. "Now, pretty young lady, I never—no, I never, said I wasn't going to help you. I just disagreed with the way Odd, here, put his spin on what you described to me ever so politely. He was tryin' to force me, but if he'd explained it as you did." Martin left his small stall with a crop of keys, "I would have been honoured to help you." He started leading us to a platform. "Now, ah, I'm more than able to help you with everything you need. No point in disturbing the manager when I can help you get this Ever to Central City. The train should be gettin' 'ere any minute now. Come on, I'll show you the way. We'll hook up an Ever carriage once they arrive."

As he passed nervously through our group, Odd smirked, raising his hands. "I'm not going to say it, Martin. Oh, don't look at me like that. You know I'm sorry for the cat thing. How was I meant to know you were fond of it? You coulda just said something when I was in Tinkette Valley."

He stumbled past Odd. "I don't wanna hear your excuses, Odd. You know how I feel about your sarcastic apologies. Hell, remindin' me hurts the most, so will ya knock it off?"

Zia and Bailey started to follow. Odd rolled his eyes and murmured, "It was over a hundred years ago. It's not my fault you're still somehow looking for the damn feline. Look, I put the whole missing cat behind me, yet you …" he mumbled to himself. Martin ignored him and continued leading Zia.

Teala crossed her arms. "What's that all about?"

Odd pushed against his eyes with the tips of his fingers. "Long story, Tea."

I smacked his back, and he jolted, straightening his posture. "We have plenty of time. How long is it to Central City again?"

Assonance and Faith were admiring the timetable, its green screen scrolling through the trains, their locations and each platform. "Twenty-eight hours! I didn't think it was that long," Assonance replied.

"*Twenty-eight?* Eight plus twenty—you gotta be reading it—no!

CHAPTER 8: TRAIN TRIPS

See, Odd? Plenty of time. Talk away, you luscious hunk of demigod goodness."

We walked deeper into Everbreen's Grand Station Hall, catching several lifts and escalators, and further down the branch tunnels.

"Martin here, he's like me, a demigod of sorts. Instead of time, he's the master of coal," Odd explained. "Martosia is his real name; he's been burdened with the sanctum of passage through the railways, kept here to enforce the peace between the people, the gods and the spirits, especially in Everbreen. There's always some third party involved in the other major cities."

We entered platform thirteen, Martin describing the ins and outs of each carving within the oak walls. We had climbed through several layers to get here and, when he finished his sentence, only one face lit up—Assonance's.

"This here is one of our eldest branch platforms," Martin said. "Inside, we're nestled between the excavation of Everbreen's fourth-oldest tree. The spirits called this Minaha, meaning *wing* in the mother tongue, as it was planted on top of Aeithalis' right shoulder."

"The giant?" Titan exclaimed.

Martin continued. "Yes, the giant."

Assonance, eyes big and round, gasped, "So, we're inside a tree branch? That's a big tree branch!"

I nodded at her. "It's like WonderWork. That's the big tree near the centre of town. That's where we found you and the rest of the group, right underneath it—you know, when Araidian and his ..."

Faith's eyes met mine.

"What?" I asked obliviously.

She gave me that look most men fear—*the don't you dare eyes*. Was it really that touchy of a topic? *Right, Assonance's brother.* Never mind!

I raised my hands.

"There's plenty of big trees in Everbreen, Assonance," Faith said. "When we return, we can take a short trip and visit the centre of town where the largest tree rests."

"You mean the Ancestor Tree," Martin chimed. "It's gorgeous, ain't it?" He tapped Dally's shoulders, "Young man, you look ripe and strong. D'ya mind helpin' an old geezer with some boxes? I'll need to empty this Ever's carriage before the train arrives."

The train tracks went from end to end, fire torches lighting the sides of the branch's walls. Dally reluctantly nodded at Martin—he didn't look that old. When they left, Titan followed. He told me he was bored, wanted to do something other than talking and walking. Odd bit his lip, "We're missing someone," he said. "Othello—where'd he wander off to?"

I muttered a few words but forgot what Othello had told me.

"*Flashlights*," Faith muttered. "Something to do with flashlights."

Odd nodded to himself. "Ah, *flashlights*. Righto, convenient. I must thank you, princess, for your amazing arguing and debating skills. You left Martin in quite the thick of things."

"Hear, hear!" I added. "Hey, Odd … What's up with you and Martin anyway, the whole—what was it? *Cat thing*?"

He shrugged. "Oh, that whole issue happened over a century ago. The guy's still complaining about his bloody cat running away. Look, it's a long story, and there's a giraffe involved and a whole bunch of other stuff. But he's helpful and we owe each other a few favours."

Occasionally someone would walk past, but besides the occasional early-bird Ever, the station was rather empty. I wasn't the only one who noticed. "Empty for a main platform, isn't it?" Zia pondered. Faith and the rest discussed the topic of emptiness as Teala wandered down the platform. She stared at the black railway and the grey rocks that held it afloat. I sauntered towards her, not sure whether to grab her shoulder or stand next to her.

"You all right?" I asked.

She flinched. *Did I wake her up?*

"I don't know. Feels like I've been falling lately in my dream … Train tracks are in it. Not these ones. The tracks are similar, passing over a bridge and a rapid river."

I stood next to her, making sure our eyes met. "You think the ones in your dream are somewhere down this line?"

She shrugged, "I couldn't even guess. No, I'm okay Perry … Do you think we'll be able to see her? Do you think she'll recognise me?"

"Who? Liv?"

She nodded.

I grinned. "Of course she's going to recognise you. She'll be proud of you for being all grown up ... What's it been, almost four years since we last saw her? I think she'll have more trouble noticing me than noticing you. Are you nervous about seeing her?"

Teala shook her head. "Do you think she'll have kids?"

"Why do you say that? The dream?" I asked.

"That's it, isn't it? It's always the dream," Teala laughed bitterly. "I just want it to be over some nights, but I don't want it to just be pitch-black forever!"

I heard the train coming. "You should write it down one day. I'm sure Odd can find you a journal like Zia's. I'd like to know more about it, who this robot-arm guy is and the Man on the Boat."

Teala turned to me. "Well, to tell you the truth, I think ——"

The train passed us, the high pitch of metal grinding down the rails. I couldn't make out a single word she said.

When the steam from the train's head stopped, I asked Teala to repeat herself. Weirdly, she put her hands behind her back and smiled. "Oh, it was silly to say. Don't worry, it's better you didn't hear it anyway. I think this is us—we should ask Odd."

"If you say so." I flicked some of the blond locks that fell slightly past her temple. She giggled as another loud rumble echoed somewhere in the distance. "Hey, Odd! Is this our ——"

"Yo! Perry, Odd, Bailey! Give us a hand, will ya?" Dally waved for us to come. He was down under the platform, pushing this brown shed-like train carriage over with Martin and Titan. It was at least three times the size of him and I was surprised the three had moved it so far before Odd and I jumped onto the tracks.

"Bailey, you coming?" I asked.

He shrugged. "I don't know if it's such a swell idea to jump so far down with Kyle strapped on my back. He hasn't mumbled a word since yesternight; I don't wanna wake 'im."

Odd tossed his suitcase to Faith and began pushing the carriage next to Titan. "Oh, jump down ya big ol' cry baby. This stupid dilemma is for you, so you might as well help us move it to the back of the express train. I'll numb the pain again if he wakes." We all stared at Odd, silently groaning at his choice of words.

"Pain?" Bailey asked.

Odd rolled his eyes. "His body is melting as we speak. Without that layer of cobblestone and who knows what else ... He's probably been in pain since the minute he started screaming."

Bailey bit at his snout. "Righto. I'm comin'." He studied for the softest areas as I leaned into the brown tin can.

It was a strange-looking carriage; you could smell hay from the back. There were four windows at its front and it looked as though it was for transporting materials rather than humans or transformed Evers. Odd smiled.

"You all right there, Perry? What? You really think Othello would vanish without telling me how to look after Kyle? He's a wise man—well, he has his moments. Do you remember what Kyle said before he started screaming?"

"Are you saying something triggered the melting?" Dally asked.

Odd shook his head. "Not necessarily. I'm just curious. It's the adventurer in me."

I nodded. "It was in one of the spare tent-lets. He was—he mentioned one of his sisters, one of the octuplets. What was her name? Maggie! Said something about a doll and afterwards, we tried asking him some questions and he sounded like the troll again screaming his head off."

Odd gazed into the back of the carriage. "Interesting. A doll. What doll?"

We all shrugged as Zia plucked at her clean nails. "Hey, don't we have a creepy old plastic doll?" she said. "Y'know, under Tea's tree, where all the other stuff is?"

Teala lit up. "You're right. It was one of the mementoes we collected before arriving in Everbreen."

Faith and I stared at each other, muttering simultaneously, "*It's from under the Cobblestone Bridge!*"

I stepped away from the moving carriage. It was really moving now, but I was so excited. "I'll get it!" I shouted.

Odd raised his hand as if it were a fan. "Wait! We need your help moving the carriage, so we don't delay the express train. We don't have enough time to fool around; I get that's your speciality, but this carriage isn't going to move itself. Dally's going to give himself a migraine if he pushes his gift any harder." He turned to Teala. "Tea, how far can you teleport now?"

She stood tall. "A few streets away. Why?"

"Go back to the house and bring the doll. Just dump it in your bag and be as quick as you can. We're counting on you!"

She paused for a bit, smiling at me.

To be honest, I was proud of her; she was so fast. Once she vanished, a red mist of ash fell where her body had once stood.

Martin mustered, "I'll be rather blunt here. I don't understand what Central City's got to do with melting, dolls and cobblestone, but Odd, I think you've found yourself a funny group of youngsters. Now, just keep pushing her forwards. I'm gonna let you know when to stop so I can lock her in onto the six o'two express to Central. Just listen out for my voice."

He strolled down the opposite railway and disappeared. We continued to push and push.

Eventually, Martin's raspy voice called, "All righty, slow her down now. Keep going, keep going, going. Just a little further ... Stop. I said STOP!"

As I lifted my hands from the metal, the whole carriage dropped an inch onto the railway. It was as though it had been floating from the moment I started to push. I climbed up, helping Titan back to platform thirteen.

"How on Hope's Light did you six manage to push this thing forward? It must have weighed a tonne!" Zia put her hands by her side.

"It sure looked heavy!" Assonance gasped.

I was about to explain how light and easy it was, but Odd objected. "The tall man with the curly mane! Dally was lifting it slightly above the railway with his mind—levitating it must have been a little too much for him alone."

Bailey added, "Explains why he needed help pushin' it forward."

Dally, too concerned with shaking his head, seemed somewhat startled. "Me?" he asked. "No, it was the train man's idea. Said he knew what I could do, had an eye for these things, I don't know. I lifted it up and thankfully Titan was there." He rubbed Titan's head. "But even the two weren't strong enough to push it. So it was—well, it was mainly me, but a group effort nonetheless."

"Aye!" Martin jumped from between the last two carriages. "I told ya you were ripe and strong." He fiddled with his many keys, tossing two he had unclipped at Odd. "I suggest you all be getting on now. The train leaves in about five minutes. Good luck with it all. Odd, best give 'em back in Central City, ye hear?"

Odd nodded. "I hear indeed. We'll buy you a cat on the way. I'm sure there's a pit stop or two."

Martin walked down the platform, ignoring Odd's wink. "Ah, shut your gob. See you kids around!"

We all thanked him for his assistance, while Odd and Bailey opened the side of the metal carriage. "It's a weird-looking thing, isn't it?" Titan said.

"It sure is. What is this metal sheeting?" Zia mused.

A metallic shuttering whizzed past. "It's not meant to look nice, you spoilt royals. It's for transporting marraboo back when they were scarcer. Just get in … Faith, Perry, *come on!*" Odd ordered.

"What about Tea?" I insisted.

"She'll make it, we got time." He clicked his thumbs and Faith and I couldn't help but smile.

Once everyone was inside, we left the side open. Faith passed Odd his suitcase. Yellow hay, dry like the desert, covered most of the floor. It smelt like my old hamster, Gizmos' cage. Towards the front half of the carriage, there was a small three-step staircase, eight leather seats, four windows, two on either side, and a crappy door that led to the next carriage over. Outside, more people zoomed, anxiously boarding the train one by one. The station got full quickly!

As the rest got comfy, Assonance sat next to Zia, discussing different ways to tie up their hair. Bailey and Dally investigated what was under the hay while Odd tolerated Titan's ingenious questions on reincarnation and I waited by the opening. At some point, I guess Faith grabbed my hand. I only noticed once her shadow touched platform thirteen's concrete.

Suddenly, Teala appeared, red ash falling around her. The doll was in her hands.

"Quick, Tea!" Faith waved her over.

She jogged inside, forty seconds to spare, but as soon as Kyle spotted the doll, his eyes bolted open. Bailey ceased his fidgeting and Odd ordered me to close the carriage's side. Kyle screamed for the doll with all his might. The train honked its horn; you could hear its wheels start to move as I closed the metal container. *Everbreen was gone!*

The Gifts Of Happinness

Central City
A. The Highland District
B. The Midcourt District
C. The Blym District
D. The Sporangia Sector
1. Hartway's Abode
2. The Sumbmossa
3. The Cyrillic Forest
4. Giea Village (Ga'takiti)
5. Daegon's Apartment
6. Central Station
7. The Tired Docks
8. Pimper's Park
9. Okata Ferry Service
10. Bouddi Park
11. The Banana Cabana
12. Parliament House
13. Drown's Fountain
14. Speckle Park
15. Riverlet park
16. The Old Silk Factory
17. Old Parliament House
18. WonderWorks Retail
19. Silk Square
20. The Shaggy Docks
21. The Flatlands
22. Lake Okata

Chapter 9
Welcome to Central City
Faith

The train carriage was cold, not as if the air-conditioning was too high, but because of the rushing air seeping through the steel ridges along its walls. Heads bobbed from side to side as Odd began to explain where the Doctor lived.

"Central City isn't like Everbreen or Kelton Whide. There are layers to the streets, little nooks and hidden details. It's a lot more dangerous than you'd all think!"

Dally groaned, tightening the rope around Bailey and Kyle. "It's the capital city, where the Regime holds order. It's nowhere near as dangerous as Fleddington, is it? And in comparison to what Everbreen was like when Araidian was under control, I doubt we'll have much trouble!"

Odd shook his head. "The most dangerous thing to a man is often right under their nose." We were all quiet. Zia's breathing was heavy as my fingers began to twitch.

Assonance stood. "He's right! There are safe places like the Highland district—even the Midcourt district, where the council members stay, is secure. That's where the station is. However, parts around the plaza and some sections near the Blym district can be harsh on people. Lots of homeless Centrillians from what I remember."

Odd bit his lip. "Unfortunately, the Doctor doesn't live in those lovely places. He's a minimalist of sorts. Likes the challenge for survival."

Assonance raised her voice. "You can't be saying we're going through the Sporangia Sector!"

Odd's eyes focused on the hay around his boots. "I'm not saying *we are*. I'm saying *I am*. And I'll need Perry and Dally; you too, Faith. Bailey, you're too much of a target. Keltons, you're both too recognisable, and Tea, it's going to be ——"

"I don't care for your excuses," Zia said sternly. "Why's this one called a sector, while the rest are districts?"

It was a walled-off section, the buildings of which were part of the original Central City, previously named Sporangia after a handsome duke who battled dragons and saved princesses. His sons were diplomatic and—as the town expanded, covering as much of the land as it could—the lords began to trade with the Farmers of Hope in Kelton Whide. Assonance said that Central City spread upwards, instead of outwards like Kelton Whide. Once relationships were established, more meetings were held between the yellow-crested sailors and fishermen of Bellows Curve in the north-west, Kelton Whide and the Sporange family, regarding the trade of salt and seafood, corn and milk, and fabrics.

I tapped Odd. "What do the others do when we venture into the walls of this ... sector?"

"What do you think, Faith?" Odd grinned. I could smell the caffeine on his tongue. "Arrangements have been made. A close friend of mine is at a hearing—some new arrangements with the increase in immigration near Drewmora. That doesn't matter, I'm not fond of politics. He's going to house us while Kyle gets the aid he needs. I believe this will also be an appropriate time to visit Perry and Tea's sister, seeing that tomorrow we'll be visiting Parliament House!"

"Sweet! Which room are we visiting? The red one or the green one?"

Odd rolled his eyes. "And that means?"

"I think Perry's talking about the House of Representatives and the Cabinet Chambers," Bailey said.

As everyone began to talk at once, Teala leapt to a window. "*There it is!*" We all gathered against the left side of the carriage, crowding the windows. "*Central City!*"

Chapter 9: Welcome to Central City

A waterfall poured beside the train tracks. Above it, where the water was still, a small oval-shaped island sat upon a perfect blue reflection. Like a giant moat, the lake offered a dark blue, painted silhouette of the bush and midday sun that surrounded the capital. Behind the lake, similar to the ancient trees in Everbreen, Central City stood on an island with skyscrapers that were almost twice as tall. In the centre, the orange beacon burned upwards into the sky, beating the heartbeat of the gods. Its light illuminated the windows and maze-like walls. The train swerved a curve. I couldn't find a single building that was one storey high. Some had gardens on their walls and green ferns that looked almost artificial. Others were glass boxes, some made from old orange bricks with billboards and glowing signs for new movies and songs.

"Dally, they made another *Cowboy Man*!" Perry gasped.

Dally smiled. "Oath, that was a pretty good superhero flick!"

"It was a western!"

"No, it wasn't. It was a superhero movie, trust me."

As the two argued, the carriage's orange ridges appeared in the still lake. Odd said it was like a perfect mirror that went on and on, only to show you the truth after all the lies in life. Beyond the lake, and past the city, a small grey-wood forest swayed in the wind.

"Trees?" I wondered.

Assonance smiled. "Yes, it's the Cyrillic Forest, where the Bywoe trees live, untouched by the kings of Sporangia and the politicians in Central City. It's dangerous there!"

The closer we got to the city, the more overwhelmed I felt. The buildings were so tall; my heart leapt a beat at how they balanced. Fifty, sixty, a hundred stories. Green, and black, and grey; light rails and trams speeding past as if each level of each building had its own circuit of roads. The people far below us were like ants, bombarding the crowded waterways, darkened by the shadows of the towers surrounding them.

Between the towers, smaller buildings hid. They were white and made from a sandy marble with ancient pillars similar to Whide's Cathedral, but not nearly as long. Bit by bit, we travelled over the water. Assonance mentioned that Centrillians don't travel by car;

they row boats and canoes through canals that are centred between footpaths within the city. More colour emerged. We had reached the capital's downtown, the Midcourt district. The buildings lost their height, and it almost felt like home, minus the abandonment of trees and imperfect patches of ferns.

Here, the train lowered itself. The bright sky vanished as my own reflection covered the carriage's window. We had entered a tunnel. The train continued to wobble, then it stopped! Steam covered the outside and, when it drifted away, I could see grey concrete platforms, white circular etched pillars, and many people and animals rushing past. I could see so many coloured crests. Not just orange, but green, blue, red and black—even pink and yellow. Hundreds of people and animals crowded the station, the sunlight staining their legs and hoofs.

Odd opened the side door and I could hear Bailey gulp. "You holding up okay?" I asked.

He stared out the window. "Dere are so many fellas ... and I'm so big. An' Kyle? What will dey think? How are we gonna get through?"

"Oh, I'm sure they'll move out of the way for you!" Perry tapped his shoulder.

"Yeah, I wouldn't mess with a panda! Especially one with a knocked-out guy strapped to his back," Dally added.

The ground began to vibrate. We all stared at one another before rushing to the carriage's side. Odd leaned on the opening, his hands in his pockets. A man with a round head, small hands and long grey hair wandered by our carriage; with each step he took, the ground would tremble. He was thirty feet tall, at least, and strangely proportioned with long fingernails, hairy ears, a big round nose and chubby knees. He passed us, waving to Odd. Odd nodded at him.

"Welcome to Central City! Everbreen wasn't the only town affected by the beacons. He's from Tinkette; a leatherworker, now too big to even catch a train." He eyed Bailey. "And he can't turn back. That's who he is now. Sometimes we can't choose who we are, we just end up being something we've always been."

Zia flicked his ear. "Don't go all prophet on us, Oddington!"

He pushed her hand away. "Never. Where would the fun be in that?

Chapter 9: Welcome to Central City

And only people who are my equal call me Oddington, princess." He winked at her and instructed us to follow.

We wandered down many simple hallways, grey and gloomy, overcome by the stench of body odour, stress and soggy feet. Orange numbers told us which platform was which; an orange skirting was the only detail that decorated the walls, besides the occasional map. It was mundane in comparison to the natural beauty found inside each tree trunk I had become accustomed to. From the minute we walked out, people were very rude and obnoxious. It was like no one wanted to be where they were the second they arrived. After a few barging shoulders, Teala tugged at my hand.

Basic instinct taught me to grab hold of her and she laughed. "Faith, I'm fine. Just wanted to talk." She waved the vinyl doll about. "People sure are busy here, huh?"

"Very! It's a lot more full than Everbreen and Kelton Whide. It's like we're swimming in a pool of people," I said.

Bailey was behind us, sighing. "Maybe I should go in front. They all seem to jump out of the way the second they see me. Why is everything so big and so full? Like, I'm used to seeing fancy buildings and concreted hallways from Kelton Whide, but this is ridiculous!"

Assonance turned around, skipping sideways until we reached an escalator. "It's not always this busy; we just arrived at a bad time. Lunch is when Centrillians are always about, too busy trying to figure out what they're going to eat. You'll get used to it. I kind of missed being around so many people."

"Really?" Zia gawked.

Assonance looked at us like we were joking. "Of course. Just hearing all this commotion, it's great! Wait 'til you see outside in the Midcourt District. There's some amazing stuff out there, I'll point it all out."

We reached the main hall. The roof was so high—almost the size of the cathedral, maybe larger. Old brown cobblestone surrounded the glass ceiling and gothic arches outlined the first ten platforms; several workers in fluro-orange vests stormed around like a catastrophe had occurred. Even though there was so much space, I felt even more squished than I ever did back in our Town of Tents.

As we went to leave, someone yelled, "*Oddington!* You're not going to forget to return those keys, are you?"

Odd's body sank. He sighed, "Martin, Martin, Martin. How good of you to find us before we left. I almost forgot, how silly of me!"

We all cocked our heads. Behind a glass box, Martin was sitting in a different uniform from before. He had the same vest on as the other workers—so bright it could sting your eyes. He didn't look fatigued like the rest of us. His hands were clean; there was no dirt under his nails, and he smelt fresh.

Odd fiddled with his pockets. "How's the station here been?"

Martin took the set of keys Odd offered through a small hole within the glass. "Rather slow of late. Not as haphazard as when Kelton Whide was attacked, but still, things have been strange since the beacons were turned on. But today's quite blossoming. The Moonlight Markets are on, just outside. Some new stragglers trying to make their mark on the politicians."

Their voices went more casual, yet Odd acted as though our group wasn't behind him, waiting. "And the Regime? Has Senator Hartway arrived?"

"Hartway left the same day as you. The new bullet trains are quite effective. He arrived yesterday. For the Regime, there seems to be some tension. Mr Kingsleigh's in town, going up against the Senate."

Odd eyed him slowly. "Fantastic, Charles. He's been wanting the Senate for months now. I don't know how a mine's going to help his reputation, especially in Tinkette Valley. Thanks for the heads up, Martin. I'll be seeing you." Before he walked off, he spun around. "Oh, has Eddy been stocking up his new shop here?"

"The two-storey one?" Martin guessed. "He's been back and forth from Everbreen to Central City since the middle of the celebration season. It's been a span since I last saw 'im, but Ophelia should be overlooking the final things. She arrived last week."

Odd nodded and walked away, noticing how distracted the rest of us had become. Teala and Perry threw their train tickets into the nearby plastic garbage bin. I was standing beside Odd.

"Who's Charles?" I asked.

Chapter 9: Welcome to Central City

He stared at Perry, who was laughing with Titan about Teala's miss of the bin. Zia was going off at them. "My old boss. Charles Kingsleigh ——"

"Alice's father!"

He looked me in the eye. "If we don't bump into him, don't mention it, okay? It's best I tell you and you alone." He yelled for Assonance and asked her about the Moonlight Markets. Her face lit up. "The election's already this close? Gah, I don't know who I'm going to vote for!"

"Wait, does that mean I have to vote too?" Perry asked. "Oh, and why is no one wondering about Martin? I could have sworn he didn't catch the train with us. How'd he get here so quickly? He can't teleport, can he?"

Odd slapped his head. "Dumb question. He's a goddamn demigod; that's a perfect excuse to make it unexplainable. Like I said, Martosia has been burdened with the sanctum of the railways. How's he going to protect the train stations if there isn't one of him stationed at every station?" Odd stumbled beside Assonance. "So, I'm not too big on the whole political propaganda. Can you explain to all of us what exactly is going on? You probably know more than me when it comes to the human part of parties, elections, all that jazz. I don't even get to vote!"

Assonance was surely in her element, describing what each of the three parties were. There was the Liberal Party, the Alliance and the Socialists of the Old. There were more than three, but to her, those were the most important, each having several representatives in the House of Representatives—or, as Perry and Dally preferred to call it, *The Green Room*. She told us that the Moonlight Market was one of the biggest events leading up to the elections for the party. However, this party can only be elected through the votes of the many.

We marched outside into the giant hexagon, where several old gothic structures walled off each side, circling a giant fountain. We left the white sandstone of the station, wandered down fifty steps that spanned for far too long and entered an abundance of colourful stalls. The smell of paper, cardboard and glue was rampant. Each stand advertised someone else who was more important than the person advertised next door. Some had taglines.

For what is true and bold

Vote for the Socialists of the Old.

Prym before Kim.

We want less global warming and more job opportunities.

Brochures and little pamphlets were thrust in our faces. I could have sworn Assonance was laughing the whole way through the market. Behind the many coloured roofs of the stands, fluttering up and down with the wind, the buildings seem to go on endlessly. I could feel the debate from each politician as everyone marched through, searching for an exit.

Perry clasped my hand, admiring the sky. "It's loud here, huh? I don't even know what any of this means. What the heck is a lefty?"

I smiled. "Left-wing. The Alliance is left-wing; it's like slang for people who are into it all."

As he began talking about Kyle and how hot his body temperature had become, this family of five stumbled towards us. There were two boys around fourteen—brown curly hair, broad smiles and blue eyes—a little girl who reminded me of Teala when we had left for Everbreen. Their father hustled them to stay close, calling to a boy our age with short blond hair spiked up to the side. The eldest brother had round blue eyes darker than his brothers' and was around Dally's height but twice as skinny.

"Ei, Harry. What d'you think of this?" The father suggested.

He had a lush brown beard and strong, skinny arms like his sons'. Each child gathered around the stand, except for the little girl. She skipped through the herds of coloured-crested immigrants, stopping only once she spotted my golden wristband.

"Excuse me ... Why are you wearing that? Do yer not like your crest?"

I smiled, letting Perry's hand go and kneeling beside the girl. She had dark scarlet hair, tied in a very dad-like ponytail; her eyes were bluer than the waterfalls in the Forest of Farbe, and her skin more tanned than mine.

Perry hopped on one leg, rubbing his head. "Ah, jeez. Kid, you lost or something?" He searched for the others. "I hope you aren't lost;

CHAPTER 9: WELCOME TO CENTRAL CITY

I don't think we need any others on this trip. It's already confusing enough with everyone talking over one another."

She ignored him as I lowered my voice. "I don't dislike my crest; mine's rather nice," I said. "I see yours is blue—a dolphin! Here," I began unclenching the wristband, the metal cogs unravelling until it was loose from my arm. I pulled it off to reveal a bright white glimmering light.

Her eyes widened. "*A dragon!* Why would you cover something so rare? I've never seen anyone with a mythical crest before, certainly not a Kelt."

A voice yelled in the distance. "Ei, Taylah! *TAY!*" The eldest brother joined us, his blond hair falling over his forehead as he grabbed his sister's shoulders. "Geez. Sorry 'bout that, guys. She didn't cause yer any trouble, did she?"

The two siblings started mumbling to each other.

Perry shook his head. "Oh, no trouble at all!"

I stood up. "No, she was just wondering about my band."

Harry's grin faded. "Yer play music. That's cool."

I raised my opened wristband. "No, I ——"

Harry laughed to himself. "Ei, she does that. A little too curious for her own good sometimes." His eyes were drawn to the whispers of light on my wrist. "Oh, white crests, huh? Been in the city long?"

Perry shook his head. "Just arrived actually. Yourself?"

"We've been here three days now. It's a wild city. Anyways, sorry about the little seasnapper. Oh, by the omens! Where are my manners?" He offered his hand to us. "I'm Harry ... And this is Taylah!"

Perry shook his hand and we introduced ourselves.

I would have loved to continue chatting, but the day was disappearing. "Sorry, Harry. We need to go help a friend. Hopefully, we'll see you again. Have a good day. You too, Taylah!"

She smiled at me, and Perry and I left to catch up with the others just outside the market.

Bailey and Zia had been watching us. "Who are dey?" Bailey asked.

Perry glanced back to the family. "Miners from Drewmora. Nice people."

Zia's face lit up. "Wow, miners. What a strange life. They look friendly."

I walked beside her. "They were. The little one was cute. Reminded me of Tea. Where are the others?"

"Odd found something he knew and got all excited." Zia rolled her eyes. "He's been acting differently lately. Do you think it has something to do with Othello?"

Perry shrugged, "He's just out of his element. Normally he's two steps ahead, but with Othello and Kyle, I think he's a step behind."

I smiled. "Whatever he's running from, I hope it's not us ... Now that isn't very Centrillian!"

I gasped at a long rectangular white building. Several flags, including Kelton Whide's and Everbreen's, rustled in the wind above a dome in the middle of the roof. As we approached it, an elderly man—his wide stomach clasped tightly by his parachute pants, pink belt and peach-coloured blazer—walked down the stairs from the main entrance. His hair was completely white, and his leather boots reflected the sun's gaze. His dark knuckles were wrapped around the handle of a suitcase. He staggered for a moment, catching sight of Odd.

After a moment's hesitation, he called out, "Odd, you devil of a boy!" Coming closer, he forced Odd into a headlock. "How long has it been since I saw your pretty, ageless face? I think I've grown older—too many white hairs since you last stayed with Fletch and me."

Odd laughed childishly, pushing against the delicate fabric of the man's suit. "Well now, Genny, I still send you letters when I can. Don't get your undergarments in a twist, you balding native!" Finally, he escaped the man's clutches.

"Odd!" Dally exclaimed. "Who's this?"

Smiling, Odd patted the man's back. "My old foster father," he said. "Generalissimo Hartway. Or, as most simpletons know him, Senator ——"

"Hartway," Assonance gulped. "The head for the Rising Rights of Indigenous Inclusion and a member of the Senate of the Royal Eight."

Hartway grinned. "Looks like you've found yourself a Centrillian,

Chapter 9: Welcome to Central City

Odd! Well, how unfortunate for you. I apologise for his poor directing skills; he's never been one for leadership. Terrible talker." He winked at us, while Odd frowned.

"Look, Hartway, we don't have much time. These kids need a place to call home for their short time in Central City. We must make haste." Odd pushed through our group, untying Kyle from Bailey's back. "Our poor friend is in need of an alchemist!"

"You're going to Daegon!" Hartway pricked one eyebrow up.

Odd's mouth slumped. "Yes, Daegon! But I need you to help the panda, the Centrillian, the curious one and the two Royals so I can visit him with the aid of the other three."

Hartway stared at Titan and Zia and bowed. "The prince and princess of Kelton Whide. Masters of Glass ... You've certainly changed since your headshots. I thought I recognised your faces."

Zia pulled back her head. "I thought everyone was going to notice us, but by the looks of things, you seem to be the only one. I guess we're not as famous as we thought, hey Tye?"

Again, Hartway laughed. "Nonsense, Your Majesty. I believe it is more respect and shock. Your faces will be on the front of every newspaper by the morrow. I'm sure a thousand photos have already been taken—the media is everywhere." He turned to Odd. "I'll be honoured to have the White Lights of Hope under my roof, although I can only supply the luxuries of the Senate."

Odd lifted Kyle from Bailey's flattened fur. He carried his body like a mannequin. "Here ya go, Dalton. Make sure you don't drop him, butterfingers—he's fragile!"

Assonance raised her hand, just slightly above her head. "Can I ask, Senator, why are you here? Especially seeing that you've come from Parliament House."

Hartway played with his scruffy beard. "The Eight are meeting with the House of Representatives to discuss matters concerning the Native Title Act—you know, the Evers and the resulting change from the beacons. Their lights have shone for three years and we've barely changed as a society. I believe tomorrow is going to be one for the history books. Some very big changes are coming, I will put my life on it!"

"Wow, the Eight are coming together! It's been a long time coming."

"Wait! All of the Eight in the Senate are going to be in the same room, including Roofus from Kelton Whide?" Zia blurted.

Hartway nodded. "Yes, the King's Hand will be arriving by the morrow."

Zia's breath was fast, bursting at her chest. "He may have insight about father, may I attend?"

"Well, of course. It's why Odd brought you here, is it not?"

We all had different excuses for him.

"Oh, I see." He stared at us, eyes wandering back and forth before finally resting on Kyle. "Best we don't waste any more time; it's a long walk to Daegons. Good luck! You'll need it in the Sporangia Sector. I wish you all a safe return." He lent his hand to Zia. "If I may, princess?"

I could hear Dally mocking him behind me. Zia took Hartway's hand, just how a princess would, despite the grime and muck under her fingernails. They linked arms as Bailey and the rest farewelled us.

Teala went stiff as she hugged Perry's side. He didn't notice at first, hugging her back. "I'll be right, Tea!"

She closed her eyes. "I know you will! Just don't lose any of yourself when you're out there, okay? And be careful of the dog!"

Perry grinned. "Dog? Sure, Tea. I can't lose any more, I promise. We'll be back before you know it and my head will be in one piece. Go, protect the princess. They need you!"

Teala knocked fists with Dally and hugged me, her tight grip strangely pleasant. Before she had finished waving goodbye, the vinyl doll tight within her hands, Odd was already leading us out of the Midcourt District.

Chapter 10

The Sporangia Sector
Faith

Old sandstone walls, pointed arches and immensely detailed winged gargoyles loomed before us as Odd stopped at a grey door. A guard was stationed outside the ginormous timber gates, which rose above the Sporangia Sectors' old medieval walls. Twenty-five feet, Perry guessed—maybe thirty. Dally began to debate how safe it was to scale the stone.

A guardsman with strawberry-blond hair and a chequered orange and black uniform pushed his hand forward.

"Halt!" he instructed. "What business do you have in the Sporangia, outsider?" Inside his scabbard was a narrow silver blade. The hollow oval Centrillian emblem was embroidered proudly above the left side of his chest.

"A military man," Odd scoffed. "We simply seek to follow the gods. And an old friend owes me a favour."

The guard stood taller. "State your business or leave, simpleton."

Odd laughed. "Well now ... Would you like papers?"

"If you got 'em!"

Odd pulled up his white sleeve. "Does this explain my business?"

The guard took out a strange gun from his side pocket, placing it slightly above Odd's crest. It hummed. He lifted the gun and observed it for a moment, biting his lips and standing aside.

Odd winked at him, passing through the grey door. "Oh, those four are with me. See you in two hours."

As we passed, the third guard at the post scanned our crests with a similar machine. On its left side, white words appeared, but I couldn't make them out. Dally had to juggle Kyle to find his crest so they could scan it. Once through, Perry, his hood over his head, tapped Odd's shoulder. "The heck was that? Why'd they scan us?"

Odd turned, pushing past the timber gates and into the Sporangia Sector. "They don't scan you in Kelton Whide, do they?" he mused. "And Everbreen's too evergreen for that type of manipulation. Welcome to the real world, Perry! Do you see that code under your crest? That series of symbols from the gods and spirits is the outline of your life. How it was, how it has been and how it will be. Those machines use Giza dust from the old rocks, mushed up and amplified, to decode what it says. Centrillians are extremely wary of the Sporangia Sector. It's overflowed with immigrants—the poor, the crazy, countless other loonies. So, to keep the peace, they place a time limit on our crests. In two hours, even if we were to split up or if one of us were to get hurt, all five of us will be on the outside of these walls."

"But ——"

"*No matter what, Perry!* They've engraved it on your code, and you can't fight it. There is no escape."

I gulped. "So they branded us?"

Odd shook his head. "No, they're protecting us from ourselves. There's a reason I made sure only you three came with me. This place is not safe, so we'll be in and out; just keep your heads down and follow me as closely as you can. Don't talk to anyone, don't run or scream. Just follow. Keep him close, Dally!"

Dally frowned as he tossed Kyle over his shoulder. "And what if Kyle wakes up? He'll do all those things!"

"He won't! It's not what Othello wrote on his code. Now, hopefully, my memory is still what it was."

As we trudged through, the sector was rather homely. It reminded me of the older houses near Jinkie's Gap. They were smaller, square-shaped cottages made from a heavy orange stone and a mouldy

Chapter 10: The Sporangia Sector

cement. Each house was stacked on top of the next as if they were bricks themselves. Sporangia was layered, with many balconies and little second storeys, but in comparison to the rest of Central City, everything was quite low to the ground. Even the roads were made out of dark charcoal, hardly like the many waterways we had to pass over just to get here.

A gentleman with black bags under his eyes and veins bulging from his hands, slouched outside a two-dollar shop which had been squished inside the sector. An overpass between two dark timber buildings reflected luminous shadows as a chill numbed my spine. Mumblings erupted from our left. "Traders, they say!" I heard. It was a raspy voice, broken from age and a troublesome past.

As we continued forward, more people in shaggy clothes, all torn and rugged, drifted around us. The only thing I could see was the top of Dally's brown mane. Hell, I wanted to hold someone's hand! My heart fluttered when a younger Centrillian, quick on his feet, snatched a bag of chips from the two-dollar shop's front stand. The larger gentleman, bloodstains smeared on his grey apron, chased after him. He gave up after a while, glaring at Dally and me.

A lady with short yellow hair approached Dally. Her eyes stayed focused on him and Kyle's missing hand, but her body swayed back and forth like a hungry serpent.

"Well now, what has happened to your little friend here? Is his heart melting? I can fix him—just let me see his arm, quickly now!"

Dally pushed her hands away. "Get back! No one's touching him." The lady continued to try and grab hold of Kyle's arm, but Dally stood firm. "Unless you want to go through that wall, I suggest you stop staring." He heaved his shoulder into her. "Don't tempt me, lady!" he snarled.

We walked past and I could hear the lady hiss, "How rude!"

The buildings eventually became more crowded. A horrific scream echoed from an alley to my left. Perry readied his staff but Odd stopped us. His hand was spread out and his face was grim. The screaming came to a halt; the smell of blood lingered. Perry pushed in front of me. "Why are there no guards in here?" he demanded. "How can they just ... Why guard the outside, but not here?"

Odd gulped, staring at the sky. "'Cause this is where they keep the leftovers. Kelton Whide had the exact same system. You remember your old neighbourhood, Dally? What happened to your father?"

Dally pushed his shoulder into Odd. "Don't you dare mention my father! You don't know us, Odd! And you certainly don't know me! Just keep walking. The faster we find this doctor, the faster we can get outta here." Dally pushed ahead.

Odd raised his brows at Perry and me. "Our society doesn't treat its people fairly," he said. "We've forgotten individual potential in favour of complete and utter hierarchical power. Don't look at me like that! I would never tell, but I do advise that you let him know before he finds out ... Onwards!"

Perry and I staggered loosely behind Dally, eyes wide open, hearts heavy. "You shouldn't have come!" he mumbled.

"How were we meant to know, Pear?" I sighed. "Odd has his ways—he didn't mention that this place was like this; neither did Assonance. You heard him—no matter what happens, we will all be outside these walls within two hours."

Perry shook his head. "Yeah! No matter what, Faith. Those two hours could be the last in your code. Or mine, or Dally's, or Kyle's. Then what? What was all this for?"

"To save a friend! And if that happens, well, at least we tried. What's gotten into you?"

Perry pulled off his hood. "I just ... I don't like it when you're in danger. Otherwise, I'd be as happy as a bean! But not like this."

I walked beside him. "A bean? You want to tell him, don't you? And that paper man, he's still in your head. Look. You and I, we have each other. *No matter what!* When this is over, and when we know Kyle is getting better, we'll talk about everything and figure it out. I promise!"

Odd yelled, "Lovebirds, this is it! We're close, I know these walls."

Dally rolled his eyes. "You better, Odd! I'm getting really sick of carrying Kyle!"

Odd read the alleyway's signposts. His fingers floated towards each one like those of a composer until the fourth caught his attention. "Bingo. Dally, pass the small albino, please. I'll handle the rest of your carrying duties."

Chapter 10: The Sporangia Sector

Dally's eyes squinted. "Albino. Kyle's a Kelt."

"Oh, for the sake of arguing. Pretty please Dal-Dal, pass little ol' Kyle-the-Kelt to me. We have an appointment with Daegon!"

Dally handed Kyle to Odd, who threw him over his shoulder.

As he tiptoed, he repeated the word *flashlights* over and over, like a spell. A loud howl ricocheted off the alley's tin walls.

"Anarchy Alley," Perry mused.

We were in the thick of it now. Odd continued his chanting, clicking his fingers.

Perry whispered, "How come you don't freeze time when you click your thumbs now? I thought that's how your gift worked."

Odd's body slouched. "I can control what click freezes time, you noodle! Gah ... *Flashlights, come here ... Flash*——"

In a flash, Odd was holding himself and Kyle up against a large, dark shadow. Muffled licking was interspersed with heels scraping the ground. The beast, dark as midnight, had short black fur and two blue collars. Long claws extended from its paws. Its four ears were bent, and its two snouts were shiny, reflecting the stale air. Two enormous tongues flicked at Odd.

Odd laughed. "Flash. Lights. I see your uncle Othello brought you two a treat; calm down." Odd straightened himself, the stench of a wet dog crisp on his chin. Beside him was something unlike anything I had ever seen.

"Is that a ... a two-headed dog?" Perry wondered.

Dally nodded, "I'm seeing two. What happened to just one ——"

"Or three!" Perry gawked.

I stood my ground as the two heads examined us differently. One was more curious, the other confused. It was a Dutch hound with two heads, each reaching the top of my chest. I gulped, bracing my feet.

"Hey there, boy! Is he friendly?" I asked, leaning down.

Odd shrugged, "They can be."

The left head began tensing its teeth, snarling at my open hand. Odd continued. "But Flash here is a girl. Very sensitive. Lights is a boy!"

I apologised to Flash. The two heads tiptoed towards me, sniffing my palm and ankles. My heart was racing; you could hear it. But Flash and Lights didn't mind. Flash tilted her head to the left.

Perry folded his arms. "Is this what Othello meant when he told us *Flashlights*?"

Odd pouted his lips, shoving past the two heads and my side. "To a degree. It was more a metaphor that he had questions for Daegon."

"Why?" Dally demanded.

Odd eyed him down. "I don't know. He doesn't exactly tell me these things. But if Flash and Lights are both this happy, it means he got what he wanted. Othello can be a cruel prophet when he wants to be."

We continued down the alleyway, past a broken metal chequered fence and into what seemed to be a tiny patio. Flashlights was drenched, although it appeared it hadn't rained in months. Odd approached a dark timber staircase.

"Did you mention anything to him? I mean, Othello?" he asked.

We all pondered, reflecting on what we had discussed. We had mentioned the Floral, Ada, her crest changing colour; that's when Odd had stopped us.

"That explains it. Come on. Daegon should be up here in his study."

We climbed the steps, Flashlights leading the way. Odd opened the fourth door down a skinny grey veranda and sang, "Ding dong, special delivery. Time's up, hombre. The doctor's orders. And rumour has it that's the kind of nickname you've given yourself, Daegon."

The room was pitch black, the walls covered in monitors and orbs reflecting projections and videos of different people, numbers and letters. The Doctor, his hair a thick black, moistened by the comb of his fingers, slid his small, round glasses to the bottom of his nose. He tilted his pointed nose at Odd, who was dumping Kyle on the orange lounge.

With a raspy, devilish voice, he frowned. "Othello mentioned I should be expecting you, Odd. How nice of you to drop in; your master just left, so on you go."

Chapter 10: The Sporangia Sector

Odd sat beside him. "No, no, no, Daegon. He's your master too." Odd picked up a prosthetic metal arm with wires hanging out of it. Shards of metal fell when he raised it over his head. "Are you making a robot or something?"

Daegon grinned, "Not necessarily. Lots of missing body parts since the beacons have been turned on. Thought I'd practise some larger, more useful inventions ... I see you've brought friends. How may I help?"

Odd gestured to Kyle. "The kid! On the lounge, you spaz! I need you to help him, but not here. In the Midcourt District."

"Are you out of your mind, Odd?" He turned his head to Perry, Dally and me. "Hello, by the way! I'm the Doctor, master of alchemy, safe and free in the Sporangia Sector."

Before any of us could respond, Odd snorted, "Safe? You're joking ... Give me your arm. Give it!" Hesitating only briefly, Daegon sighed and pulled up his sleeve, revealing the orange glow of an octopus.

Odd rolled his eyes. "Gah, you have less than an hour. The exact same time as me!"

Daegon's face dropped. His cheeks flushed pink and his left hand whipped towards his face. "By the silk, Odd! I've done the math, and I'm ... I'm not meant to leave for another five years; I swear I used the right formula. I couldn't be." His eyes went wide, his mouth shut tight and his cheeks stopped moving. "Othello, that bastard. Silking!"

Odd smiled, "Whoa, language! Now look at the kid, will ya. You got fifty-five minutes!"

The Gifts Of Happinness

Chapter 11
The Drowning Girl
Bailey

Jeepers! Central City sure is tall. There are a lotta wild things in here; I can't even fetch the words to describe half of what's goin' on. So much commotion an' little to no silence when ya trek by so many different types of shops an' food joints an' service areas. *I can't even hear any birds!* Senator Hartway had a dandy apartment-house-thing. I don't know where to start, I was gobsmacked the whole time.

While Zia was treated to a first-class tour from Senator Hartway himself, Assonance explained that the Midcourt District was the largest of the districts. It's where the court an' councils come together in a sorta town square with a magnificent fountain at its centre—this was the fountain we saw in the markets. Hartway only took us three blocks west from the fountain an' opened a mahogany door to a four-storey complex. Old-fashioned orange bricks covered the walls of the shack; its roof was a perfect dark oak triangle. When the senator led us inside, I could smell pollen as rich as the Flowers of Memory.

Teala an' I struggled to get inside. Everythin' was so warm an' neat. No tree roots pierced the carpet, and no branches or leaves leaned on the opened windowsill; in fact, each window had an orange an' red curtain as though we had travelled back to when the gods trekked Euphoria. Most walls were white, and the lounge was a dark, crispy grey, reekin' of leather.

"Here, my favourite artwork from Pocassi herself," Hartway said, showin' us an art piece between the lounge room and front door.

"Such a tragic tale. One of the smaller towns where the brownies lived was bombed during the Echo Wars just a few miles west. 'Tis a stunning mural, isn't it?"

Zia paused, starin' at the strange collection of shapes. Titan rolled his eyes. "So sad!" he murmured with a sarcastic sigh.

We reached the staircase an' ... *by the Spirits under my paws*, these rinky-dink ol'-fashioned houses get my blood pumpin'. Teala turned to me as the senator led Zia up the marble staircase. Ye could hear his boots bounce. "Why'd you stop?" Teala asked.

I sighed. "I'm not gonna be able to fit up dere. It's dandy, I'll wait here; you go explore. Maybe ya can get de royal treatment like Zia!"

Senator Hartway lifted his noggin. "Are you okay there, panda?"

"Yes, sir," I grinned. "It's just, I ... I don't wish to ruin any of de senate's lovely walls an' artworks 'round ya staircase. Would it be swell if I waited 'ere?"

"Bollocks!" Hartway whispered to himself. He began leadin' Zia down the steps. "I apologise, Your Majesty. It wouldn't be fair to experience the spas and trained masseurs without you all up there. The hot tub's being freshly prepared as we speak."

Zia's mouth dropped open.

Hartway continued, "And don't get me started on the all-you-can-eat buffet. We have all kinds of foods, from buckhorn to chicken, and even some exports I delivered myself from Tinkette Valley." Titan mirrored his sister's expression.

Zia pulled her hand away. "A warm, relaxing spa, you say?"

"And all-you-can-eat ... FOOD!" Titan added.

The senator nodded, smiling glumly as the two royals prepared to skedaddle.

Assonance cheered, "That's okay, Zia. You and Titan should go and enjoy yourselves. I was just going to visit my parents, that's all. Would you like to join me, Bailey? Teala—can I call you Tea?"

"By all means," Teala smiled. "We'd love to come. Whereabouts do they live? Oh, I just gotta find a safe place for the doll first." Teala trekked 'round me, pattin' my side. She placed the doll on a spruce cupboard inside the main living room.

Chapter 11: The Drowning Girl

Assonance played with her honey-coloured hair. "Just south of here in the Blym District."

The senator's noggin went up, and he stared at Assonance. "The Blym District is not as safe as it used to be. I'd discourage you from going there in such a small group."

"But Senator, my parents haven't seen me in several years. I really need to see them!"

The senator frowned. "What happened to you, girl?"

Assonance gulped, grippin' at her hands. "It's not a happy story, Senator." She turned to me. "Can we leave sooner rather than later?"

I nodded, watching Zia an' Titan, who were gettin' lured by the scent of lavender bath bombs an' crisp battered schnitzel. They trekked up four steps before Zia stopped herself, sighing an' tuggin' on Titan's sleeve.

"We'll go with you, Assonance!" she said. "It's better we stay together than split apart. And besides, I'm kind of curious what a normal Centrillian household looks like. No offence, Senator Hartway. This complex of floors is certainly impressive—an obvious indication of your achievements—but I'll have to take that spa another time ... Can you keep the water hot for me? *Titan!*"

Titan climbed a fifth step before bein' dragged back by Zia. "Yes, yes!" he whinged. "We'll go meet Assonance's family. I wasn't hungry anyway!"

The senator grinned, his hands tightly clasped together. "No, this is just primitive—and that's coming from a native. You all must come and visit my daughter and I up in Tinkette Valley. It's much more magical than these walls. They've no history to them, no stories to tell!" He trekked with us to the front veranda. "I tell you what—I'll make sure this complex of floors is ready for all of you when you return. Do be safe out there."

He fiddled inside his blazer pockets an' waved over Teala. "Oh, and curious one, that's what Odd called you ... Keep this close. I hear you're having trouble sleeping." He handed her a web of Redmer twigs, all connected with beige strings an' white feathers. Each timber stick of the dreamcatcher had the engravings of Othello's alchemy etched red like blood. "This should help, but keep it far from Kelton Whide," he warned.

"Why?" Teala asked.

"They're taboo in Kelton, Tea," Zia scoffed. "Our wretched royal blood doesn't agree with such creations. It'd burn us if we got too close!"

"Really?" Assonance gawked.

"Yep. Tinket totems are what drove my great, great, great—a thousand times over—great grandmother Hope to madness before she became the beacon."

"Before she was Teleios?" Teala asked. "I know the story."

The senator bowed his noggin. "Keep it close, my dear! I've given it my blessing; a curious one! Just for you."

The Edath Road—which was more of a waterway than a road—was full of buildings fifteen storeys tall or more. Teala fiddled with her wooden totem. It was the size of Assonance's hand, schmick with the scent of fresh craftsmanship. "This is it!" Assonance cheered. "The Blym District."

"The buildings are so tall! How'd you live here? Especially in a house!" Zia asked.

"I didn't live in a house, Zia," Assonance giggled. "My parents and I lived in an apartment building, which I hope they still rent. Maybe they've bought it by now ... Trust me, these aren't even that tall. The buildings get taller the further away you get from Lake Okata."

I crawled behind Titan, gazing at a passin' airship. A zeppelin-like machine was overhead; on its sides, where the balloon reflected the beacon's orange light through the many windows of each buildin', advertisements for a soft drink played.

"Dat's a bonkers airship!" I gasped.

Teala lost focus on her totem. "Sure is. It's like half the size of Araidian's one!"

"Well, I can tell you that there are no giants around that can knock these zeppelins down!" Assonance cheered.

"*Zeppelins.* As in plural?" Zia exclaimed.

Assonance nodded, waitin' for the set of lights to turn red. "Yep! Tons of 'em. When I was learning business in school, they said it was best to learn it here as Central City has the highest consumption rate in all of Oberon."

Titan picked his nose. "I was wondering why there were so many screens."

"Screens?" I asked.

"Yeah, advertising screens," Titan pointed at the next zeppelin over yonder. "Like on the side of those zeppelin things. It's kind of clever."

The passing canoes an' hovercrafts came to a sudden halt. The waterway pulled apart an' the sound of gushin' water sounded as a bridge formed with several concrete pieces protruding from the water. *Five, six, seven!* Seven dark orange slabs appeared an' floated above the water, connectin' the two sides of the waterway. A giant herd of fellas migrated from one side to the next. We made it across an' the bridge was empty. The seven pieces sunk back into the waterway an' the traffic continued.

The buildings must a' grown from fifteen storeys to maybe sixty in the space of four blocks. There were lots of fellas, mostly Centrillian; however, I did spot a Fledding, a Drewan and an Islander strollin' with their red, blue an' black crests. I even saw other Evers like me. There was yellin', cigarette smoke, strokes of water—far too much commotion an' it was all too fast!

The more we trekked the more construction seemed to be underway. This differed in Everbreen—the new infrastructure for Evers was barely underway at home. Men in orange hardhats hung off human-made glass cliffs, movin' details of each building 'round. Doorways were gettin' larger, new elevators an' escalators were bein' put in, an' half the sidewalks had grown to fit me an' another three fellas. If I'm frank, I thought I'd feel more overwhelmed, but it's not too nutty here. We reached a triangular building, forty-seven storeys tall, called the *Sumbmossa*. Named after the God of Ice, Sumbria, I think. Assonance started to bloom. Her eyes sparkled as the glass lobby door split apart.

"This is it, I'm home!"

Inside, there was a fish tank, silver an' orange chequered tiles an' a chilly air-conditioner. I could smell sanitiser as if the janitor had just mopped.

Zia stared upward. "Wow, that's a lot of elevators. Do you think Centrillians know what stairs are?"

"Would you walk thirty flights of steps every day just to go home? And then thirty again when you leave for school?" Assonance smirked.

Zia undid her bun, straightenin' her hair before tying it up again. "Fair point. Thirty flights of steps, how many is that in total? Bailey, what's twelve times thirty?"

I lowered my brows before stuttering, "I ... I'm not sure. Math was neva' my strong point. Uh ... Let me think. Three hundred an' ninety steps."

"You walked four hundred steps every day! Now that's commitment." Titan laughed as an older couple stepped out of the second elevator.

Assonance turned to Titan. "I didn't walk up any staircases, Titan. There aren't any stairs to begin wi———"

The couple passed us and the golden walls of the lobby. Under the lights, the miss was pale; she had similar rich honey hair like Assonance an' familiar brown eyes. The fella was well dressed an' had a thick beard similar to many Drewans we'd met before. They held each other's hand.

Assonance stood tall an' called, "M-M-*Mum! Dad!* It's—I'm home!"

The couple turned 'round. The miss lit up the second her eyes caught Assonance.

"Ona!" she cried. "It can't be you—you ... they said you and your ..."

The two collided, huggin' for a moment. Teala stopped starin' at her totem, placing it 'round her neck, an' Zia leaned her elbow on my fur.

"Well this is nice, isn't it?"

"What should we do? It's kind of awkward if we just stand here and watch." Teala whispered.

"Let's take three steps back an' act like we're just visitin' de complex," I said.

We all took a few steps back an' whistled away from the laughter

Chapter 11: The Drowning Girl

an' excitement. Assonance held her pa's hand an' then her ma's. She was so busy smiling, she almost forgot we were there 'til Titan whistled louder.

"Oh, mum, meet my friends from the town we made." She dragged her ma toward us. "This is Teala. She has this crazy dream she sees every night and it builds up and up and ... Oh! This is the Princess of Kelton Whide." She put a finger on her ma's mouth. "Shh! Don't tell anyone, we can't let anyone know just yet. And this is her brother, the Prince. He's a cutie, isn't he? They can manipulate glass. Like without fire and stuff. And it just moves. It's crazy ... Oh, and I can't forget. This is the one and only Bailey. He's an Ever who turned into a panda when he was like fifteen. How crazy is that!"

We greeted her ma an' her pa came an' shook everyone's hand. He thanked us an' patted my forehead. *Just how I like it, I guess.*

After discussin' where Assonance had been an' how she had been taken captive inside Irene's Family's Lair three years prior, her ma almost couldn't stop cryin'. Her pa wanted to tell the military an' search for the lair, but we explained what happened to Irene an' Araidian. Between all the dilly news an' the happy smiles an' tears, Assonance's pa asked, "And what of your brother?"

Zia's eyebrows clenched. "You have a brother? Why didn't you ..."

I nudged her shoulder.

"Oh ... Not my place to say. I apologise," Zia said.

Assonance's ma bit her lips. "A princess apologising to my daughter. Don't be so nonsensical, Your Majesty. You have a right to place your voice above any person. We may be Centrillian, but your ancestors did help build Central City into what it is today."

"Yuri ran away!" Assonance gulped. "I couldn't—he ... They hurt him! They changed him, Mum." Assonance had tears fallin' from her eyes.

Before either her ma or pa could comfort her, the receptionist interrupted the reunion. "Mr and Mrs Milk. I apologise. Especially under such ..." the receptionist sighed. "I'm sorry, it's just my manager called. We have other guests arriving soon and plenty of visitors. He requested that you all move into another part of the complex. I'm sorry to do this."

Assonance's pa wiped tears from under his eyes. "That's okay, Bec. Thank you for letting us know, we wouldn't want to get in the way of your manager's business, especially during this busy time of year. Why don't we take this upstairs? Would you kids like to join us? We'll make you some tea, isn't that right, honey?"

"Yes, I believe we have some crumpets and cupcakes, fresh from the bakery."

We all agreed.

As we approached the elevator, I stopped, sighin'. "I think it's best if I stay down 'ere. It was lovely meetin' ya fellas. I don't think it'd be a dilly idea if I got in the elevator with you all. I'm too ... *y'know*."

Teala whispered somethin' to Assonance an' they both smiled. "I'll wait with you, Bailey," Teala said, strolling towards the exit. "But if you guys could bring some cupcakes out, that would be lovely. I'd like to hear some more of Mr Milk's stories."

"Dat makes two of us," I growled. "We'll see ye fellas 'round. I'm glad we could bring Assonance back home!"

Outside, a yellow ferry burst steam from its chimney. I admired the many adverts for some new blue hat. Teala flicked my green cap, my ear hairs rustlin' from her palm. "Hey, look at that! Aren't those the same brand of shoes you like—you know, the pair you lost in the Holiday River?" she asked.

I stared at this sizeable rectangular poster. "Yeah. It is! They got new ones now." In the corner, under the advert's tagline, *Crokkies ... More than just a shoe*, I could see a familiar logo. "Wow, Alice's father is promoting 'em. I didn't know dey owned property in Central City."

Teala sat on a bench, kickin' her feet back an' forth. "I think WonderWorks owns property in most major cities. There are only two towns that don't have their towers ... You think that's why he's here?"

"Why who's here?"

"Alice's father. Do you think he's trying to get property in Tinkette Valley and Kelton Whide?"

I shrugged, "I couldn't tell ya. I'm no business fella. But it's a dandy guess ... How'd ye know he was 'ere? Ya dream?"

"Kind of." Teala suppressed a laugh. "I overheard Odd mentioning it to Faith. But it's not him who was in my dream."

"If it wasn't him, who'd ya see?"

Teala gazed at the sky. Her eyes were round. "A man covered in paper, with two swords an' no words."

I raised my eyebrows. "Poetic ... Does it mean anythin' to ya?"

She shook her noggin an' giggled. "No. It's just my dream ... How long do you think they're going to be?"

I glanced at the *Sumbmossa's* maze of windows. "As long as dey need. Not seein' someone for a long period of time—I'm sure it's hard to see family again. I know it can be."

Teala patted my noggin. "A while then," she said. "That's okay, you're probably the only person I'd like to be stuck outside with anyways! You're happy, aren't you?"

I scrunched my face. "Uh ... I guess. I'm not *not* happy. Why do ya ask?"

Teala leapt from the wooden seat. "Just curious. It's a funny question, that's all."

I followed behind her. "Wha'? What makes ya happy?"

"Yeah. Like dancing, family, swimming in the ocean. All sorts of things. It's a good question 'cause people act funny when you ask it."

"I guess when ye put it like dat! Let me guess, ya not happy 'cause we have to wait?"

She stopped and turned to face me. "Nope. I volunteered to be here. I don't mind. I'm not happy because you don't have any fun ideas or plans for us. All you want to do is look around. Let's go exploring."

"Oi! I do have ideas an' ... plans. An' you can offer some ideas as well—I'm all ears!"

Teala continued gigglin'. "My idea was to ask for your ideas. Are your ears happy now?"

I sat my bottom down on the cold sidewalk. "Dandy ... Hmm. Wanna play *I Spy*?"

We played a few rounds. First round, Teala spotted an owl. The second I noticed a purple crest—a person from Bungonia. The third was a unicycle an' the fourth an orange sweater. We walked 'round the side where another fountain had been dug into this tiny town square, spurtin' water into the sky. The flying water dropped an' landed in a deep pool. The shapes etched in the fountain's side reminded me of the old symbols of the spirits found in the Heart of the Forest in Farbe. I was sittin' beside it, facing Teala as she picked another object. Her eyes were tight as she examined the smells of chlorine an' the taste of the hotdog stand two-metres behind her. As she gandered, she muttered, "I spy with my hopeful eye. A-A-A ... *A drowning girl?*"

I titled my noggin. "Tea, ya not meant to say it aloud. We've been through this like three times now. I can't believe ya albinos don't play I Spy in Kelton Whide!"

Teala's face was now white as snow. "No, I'm serious Bailey. Behind you! There's a drowning girl, she—we need to do something."

I spun 'round an', sure enough, a girl was face-first in the fountain. It was as though she was possessed. I threw myself into the water. *It was freezin'!* Teala was behind me. The crowds of commuting fellas that surrounded the fountain stopped what they were doing to watch us.

I nudged the girl as hard as I could with my snout. I heaved an' heaved 'til her body flipped 'round. Her face was above the water, eyes shut tight, face a cold white an' lips dry. I could smell her soul, smell it weakenin' inside her chest. Teala picked up the little girl an' threw her onto my back. We skedaddled out of the fountain an' once we reached the concrete city, the fellas watchin' returned to their hustle as though nothin' had happened.

Teala, outta breath, stared me in the eye. "Told you I saw a drowning girl! Why does this crap always happen around us, Bailey?"

I grinned, water drippin' past my eyes. "I have no idea, Tea. Maybe we're cursed."

"Is she still ——"

"She's swell," I said. "I can feel her heartbeat an' her crest is alight … Best we lay low for now. Can ye teleport us somewhere sunny? A rooftop?"

Teala analysed the region behind me. "I have an idea."

I sniggered, "'Bout time. On my mark." I began breathin' deeply.

Chapter 11: The Drowning Girl

I could hear the sounds of canoes driftin' past, the sizzle of the hot dogs, my heartbeat an' the water dripping off Teala's pants an' my fur. The street became cloudy, a subtle mist covering the streetlights, journeying towards us 'til the only thing ye could see was a wall of grey fog and the fountain's water. Teala held my fur. A red light glistened. All that remained was fallin' red ash.

Chapter 12
Mr Bear's Reunions
Bailey

The fog began to disperse once we laid the little girl on a large generator—I think it was for the air-conditioner. The sunlight was refreshin', a welcome change from the crowded streets an' clustered alleyways. Teala glanced to the streets, her noggin stickin' out like a meerkat.

"Do you think anyone noticed?"

I watched with her. "No, it was just a foggy moment in time."

Down the street, Zia an' Titan emerged from the crowd. I nudged Teala. "Well, someone noticed. Can ya tell 'em what's goin' on?" Teala nodded. Before she vanished, I said, "Make sure ya don't get seen, Tea! I'll look after the lass, make sure she's not shook when she wakes."

"Don't worry about me, Bailey! I'm not Perry. Besides, I brought my earphone. Hopefully, Zia decided to wear hers. We can stay in contact."

I nodded, showin' her my left ear. A grey device was wrapped 'round the black hairs an' Teala's voice projected from its microphone's end. "I neva' leave home without it!" I laughed. "Now get goin'."

When Teala disappeared, I tried to get in contact with Zia. Fortunately, she was one step ahead of us. At first, her voice was fuzzy, but it eventually cleared. "Bailey! Bailey, come in. Can you hear me?"

"Loud an' clear, mate!" I said.

Zia sighed. "Why'd you fog?"

CHAPTER 12: MR BEAR'S REUNIONS

"I didn't fog. That's not what it's called!" I paused, scoping the concrete jungle. "Teala an' I ran into a dilemma. Dere was a girl. Look! Teala will explain everything. Turn left just up ahead an' make sure Titan doesn't do anything goofy, right?"

Zia glanced up. Her eyes examined all the roofs, tower to tower, 'til she grinned at me. She put her thumb up an' pushed Titan to the right. I could hear Teala appearin' and then a moan behind me. *This wasn't from my earphone! It was the girl!*

My paws clenched at the gravel as the little lass, dark red hair drenched in the shade, raised her noggin. She rubbed her eyes, moanin' at the intense sunlight. *Musta had a headache!* It wasn't long before she noticed me. She squinted, then her eyes widened.

"Excuse me. Mr bear ... are you okay?" she asked.

"Hmm? Am I okay?"

The girl smiled. "Oh, he can speak. You're an Ever—I've met one of you before. How did I get up here? Do yer know, Mr Bear?"

I moved closer to her. "Aren't ya scared of me?"

She shook her noggin. "Why would I be scared of you? You're an Ever. And I'm a Drewan; we're cousins."

"Sounds 'bout right if ye ask me!" I smiled. "Me an' a mate, we saved ya. Do ye 'member what happened?"

The girl scrunched her face again, bitin' her lip. "No! I'm not sure. I remember there was water and ..." She began pickin' herself up. "Well." Her feet were not as strong as she thought, "I'm not much of a fan when it comes to water, 'cause—Ah!" She fell back.

"Oi, now! What kinda Drewan doesn't like water? Ye must be a very special kind a' Drewan to be sayin' things like dat!"

The girl leaned on me. "Please," she said. "There's lots of Drewans like me! And anyways ... What kind of Ever is black and white? I've never seen a bear like you before."

I made sure she was stable before movin' away from her side. "I'm a panda bear. But you can call me Bailey! What's your name?"

"Taylah. Have you seen my brothers?"

"Ya brothers?"

Teala an' Zia appeared on the roof.

Titan fell to the ground behind 'em. "Let's never do that ever again!"

Taylah hid behind me. "Taboo! You broke the rules. Bailey, they used their powers inside the city!"

I put my forehead on Taylah's. "It's dandy. Dese are my mates. They're not gonna hurt ya. We're 'ere to help!"

I took a deep breath, turning to Zia. "How's Assonance?"

"She's good," the princess said. "Give her some time. They need it. I think she's going to sleep the night. So this is the girl, huh? This little one was at the markets today. I remember you—the mining family."

I turned. "De ones Faith an' Perry met."

"Precisely," Zia cheered. "Are you lost?"

Taylah nodded as Teala barged through. "We'll help you find your family." Teala offered her hand. "We've got nothing else to do!"

Titan lifted himself from the pebbles. "There's an all-you-can-eat buffet with my name on it." Everyone turned towards him, glarin'. He gulped, "Which, is going to be warm when we get back *after* finding this girl's family. I'm sure of it! Would you like some food?"

Taylah shook her noggin.

Titan cheered, "Great! More for me. All right, let's make this quick. Down the fire escape we go. Let's move, Team Titan!"

Zia shook her noggin. "No! No *Team Titan*. But he has a point ———"

"That we're a team and Titan is in it!" Titan blurted.

"No, not that, Tye. It's a royal promise." She winked at Taylah, who took hold of Teala's hand.

Teala was about to head to the fire escape's door, but before she pulled on the doorknob, she turned to me an' pushed her lips tightly together. She yanked Taylah over to my side. "Yeah, yeah, you're too big. I know, I know. Every time, Bailey! When are these cities going to finish their renovations so Evers can finally fit inside their hallways? Hey, little one, what's your name?"

"It's Taylah!" I said.

Taylah admired Teala. "Okay, can you close your eyes for me please?" Teala asked. "Just real quick! On the count of three ... One. Two. *Three!*"

Chapter 12: Mr Bear's Reunions

We were back in the middle of an alleyway. I'm not a hundred per cent sure, but it seemed to be close to the fountain. Teala's breath was heavy, her lips dry as her eyes flew from side to side. *Lucky!* No one was around. Even the homeless seem to be dangerous when it comes to using ya gifts within the perimeters of a major city.

"You guys coming or do I get to eat back at the Senator's place?" Titan exclaimed, exiting the fire escape with Zia.

We searched the capital for what felt like almost a whole leap. We trekked past the Sporangia Sector's archaic walls, their sharp sandstone arches an' gargoyles the size of—*well, me,* an almost fully-grown bear. Past the eerie walls that scaled far too high, we approached a shoppin' district. Towers shrunk from twenty-storeys to five. Familiar brands from both Kelton Whide an', surprisingly, Everbreen glowed above us on the fronts of each complex. There was the Kelton company, SHOE—they sold clothes an', ironically, no shoes—a round building with a large wavy *M* an' the smell of deep-fried chips, an' a rather small two-storey concrete shack with an orange imprint above its main entrance—*EDDY'S*.

We glanced inside, but there was no one there. No Ophelia, no Eddy, no potted plants or herbal incense. Teala moaned as we continued down the aisle. "Gah, he'd know what to do. I think he'd say, *oh just turn left, then right and you'll be able to find the little one's family in no time.* I'm sure. And if it was Ophelia, she wouldn't know anything, but she'd try her hardest to help."

Taylah glanced at the orange sign, which was reflected in her ocean-blue eyes. "Do you know him, Eddy?" she asked.

As we explained who Eddy was, Zia stormed in front, swindling a newspaper from a shop we passed. She chewed on a green apple, her eyes scrollin' an article. She sucked on her lower lip as her eyes jumped from the newspaper to me. "Bailey, do you want my core?"

I glanced up. "Sure, I'll eat it if ye don't want it ... Hey, Taylah! Where are ya brothers again?"

Taylah tugged on Teala's hand. "I'm not sure. We're staying with a family friend."

"Is this family friend a part of the council or any parties?" Teala asked.

Taylah shrugged. "I don't know, sorry. It shouldn't be too hard; they'll be on the lookout for me, I promise."

Titan rolled his eyes. "Oh, boy! There goes the all-you-can-eat." He approached Zia. "Any word on Father?"

"No. He's still missing," Zia sighed. She threw me the core of her apple an' we resumed our search.

Past more shoppin' brands, a cinema, an old lookin' motel called the Spor Spor Inn and the dockyard, where the water reflected the orange hues of the sunset an' the beacon, we approached the Highland District. The difference between the two districts was immense. Buildings again grew, but this time, at the foot of the Highland District, the towers bent. Some spiralled, others had larger, more rounded roofs with green grass an' ferns planted on their sides, below their many windows an' the giant televisions, which flashed all sorts of propaganda—one even mentioning the attack in Kelton Whide.

Before we entered the district, a male voice emerged. "Taylah! Hey, Tay …"

Two others, slightly younger but with a similar pitch, echoed, "Is that Tay?"

"I don't know. Why don't you ask?"

"I don't wanna ask. You ask!"

"Are yer scared? What if it isn't Tay?"

"Well, it looks like Tay. How many guys do you know look like Tay, huh?"

The older voice erupted. "Shut up, yer hosers. I'll ask!"

This blond boy, 'bout Perry's age, approached us. "Excuse me, Mr Ever. I don't mean to barge in. But have any of you seen my _____"

"*HARRY!*" Taylah dropped Teala's hand an' skedaddled to her brother.

The two siblings hugged. Harry yelled to his brothers. "James! Leo! Come here. We found Tay!"

Chapter 12: Mr Bear's Reunions

Everyone collided, Taylah gaspin' about the whole afternoon. She talked 'bout the drowning an' teleportin'.

When they settled, a familiar voice laughed behind the family. Odd, the rest of our group an' a two-headed critter behind 'im, put his hands on his hips.

"Well, isn't this a nice reunion!" he cheered.

Chapter 13
Omahwei
Perry

After Odd explained everything to Matthew Doubtson, Harry and Taylah's father, we left the family with smiling faces and a concern for the meeting tomorrow. Matthew raised a question about the senate disagreeing with the integration of a WonderWorks' mine inside the borders of Tinkette Valley's national heritage. It'd be against both the spirits and omens if they built such an exploitive, resource-consuming factory inside such a naturally preserved area.

Odd smiled. "No need to worry, Mr Doubtson. Just look after your family. I promise you that Tinkette Valley won't end up like the Old Mine in Drewmora. WonderWorks has power, but not enough to disturb the peace of the gods and spirits. We don't want another Echo War. Senator Hartway won't budge and, with Senator Carvanah, the King's Hand will make sure the farmland in Kelton Whide is secure. Especially after the attacks and, most importantly, when the prince and princess of Kelton plan to attend."

Matthew glanced at Zia and Titan. "I thought I had seen you two before." He bowed. "Yer Majesty. Highness. Simpalo."

Zia lowered her eyebrows.

Matthew grinned. "It means good fortune, that yer both matter."

On the way back to Hartway's, I felt kind of bad for Bailey. The poor guy had to support the crinkly weight of Daegon on his backside.

"Is no one going to acknowledge the two-headed dog?" Zia blurted.

Dally mused, "It's half dog, half marraboo. Daegon's somehow kept it alive." Daegon laughed, his eyes stuck on Kyle, orange symbols floating above his slumbered body. "Flash and Lights are a cultural privilege in Sporangia!" The Doctor said. "I'm certain that when Odd used to walk on this island with Othello way back when pimpers walked upon Euphoria, most people would likely have a wairith beside them ... You've certainly brought a lot of uneducated people with you, Odd!"

Odd laughed, "They don't travel much. You've met albinos before—they stick to their patios and crops, not wanting to leave."

The senator was going through an immense amount of papers on the front veranda. He was reading them out loud, yet when we arrived, he stopped to look at us. "Well now. The food and baths are still warm. Come in, come in. I'll give Kyle and the alchemist my bedroom. It's the largest and probably the most secure and safe for Daegon's practice." We entered the white marble mansion and I finally got to chill. When our skins were clean, our bellies full, and Bailey's fur combed and unknotted, I woke the next morning next to Faith.

Her face was so still, and she smelt of strawberries and coconut. I wanted to seize the day and not look back. The orange orb behind Faith said one past six. When I read it, I knew a smile lingered in the corner of my mouth.

"Morning," Faith murmured.

I shoved myself closer to her, our noses almost touching. "Morning. How'd you sleep?"

"Like a baby!" Faith laughed, "It's nice to be in a warm bed under such nice sheets."

"Do you mind explaining how nice they feel?"

She grabbed my hand, wrapped hers around mine and smiled. "Like holding someone's hands on a beach. Or ... Eating chocolate with strawberries."

I leaned in closer. "Is that right?"

Faith listed more sensations. "Maybe more like the sound of the piano when the person playing knows the perfect tune. Or the smell of a fire after a long day. Or even—and maybe I'm exaggerating a little—but that feeling I get inside when I'm with you."

I kissed her, the taste of her lips perfect. I breathed in as I pulled away, hearing Odd thumping about above us.

Dally walked into our room, gulping at the sight of our closeness.

"Um ..." He began closing the door, apologising for the intrusion.

Faith picked herself from the white linen. "It's okay, Dalton. What's the word?"

He leaned on the door. "We're leaving soon for Parliament House ... Pear, you should see the smile on Tea's face. Hartway said that Olivia's there. She doesn't know you're in town ... I'll give you two some space."

"Thank you, Dally. We'll be out soon." He closed the door gently and was gone.

I bit my lip. "Wow ... *Liv!*"

Faith nuzzled me. "Are you nervous?"

I shook my head. "I don't think so ... It's just ... If I've lost my feelings and Teala's lost her dreams, what do you think Liv's lost?"

"I suppose we'll find out. Gosh. Maybe she's like me and hasn't lost anything!"

I nodded, "Maybe ... Have you seen my hoody?"

Odd and Hartway were arguing their way downstairs.

"Genny, I'm not insisting that you do anything, just wear the vest in case. Who knows what could happen today?"

Hartway stopped at the end of the staircase. "*I* know what's going to happen. Trust me, Odd. If I were in any danger over a meeting with the eight, someone like General Ko would have intel. His militia have been stationed, guarding each member of the senate for the past week; they'd know if anything was suspicious."

Odd waved his arms about. "Yes, but with what Daegon and Othello discussed and with Charles Kingsleigh organising this whole ordeal ... I know him." Odd began adjusting Hartway's tie. "He's got a lot of enemies. And it's not you I'm worried about, it's him. I don't want you to get involved with his insanity, let alone *end* simply because you were in the way."

Hartway smiled. "Othello will be there, as will you. There will be mountains of militia stationed at every wall. The Centrillian guard gets trained just outside its walls, so if anything happens to either Mr Kingsleigh or me, it'll cause a war—well, maybe not a war, but a big fuss. Trust me Odd. *Kimpotium na-la!*"

Odd sighed, nodding.

He turned his head and noticed us watching. Eyeing me down, he raised an eyebrow "What? Oh, your jacket's upstairs. I think Teala had it last, got cold last night."

Hartway approached us. "Are you excited to see your sister? She's a good lass!"

I nodded, "It'll be nice. I don't really know what to say to her."

Hartway laughed, approaching the front door. "Oh, I'm sure you'll do fine. It's not what you say that counts, it's how you feel! Now I have to practice my argument against the WonderWorks mine in Tinkette Valley. I'll be outside where the world's nature can hear me." He winked at me as Odd slouched on the railing.

"What's wrong with you?" Faith asked.

Odd stared at us. "Not much. It's just Daegon. I'll have to go through it with him again when we get back. For now, breakfast!"

We followed him upstairs. Teala jumped on me the minute we entered the dining room. She had my jacket, its white sleeves dangling past her hands and waist. Hugging my side, she cheered, "Did you hear the senator? He said Olivia's working today in Parliament House. Odd's going to take us to see her!"

"Really! Is that how this whole thing works? What about the meeting? With the senate? Don't you have to attend, Odd?"

"Since when did I say that?" Odd asked. "I guess I'll attend, seeing that my old foster father and boss are there, but I don't legally have to be there when it happens. And don't worry, I'm a man of time. It'll work out. We'll visit Olivia a few hours before the meeting. And you'll be fine. It'll be like visiting Zia and Titan in the Castle of Glass!"

"I've never been inside the Castle of Glass before," Dally objected.

"Neither!" Bailey added.

Odd rolled his eyes. "Don't worry. The meeting isn't 'til this afternoon. Hartway wants us there early so he can prepare for the meeting and file some more papers. I don't know, some legal mumbo jumbo!"

We ate like kings and queens; I certainly know how Titan and Zia felt back in the Castle of Glass. I gobbled some bacon and eggs, having a competition with Dally to see who could make *the best breakfast roll muffin thing*. Turns out Titan was better than both of us. Before our plates were dry, Daegon, black bags under his eyes, stepped out of Senator Hartway's ensuite. He smelt as though he hadn't washed in three years and joined us in the kitchen, grabbing a red apple.

"So how's Kyle?" Zia asked.

Daegon bit into his apple. "Well, princess. Your friend has been an absolute nightmare. Reversing such a polarising issue, so deep within his body has had me restless. His whole muscular system, his entire structure of blood and bone was decaying." Daegon sat next to me, rubbing his eyes. He searched everyone, biting again into the apple. "Can someone please explain to me why he's even like this to begin with?" The Doctor asked.

We all examined the room, avoiding his eyes.

Titan shrugged, "'Cause he was a troll like not even two days ago, you stale corn."

"A troll?" Daegon queried. "What, like the ones in Tinkette Valley? Like when they tell kids about Gieas turning naughty children into beasts of stone and gargoyles?"

"I'm sorry. I didn't understand half of that," Teala admitted.

Daegon laughed at himself. "Oh, that's right. You're albinos—well, the majority are." He admired Bailey. "Don't worry. Evers are much more preferred than bloody white-bloods with their invisible fields and cow crops. Pesky farmers, you lot! Oh, I remember you, young lad. You lost ya stomach."

Titan groaned.

Odd stood from his seat. "That's enough, Daegon. They may be albinos, but they're the best you'll meet for the next million miles."

Daegon licked his apple and grinned, "No, no, it's fine ... Your friend should be back to normal by the morrow; however, there may be some alterations."

"Alterations? What exactly are you implying?" Faith asked.

"Well, it's hard to recover what is already lost. The best way for me to make him as normal as Perry or—let's say—the prince, is if I let the body melt and reconstruct it based on what is left over through a gravity lens."

"A gravity lens. What, like the things they use in orbs?" I asked.

Daegon nodded, "Precisely. Your friend will still be alive, and he'll be able to eat and sleep, however, he'll be a little ... *mooshie*, for lack of a better word. The gravity lens will hold his fragile goopy-self together in a solid form that reflects my own. And yours, Odd's— every person who hasn't been affected by the beacons."

"So you haven't stopped the melting?" Dally snickered.

Daegon laughed. "Of course I have. I've just got other larger projects on my mind if I'm honest. He should be fine, it's just what has melted is gone forever. Hence why I explained everything beforehand. Any more questions?"

Dally slammed his hand on the table. "Kyle better be the most important thing that's on your mind. Otherwise, Imma have to ——"

"Dally! Enough!" Odd ordered. "I promise you, Daegon is going to be doing the best he can for Kyle. 'Cause if he's not ... Well, we don't have to linger on that ... Quick, eat up. We leave on the hour."

Daegon stayed behind, smashing the orb in the living room before preparing for his alchemy. He took a bunch of items, including vinegar, lentils, a glass jar, the gravity lens, nail clippers and a toothbrush. He said the latter was for himself as he wanted to test Senator Hartway's bathroom. We left, Bailey and Odd leading the pack with Hartway. Faith and Dally were discussing how similar Evers and Tinkettes were. Bailey and Hartway even knew the same slang, like *schmick*. *Who'd have thought?*

As they headed towards the centre fountain, they noticed that the Midcourt District had changed. The smell of expensive brochures, the constant sound of debate after debate, the timber market stands and the people who supported each party were gone. Unlike yesterday, the Midcourt District was almost underwhelming. We approached the building Senator Hartway had walked out of yesterday.

Parliament House was very Keltic in its design, matching the architecture of Whide's Cathedral and Kelton Grammar. Its hallways, from the entrance to its many nooks an' crannies and the sporadic mix of elongated offices, had cream-coated walls, orange skirtings and an abundance of clustered artworks similar to Othello's house. Bailey's paws were a perfect fit inside the places Hartway took us. He said that Parliament House had gone under countless renovations to improve the quality of life for Evers after the green beacon was turned on.

Zia laughed, "Every place we go there seems to be scaffolding, tradesmen, new doors and elevators. Is that something the senate have discussed?"

"Thoroughly, my dear princess," Hartway mused. "After the attacks in Kelton Whide, we had a meeting. 'Tis hard on our parliament now that the beacons have become a part of our daily lives."

Faith's eyes lingered on the senator. "If my memory is correct, Central City's beacon was the last to be turned on. Araidian never reached the capital, did he?"

Hartway shook his head. "You're correct, Faith. Araidian never stepped on this island. The Regime made arrangements with him. They turned the orange beacon on for the freedom of Kelton Whide. He did what he agreed to; however, we had no idea how powerless Everbreen had become. Before the Regime had any control over the situation, Araidian was on his way to begin a war. However, he never set his giant beast upon the Centrillians. He was found unconscious inside Everbreen's WonderWorks. That's another reason why today's meeting is so difficult. Charles is using the capture of Araidian under his property as a point of argument."

I rushed to Hartway's side. "And what of Araidian? Is he in Golden Time?"

"No, he's being dealt with. Isn't that right, Odd?" Hartway said.

"Wait! Odd, Araidian isn't in Golden Time?" I blurted.

Dally rolled his eyes. "You've got to be joking!"

Odd put his hands up. "Easy now. He was taken under the command of the Drewan Army. He's one of the seven inmates inside the Honeycomb."

"What? The big hole in the Jackson-Lee desert?" Bailey asked.

Odd nodded, "Spot on. He's more secure than a vowed monk's virginity!"

Chapter 13: Omahwei

Titan snorted, laughing.

Zia growled, "Really, Oddington!"

"What'd I say about using that name, princess!" Odd scowled.

Hartway smiled, turning to face us. "It's time I leave you all for a few moments, while I prepare myself for this afternoon. I wish you all good fortune. Omahwei."

Teala licked her lips. "What does that mean?"

Hartway laughed to himself. "It's a fun word. It means *I see you, I hear you*. We'll meet again."

We all said it back to him.

Teala laughed, "Well, I guess *omahwei* to you too."

Hartway turned and entered his office.

Odd clapped his hands. "Fantastic. Who wants to go see Olivia?"

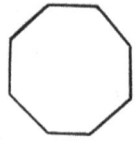

Chapter 14
Once Eight, Now Seven
Perry

We journeyed down three hallways and stumbled into a little rectangular room with two desks diagonally facing a glass door. Two secretaries typed rigorously, their eyes focused until Bailey entered the room. One, with permed brown hair and a fringe, gazed at us.

She smiled, "Oh! An Ever and a room of Kelts. What a benign crowd of people."

Odd grinned, "Well, isn't that just all groups of different people from different cities? Mrs Caduca is expecting us. Well, she's expecting me, but my siblings wanted to tag along. And our ... Ever servant!"

Bailey raised his eyebrows.

Odd waved his hand at us. "Senator Hartway gave us clearance. Is she busy?"

The secretary examined her computer. "That's perfectly fine, Mister Odd! Such a peculiar name."

Odd winked, "Imma peculiar person ... May I enter?"

The lady stared into his eyes. "One moment please." She picked up a phone and said, "Hi, Liv! There's a Mister Odd to see you just outside. Yep, I'll send him in. He's got some tagalongs, I thought I'd warn you ... Yes. Uh-uh ... Senator Hartway. I thought as much. Okay. They'll be in soon." She hung up the phone and leaned her chin on her palm. "You can enter now!"

We marched forward, crowding what I assumed to be Olivia's

office. It was quite astonishing. Teala and I gasped, seeing photos of us when we were little. As Bailey covered the front desk, I heard Olivia's voice. My heart jolted, my fingers shook, and I couldn't swallow. It was like being in the presence of an angel, but all I had seen so far was Bailey's behind. I shoved past his black fur, Teala following.

"Mister Odd! What is the meaning of this?"

Odd shrugged, "I have a few people I'd like you to meet."

Olivia raised her voice. "I did not accept your invitation to be bombarded by ... by ... *Tea* ... *Perry*. You—you. How on earth?"

She ran past her desk and collided with Teala, hugging her. I folded my arms, and something inside my belly made me grin for way too long. Even though I couldn't stop smiling, I could smell Mum on Olivia; I could hear her voice too. She was an older version of Teala with the same blond hair and emerald-green eyes. Her lips were a deep red, her skin a rough olive like mine. When her arms wrapped around me, I felt nothing. Her head, for the first time ever, rested under mine. She dug it against my chest, most likely squeezing me with all her might.

"Mum said you were gone!" she cried. "That you'd gotten lost on your way to Everbreen! How is this possible? Why are you here?"

Teala jumped, "Oh, boy! Do we have a story to tell you."

I gestured to Odd, "We have him to thank, sort of. It's been a wild couple of years, that's for sure."

Olivia examined Odd. She then searched everyone else. "Holy— by the tits on Hope's Light, Faith! Look how gorgeous you've gotten. And Dalton. My word, have you grown, and look at all this hair ... Oh, and the princess and—AND PRINCE. Why are you two here? I read that you two were in Central City, but I ... I didn't believe it. And an Ever—*No!* B-B-Bailey? Is that you?"

Bailey nodded, "I got a little hairy, didn't I?"

Olivia hugged his head. "No, you're perfect! How are you all? Why the heck are you here? What took you so long? I ... I don't have time for this! I ——"

Odd clicked his fingers. A blue tint covered the walls of Olivia's office, the sounds of the city outside stopped, and Faith grinned.

Odd eyed my sister. "You've got plenty of time, Liv!"

Olivia pointed at him with shaken hands. "You used your gift. You'll get in trouble, that's taboo here."

Odd's face was numb. "It's taboo everywhere ... No one's going to know, so there's no taboo—simple!"

Olivia's eyebrows scrunched. "What did you do?"

"Everything and anything!" Odd raised his arms. "As much time as you need, because here, seconds are minutes, minutes are hours, hours are days. Well, give or take a few thousand whatnots!"

Olivia's mouth stayed open. "Whatnots? ... Tea! Perry! Who the heck is this guy?"

She went to her desk and pulled out a device from her side draw. It was similar to the scanning machines the guards had at the Sporangia Sector's gates. Odd raised his hands. "Whoa! You're going to scan me! That's private information, hun. And I'm not really in the mood to be tagged!"

I pulled her back. "Liv! It's fine. He helped us. How do you think we got here!"

"Odd's not too bad. Well, not tagging-worthy bad. You'll get used to him ... eventually," Zia blurted.

Teala grabbed Olivia's hands. "You don't have to ... scan him. He just froze time for a while. I'm sure he'd be happy enough to turn it back on."

Olivia and Teala faced Odd.

Odd bit his lip and smiled. "Anything for you, Tea. I thought it'd be best if we wait in here for a while, so everyone can catch up. I'm sure Olivia's busy with all her paperwork. Especially for Mr Kingsleigh and his looming meeting with the Eight!"

Before Olivia answered herself, I had to clarify something. "Wait a second! You work for ... Actually, who the heck is Mr Kingsleigh, Odd? I've heard his name more times here than my own. And what the heck does he and WonderWorks have to do with the Senate of the Eight?"

"Mr Kingsleigh's the owner of WonderWorks Incorporated. He's one of the leading technicians in communications, entertainment and outdoor gear. Mr Odd works under him, does he not?" Olivia asked.

Chapter 14: Once Eight, Now Seven

This can't be true! "ALICE'S FATHER?" I groaned. "Why the heck are we in the same place as Alice's father? He'd ... He'd ———"

"He'd wanna kill us if he knew we were here!" Dally interjected.

"Oh, Perry! I wanted to tell you last night. Gosh. Stop overreacting, Dally!" Faith sighed.

"Home? Where *do* you all live now?" Olivia asked. "Why haven't you returned to Kelton Whide where it's safe? And what on earth do you mean by Mr Kingsleigh wanting to kill you? You have one of his CEOs leading you into Parliament House ... Oh, and the meeting! On Hope's Light, it's in two hours."

Everyone argued for a second. I *swear I couldn't tell who I was more pissed off at,* Olivia, Odd, Faith ... *Argh.*

"I want answers!" I yelled. "Did you know he was going to be here, Odd?" I pointed at Olivia. "And since when did you work for Charles Kingsleigh? I thought you were under the command of Othello, assisting with the ecological laws for the Socialists of the Old."

Odd and Olivia answered in unison. "*I did. But things changed.*"

I threw my hands in the air. "You both did not just say the same stupid line!"

Olivia tugged on Teala. "How do you all know Mr Kingsleigh and his daughter? ... You really did make it to Everbreen, didn't you?"

Teala nodded, "Yep. We lived there for about a year under the control of Araidian's Warriors."

"The A.W.. What a joke!" Titan laughed.

"What do mean joke, Prince Kelton?" Olivia eyed him down.

Zia slapped the prince's head. "Let me explain, Olivia. Titan and I were captured during the attacks in Kelton Whide. Araidian kept us as bait for our father, who is still missing, and abandoned me under guard in Everbreen. Without your brother, Kingsleigh's idiotic CEO, Faith, Teala and Bailey, I'd still be a captive."

"I had to jump on a frickin' van for her!" I clarified. "Which is beside the point. Odd gave us shelter in Everbreen. We crashed at Othello's house ... Whoa, Odd why aren't you blabbering about explaining things *properly*?"

Faith took a step forward. "Kyle's not the only reason for why we're in Central City. Othello told you something, didn't he?"

Odd shook his head. "No. Othello didn't say anything. I just had a bad feeling about today's meeting."

"Why, Odd? You saw de guards," said Bailey.

"And the military is just outside these walls. You know how protected this district is!" Dally added.

Odd scratched his chin. "Just a feeling. Don't worry about poor ol' me. I just need someone to get me into that meeting. Kyle was a coincidence, Zia's an advantage, and Olivia is the ticket. I need to make sure no one gets hurt!"

Olivia tensed. "And who would want to hurt the senate?"

Odd's face was grim. "It's not the senate I'm worried about. Olivia, I know we don't know each other, but can you please help me?"

Olivia looked down to Teala. Teala crossed her arms. "You can trust him, Liv!"

I nudged her shoulder. "And we kind of owe him a few favours. Just keep him quiet. He asks a lot of dumb questions."

Odd laughed sarcastically. "You're hilarious Perry." He leaned on my arm. "What do you say, Councillor Caduca?"

The next two hours outside Odd's timeless dimension were rather refreshing. I smiled throughout every second and so did Teala. Heck, everyone had a grin on their face. Olivia had some crazy stories about after the attacks in Kelton Whide. Apparently, the city was still rebuilding; we even had a Day of Memory for the people we lost. She told us new stories about Mum. It was like music to my ears, hearing that Mum was still oddly sporadic and mystic in her own unique prophet way.

She told us of Lady Vivian Kelton, how she and Senator Carvanah, her Hand, were rebuilding homes, farmland and families without the protection and invisible walls of the Floral. *Yep, you heard it right.* Zia's mother had abandoned the Floral because every day a new white-crested citizen returned to Kelton Whide with a new story to tell. *I guess they were just waiting for the royal family to come home.*

Chapter 14: Once Eight, Now Seven

Odd pointed at me, then Teala and, finally, Olivia. "So, we have the loss of feeling. The loss of dreams. And the loss of ..."

"Taste. I can't taste a thing and it's dreadful during dinner!" Olivia said.

Titan gasped, "I'm so sorry. May the Light of Hope guide your belly."

"I like the sound of that," Dally snorted.

Olivia picked her head up. "What did you all lose?"

Titan mused. "Me—well, my belly. Doctor Daegon had to put a new one inside of me before it disappeared forever. Someone better check on Kyle soon."

Zia hugged his side. "Don't worry, Tye. As soon as the meeting is finished, we'll rush over to see him. Odd'll make sure the Doctor goes back to his captivity in the Sporangia Sector. I lost my thoughts. Odd gave me a writing journal so I could ... I don't know. I just write things and it feels relaxing."

Bailey shoved through next to Zia. "It's also a dilly way to check on what we're doin'. She writes everything in it!" He glanced at Zia's revolted face as she clenched her teeth together. "What?" the panda asked. "It's not my fault ye read some of it to me!"

"No, he's right. It's a great blog. I'd even recommend uploading it ... Faith and Dally are a little more complicated," Odd said.

Faith faced the ground. "I haven't lost anything yet, and neither has Dally."

"That's fine," Olivia cheered. "There's plenty of people in Central City that still haven't lost anything. It seems lately that every day passes with another scream or big dilemma when someone does in fact lose something. Do you know why it varies within different people, Odd?"

Odd pointed to himself. "Well, Councillor. I'm more interested in your thoughts."

Olivia pouted. "Obliged. My guess is it's dependent on the age of a person's blood. The prince and princess have a royal bloodline close to the gods. Heck, they have the blood of the gods. Us white wolves were one of the first to ever help the Mother Light and Bailey's an Ever. His whole culture is enriched by the blessing of the spirits and that leaves his blood closer to nature. It'd be the same with the Tinkettes ... Do you agree?"

Odd played with his fingernails. "Somewhat. It's an amazing theory, though. Keep at it, Councillor." He laughed to himself and stood. "Look at the time. We'd best attend this meeting."

Olivia folded her legs. "I never once agreed to your scheme, demigod! But seeing that the princess needs an escort, I'd be happy to show her royal flunky the way to the House of Senates."

I had to know! "What colour's that room?"

"It's de eight colours of de major cities," Bailey explained.

Olivia searched Dally and me. "Don't do anything stupid. Perry, Dalton! Faith keep them in check, please. You too, Bailey. I don't want to hear any complaints when we're gone. I would still like to introduce you to someone very special."

No way! She hasn't met someone, has she? "Get out of town! You haven't got a boyfriend, not with those looks!" I smirked.

"Perry, I swear to the Light!" Olivia growled. Odd and Dally laughed.

"I want to meet him. I'm sure he's lovely and awesome and stronger than *Perry*," Teala argued.

"Just my opinion. We all know I'm the alpha male!" I shrugged.

Dally slapped my hood, "Get over yourself!"

I glanced in Olivia's eyes. "Go. Please, we have all the time in the world to talk after the meeting. Hurry and escort Her Royal Majesty, Princess Zia Glassion Kelton and her primitive degenerate demigod before they get bored."

"Between the two, they have the patience of a fish in the Holiday River," Dally mumbled. Titan wheezed at his humour.

Zia's face went red. "You two, I swear on ... Huh! Must keep composure—lots of royal talking. Important people ... We'll see you soon!"

Olivia put her hand on Zia's side. "It's okay, Zia. You'll do fine. The House of Senates is this way."

I followed them to a doorway where two guards were stationed. Master Othello waited with the guards and his arms flew into the air when he saw the trio. "Olivia. Odd ... *Princess?* Are you all attending the meeting?"

They discussed things further. Othello turned to the guards. "These three are with me. Please be respectful in front of royalty, fellas. Like this," Othello bowed to Zia. Zia ordered for him to stand and so he did. The guards repeated his movement, and they entered the House of Senates.

Dally and Titan lingered behind me. "Why aren't you going in?" Dally asked.

Titan shrugged. "I don't really care. Like, what am I going to add to a debate with a bunch of oldies and my annoying sister? Plus, I'm not too keen on Roofus, he's obnoxious."

Dally's eyes lit up. "I'm surprised you know what that word means. Just given the whole *globalisation* thing before. What if they start talking about climate change?"

"Well, then I'd have to go," Titan said.

"Tye, they're talkin' about a mine, most likely coal, which produces fossil fuels an' only de spirits know what else," Bailey explained, sitting on his arse. "De whole meeting will be 'bout de future an' climate change an' stuff like dat. I wouldn't be surprised if dey didn't start talkin' about investing in one near Everbreen."

Dally leaned on the back wall. "But that land's owned by the spirits—they can't. Tinkette Valley's different. That's where the gods are from. There are different rules to follow."

"Fair dinkum, but still," Bailey sighed. "If Alice's pa really wants a mine dat nuttily, what's stopping 'im? He's got more power than Araidian!"

"But why Tinkette Valley?" Titan asked. "Father says that place's a dump. The natives have taken everything, and the resources are malarkey. He said it's like a totally new continent, with different materials and ores. I wouldn't do it."

"But you're like thirteen," Dally quipped. "What do you know?"

"I'm a royal thirteen-year-old. I know more than most simpletons at the age of fifty. Like you said, shouldn't I be in the meeting? I'm of the younger generation. Those oldies don't care about me, even after my bloodline and title. So yes ... Climate change is good, but I have no power. Zia's the same!"

"Then why'd she go into de meeting?" Bailey wondered.

Titan rolled his eyes. "Roofus. Our mother's Hand. He might know something about Father. That's all she cares about at the moment. I hope he knows something too!"

The three continued their debate behind me as I sat near the entrance to the House of Senates. Faith leaned her head on my shoulder. We watched Teala tug on the sleeve of one of the guards. "Excuse me, do you know Olivia Caduca?" she asked.

The guards looked at her, confused. The one she tugged on smiled. "Sure I do. Liv's great! Hey, Terry, we know Olivia. Y'know, Councillor Caduca!"

"Aww, she the best. Such a lovely spirit," the other guard cheered.

Teala laughed with them. "That's good. I'm her sister. You wouldn't be her special someone, would you?" The two looked at one another before answering as honestly as they could, red cheeks and shocked grins.

Faith blocked their conversation from my ears, her freshly brushed teeth still reeking of mint. "I forgot the gift!"

I leaned my head on hers. "What gift? Oh, you mean ——"

"Yep. Do you think it'll come in handy?"

I shook my head. "No. Not here. Not unless something bad happens. Hey, can you smell like ... I don't know, *paper*, just before? Like the expensive stuff you make brochures and pamphlets with?"

"No ... Have you heard bells?"

"Can't say I have. I guess we're both losing our marbles. Ever since we got here, it seems more dangerous than the Forest of Farbe. But we're surrounded by guards, people, manmade things. It's ... It's ——"

"It's yuck. Seeing it all. Gosh, maybe that's not the right word. It's just strange. In comparison to Everbreen, Central City feels like a mousetrap. Does that make sense?"

"Perfect sense. It's a maze!" I said.

"But we're safe, aren't we?"

"I don't know, Faith! I'm smelling paper, you're hearing bells.

Chapter 14: Once Eight, Now Seven

Titan's talking politics with Dally and Bailey. And Odd doesn't know everything here. A mousetrap's not a bad way to describe it."

Faith paused. "Oh my … Maybe we're just overreacting. Kyle's getting better. We'll be able to talk to him soon, have another Kelt, someone from school … We need to look at the positives, remember?"

"Don't worry, Faith. I'm smiling. What do you think they're talking about in there?"

Faith thought to herself. "Global warming, the future, resource management, Charles Kingsleigh, Araidian. How silly the two are!"

I laughed. "Amen, sister. Stuff those guys."

Teala nudged my leg. "Hey, Perry. Have you seen my totem? The one Senator Hartway gave me? I can't find it any——"

Screams erupted from inside the House of Senates. The guards lifted their guns and stormed inside. I stood, holding Teala back. The slicing sound of metal ricocheted past the open doorway. Before either Dally, Faith or I could intervene, more screaming and ordering came from the chamber. As I stepped forward, the man dressed in paper clothes exited the House of Senates. The white of his bandana coloured his blue eyes even more. His gaze pierced my heart, and without a second thought, I bolted towards him. Faith tried to stop me, but I needed to get him.

"Perry! Wait! Dally, we have to go after them!" she yelled.

I followed him down hallways, past secretaries and artworks. He was fast—more agile than anyone I had ever met. I ran through walls, pillars and a fire escape just to keep up, but he knew the ins and outs of this place better than I did. I swear he was always one step ahead. But as we ran through another corridor near Olivia's office, there was a dead end. He shoved a councillor out of his way, her workpapers flying into the air, and when we reached the hall's end, he turned to me.

Behind his bandana, I knew he was smiling! He caught one of the pieces of paper and made a plane out of it patiently. I was too late. He threw the paper plane and black ink sparked. He disappeared! The plane flew into the ventilation system. *It was him! It had to be!* I turned back the way I came and entered the fire escape. Who needs to use doors when you can just faze through them? I teleported up each staircase until the blaze of the afternoon sun was upon me.

The paper plane flew out of its vent. I watched it closely as it passed my face. It began to unfold itself in front of my eyes. A large paper foot about the size of mine unfolded itself and kicked me in the chin. I regained my footing and pulled out my staff. It extended into the long staff as the paper plane finished unfolding to reveal the ninja person. He pulled out the two swords from behind his back and, to be honest, I gulped. I had never fought anyone with real swords before. His swords were very thin—they were made out of paper! He cracked his neck, left and right, pointing his left sword at my chest. He was ready. I positioned myself, holding my staff firmly. And with one deep breath, he attacked!

Chapter 15
Paper Thin Consequences
Faith

When he examined us, I knew I had seen him before. "Dally! We have to go after them! Bailey, Tea, Titan—check on the others. Make sure they're okay. We'll meet back here when we find Perry! Come on, Dally!"

The screaming and crying continued outside the House of Senates. I forced myself to ignore them. If Perry got himself killed chasing down this lunatic, I'd only blame myself.

Dally and I ran until Perry jogged past us. *The paper man was missing!* We yelled his name, but he didn't notice. He collided with the fire escape door and we followed. Dally turned the doorknob.

"Lucky bastard doesn't have to worry about doors anymore," he joked. "I'd kill to do that! What? It's cool."

I rolled my eyes, running up the stairwell. "You could probably lift this whole building with your gift. Maybe even the island if you gave it your all. Come on. I see white ash!" I said.

The ash was everywhere. Every second staircase had Perry's teleportation residue sprinkled on the grey concrete.

Then the lights went out.

The only glimmer came from our crests—the white glow of the dragon and tiger under our arms. "Where's your band?" Dally asked.

I kept tiptoeing forward. "Could ask you the same thing!"

"We're in Central City, Faith. No need. If memory serves me right, you had it on yesterday!"

I rolled my eyes again as orange emergency lights illuminated the stairwell. "I'm just letting my wrist breathe!" I heard something metallic slap against a timber staff. I clasped the doorknob. "Do you hear that?" I asked.

We ran out into the battlefield. The paper warrior kept flipping and twirled around Perry. Perry blocked all of his attacks as best he could, teleporting out of his katanas' range. It was like watching two dancers waltz around one another; a performance as clear as day! Dally ran into battle, lifting rocks from the ground with his mind and shooting them at the paper warrior. The man swept Perry's feet, cutting the rocks in half with his katana. Perry teleported behind him. They tussled for a moment, paper sword on staff, the smell of wood burning.

The paper warrior threw one of his swords at Dally. The sword caught his sleeve and held him against the ventilation system. I braced myself. All of a sudden, a small paper plane had flown to my side. It landed next to me—so relaxed and pretty, but Perry had something else in mind. He screamed my name and the plane unfolded itself, becoming the warrior. He clasped my neck and Perry slowed. I grabbed his hand and saw a wooden cabin in the middle of a forest, test tubes in a lab, a silver liquid; I heard screaming, talking of experimentation, a white glow and a piece of paper falling to the ground.

The paper warrior grew another sword from the paper of his hood. His fair brown hair was long, as though he hadn't cut it in years.

Perry put his arms up. "You don't have to do anything! Hurt me, not her! You know who I am. Don't you? I'm the white wolf."

The warrior took a deep breath and placed a card in my hand, then he vanished. A paper plane flew into the sunset.

Perry hugged me and I felt his warmth. "He gave me something!" I showed him the cue card. Inscribed in black ink were the words *I don't want to hurt anyone. I'm Papercut.*

Perry scrunched his face. "Is that his name? Papercut?"

I focused on his eyes. "I'm not sure. He didn't hurt you, did he?"

Perry shook his head.

"Hey! Can someone please get this sword off my shirt?" Dally yelled. "I can't move. He's got a good throw. I can't get up! Please ... Perry? Faith? I'll love you very big much!"

Chapter 15: Paper Thin Consequences

When we returned downstairs, the orange lights still highlighted the hallways. Parliament House had a cluster of National Guards strolling through the halls. They asked strange questions for strange reasons. By the time we reached the House of Senates, a cold sensation lingered in the air. Bailey waited outside. He looked half asleep, sitting on his bottom with his legs folded. I rubbed his side.

"I don't think it's an appropriate time to be meditating, Bailey!"

Bailey opened his left eye. "I'm prayin' for de souls dat have passed. I'm makin' sure de spirits guide 'em to de white ceilin'. Othello asked me to."

Perry glanced inside the chamber. "The heck happened?"

"A senator's been murdered!"

Dally pushed through. "And that Papercut killed them!"

Blood dripped from Dally's shoulder. He covered it up, glancing back at me. The room was an octagon, and each eighth was a different colour, like a rainbow pizza. Red, orange, yellow, green, blue, black, white and pink. There were several chairs inside each section and many guards talking to the panicked councillors and representatives. In the centre of each section, there was one chair pillared above the rest with a platform for the senators to stand on. Pieces of paper, some with splatters of red and sporadic scribbles of black, covered each eighth.

Olivia was talking with Teala and Othello, discussing the possibility of someone sneaking inside. Othello mumbled, "I told them to cover the vents. They never listen."

Olivia turned to us. "You guys are okay!" She hugged Perry.

Teala crossed her arms. "I knew they'd be fine."

"Did you see this in your dream, little one?" Othello asked.

Teala shook her head. "No. I saw a piece of paper with blood on it. And then blood on your face. You were missing an eye. Just last night, actually!"

"Oh, peculiar indeed," Othello laughed.

Perry leaned on Olivia. "We tried to stop him! He got away."

Olivia held him tighter. "Don't be foolish, Perry! That maniac could tear right through you. Why would you …? Promise me you won't do something like that again!"

Perry pulled away. "I can't promise that! I'm not the same boy you knew in Kelton Whide!"

Dally barged between them. "Can someone explain to me what happened in here?"

Othello came closer. "Death, young master. And the death of the powerful is always more tragic!"

An uproar emerged from the centre of the octagon. An older man barged through. *"I've had enough!"* His face was tanned, and he had dimples, even when he shouted. His grey suit had bloodstains. He marched through the crowds of mourners, palming away military men, officers, senators, councillors and everyone else who had snuck into Parliament House. His black hair was pulled back and his hands had been overworked. His blue eyes searched us as he stormed outside.

"I almost died today, General Ko!" he shouted. "And if memory serves me right, your men were meant to report back to Drewmora today at o'five hundred. So, please … I don't want to hear it. I am leaving for my room with the safety of my own men!"

General Ko, a grey-bearded military man twice his size and age ran after him. His uniform was crisp—a blue jacket and cap with several medals over the left side of his chest. His skin was wrinkly and pale, his nose stubby, his thumbs too large for his soft hands. "Sir, I was ordered by the prophet to abandon our orders until this evening's meeting had concluded."

The two collided with Othello. "And how fortunate it was for me to tell your men."

The rich man stared Othello in the eye. "Get out of my way, pig! Your ways are dying in this world! Don't act like you saved my life, telling *my* men, the Drewan General and his men to stay back! You are scum!"

Othello's eyes twitched as some spit landed on his cheek.

"How primitive for a billionaire who almost got assassinated, Mr Kingsleigh!" he chuckled. "You should be thanking the recently passed senator … My ways may be dying, but this scum allowed you to avoid that maniac's sword! It's been two hundred and thirty-three years since someone was last killed in these walls. And if you didn't

Chapter 15: Paper Thin Consequences

order your men to go against what I had asked, we could have made it to two hundred and thirty-four!"

Mr Kingsleigh pushed Othello aside. "Don't you blame all this on me! You knew this was going to happen, no matter whether I told my men to cover those salty vents in the ceiling! Get out of my face!"

Mr Kingsleigh and General Ko stormed out, arguing about leaving for Drewmora as soon as possible.

Perry folded his arms and we stared at them. "So that's Mr Kingsleigh!" Perry grinned. "I'm guessing it's his award-winning personality that's made him so much money!"

I picked up one of the many pieces of paper and clasped it in my hands. Closing my eyes, I felt a rush. When I opened my hands, the paper was a white handkerchief. I handed it to Othello. "Maybe it's his magical awe for inside manners and spit!" I joked.

Othello smiled, wiping his cheek. "You may be onto something there, Faith. He's a hard man to please. An even harder man to argue with. Why do you think the senate was involved to begin with!"

In the corner of my eye, I could see Zia. Her arms were crossed; several men in white surrounded her and Titan. She was looking at a man with not a single hair on his head. He wore a white suit with a crown emblem on his collar and stood at the centre of their guard. Titan saluted me, his face glum.

Dally blurted, "Yo, Zia! The hell's up with the paparazzi?" Honestly, both Perry and I could have strangled him then and there.

"Actually, do one of the guards know how to do stitches? Dally's arm won't stop bleeding!" Perry called.

Dally's eyes lit up. "That's the guard! What's up with the suits, boys?"

Titan plunged his hands into his pockets. "It's a formal event, you knobhead."

Zia waved the guards away. "Please, gentlemen. It's fine. These are Kelts, just like us ... Roofus. I'd like you to meet my saviours."

The bald man waved at us.

"I remember you. *Roofy!* You were under my dad's command when I was little!" Perry gawked.

Roofus looked at us. "*Perry?* Zia, the White Wolf's son is your saviour. There must be a misunderstanding!"

Olivia smiled at the guards. "Gentlemen. Your Majesty. Prince. Are you okay?"

Zia admired her nails. "Never better. That paper freak would have never come close to me with all these men."

"Any word on your father?"

Roofus stood. "It's ... complicated," he said.

"Complicated words are better than no words," Othello chimed.

Perry shook his head. "You're right ... Speaking of words—where's Odd?"

We all searched for him. Tumbling out of the blue section, through the black and into the white, I found him.

He was slumped on the ground alongside Senator Hartway, a red hole in his chest, his right arm severed clean off. Odd wasn't crying. He just held the Tinkette, staring at the ground. He shook his head and stood, dropping Senator Hartway's lifeless body. He nodded to two men dressed in coats. "You can take him now. His spirit's safe. Thank you."

"Odd! Are you okay?" I asked.

He took a seat in the white section. "Not really. He was a good man. Didn't deserve to die! There shouldn't be blood on these floors. It's my fault. I knew something bad was going to happen! He should have ——"

I reached out for him. "I'm sorry. But you don't have to blame yourself. You didn't do this. That fiend, that ... *monster* did this."

Perry crossed his arms. "His name's Papercut! And we'll get him!"

Odd shook his head, standing. "You saw his eyes. Whatever the name is, he wasn't alone in this! And I'm not after revenge, Perry. I ... I'm just sick of people dying around me!"

Dally joined us. "So what happens now, Odd? Is there gonna be a war?"

Odd raised his brows. "Maybe ... For now, we mourn. I'm sure there'll be lots of meetings, lots of adults and oldies talking and theorising." Odd stared at us, his eyes tired. "He didn't deserve to die as a casualty in an assassination attempt!"

Chapter 15: Paper Thin Consequences

"He wasn't meant to be killed? Then who was Papercut here for?" I asked.

Odd searched the blood on the floor. "Charles Kingsleigh. That sword went through him. He should be dead. Instead, one of our senators got the end of the blade."

Dally pointed to the exit. "We just saw Mr Kingsleigh. He didn't have a single scratch on him. He was fi———"

Odd's voice tightened. "I saw the blade plunge through his chest. He should be dead."

A brusque voice emerged behind us. "I saw it too! But the aftermath does not always reflect the event!" Roofus stood with Zia. His eyes were on Senator Hartway's remains as the military men covered his body with a tarp.

Zia interjected, "I didn't see much. Mainly the general from the militia. But he did put himself before Mr Kingsleigh. The murderer pulled his blade away. It was as if he didn't mean to do what he did! His eyes bulged and blood began to pour from Hartway's shoulder. It's just ... He has a daughter!"

Before I could offer my condolences, Odd began moving. "Where is he, the bastard? Where did Kingsleigh go?"

"Outside," Perry said. He and Dally pushed Odd back. They both yelled at him to not do anything stupid.

Odd pushed through. "I'm not gonna do anything stupid," he said. "I'm just going to have a little chat with my boss."

Perry screamed my name. "Faith, you gotta do something. This might not have caused a war, but he might!"

I was this far away from blocking the doorway with carpet or closing the walls before Odd, but as my hands tensed and my crest burned, Othello grabbed my wrist. "Not here, dear! The handkerchief was more than enough! Eyes are everywhere."

I nodded, noticing that Roofus was staring at me. It was as though I'd offended him; his eyes stayed on me as we retreated outside.

Bailey opened his eyes when Teala and I ran past, eight Kelton guards rallying behind us.

"What de whip's goin' on?" he wondered.

"A fight, a fight. Come on!" Titan cheered.

Zia complained as Bailey joined the herd. "It's not a fight, Titan. Don't be ridiculous. Odd's just a little worse for wear!"

We were right on Odd's tail as he stormed out of Parliament House. Mr Kingsleigh was ordering his men in blue different instructions, still arguing with General Ko about Drewmora.

"The city is obviously not safe, General. That salty assassin may still be here watching us as we speak." He noticed Odd in the corner of his eye. "Odd! What an unexpected gift. How long has it been? Almost a year. I have some good news for you. Seeing the numbers you found last year, I believe the mine in Tinkette is right under our grip. A few more meetings and we'll have it. And the omens are upon us. I'm feeling good about this one!"

"Shut your mouth, Charles! Who the hell did you piss off to get Hartway killed?" Odd yelled.

Mr Kingsleigh searched his men, then Odd. "*Senator Hartway*. You were at this evening's meeting? How come I was not informed of this?"

Odd's eyes were locked onto Mr Kingsleigh's. "Self-invite. Why was there a goddamn assassin after you? The hell did you do?"

Mr Kingsleigh raised his hands. "Oh, please. The senator was a minor inconvenience. He was going to get elected out of parliament next year anyway. Tinkette Valley will move on, Odd ..." He noticed Odd's face. "Oh, I forgot. You two were close. My apologies. But I've always told you, work and family are two we cannot make one. Think about the positives. With that old fishtail out of the way, we can really get a move on with this mine. I'm talking more resources—we can work on that Lupo ——"

Mr Kingsleigh staggered back, his cheek red and slightly bloodied. Odd's knuckles were so tense, I thought a vein was going to pop. General Ko held Mr Kingsleigh on his feet, but the businessman seemed rather amused. He put his hands together, chuckling. "Oh, Oddington! Why would you go and do something like that?"

Odd shook his head. "This has nothing to do with business. Not that stupid mine! You caused an innocent, righteous, good person to die today. You made his daughter an orphan." Mr Kingsleigh tried

Chapter 15: Paper Thin Consequences

speaking, but Odd reiterated. "She's fifteen, Charles. That's a year younger than Alice!"

Mr Kingsleigh scowled at Odd. "Don't you dare mention Alice, Odd. Remember who has more power here!"

Othello patted Mr Kingsleigh's head. "I believe I do. Well, I'm equal to the White King's Hand, Senator Roofus Carvanah. Am I not?"

Odd stepped away. He eyed General Ko. "General. I want all your men guarding Mr Kingsleigh. I want four stationed at his door, three on the roof, and I need the ventilation ducts covered. Do you understand, General?"

General Ko stood tall. "Yes, sir! You heard him, men. I want a perimeter sweep of the Midcourt District. You four stay with Mr Kingsleigh, you two with Odd!"

Odd palmed them away. "I have my own people, General. Thank you for the offer." He glared at Mr Kingsleigh. "Charles. I'll be seeing you!"

Mr Kingsleigh pointed at Odd. "I want answers, Odd, or you're fired. I'm serious this time. I want a meeting!"

Odd wandered over to us, smiling. Perry raised his brows. "You feel better now?"

"How'd you not get fired?" Dally asked with a smirk.

Odd continued back into Parliament House. "Because WonderWorks needs me as much as I need their six-digit income!"

Bailey crawled into the building. "Ye make six digits an' we've been livin' in a prophet's house all dis time!"

Odd stared back. "How do you think I could afford the renovations, especially the ones for you ... Wow, what a crowd we have here!"

He searched the Kelton Guard, Roofus and Olivia.

Placing his hands behind his back, Odd stood tall. "Senator Carvanah! Councillor ... I apologise for showing such aggressive tendencies, I believe it's time for us to head home. We were being sheltered by Senator Hartway."

Roofus faced him. "My condolences. He spoke highly of you, demigod. I have some errands to attend to regarding Mr Kingsleigh and the train station. We must catch this assassin as soon as possible. The Drewan Militia return home in two days. Mr Kingsleigh plans to go with them. I'll try my best to delay their transport, seeing that the investigation is still underway." He turned to Zia and Titan. "Your Majesty, Highness," he bowed. "May the Mother's Light shine upon you." He instructed the troops behind him from the Kelton Guard. "You six stay with her at all times."

Titan raised his hands. "Roofus, it's okay. We've spent years by ourselves; I'm sure we'll be fine for a few more hours. You do what you need to."

Roofus pointed at Titan. "Make sure the prince doesn't do anything ill-advised or childish. Their lives are far more important than yours."

Zia raised her hand. "Senator Carvanah! I appreciate the concern and your men's willingness to act as my guard. But after the information you gave me, we will not be returning to Kelton Whide with you."

Roofus tried explaining himself.

Zia demanded, "Which is exactly what you are alluding to by stationing these men by our side. I want to go home as much as you and the rest of these Kelts behind me. But for the time being, I am not returning home until I find my father. And with the information you have provided, I believe my best course of action is to stay with Mr Kingsleigh's CEO, Odd. He and Faith are more than enough protection!"

"But, Your Majesty ———"

Zia smiled, "And if you think this is ill-advised, call my mother. I'm sure she'd do the exact same if she were in my situation. Kelton Whide is in good hands under her protection, and I'd much prefer that you and your men protect her than me while I search for the king!"

"Your Majesty, your mother would request ———"

"That's an order, Senator Carvanah!" Zia smiled. "Next time you see Titan or me, we will have our father with us! And that's a promise I make to Hope, to the white beacon, to you and to my mother!"

"You've grown, princess," Roofus grinned. "Your wish is my command, you know that. It's been like that since you were a child. I'll let your mother know. She'll be proud. But before I go, can I do one last thing?"

Chapter 15: Paper Thin Consequences

Zia nodded and Roofus looked at us. "White Wolf! And friends. Could you come here? You too, Ever!" We approached him and he looked at each of us in the eye. "Although I cannot make this as formal as it should be, I'd like to make you all members of the Kelton Guard."

Perry knew what to do. He stuck out his wrist and I followed suit with the rest.

Senator Carvanah rubbed Perry's crest, reading its code, and continued down the line. "Perry Caduca, the white wolf. The reaper that leads the pack. Dalton Lee, the white tiger. The virus that protects the pack. Teala Caduca, the white wolf. The rose that holds the pack. Bailey Giggles, the green panda. The Ever that understands the pack. The first Ever to be initiated into the Kelton Guard. You should be proud ... And Faith Brooks, the white dragon. The heart that keeps the pack afloat. Welcome to the Kelton Guard. When you return to Kelton Whide, I expect the prince and princess to be in the best shape possible. That goes for you too, white rabbit!"

Odd chuckled, "Don't read my crest, Senator. It's no fun that way! You won't find anything worth reading. And that reminds me. I need to talk to the reaper and the virus when we get back to our temporary house."

Olivia stayed behind. She hugged Perry and Teala and told us that'd she'd be happy to meet when she had the time. We gave her Senator Hartway's address and Olivia smiled at Zia. "So why would a princess stay with such a strange group of people?" Olivia asked.

I stayed next to Zia. "This group of people are like family," Zia admitted. "And that demigod plans to go to Drewmora. That's where my father was last seen, according to Roofus' lastest report!"

"I suppose we're not going home anytime soon. We'll see you tomorrow, Liv! You must have plenty of work to do," I said.

Olivia shook her head. "No. I'm done for the day. I'm going to collect my things and go home."

My eyes widened. "Gosh! You do have that special someone!"

"Will we be meeting him tomorrow?" Zia added.

Olivia winked at me. "Maybe ... I'd like to know what's going on with Faith and Perry first. He must be a headache!"

I rolled my eyes. "Oh, all the time! He's mood-swing central!"

"It's why we love him," Olivia laughed. "I look forward to talking with you. Stay safe. Especially you Zia ... And Faith. I'm glad you two are together! Keep him smart."

We said our goodbyes and left. Some of us had blood on our clothes, others had bags under their eyes; we exited Parliament House the same way we had entered, but with one less soul—one less friend!

Chapter 16
Gravity is Weird
Bailey

When we returned to Senator Hartway's shelter, Odd forced the door open, mumblin' to himself words I couldn't make out. He clapped his hands an' the lights came on. Without a word, Odd trekked upstairs, half dazed.

Faith watched him and mumbled, "I've never seen him like this before."

I nudged her with my snout. "Do ya think we should be shook?"

"Beats me," Perry snorted. "He hasn't said a cohesive sentence since we left Parliament House."

"Why do you think he wants to talk to just you two?" Faith wondered.

"To be honest, I don't even think he knows," Perry said.

Dally laughed, "Probably some prank he wants to pull on his boss. What was his name? Charles?"

Teala began throwin' the couch cushions from side to side. "Has anyone seen my totem? The one Senator Hartway gave me! I can't find it anywhere!"

Before anyone could answer, there was a knock at the front door.

"Who on earth?" Zia sighed. "I swear to the Mother Light, if Roofus is behind this door, Imma slice his nose off!" She readied her green stained-glass shard.

"Crap! She's serious," I gasped.

Zia threw the door open. On the white veranda, Assonance

135

shielded her noggin. Her body had shrunk from a girl to a bird in seconds. "Whoa, whoa! Princess, please don't! Silking hell! It's me, Assonance!"

Zia placed her shard in her satchel an' spread her arms out. "Ona! I almost forgot you existed."

Assonance returned to her two-legged self an' the princess hugged her. Assonance's eyes jumped, one brow droppin' as Zia moved her inside.

"Great timing! We just got home ourselves," Faith said.

"How are ya folks?" I asked.

"Great!" Assonance smiled. "They're still almost the same as I remember. But without my brother, it's still not what it was!"

"Huh? Is your brother back with the others?" Titan blurted, his finger half inside his left nostril.

Teala analysed the grey carpet 'round as she walked past.

Assonance shook her head. "Twin, actually. And no, Yuri is not back at the Town of Tents."

Dally waved his right hand. "You know you don't have to call it that. It's just ... Wait! If he's not back at the tents, what happened to him?"

"He was with us at one point," Assonance's voice was cold as steel. "Irene's Family found us on holidays. We went a little too far west and they snatched us up just a ways off Liverrum! I don't ... Sorry, I just ..."

Perry put his hand on her shoulder. "It's fine! Irene was an evil bastard. If you don't want to talk about it, you don't have to. No one's going to force you."

"But if you have anything on your chest about Yuri, let us know," Faith said. "Your words are safe in this group!"

"Oh, yeah! How like Teala's worried because her birthday's in two days!" Titan laughed.

Teala stopped her search and growled, "TYE! I tell you one thing!"

Titan raised his hands, "What? It stayed in the group, didn't it?"

Perry watched Teala. "Tea! Why are you worried about your birthday? Did you think we'd forget?"

Chapter 16: Gravity is Weird

Teala shook her noggin.

"We couldn't forget about you, little dude!" Dally cheered.

Faith was 'bout to join in, but Teala placed her hands out like two fans. "Whoa! Let's calm down. I'm only turning thirteen. Gah! Look what you did Tye! I lost my train of thought. Where the hell is that stupid tot——"

"Is this, by any chance, what you're seeking, birthday girl?" Daegon's voice erupted from the top of the staircase.

Assonance searched us all. "Who the silk is this?"

"The alchemist! Don't touch our stuff!" Titan growled.

Daegon looked down to the prince. "Oh, please, prince. Are you still angry over the little cuts I had to perform? Don't you remember who saved your life?"

"YOU MADE IT WORSE!" Titan roared. "You're the reason why I have a metal stomach."

Daegon rolled his eyes as Teala approached him.

"What do you want, Daegon?" Zia insisted, guarding her brother.

Daegon laughed, passin' Teala her totem. "Don't you want to see your friend? He's awake! Very handsy."

I squeezed my way through the narrow staircase. My hairs got caught on the picture frames as we skedaddled towards Senator Hartway's ensuite. Titan grabbed hold of Teala's totem.

"Hey! Why'd you take my catcher?" Teala cried.

"To see if he did anything to it!" Titan scowled.

Teala tossed her hands at the dreamcatcher. "Give it back, Tye! It's not funny."

"I'm not messing around, Tea."

I turned 'round at the top of the staircase. "Can ye two stop arguin'? Today's been exhaustin'! Y'know, it might be swell to see Kyle's face! Something dandy for a change. So just stop!"

Titan stared at me, a grim flatness to his lips. "I'm just making sure we're safe," he said. "You don't know what he did to me. He cut me up an—*Argh!*"

He tossed the totem to Teala as though it was burnin' him.

"Are ye right, Tye?" I asked.

"Just a little sting." The prince sucked on his finger. "The totem seems fine, but I'd get Odd to look at it. Just in case." He trekked into the ensuite. "Oh, and Tea, I'm sorry I told everyone. I should have checked with you beforehand!"

Wha'? I've neva' seen Titan care for anyone but himself an' Zia before. Crickey, I hadn't heard him speak all that much 'til we arrived in Central City. Teala was obviously thinking the same thing.

We entered the room behind Assonance. Instead of cheerin', the Centrillian dropped to the ground, screaming. "*What the?* Why is there a two-headed dog in here? Holy silk, is that a wairith?" she asked. "They're meant to be extinct! How'd you get your hands on one?"

"Where the hell have you lot been keeping her? She's got more brains than, like, literally all of you combined!"

"A girl and a boy! How on the island did you manage to pull this off?" Assonance asked.

Daegon admired his hound-like creation. "Oh. Flash was originally a marraboo. Lights was its original form when the hound was alive. I spliced the two forms together through the strength of Light's soul and it kinda just happened!"

A cough sounded beside Daegon. "It's pretty cool when you think about it. Half dead, half alive … It's relatable!" Kyle wheezed on his bed, liftin' his noggin up from the pillows Dally had just adjusted.

"Hey, bud!" Dally mumbled. I reckon every fella had a grin on their face, even Daegon.

Perry stood by his side. "How're you feeling?" he asked.

Kyle kept liftin' his noggin against the pillow. It was as though something had pinched his hair, pullin' him back to the bedhead.

Kyle nodded, puttin' his thumb up. "Good, good. It's just m-my head's a l-little heavy, that's all."

"Heavy? How can we—*your hand!* It's back. Your hand, it's—it's …" Faith lost her train of thought.

Daegon shoved everyone aside. "A minor adjustment I decided

to make," the Doctor bragged. "His hand had previously been melted by something extremely powerful. It sped up the melting process; I simply reversed it."

Zia reached her hand out to Kyle's pillow. "Is everything okay?" she asked. "You seem like you're being pushed back by something."

Daegon slapped her hand away, "Tsk, tsk, tsk! He's lying on his holder. Who moved these pillows?"

Dally eyed Daegon. "I did. What about 'em?"

Daegon swiped the two white cushions from behind Kyle. It caused Kyle to swing forward. When he was adjusted to the mattress, a little metal device shaped like a spinnin' top drifted up an' up from behind him. It stopped, floatin' above his scalp. We all took a step back as the little reflective device made several buzzin' noises. Ye could still smell the freshly cut metal as it spun, movin' when Kyle moved as if they were one.

"Doctor! What the hell is that above his head?" Zia demanded.

Kyle pulled off his blanket. "Oh. It's what's holding me together. I call him Holdie!"

"*Him?* That's a little sexist," Assonance objected.

Kyle raised his hands. "Hey, look, whoever you are. That's how the Doctor created it. As a he."

I was baffled. "So what does Holdie do?" I asked.

Daegon trekked up to the machine. "I'll demonstrate."

Kyle put his hands up an' begged, "No wait! Doc, no! Not aga——"

With a click of a button, Holdie dropped onto the mattress. Kyle melted an' became a wet blob on the bedsheets.

Dally an' Perry pushed Daegon against the sidewall! "What the heck did you do?" Perry ordered.

Teala screamed. The beige blob stained the mattress, bubblin' as we argued. It smelt like burnt milk, oozin' onto the floor.

Dally levitated the chair behind him, holdin' back Daegon. "You better explain to us why you'd do something like that, or this chair's going up your arse!"

"He isn't joking, Daegon! And think of the children," Perry grimaced.

Daegon's eyes opened wide and he raised his arms. "Fellas. Guys. Bros. You don't have to shove that whole piece of furniture in me. I can explain everything. You just have to give me a moment. How much chair are we talking about?"

"The entire thing, asshat!" Dally clarified.

Daegon smiled, "I could work with that!"

Perry let go of the Doctor's arms. "Dude, gross! No chair for you!"

Dally dropped the chair. "Agreed," he said. "No chair. That's … You're a sick piece of work!"

Titan began examinin' the sludge as it slithered down the bed leg.

"What are ya doin', Tye?" I asked.

His hand gestures were crazy. "Where did the flying thing go?"

We discovered it behind Senator Hartway's pink blanket. "It's on de other side of de bed."

Titan skipped 'round, pickin' up Holdie.

"What should I press first?" he asked.

I looked him ova'. "Nothin'. Only de spirits know what dis thing can do. Is it like ya stomach?"

"That's it!" Titan's eyes widened. "The stimulate button."

He pressed a white button on the lower side of Holdie. It began making noises again. It flew above the sludge puddle and the sludge boiled an' steamed. Before we knew it, Kyle was in front of us once more.

He searched his belly. The smell of burnt milk lingered an' Holdie continued to hum under his voice. "I t-told you to s-stop doing that! Great! N-Now I'm cold," Kyle said.

Faith was havin' trouble breathing. "Can someone please explain to me what just happened?"

"And quick! I think I'm going to be sick," Zia blurted, eyes waterin'. "I can't get the smell out of my nose … Even the two-headed dog's grossed out!"

Teala pulled at the bedsheets. "You're the goo. That explains so much! I was wondering when that was going to happen!"

Chapter 16: Gravity is Weird

Kyle searched the room stoppin' on Zia. "I-I apologise for the smell, Your Majesty. I understand m-my natural form isn't t-the most beautiful thing t-to look at, b-but I can still kind of move around in it."

"Wait!" Perry roared. "That's what you normally look like? So like how Bailey's a panda or how Assonance can turn into a bird, you look like that goo!"

Kyle skin went dull. "D-Dude, I melted. What'd you expect? Holdie i-is holding me together so I stay solid."

I guess some fellas do have it worse than me.

"He's right," Daegon cheered. "I had to make Holdie from scratch. It's a *Pseudosphic Gravity Compressor.* Basically, it pushes the gravity around his body's circumference ever so slightly that it not only holds him together, but it also allows him to walk and sleep."

I placed my paw near Kyle's body. The hairs 'round my claws got sucked into him as though he were a vacuum.

He smiled at me. "An Ever! Don't suppose we've met before!"

"Once," I grinned. "Back when I trekked on two feet an' ye didn't have a metal ball 'bove ya noggin—I'm Bailey."

"I remember you," Kyle smiled. "You went to Tom's party. Argh." He took hold of his chest an' laid back on the bedhead. "I'm sorry. I just got super tired all of a sudden."

Daegon felt Kyle's moist forehead. "Your body's still adjusting to the gravitational pull," the Doctor explained. "It's best to rest." He looked at Faith an' Zia. "It's also best for you lot to get some as well. I believe it's well deserved after the events at Parliament House ... How's Odd coping?"

Perry gave it his best guess. "Pissed off. Probably sad. I never know when it comes to him."

Daegon nodded, placin' a blanket over Kyle. "I'll stay by his side. I've still got tests to conduct. I'll make sure everything's sound. Just the little bits, but Kyle should be ready to leave in about two days."

"Well, what a coincidence. I'll be leaving in two days," Zia blurted.

"Oh, princess. We'll all be leaving in two days ... Wait! Where are we going?" Teala asked.

Zia patted Teala's noggin. "Titan and I are going east. To Drewmora. To find our father!"

"DREWMORA!" Perry gasped. "You can't be thinking of going on your own."

Another voice came from the doorway. "She's not!" Odd leaned on the door's frame. "I'm going with her. You're welcome to join. But someone's going to have to protect Charles. And as much as it burdens me to say this, I'd rather if he were alive than dead."

Perry took out his staff. "Well, if you're going, I'm coming along. I want to solve this whole dilemma with Papercut!"

"Papercut?" Assonance uttered.

Odd rolled his eyes an' sighed. "I've had enough talking and debating for one day. Can we please discuss things in the morning? I'm sure you're all eager after today, and I appreciate that, but I've had enough. When you have some time, I'd like to discuss some things with Perry, Bailey and Dalton. It's a guy thing! Sorry ladies."

"What about me?" Titan urged.

Odd strolled into the kitchen. "You're too young!"

Chapter 17
Odd Explains
Bailey

We left Kyle under the supervision of Daegon. Although it didn't feel right—he reeked of misery—I reckon he was the best fella we could have visited under such whack circumstances. Zia began eatin' with Titan on the island bench. Faith an' Teala tried their hardest to explain everything to Assonance an', with each revelation, Assonance gasped an' tears dripped from her eyes. *Bless her soul.* We eventually wandered to Odd's room.

Dally rubbed his neck, "I swear on Hope's Light, this better not be stupid." He mimicked Odd's voice. "*Oh, go climb a cliff and kill a dragon so I can create a spell in my office and reformulate Senator Hartway's body through the power of alchemy. Just kidding. You don't need to know. Now get going!*"

"That's a very specific situation, but I wouldn't be surprised," Perry said. "No offence Bailey, but it's weird that he asked to see you too."

I looked up to him as we strolled through the main hallway. "What do ya mean by dat?"

The two laughed.

"Tell me what's funny!" I insisted.

Perry raised his hands. "Fine! Don't worry. It's just … Over the past few months, Odd's made us do some pretty ballsy stuff."

"We've broken into buildings for him, stolen countless little bits and pieces," Dally said.

I had to clarify the applesauce before my brain went whack. "Is dat what you've been doin' every time ya drift from town? Stealin' jewels an——"

Perry waved his hands, "No, we didn't steal anything precious. We just did what Odd told us. It sounded interesting when he explained it. We only took papers, files and some photos. We did it to make sure everyone was safe. Nothing bad."

"Yeah," Dally agreed. "Never anything bad. I think that's just a silent rule. Odd knows it, so do we. Like, no one's died!"

"Dally! Of course no one's died," Perry argued. He took a deep breath and admired my fur. "Look, Bailey. It hasn't been easy, but everything we've done was for our people—for you, Tea, Faith, the princess. Everyone. And if he asked us to do something completely ridiculous, we would have said no. Wouldn't we Dally?"

"I would—you wouldn't! You're his slave, bro!" Dally laughed.

Perry slapped his shoulder. "I'm not his slave! I'm no one's slave."

"Neither am I," I giggled. "So then why de heck would Odd need me? Especially if he wants us to steal somethin'."

Perry shrugged an' opened Odd's door.

Odd was rushin' from his bedside to his cupboard, takin' out different suits. One was a light blue, a second was grey an' a third was a sort of creamy white. He placed each on his bed an' turned to us, beckoning for us to come.

"Yes, yes, yes. Come in, come in. I've got a surprise for you two. Oh, and Bailey, you're the most important piece of the puzzle." We crowded his bed. The suits were crinkled an' their ties were missing.

Dally picked up the blue one's sleeve. "And these are for …"

Odd clapped his hands. "Preciously. I am thrilled to invite you to a little club I like to call the *Banana Cabana*. There's dancing, pretty ladies, alcohol, a whole lot of lots. And it's best we go tonight before the news of Generalissimo gets out."

Perry put his hand on Odd's shoulder. "Hey, Odd! You're taking this mourning thing a little weirdly, don't you think? You sure we can't sit down and talk things through?"

Odd moved his hand aside. "Perry, I'm fine! I'm more worried about you. We get to go clubbing, experience the city life, and you're worried about little ol' me! Please ... What's wrong with you?"

"What's the catch, Odd?" Dally folded his arms.

Odd shimmied across the room with a skip in his step. "The catch? Nonsense! I just want to take a load off with my two best buds ... I also have some business to attend to and I thought it'd be nice to experience the night-time orchestra we call clubbing."

"That didn't really make sense," Perry frowned. "Look, Odd, we're happy to help. It's just, after today—what happened. Are you sure your head's in the right place?"

"Of course my head's in the right place," Odd harrumphed. "It's above my shoulders. That's where it should be, isn't it? It'll be fun, stop whining."

"Odd, pal, I don't think this is a good idea," Dally urged.

Odd waved his hands, dismissing the two Kelts. "Dalton, don't even start with me. Otherwise, I'm gonna let Titan piss in your morning coffee."

Dally stuck out his tongue. "You wouldn't!"

"Don't tempt me."

I was balled up. I'm an Ever; clubbing's not really my forté, an' well ... I don't reckon I'll be allowed in just yet. "Ease up. If they're goin' clubbin' with ya, what am I doin'?" I asked.

Odd gazed at me with a smile. "Oh, something very special, Bailey. You're the lookout—the eyes and ears. The whole nine yards for this plan. We may collide with dangerous obstacles, but if a bear like yourself came to our rescue, I bet those scary threats won't trouble us anymore."

Perry picked up the cream-coloured suit. "So, what's the plan?"

Odd rubbed his hands together. "Simple. We enter at the front—security already knows me, lovely guys—Bailey will wait just across the street, so he can see the front and side exits. It's an alleyway. We'll do our thing, enjoy the city life and meet him at the side exit. If all goes well, we won't need Bailey to scare anyone off, but otherwise, you can scare as many people as you want. Then we go home, eat some rice cakes with Kyle and call it a night!"

Dally still wasn't budging. "And what exactly might trouble us inside the club, Odd?"

"Do you really have to ask questions every time I explain something?" Odd sighed.

"Yes. 'Cause you're bad at explaining things!" Dally stood his ground.

"I am not bad at explaining things, I just have a way with words! And you don't appreciate the way I say things."

"No one appreciates your orders, Odd! Just tell me what the danger is, and we can head off!" Dally's face was tight.

Odd groaned, "Fine! But you better work on that smell of yours!"

"My *smell?*"

"The danger is the security and the people I'm meeting with. They're contractors for Charles. A side project if the mine backfired. He's a little annoyed. So I don't lose my job, I have to get what they possess. Before we depart for Drewmora, I thought it'd be better to be in his good books than on the bench." Odd rolled his eyes. "Don't worry. I'm meeting with the men alone. You two are just going to be on the dance floor—just guests inside the Banana Cabana. Does that clarify things?"

"What are you collecting?" Perry asked.

Odd threw the blue suit at Dally. "Enough talking. Just put these on. I'll

explain whatever else on our way to the Cabana."

I waited outside in the hall for the three spunks to change. I could hear laughin' in the kitchen.

"Omahwei!" Titan exclaimed.

I turned to him. "Omahwei?"

"Yeah. Omahwei. The old guy said it. The senator. It means uh ... I see you, I hear you. I think."

"An' what'd ye hear, Tye?"

"Oh, this and that. What's a Banana Cabana?" Titan chuckled.

I growled, "Ease up! If Odd hears ya, he'll ——"

"He'll what—ground me? I'm coming with you, Bailey! I'm not

staying here with the girls. I'll go mad, looney—how do you say it? *Whackers?*"

"Whoa. Steady up, prince. I would let ya, but it's not my choice."

"Oh, I beg to differ! I'm coming."

"No!"

"Yes!"

I searched the room. "Right! Ye can come, but we can't let de demigod know!"

Titan rubbed his forehead. "And how are we going to manage that?"

"Do ya have an earphone?"

"An earphone?"

"Yeah, one of dese." I showed him my left ear.

Titan's eyes bulged. "Oh, those thingies! I never got one ... I'll just borrow Tea's. That'll do it." He trekked off. *Crickey! That's gonna be so suss if he just asks.* I skedaddled ahead of him, his body bouncin' back with black fur on his cheeks.

Perry yelled from the bathroom. "Hey, Bailey! Why are you jogging? It's already hard enough getting changed in here, I don't need the floor bouncing please!"

Odd yelled through the spare bedroom's wall. "Perry! Don't be rude about his weight. You know he's sensitive!"

"Argh, nuts," Perry scoffed. "My bad. Keep doing you, Bailey. Be out soon."

Faith asked if I was dandy. I told her Titan an' I were just racin' 'round in the hallway. Zia laughed at us.

Titan whacked my side. "The hell d'you do that for?" he demanded.

"Don't just ask Tea. She'll know we're up to somethin'!"

Titan rolled his eyes. "Dude, as if I would just ask her."

"What do ya mean—ya not gonna ask her?"

Titan shuffled 'round me. "Let me demonstrate!"

He wandered into the kitchen an' raised his voice. His arms were by his side as he pouted. *"ZIAAAAAA! IT'S NOT FAIR! WHY DO YOU ALL HAVE EARPHONES, BUT I DON'T!* Even Teala has one. Why didn't Odd get *me* one?"

"Oh, don't worry Titan. I don't have one either," Assonance said.

Titan cried again. "YEAH, BUT ... But I don't have one. And I've been part of the group since before the Town of Tents. Why don't I have one? TEALA CAN I USE *YOURS* FOR TONIGHT? I'll give it back, I promise."

"Sorry, Tye," Zia uttered. "You can't just take Teala's things. We're not in the Castle of Glass anymore. You can't just take what you want, especially from our friends."

"No, it's fine, princess. He can borrow it if he wants," Teala said.

The princess wasn't having it. "No. He always does things like this. Titan, you have to understand that we're not kids anymore and we're certainly not royals. We don't get things when we complain."

"Don't treat me like a spoiled brat," Titan scoffed. "I just want to borrow it. And if Odd does eventually get Assonance and me one sometime soon, I'll know how to use it. Please. Pretty please? I'll give it back in the morning! I promise, I promise, I promise ..."

Titan trekked back to me, throwin' an' catchin' Teala's earphone in his cupped hands. I eyed him down.

"How was dat not askin'?"

"Dude, that was pretty much complaining," Titan smiled. "How annoying ... So, what's the plan?"

After explainin' to him that I'd fetch him once Odd, Perry an' Dally were safely inside the Banana Cabana, he nodded an' put the earphone in. I told him that the earphones were how we were gonna stay in contact an' that he couldn't tell the girls what we were up to. He saluted me an' then jumped at something. It had me schmooked.

I turned 'round as Odd adjusted his grey suit's cuffs. He pulled my hat off as he led the pack through the hallway.

Perry threw his arms out, "How do I look?" He had his white hood beneath his blazer.

I grinned, "Schmick! Very schmick! You too, Dally! Quite gussy."

Dally bit at his gums. "This better be worth it. Otherwise, I'm head-butting Odd."

They strolled into the kitchen. The girls whistled as they trekked past.

CHAPTER 17: ODD EXPLAINS

Odd silenced 'em. "Thank you, ladies. We'll be home in around two hours. Business meeting for Charles, unfortunately. I need to look my best with my two awkward-looking security guards and panda bear. Just a precaution. We'll see you soon. Stay safe!" Everyone was baffled. Odd had never told anyone to stay safe. He left my hat on the staircase's railing as Perry an' Dally waved goodbye.

We had no idea what kind of mess we were 'bout to stumble into.

Chapter 18

The Banana Cabana

Perry

Loud music emerged just down the waterway.

Bailey slumped. "Crickey! Dat's a colourful club!" he said, awed.

Fluro yellow and orange lights glistened, reflected in the rippling water and windows ahead. It looked as though the ground was jumping to the music. Barely balancing upon it was a herd of people, all dressed nicely with orange glow sticks wrapped around their arms. Behind them was the end of the island. The lake jolted to the vibrations of the club. As we stumbled further along, Odd diverted into an alleyway. We turned left and faced the yellow flickers of the club's nightlife. The beat dropped as Odd huddled behind a large metal waste disposal bin. The smell of fish and onions was so fresh, Bailey stuck his tongue out in disgust.

Odd peeped over the bin. "Bailey, you stay here. Okay?" He pointed forward. The side of the Cabana was terribly lit with a flickering streetlight and no neon orange, just grey brick walls and posters advertising the Banana Cabana's next big shows.

"Jus' keep an eye out. Dat's all I gotta do?" Bailey asked.

"Pretty much," Odd said. "If you see, or hear, or even smell anything suspicious, you let Perry know. Worse comes to worst, just call for all of us."

I smiled at Bailey, tapping my earphone.

"See ya all on de other side den!" The panda cheered.

Chapter 18: The Banana Cabana

Odd stood, adjusting his own earpiece, and wandered around the bin. Dally and I caught up, but *man*, was I confused. *What's he so worried about?*

The world got louder as we were consumed by the crowd of intoxicated Centrillians. Odd was patient. He stumbled through the herd, splitting the people around him like a prophet, and led us to the front of the line. Some lads without shirts argued; others faced Dally and me with grim faces, their breath reeking of cigarette and vodka. Fortunately, the security guards knew Odd. They shoved the lads off us, and we reached the head of the line without any trouble.

"Hey, Dally. Am I sweating?" I asked.

Dally surveyed my face. "A little. Don't worry about it, man. This is definitely a different vibe from Everbreen!"

I raised my eyebrows. "Kelton too!"

The security guard at the front stopped Odd. "I didn't think you were gonna show," he mused. He had a red viper tattoo along his bald head and down his neck. It was a similar snake to Kate's green crest back in the Town of Tents.

"I didn't think your boys were going to pull off those party animals. We're all surprised. How's the night?" Odd asked.

The guard smiled, "Splendid. Just splendid." He turned around to a lady at the entrance. She had a desk with a deck of cards and a stamp. "Get me a special," the guard said.

"The two in the suits are with me," Odd said, pointing at us.

The guard sighed, "Get me three specials."

Odd strolled past the guard. Dally caught on and followed.

Entering, I gave the lady my crest hand, and she slammed her stamp against it. My hand dropped down. An orange symbol was painted onto my skin. The words glowed: *The Banana Cabana VIP*. It sparkled as if it was made from stardust. We walked through the main entrance and, for a bit, I couldn't see any security. "Hey Odd, did you ——"

Odd put his finger on my lips, "Shh."

I shoved his hand away. "What'd you mean, *shh*?"

Odd kept his pace. "No time for questions Perry! This way."

Dally rolled his eyes. "Security's tight here. Some shady business must take place behind these walls."

The music got louder, and the further we walked, the more the chequered walls and red carpet bounced. We strolled past the front bathroom where two girls about our age stumbled out, laughing their heads off and chatting away in slurred voices. *Huh! Weird.*

"Where's the male's toilet?" I asked.

Dally looked at me and shrugged. "What the …? That can't be right."

"It's a Bellcurve's tradition," Odd grinned. "They keep their female and male toilets separate from one another. The privacy of the sexes is important in their culture."

"So this place is owned by a Bellcurve then?" Dally guessed.

"Like Waldo. He had a yellow crest," I added.

Odd stared at me and continued to another opening.

The inside of my mouth was dry as we entered the main part of the club. The yellow lights vanished, soon replaced by the flashing blues and greens of the DJ's stage and people hoarding the dance floor. The beat dropped a dozen times as we reached the bar. I could barely hear myself think, let alone hear Dally and Odd—not to mention that Bailey thought it'd be a good idea to ask how we were.

"Perry! What de whipper's happenin' in dere? It's so loud."

Another voice mumbled something before Bailey raised his voice. I could have sworn it was Titan, but there was just no way.

I pushed down on my left ear. "Huh? What, Bailey? It's just the music. Can you hear me?" I asked.

"Why are ya yellin'? Ya gonna get my cover blown! Tye, I swear by ──"

His voice faded. "What'd you say, Bailey? … Bailey?" *Why'd he …?* He had turned his earphone off. I didn't even know he could do that. Must be getting better at using his paws.

Dally faced the bar, reading the drinks menu. I sat next to him. Odd came in close—I think he was touching our backs as he mumbled, "You two stay here. I've got some business to attend to. Stay out of trouble. If you see anything suspicious, you let me know asap. See

Chapter 18: The Banana Cabana

you on the flipside." I could hear him patting us. He turned around and walked up a staircase into another section of the club where three security guards dressed in black suits stood. They checked his blazer before letting him pass.

Along the floor, there were a handful of little gazebo-like rooms with orange and yellow curtains. Inside each gazebo, girls danced half-naked. I'd never been in a place like this before. Surprisingly, Dally wasn't all that fazed.

"You need to stop looking, Pear!" he groaned under the dance music.

I looked at him. "How come you're not overwhelmed? Why are you so calm?"

Dally played with a toothpick. "Perry, how long was it when we were separated after the attacks in Kelton Whide?" he asked.

I sat, staring at the bar. "Bit over a year and a half. Maybe less."

Dally crushed the toothpick. "A lot can happen in a year and a half." His voice was raw. "Especially when you're out in this world surviving ... Let's just say this isn't my first rodeo in a place like this. Don't worry 'bout me. How are things with Faith? I didn't walk in on anything this morning?"

I licked my lips. "No. No, don't be stupid. We were just talking."

"So you had pants on?"

"Yes, I had pants on!" I said that a little loud. "We wouldn't, we haven't ... Not in a place like ——"

"Wait, you haven't? Like *nothing*? Not even a little hand stuff?"

"Not really. Like, a little, but ... Things are complicated with my touchiness and well—I don't really want to go into it. Not here! Like you said, a lot can happen when you're trying to survive in this world."

Dally paused for a bit. "Apparently too much sometimes ... What do you think Odd's meeting's about?"

I shrugged. "Couldn't tell you. I'll see what I can hear!"

Listening in, I could clearly hear Odd's calm walking and breathing. He raised his voice. "Gentlemen. No need to check my suit. I just bought this beaut——"

The sound of patting trickled in. Another deeper male voice said,

"He's clean. Come on through, Mr Odd!"

Odd laughed, "It's just Odd. *Just Odd.* No mister insight, I'm afraid."

"By the bullock eater beneath my shaft, I can't believe my own gruesome eyes!" A woman's voice echoed through the earpiece. "Oddington, you sick Half-a-Pimper, d'hell d'you get here? Please, please. Move over will ya? Let the man sit. Please have a seat, right here. We've got a fair amount to discuss, now don't we?"

Odd's pants crinkled as he sat. "We do ... Charles has been missing you of late. Says the mine's integration in Tinkette is on you."

The lady responded. It was sluggish as if the women had a lisp. "On me? Oh, for the love of a Pimper, why the hell is that fool blamin' me? What? Because he decided not to show! If he wanted the bloody milk, I'd have given it to him. Oh ... this is about that paper fellow, isn't it?"

Odd let out a sigh. "To a degree. You've worked with Papercut before. Why would he try and assassinate Charles? Why now?"

"Now isn't that the question. Look, I didn't work with the kid," the lady laughed.

"Yes, but you were there when they injected him."

"I didn't see half the crap they did to that poor kid. His voice box stopped working when the beacon took effect. If you want my opinion on the whole assassination, maybe Charles wasn't the only target."

"You're not suggesting that he purposely killed Genny?" Odd gasped.

The woman giggled. She took a sip of her drink and continued, "You haven't seen what I've seen. That boy isn't human. I saw him wipe out a whole room of trained Fleddings, just with two straps of paper and that hunger in his eyes."

"Who else was he there for, Heb—my apologies, that name's taboo in most cities."

The lady laughed, "And it's best we keep it that way. This facade can only last so long, Odd ... From what I've heard, Papercut's contract was for three people. An ape from Everbreen, a senator, and

Chapter 18: The Banana Cabana

the third I cannot say. But knowing the source, take it with a grain of salt. There's a lot more deception these days."

Dally nudged me. "Man, I gotta dump a log. Here, I'll shout the first round and you can meet me up the stairs Odd walked up. I think the male toilets are down there." He pulled the cash from his blazer and the bartender came running. "Two Tinkette Clubs. With Sugar Fill. Thanks." He handed a twenty over and took hold of his drink. He passed me mine, took a sip and dropped off his seat. "Don't go dancing without me."

I shoved him back. "Wouldn't dare cut up shapes without you."

He grinned, placed his drink on the bar and scurried to the security guards. The music changed and I took a sip. It tasted salty, like the old parties we used to venture to back home.

Odd's voice grabbed my attention. "This is nice," he said. "The following you have here. Reminds me of before. Back when Hope ____."

The lady's voice was different now—more ladylike. "Please! Not tonight. I'm happy to hear you still remember, but not her name."

Odd stayed quiet. "I'm sorry ... I think it's time we move on."

"Yes, let's ... Are you sure you want to go through with this?"

Odd's voice was calm as he gulped on something. *Was he drinking?* "I have no choice in the matter. Rules are rules, right? You know."

There was some clambering and clicking from the earphone.

"So that's what it looks like. Lupo."

The woman's voice went back to the way it was before. "The Pimper's Milk. A bizarre request, coming from Charles. But as you said, rules are rules! Hold it tightly."

"And why's that?"

"Oh, it's simple. I had a dream last night. So Odd ... You wouldn't know who Teala is ..."

Argh. My ear! Where'd this stupid static come from? Why'd she ... How'd she know Teala's name? Where the heck did Odd go? I snatched Dally's drink and finished mine off before storming out onto the dance floor. The music got louder and louder the further I got from the bar. So many people were jumping up and down, I almost tumbled. To balance, I placed my free hand in my blazer pocket. The guards glared at me as I approached them. They stopped me with their palms outstretched.

"Sorry, bud. You can't come through. We need to see some identification."

Are they messing with me? "But I'm already in the club!" I argued.

"Look, we don't want to kick you out. Identification or you can go back to the bar," the guard said.

I pointed at the one giving me the orders. "That sentence doesn't work. Don't I need identification to sit at a bar? I'm only going up to find my friend—he went to the toilet."

The quiet guard slowly reached for his pistol. I calmed my voice. "Wait! I'm sure it's somewhere. Give me a moment." As I leaned down, Dally threw himself out of the doorway at the top of the staircase. He slammed one of the guards into the wall and threw another over the railing using his mind. He screamed my name, and I threw the drink into the air. *What a waste of ten bucks.* As I did this, the DJ dropped the bass, and I pulled out my staff. The guards were one step ahead of me. Fortunately, bullets go through me. None of the dancers were fazed.

I knocked the bossy guard and the quiet guard to the floor, kicking their guns away. When I turned, the DJ, the bartender and the dancers were all wearing half black and half white masks—simplistic versions of the Hebi mask Dally was accustomed to wearing during heists. Each mask glowed under the fluro lights. All the dancers stopped and stared at me as the music continued to play. Dally and I observed their eerie gaze and one started to move. Another started to vault towards me. I swung my staff and he crashed into the DJ's speakers. When I looked up, the whole crowd veered toward me.

I flipped around, putting my hood on, and Dally screamed, "LET'S GET OUT OF HERE!" He headed back through the door upstairs. The masked ones chased me and grabbed onto my legs. *Holy balls!* I fazed through the wall next to me, and when I re-emerged on the other side, Dally's shoulder rammed into another guard. This part of the club was a lot brighter and there was way more security. I ran to Dally, using my staff to send another guard flying against the doorway. The doorway was filled with a cluster of masked intruders.

Chapter 18: The Banana Cabana

The sound of Dally's fist hitting one guard after another was constant. "Odd owes us big time for this. PERRY! Watch out." The bricks that held the Banana Cabana flew out of the bathroom's wall, breaking through the cement to collide with a masked women's body. She fell back, bricks half lodged into her side. I grabbed Dally's arm as the doorway began creaking. *Oh! It's gonna break!* A white light took us.

When the light vanished, we were halfway down the hall. White ash fell and burnt the orange carpet. The doorframe had fallen, and countless white and black masked ones and security guards had begun chasing us.

"Quick! Get 'em!" a guard ordered.

"No, you don't!"

Dally and I bolted into one of the gazebos as the guards narrowed our escape. We flung any hands or tasers away from each other's sides.

"Where the hell is Odd?" Dally shouted.

I was halfway fazed through the main back wall of the hexagonal gazebo, yanking a guard with me. I thought I'd just freak him out, but when I re-emerged on the other side, he was missing. I returned to Dally. The guard was still there, unconscious, his head against the wall I had run through.

"I don't know. He's not answering. Neither is Bailey," I said.

Dally whacked another masked dancer. "That idiot's gonna get us killed in here. Where the hell did all these maniacs come from?"

I shrugged, spinning my staff into the bellies of the DJ and the bartender. "Sorry guys! I prefer my mix tracks shaken not stirred!"

Dally flicked his pinky finger. The lightbulb in the gazebo fell and drifted to the motion of his flick, smacking another guard in the forehead. "Really Perry! That didn't even make sense." He looked at the guard with the bulb shards covering his head and chest. "Lights out!" he smiled.

I yanked Dally and spun. The white of my crest glowed. We faded into another room, white ash falling to our feet. "That was cheap, Dally." I clicked in my earphone. "Hey, Odd! Where are you? I think it's best we leave now!"

Odd rushed past us, yelling, "That might be the best suggestion you have ever had. But I'm a little preoccupied!" He swung a steel suitcase at another masked dancer who was shirtless, glowing orange with a fluro wristband and necklace. We ran to his side. Odd knocked the dancer over.

"The hell is happening, Odd?" Dally asked. "I take one crap and this place goes ———"

"Yeah, yeah, yeah. Save it for later, smelly ... Look! You buy one bit of fluid from a spirit; these things tend to happen. Blame Charles when we see him. He's the reason we're in this mess."

I leaned on my staff. "So how do we get out of here? Did you get what you were after?"

"Indeed, I did! But I've never been here before," Odd smirked.

Dally's eyes bulged. "What do you mean you've never been here before? Aren't you thousands of years old? You don't know anything, do you?"

"I know enough," Odd sighed. "But this establishment's not normal. I hadn't heard of it until Charles mentioned it during our phone call about an hour before we left."

We began marching through the silent halls of the Cabana. *Huh, where'd the screaming go?* Dally flung his arms about. "So why the hell are you doing so much for that douche? If I remember right, you punched him in the head a few hours before this amazing phone call."

Odd stayed quiet—one with the hallway. "There are things you don't need to know about me, Dalton." His voice was mellow. "Just know that we, as people, have rules to follow. I hate Charles. I'd much prefer if he died in a dark hole, but alas, he's intrigued me with this project of his."

"What, the mine?" I asked.

"No, not the mine. Something more ———"

Suddenly Bailey's voice echoed in my ear. "Bailey! Is that you?"

"Perry! Why'd ya turn ya earphone off? I've been waitin' outside de Cabana for almost three hours."

He can't be right. "Three hours? How on ..."

Bailey continued, "Look, it's gotten quiet. No one's 'ere. It's empty. Dere's no music. I'm gonna head for de back exit."

CHAPTER 18: THE BANANA CABANA

"Yes, Bailey," Odd cheered. "Open the side gate if you can—Ah. That's a lot of masks."

The masked ones emerged from where we were heading, covering the hallway's corner and climbing over one another. We turned and ran. I can't believe my legs took me so far. I remember Odd threw one masked dancer off Dally's back and then a blue light emerged. The moon! The smell of the fresh Central City air. Leftover hovercraft exhaust, the mould of the water behind the Cabana and that incense smell Bailey's fur has. As we plopped out of the exit, two guards came rushing behind us.

The sound of crickets echoed as I picked myself up. All three of us were slouched on the floor. Odd was on his feet first. He chopped one of the guard's Adam's apples and then a roar startled my ears. Bailey, with all his might, growled. It echoed down the alleyway, almost knocking me back down. But even though it made my heart race, the guards kept coming. One had *BCS* imprinted on his hat. He ran towards Bailey. A glass shard slapped his wrist and he flew back into the skip bin next to Dally. The glass had not pierced his skin; instead, it melded around his arm and, like a handcuff, locked him in place against the bin's metal. Dally stood, searching for Zia.

A high-pitched laugh erupted behind Bailey. "See! I told you I should have come. He's not going anywhere!"

You got to be kidding me! "Titan! What are you doing here?" I asked.

Titan put his hands behind his back. He had Zia's green stainless glass. Dally sighed, "Oh, Zia's gonna kill us! Especially you, Titan!"

"Wha'? She ain't gonna do anything," Titan grinned. "And besides, Bailey invited me ... I mean—look! I'll explain everything. Zia won't budge if it comes from me. As long as her precious shard doesn't break, she'll be happy! It's bloody hard to hold anyways. I don't know why she brings it everywhere!"

Odd took the guard's hat off and put it on Titan's head. "That should probably explain to you why she wears that white glove of hers ... Do any of you hear that?"

Bailey stuck his head into the Banana Cabana's back entrance. "I told ya not to be a simp, Tye! Now, look what ya done!" the panda cried. "Why would ya bring Zia's shard? Gah ... No, I can't hear anythin'!"

Odd looked Dally and me in the eye. "Where'd the masked ones go?"

Bailey sneezed, retreating onto his back paws. His face was drenched. "Eh! Some got in my mouth! Yuck, yuck, yuck!" He licked his snout. "Oh, neva' mind. It's jus' water, I think. D'hell was dat?"

Suddenly a black-gloved fist with an orange fluro band emerged from the wall. The bricks crumbled around the fist as Bailey hurried to my side. Then the sea of masked ones flooded out of the side entrance. Bailey growled at them.

They didn't stop.

He growled again, his fury piercing my ears. Bailey turned to Odd. "They're not scared of me! Odd, they're not scared. Why am I even 'ere? What do we do?"

Odd ran towards the water behind the Cabana. "Looks like we're going swimming!"

Titan ran behind me. "What are you guys talking about?"

I shoved him ahead. "Speed up, Tye! Can't you ... *Just run!*"

We ran into the water and the noises stopped. The masked dancers had vanished! Titan whinged about how cold it was and how stupid we were for running away from a few curious guards. Bailey snorted, paddling through the water, his fur splayed out around him.

"Yeah, sure. Curious is a way to put it. Dat fist almost conked me!" Bailey uttered.

"It wasn't that bad!" Dally said, leading the pack.

Bailey zoomed behind him. "It went through a wall, Dally! A whippin' wall."

Dally shrugged it off. "Well, they've stopped chasing us! For now. I can't see any of them. What the hell's the plan, Odd? What are those things?"

"Games, Dally. They're playing with us. We're going to camp out by the forest, catch a ferry back to the mainland in the morning. If they reappear, we'll need to leave for Drewmora tomorrow. The further from the Cabana we are, the further they'll be."

I splashed the water with my fists. "You gotta be kidding me! That's at least five kilometres away. Plus, we don't know how deep the water is! What if Titan can't swim?"

Chapter 18: The Banana Cabana

Titan shoved me. *"I can swim!* I may be of royal blood—doesn't mean Father didn't make me attend swimming lessons."

"Well, Perry," Odd murmured. "If you want to fight all night, be my guest. The Banana Cabana is just behind you!"

I kept trudging through. It took forever. The water got deeper the further we walked until suddenly my feet weren't touching anything. Titan had to lean on Bailey's back when we got to the deeper parts. He was shaking by the time the land became shallow enough to walk on again. Surprisingly, for such a long stretch, the water here was quite shallow. Not like an ocean, becoming deeper and deeper; instead, it was bumpy and unreliable. Your foot would get caught under rocks and little gaps. When we finally climbed under the trees of the grey wood jungle, I could have passed out.

Bailey leaned his back on a tree, Titan next to him as Dally shook the water out of his pockets. "So much for these suits. Let's rest for now. I can't see any masked people," Odd sighed.

I stood next to Bailey. "How does the grass feel?"

He grinned, the wet hairs on his snout dripping with water. "Dilly. Almost like home!"

Odd cursed at the top of his lungs. "Not today! Gah, I can't take you guys any——"

I spun around. Odd had dropped to the ground, face first. His suitcase slapped the grass and he began snoring. Dally ran up to him. A dart was hanging out of his neck. He started to wobble, and I braced myself, running to protect Titan. But by the time I reached him, these small creatures with orange tattoos and leaves in their hair had surrounded us. My breath got heavy, something tasted stale, and the world went black as my head hit the ground.

Chapter 19
Boys Will Be Boys
Faith

"Would you look at that!" Zia mused. She leaned on a spruce tree branch high above the evergreen soil. The grass swayed and the stench of sweat and dirt lingered anxiously. I clasped onto another tree branch as its atoms swayed to my will. The whole tree bent backwards for me, the sound of its leaves rustling. When it lifted me, returning to its upward self, I gradually swayed over to Zia. The tree dropped me off as the branch she stood upon reached out and caught me, holding me like two wooden hands with leaves for fingers. The branch hand pulled me inwards. I slumped my head down beside the princess and grinned.

It didn't feel right, but this whole thing was mildly amusing. "How on earth did they manage that?" I pondered.

Teala appeared in a ray of red light that flashed as fast as it vanished. Red ash fell down the branch as she sat admiring Perry, Dally, Bailey, Odd and Titan, who were tied up with vines. They were being carried like roasted chickens by several smaller creatures. The creatures mumbled to one another in high pitched voices, their fluffy, rust-coloured fur fluttering in the breeze.

Assonance flapped her wings behind me; the wind from her flight cooled my arm. "Thank the Pimpers! You were right, Zia!" she cheered.

"Of course," Zia snorted. "These idiots can only go so far before they end up tied up. I'm kind of glad Titan took your earphone, Tea."

Tea shrugged, dangling her legs. "I'm just surprised Odd's tracking system still worked. We haven't used it in ages."

Chapter 19: Boys will be Boys

"Not since WonderWorks!" I added.

Zia rubbed her head. "No. We have. Odd makes sure when he sends out Perry and Dally that they're wearing their earphones. It's normally through his computer so he and I can track them. Make sure they're not doing anything stupid. But ... Well, he only put the system on his laptop a few days ago when we stole some files from the new WonderWorks CEO in Everbreen. We're pretty lucky he brought the damn thing!"

"Do you think he knew? To do all this? To bring his laptop?" Assonance asked, hovering lower.

Zia shrugged, "You just can't tell with Odd. Especially nowadays."

I leaned down beside Teala, watching carefully. The little creatures dropped Bailey. They argued for a moment, six of them picking Bailey's stick up and shaking it. Teala's crest was blinding, but through its light, the little creatures, one foot at a time, carried the boys further. They were shaped like eggs, with paws similar to Bailey's but smaller and darker. They had eyes like a slow loris, round and reflective in the forest. I tasted my dry lips. "The real question is how do we get them out of this?"

Zia threw another glass shard she had stolen from Senator Hartway's house. As it flew, the princes began to go see-through. The shard collided with another tree stump. Zia's legs floated as though drawn by the shard. She glided through the trail the shard had created, like a glass angel on a Christmas tree. Almost fully transparent, her body floated, vanishing amid the orange and red canopies. When I focused on her shard, she stood beside it, yanking it out of the branch, and waited for us to reach her side.

I joined her, making the branches of the forest my swing. Each tree bent down for me or caught me or held me as I catapulted towards Zia. When we joined up, Teala appeared beside us with Assonance flying furiously through the changing forest.

"Crud, I'm getting tired," Zia groaned. "I don't think I can meld myself into this shard again. Maybe one more time, but I don't want to get stuck halfway from being skin and flesh to glass. If we don't do something now, we might lose them."

Teala sat on a canopy. "Agreed. I don't think I can teleport much further either. I've never done it this much before."

The creatures had carried the boys for what felt like hours. However, when I admired Perry, drooling in his sleep, a bongo drum echoed throughout the forest. *Where on earth was that coming from?* Assonance's wings fluttered sporadically. "Don't worry guys. I'll have a look!" She zipped off into the red leaves ahead. Zia caught her breath. "Gee, that girl, I tell ya!"

We paused for a moment. Assonance came flying back, almost knocking us out with her brown feathers. "GUYS, GUYS, GUYS! There's a camp not far ahead. We can probably walk the rest of the way!"

Teala stuck her head over the branch that held our weight, gazing at the grass below. "Well … We just need a way down, don't we?"

Zia held her breath. "Here we go again. One last time!" As she threw her shard and it hit the ground, we were all off the branch.

Colliding with the grass below, we all met at the same place, eight feet stomping on the ground. Assonance flew, transforming back into her Centrillian self, complete with two legs and a button nose. A spruce tree bent and placed me beside her. Teala appeared; red ash fell beside our boots. The shard grew and grew until it resembled Zia; her colour returned as she gasped for air. The bongos echoed.

The breeze scorched my skin, it was so cold. Recovering, Assonance surveyed the forest.

"So what exactly is this place, Ona?" I asked.

Assonance searched ahead. "Tribal land. Sporangia made a pact with these beings. They're called Gieas. Natives to the Cyrillic Forest. It's why there are no buildings here!"

Zia eyed the dark grey bark of the tree stumps. "You're right. There are no signs of settlement or even immigration."

I leaned down, feeling the damp dirt between my fingers. "There's no signs of anything! Just the creatures. Even Jinkie's Gap had a few farms and crops. It's bizarre. This dirt's perfect for most crops; it's cool and light, damp enough to act as manure. Depending on the rain, this forest would be an amazing place to start a wheat farm, even cocoa bean."

"You sure know a lot about dirt and crops," Assonance said.

"Of course we do," Teala giggled. "We're Kelts. Farming's everything at home."

Chapter 19: Boys will be Boys

"If my dad had access to land like this, they'd have taken it!" Zia smelt the fresh air. "So why has Sporangia been so patient with these ... Gieas?"

Assonance looked to the camp. "Because of what they do ... You know, the old Pimper stories."

"Pimper? What's that?" Teala asked, picking up a blue flower.

"Ah, what do you guys say for it? Gods! *Pimper* is Centrillian for God. We call their tales of old Pimper's Dreams. There just ol' stories they used to tell us when we were younger. Like how if you got stuck in the Cyrillic Forest, Gieas would find you and turn you into stone. And those who fell victim, the Gieas would return them to the mainland. The town put the stone statues up like gargoyles on the outer walls of Sporangia to warn visitors and day-goers to stay away from this forest. But it can't be true. Those old walls are just ancient Centrillian architecture. I've never seen anyone come back frozen in stone."

Zia pushed forward. "So it's not true. Perfect! Even if it is, we might as well rescue the idiots sooner than later so we can go home and sleep. I'm wrecked! Plus, this place is giving me the heebie-jeebies."

We ended up at the entrance of a wooden paradise—a strange mix of weak timber bridges stretching from one tree to another. Between them were dark wooden shacks of varying sizes, each sheltered by a roof with leaves for shingles and cream-coloured curtains for doors. Each house was small and always a few metres above the darker grass and tree roots. The smell of fire wafted in the breeze as we scampered further into the treehouse village.

The bongos got louder the deeper we ventured; as my ears began to ache, a sort of didgeridoo joined in. High-pitched cheering came from the Gieas as they danced around the boys. In the middle of a fenced-off area surrounded by paths, makeshift fences made from branches and bark, and a larger building with peculiar masks hanging on spears at its front door, they placed the boys down. The Gieas were two-legged with grey paws. The ones carrying the boys had feathers in their fur. They joined the others in their dance, shoving their arms into the air.

"Is it me, or are these things a lot cuter on the ground?" Zia chimed.

"They are really small now that you mention it. I've never seen so many this close before!" Assonance whispered.

"Do you think they're going to eat them?" Teala mumbled.

I looked down at her. "Why do you say that? Did you see it in your dream?"

She shook her head. "No! It's just … why else would they be celebrating like this?"

A groan came from the centre of the crowd. Dally stirred, rubbing his head. He mumbled, "Gah, damn! What the fu——"

Odd put his hand out like a gentle fan. "I wouldn't speak too loudly, Stinky. These are Gieas. And they're telling a story."

Dally searched around, growing suspicious. "Okay. Why would they be telling us a story if we're all passed out?"

Odd pointed at the big shelter. "They're not telling us anything. They're telling her."

A woman stood at the front of the main building with a mask over her head. It was shaped like a love heart with several shades of orange, hints of blue and two giant white eyes; it matched her white dress. She walked elegantly in comparison to the Gieas. The small creatures appeared to worship her. Perry picked his head up; his hood had fallen off.

"Dude! What the hell is going on?" he asked. "Damn, another masked lunatic!"

The woman raised her right hand into the air. The music stopped and so did the storytelling. The Gieas stared at their god, their spears, bows and arrows freezing. She was almost shining in her white dress. You could even smell her purity from here.

Zia wanted none of it. She gripped at her new shard as Teala clasped her wolf crest. I leaned down to her. "Are you okay, Tea?"

Teala searched my eyes. "Is yours not stinging?"

Truth be told, mine was burning. I smiled, "I'm sure it's fine!"

The Gieas took my attention. They chanted *Gah Ma, Gah Ma, Gah Ma* over and over until they were out of breath.

Chapter 19: Boys will be Boys

Bailey rolled over. "Crickey!" he sighed, tapping an unconscious Titan. I think we were all ready for a brawl.

The masked lady began to laugh. The Gieas copied her in a higher pitch. *What was so funny?* The masked girl reached for her mask and the Gieas gasped. The laughing vanished like a storm in the sunshine. She lifted it over her head and, would you believe it, *said Perry's name.*

"I did not expect to see you here," she cheered. "Dally, is that you? And the prince?" Her tone changed. "Gek ohi nokala. Felti gep! Gumo! Quelto gumo. Felti gep! Gelhi Gah Ma's nokala!"

The Gieas untied the vines around Bailey's paws. Their *Gah Ma* rushed down a timber ramp that swayed from her podium to the ground. She slid to Perry's side. *Gosh!* The Gieas are tiny. *Were they always this short?* They were only half the height of their Gah Ma, reaching her tummy. Dally looked like a giant beside them. Perry said a name I couldn't quite catch. Her face was still blurred behind a bundle of leaves.

"Can you see her?" Assonance asked.

I shook my head.

Zia was ready to charge. "Well, I don't like this *Gah Ma*. She's not one of us! We can take these Gieas. Look how small they are!"

"Wait a moment, Zi!" I held her down. "There might be a better chance to get them if we just wait. Five more minutes. Trust me." Zia shook her head.

When I looked up, the masked lady had let go of Dally.

"It's so good to see you both," the Gah Ma said. "And you, prince. Gosh, so much has changed, hasn't it? You two have become quite the gentlemen, I see! But if you're here, it means she was correct ... Gelti ohi pardo. Timin faw!"

The Gah Ma's body turned to our spot behind the shrubs. Zia growled under her breath and I heard Teala attempt to calm her. The masked lady tiptoed toward us, pointing in our direction.

"Faith. Your Majesty. Teala."

The Gah Ma knew our names. How?

"There's no need to be wary of my mask. They have lots of meanings in this world. I'm sure Odd can tell you all about it!"

Zia stood, storming towards her. I tried stopping her, but she wouldn't listen. She opened her mouth to roar, but something caught the princess' tongue. I joined her as quick as I could.

Felicia stood before us. Her blond hair was still as beautiful as ever, her brown eyes like the dirt of the Cyrillic Forest, and her smile as perfect as it had been in Kelton Whide. She looked at me. "Hey, Faith. Long time, no see!"

I marched up to her and felt the warmth of her pale skin. She was still so smooth, even though she had dirt under her fingernails. *As If … How is she even like this? She's so dirty.*

Teala hid behind my back. She pointed at Felicia. "I remember you. You're Gracie's big sister."

"Now that's a name I haven't heard in a long time," Felicia smiled.

Zia tapped her shoulder. "Don't worry. Gracie should be safe. If she's got half the talent you have, she'll be—what? Leading a pack of Gieas."

"How'd you know we were there?" I asked.

Felicia looked to her followers and Titan picking his nose in the middle of the crowd. "I'm just a Gah Ma in this village!" she admitted. "I'm not the wisest here. Come. We have much to discuss."

We met with the boys, half asleep and smelling of a freshwater lake.

"Big night, boys?" Zia mused. "Don't even start with me, Tye! Just give me back my shard!" Titan fumbled, handing Zia her green shard. She placed it firmly before her grey eyes, her white glove numb to its sharp bumps. "Gah, look at what you've done! It's all squishy. This better be your blood on it!"

Titan raised his left hand, showing a few slices down his palm. The smell of blood was fresh on all but Bailey.

"Yeah. That thing's sharp as," the prince cried. "I'm never stealing that crap again. Didn't even really help."

Zia put her nose in the air, sighing as she walked away. "And give Teala her earphone back. She needs it more than you."

Titan took the earphone out of his ear. He held it out to Teala. "Sorry, Tea. They're kind of cool."

Chapter 19: Boys will be Boys

Teala stuck her tongue out in disgust, surveying the bloodied, sticky device in Titan's palm. "No, you can keep it for now. I'll be fine 'til we get home."

Assonance had her arms out wide. "Are you guys okay?" she asked. "What the silk happened to you? How'd you end up on the other side of the river?"

Dally rolled his eyes. "We walked and swam and then walked again. Rather refreshing at one in the morning. And I'm starting to get a kick out of Oddy-boy's plans! This one's done us well."

"When we needed to act, you were as quiet as a fiddle, Stinky!" Odd mused. "At least I suggested something, instead of just staring at the ground."

Dally pointed at him. "Stop calling me that. And I wasn't staring at the ground. You saw how many of those masked freaks there were. You lying sack of ——"

"We're still alive, aren't we? Why the hell are you angry? The whole group's even here. I think my plan worked better than what I had originally thought." Odd turned to Zia, ignoring Dally's cries of protest. "Thank the heavens someone's got a brain. I am so glad I showed you that new tracking program. I hadn't even unpacked it yet."

Before Zia could respond, Dally's interrupted. "On Hope's arse, you're really starting to piss me off!" he yelled. "I'm really starting to think that you actually know nothing, Odd. Over the last six months, you've gotten Perry and I almost killed at least a dozen times."

"Hey! Give it a break, Dally," said Perry. "He didn't do anything that bad. We're here, no one's injured, Kyle's doing well."

"Bro, I don't even know where I am at the moment, let alone how the stale girls got here!"

"Language, mate. We don't know how old dese little critters are," Bailey said.

Dally observed the crowd. "Fine. I apologise. But I am done helping you, Odd!"

Odd smiled. "Why? Because I called you Stinky?"

I turned to Odd. "Really, Odd. Why'd you go and say that?"

Dally's face turned red. "Oh, I'm gonna ——"

"Omahwei! ... Omahwei, Dally! This is a place of peace. And I will not have you fighting under the Bywoe trees." Felicia pointed a long walking stick at him.

Odd watched her closely. "How do you know that word? It's ——"

"Tinket!" Felicia answered. "Right? There are many ways the Gieas live. They serve under the pink beacon."

Odd folded his arms. "Yes, but these Gieas are different from the ones in Tinkette Valley. They're smaller and have different-coloured fur. I had no idea there were so many down here." He looked to Bailey. "Very protective creatures. I think they like you!" A Giea patted Bailey's side. His eyes widened.

I finally reached Perry and hugged him. His back straightened from the impact of my arms.

"Whoa! Faith. It's fine." He hugged me back.

Letting go, I picked leaves from his hair. "You almost got me saving you again. Are you okay?"

He smiled, kissing my forehead. "I'm fine. And you've only saved me once."

"Please. I can name at least three or four other times. Like back when Kyle was a troll. Huh, it's so strange, saying that now." I clasped his hand. "I'm just glad you're okay."

Dally was staring at me, still fuming. I looked up but he avoided my glance.

Felicia approached us. "Well, how *not* shocking ... Perry and Faith, I calculated it! I believe Zia, you owe me ten for that bet we made in Kelton Whide. Remember?"

Zia put her chin up. "Gah. Now that's a blast from the past."

"I'm only joking," Felicia smiled. "Haven't you all grown. And you've brought an Ever and a Centrillian."

Assonance offered her hand. "I'm Assonance."

Felicia grinned, shaking it. "An orange raven. I look forward to walking with you ... There's someone I'd like you all to meet. But there's a story I must tell you before you see her!"

Chapter 19: Boys will be Boys

"And who is *she*?" Zia demanded.

Felicia rubbed at her blond hair. "I was visited by a man on a flying carpet. He told me to expect a panda bear and four albinos. He did not disappoint."

I wondered aloud, "How'd Othello know?"

Felicia answered before Odd could give it a guess. "Because he saw them crossing the river when he flew over to interrogate Ma Ankhalo."

Odd searched the camp. "And why would he interrogate someone like that? You live with Gieas."

Felicia bowed. "That is exactly the story I must tell you. I've been here for over two years. I've calculated the perfect heights for the treehouses, the exact amount of timber needed to shelter each and every single one of these Gieas, and I've also made room to shelter other stragglers lost in this world. Some old friends." She looked at Dally. "A girl in a black hood who sought answers on the man who betrayed her." She turned her attention to Assonance. "A crazed gentle spirit obsessed with Hope's Light in search of redemption." She stared at Perry. "And a boy made of paper who told me he was scared of what he was about to do."

Perry mumbled Papercut's name.

Felicia continued, "The Prophet Othello was interested in discovering why we had welcomed such damaged spirits. And although one was my fault, it was fortunate my downfall led to your safety."

Odd took a deep breath. "Have one of these damaged spirits you've kindly sheltered experienced a berserk?"

Zia and Bailey gasped. "You don't seriously mean that, do you Odd? There hasn't been a berserk since the start of the Echo Wars!" Zia exclaimed.

"And even if there had been, we'd have heard it on de news, or on an orb or somethin'. We'd know about it! They're not somethin' ye can easily cover up," Bailey added.

Odd bit his lip. "Well, why else would Othello come here, of all places? When people go berserk according to him, it's often because of the beacons. What did he ask you, Felicia?"

Felicia shook her head. "I'm not the one he asked." She examined the Gieas. "Lamalayo! Peporious layi'demo ra toi nokala. Li tlihi gi Ma Ankhalo!"

The Gieas who were infatuated by Bailey's fur stopped their patting and instead wobbled eastward, singing and dancing like before.

"*Ma Ankhalo! Ma Ankhalo. Li tlihi gi Ma Ankhalo!*"

The rest of us smiled. Teala swung around with an older Giea, but Dally and Odd were both unamused. Dally adjusted his cuffs. Odd snatched a suitcase from a smaller Giea, brushing mud from its side. I inhaled, tasting the rich warmth of pollen as we followed Felicia deeper into the Bywoe trees. A Giea with a black fur patch over its left eye clasped my hand. It smiled and led me forward.

Perry laughed, "Looks like you got yourself a new boyfriend!"

The grass we stood on became thicker and more evergreen. "They're cute. Don't tell me you're jealous!" I teased.

He winked at me. "No, you go on. I'm just going to check up on Tea."

"Ma Ankhalo," Odd said. "A One Mother lives here? There is a sort of sense to your story, I will admit."

Felicia looked back at the demigod. "Is that what makes you happy? When things make sense to you? When you understand everything and anything?"

Odd paused. "No. No, things never make sense. Not in this world."

"Then why do you frown?"

Odd searched for ants within the green strands below. "Because I've been lied to ... Does this make you happy? The little ones? Protecting them?"

Felicia carried a baby Giea in her arms. As she cradled the ball, she stared into its blue eyes. "I'm not sure. I could do the world a justice by leaving this place. With my brain, I could change the world. But I'd feel empty either way!"

"Curious," Odd smirked. "A girl who's as wise as a prophet. I never knew Gieas could create such extravagant architecture. But you lack ——"

"I lack nothing, demigod. Happiness, sadness, the damaged souls—those three did not just have emotions. Happiness is more than just an emotion!"

The black-patched Giea slowed as I approached Bailey and Assonance. It leapt up and down like a child. I felt a peculiar weight on my shoulders—its furry paws were ticklish against my hair. Titan was teaching a Giea half his height how to count his fingers. Teala was picking flowers, one orange rose at a time, with a whole herd of them.

Perry walked over to her. "Are you feeling all right?"

Teala stood beside him. "I'm fine. A little drained, but I'm managing. We're gonna need a memento!"

Perry rubbed her head. "No doubt. Keep an eye out while we meet this—what was it?"

"Ma Ankhalo. I think she's going to be rather surprising!"

"And why's that?"

Teala held onto her dreamcatcher. "Why do you think?"

The two laughed, Gieas climbing, pulling at them and dancing.

I relaxed my shoulders to the weight of the Giea. Bailey had a half a dozen sitting on his back as if he were a horse. They slid off his side and switched places, laughing as he and Assonance talked.

"An' dat's when I roared—an' Odd said they'd be shook of me ... but they weren't. So den I got splashed on de noggin with dis water, I think, an' a whole bunch of zozzled masked fellas came runnin' out of de building, throwin' their meathooks at us. But it was dandy. We skedaddled into de water an' now we're here."

"I'll be dang!" Assonance said. "Sounds like a silky night! We just stayed up late, talking. Zia cracked open the wine cellar."

"De wine cellar? Well, I'll be a crackpot."

"I was surprised too." I chimed. "I had no idea that Tinkets were so into their alcohol!"

Dally was ahead of us, alone. He walked with a hand in his left pocket and brown smudges on his blue suit. He looked at me. "Surprised! What, d'you forget about your favourite cider at home? What was that stale corn called again?"

I laughed at him, "It wasn't that bad! *Somvaltey*. The next cheapest thing from a goon bag."

Dally chuckled as Assonance tapped my shoulder. "Somvaltey. Now that's a riot. Back in the cult, I stole a whole ten-pack with a few of the girls. By the time Irene noticed, we'd passed out in our rooms! They thought we had gotten a virus or something!"

"Ah, cider's never been my thing," Bailey grimaced. "My ma used to drink red wine. It was cheap."

Assonance and I giggled at the same time. "*Velvet Red Minot!*"

"It featured heavily in Senator Hartway's cellar," I laughed.

Dally's whole body was off, as though someone had blown out the small white fire inside his crest. I wandered up to him, "Are you holding up?"

He turned to me. "Just over it! I wanna have a shower."

The Gieas seemed to be avoiding him. "You didn't get hurt, did you?" I asked.

He shook his head. "No. And even if I did, you'd be able to fix it. It's just, this place. Felicia, she's ... Do you think she knows anything about Ada?"

"Why don't you go ask her? What happened to you two?"

Before he answered, the grass beside my feet grew in size and girth. Tree branches cracked; leaves and flowers burst into life. The Gieas began to chant again. Everyone slowed. The smell of nothing laid ahead, as though the air was pure. The Bywoe trees became denser.

Dally stared at the growing grass. "You see that, right? Is that you?"

The grass around my boots sprouted as though I was giving them life. But I didn't feel drained or as though the light on my crest was feeding them. "It's not me! What is this place?" I asked.

Bailey approached us, roses of orange and blue sprouting around his paws. Here, we all had this gift; when my foot moved away from the grass strands, they returned to their previous size. Felicia handed the baby Giea back to its mother. "This," she inhaled. "This is the sanctum of the Ma Ankhalo! The One Mother!"

Zia held onto a dying shrub, its leaves growing to great extremities purely from her soft touch. "And that means?"

"A Good Spirit! Your One Mother is a Good Spirit!" Bailey grinned.

Assonance gawked and Odd licked his lips. Perry folded his arms, a branch building itself as he leant on a large Bywoe tree. "Now I'm no genius ——"

"That's for certain!" Zia cracked.

"But!" Perry sniffed. "If I'm correct, that's a whole lot of things, isn't it!"

"Precisely," Odd nodded. "Half-marraboo, half-god. Serenity? Am I correct? That's who's hiding just ahead."

Felicia giggled, "Oh, not hiding. *Being!* She's been expecting you."

Perry looked me over. I made sure our eyes met. "I thought Good Spirits were extinct," Perry said.

"And I thought humans weren't wise," Odd laughed. "Have you ever wondered why each major city has one prophet? Have you ever just once questioned their wisdom? Of course not. They're prophets! They can't be wrong. It's 'cause they're not wrong! We were meant to come here today!"

Assonance stumbled forward. "Why?"

Felicia pouted. "If I may. Odd, there are eight Good Spirits known to man. In the heavens, I'm sure there are more. Perry, Tea. I've learnt a lot from being here. I can tell you why she knew so many things!"

Perry bit his lip. "What things? Who?"

"Your mother. Prophets are chosen through their blood—their connection with the Good Spirits."

"So prophets have a spiritual connection to these Good Spirits?" I asked.

Odd continued to explain. "They do. It's why they can foresee things. It's the reason for their wisdom. Bad for the brain, I hear."

Zia let go of her shrub. "Well, if Othello's already connected to one of these Good Spirits, why'd he fly here to meet with this one?"

"Now that's the question, isn't it?" Odd smirked.

Dally pushed ahead. "Enough with the exposition dump! Let's just see the chick and get the hell out of here! No offence Felicia, but I'm tired, and I don't really care about all this who's wise and who's not!"

Felicia tossed her stick before Dally. "'Tis not you she seeks." She searched him up and down. "Under the Bywoe trees, we follow me. Understand? You are only welcome here because I have allowed it."

Dally retreated. "I'm sorry!" He smiled, "Look who's *Miss Responsible* now. I remember when you'd act stupid to impress knobheads at school. Wasn't really an act, was it? No, no. No, this is more like it. The real Felicia! Please. Lead us. I wouldn't want to get in your way. Same book, huh?" He winked.

Felicia grinned. "How mature of you. We all grow up sooner or later! It's good to know you're still the same as before. There was never anyone like Dalton Lee back at Kelton Grammar!" She looked at the rest of us and bowed. "I welcome you all to the serene lands of Serenity." She closed her eyes, took a deep breath and walked ahead, grass and ferns growing around her. "Follow!"

Chapter 20

Serenity

Bailey

The air was so vulgar here. I was bamboozled the second the grass 'round my paws began sproutin' in size, becoming thicker and longer. Followin' Felicia, a face I somewhat remember, was dandy. She was a dynamite, leadin' the pack with a sense of pride. Her blond hair was as soft and shiny as the silk they sold in Central City; the scent of peppermint drifted behind her as she walked. Her mask had fallen back, and it stared at me as she trudged forward, swinging to the rhythm of her hips. Suddenly I couldn't feel anything. *The Gieas had stopped.*

The Bywoe trees were unlike anything from Everbreen: large, dark grey trunks with heavy amounts of resin seepin' from their sides. The deeper we ventured, the less sunlight there was—just a maze of dark grey an' green. The cicadas began to chirp. Sweat was gushin' down Dally's forehead and the hairs on my belly dripped. Then a hypnotic hum like my ma's singing voice washed over me, leavin' us with an overwhelming sense of calmness.

Spirits appeared, like ghosts in a movie, starin' at us with their infinite gaze. Their hollow black eyes, ranging from small circles to large ovals, peeked into our souls. Some, larger than life spirits the size of myself stood beside Bywoe stumps. Others, smaller an' more agile, peeked from the treetops. We were slowly being caged in.

The Bywoe branches cracked an' leaned, pushin' closer to my side. As I stumbled behind Assonance, a little bug—so cushy an' dilly— flew above my snout. It had large wings an' a bonkers see-through elongated ball under its tummy like a lightbulb where its tail should be. It gandered at me an' I could have sworn on my own soul, it waved. The little lightbulb lit up with a yellow an' orange glow, like the lights you'd decorate ya shack with during the Celebration Season. The bush became a place of utter disbelief. Just like the time before when we bumped into the troll from under the Cobblestone Bridge, fireflies lit up the Bywoe trees as if they were yellow raindrops frozen in time.

Teala let out a relieved smile. A firefly touched her nose. "Let's hope there's no troll at the end of this forest!" she said.

"That would be a travesty!" Faith laughed.

Odd was baffled. "Travesty?" he queried. "Fireflies are special creatures. I'm surprised they're even here!"

A yellow glow glistened in his eye. Perry had a few yellow shimmers land on top of his crest arm. "I don't think they're that special, Odd!" the hoodless Kelt said. "We saw them a while back on our way to Everbreen!"

Felicia chuckled to herself. "How peculiar."

"And why's that, Felicia?" Zia asked.

Felicia had a herd of fireflies light the tip of her stick. "'Cause I've only ever seen them here. Near the Ma Ankhalo. She's close."

We hushed ourselves; even Titan an' Dally stood tall an' wary. The whispers of water gushed ahead as what seemed to be a cavern darkened the leaves of the Bywoe trees. The Gieas' weight left my back as they hurdled towards the cavern an' bowed. Felicia slammed the bottom of her stick down. When it thumped the grass, the fireflies' light twinkled upward in a yellow flurry as though a firework had been blown into the canopies above.

Perry pulled his hood over his noggin. All that laid ahead was a cluster of green an' grey vines as thick as custard, an' leaves so evergreen I thought I was home. An' silkworms—so many silkworms—climbin' over the Bywoes' branches. I could hear Odd gulpin' as we entered the cavern one by one behind Felicia, not a word said between the ten of us. The green vanished as my eyes adjusted to the cavern. Fireflies lit up the ceiling like starlight. *On the spirits, we had reached a sanctum!*

To my left was a waterfall not as large as the ones in the Forest of

Farbe but just as pure an' sweet. The crashin' water was a symphony under the hums of the spirits. To my right was something quite bafflin'—simple paintings, as though the Gieas had drawn orange an' blue pictures on the side of the cavern's rocky wall in crayon. In the grey bumps an' creases there was a panda. One image stuck out to me: a woman who was missing the top half of her noggin. Her hair, her forehead an' her eyes had been replaced with ferns, grass, flowers—all sorts of blessings from the spirits. It was as if her head had been sliced in half so that a forest could be planted above her nose.

As I gazed at the paintings with Zia an' Titan, a woman's voice echoed in the cavern.

"I feel an urge to listen to the Hopeful Mother's White Light. But that would be certainly malarkey, wouldn't it, White Rabbit?" Odd seemed unsurprised by the voice, grinning with his suitcase in-hand. He searched the cavern, "Your voice is just what I assumed it would sound like, Serenity. How long have you been waiting?"

I wandered behind him with Faith an' Perry. Perry opened his mouth, "Who's he talking t——"

The woman's voice became louder. "Don't be so impatient, White Wolf. I'm right in front of you. The Ever can see me!"

She was right! I could see her as clear as day.

She was exactly like the drawing—a woman sittin' on the soil with her legs folded above a dark blue mat. Grey tree roots had grown over her feet an' spread from her mat to the walls, clusterin' like spiderwebs. Leaves covered her shoulders like nets. Although she had no eyes, she looked at me with a gaze of knowin'. Behind her, there was this tree, fat an' wide with pink flower petals falling 'round it. Green ferns, grass an' flowers were indeed growin' above her nose where her eyes, forehead an' hair should have been. Her blood-red lips smiled at me and I could taste the pollen from the garden inside her skull.

A pink leaf dropped from a branch an' landed in her hand. When she caught it, her lips widened, revealing a perfect smile. I could feel a coldness slither from my tummy an' out of my breath.

Perry prepped his staff, Dally cracked his neck, an' Zia wielded her green-stained shard. The half-headed spirit spoke softly. "I've been waiting for a while. I would like to tell you all something. But before that, I must offer my condolences for Senator Hartway. The Ka'Bywoe Tree bleeds for him."

Felicia gawked, leanin' down next to the large tree behind Serenity. "Gosh!" she cried. "That's why its leaves have turned pink. Its sap has been thicker than normal as of late."

Zia steadied herself, smiling. "And what is it you'd like to tell us, Ma Ankhalo?"

Serenity laughed. "It's kind of you to be so formal, Your Majesty. I am no Ma Ankhalo to you. I'm Serenity, the Good Spirit of Nature."

Why is she 'ere of all places?

Dally had the same idea. "Then should you not be sheltered in the walls of Everbreen?" he asked.

Serenity rubbed the grass in front of her folded legs. "I am where the Bywoe trees spread and grow. And I am not the only Good Spirit in this world. The way I see things, Everbreen is more beautiful after the eradication of Araidian."

"Agreed!" I chimed.

She titled her noggin slightly to the left. We huddled closer behind Odd. Serenity gazed at us; I could feel her non-existent eyes on me. "The gods are waking, and you will all be there when they battle." Her voice sounded deeper. "A prophet visited me last night."

Odd kneeled beside Serenity. "And what did he ask you?"

Serenity turned her half-head towards him. "That is not what I have been waiting to tell you. But it is best you learn from me. It is curious Fæh's prophet would want to visit me."

She paused an' searched our faces before focusing on Teala. "Curious one. May I hold your Tinket Totem?"

Teala nodded, takin' it from her neck an' handing the dreamcatcher to the Good Spirit. "Of course."

Serenity smiled, feelin' the dreamcatcher in her hands. "Do you know my face, White Wolf?"

Perry mumbled to himself as Teala answered, "You're in my dream. You and another."

"Another? Was this other you speak of accustomed to wearing a cloak—a cloak as dark as midnight? And a face of nothingness?"

CHAPTER 20: SERENITY

Teala nodded and Serenity grinned. "Fæh Jiwa! Another Good Spirit ... Your dream must be very important, little one. Strange how he keeps colliding with my life. I would love to discuss this dream of yours further, but unfortunately, my time is short."

Another pink leaf landed beside me. I leaned an' crossed my legs beside Perry; the grass felt wet beneath the hairs on my bottom. It was like the beginning of rainfall when the pink leaves lose their hold on the Ka'Bywoe Tree. Felicia stood behind her Ma Ankhalo an' looked to the King of the Bywoe trees. "She's not lying," Felicia mused. "Once the Ka'Bywoe Tree runs free of its leaves, and the last one drops onto the grass, she'll need rest."

Serenity pointed at Assonance an' I. *What did we do?* "Gah Ma Fel, I would like you to accompany these ... adventurers to Drewmora."

"But Ma Ank——"

"There is no need for argument or debate." The Good Spirits' lips were tight.

"But what about you—the tribe—what we discussed? I can't leave you alone. What about the Regime?"

Serenity looked ahead. "The Regime will not touch me. Nor will any politician. I will be fine under the protection of Bywoe trees and the fireflies."

"But ——"

"You will understand later! Dragon, Wolf, Koala, Tiger, Raven, Panther, Rabbit and Panda. You will all experience things in this world that I will not be able to foresee, and neither will any other prophet. And although I believe my warning to abandon your mission to Drewmora will be fought ferociously by the princess, the hooded reaper, the demigod and the dying soul, I would like to say my piece: I've already given you an old companion for your journey. Someone I trust with my life, my Gah Ma Fel!"

"Thank you. I'd offer my soul, but we both wouldn't want such a damaged spirit. What is this piece you speak of?" Odd asked, pink leaves falling 'round him.

Serenity raised her hand to the grass that grew above her nose. A ladybug emerged from her head garden an' climbed onto her fingers. She let it crawl down her hand an' onto Teala's dreamcatcher. "There is death in Drewmora," she said. "Immigration from Kimeria has led to crueller times under its glass walls. If you enter its hexagonal doorways, there is no returning."

"Returning from what?" Faith asked.

Serenity frowned, "Call it *reality*. Everbreen was just the beginning. I see you are all along for this journey. I have been waiting to tell you one thing and one thing only."

We sat quietly. Serenity took a long moment to examine us. Well, I think she was examinin' us; otherwise, I got no clue.

She handed Teala her dreamcatcher an' sighed.

"The gods are waking, and you will all be there when they battle … One of you will fall so hard, you'll see another world. Others will become leaders, rulers, fragments of the past. And some will die. Do not close your eyes when under the dome of Drewmora! The truth will not reveal itself otherwise."

Perry looked at me, then at Dally an' Faith. "Is that it? What does that even mean?"

Odd stood an' the last pink petal fell, landing beside my paw.

Serenity gazed at me again. "Be wary, Ever. The world is not fighting against you. You need to let it, ah ———" A gush of air howled in the cavern. Like a lion growlin', the wind pushed me onto my four paws.

Felicia raised her stick. "Tiki nah lo. Ma Ankhalo bevosa!"

The branches 'round Serenity began to peel back. The cracklin' of their bark sounded like crying as Serenity's half-head slumped down.

Felicia stormed past us. "She is resting now. I will have the Gieas tend to her."

"And what about us?" Zia asked.

"I believe we have a ferry to catch!" Felicia said.

Teala put her dreamcatcher 'round her neck. Assonance stood beside Felicia as they trekked toward the cavern's rear.

"The ferry is far from here!" Assonance said.

Felicia winked at her, "Do not fret, Centrillian. Shouldn't take us any longer than an hour and a half. I've got it calculated!"

Chapter 21

Home Away From Home

Perry

Tap, tap, tap! I was tapping my hands against my—argh! *Is that a horn?* Guess we're reaching Central City's docks. About time! I yawned, spinning my staff. My tongue tasted dry and I could smell the fumes above the freshwater lake. Faith sat next to me, her eyes stuck on Felicia, Dally, Titan and Zia. They laughed as the passing water journeyed away from the ferry.

We were a few hours out from the Bywoe trees. The Gieas guided their Gah—whatever it was—*Felicia* out of the forest, and we cruised to the port with smiles and a surprising amount of calmness. Faith leaned back on the tin walls of the ferry. The dome windows stuck out like sore thumbs, one bumping my scalp as I leaned next to her.

"It's like we're always finding someone these days," she uttered.

"Kelton Whide's coming to us. I don't think we ever have to go back at this rate!" I said. Faith put her hand on mine. I guess she wanted me to stop fiddling, so I took hold of her, our fingers intertwining.

"Do not close your eyes when under the dome of Drewmora! The truth will not reveal itself otherwise," she repeated. "What do you think Serenity means? Do you think it has something to do with the gift?"

I shook my head. "Probably not. But she is a Good Spirit! I say we worry about it once we reach Drewmora. It's just a train ride away. We'll be there in no time."

"And it's Teala's birthday, the day we leave."

I raised my head. "It is, isn't it? Thirteen. Give Liv a heart attack, tellin' her that! Might as well save it for this afternoon."

"Afternoon?"

I nodded, "I'm meeting her *man*. Some stud she met from her days back in the labour party! You should come."

She pouted. "I don't know. It's your family, I'd just get in the way. And besides, we've found two Kelts in the last week. I think it's time we celebrate. Maybe organise something before we leave. Celebrate Teala's birthday. Just something Zia and I were thinking about."

I rested my head again. "It's only going to be this afternoon. An hour after we get back. After, we can go to the shops and buy whatever Teala wants for a little party with everyone. That'll be fun. I heard Eddy's in town." I leaned my forehead on hers. "And who said you weren't family?"

She smiled, searching me up and down. "Well, in comparison to a stud, I don't think I'll be able to beat such a title."

"I think you're much better than a stud!" I laughed.

"And how's that, White Wolf?"

I leaned closer. "Because you're smart. Brave. Beautiful. You probably have really smooth skin."

"Oh, it's super smooth. Been moisturising. But you forgot something," she laughed.

I was seconds away from tasting her. "Oh, yeah? Do tell?"

"I'm always saving you." She kissed me. I closed my eyes and this sharp metallic pinch echoed. It was like the ferry was holding in a fart.

I jolted up, turning my head to see Dally and Titan giggling. The glass dome window was in shards. Everyone was staring at us.

Felicia rested against her staff. "Now, who saw that coming?" She sat next to me. "Look at you two. I don't think anyone's surprised."

"I was …" Faith had lost her words. "What happened to you, Felicia? How'd you end up with Serenity under the Bywoe trees?"

Dally and Titan went back to watching the water. Zia and Bailey discussed what was inside Zia's journal, and Odd, Assonance and Teala sat close by, throwing their hands in a debate of dreams.

Chapter 21: Home Away From Home

"I suppose as much as you." Felicia looked ahead. "I stayed alive because I was always taking a moment to be calculated."

"What do you mean by that?" I asked.

She raised her staff. "Did you know that panthers are incredibly intelligent, yet at the same time, incredibly lonesome. Ironic, I suppose!"

She showed us her white panther crest. "We are what we are. The beacon looks beautiful from these parts."

"We're so close to home," Faith grinned. We all admired the white light piercing the southwestern clouds.

"Well, we're only five hundred and twelve kilometres away. Give or take a couple of centimetres," Felicia laughed. "It's hard to estimate with the ferry rocking so much and the clouds being so frequent."

I raised my eyebrows. "Did you just figure that out now? Or did you just have that number memorised for this kind of situation? 'Cause that's nuts!"

She looked at us with a grin. "Oh, I'm just good at numbers now. A minor effect from the beacon's light ... What have you learned since the time our crests began to glow?"

I trudged into Hartway's complex—whatever the building's called—and sat on the lounge. Dally joined me, groaning as his arse collided with the cushions.

"What are you whinging about? You can't feel anything." He threw his blue blazer onto the lounge's footrest and rubbed his face. "I am so sticky, it's not even funny."

Zia, grinning, jumped between us, her hands slapping the backrest. "Then have a shower, you dingus. And I thought I whinged! Gee. And be quick about it, I was thinking of spraying Bailey with the hose, seeing how he's all big. Who knows what those Gieas left behind."

Daegon strolled by with a bowl of cereal and a milky spoon. "Gieas, you say," he said. "Now why the salts are ye with silk'n Gieas? Rather have my hide cut off than be with them halfunts."

Zia rolled her eyes. "Odd why the hell is this knobhead still here? Isn't Kyle better now? We don't even need him or his deranged Centrillian voodoo."

Daegon pointed at her with a stern middle finger. "I'll have you know that alchemy is not a form of voodoo. It's a science—a science that is keeping your poor lil' brother together. Not to mention that boy upstairs." He searched the room, his arms spread wide. "Is there anyone else who would like my voodoo to assist them? I'm all ears!"

Odd waved him down. "Settle, Deagon, before I put another Sporangia mark on your code. You got any idea why Othello would be visiting a Good Spirit apart from his own?"

Daegon chuckled, "The prophet didn't mention anything to me. He's probably looking for something. Why else would he be visiting another Good Spirit?" He eyed Titan. "What do you want, prince?"

"Nothing," Titan grinned. "Just wondering what makes you tick! I'm going to have a shower."

He wandered upstairs as Faith, Assonance and Felicia strolled inside. Assonance pointed to the walls and the staircase. "And here we have it. Our home away from our tent-lets. It's still a work in progress."

Felicia had something caught in her throat. "You're living in a senator's abode? How peculiar."

I stood, my stomach churning at the sudden realisation. "So that's what this thing's called. I was just thinking of calling it a house-thing."

"Aye, abode," Bailey laughed. "Don't think I've eva' heard of dat one before." Next to him was the red vinyl doll. I grinned, picking it up. "It's not the worst place to take shelter. We should check on Kyle. You remember him, right Felicia?"

It looked like she had just woken up. "Kyle. *Kyle Matthews?* Is he with you? I didn't see that coming. Where is he?"

Daegon pointed to the staircase. "Just there, my dear!"

Titan was escorting a very pale and black-eyed Kyle down the stairs. Holdie floated above his head, spinning like there was no tomorrow. He was as shocked as the rest of us.

"Felicia?" Kyle gawked. "Well, it's like the Celebration Season has come early this year!" When his foot reached the floor, Titan let go of his elbow. Kyle nodded to him, "Thank you, Your Highness."

Odd put his arm around Daegon. "I'd like a word. I'm curious

Chapter 21: Home Away From Home

about the Centrillian belief in Good Spirits and Gieas. Who better to learn from than not only a Centrillian but a master alchemist?"

Daegon laughed as the two wandered around Kyle. "Well, that is why they call me the Doctor." They left, Odd's grip still firm on the suitcase he had taken from the Banana Cabana.

Faith rushed over to Kyle. "How're you feeling?"

Kyle watched his feet. The sound of Holdie spinning hummed under his voice. "Better. W-well, I'm not melting anymore a-and I'm not a troll."

"A troll?" Felicia mumbled.

"It's a long, long story." Kyle laughed.

Dally jumped, joining them. "So, you remember what happened?"

Kyle searched for ants. "Uh! Remember what? D'you mean the attack in Kelton Whide?"

"I believe the idiot was wondering about how you turned into a troll," Zia mused. "Do you remember any of that?"

Kyle felt his heated forehead. "Maggie! I was ... I was with Maggie and there were ..." He took a deep breath. "W-we got a ride, a shuttle. It crashed on its way to Everbreen. It was just Mag and me; I don't know what happened to the o-others. Have y-you guys seen anyone else? I'm pretty sure my family's s-safe but—man! I can't remember. I just ... *Maggie*."

I handed him the doll. "Does this ring a bell?"

He scoffed, shaking as his hands took hold of it. He had tears in his eyes the moment he touched it. "Oh, now that's a sight. This was hers. It was Maggie's. Thank you."

I raised my eyebrows. "Well, I did take it from you. Even as a troll, you kept good care of it. Under that bridge."

Kyle was admiring his doll and his recovered hand. "You were there. I-I'm so sorry. I couldn't control myself. A-all I wanted to do was protect *this*. This doll. And you took it. And I hurt you!"

"And I tore your hand clean off. It was missing less than a week ago," Faith said.

Kyle nodded, "And now it's back."

"And so is that doll!" I argued. "Don't apologise for hitting me over and over and … well, you hit me a lot, but that's … that's not the point I'm trying to make. And I kinda didn't feel it. Except when I started bleeding."

Kyle was still in awe. "I … I couldn't stop myself. You were just defending yourself; I wanted to kill you." We all paused for a bit.

Assonance intervened. "Hey, why don't we relax. It's been a heck of a week and I'm sure Perry and Dally and the prince all want a shower."

Bailey crawled to us. "Schmick idea. So, who's gonna hose me down?"

While Zia, Assonance and Teala scrubbed and sprayed Bailey at the back of Hartway's Abode, I rinsed myself off and changed back into my hood and boots. I walked downstairs to see Dally, Kyle, Felicia, Faith and Titan laughing about the time Felicia got told off by Mrs Mackenzie on sports day for not wanting to play tag football.

"Hey, there he is!" Dally cheered as I stumbled in.

I pointed at myself, "Me?"

Kyle roared his classic laugh. "Yeah, you. The one and only."

"I'd join in, but duty calls," I said. "I'll be back soon. If you guys would like, I heard Zia really wants to do something special. And Teala, Faith and I are going to be a little bit. Mind helping out?"

"With what?" Felicia asked.

Faith grinned, lifting herself from the lounge. "It's Teala's birthday tomorrow and we've all found each other. We wanted to have a little celebration before we head to Drewmora."

Kyle nodded, holding the vinyl doll close. "Sounds fun. Y'know, I-I haven't really eaten anything but marraboo and raw rabbit meat over the last few years. Wouldn't mind some sweet chompers or who knows what else they got at the shops here."

Dally nodded, "We'll go shopping, set up the—what's it—*abode* and make it real special for the little dude."

I couldn't help but smile. "Thanks, guys. It means a lot. She's turning thirteen, so I don't know, maybe Felicia can calculate how much everything will cost. Oh, and make it girly."

"Easy done. I'll be needing a change of clothes though," Felicia smirked.

Chapter 21: Home Away From Home

Faith stood next to me. "Eddy can probably help with that one."

Dally crossed his arms. "Eddy's in town. 'Bout time that old geezer gave us a hand. I ain't buying food from him, but if we pass his shop, I'll get some extra clothes for you, Felicia."

After we planned what to buy, I handed over the money. Then we went our separate ways.

Chapter 22
One Last Day

Perry

Teala was kind of fidgety. She held onto her dreamcatcher. "... What if he's evil—like, I'm talking Araidian evil?"

I shrugged, leading us down a waterway. "And why would she date someone like that? Olivia can be dumb, but she's not that dumb. Did she ever have a bad boyfriend in Kelton?"

Teala skipped ahead. "No, but who knows what can happen in three years. Like you're dating Faith!"

"What does that mean? Faith's not evil."

"I never said Faith was."

I nudged Faith, who was staring at the ripples of the blue Centrillian water. She shook her head as though I'd woken her. "Sorry?"

"Are you hearing this?" I asked.

"Gosh. Didn't you know? I'm evil," she laughed.

Teala gigged with her. "See. Don't be so serious, Perry. None of our friends are evil ... Where'd Liv say she was meeting us?"

I searched the water, the blue lights from under the waves reflecting on our faces. A canoe passed us, the rower's strength clear in her paddle. There were at least a dozen in the water. One of them spoke.

"Ahoy! Perry. Tea. Over here!"

Olivia was on this large, narrow, dark wooden canoe. The rower pushed her and another forward. A hovercraft floated past as her

Chapter 22: One Last Day

canoe docked just ahead of us. It echoed in the distance as we approached the bobbing timber.

I held Teala's hand as she shimmied onto the orange silk chairs. She spread her arms, rocking back and forth. Olivia sat with a smile as white as her crest. Next to hers was another almost perfect face. His eyes were a rich blue, his skin a dark olive, and his frail beard and hair a pure blond I'd only seen on Gabe. His crest was a blue sea lion. After Faith found her footing, I joined them. My heart jumped and my ankles rocked to the ripples of the waves. Olivia laughed. Before I knew it, the canoe, like a fancy floating lounge, glided down the waterway.

"Name's Giuseppe. It's nice to meet yer, Perry. I've heard a handful of stories."

I took care, examining him from his boots up to his fine military wear. "Drewan," I surmised. "A native name?"

He nodded, "Yes," and offered the silk lounge to me. "Please, I didn't mean to bother you. Yer seem to be having trouble balancing."

"I can't really feel much," I laughed.

"Have a seat."

I sat next to Teala.

"I'm glad you could make it. Did something happen?" Olivia asked.

Teala scratched her head. "Besides the senator ... It's been a crazy few days."

Giuseppe sat next to Olivia, his hand rubbing her knee. He noticed my glare and moved his hand away. "So, Teala, Olivia has told me that yer have all been residing in Everbreen. How was it? Did yer visit the museum?"

Teala's eyes lit up. "A few times, actually. Have you been?"

We passed under a small bridge. Giuseppe smiled, "It's been a while. I used to have family from there. Other sea lions." He noticed Faith, "I don't believe I've been told about yer other sister."

Olivia rubbed his chest. "No, this is Faith. A very close family friend and Perry's ... girlfriend?"

"Yes. That's correct," Faith giggled. "Perry thought it would be nice if I tagged along."

Giuseppe raised his eyebrows. He noticed her crest, "A dragon, how precious."

I leaned forward. "So, Giuseppe. What do you do?"

"Ei, when I'm not travelling with my battalion, I'm either defending Parliament House, shooting things or being distracted by Olivia, here." I wanted to gag. Both Faith and Teala grinned like it was cuter than a baby Ever.

Olivia slapped his side. "I don't distract you. You've distracted me for the last five seasons!"

My mouth dropped. "You've been here for five seasons? What happens when you're sent home or somewhere off the continent?"

Giuseppe looked me in the eye. "Then I go. There are such things as long-distant relationships. And when I'm sent home, Olivia can come. WonderWorks enterprise facility is under our guard." Giuseppe raised his arms. "Enough about my salty self. Please. Tell me about yourselves. You are exactly how Olivia described."

Teala went on and on about Everbreen and her dream. Giuseppe admired her dreamcatcher. Faith talked about the time before in Kelton Whide and how different things had become. I added my part. Surprisingly, Drewmora also got attacked. However, the Drewan Militia caught three of Araidian's Warriors before they were able to plant several sticky bombs in the main two hexadomes within the Upper Hexadome.

"How'd the beacon get turned on?" I wondered.

Giuseppe shrugged, "It was the will of the dead prophet, Othello. The blue light turned on and he was resurrected to study with Malaysia. From what I heard, the wise prophet came back to learn Malaysia's mother tongue—the ancient Drewan language founded from Euphoria's heart and the blue beacon."

"Malaysia the Weary. A descendent of Happiness, the women who saw the heart of the world. She's a prophet herself, is she not?" Faith asked.

"Sort of," Giuseppe said. "After Happiness mined too close to the planet's centre, that part of the mine was restricted for only her and other prophets. General Ko ordered extra protection in that mine the day we turned on the beacon. A day later, my battalion found Othello

Chapter 22: One Last Day

the Wise, naked, admiring the symbols inside the mine. He'd been dead for months. Strangest day of my life."

Teala admired the orange beacon only metres away from our canoe, beaming into the air like a line of orange fire.

"Is it as beautiful as the orange beacon?" she asked.

Giuseppe grinned, "Just about, I'd say. How many beacons have you three seen?"

I leaned back. "Three. The white one, the green one and now the orange. We're heading to Drewmora tomorrow. It's Teala's birthday, Liv."

Olivia's face burst with light. "Birthday! Oh my, it really is, isn't it? How ... You're not ... you're not heading to Drewmora with Mr Kingsleigh's CEO? Are you?"

We all explained what we thought we were doing on the train to the underwater city.

"Well, that's okay," Olivia muttered. "I'll give you something tomorrow then. Being part of Kingsleigh's council, I've barely had time for myself. But I can manage some time to get you a gift. And if that means we'll be on the same train, we can talk the whole way to Drewmora."

Teala was baffled. "You're ... You're going to Drewmora?"

Olivia grinned, pointing to herself and Giuseppe. "We both are. Sep's whole—what do you call it—unit? The whole Drewan militia are going there and so am I to establish a few things for Mr Kingsleigh. Especially after this last week and the mine's failure."

"It's a date then," Giuseppe cheered. "If it's anything like tonight, it'll be a quick train ride! You'll all love Drewmora. It's a lot different to here!"

Olivia couldn't stop smiling. "It'll be amazing. Gosh, if it's your birthday and you were nine when I ... How old does that make you now?"

Once we were on solid land, Olivia hugged Teala and me. Giuseppe threw the canoeist a few Drewan silvers and off she went to pick up another round of people. *I wonder how many crests she sees—how many colours and types of spirit animals?*

Olivia smelt like trimmed grass, but not Ever grass or Centrillian. Just trimmed grass from home, like she had never left in the first place. It almost brought tears to my eyes. After a few moments of silence and smiles, we left each other again. She said she'd be waiting for us, bright and early, at the station. I didn't want her to go, and neither did Tea, but under Giuseppe's arm, she seemed happy. I guess that's what makes her Olivia. She was happy! And because of that, I had this feeling inside, not of numbness, but a subtle calmness. Seeing her smile just made the world smell better and the air fresher.

On our way back, as we discussed Giuseppe, a familiar shop caught my eye. On a concrete wall under a tower of other similar-sized shops, there was a yellow light. A small old man drank a litre of milk with an orange sign above his head: *EDDY'S*.

"You sure are everywhere, aren't you?" Teala said.

Eddy rubbed his milk moustache and grinned, "Well, well, well. If it isn't de dynamic trio. Aren't ya missin' de one with de hair?" He paused, examining the waterway. "What do ya think of de expansion? Ophelia an' I have been workin' hard to get dis joint up an' runnin'. I think it's quite homely."

"It's perfect. The orange suits your name," Faith laughed.

We approached him. I rested my arms on his open front counter. "Who's looking after your other shop in Everbreen?"

He looked at me like I had a missing nose. "Who d'ya think? Me, of course. An' Ophelia. Gah, Odd was right. He said you'd ask dat. What can I do for ya?"

I looked at Tea and gestured for Eddy to come closer.

He giggled when I whispered in his ear.

"Is dat right?" he murmured. "Well. I'll see what I can whip up. An' happy birthday, little one. Well, I'm gonna miss sayin' dat soon. You're growin' into a lady."

"Yeah, she is," I smirked.

"I think I can make an exception," Teala blushed. "You can keep calling me little one until I'm grey and old."

Eddy chuckled, leaning back in his seat. "Oh, I don't think I'll be 'round dat long. Anythin' I can get for ye ladies?"

Chapter 22: One Last Day

Faith requested some new clothes for Felicia. Teala, a new hat for Bailey. Eddy gave us three paper bags and we went on our way. "Don't be strangers, ye hear?" the old Ever called.

Teala fiddled with her bag.

"What's wrong, Tea?"

Teala pulled out the hat she got for Bailey. It was blue nylon. Her face slumped. "Eddy forgot to give Bailey ear holes for his hat. How's he going to wear it now?"

Faith's voice was calm. "It's okay, Tea. I'm sure we can all chip in and put a band at the bottom so he can wrap it around his head."

"Or we could ask Zia to cut some holes in it," I mumbled.

She noticed my bag. "Maybe. What'd you get me?"

I pulled it away from her. "It's a gift. I'll show you tomorrow—on your *actual* birthday. Come on. We're almost at the abode."

When we arrived, the lights were off. I wanted to laugh; it was so obvious. Teala didn't seem to notice. She wandered inside like we were heading to bed. The moment the door creaked open, everyone shouted, "HAPPY BIRTHDAY!" Teala was speechless.

When the voices settled down, Odd stumbled downstairs. "Da hell's all this nois—huh?" I guess he noticed all the balloons and the makeshift birthday banner, which was surprisingly well crafted. There was food everywhere. Zia had snuck into the cellar again—wine bottles appeared left, right and centre. Teala's cheeks almost tore into two.

"Is it that time of year again?" Odd laughed.

"Thank you, everyone," Teala said bashfully. "I … I don't know what to say." She took a deep breath.

Dally leaned on the couch. "Well, it was Perry's idea. We just—y'know. Set everything up."

We played music, talked and just took a breather. Even Odd and Daegon joined us—well, Daegon came downstairs, stole some food, examined Holdie and then went back into Hartway's ensuite. Felicia got changed into her new clothes. Titan made fun of Teala, Dally made fun of Tye, and there were a lot of happy faces. Everyone told stories. Kyle told of home. Felicia told of Good Spirits. Assonance told of Sporangia. Teala told of her dream. Bailey told of the Town of Tents. Zia told of the royal kingdom. Titan told of food. Dally told of Ada. Odd told of the time before humans. Faith told of the new maps she had drawn. And I told the story of now—of how glad I was that we were all together.

Towards the end of the night, Assonance left to visit her parents. Teala hugged her goodbye—heck she had pretty much hugged everyone, except Odd. He sat alone, half asleep. His eyes were pensive, his nose half-flared and his hands tightly tensed.

Teala approached him. "Are you okay?" she asked.

He smiled at her as I watched with Bailey. "Huh? I suppose, Tea. You shouldn't worry about me. Are you having fun?"

"I'd be having more fun if you were happier."

He took a moment. "Really! That's stupid, Tea. But I appreciate the thought." He looked her up and down. "And who said I wasn't happy?"

"Your friend died."

"That he did. Doesn't mean I won't see him again." He admired her green eyes. "Doesn't mean I can't be happy, Tea. Happy birthday."

Odd jumped when she latched her arms around him. At first, he was baffled, but I grinned once his shoulders loosened and he hugged her back.

She laid into him for a bit and Bailey looked at me.

"That's dandy," the panda said. "He seems relieved."

"He is," I patted Bailey's head. "Come on. I'll show you the chompers, they're sweet as."

"Chompers?" Bailey asked.

"Yeah, chocolate. Hey, Dally, get us a chomper. Bailey's never had one."

"What?" Kyle blurted. "Bro, you're missing out! Chompers are better than rice cakes."

As we introduced Bailey to chompers, and Teala let go of Odd, it was nice to be surrounded by the people that made me happy. These days were coming to an end and none of us knew what dangers were ahead. It'd be a long time before we could celebrate like this again.

CHAPTER 23
ANOTHER REALITY
Faith

I still smell wine! *Fruity.* Oh my, and Perry. His scent, a linger of oak bark and moisturiser fresh atop our bedsheets. Lifting our white bedsheets, the feeling of silk between my fingers, I noticed him shirtless at the bed's end. Holding my head up, I tapped him with my foot. He remained preoccupied. "I nudged you," I giggled. "Are you okay?"

He turned his head, smiling. "Me? Just a bad dream."

I shuffled over to him, our knees touching. "Do you want to talk about it?"

He shrugged, "Nothing to worry about. Was just a dream." He paused, and for a moment, I suppose he got lost. Then he smirked, "I love you."

I rested my head on his shoulder; he was so warm. "I love you too."

After a few moments of staying still, talking about nothing and laughing, we left the white-walled bedroom for the last time. Outside, where the lounge room was, Perry rushed upstairs to give Teala her birthday gift; a white, green and orange bracelet made from bark and quartz. I saw Kyle, who was mindlessly sitting with Holdie. He had propped the metal spinning-top device above his hand—the hand I destroyed. It floated, swaying to the subtle shakes of his palm.

"Morning, Kyle," I said.

When his attention turned to me, Holdie returned to its usual position above his scalp. "Morning, Faith. It's been a while."

I sat beside him. Between us, the vinyl doll watched me.

"That it has. How's your hand?" I asked.

Kyle clenched his right hand. "It's like it was never gone in the first place." He gazed at me. "Don't blame yourself, Faith. Look, w-we didn't really know each other back in Kelton Whide, but th-that troll you fought. What did you do to it exactly?"

"Do you not remember?" I asked. "I changed the structure of your atoms and turned your hand into sand. I didn't know what would happen. I could have turned your whole body into ..."

Below his hand, his white crest of an armadillo glistened against his chin. "But you didn't," he said. "And I didn't know what I was doing. I hurt you and Perry. And look," he showed me his palm. "It's still here. It hurts, but it's here. And you saved me from the curse. From everything."

"Curse?"

He nodded, "That's how I would put it. It infected me, my light, my connection to the beacon. It was like witchery or something. A silver liquid."

"Are you saying someone did this to you?"

"Not someone—some*thing!* I-I don't remember, but I was w-with Maggie after the crash and there were fireflies and ———"

I turned to find Bailey on the staircase, sneezing loudly. The paintings on the wall next to him shifted as he shook his head vigorously, nose running. "Sorry. Didn't mean to disturb ya. I think I'm allergic to de carpet 'ere," he said with a clogged nose.

I smiled, "It's okay, Bailey. No harm. Are we leaving soon?"

Bailey crawled to our side. "Jus' about. Felicia's try'na lure Zia outta her mornin' spa."

"Of course she's having a morning spa. And what about Assonance?" I wondered.

"Still with her folks in de Blym District. Said she'd meet us at de station."

"She doesn't have to go. But it's not my choice. Have you seen Odd?"

"He's dandy. Got his laptop, de suitcase from de Cabana an'

everything. Dally an' 'im are arguin' like usual, 'bout Charles I think."

"Who is this Odd guy?" Kyle asked. He stood, packing the vinyl doll into one of the bags that'd been dumped in the room. We laughed, telling him all we knew about the demigod, Oddington, while we waited for everyone.

Before we left, Daegon bid us farewell. He wished to never see us again. Titan smiled at him glumly, while Teala yawned, searching for her dreamcatcher. Of course, Daegon found it. He said he didn't want it to get crushed during our celebrations, so he'd kept it safe 'til morning. Teala smiled and thanked him. Finally, he turned and left the house with Flashlights' two heads by his side.

"So, how's the code thing work again?" Titan asked.

Odd crossed his arms. "Well, if I got the symbols right, he'll be trapped there for—what'd you say last night?"

"Three days. That's how long it took for him to replace my stomach."

"I think I did three days—unless it's years. Oh, well," Odd smiled. "Looks like the *Doctor* is going to have some fun. It was a good idea, Tye. Clever kid."

Titan yelled to Daegon as he and Flashlights journeyed back to the Sporangia Sector. *"Have fun with the Gieas!"*

Daegon looked at his crest and his eyes widened. He screamed, turning his head, however, his body continued forward. "No! Odd. What'd you do? I swear on a pimper's silky arse, if you put something on my code last night, Imma kill ya next time I see you! You hear me?"

Odd looked at Titan and shrugged, "D'you hear that?"

It was a fantastic day. Not a cloud in the sky and a cool breeze against my forehead. Too bad we were only walking to the train station. I wandered with Perry, Teala and Bailey when something peculiar happened. We crossed a waterway, the sound of the lake slushing beneath our feet, and before us was a torn-down wooden warehouse, unused and dusty. We passed an alleyway beside the warehouse, and Perry gasped, "Hey, Bailey, isn't this ——"

"The Banana Cabana!" Dally finished. "I swear it was here too. This ... This is where we got swarmed."

Titan approached them. "You're right, this is it. What happened to that big ol' banana and the yellow lights?"

Bailey examined the sides of the light-grey oak. "Do you think those people are still here? *Those things?*"

Odd, with his hands behind his back, bit his lip. "How elusive," the demigod mused. "It is everything and anything that is nothing. A mind game."

Dally tensed his shoulders. "Don't start that crap, Odd. It was right here. We were inside with the two toilets and the masked freaks. The hell's all this?"

Odd smiled, "My guess is we entered another reality. Which makes sense with what I was getting and who I was meeting ... The question is, who controlled those masked ones? And why did they let us leave?"

Odd explained the tale of the masked ones. Dally took Hebi's mask from his backpack to demonstrate what they supposedly looked like. Odd was right. If someone had enough power to seamlessly transport all five of them into another reality, why would they let them leave?

We reached the station. Piles upon piles of Drewan militia escorted businessmen and women into the four trains. The two platforms were full. Martin swung his keys around, eyeing the crowd with a pale face. "Oddington!"

Odd gave him a nod. "Martosia. What's the word?"

Martin examined the trains. "The Drewan Militia are reporting home after their services in Parliament House were retracted," he explained. "Lack of funding, I hear. I've acquired boarding passes for you all, including the two extras for the fifth and last train."

"I appreciate the help, especially after such late notice. Have you heard from Othello?" Odd asked.

Martin scratched the back of his head. "Passed through yesterday. Said he was going nowhere."

Odd chuckled, tapping Martin's shoulder. "Sounds like Othello. Thank you. I'll be seeing you in Drewmora. How are the hexadomes?"

Martin grinned, "Very, very wet. Safe travels." We all waved at him and thanked him for his services. *A kind soul, that Martin.*

CHAPTER 23: ANOTHER REALITY

When we reached the third platform, the fifth train arrived. The screech of its horn echoed through the ginormous station and the white concrete beneath my feet wobbled from the militia's boots.

"Oh, there they are! Do you see them, mum?"

What a familiar voice. Assonance approached me with a smile. Mr and Mrs Milk were behind her, bright-eyed and relaxed.

Assonance looked at her parents, "See, I told you that we'd make it."

Her mother rolled her eyes.

Her father, brown-eyed like his daughter, waved to us.

"Excuse me! Mr Odd. Are you Mr Odd?" he asked.

Odd pointed at himself. "Me? Well, of course I am. You can just call me Odd. You must be Assonance's father, Mr Milk. I've heard a lot."

Odd approached him with Perry and Zia by his side. Mr Milk greeted the princess.

"My daughter would like to join you on your voyage to Drewmora," Assonance's father said. "And although I dread the sight of her leaving, she has reassured me that you are a very capable and protective guardian. I trust that she will return to Central City safely." He pulled Odd close—I had never seen Odd so white-faced before.

"Of course," he responded. "It'll be my pleasure to protect your daughter and ensure her safe passage. I'm sorry we've dragged her into this. But I can assure you that she will return within the season's end. That is an oath, Mr Milk." Odd put out his hand and Mr Milk yanked it so hard it almost fell off.

"Thank you, Mr Odd. I wish I could convince her otherwise, but she is like her mother. She is determined to see this through with you, and I appreciate your kindness. She holds you and your companions in high regard. I look forward to your return."

Odd nodded.

"Oh, and one last thing. Just make sure you're doing the right thing. I don't want to see my daughter as something she is not."

"You don't have to worry about your daughter," Odd said. "She's got a good soul. She knows who she is. I'm guessing she had good role models growing up."

201

The train's horn howled again. Its doors slid open as smoke billowed onto the platform. Mr Milk joined his wife as Teala and I shimmied away. Assonance hugged her parents as though it was the last time she would, and they kissed her forehead. Her mother almost didn't let go of her hands.

"Mum, I'll be fine. And look on the bright side. This way, maybe I can find Yuri, and we can be a family again."

They hugged again and again until Assonance was beside me, staring at her parents from afar, waving to them.

We wandered to the back of the train. Bailey was entering his own carriage, the final one on the eight-carriage train. As he and the rest entered, another familiar voice roared, "*Odd!* How many times must I say your name? You good for nothing ——"

Odd sighed, "Good for nothing *what*, Charles?"

Mr Kingsleigh, escorted by General Ko and Giuseppe, reached us. Olivia rushed behind them, piles of paper in her arms. She hugged them as though they were keeping her alive and, without hesitation, dumped them into Odd's hands.

"These are yours, Mr Odd," she said.

Odd raised his brows, holding everything on top of his laptop. He was unimpressed by the entire situation. "And these are, Councillor Caduca?"

Before Olivia could answer, Mr Kingsleigh spoke. "Paperwork. For our little incident the other afternoon. And some other minor deliveries I believe you and I are conducting. General, could you kindly." General Ko towered over Odd with a frown. He snatched the black suitcase Odd had recovered in the Banana Cabana.

Odd readjusted himself, still holding the papers. On top of one sheet, I read *Project Lupo*. "How fortunate," Odd grinned. "I'm glad I could offer my services. Will you be joining us, Charles?"

General Ko returned to Mr Kingsleigh's side. The latter laughed.

"No, I will be on the first train with General Ko. However, his best lieutenant, Officer Malvitch," he gestured to Giuseppe, "will be looking after you and your train. I just wanted to make sure everything was in order and that I had my delivery."

Chapter 23: Another Reality

Teala tapped Olivia. "Are you catching this train?"

"You've made yourself a friend, Olivia? How particular. What's your name, curious one?" Mr Kingsleigh smiled.

"This is Teala, my sister," Olivia answered. "Mr Odd, here, helped me acquire a boarding pass for her. Everything's been paid for. I just ... I want to keep her close for when we return to Kelton Whide. After the arrangements in Drewmora, of course. It's just, after the attacks in Kelton, things have been quite difficult for our family."

"Family! I believe you mentioned you had a brother as well. A similar age to my ... *Alice*." Olivia watched her feet as Mr Kingsleigh examined our group.

Dally ducked his head out from inside the back carriage. "The hell's the hold-up? Wait, is that ..."

Perry pushed past Odd. "Tea, are you all right?" he asked, fear in his voice.

Mr Kingsleigh grinned at the trio. "There he is. What a nice-looking family. Your sister's been a great help in my plot to safely acquire property in Tinkette Valley." He turned to Perry. "You look familiar, son. Have we met before?"

Perry tensed his jaw. "I don't believe so. I just have one of those faces. Nice to meet you, Mr ...?"

"Kingsleigh. No, I think I'd remember a face like yours. It's the scar on your lip ... Oh, maybe it was something my daughter mentioned. Memories! They're the worst drug of 'em all. Much worse than dreams, curious one. May I see your dreamcatcher?"

Teala nodded, "Of course, Mr Kingsleigh. It was a gift." Mr Kingsleigh took it from her and smiled. "How poetic," he murmured. "I hope you have good dreams." He raised his hands as though to hug the two Caducas. "And safe travels. I look forward to understanding a little more about Olivia. A fantastic council ——"

"*Hey, asshats!* Can we hurry it up?" Dally yelled. Everyone on the platform stopped to stare at him.

Zia punched his shoulder. "Really, Dalton! Not the time."

Mr Kingsleigh handed Teala's dreamcatcher back. He eyed Dally and then the princess. "Your Majesty." He turned to Odd, snarling.

"Odd, I expect those papers filled out and on my desk in Drewmora when we arrive. What was it that old fool said?"

"Senator Hartway?" Assonance asked.

"Yes. Hartway. Odd, you'd know. That salty *I see you* Tinket word?" Mr Kingsleigh wondered.

Titan blurted from inside the carriage, "Omahwei?"

"Omahwei!" Kingsleigh clapped his hands, "That's it. Omahwei to all of you. I'll see you in Drewmora."

I ran to Teala. "Are you two hurt?"

Zia folded her arms. "Yeah. What'd that nutbag do?"

"Nothing ... Let's just board," Perry mumbled.

Teala examined her dreamcatcher closely as we boarded Bailey's carriage.

The smell of hay tickled my nose the moment we entered. The yellow lights flickered on and Giuseppe left the carriage. He walked out through the only exit and up a staircase where there were three vacant seats.

"What's he doing?" Teala asked.

"Making sure the train's safe before we leave. After Senator Hartway's assassination, the Drewan militia have been on high alert," Olivia explained.

"Same with the Kelton Guard. I'm surprised we didn't see any of them at the station," Zia added.

Titan folded his arms, sitting on one of the seats. "Don't keep your hopes up, Zi. There's probably one spying on us right now ... Well, maybe not on this carriage."

"No, there's been one spying on us since we left Parliament House. I just know it!" Zia smirked. "How long is this ride again?"

"Forty-two hours," Olivia uttered. "I know it's long, but trains are the easiest way to travel to Drewmora these days. With all the immigration from Bungonia and the Charltum Islands, it's hard even for a Drewan to enter its hexadomes."

"There are much worse things than forty-two hours on a train," I cheered. "We can do it, gang!" The boys gave an unenthusiastic and sarcastic hurrah, and the carriage began to move. *Next stop, Drewmora.*

Chapter 24

The Sudden Express
Faith

The first twenty hours went rather fast. It seemed we were always walking back and forth to the beds on the fourth carriage, and in between the two before Bailey's carriage. Someone was always sitting down, ready for a talk. I learnt about Assonance's brother, Yuri. Perry told me that they had called him Milky back in the days when we were trapped in Irene's Family.

I also learnt about Assonance's time in captivity. She remembered me, being *Kygo's favourite. That name!* I just wanted to curl up in a ball and cry at the thought of it. Assonance had been trapped there for two years before the Town of Tents; in that time, not a single guard had given her any sexual attention. Turns out, she was always too busy helping the newborns and nurses with feeding. However, that was not to say that she didn't get hurt. *But neither of us wanted to remember those days.*

Zia believed she'd found the Kelton Spy, although so did Titan; each thought it was a different person. *It was chaos.* Dally almost got into a brawl within the first hour, but he was only defending Kyle and Holdie. Unfortunately, Kyle did get some strange looks, so he spent most his time with Bailey. Felicia was often with me, Olivia and Zia, while Assonance and Teala interrupted Odd's paperwork to discuss Drewmora. And Giuseppe walked from one carriage to the next, spending too much time being preoccupied with Olivia.

It was early morning when I went to check on Bailey. He'd been sleeping more and more of late. He was still sneezing, and his temperature had risen overnight. He opened his eyes when I kneeled beside him.

"So, what'd he say?" the panda asked.

I rolled my eyes. "You know Odd. Just talked about rules. Said he'd check on you this afternoon when he's done his paperwork. He promised."

Bailey nodded, "Dat's okay. Thank you, Faith."

Perry laughed as he and Assonance peeked their heads through the window. "I'm telling you, I don't feel it. No wind, nothing!"

Assonance was bewildered. "So if I were to slap you, you wouldn't feel it?"

"You're not going to slap me, are you?" Perry asked.

"No, just theoretically."

"Uh, no. Unless you made me bleed, then I'd get all sore. What'd you lose?"

Assonance grinned, "My appendix."

"Get out of town!"

"Yep," the bird girl laughed. "That's what the nurses said when they gave me an ultrasound. That was a few days before we left for Everbreen. I'm pretty lucky."

Bailey put his head up. "That is really lucky."

Assonance's face went stale. "Well, that's not all. I still feel my bones crack and mould every time I turn into a raven. It burns like salt when I have to do it a lot."

I stood beside her, "Wow. I'm sorry."

She smiled, "What did you lose, Faith?"

Perry went silent as I turned to the door. "Ah ... Nothing special. I'm going to look for Felicia and see if she can help Bailey."

Perry stood. "I'll come with you. You wanna join us, Assonance?"

She shook her head. "No, it's fine. I'll stay here and keep Bailey company. I haven't gotten to know Felicia. Got any topics to talk about?"

"She's changed since we knew her in Kelton Whide," I admitted.

"Maybe her phone?" Perry joked.

I pushed him out of the carriage. "You doofus. Just be yourself, Ona. She's kind. I'm sure she'll like you. See you soon."

Chapter 24: The Sudden Express

Perry barged back inside. "HEY, BAILEY! We're getting you help. You'll be back to normal in no time, bud."

"Cheers, Perry. I'll see ya fellas soon."

The Ever had his head on his paws as I waved goodbye.

When I entered the second carriage, Felicia was already heading towards Bailey. "Hey Flic, could you have a look at Bailey?" I asked. "I know you're a numbers lady, but you're the best we've got. He's got a fever."

"I was just on my way to see him. I was curious about how much he weighs."

"Weighs?" Perry mused. "He's a bear. How much do you think he weighs?"

"In kilograms?" I didn't know whether to take her seriously or not.

She giggled. "Oh, don't worry. I'm curious about Ever culture. It was always on my bucket list at home and seeing how he's an Ever, I might as well take the opportunity. I'll see what I can find out, but I'm not an expert when it comes to fevers. Okay?"

I put my hand on her shoulder. "Thank you."

Titan was sitting alone in a crowd of randoms, including many Drewan militia under Giuseppe's command, simpletons covering themselves in hoods and employees from WonderWorks. He was playing with a dreamcatcher; it looked like it was burning his fingers. Every few moments he'd pull his hands away and flinch. Groaning, he noticed us and waved.

"What's up with everyone having dreamcatchers? Are they like a trend or something? Gee, I think I'm getting old," Perry whispered.

"Can't say I get it," I said. "We're not in high school anymore."

We entered the third carriage. "Yeah—whatever happened to the crappy dance moves or that challenge trend? Kids are weird now," Perry admitted.

I laughed, "Kids are very weird."

There were fewer strangers on this carriage. Dally and Kyle sat together, Holdie floating above Kyle's head. Two Centrillians across from them gazed at Kyle as if he were an alien. Odd was hunched over a desk. Piles upon piles of paper consumed his table. He put his middle finger up at Perry.

Olivia, a seat down and across from him, spat, "Mr Odd! I understand you and Perry have a past, but that is no way to treat someone. Besides, it's your fault for punching Mr Kingsleigh."

Odd slouched, staring at her. "No, it's his head's fault for being in the way of my fist." He gestured towards Perry, "He's a tough young man, he'll live. Trust me."

Perry wandered to Olivia, who was sitting with a laptop. He began talking about the time Odd knocked him out by accident.

I approached Kyle and Dally. "How are you holding up, Kyle?"

Kyle pointed at himself. "Me? Fine. Wish people would stop staring, but I'm peachy. R-r-really hungry now that you mention it."

Dally tapped his shoulder. "He even got his big boy talk with Odd." He stood, holding the ceiling bars. "Told you he's a piece of work."

"He was okay," Kyle grinned. "He was more curious about Holdie and what Daegon and I talked about. Seems to really care about you lot."

Dally sniffed.

I stabilised myself using the next row of seats. "Who knows with him," I said. "Don't worry, Kyle. We should arrive soon. Just a few more hours."

He smiled at me as I left, and Dally joked about my optimism.

I sat beside Perry.

"I don't like the way he's treated you, Perry," Olivia argued.

Perry put his hands in the air. "It's been for my own good. If he went too far, Faith and Teala would do something. Same with Bailey. Look, I don't feel anything, he hasn't really hurt me. It's fine, Liv! Isn't that right, Faith?"

I rolled my eyes. "Don't drag me into this. I've told you and him to relax countless times. It's like you're both trying to prove something to the other."

Olivia shook her head. "Men! I'll never understand why they boast."

"Do I really boast? I always thought I had a good smile, but a lady as fine as you would never lie." Giuseppe had entered the third

Chapter 24: The Sudden Express

last carriage with his rifle. His face scrunched up; it was like he was blushing.

Olivia's mouth slid open. "Well, you're a different breed in comparison to Perry and Mr Odd ———"

"It's just Odd, Olivia. You don't hear me saying Miss Olivia, do you?"

Before Olivia could argue, Giuseppe put his hand between the two. "Ei, enough of that. There's no reason to be creating conflict. Now, I get paperwork can be stressful Mr ... Odd. But that is no reason to be rude."

Odd leaned back, smiling. "Whatever you say, Sep. Just keep your pants on, okay?"

Giuseppe towered over Odd.

"Do you mind?" Odd asked, smelling the peppermint on the Drewan's breath. "I have lots of paperwork to read. I hear it can be very stressful, according to your battalion." Odd winked, and Giuseppe stood tall, holding Olivia's hand. "I think when we reach home, we should create some distance between Odd and us. You'll all love it. The hexadomes, the people, the salty station. We just have the Pilum Bridge to cross before we reach Drewan land."

"I thought Drewmora was underwater," Dally blurted. "Ain't that enough land for you bluies?"

Giuseppe kissed Olivia and took patrol down the carriage. He tapped Dally's shoulder—they were the same height. "Dalton, right?" The commander asked. "Perry speaks about you in high regard. We *bluies* are mainly miners. A lot of money in that kind of business. Drewan land covers most of the south-eastern corner of Oberon. You'll see. The Kuni Plateau is a little different from the farms in Jinkie's Gap." He winked and left for the second carriage. Dally rubbed his shoulder in disgust, joining us with Kyle. They sat across from Odd discussing Giuseppe's charm.

Zia burst from the fourth carriage, her finger pointed upwards as though she had dust on it. "I think I've figured it out?" She cheered.

Dally rolled his eyes. "Not this again. If you mention the Kelton Spy, I'm gonna ... You know, I think screaming about them isn't all too bright."

Zia was flustered. "Well, they're obviously not on this carriage, knobhead."

"The knobhead has a point," Odd argued. "Your theories have been rather excessive," he rubbed his forehead. "Hmm. I think this paperwork is getting the better of me."

Kyle leaned over, "What'd you find, princess?"

"Anything we should know. I can inform Giuseppe." Olivia insisted.

Zia waved away her concerns. "Oh, please. Commander Malvitch is fine where he is. No need to get the Drewan militia involved. I saw a very suspicious elderly woman. Reminded me of Titan's carer. Where is he? Titan?"

Perry pointed at the carriage behind us. "Back there, playing with some dreamcatcher. Maybe you should chill out for a bit. We've only got what?"

"A few more hours," I added. I looked Zia in the eye. "Perry's right. Maybe you should relax. We can figure this Kelton Spy business when we're safe in Drewmora."

Zia patted my head. "You two are cute. But if that spy isn't resting, neither am I. I want to ask Titan what he remembers of his carer, Gigi. I think that'd be the key."

Zia scurried down the line with a smile.

Dally laughed, "You think she'll ever stop?"

"Who knows?" Perry shrugged. "What's this, the sixth suspect since we left. Gah, we gotta get off this train."

"Agreed. I'm getting really claustrophobic in here! Gosh, not to mention the constant shaking," I yawned.

Teala, her hair still tangled from sleep, wandered by, asking if anyone had seen her dreamcatcher. Perry answered straight away, "Oh, Titan was playing with one before. He's just back there ... *I've said that too many times today.*" He pointed to the second-last carriage and off Teala went with a frown and a grunt.

"She's gotten quite close with the little prince, hasn't she?" Olivia laughed.

"I suppose. They do spend a lot of time together," I said.

Chapter 24: The Sudden Express

Olivia watched the passing Flatlands. "I remember when she used to have a tantrum every time we had to go to the castle or the cathedral."

Perry snorted, "'Cause every time she had to sit next to Titan! Yeah, they're tight. Always bickering, but he looks out for her."

Suddenly, the sound of footsteps interrupted us. The middle lane swayed as Titan emerged into the third carriage, clutching Teala's dreamcatcher. Teala screamed at him. The two barged through, making some of Odd's papers fall.

"Gah! Tye! Tea! Can you ———" Something had caught the demigod's eye. He frowned, examining Teala's dreamcatcher as they proceeded into the next carriage.

Odd stood up—the first time I remember seeing him stand this whole trip. He yelled for Teala, but her dreamcatcher was her only concern. "Tea! Teala! Gah. Let me look at the freakin' ..."

He barged passed Kyle, knocking Holdie. Holdie spun to the ground. *Clonk!* Dally and Odd held Kyle upright as his cheek began to melt.

"Sorry about that, Kyle," Odd said. "I didn't mean to knock Holdie from you. It's just ..." Odd eyed the fourth carriage. "I need to have a look at that dreamcatcher. Look after him, Dalton."

Dally saluted Odd as he ventured to the next carriage over. "Eye eye, captain ... You good?" he asked Kyle as Holdie returned to his post.

Kyle was hunched over, his hands holding his stomach back. "Just a little queasy. Shouldn't take long to recover." He leant back, ignoring the stares of the other passengers.

I could see the Pilum Bridge, its sandstone holding it above a rapid river. *Maybe the Holiday River?* Before our line of carriages, several more trains were crossing the rapids, shaking the ground as their steel heaved against the railways. The grass in the Flatlands was yellow, almost dead from the lack of rain. The trees were sparse, similar to Jinkie's Gap. As the second train toppled over the Pilum Bridge, Kyle groaned. He gagged, holding his stomach further back.

Dally leapt to his side. "You all right, pal? What's the matter?"

"N-nothing man. It just hurts. I-I just need a second. Argh!" He stood, limping forward into the second carriage. Dally was ready to follow.

Perry leapt and pushed him back. "I got it, Dally. You rest. I'm sure looking after both him and you can be exhausting."

Dally tapped him. "Thanks, Pear."

Perry entered the second carriage.

Odd and Teala had grown louder. The carriage door caught my eye.

In between our carriage and the fourth, the passing railway seemed like a black sludge. A tight thud sounded. Giuseppe entered, making his way back to the head of the train. Everything became silent. He smiled at me; Dally folded his arms as he ventured towards us. He began talking to Olivia—something to do with General Ko's new orders—and I saw it again. As we approached the Pilum Bridge, the black sludge climbed the side of the carriage, crawling just outside like an infection.

Holding on for dear life as the wind knocked the sludge back, Odd opened the fourth carriage's door. He ripped at the air and threw Teala's dreamcatcher. It sparkled with more black sludge. The smaller chunk, I'd been eyeing, leapt onto the dreamcatcher. It vanished into a pool of darkness. Odd tackled Teala and Titan. A yellow light glistened brightly as the sound of metal popping and piecing filled our ears. It left us in shambles. My ears rang as I thought I'd vomit. After the colours returned, the weight of the carriage shifted downward. The sound of the rapids became closer and closer until Dally's head smacked against the window. *We were sideways!*

The train had toppled over; the last four carriages were hanging down above the rapids. *BAILEY! I had to do something!* I could see Odd in the next carriage, Teala and Titan in his grasp. As we swayed back and forth, Giuseppe vanished. The sound of metal creaked like a door and, before I knew it, something large had splashed into the water.

Olivia's eyes were wide as she reached her hand out to mine. Dally discovered a new bump forming atop his crown as the glass behind his bottom began shattering. The wind was horrendous as it pierced the growing cracks. Like a rollercoaster, the carriages shifted down.

Chapter 24: The Sudden Express

Screams echoed through its chambers. It was getting hard to breathe. Dally fumbled over my chair as his body began falling through the carriage as though into a black hole.

Blood rushed to my head. It was hard to maintain my grip on the chair. The metal churned above us, igniting with sparks. *The dreamcatcher was gone!* The steel of the train still rang. My heart leapt as vertigo kicked in. And when the water touched my neck—Teala, Titan and Odd a world away—my brain went numb and everything went black.

Chapter 25
The Man on The Boat Waits
Bailey

The water was so chilly! My noggin was boilin', spinning in every angle imaginable. I wanted to barf, but I was distracted by a scream. Even though my sinuses were clogged, I knew the voice. *Assonance!*

I took a deep breath, holdin' back the blurry fatigue, an' managed to pull myself onto my four paws. Liftin' my eyes 'bove the sand, I could see that carnage laid all around. Two train carriages had been smashed into pieces. A dry forest surrounded us with similar trees to the ones in Kelton Whide. The smell of smoke lingered behind their dry eucalyptus. My stomach churned; the taste of salt on my warm tongue made me groan.

Chunks of glass covered the damp shoreline. I couldn't see the Pilum Bridge. Before the explosion, Assonance had been amazed by its architecture, its height an' size. *Crickey! Assonance.*

I tumbled ahead, smackin' into a train seat. The scream echoed again!

I was alone. But I knew there ought to be others. I tried the one thing that normally worked. "ASSONANCE? Are you out dere?" I yelled. "Hey, Assonance? Ye hear me?"

It was quiet. The rapids splashed against the wreckage; it felt like they were being drained. Red sprinkled throughout the ripples an' another scream sounded, "Bailey! Is that you?"

I skedaddled towards the voice. "Yes! Assonance where are ya?"

Chapter 25: The Man on the Boat Waits

Assonance's voice was to my left. "My arm, it's stuck!" she cried.

I ran over a mountain of rock before finding Assonance behind a burnin' table, alight even though the water was runnin' over it. I almost fell on top of her. A train wheel was coverin' her left arm. "Is it hurt?" I asked.

She shook her head. "No, no it's not hurt. I just ... I need you to get it off. Please! Is there anything you can use to push it off?"

I looked 'round, findin' a piece of timber from inside one of the carriages. It was half on fire, so I dipped it in the water. It was still warm on my teeth when I tried shoving it under Assonance's arms, under the wheel, under the sand. *Nothing!*

Assonance was gettin' teary-eyed. "Is there anything else?" she begged. "Maybe there's a town nearby—they could help."

"I can't leave ya 'ere, alone! Who knows what's out 'ere. We're gonna have to try somethin' else. Hmm." I had another gander, seeing more flames, more blood an' a pair of boots that made the sand jump.

"Oh, thank Hope's Light, you're alive!" Felicia cheered.

She strutted down the mountain of rocks an' I felt her hand caress the hairs in the space where my eyebrows used to be. She was freezin'. She examined Assonance an' gasped, "That's not good! And that stick's not going to work. We're going to need something longer. How heavy would you guess that wheel is, Assonance?"

Assonance went red in the face. "How the silk am I meant to know? It's squishing my hand ——"

"But her hand's not hurt, right?" I asked.

Assonance nodded, "Well, it's not broken. I can still feel my hand."

Felicia, like a crazed scientist, pointed a finger in the air. "Good, good, good," she said. "We can work with that. Bailey, we're going to need a bigger plank."

A bundle of rail was making its way down the river. Felicia leapt for it. "Bailey, that bit there, going down the river—it's perfect."

"Wha'? De bit of rail? Won't it be too heavy?"

"Not for you!"

What the whipper does that mean?

I followed her. We caught the black half a' rail but I couldn't even see Assonance anymore. I stopped the flippin' thing with the side of my belly. Felicia said it was a swell idea an' so I pushed myself down the river as though I was dog paddling. The next thing I knew, my tummy was bubblier an' it hurt when I breathed in too deeply. Felicia somehow dumped the black metal log on top my back, holdin' its end as we ventured towards the crash site. It looked so small.

Had anyone else survived? What 'bout the others? Did they make it out? By the spirits ...

Assonance was relieved when we returned. She said the rail was freezin' when we jammed it under the wheel. Felicia pushed a small rock between the rail an' myself an' made a seesaw. When the rail rested on the rock, I tilted my noggin, "Now what?"

Felicia looked at me an' smiled. "You jump!"

The rail was stuck at a ninety-degree angle. I couldn't leap on that even if I gave it my dilliest effort. An' my gifts were just as useless. But once Felicia admired the burning table, I knew what she had in mind.

It took us forever to get the wooden table. The smell of burnt hairs was pungent as we dumped it down the river. Crickey, the rapids took it. I ran after it. "Let's not let dis one skedaddle, huh?" Before the table could get as far as the rail, we saved it at the rear of the debris. Felicia an' I shoved the table at the high end of the rail seesaw. I climbed up, each paw slippin' when I attempted to lift my heavy body. An' low and behold, I leapt on the rail, twisting my gut, an' the wheel flew off the sand.

Assonance stood, huggin' Felicia. "You guys did it, thank you!"

They searched each other's eyes for a long moment. I rolled on my butt, sittin' with my legs folded, and sneezed, blowin' away the sand.

Felicia grinned, "Just as I calculated. I knew Bailey would be heavier than that bloody wheel. Come on, we should check for the others."

Assonance let go, "You're right. Thank you again. Maybe there is something that we could use for shelter."

I stood. "It's a dandy idea, but I think everything worthwhile has been burnt or washed downriver. It doesn't look like it'll be rainin' anytime soon. Let's be quick. I reckon the others are out there somewhere!"

Chapter 25: The Man on the Boat Waits

It was nightfall. Felicia finally removed the final piece of broken earphone from my ear. She chucked its wires into the fire. Assonance's arm had become wearier. The crackles of our fire echoed under the eucalyptus; their minty scent warm as the orange lights played with our shadows. We were lost for words. We managed to scavenge the hat Teala had gotten me before we left Central City, two drenched backpacks from the Town of Tents, an' some burnt paperwork. Assonance wore the blue hat, holdin' her left arm against her right palm.

"Are ye right?" I asked Assonance. We had travelled a few hours into the woods. Even though the Jakoo River was long gone, I could still hear water. "I think it's just bruised," Assonance said.

Felicia sat with her staff, admirin' the dry canopies above. "We're near the desert. You can tell by the trees."

They were a lighter green to the Bywoe trees, almost yellow in comparison to the ones coverin' home.

"They're pretty dry, aren't dey?" I mused.

Assonance stared into the waverin' flames. "So are we really going to walk all the way to Drewmora? How do we even know where it is?"

Crickets had begun chirpin'. "De sun," I explained. "Drewmora is somewhat on de opposite of de continent to Everbreen. So, if de sun rises in de west, where Everbreen is, Drewmora should be where de sun sets."

"Bailey's correct," Felicia added. "And although it is not exactly where the sun will set, once we reach the Full Sea, I can probably calculate how far we are from the big blue city."

"And the others? Do you think they'll have the same idea?" Assonance asked.

I nodded.

Felicia was more confident. "It's the only logical assumption." She threw an earful of leaves into the fire. It burst, spreading embers into the sky.

Assonance smiled at both of us. She wiggled her finger in the dirt. "Well, this sucks!"

Felicia shimmied over to Assonance's side. "Bailey, you're an Ever.

Why don't you tell us one of their tales? I've never heard one from an actual Ever before, and it'll keep Assonance distracted while I examine her arm."

My voice was still sticky with phlegm. "A story? Which one?"

"How about the ones about the Good Spirits?"

Felicia took Assonance's arm and she groaned. "Sorry ... I agree, Bailey. Do you know any on Fæh Jiwa?"

I thought for a moment; Fæh Jiwa, the Good Spirit who was connected to Othello the Wise. Of Everbreen descent, Fæh was the bastard of a god unknown to man.

"I have one, I reckon. Fæh Jiwa's pretty prominent in dis story. Jus' look into de fire an' I'll talk away."

Assonance chuckled.

Felicia was more hesitant. "Is this some sort of Ever magic?" she asked.

I laughed, "Nah. Magic doesn't belong in dis world. You of all fellas should know dat. Trust me. Look into de fire." I concentrated on the ash inside the flames an' made a dark wall of smoke inside the orange rhythmic beat.

Like a movie, it played—an illusion that never gets old, even after tellin' thousands upon thousands of stories. A little gift that made me happy, never burnin' my crest even when the green beacon was turned off. I told 'em about a time before man, when Aeithalis walked on the lands of Euphoria, hand in hand with the spirits. Their smiles glistened as Assonance slowly drifted off to sleep, leaning her noggin on Felicia's shoulder. At first, the white panther was startled, even hindered, but was soon absorbed by my story. She listened 'til the very end.

The smoke of our fire billowed in the west. We'd been trekkin' for some time now, led by Felicia. It was quite a scorcher, but the shrivelled shade of the eucalyptus kept us from overheatin'. Felicia wandered ahead with her stick.

"So Fæh Jiwa has no face," she mumbled.

She was kinda right, but not really. "Oh no, dat's jus' how de story goes. I suppose we lesser beings wouldn't be able to comprehend

CHAPTER 25: THE MAN ON THE BOAT WAITS

his appearance," I explained. "It's why he wears a black coat. How Othello writes, it seems his face is a swirl of nothingness. A pol—Ah, what is it?"

"Polarising?" Assonance guessed.

"Yes. A polarisin' vortex of colour dat can make men go nutty an' can even turn ya soul into a marraboo."

I sneezed as Felicia admired the shimmer of sky behind the fair canopies. "Bless you! Serenity didn't wear clothes. The plants in her cave protected her. It's strange how much the Good Spirits vary. They're so different."

Assonance walked beside her. "Well, so are we. An albino, an Ever and a Centrillian. Can't get any more different than that."

"Oh, if we had a Fledding it'd be fascinating," Felicia laughed.

Assonance nudged Felicia playfully. "You don't have to be so rational. I think it's rather interesting right now. Why do you even want to know about this Fæh person?"

"He's not a fella. He's half-spirit, half-god," I said.

Assonance smirked at me an' went back to starin' at Felicia. "I know that, Bailey. There used to be stories of him in Central City."

I was curious myself, but the two seemed more interested in each other. Felicia cut me off, "You don't say. Is he not of Everbreen descent?"

I tried answerin', but Assonance interrupted. I sighed, smellin' my own sick throat.

"The story is more about wairiths and how they were created."

"Wairiths?" Felicia asked.

"De two-headed dog dat Daegon owned. What's so special 'bout em?" I finally got a word in, but it felt half-ignored.

Assonance twirled her finger through her hair. "Well, the story begins when Central City was Sporangia. Back when political intrigue hadn't reached its peak. They say the original leaders were those connected with the Good Spirits—the middle tier between the righteous pimpers and the sustaining spirits."

The sound of water caught my ear. I reckon we were rearin' towards the Jakoo River. *Where was Felicia takin' us? Weren't we supposed to be headin' towards Drewmora?* I tried breaking the two chatty-birds up, but they continued.

"Yes. Serenity mentioned a time like this to me," Felicia cheered. "She said it was better, although less structured and harsh. She despises technology, flying ships, all that. What of the wairiths?"

Assonance began fiddling with her hands behind her back. I could smell the damp sand where the riverbeds were, an' although my voice was thick, almost bear-like, Felicia remained preoccupied.

"Oi, Felicia! Ye sure we're goin' de right way?"

Felicia rolled her eyes. "If you're worried about the Jakoo River, I can assure you that if we continue on this track, we should pass its end and the dam that accompanies it."

I bit my tongue in surprise. She was much smarter than she looked. Assonance's voice was chirpy. "Gee, you are a clever one, Felicia ... About the wairith, they're Sporangian born. They're oddities created when a living thing passes into the afterlife. We humans—like the birds, butterflies, ants and even roses—have our alive spirit and our marraboo spirit. And although I believe Evers do not believe in this particular way of the afterlife, we ———"

"Nah, we don't," I roared. "Marraboo are born when a soul stays on this earth in search of something. They say they're the minds an' hearts hiding from the grim reaper himself. The Forest of Farbe, however, was entrusted to de spirits after de War of Flowers. It's de one haven for all marraboo in dis world. But Good Spirits, I hear, have de power to protect 'em from de deliverance of de afterlife."

"That's all well and good," Assonance argued. "But it does not mean that an alive soul and their counter opposite, a dead soul, would be the same thing. They're different."

I shook my noggin, "Nah, they're de same! How could a soul completely change into somethin' it's not when it passes from de land to de white ceiling? It wouldn't make sense."

"I never said that it completely changes." Assonance's nose flared. "I said that the structure of the soul changes when it stays out of a human body. This is to hide from the heavens and the pimpers."

Before I could speak, Felicia cracked up laughin'. My mouth dropped an' I could hear her snort beneath my breath.

Chapter 25: The Man on the Boat Waits

"What's so funny?" Assonance wondered.

Felicia pointed at the two of us. "You're like an old married couple. Now I've never heard of a Centrillian and an Ever before, but there's been weirder, trust me. Come on, enough now. I get the story. Fæh, most likely to prove himself or to impress another, accidentally combined these two-in-one souls together and made a wairith. That's why that dog had two heads—it was, in fact, two souls." She reached a halt.

Assonance's noggin dropped to the ground. She searched for ants an' whispered something. I think it was *I don't want to marry Bailey!* An' if it was, well, I didn't wanna continue to Drewmora anymore. The blues conked me hard, but Felicia's grin was wholehearted. "In a sense," Felicia chimed. "I gotta admit, Bailey, Assonance has more proof than yo——"

As I crawled behind 'em, the two girls were launched up into the canopies in a big ol' chain net; it smelt like moist steel. A pulley lifted 'em above my noggin. My heart pounded against my chest. Both of the girls had been jammed inside, cheek-to-cheek, fidgetin' as if they could cut themselves out. I heard a horn. It was so loud, my ears felt like they were bleedin'.

Felicia fiddled with her stick, "Okay, I'm going to try and download the chain."

Assonance pushed her hands against the silver steel. "What are you on about? I'll just fly through it. Give me a moment. The holes can't hold my raven form."

Her orange crest glimmered. As it glowed, a shimmer shook the chain. Assonance jumbled back. It was like she'd been electrocuted. I stared at 'em, so high an' helpless, an' searched for the branch the net was hanging from.

"Nice going, Assonance!" Felicia gawked.

"Are ye fellas dandy?" I begged, tastin' the dry eucalyptus.

Assonance groaned, "Ah, the silky net stung my crest. Bailey you're going to have to ——"

"Look what we have 'ere!" A man leapt above a branch two trees away from us. He was dark-skinned with a shiny bald scalp, a sharp tooth hangin' from his neck an' a red salamander crest glowin' under his wrist.

Felicia threw herself against the net a few more times. However, when her white light shined like a firecracker, she screamed. The net wobbled again as the dark-skinned man laughed. "No use trying to get outta there, girlies. I've never lost anythin' in my net, not even those with powered crests." He stared at me. "Oh … I missed one." He whistled an' a sort of barbaric cheer echoed behind me.

Assonance wiggled, hangin' like a chandelier. "Go, Bailey! We can deal with this. He isn't scary."

Felicia nodded, leaning back on the chain. "She's right. It's just a little bit of metal. We'll meet up with you once we're done with this mess. I promise you, we will make it to Drewmora. Just go!"

"But I can't leave ya!" The shrubs behind me rustled as the sound of chargin' feet became louder.

"Just go, Bailey!" Felicia ordered.

"Run, Bailey! *Run!*" Assonance screamed. As if I was hypnotised, I began sprinting, hearin' the dark-skinned man laugh above me.

As I skedaddled, Assonance yelled in pain once more. I wanted to turn back, but the marchin' feet were on my literal tail. I brushed past leaves, branches—all sorts of sharp stones, cuttin' my paws. An' even though my body burned, heating up the more I ran, the howls of Felicia an' Assonance stayed with me each leap I took. A hiss growled near my ear. A yellow light flashed as I pushed past another eucalyptus. An' then thunder struck. To my left, after the blast tore through the tree, the trunk groaned. The tree split in half an' fell in front of me.

I diverged towards the sound of water as the ground jumped from the impact of the fallin' eucalyptus. Its leaves rustled. A girl about my age with curly pitch-black hair called, "Ghad! You almost got 'im, Spice! Quick, he's heading to the river." More footsteps sounded as more of them joined in their battlecry. I could smell the sweat an' blood mixed on my fur. *Why did I have to be so heavy!* There was lightenin' all 'round me.

I took another leap towards the Jakoo River and felt the wind spray against my snout. Grey fog emerged behind the eucalyptus 'til the path ahead was pitch-grey. I stumbled towards the sound of water. The marchin' feet came to a halt.

Chapter 25: The Man on the Boat Waits

I heard their confusion. "Where'd he ..."

The girl spoke up. "There shouldn't be fog 'round these parts. This was him!" She paused a moment. "Ritesh, he's gone! We can't see anything, but we got him trapped."

Ritesh did not respond, however, the girl continued, "Aye ... You two scout down towards Kattagow, you three check the river and Murry, Spice, you two come with me. I have a feelin'."

Her voice faded as my fog dissipated towards the riverbeds. The soft sand soothed my boiling paws. I felt like I was melting. But as the shade of the canopies loosened their hold an' the heat of the sun caught me, I saw something that almost made my heart stop. The Man on the Boat had been expectin' me.

They sat there with their straw hat directing the sun away from their dark, colourless eyes. A guitar and a fishing rod sat beside them. I approached the shore an' my legs gave out. They continued to sit, smilin'—a smile so peaceful, it could stop wars, heal the dying an' put back together what had been broken. They put their hand out towards me.

Chapter 26
Kattagow On Fire
Perry

"Oh, this is just great, Perry! I'm all wet, I can't find my bloody shard, and we've lost everyone!" Zia complained.

My head was about to explode. *One more word and I swear to the Mother Light, I'll*——

"*Perry*, are you even listening? What the crud are we going to do?"

I sat my arse on a dead tree stump that'd been cut the year before. The smoke drifted southwards, towards the Jakoo dam—the dam Teala was so anxious about last night. I pulled out a broken earphone from my ear and my stomach gurgled; I could almost taste the princess' vanilla breath.

"PERRY!"

I leaned back, "I don't know, Zia!"

She lowered her voice and took a step closer to me. "Should we go to the smoke? See if anyone else survived?"

I examined the rising black cloud in the distance. It was from the remaining carriages. But the cloud of chaos was pretty small. I looked at Zia. "That could take at least a day. By the time we get there, the people who'd have survived most likely would have moved on."

I admired the swaying river. Chunks of the Pilum Bridge's sandstone, metal rails and the leather seats of each carriage were scattered throughout the rapids. Zia flicked through her damp journal. She mumbled curses and began writing furiously with a dry pen.

"What are you thinking about?" I sighed.

Chapter 26: Kattagow On Fire

"Shh!"

Did she just tell me to shh? I opened my mouth, but before a single word emerged, Zia whipped her finger onto my lips.

"Don't even start with me, Perry! I have so many things I need to write down and none of it is processing in my head. I don't know if I want to cry, scream or jump for joy because we've probably lost that stupid Kelton Spy Roofus sent after us. My heart feels like it's about to burst. And the only thing I can manage to write is Titan's name. So please, I beg of you, give me a few moments to process what I'm feeling. I'm sorry I can't think like you, but I'm trying my hardest to keep myself sane."

She paused, tears rushing down the sides of her cheeks.

I calmed a little. "I'm sorry, Zi! I'm worried about the others too. Especially Teala and Olivia. And Faith! Everything was going so ———"

"Perfectly?" she suggested. "For once things would have worked out. It was too perfect." She pointed to our half-submerged carriage. "How the crud does something like this even happen, Perry? Who the hell would bomb a train?"

I sat upright, "Maybe it was Papercut? Maybe he assumed Kingsleigh was on our train."

"No! You didn't see him in the House of Senates. He was precise—accurate with every swing—until Senator Hartway pushed Charles out of the way. If you'd seen what I saw, you would know that this isn't that paper kid. A monster did this!"

"Papercut *is* a monster! And either way, someone attacked the train. Which means someone will be searching these wrecks for survivors. Just like ———"

"Araidian!" Zia's voice was raw. "I remember. He checked the entire Holiday River. If these attackers think anything like that madman, I'm sure they'll be here within the hour."

I stood, stretching my back. "Then it's best we head into the forest. We can probably figure out where to go next if we visit a simpleton village."

Zia leaned over into the water. I wondered how it felt. Was it cold and soothing on her overworked fingers? Or was it warm and heavy, thick from the losses of the train wreck? I approached her as she threw me a bag dripping with vines and water. She smiled and wrote in her journal. I reached her side, dragging the strap of my bag over my shoulder. The Jakoo River sounded so peaceful.

Zia's white glove stopped moving and she put her pen in her ear. In her journal, I read, I need a weapon!

"Do you have your staff?" she asked.

I pulled the carved oak from my hood. The golden symbols etched on it reflected in Zia's grey eyes. "Always." I put my hands in the air and stumbled backwards into the water. "You do whatever you have to. I'll scavenge what I can. Maybe find another bag."

The Jakoo River was a dark blue, much darker than the Holiday River. As I fished for another bag, something emerged from behind a rock. Seconds later, glass whooshed past my ear, *fast*. Another see-through shard narrowly missed my head.

Thousands and thousands of blue glass shards peeled off the train carriage like floating raindrops. Zia had her eyes closed, holding her gloved hand out as though she was summoning them. Her hand was flat, her palm facing out, and the glass shards swirled as though a tornado had taken over, ruffling my hair.

When Zia opened her eyes, a blue shard of glass was perched on top of her white glove. She giggled at my astonished face and the two bags I carried.

"I think it's best we go now. I'm ready!"

The ground in the forest was harsh, covered in a layer of dried and dying leaves. They crackled as I walked, searching my bag. Inside, I found the doll Kyle had kept under the Cobblestone Bridge.

Zia brushed past my shoulder and I put the doll away.

"Are you all right?" I asked.

She clutched her new blue shard as though it were her baby. Walking ahead, she watched the eucalyptus leaves. "I don't know. Perry, what if we can't find the others? What do we do?"

I took a deep breath. "We continue to Drewmora. That's the goal, isn't it?"

"But what if they're ———"

"They're not, Zi! We'd feel it if either Teala, Titan or Olivia were to pass to the White Light. And if they haven't, the others are bound to be fine! I think we just gotta regroup and figure out where we're headed!"

She spun around, walking backwards. "You're right! It won't be easy, but then again, it's never easy. It's not like one of the others are going to fall from the—Argh!"

Clunk!

A small metal pseudosphere fell like a walnut. It looked familiar. We stopped to examine its steel complexities. It smelt like a coin that'd been passed from one to another a few too many times. Sweaty, almost.

Zia patted her hair down, groaning, "The crud is that thing?"

I held it close to my eyes. "I've seen this before. Didn't ——"

I jumped, hearing a slither. Sludge, the colour of human flesh, dribbled down the white bark of the eucalyptus. I held the device tightly as Zia cried with laughter.

"Oh, by the Light. That thing reeks!" she said, pinching her nose in disgust.

Our eyes lit up as we regained the scent. "*KYLE!*"

I ran to her, fiddling with Holdie. "How do you turn this thing on, Zi?"

"I don't know, maybe we should ask ... never mind, he's all gooey!"

I glared at her. "Doesn't Titan have a similar device on his stomach? Don't you know how to use that?"

Zia snatched Holdie from my hands. "Yes, yes. We need to find the stimulate button. Crud, who do you think you're talking to?"

I pouted my lips. "The Royal Majesty of Kelton Whide?"

Her eyes bulged; I thought they were going to fall out. "Perry! What'd I say about starting with me?" Her eyes loomed on Holdie. "There it is!" She pressed the metal's side and a sparkly noise echoed from the UFO.

Holdie started spinning and spinning as though it'd just woken up. It spun so much it began to hover above Zia's palm. It drifted away from her and gradually stopped above the sludge. The sludge started to boil and pinch. Kyle's body formed like a clay sculpture. Before I knew it, Kyle sat on his arse like he'd just fallen out of a tree.

"Ah, my back," he whined. He rubbed his eyes. "Perry? Princess? How the ...? Where are we? And why am I on the floor?"

I helped him up as we both explained the explosion and the train wreck.

"How'd you end up in the tree?" Zia asked.

Kyle's breath was heavy. "I w-was kind of thrown up there! I ... I d-don't know. But i-if I didn't turn Holdie off, I'd be dead right now." He leaned on the eucalyptus trunk.

"What do you mean *dead*?" I asked.

"I r-remember being splashed with water," Kyle stuttered. "I-it hit me so hard, Holdie and I smacked the head of the carriage. Then, b-before I knew it, something forced the carriage upward, and we flew out. I was thrown into the sky, the trees rushing below me. And then I started falling back down. I would have been impaled or s-something, man! That crap was ridiculous. So I turned Holdie off and I smashed myself against the t-top of the tree."

Zia scratched her head. "How did you end up flying out of the carriage? Sure, it jolted around, but to the extent of throwing you into the forest?"

"I think it was my fault. I could have hurt you guys. Geez, lucky you weren't. I'm not used to controlling my gifts."

"Your gifts? If I remember right, Kyle, you armadillos could control the earth," I noted. "How'd you make a train catapult you across a forest?"

"I-I don't know, man. I don't have an explanation. I just got thrown into the air!"

"All right. It's fine!" I patted his back. "It's good you fell out when you did. Maybe someone upstairs is watching out for us?"

Zia laughed at me. "Oh, please! No god is watching us, not even Hope. I'm glad you're okay, Kyle. I remember your mother was very proud of our home."

Kyle's sweaty face went white. "Oh, yes. My mother." He gulped, watching the leaves below.

I put my hand on his shoulder. "Hey, dude! I'm sure she and the others are all right. Your family's tough."

Chapter 26: Kattagow On Fire

He sniffled, "You're probably right. There was ten of us. Mum and Dad made twelve. I know Maggie isn't all right ... I think." He wiped the sweat from his head. "Don't mind me. What's the plan? Where were you two going?"

After explaining our thoughts on regrouping at the nearby simpleton village, Kyle's face brightened. "I think I may be of service!"

Holdie span down to his open palm, hovering above his palm. Kyle fiddled with the device. After some beeps, a blue light emerged from the top of Holdie's spinning top. *A hologram? ... No, a map.* It had a white dot on it.

Kyle was more amazed than both Zia and me. "That's nifty!" I mumbled.

Kyle examined the map. "So we're here in the Driwood Forest. By the looks of things ..." The map began scrolling through different landmarks, canopies and mountainous terrain. It halted at a small complex of squares and triangles. Kyle smiled, "Here. Kattagow!" He pointed down to the north-east. "If we head that way, we should make it there by nightfall."

Zia stretched her back. "Nightfall's better than nothing." She pointed in the same direction as Kyle. "This way, huh? Well, let's go visit Kattagow."

The sun was setting when we managed to reach the end of the Driwood Forest. The eucalyptus trees had spread rapidly; their dried leaves stopped crunching beneath our boots. Zia led the way, writing in her journal. Kyle followed her with a contemplative face—it was like he was in pain, thinking so much. I guess a light breeze had made his jacket wobble.

Zia twirled around and wondered, "Maggie? Sorry, I ... I have trouble thinking. Would you like to talk about her?"

Kyle shook his head. "What's there to talk about?"

I stumbled behind him. "Plenty." I pulled out the vinyl doll and offered it to him. "Here. I thought it'd be best if you kept it."

He eyed it down like it was the one who had cursed him to be a troll. He palmed it aside. "Perry, I don't want to look at that thing. There's nothing to talk about. Let's just keep walking towards Kattagow." He scurried ahead of Zia.

"It's okay, Kyle," Zia grabbed his hand. "We just want to help. The way you mentioned her name before, how you said it. What happened?"

Kyle shoved her away. "My gifts triggered something, okay?" he shouted. "I made the sand in the river grow into a mountain within a second. It was so fast you two didn't even notice. But I felt it. I felt the sand. So can we please drop Maggie. She's dead!"

He trudged forward, tears falling from his eyes. Zia complained, apologising and telling him we didn't mean it. But he ignored us. It was silent until the stars started to sparkle. The smell of fires and home cooking lingered eastward as we approached a ball of orange light. It was amazing for a simpleton village. Kyle led us, still red in the face and too stubborn to talk. *What the heck happened to the poor guy?*

The buildings here were cosy and small in comparison to Central City, however, they were clumped tight together. We crept behind the walls of the village, which were at least two storeys high and crafted from a light-grey timber similar to the eucalyptuses in the Driwood Forest. Each building was a similar colour with fire-lit lamps and glowing brown crests. Our white crests stuck out like a blood blister. However, unlike the Sporangia Sector, these simpletons smiled and greeted us as though we'd lived here since the village's beginning.

Beyond an abundance of grey timber posts, we wandered past a familiar family of Drewan Miners searching for shelter. Harry and his little sister looked at us with curious eyes as the two brothers pulled a long wagon full of bags and minerals covered by a blue tarpaulin. Their father waved to us. "Yer Majesty!" He faltered for a bit, registering Kyle's scowl. "My apologies," the Drewan bowed. "You must not remember. We met in Central City. You returned my youngest to us, yer did. I am forever in your debt."

Kyle sighed as Zia shoved herself in front of him. "That's kind of you," she smiled. "I do indeed remember your family. You are Drewans, correct?"

Mr Doubtson nodded, "Yes. We be Drewan by blood. Blue-crested for generations."

"Will you be sleeping the night here in Kattagow?"

He smiled at us, sweat glistening his nose. I could smell the coal on his clothes. "Unfortunately, we cannot afford such luxuries. We'll be camping just southward of the village."

Zia's faces dropped. "Is that so? If I had the appropriate travel funds, I'd have offered you and your family shelter. You do not owe me anything, Mr Doubtson. I do hope that you keep well. You and your family. By the Light itself."

He bowed again, "We'll certainly try, Yer Majesty. Thank you for your blessing. I be hoping our paths cross again. The debt I owe shall be repaid." He gathered his kids as they journeyed towards the village's exit. I nodded to Harry as he grinned at me. Taylah waved to the princess with pink cheeks. They all had that coal taste to them. When they left, I was curious as to where we were going to sleep ourselves.

Zia strutted towards the most spectacular building she could find. It was masterfully crafted using the signature grey eucalyptus trunks as posts for each wall, a tipi-like roof that reminded me of all the fires we used to have in the Town of Tents and a sign with a sheep eating a sprout of grass. The sign at the front read *Medok Inn*.

Zia entered its racked doorway, walking ahead of the people who were waiting for a room in the lobby. A fresh fire under the chimney gave a calming scent—it was like Odd's house. Kyle stood, groaning at the gasps and stares he received from the small crowd.

Zia's voice would make your ears bleed if you were to ignore it. "Good sir," she said at a bald simpleton. "Yes, you good sir, behind the counter. Do you not realise who I am?" She slammed her hand on the front counter. Why was she being so full-on? The couple behind her took a few steps back. She smiled, turned to me and winked. "It's my appearance, isn't it?" she asked the receptionist. "Oh, by the Light, can the Princess of Kelton Whide not get service when she wishes? When my mother hears how dreadful you lot in Kattagow have treated me, she'll fork your farms away and steal your sheep. This inn will be a shamble of its older self and I'll turn it into a shack for my pets. We've plenty of koalas that need shelter, and I'm sure Mother would like to get them out of the Castle of Glass and into a homely eucalyptus shelter."

The simpletons, the travellers from other major cities with yellow, black and red crests, and Kyle all dropped their jaws in a frozen awe.

It was dead silent until Zia rolled her eyes. "Well! Do I have to ask again? Your best room, sir! Now and quick. I'd hate to give the Medok Inn a terrible rating during my visit to Drewmora!"

The bald simpleton gulped. He fiddled behind the counter, and before I could say *damn*, we were tucked into their most excellent room five storeys up from the lobby.

One of the workers closed the door behind Kyle. He scratched his shoulder. "I-I'm guessing you've done this before?"

I propped myself by the window, peeking out to see if anyone familiar or suspicious was outside. I think it had become a habit after all the times I had waited for Araidian's men to leave Odd's street. But Kattagow was void of any threat. There was no one around.

I stifled a small laugh. "Oh, she does that every day! It's going to bite you in the arse soon, Zi!"

Zia scoffed, sitting on the master bed. "Oh, shush! Who'd hurt a poor ol' princess for throwing her weight around? I'm using my royal blood to our advantage. We could have slept with those miners from Drewmora."

Kyle wandered to the fridge, opening it. "What? The family that reeked of coal. I'll pass. A bed's better than a tent-let. A b-bloody paradise in comparison to under a bridge."

"You're starting to remember, aren't you?" Zia asked.

Kyle nodded, "Bit by bit. Flashes, that's all really."

I sat by the window as my white hood crinkled against the sofa. "Do you remember me?" I asked.

Kyle shook his head. "Like I said. Just little flashes … Was that a horse and carriage that just went by?"

"Yeah," I nodded. "They're not kidding when they call them simpletons. Old fashioned, I guess." A car horn honked behind the inn. I rolled my eyes. "A *little* old fashioned," I clarified.

Zia moved one of the pillows and tossed me another. "If you're on lookout, I'm getting some shut-eye. I'm a burnt crop after today's crash. Oh, and don't wake me unless you're certain you've seen someone! Okay?"

Chapter 26: Kattagow on Fire

I put my thumb up as Kyle crossed his arms. We turned the lights off as more cars and trucks crossed the dirt road. It'd been an hour and I hadn't seen anything. No Faith! No Teala! No Olivia. Not even someone as big as Bailey. *Nothing!* Zia's snores filled the room like an orchestra; beneath them, though, I heard a sigh. "Can I-I have a look at the doll?" I turned my head away from the bright moonlit streets to the darkness of the ensuite.

The red curtains next to Zia's bed glimmered gently behind the shine of Kyle's white crest. He was sitting, legs crossed, on the beige carpet. I smiled at him, tossing my bag. He caught it, pulled the doll out and grinned. Holding Holdie above its wooden head, Kyle laughed to himself. *The doll was a little him.* He sighed again. "She loved this thing. Mum always got angry at her each time she took it to school. Y'know I miss them all, but Maggie was ... She always looked up to me." He paused, sniffling away his dry tears.

Holdie returned to his head and our eyes met. "How'd you get that scar?" he asked. "I remember it was more swollen when I beat you senseless at the Cobblestone Bridge."

I raised my eyebrows. "Senseless? It was more like you cobbled me a little; *beat* is a bit much, don't you think?"

I made him chuckle.

"I was forced to fight an Ever to the death! It was for a sacrifice. He was Zia's age."

Kyle's eyes widened, "I'm guessing he lost, huh?"

"I don't know," I shrugged. "He just ... someone intervened after he cut my mouth half open."

I stared out the window. *Still nothing. No cars even.*

"How'd you get out of Kelton Whide?" I wondered.

Kyle bit his lip.

I watched the moon's reflection inside a puddle of water. A foot splashed into it. It was a hooded man. He covered himself under a wet brown cloak. A white spark flashed in the sky. Thunder struck.

Kyle stood and trotted toward me. "Evacuation shuttles. There wasn't nearly enough, but as soon as the first sign of gunfire hit the festival, my family were split apart. Maggie had to go grab this stupid doll from the house. She ended up leaving it and Mum forced me to go back home with her. Forty minutes later, when she picked it up, and I closed the front door, screaming just … *screaming, man!* Then the trees near our house were on fire. The whole festival was alight. I grabbed Maggie and pulled her towards the Castle of Glass. But it was too late. The whole castle had been—I don't know. It was like the glass that made it had been shape-shifted. I did the next best thing: I ran to Juice's house. It wasn't far from the castle and I knew his parents would know what to do."

He stuttered for a bit, breathing in and out. "It's blurry, man. I … I remember holding Maggie's hand like it was the only thing making my heart beat … Uh, and …" He looked me in the eye. It was like he was about to cry again. "*JUICE!* He got captured, tackled by some bozos in an A.W. uniform. I just … I hid man! They were putting cuffs over Juice's wrists. He bit one of them, an older-looking guy with greying hair. The guy flinched. He looked like he was authorising the attack, but ——"

"Did he have a white suit, a top hat?" I asked.

Kyle was taken aback. "No. No, I just said it. He was wearing the same uniform all of them were … Juice looked me in the eye, and I could see it in his face. He didn't want me to go in there and get hurt. His blue eyes, man. Like a *stay back* kinda thing. I ran into his house, got Sam and Gerard from under their beds and took them all to Hilly Park. That's where the shuttles were taking off."

Tears fell from his eyes. He sniffled, wiping his red face.

I sat up, "What happened next?"

He shook and stuttered some more. Holdie spun above his head with each word he said. "Kyle, what happened next?"

He scoffed, "I don't know. They split the WoodWood brothers and Maggie and me apart. I haven't seen them since they were launched towards some simpleton village in the east."

"Near here?" I suggested.

"I don't know. Around here, maybe." He paused again, calming down and watching the moonlight. "Gah, it's getting hot in here! Maggie and I were also launched eastward towards Everbreen. The shuttle got shot down; there was blood, Perry! Lots of it." He groaned

Chapter 26: Kattagow On Fire

and played with his forehead. Grunting, he searched the carpet. "I remember fireflies. So many in this little forest. And the sound of water. And a hooded man."

"What'd he look like? Did he do something to Maggie?" I said, vaguely tasting the smell of smoke.

Kyle avoided my eyes. He had a layer of sweat on his forehead. "That's the thing. He didn't have a face; it was just *nothing*. All these colours. It was like the fireflies were lured to him. He took Maggie. He ——"

An orange light erupted. It blinded us both, waking Zia. The smoke suffocated me as black fog covered the ceiling. The door was on fire. I pulled my staff out. Holdie spun, lighting the smoke with a blue torch. Zia jumped from her bed as the floor steamed.

"What the hell is going on?" Her hair was in knots.

Kyle itched at the small pinches of black hair beneath his chin. "A fire! The inn's on fire!"

I approached the burning door. "Yeah, but who'd burn down an inn. Why?" Next to the door, down the hallway of orange and black, the man in the brown-soaked cloak waited for us. It didn't look like him—his stance, his lack of swords, his covered-up body, but I was sure it was him! It had to be. *Papercut!*

Harsh screaming erupted from the many who'd taken shelter in the Medok Inn. Their voices ricocheted off the timber floorboards as I faced my opponent. I pulled out my staff, its ends extending from its smaller self. I could see sweat drip down my eyebrows. *Was it really that hot?* I could taste the smouldering timber. The doors of each room melted from the wavering flames. Papercut wielded a khopesh, a heavier sword in comparison to his slender paper-thin katanas. I could see the end of the sword glimmer as his faceless body arched perfectly, awaiting my strike.

DING! Zia pegged a shard of glass toward his cloak. He deflected it with his ... *his metal sword?* She threw another, face red and shining with sweat. The cloak swung his sword. The small blue shard bounced off, leaping into the elevator's door. The sound was hard, metallic. That couldn't be right. "Never wake a princess up when she's getting her beauty sleep!"

I looked into her grey eyes as Kyle ducked under a fallen piece of burning timber. "Hey guys, we gotta get outta here! Guys!" he pleaded.

I drew my staff and ran towards the flames. "Kinda working on something, Kyle. Give me a second?"

The timber of my staff pummelled against his sword. His strikes seemed heavier as I fazed through him. He murmured as though surprised. *I didn't know he could speak.* Zia groaned, half asleep as she moulded her shard of blue glass into a chain and ball. She swung the see-through chain like a catapult, but Papercut was good. He knocked away her glass ball and it crumbled like a tower made of rocks.

Argh! He swung his sword at me. I teleported to his right side, smacking his head with the heavy end of my staff. He groaned again. Zia yanked her glass chain, almost hitting my side. It fazed through me like a bullet and smacked another doorway. The sound of burning lingered all around. Kyle screamed as Zia went for Papercut's feet. The brown cloak dodged her. *Why wasn't he using his gifts?* He was simply avoiding us, barely putting in the effort. As though he was just entertaining us.

Kyle squealed again. Holdie got knocked back by a falling piece of timber. The metal frisbee flew as though someone had scored a six in cricket, colliding with Papercut's brown cloak. Like a wasp hitting a windscreen, Papercut looked down. Holdie dropped to the ground. The cloak raised his foot above the jiggling metal. Yet before his foot crushed Holdie's circuits, Kyle's body knocked him to the ground.

All I could see was Kyle sitting above the brown cloak. Kyle rubbed his temple, half dazed. Another chunk of ceiling dropped into the burning abyss of the lobby. Holdie returned, floating above Kyle's crown. He watched our shocked faces. "What?" He glanced down and jumped to my side. "Argh, is that ... that's ———"

"Papercut."

"Papercut?" He sounded like he had heard the name before. He stuttered a moment and searched the brown cloak. "Don't worry about him," Kyle suggested. "We gotta get out of here!"

Kyle ran the opposite way to the elevator and the steps. I propped my staff into the air, preparing a finishing blow for Papercut. Zia's shadow stood close to mine behind the lights of the fires. "Leave it be, Perry! You're better than that," she said.

Chapter 26: Kattagow On Fire

She was holding onto my forearm. "Let fate decide!"

"But what if he comes back?" I asked.

Zia melded her glass ball and chain into its previous form. "Then he comes back. We shouldn't decide if someone is to live or die."

"It wouldn't make anyone happy," I chirped, watching his cloak. "Come on. This is no place for a princess!"

Zia led the way back into our room.

We were on the highest floor of five. We'd need at least a staircase to get out of this place. Kyle smashed the window in our bedroom. "This way!" He crept over the sharp broken glass. Zia waved her hand downwards. As her hand moved, the sharp shards around Kyle's legs shrank downwards and vanished.

Kyle propped himself on the Medok Inn's roof. "I have an idea. It might work!"

Zia followed him as the moonlight of Kattagow blinded me. Sirens howled like fireworks, and when I realised how high we were, my stomach heaved.

"Well *might work* sounds better than any of the other ideas floating around." Zia gawked, surveying the blue concrete roof slates. They were placed diagonally, so my boots slipped the moment my head touched the starlight. Kyle crawled a few steps away from the window and raised his hand as though he were summoning something. As he did this, the dirt road where the red fire trucks arrived grew upwards. The dirt pillared up until it towered below Kyle's feet. The dirt stopped. All the simpletons, the firefighters and ourselves witnessed the birth of a hilly mound.

Kyle had his arms in the air. "Yes! I hope that isn't where the exit is."

Zia peeked down, her head vanishing behind the roof. "Nope, you're good."

Kyle looked at me with a deep breath. "Told you I can make the ground grow. Quick now! I don't know how long I can hold it." Men in orange soldiered, hosing the fire. Zia tumbled down the hill first, then I nodded to Kyle and dropped down myself. Kyle stood on the hill's peak and raised both his hands again. Holdie spun above his head as he gradually descended. The hill began shrinking and shrinking until the dirt road had returned to the one I had watched before the fire.

A few firemen asked if we were all right. Zia did most of the talking. If this was Papercut's fault, then this fire was on us. She ordered them to inform her of any injuries—no one was hurt. Thanking them for their brave work, we travelled towards the southward exit, trudging against the heavy main road. The sound of the water was satisfying.

The fires were still dancing in the background, lighting our journey. A smoky scent was still pungent under my nose, and, in the distance, I spotted a brown cloak once more. *What? Already?* This psycho was still on our tail. The moonlight glistened against the southward gateway to Kattagow as I readied my staff once more.

Zia rolled her eyes. "Oh, not this idiot again. Didn't we teach him enough inside the inn?"

The cloak turned away like he hadn't seen us.

Maybe it was a trap?

Kyle scratched his head. "Is he trying to rob that store?"

"No time like the present," I laughed, vanishing under a white light.

When I reappeared, the brown cloak was fiddling with a locked glass door.

White ash fell around us. "Hey, are you having trouble entering this locally owned business," I quipped. "I hear Kattagow have some amazing tourist attractions. Like a burning inn!" I swung my staff; however, instead of blocking it with a metal khopesh, he parried the oak with his bare hands, over and over again until he pulled down his hood.

"Whoa, whoa, whoa!" he cried.

Wait, this isn't Papercut.

Harry had his blond hair slicked back and was huffing as though he'd smoked a whole packet of cigarettes. Zia and Kyle arrived on foot. Harry put his hands out towards us. "Please don't report me!" He was about to say more but something caught his eye. The orange flames ignited his blue irises and his body dropped. He let go of the lock and gasped, "What the salt happened here?"

Chapter 27

The Day That Followed
Faith

"Can you see anything?" I called.

Only the lorikeets replied. It seemed we'd gotten ourselves lost in a maze of withered gum trees. Their fragile branches, ripe from the drought, made the breeze hollow—it was as if a ghost was eyeing us. I pulled my arms back to my side. It was silent. A flash a blue light glimmered beside me as an uproar of leaves took flight, forming a mini-tornado.

Olivia's white skirt had muddied patches that looked as though the water from the Jakoo River had never dried. Her white and blue cardigan had several tears and rips around her waist and elbow. Her Kelton Whide badge, the crown emblem of our home, had been pinned perfectly on her chest—it now sagged from the days following the explosion.

Her breath smelt bitter. "Train tracks!" she huffed. "I saw train tracks up ahead and a cloud of smoke."

I smelt the air, "I don't smell any smoke."

"It's close. A few hours' walk."

I stared at the forest. Even here, the sun was boiling.

"Do you think the others had something to do with the smoke?" I wondered.

Olivia shook her head. Before either one of us could speak, a laugh crackled behind me.

Dally had been sitting on a fallen gum tree; it was shrivelled and black from the heat of the plateau. His boots were firmly set into the layer of leaves that had drowned the bushland. Tightening his windbreaker around his waist, he held the mask of Hebi, its black and white shades almost a part of his fingers. "Oh, of course it was one of the others!" he mused. "Probably Odd luring us to Drewmora." He glanced up at the canopies. "What are we even doing out here? Olivia, please don't tell me you want to go towards the smoke?"

Olivia crossed her arms. "It's the best sign we have. Especially now that Faith's earphone's not working. And what happened to yours again?"

"I don't know, it's gone!" Dally shrugged.

"Well, even if the others didn't cause the fire, Her Majesty may have seen it," Olivia said. "And if she's drawn to it then we might end up finding her."

I lowered my brows, "Her Majesty? What about Pear? Tea? The prince? Felicia? Asso———"

"I can still feel Perry and Tea, okay!" We both looked at her like she was crazy. She clapped her hands together. "Oh. You two don't have siblings. Let me explain. I have this notion in my gut—in my crest. It started last year. I believe it's from the beacon's light in Kelton Whide. Because the light has stayed on, I feel closer to Perry and Teala. From what Master Othello has told me of this feeling, it's similar to the sense our parents have for us. It's an inner tether that connects them to us. Being part of the same womb, Teala, Perry and I are always connected. That's why mother and I never lost hope. We eventually could feel them, in here." She touched a fist against her chest.

My shoulders relaxed. "Good. He's okay. Hopefully, the others are as well."

"Speaking of beacons, what about Drewmora?" Dally asked.

He leaned back, groaning as he held his left kidney with one hand, and pointed to the blue light shining in the far-off distance.

Olivia felt the bark of the fallen gum tree he sat upon. "Where there's a fire, there's usually people. We need water if we are to make it to Drewmora. Especially here!"

"Here?" I pondered.

"Yes, here. The Kuni Plateau."

CHAPTER 27: THE DAY THAT FOLLOWED

I rolled my eyes. "The driest bushland in Oberon!"

Dally stood, pressing his lips together as red seeped through his black shirt. "Argh! We should get going then, huh?"

I pulled him back. "Hold on. Let me re-bandage your wound. It's seeping through ——"

"Faith! I don't need your help. If I did, I'd ask."

I waved my arms about. "Ah, you're just like Perry, you know that!" I pulled out my hand and reached for his shoulder. "I just want to help and ——"

For the first time in a long time, Dally hit me. He slapped my hand away so hard I thought my fingers were going to go black. My heart heaved as the pain swept through me. I clasped my hand away from him as his face turned red. His brows squished together. "Don't you dare compare me to Perry! I'm nothing like him. Now, if I needed your help, I'd ask. So please." His voice relaxed as he sighed, "I'm fine ... Which way was that smoke?"

Olivia pointed, lips pursed.

Dally nodded and stormed off into the forest. As he adjusted his bag, holding the mask of Hebi, Olivia grabbed my hand. She looked me in the eyes. "Are you okay?"

I nodded, "Yes."

She glared at Dally. "What the hell happened to him?"

I looked with her. "That isn't him. You know that as much as I do. He's just ——"

"Being a doofus?" she suggested.

"Something like that." I took a deep breath and followed Dally's footsteps.

We continued until the gum leaves—red, green and orange—disappeared completely. The dirt in the plateau was almost orange as the sun's full force burnt us. Dally soldiered forth as I began tasting my sweat. A metallic shine teased us and, all of a sudden, we had reached the train tracks.

Standing on their heated metal, Dally admired the giant smoke balloon that covered the sky. Beneath it was a simpleton village no larger than the perimeters of the Castle of Glass. Dally rubbed the sweat off his forehead. "Y'know, Olivia. I think you're right," he said. "That was definitely a person. We should be there within the hour, you think?"

Olivia stood beside him. Dally was only a fraction taller than her.

"Less," she said. "If we continue at your ridiculous pace. I say we slow down. Catch our breath."

I sniffed the air. "Smells like smoke. It doesn't look too thick though. I can see the clouds behind it."

Olivia nodded. "That means the fire's been out for some time now. Hopefully, they're open for business." She stepped off the tracks, Dally behind her. "Whoa, whoa! Look, Liv. Hold on a moment."

She turned to him.

Dally pointed to the tracks. "You see these tracks? They lead to Drewmora. If we follow them, we'll be there by the end of the month. Now I'm not saying I'm an expert on the others, but I'm positive Perry, Bailey, the princess, even Odd would have thought about meeting in Drewmora. Why don't we just follow the tracks?"

Olivia examined him from top to bottom. "I love the enthusiasm, Dally, but there are ... faster ways to Drewmora. Especially with this." She pulled out a *Central City Labour Identification Card*.

"Your old Labour Party ID?" I clarified.

Olivia nodded, "Parliament benefits ... You just have to trust me. I'm all for walking towards Drewmora. However, if the others are—like you said—heading to the blue city, I might have a few tricks up my sleeve. And Her Majesty and Perry aren't daft enough to follow the tracks." She pointed to the smoke. "If I'm correct, that's Kattagow. Beyond the village, there is a swamp and a ferry service that'll take us to the Full Sea. Now, which do you prefer? A ferry ride or a month of walking?"

"You don't need to ask me twice!"

Dally followed me hesitantly.

Olivia walked ahead as we approached the grey walls of Kattagow. Dally walked mindlessly behind me. I softened my pace until we were side by side. "Can we talk about what you did before?" I asked.

He shook his head, eyes focused on the village.

Chapter 27: The Day That Followed

I stared at his smudged face, a warmness growing inside me. "It's been a long time since you last …? Why were you so angry before?"

He ignored my eyes. "I'm not angry. I'm just sayin', if I needed your help, I'd ask. Do I have to repeat myself?"

"No, you don't! It's just two days ago when we were in Central City, I would have never of thought you'd be someone who'd ———"

"Faith, drop it!" His voice was stern. "I'm done complaining, arguing, whatever it is. We ain't kids in Kelton Whide anymore. We're out here, by ourselves."

I stopped, "I'm not arguing with you."

He turned around just before the walls of Kattagow. "You are. And I'm done. Just … *Enough!*" He threw his arms in the air. I bit my lip and stared him down. He walked backwards, into the village, the grey walls casting a dark shadow down the left half of his face.

Olivia led us towards the smoke. I shuffled behind Dally, observing the small amount of protection this village had. Not many guards for a populated homestead. Like most simpleton villages, similar to Glenstone and Liverrum, the majority of residents had brown crests in the form of mythical animals. Before we reached the burning leftovers of black eucalyptus and the blue and red sirens of the firefighters, I noticed Dally examining his wound. He slapped his kidney as if the pain of his slap would cauterise the bleeding. I quickened my pace. Olivia was so concerned for Zia and Perry, she continued towards the black carnage. I jabbed Dally's wound, pushing him into the closest alleyway to our right.

His eyes were furious, and he bared his teeth. I put pressure on his leaking wound. He groaned, pushing me away.

"What the hell is wrong with you? What'd I just say!" His voice was firm, but each word came out as a whisper.

I closed my eyes. "I'm helping you! Give me a moment, this might work."

"Might work! Might work … What are you? Fricken ———"

His voice became a blur. I began to feel the cotton and polyester of his shirt. Through it, I could sense his skin, how hot it was and how it throbbed to the cut. I felt his blood cells, white and red, working to heal him, but too much blood was seeping through the bandages.

I grabbed hold of what was familiar about him, about his past self before the train window cut deep into his side. All of a sudden, the throbbing lessened. The atoms in his blood returned to their usual flow inside his body. The skin that had been brutalised repaired itself. When I let go, the wound had been healed.

Dally was staring at me with a thrill in his eyes. It was like I'd scared him. His breathing slowed. I looked up; his arm was raised above my forehead. Was going to hit me again?

"Don't you dare!" I shouted.

He lowered his arm. "I … I wasn't going to do anything. How'd you … How'd you do that?" I could smell the ripe odour of his sweat.

"I reversed what had happened to you by changing the types of atoms inside the cut. I just made everything based on memory. Happy now?"

I could feel his chest heave in and out. His brown eyes reflected my gaze. "Why would you … after what I said?" he asked.

I pushed him aside, stepping out of the alleyway. "Because you don't scare me, Dally! Everyone needs help, even you!"

When I returned to the main dirt road, Olivia was midway through receiving the news. Dally staggered behind me as I approached her and what seemed to be a manager of sorts. "Thank you so much for your time. Just to confirm, you did in fact see Her Royal Majesty and two Kelts accompanying her? One with a strange metal objecting floating above his head?"

Before I reached her side, Olivia thanked the man again and walked towards me.

You could hear the excitement in her voice. "He was very helpful … Where'd you two rush off to?"

I shrugged, "Just browsing a few of the shops. Someplace to buy water."

Olivia pointed to the man. "Well, the lobbyist did mention a convenience store just down the main road."

Dally reached us. "What was this place?" he asked.

All three of us analysed the black slump of burnt timber, beds, half-singed doors with room numbers, clumps of burnt clay and

Chapter 27: The Day That Followed

charred red curtains. Olivia took a moment. "It was one of the town's most prized buildings. *The Medok Inn*. The gentleman said that it was the perfect resting place for people who were travelling from Ptak Isles to Kelton Whide or Central City to ——"

"Drewmora!" I finished. "What else did he tell you?"

After she explained that Zia and Kyle and another Kelt boy were here, we reached the store. Its front lock had been prised open; however, when we entered, the cashier was almost grateful. The smell of window cleaner was pungent as the cashier scanned our water bottles. Her skin was rather dark and her fingers brittle almost to the bone.

She explained to Dally that nothing had been stolen. "Yes, yes!" She cheered. "I came to work and saw the door." She flicked her brown hair back. "And I prayed to the gods that those bandits out east hadn't come and stolen our goods again. After checking the stock, I realised that nothing had been stolen. And so, for such a splendid day, I'm going to give you the waters for free."

Dally smiled, "They're only a few dollars. You don't need to! It's okay, we'll pay."

She waved her hands above the counter. Her crest was a brown imp, so strange. "No, no. I insist. Please, take the offer. The gods work in mysteries ways and I must repay my fortune onto others."

Dally was about to argue. Olivia stomped on his boot. "Sounds good," the councillor said. "Thank you kindly, Shimali. We'll use the money you saved us wisely." Shimali waved us goodbye as Dally carried the bulk of the bottles outside.

"She could have used the few extra dollars, Liv!" Dally groaned.

Olivia stormed ahead towards the eastward exit. "It was very considerate of you, Dalton, but we're going to need it for the ferry."

"So you really want to leave the others? We're not going to wait for them here—not even for a few hours?" I asked, reaching her side.

She stopped, "Faith, don't worry yourself. The others will be okay. We'll see them in Drewmora, maybe even along the way. I can still feel Perry and Tea!"

"Do you think that means my dad can feel me? Now that the beacon's been on for so long?" Dally smiled, joining us.

"Maybe. If he's out there, then yes. The same goes for your parents, Faith!"

A smile scrunched my cheeks as my dimples creased inward. It felt like I didn't mean to, but the news warmed my insides.

Unfortunately, Olivia continued talking. "We're going to have to be careful once we leave these walls. The Oogali Swamp is dangerous. It's very humid. I'd advise we get rid of that packaging for the water. Put as many as we can into our bags." She paused, biting her small lips. "If only I had a map!"

"What do you mean?" I asked.

Olivia admired the walls of Kattagow, their gums shimmering in the wind. "Just a precaution. Just so I could figure out how many days it'd take before we get to Drewmora, the princess, Mr Odd. Everyone!"

I shrugged. "Well, lead the way. We'll get rid of the cardboard. Don't want to litter."

She grabbed five bottles from Dally and walked off.

"You think it's true?" Dally asked.

I looked at him, "True?"

"The feeling thing. With Perry and Tea?"

"I suppose," I nodded. "If I can heal that scar of yours with a few years under the beacon's light, anything can happen."

He passed me a water bottle and stood. "Yeah, the world's changing, huh? Changing fast … You go on ahead."

I eyed the cardboard. Dally smiled, "I'm not gonna dump a whole …" He examined the cardboard and rolled his eyes. "All right, let's go find a bin … *together*. We have a ferry to catch!" Dally stuffed the cardboard into a small circular bin. We continued behind Olivia, not aware of the familiar dangers that lingered inside the Oogali Swamp—dangers that would change our lives forever.

Chapter 28

Milky Complications & A Lack of Fur

Bailey

The sound of the waves crashin' against the shore soothed my noggin. There was sand all over my face an' a fella's arm buried under a slimy clutter of seaweed. It twitched as I watched it, its pale freckly skin burnin' as it rubbed itself deeper in the sand. Its nails had been chewed on like a dog's play-toy. My heart rushed with excitement. *Was I movin' this hand?* Its fingers moved out, then back into a ball. My mouth dropped open, shocked by the familiar nature of the hand. 'Twas like mine before I transformed—before I changed forever.

A crackle echoed above me. I heaved myself up, seein' two hands, two arms an' a human shadow. My breathin' and my sense of smell had faded. I searched upward. Things were so blurry. The dryness of the trees, the crops of tall grass, the darkness of the canopies—it was all so hard to see. I leaned on one arm an' grabbed at my chest. My heart, it was so soft! *Wait!* I grabbed my chest, with four fingers an' a thumb. I licked my lips an' rolled in the sand, feelin' the rest of my body. It was skin, rough an' soft pale skin. My eyes had sleep under 'em. Tears dripped down my cheeks, but before I could wipe 'em away, screams erupted nearby.

Three fellas landed on the sand. A girl with curly black hair an' a scar across her left cheek eyed me down with a bow an' arrow. Her blue eyes squinted. The two other fellas joined her, one with a spear, a long strawberry-blond mane an' tanned skin, the other missing two teeth and red in the cheeks with very little hair above his burnt scalp. The strawberry-blond lowered his spear. "That ain't a panda."

The girl raised her bow, "No, that's a pervert!"

I raised my two human arms. It felt like heaven, raising 'em so high! "Whoa!" I pleaded. "Don't shoot, I'm not one of 'em perverts. I swear by de sprits, I'm de panda. I swear!"

The girl approached me, turnin' the sand with her boots.

The red-cheeked fella held her shoulder. "Hey, slow down, Georgia! We don't know what he's ———"

"He's naked, Murray. What's he gonna do?" Georgia chuckled.

I looked down … *she was right!* I dropped, coverin' everything I could. Georgia continued towards me as Murray rolled his eyes. "He could be one of those changing ones. Like Milky!" he called.

Georgia was a foot away from me, still smilin'. "You heard his accent. He's an Ever." She leaned down an' stared me right in the eye. I could smell roses on her neck. She admired my dry sandy self an' licked her lips. "And I don't know what the hell happened to him. But he's coming with us."

I took another deep breath. "I don't wanna hurt ya!"

She leaned so close to me, I almost coughed. "And how are you going to do that, Ever?"

As I stared at her, I could feel a saturation of fog in the air. It didn't form like ink in the ocean; instead, it made me sweat. I had neva' felt it so powerful and so focused before. It was like a canon, locked an' loaded, ready for its target.

I smiled at Georgia, "Well, by cleanin' up someone else's mess."

A combustion of fog, grey an' cloudy like a thunderstorm, flew into the air an' knocked Murray off his feet. The fist of grey distracted Georgia for only a moment. I was shook when she rolled her eyes at me.

"Naked *and* dumb!" she said.

She clenched her fist an' my eyes went blurry for a second. Then everything went black.

I could feel underwear when I came to. It was dark an' above me was a mountain of grey stone. Firelight guided whoever carried me

CHAPTER 28: MILKY COMPLICATIONS & A LACK OF FUR

like a young'un. Murray's voice rang loud near my ear. "Can someone else carry the Ever now! He's not light, y'know."

I could hear Georgia hummin'. A tiny melody, so calm it made the darkness 'round us blossom. She stopped. "Oh, stop your crying! We're almost there. Ritesh and Milky can deal with him. I'm kinda curious about the two girls we caught today." She continued hummin'. It made my noggin all warm an' fuzzy.

I groaned.

"Oh good, he's up! He can walk himself," Murray cheered.

My face conked the ground an' my cheeks went red. As soon as the pain dulled, I tried liftin' myself. Georgia cried, "We're right here, you ——"

My legs were so wobbly. It was like tryin' to stand on noodles. I heaved an' heaved 'til the cave was upright. My arse got another beatin' as I lunged backwards to the limestone floor. Murray an' Georgia's voices spiralled in tone, gettin' louder an' louder.

"Oi! You two are like a gauze mat under a burner. You're lucky Spice ran up and got me." It was the darker-skinned fella from the tree. He was a lot shorter, maybe five foot three on the ground. His hair was so short around his scalp, it was like it couldn't grow, an' his eyes were a dark brown like crystals on salt. Red glimmered from his wrist, a salamander crest that burned bright within the cave.

He glanced at me, then back at Georgia. "This is the panda? *This!* Are you thick, you dummies? I asked for a bloody bear twice my height with four paws and black and white fur. You give me this, an ... an *Ever?*"

Georgia slapped away his hand. "Oh, for crying out loud. Look at his crest, you noodle." She heaved onto my arm, shinning green light into Ritesh's face. "That's as panda as you're going to get."

Ritesh stood back. His eyes were so wide, I thought they'd pop. "Wha'? How can a ... How can an Ever change from their ... That's ——"

"Unheard of?" Murray mused, foldin' his arms. "Well, he ain't no Milky, that's for sure. What of the other two?"

Georgia shoved me down. Ritesh rubbed the sleep from his eyes. "They're talkative," he whined. "Too talkative. Especially the blond.

A few of the others are out huntin'. We'll wait 'til the whole group's back to decide what to do with them."

I tried pickin' myself up once more, but my legs wobbled like jelly. Murray grinned at me. "Not too solid on ye legs yet, huh, panda?" He grabbed hold of me, sendin' pain through my shoulder blade, an' yanked me forward. Before I could protest, he dragged me into a little paradise.

Similar to the Heart of the Forest in Farbe, this small cave was an inlet for a village. A rapid sprinkled inward from the dam an' trees bloomed on the far left side 'bove a sprout of dark grass. The greenery went on 'til dirt an' limestone like the cave's entrance replaced it. Little tent-lets an' leaf buildings covered the dirt. In the centre of their hideout, there was one of those zeppelins. It was just like the ones flying 'bout in Central City, but dingier and covered by a deflated grey an' orange balloon. Its cockpit was a bronze steel that had scratch marks and silicone covering its sides. Where the controls were, the steel seemed rather empty. They were missing parts of its engine. The balloon itself was sloppy like out-of-date custard, covering most of the village's centre with orange stripes along its bland grey plastic.

Murray pushed me along. "You ain't talkin' much. What's wrong, Ever? Something hurt your feelings?" His black crest shone; it was a grinning cockatoo. I fell to the ground, smellin' the barramundi under the inlet. The dirt tasted bland. I wiped it from my mouth an' glared at him.

"I'm actually havin' a dandy time," I smiled. "I've been a panda for almost three rotations. It feels swell to have skin again an' to be able to stand on two feet."

Murray scratched his noggin. "Gee, three years, ye say? That be a long time. I'm sorry, chief."

I relaxed a little. "Don't be. It's ———"

Loud bells rang as if we were at the Whide's Cathedral with Perry's family. Their clutter of metal echoed against the cave's stalagmites. Another gatho of fellas similar to my age crowded the entrance I was dragged through. They all had spears, rifles, axes an' other weapons. This one fella with curly fair hair had a deer over his shoulder. Ritesh walked over to 'em.

Chapter 28: Milky Complications & a Lack of Fur

"Good huntin' boys?" he asked.

A scruffy-faced an' dirtied nailed fella threw his arms into the air. He had dark oak hair, soil-coloured eyes that could pierce ya skin an' an uneven malicious grin so manic it made ye stomach heave. His pale Centrillian skin was the spittin' reflection of Assonance's. They almost had the same amount of freckles over their button noses. I'd seen his eyes before. Dirtier an' bloodied, but indeed somewhere else—*where?*

"Not bad at all, Teshi! Pleffin kicked that deer's arse like a soccer ball, we killed some birds and ..." He eyed me down, a familiar craziness deep within his gaze. He smiled. "By the Light of the Hopeful Mother! An outsider. Where'd you find him?"

Georgia stood in front of me. Her arms were crossed an' strong. "He's mine, Milky. You're not allowed to touch him, understand?"

I've heard that name before? But where?

Milky raised his hands, smilin' in approval. "That's fine with me, Georgia! No need for any——"

Gigglin' erupted behind me under the cave's grass fields an' trees. Milky eyed his friends. "What the silk is that?" he barked.

White flower petals began to fall like raindrops. I could smell their fresh pollen, taste it under my tongue like a bee in spring. Ritesh led us. When the trees started to spread, he began to skip. He frolicked towards the sound of laughter, playfully shoving Georgia's shoulder.

"Oh, I forgot to mention," he said. His voice was a higher pitch, almost lady-like. "We're keeping the new girls. You three are going to love them."

Murray an' I made eye contact. *What the spirits is goin' on?*

"New girls? The hell happened to you when the net went off, Teshi?" Milky asked.

The further we trekked, the more my mouth dropped open. Ritesh began chucklin' to himself. Then I stood on one of the flower petals an' saw Assonance an' Felicia, their dandy smiles, above a fallen log with a fire beside 'em.

Ritesh skipped to 'em, his hands waving to the two like they were besties. Milky an' Georgia rubbed their foreheads.

"Oh, no. Remesh is out!" Georgia sighed.

Isn't his name Ritesh? Have I been hearin' it wrong this whole time? Milky stretched his back an' pushed past me. "I'll deal with him. He let the captives go again. What'd I tell you abou———" He saw what I saw an' stopped, frozen. Assonance looked away from the fire, the blue hat still firm on her noggin. She stood an' the two admired one another from afar.

Milky whispered, "*Ona?*"

I'd never seen Assonance's face so red before. Tears gushed from her eyes. She ignored everything 'round her as Remesh began plaiting Felicia's long blond hair.

Milky took a step forward. "Ona, what are you doing here?" he mumbled.

Assonance's hands stayed stiff by her side. "Yuri?" she cried.

Murray an' Georgia stared at each other, puzzled.

Milky tiptoed towards the fire. "I swear, I looked for you in that cave!" he cried. "I tried to rescue you. From Kygo. Irene. All of them!"

Tears flooded Assonance's face. "Please, just hold my hand!" she sobbed.

Milky sprinted across the grass like a hurricane, leapin' into her arms like how Teala used to when she was mopey. They held each other's hand for a moment, then hugged, leaning in so their foreheads were pressed together.

Remesh clapped, "Oh, I love reunions! They're so pretty. Huh, Fe Fe!" His voice sounded like he was puttin' it on. Felicia lent her noggin on Remesh's shoulder.

"There seems to be a lot of them as of late. But this one's sweet," the Kelt chimed.

"What's going on?" I asked.

Murray looked at me. "If I knew, I'd tell you ... Can you stand?"

I shook my noggin.

"You're cute for an Ever!" Georgia grinned. "Ona's what Milky's been calling his sister. She's the whole reason he joined us in the first place."

CHAPTER 28: MILKY COMPLICATIONS & A LACK OF FUR

"To find her?"

Georgia nodded, "Yep. On the other hand, Ritesh was lost when the red beacon turned on. Remesh is his more ... *flamboyant* personality."

Our eyes met. "And you're tellin' me dis why?" I asked.

Georgia stumbled towards the fire. "By the braids in the blond one's hair, Ritesh thinks she can help us. I'm telling you 'cause you're not captives anymore." She pushed at her curly hair to show a black braid hidden under her long locks.

Murray escorted me to the fire. Felicia examined me, leaning away from Remesh's shoulder. Milky an' Assonance separated but stayed close, sittin' on the timber with the rest of us.

"So what happened after Irene left me behind in the cave?" Milky asked. Assonance stared at the grass, biting her lip. "We went to Everbreen," she said. "We went, and just how they planned it, they snuck us under the WonderWorks there. They tried hurting the green beacon and we ... we were saved, Yuri. By a boy in a white hood, a princess, a demigod, a little girl, some tough guy, a talking panda and an angel. We got saved and we lived under the trees until Kyle was found ... What happened to you?"

Milky stared at the limestone behind Assonance. His eyes were blank. "When I awoke, my cell was still locked," he sighed. "I thought I was going to die, Ona. I screamed and screamed, yet no one answered. I even thought I'd lost Hope. The Light ——"

"Don't speak like that!" Assonance cried.

Milky looked her in the eye. "Sorry. It's just ... I tried so hard looking for you! I swear I did. A few days after being trapped, Ritesh and Georgia knocked on my cell bars. They were trying to scavenge some food and meds. We spent all day trying to break into the stupid cell."

Georgia laughed, "We did! Almost broke Teshi's wrist!"

Remesh placed his left hand above his chest. "Oh, my. I remember that." He slapped Felicia's leg. "Hurt like hell, girl."

Milky looked at his friends. "Been with them ever since."

Felicia pulled back an' pointed at me. "Who's he?"

Georgia rolled her eyes. "You don't know? You're joking, right? You've never seen this Ever in his human form before?"

Felicia stood, "Not many Evers have human forms these days." She examined me again from top to bottom. She pointed at my chest. "You know Perry! Dally too, don't you?" She paused for a moment and clicked her fingers, "Bailey? Is that you? How'd you ——"

Assonance glanced away from her brother. "No silk'n way are you Bailey. Evers don't have human forms. Wait, have you always been able to do this or was it your illness?"

I smiled. "Okay, okay! It's me. An' no, dis is not an aftereffect from the sickness. I … I met a man on a boat."

Assonance was interested to learn more, while Felicia sat back, lips pursed as though the image of the man on the boat had haunted her before.

After I explained this morning's events, Remesh an' Milky dragged me to their tent-lets so that I could borrow a shirt an' shoes. Halfway down the forest, Remesh's voice deepened an' he stopped. He laughed. Milky explained that he had switched back into Ritesh, who was the more frequent personality of his—the leader of the pack.

Milky asked a few questions about Assonance an' how we had ended up in the Driwood Forest. Once I had my shirt an' handmade shoes—hand-sewn with grass leaves an' tree sap—I sat outside. The inlet of water was gentle, echoin' in the cave. I admired the glassy reflections on the cave's walls. They looked like blue ripples in the rock, growin' an' shrinkin'. The sound of soft feet blocked the calmness.

Assonance pushed her side into me, sittin' on the dirt. Her eyes reflected the twinkle of water. "What a day!" she sighed.

Our eyes met. "Yeah! It's been bonkers," I nodded. "Ya brother, huh?"

She looked at my scrunched up arms an' legs. "Your human body, huh? I'm worried about these people."

"Why?" I asked.

"Yuri told me that without that zeppelin, they could be in trouble."

I leaned forward, closin' my eyes. "What would we be able to do?"

Chapter 28: Milky Complications & a Lack of Fur

"I haven't thought that far," she shrugged. "Been preoccupied with Felicia."

I squinted my brows. "Felicia? What do ya mean?"

She rolled her eyes an' giggled. She took the blue hat off an' slammed it on my noggin. "I'll have to tell you another time. I wanna see where things go first."

I adjusted the blue hat. "How do I look?"

"Like a person."

A flick of pain burned my lower back. I lunged forward an' turned.

Georgia stomped her boot on the ground. "Hurry up googly eyes," she ordered. "We need to … Where's the blond one?"

Behind Georgia, the zeppelin laid flat on the soil like a deflated balloon. Ritesh was escortin' Felicia 'round it as if it were a display. Felicia nodded an' twirled her hair. She bit her lip, admirin' its shape an' size.

I pointed to her. "Behind ya. Why'd he put de braid in her hair?"

Georgia scoffed an' turned towards Ritesh. I picked myself up, skippin' to the machine with Assonance.

"So where do you plan to find the parts for it?" Felicia asked.

Ritesh pushed some of the balloon aside. "Well, we've done ourselves pretty well. We only need one more part. And I know exactly where to get it. It's part of the engine; it'll help filter the air when the balloon is full."

Felicia nodded, "I could calculate the right measurements to get this thing afloat. Trust me, I'd be your best shot."

"And why's that?"

Felicia grinned at Georgia. "Because I can download the parts and reconstruct them without any injuries. Might take a few days though."

"Download?" Georgia asked.

Felicia's arms drooped like flailing candle wax. She searched her hands, then Ritesh, Georgia an' myself, and behind the sleepin' zeppelin.

"Who has my staff? My walking staff? Please don't tell me you've lost it!"

Murray came walkin', half-dazed, with Felicia's stick. He leaned on it, starin' at us. Felicia's face turned red.

"The staff please!"

She bit into her lip, eyes wide like my Ma when ye ticked her off.

Murray glanced between her an' the stick. He shook his head. "Oh, you mean this thing we found?"

Felicia glared. "You found it on me! Just give it here."

He passed her the stick. Her smooth, pale skin contrasted with the dark etched Bywoe branch. Her eyes closed and there was silence as Felicia became calm once more. My panda ears were so much better, an' although my vision was still faded, I could still see the white numbers appear. There were seven, maybe eight floatin' 'round the stick like bubbly clouds. Each faded in at different times. The stick eventually hovered like a shadow above her hands. Felicia opened her eyes. The numbers popped like bubbles an' the stick was gone.

"So that's downloading!" Assonance gawked.

"And it went ... where?" Georgia pouted, eyes searchin' Felicia. Felicia pointed at her crest, where a white panther shone, fierce an' ferocious.

Ritesh rubbed his chin, poking at her crest. "So you could build the engine in your crest and then ... what?"

Felicia framed the zeppelin with her arms. "Put it in the right spot. You'd be good to go ——"

"We just need the final part! And it ain't easy, lass!" Murray groaned.

I licked my lips, walkin' 'round the soggy balloon. "So why haven't ya returned de staff?" I asked.

Felicia glared at me. "What do you mean?"

"Why are ye keepin' it in ya crest?" I reiterated.

Felicia stared at the cave's ceiling. "Oh, it might come in handy later."

"You can't return it, can you?" Georgia argued.

Felicia smiled, "I can. What? You don't believe me?"

CHAPTER 28: MILKY COMPLICATIONS & A LACK OF FUR

"No, I don't! I want to see you do it before we let you just take our whole engine and lose it forever." Georgia stood tall, blockin' Felicia's gaze.

"I don't have to prove anything to you!" Felicia argued. "My word should be good enough."

Georgia pointed to the zeppelin. "This is our one ticket to safety. I am not letting you or your lies hurt any of our people. Not Ritesh, not Milky, not Murray. My sister does not deserve the pain we've endured. So prove it, or you can leave!"

Felicia's face returned to its pale state. Her eyes reflected the firelight like glitter. She raised her right hand an' clicked her thumb. White flower petals began fallin' again like raindrops.

"I've felt pain too," Felicia said. "There are over twenty thousand of these white blossoms. Each have been downloaded into my crest, one by one. It hurts every time ... I promise you, Georgia! I will fix your engine. All I ask in return is that you fly us to Drewmora so we can help our friends."

"She can do it!" I cheered. "I might not be an albino, but she's a Moore. I've heard stories of 'em from many Kelts. They can move a two-storey house down the street an' make it five times the size. Even her little sister had dat magic panther spark in her."

Georgia nodded, "Okay." She admired the fallen flower petals. "They're lovely flowers!"

There was a smooshin' sound above Ritesh. Milky threw down a rope. "If Ona trusts this blondie, then so do I. And if she can fix Winnie's ol' engine, we might as well use what we can get."

Ritesh pulled back, grabbin' the end of the rope. "That's all well and good, Milky, but what about the spare part? You know more than anyone how dangerous it'll be getting it."

"And we'll get it!" Milky said. "It ain't that dangerous. Ona's not allowed to come, but we should be okay. We just need a plan." Milky tied the rope to a hook on the balloon.

"What kinda danger are we talkin'?" I asked.

Milky, Georgia, Ritesh an' Murray stared at me. Milky jumped, hittin' the ground. "Dumb kind of danger!"

Ritesh crossed his arms. "And we're low on time. So that's going to make things more ———"

"Anxious!" Georgia sighed.

Ritesh folded his arms an' admired Assonance, Felicia an' I. "We need to rob a ferry. It has the last piece of the engine. Without it, we're little better than dead."

Milky walked 'round us. "It's in the Oogali Swamp. It's humid, sticky and full of bugs. Oh, and it's heading right to the Full Sea.

Near Drewmora. So if you want to help—the more, the merrier!"

Chapter 29

The WoodWood House
Perry

The sound of water was becoming a familiar one. We'd been walking along a secret skinny waterway, the Bluway Creek, which according to Mr Doubtson, would take us from Kattagow to Drewmora. He laughed the second day we travelled with him, saying that the Oogali Swamp was much too dangerous for Drewans.

Leo and James, the twins, were always laughing at something, continually being held back as they struggled to pull the wide one-wheeled wagon made of bloodwood with mossy green handles. The grip around the handles was old and weak, crumbling at the slightest of pulls. Harry would help them, but most often he'd hunt, sing Drewan nursery rhymes with his father, and tell Taylah and Zia stories. Kyle's awkward stutters had almost disappeared entirely. His smile was almost too perfect, soothing after the train and Kattagow incidents.

I watched the forest on our left. *Papercut could be anywhere.* Harry's shadow lingered close behind me. I turned to him, his hand moving away from my shoulder. I rubbed at it, not feeling anything.

"Sorry!" I mumbled.

"Sorry for what?" he asked. "Are yer right there?"

I smiled half-heartedly. "It's been a while since I was right. But I'm staying strong."

He smiled back. "It's something you lost, isn't it?"

"It is. A few days after the attack on Kelton Whide. I don't like touching."

"You don't talk much about yer gifts," he said.

"Neither do you!" I mused.

Mr Doubtson stopped Leo and James. He pulled out a fishing rod and walked towards a rock near the creek. We'd reached a small inlet, lush with grass and solid orange rocks that could knock you cold if you slipped. I stopped next to Harry. He leaned down to tie his shoelace and chuckled, "Oh, I'm saving my gifts."

Kyle joined us. "Did I just hear *gifts* and *saving* in the same sentence? You're not a Fledding, are you?"

Harry chuckled, continuing his knot. "Not like money-saving, Kyle! I've been saving my gift, so I don't be draining my crest."

I crossed my arms. "All right, *one*, you can't drain your crest. You can hurt it if you use it too much, but you can't drain it unless you ... you know, die. And *two*, what could you be saving it for?"

Harry finished his knot and stood. "The Drewan militia."

James and Leo cracked up, unloading their crab cages and tuna nets. "Good one, Haz!" James remarked. "Yer meant to save them for things that are going to pay off!"

"No point in saving if they're just gonna reject you again! What does it make it now, James? Five?" Leo mocked.

"Six, I think?" James stepped into the river, his grin twice the size of Leo's.

Harry rolled his eyes. "I've only been rejected three times. And they can't say no this time. I'm gonna blow them away with this new trick I learnt."

"If you keep getting rejected, why do you keep trying to get in?" Kyle asked.

Harry shrugged, "I've always wanted to join the militia. Protect my dad, my brothers. My sister. It's what Mum would have wanted. And it's what I want. I just wanna make the world a little bit safer, even if it only helps one person, I'll be happy."

I couldn't help but smile at the fool. "Following your passions, huh? I guess I'd be doing the same if we were in Kelton Whide."

Kyle's chuckle left me speechless. "We'd be farmers, shovelling crap and chewing on hay, which is a huge stereotype."

Chapter 29: The Wood Wood House

"We only chew hay on Tuesdays," I laughed. "I don't think farming is for me. I'd probably move to the Ptak Isles with Faith, study something up in the sky and come home with a stupid degree."

Kyle's eyes lingered on Zia and Taylah. They'd been stuck together like glue ever since Harry had persuaded his dad to guide us to Drewmora. "Yeah," he said. "Zia'd be queen by the time you got home."

Harry watched them with Kyle. "Zia! Queen? Yer think?"

I joined them. "She has to be queen. She doesn't want to, but that's life sometimes. Rules are rules, right?"

Zia glanced back at us and put her middle finger up at me. Kyle skipped to her. "Your Majesty, there are children around!"

Taylah put her hands by her side. "I'm not a child, thank you very much!"

"I agree. She's a grown lady, Kyle!" I laughed. "How dare you call little Taylah such things. She's only nine."

Kyle gawked. "That's true. She could be Flower Carrier this year."

Taylah pumped her fist in the air. "Yep, Flower whaddya-call-it." Her eyes focused on me. "Who are you calling *little*? I'll be bigger than you when Harry gets into the military."

Harry approached her side. He grinned, patting her head. "Thanks, Tay! See, I will get in this time." He stared at the river, its ripples so still. "Just don't go too close to the water, okay? I don't want to lose you like at the fountain." Taylah rolled her eyes.

Zia offered her white-gloved hand to the little Drewan. "It's okay, Tay!" she cheered. "You can walk on the riverbeds with me. I can tell you some of the stories from home. About kings and queens, gods and spirits—all sorts of things."

Taylah and Zia strolled into the waterbeds. The sound of their feet splashing in the creek echoed.

"Harry!" Mr Doubtson called. "Can yer fetch the package from the wagon? The fish and bread we've been saving."

Harry jogged to the wagon, returning with a small oak box in his arms. It smelt of salt, fish and cheese. His father looked at us, casting a fishing rod from a high rock.

"Have we reached Timberpoint?" Harry asked his father, tiptoeing down the creek.

"We've reached it and the two boys are going to need their rations. You can take Perry and Kyle." I believe both Kyle and I were ready to do anything Mr Doubtson ordered. However, before Harry led us into the forest of darkwood, Mr Doubtson removed his trigger finger from his fishing line. "Oh. One last thing. Stay awhile. Those two don't get many visitors. We'll head off when yer return."

Harry bowed again and saluted his father with two fingers. His father saluted back with one finger. They'd do this whenever they said goodbye.

Our boots fought through thick grass. Dried pollen and manure made my nose flare. "So what exactly is Timberpoint? And why's your dad sending us out this way? Isn't Drewmora in the east?" I asked.

Harry's eyes were focused on his feet. "It's kind of complicated. Dad travels from Kattagow to Drewmora and back to Kattagow on the regular. It's to help the people in the cages."

"Cages?" Kyle uttered.

"Since the Echo Wars, Drewmora's shoreline has become an attraction for those escaping the old-fashioned lands of Kimeria. Dad hasn't mined in years because of it ... He's trying his best!"

Kyle stopped. He put his hand out like a cup and Holdie flew down, spinning above his palm.

I turned to him. "Kimeria's a big continent. They've got what—twelve major cities?" I asked. "And that doesn't include simpleton villages. How many people are stuck on the shoreline?"

Before Harry had time to answer, a blue light glimmered above our eyes. It was so fast and bright. I squinted and saw a blue map of Euphoria.

Holdie projected the map from his top tip, spinning at a rapid speed. The three major continents were there. Kimeria, the largest of the three, with South Kimeria holding many traditionalist nations and the more developed North Kimeria, which was infatuated with a long history. Bungonia, the smallest continent, had only five major cities and was close to the size of many minor islands. Finally, Oberon had one white dot towards the south-east of its landmass. *That's where we were.*

CHAPTER 29: THE WOOD WOOD HOUSE

Kyle zoomed in until the Full Sea and Camel Hump Shore covered the blue hologram. We had a satellite view of the entire shoreline; you could hardly see sand. It was covered by tent-lets and little huts. *Cages!*

"So that's what all these squares are," Kyle mumbled.

Harry nodded, "It'll be worse in person." His arms began shaking.

I offered my gloved hands. "Pass the box! I'll carry it the rest of the way."

"Are you sure, Perry? You don't have to." Harry pulled away.

"Everyone needs help ... We're not too far, are we?"

It was as if a ghost had caught Harry's voice. Speechless, he handed me the box and lowered his arms. "Thank you," he said. "We're not far. Another five minutes. This way."

Kyle turned off the projection. As Holdie returned to his usual spot, we wandered into more greenery. It was a different green from Jinkie's Gap's dry olives and Everbreen's magical hues of sage, mint and emerald. It was very light, similar to the eucalyptus, but healthy and vibrant. The manure scent was strong here; behind the darkwood there was a timber cabin. "Timberpoint!" Kyle exclaimed.

I noticed the dark oak trees. Their bodies didn't go straight up. No, these trees had been bent and distorted like spirals, arching like candy canes and zigzagging like train tracks. The inside of my mouth clenched at the cabin's perfection. Each timber slate, each strand of hay within the roof, each meticulous detail would have taken the best craftsman decades. I readied one hand on my staff, now sheathed diagonally on my back.

"Harry, who lives here?" I asked.

"Two brothers! You might know them." Harry approached the front door. His hand reached for its silver knob. However, something else pulled the door open. Harry's hand froze as the timber was pulled back into the house. Darkness was the only thing inside.

I could hear whispers—familiar whispers. "Why'd you open the door?" a male voice said. It sounded quite young.

"'Cause they have a box. Look!" Another similar voice argued. This one was younger.

"And so you open the door. There's a lot of boxes in this place!"

"What place? When was the last time someone gave us a box?"

"Oh, let me look at the thing. By the Light, you have no self-control."

The voices stopped.

The older one spoke once more. "Huh? It's Harry."

"Harry?"

"The blond guy who wants to be in the military, you pickle! His dad gives us fish."

"Oh! Harry! He's ——"

"Keep your voice down! There are others ... On three, I'll tell them to come inside. One. Two. *Three!*"

I guess the older one enjoyed yelling; his voice was so loud.

"Um. Hey, Harry! You can come in."

Harry staggered to the door. "What about my two friends? Are they also allowed inside?" After a few more seconds of bickering, we got the all-clear from the older voice.

Kyle almost fell backwards, the timberwork inside was so impressive. The shape of the cabin was similar to a regular house in Kelton Whide, but the moulds and arrangements of the walls were unreal. *How could someone bend timber like this without it breaking?* As if entering a wizard's castle, the cabin seemed to grow twice its size when we entered. There was no sign of the two brothers.

We walked past a circular dining table for three, a fireplace, three little cacti, and a handful of dandelions Teala would have stolen if she were here. The crackling logs under the fire were comforting. I dropped the box on the kitchen bench. It was small, similar to Odd's kitchen, with handmade frying pans and a kettle above the stove. Harry sat on a mahogany stool, his legs straight down and his arms falling to his side. I began tapping my fingers against my staff.

"Hey! Yer guys wanna come out? Dad says we have to check up on you."

Harry paused. The top of the timber box began moving on its own. It was like an invisible being had pulled it and melded it upwards, twirling it until it couldn't twirl any longer. Each slate of timber that covered the top of the box started to undo itself. It was like it was

Chapter 29: The Wood Wood House

unbuttoning its own timber shell. When each popped, splinters of wood ricocheted onto the timber floorboards. Kyle and I turned to see a burning white possum crest.

I know that crest.

"Sam?" Kyle mumbled. "How'd y-you get here?"

I moved my arm away from my staff. Sam's left hand was raised, his fingers cuffed, as though he was about to use his powers.

I spread my arms. "Where there's Sam, there's ..." I paused. "Where's your brother?"

Sam pointed at the box, "With Harry!"

We turned to see Gerard unloading the box. "Oh, hiya," Gerard waved. "Kyle, is that you? And Perry? What's that thing above your head?"

"It's a long story," Kyle said.

I approached the kitchen with Sam. "It sure is! How the heck did you two end up here, of all places?"

Before they could answer, Harry interrupted us. "Wait, you guys do know each other? So it be true what they say. Every Kelt knows a fellow Kelt."

Kyle shuffled next to Gerard. He rubbed his head, and Gerard laughed, pushing Kyle away.

"Oh, these two dried wheats escaped with me," Kyle chuckled. "You two are really taking that WoodWood nickname to the next level, huh?"

I could taste the stench of the two-day-old fish from the box. I held my nose.

"How many people give you two boxes?" I asked.

Sam sat down. "We have our ways," he grinned. "What brings you all this way? There are bandits around these parts."

Kyle leaned his elbows on the kitchen bench. "We're heading to Drewmora!" he explained. "I think we're trying find Lord Kelton. But, there's also an assassin that we need to stop. Look, I've been melting, and there was an incident on the train. It'd be best if you ask Perry."

The four stared at me. "It's complicated. If we had a few hours and some ———"

I heard tapping above me. It was like someone had run across the hay roof. "Did anyone hear that?" I asked.

"Hear what?" Sam squinted at me.

"I haven't heard a thing but the fire all morning," Gerard mused, his face focused on his box of goodies.

I took a step back. "All right. Maybe my hearing's playing up."

Kyle sighed, "I'm glad you two got out safely. You look like you've done well ... Wish Juice could see you two like this."

Gerard lost his focus on the box. "Juice? What are you talking abou——"

Sam clapped his hands over Gerard's mouth. "Stop talking about your dreams, knobhead," the older brother laughed. "We wish we could see Juice too."

"Juice? Who's Juice? What kinda name is that?" Harry wondered.

"It's short for Juiceton! It's Bungonian. Mum and Dad were very particular with names," Sam explained. He clapped his hands. "So an assassin and Lord Kelton. What does that entail?"

I stayed quiet and, as expected, Kyle recounted our adventure so far.

Harry stood, "Are you right, Perry?" I heard another scattering noise. A rush of air, like a window had been opened. I crept, reaching for my staff. Behind the fireplace, there was a staircase leading to the next floor.

"So, Sammy." Everyone stopped talking. "You two are here by yourselves, yeah? No one else is gonna make the timber ... *move?*" I asked.

Sam moved closer to me, shrugging, "Not that I know of. We've been here by ourselves almost five months now. Drewans like Mr Doubtson and Harry have often brought us food, but besides that, we're all alone."

I took a step near the fireplace. "And Harry. How do you know about this place? Was there anyone else here before the WoodWood boys?"

"Ah ..."

Another sound. Timber being shoved together, and drawers being

Chapter 29: The Wood Wood House

opened. It muted Harry's answer. This was his fourth visit. I pulled my hand away from my staff and smiled at Sam, Harry and Gerard. "Hey, boys," I uttered. "Mind if I have a look upstairs? Just wanna see what you two have done with the place."

Sam rushed to my side. "Oh, this ol' hut. Nothing to get yourself worked up about, Perry! Come, we'll cook up a roast or something—the fish smells great."

"That's right. Sam and I are chefs, y'know! Aren't we, Sam?" Gerard winked.

"Well, I wouldn't say chefs, but we can boil a mean pasta. No need to go up there where all the dust is. We barely go up there ourselves."

Sam pulled me into the kitchen. I rubbed his head. "No need to go all red, Sammy," I grinned. "Kyle's got a few too many stories to tell and I'm sure it'd be good for you three to catch up. Harry and I are just gonna hang by the fire." I winked at Sam and he lowered his arms. His cheeks had flushed red, but their colour soon faded.

Harry strolled behind me, admiring the stone of the fireplace. It was the only part of the cabin that wasn't timber. It was sandstone like our school in Kelton Whide. Each brick had been glued together with paper-thin concrete. I rubbed my hand along it; the cement was quite weak, crumbling at my touch. It was as though they had used paper maché. Another sound caught my ear. Something was being pulled along the timber ceiling above our heads, creating a grinding noise that made Harry's eyes flicker upwards.

"You heard that, didn't you?" I whispered. "Who's up there, Harry?"

Harry whispered in a panic. "I don't know. I thought it was just the two brothers. There shouldn't be anyone else, I swear. Not many know of here, not many outsiders."

I pulled out my staff. "A Drewan then?"

Harry shook his head. "Bandits! Homestealers!" He stared at the ceiling. Gerard jumped out from behind the kitchen. "No! No, it's ... it's my pet giraffe. He's from Everbreen."

"Giraffe is what you come up wi—*Yes!* Our Ever friend, the giraffe! He's probably just woken up."

I stared at them. "I'm sick of these games. I'm going up there."

Sam begged me to stop, while Harry nodded, staying close to my staff.

"Wait a tic, Perry," Kyle said. "Let the boys explain themselves first, will you? Perry!"

I turned to face them before the first step. "This house has been freaking me out since we arrived and I wanna know why!"

Gerard, wide-eyed, swiped his arm from right to left. A flurry of wind seemed to blow the fire leftward. Harry jumped. I turned to see that the stairs were gone, replaced by a new timber wall. Gerard had blocked my path.

I grinned, "I'm not going to hurt them, Gerard. That much I can promise. I just want answers!" I walked through the new timber wall and climbed the staircase, which was shrouded in darkness. Each step creaked. The further I journeyed, the more scraping there was. A flurry of wind roared behind me. The light of the fireplace brightened the staircase, and I reached the top.

In his paper cloak, Papercut sat in a small triangle timber room, sharpening his two paper katanas. Unhooded and unmasked, he sat there, eyes down as though searching for ants. I raised my staff, ready to attack, then my heart tore itself into two. *I knew him. I knew the face behind the mask.*

"Juice?" I gasped. *It was him!* Scarred from top to bottom, blue-eyed and miserable like someone had beaten the life out of him—he was twice the size of what he was at school. I repeated his name to make sure.

"Juiceton!"

He glared at me. A paper card flew towards me. It phased through my chest, hitting the wall behind me. Before I could move, Papercut's katana was at my throat. I pushed its sharp side away with my staff.

Harry rushed up first as I deflected Papercut's fast jabs and stabs. The room was full of brewing stands, empty test tubes, engine pieces for a flying machine, schematics for a zeppelin named Win Dixie and a miserable mattress. Of all the weapons he could have used, Harry seized the blankets on the mattress and threw them at Papercut. They were immediately torn in half by Papercut's katana. They hovered for a bit like a magic carpet, shocked from being sliced. Harry's blue

Chapter 29: The Wood Wood House

dolphin crest was alight. A dark figure in the shape of Harry jumped from the wall and threw its fist at Papercut. Papercut retaliated with his katana, but before it struck the black figure's side, the black figure vanished. The paper sword smashed into a glass jar. Green goo sizzled, covering Juice's paper arm. He jumped. A test tube dropped from the study table and rolled to my feet.

Sam and Gerard reached the top, screaming for Juice. Papercut's arm was on fire. The WoodWood brothers tackled him, pushing down the dancing orange lights. Harry leaned back onto the greasy mattress, narrowly dodging one of the katanas as it whooshed past him and hit the wall next to his head. Juice stood, smoke flowing from his cloak. One of his sleeves was now black, covered in holes and blood. He was bleeding. Juice cracked his knuckles, eyeing Harry. I tried screaming, but someone else's voice filled the room.

"JUICE!" Kyle yelled. He stood on the top step, his arms tight by his side and Holdie floating tall over his head. "Don't hurt him! That's not you. What the hell happened to you?" Kyle asked.

I finally got to my feet. "Don't go near him, Kyle. He's dangerous. He killed Senator Hartway."

Sam turned to his brother. "Juice, did you? You told us they didn't control you any——"

Juice hushed his brother with a wave of his arm. A piece of paper dropped from his hand and he walked towards us.

I readied my staff in front of Kyle. "Who did this to you, Juice?"

He kept walking, pointing at Holdie. *His eyes were set on Holdie alone.* Blood dripped down my forearm. It stung! I froze as more blood started trickling down the left side of my chest next to my nipple. I tried blocking Juice's attacks, but he was too fast. I could feel the coldness of the room. *It was chilling my inside.* The world turned black for a quick moment, and I was on the floor.

I glanced up to see Kyle screaming at Juice. Papercut snatched Holdie, taking Kyle's head with him. He pressed the stimulate button and Kyle dissolved into a brown sludge. It bubbled. Juice lifted the test tube from the floor. He grinned and collected the sludge into the empty glass capsule. Once full, he closed the tube with a cork, admired my wounded body and smiled.

Sam and Gerard cried his name; they were so wounded and sorry. Papercut flicked a card at my chest and jumped. A black spray of ink appeared like smoke. When it faded, a paper plane holding the test tube flew out of the circle window, taking Kyle with it.

Harry ran to my side, applying pressure on my dripping wounds.

I held his arm, "It's fine, Harry! It's fine." A rush of pain shocked my left side. "Argh!"

Sam rushed downstairs while Gerard picked up the card.

He read aloud, "I'm sorry!" and looked at Harry and me. "He hasn't been the same since the experiments. The beacon took his voice. But *they* took his happiness."

"Who, Gerard? Who did this?" I asked.

"The masked ones who were hunting our friends."

Sam returned with a box of medical supplies. It smelt of tea tree oil and band-aids. As I lifted my shirt, I read my card.

"What do we do?" Harry asked. He was sweating.

"We keep going," I told him, shivering for the first time in years. "We keep moving forward. Will you two be all right by yourselves?"

Sam joked that they'd always been by themselves.

I nodded, "Good. I'll bring the whole gang here and you can come with us. Back to our Town of Tents. I just gotta go somewhere first. It's not safe, all right?"

Harry was out of breath. "How do you …? Where are we going? Where's Kyle?"

I held up the card and showed him. It read, See you in Drewmora, Perry!

Three entered the forest, but only two returned. Zia was full of questions, of course. *Now Drewmora was twice as important.* I just hoped the others were having an easier time getting there.

Chapter 30
The Oogali Swamp
Faith

Our second night aboard the Bucketeer was humid. Olivia decided on the more trusted ferry service from the three that ventured through the thick bottlebrushes and green patches of duckweed. Dally's body odour was pungent and, I'll admit, I probably smelt worse. The air was thick, rich with mosquitoes and flies. Crickets sang around us to the splashes of jumping fish and the calls of owls. I'd never been in such a bustling forest. The Bucketeer's steel mast broke through dark green canopies and vines that could tickle your neck they were so long.

I rubbed the sweat from my eyes, trudging up the inner cabins' main stairwell. At the top, there were orange timber panels similar to the inside of a Bywoe tree. The sound of my boots bounced off them, waking a half-asleep Olivia. She leaned on the Bucketeer's barricade, a white alloy that wrapped itself around the boat's hull. She turned her head to me and smiled, "Can't sleep?"

I approached her, the scent of mould covering the dark-coated midnight swamp. "No. Sleep's hard to come by," I admitted. "What are you doing out here so late?"

Olivia admired the patches of olive land, the thick oak that held the willows and one red rose that sprouted in the darkness. "Enjoying the scenery." She looked at me. "It's not every day a councillor like myself gets to visit the Oogali Swamp, let alone Kattagow, the Pilum Bridge or the Jakoo River. I don't get out of the office as much as I'd like."

"I suppose you're right! It's not for everyone, but it's different." I smiled, tasting the thick heat. "How bad can a councillor be? You've travelled from Kelton Whide to Everbreen to Central City and now to Drewmora. And you've gotten to meet some amazing people, like ... like Giuseppe."

Olivia suppressed a giggle. "Oh, Sep! Now he's one to worry about!"

We watched the land pass by as though we were on a conveyor belt. "He'll be okay, Liv! He's big and tough; besides, he probably knows these lands better than any of us. Like he said, we're on Drewan land. It'd be like if we were to get lost in Jinkie's Gap!"

"It's not him I'm worried about," Olivia sighed. "It's his orders. Half the time I'm with him, I don't know if he can even think for himself. They say go one way, he goes. But I don't believe he wants to listen any longer."

"Do you think the militia will make him do something dangerous?" I asked.

Olivia shook her head. "No, not the militia. Nor his battalion. Those in charge. He's told me stories of General Ko, their near-misses with death and the crazy antics he forces them into at the worst possible times."

"So he does whatever the general tells him?" I asked.

"They all do, Faith! It's how they're taught to be soldiers. Sep's told me that he does it 'cause he believes in the man. The general was one of the leading forces in the Echo Wars, right beside my father and Araidian. He'd risk everything for his people, and even more just to make the world a better place ... From what I've seen throughout his protection of Mr Kingsleigh and Parliament House, the general has a good heart, but his ways, they are sometimes dangerous. I think he saw Senator Hartway's death as a success!"

"A success?" I questioned. "That was the first death inside Parliament's walls since before ———"

"Yes, it was! But it was only one death. Not ten, not a hundred. Just one. That's what Sep told me. He said the general was proud of their achievement."

She flicked her honey-coloured hair away from her eyes. The wind

Chapter 30: The Oogali Swamp

was very subtle; you could barely feel it. "Enough about the past," Olivia mused. "Have you thought about what we could do once we reach the blue city?"

"Gosh, no. We could visit Mr Kingsleigh. That's where Odd would go and he'll most likely know what to do after that."

"You shouldn't rely on Mr Odd! From my experience, people who think they know everything can lead you into tough situations."

I laughed, "I don't need Odd to find the others. I think it's just the familiarity. Perry will most likely think the same. So will Bailey and Teala."

Olivia's voice was firm. "We're our own familiarity, Faith! It'd make me happy to see the others, but right now we have each other. And until that day when Teala's under my arms and I know that Perry, the princess, Giuseppe and everyone else is safe, I'm happy to forge my own path."

I admired Olivia. "Is that why you've become a councillor? To make this path for others to follow?"

Olivia's green eyes met mine. "I think I do it so I can tell myself that I'm helping people. Although there are other prior commit——"

Dally yawned loudly. "The flip are you two doing up here so late?" he asked. "It'd be early morning now and well ... I can't see anyone else up this late."

"And why might you be up this late, Dalton?" Olivia asked.

"I had a nightmare," Dally groaned. "And when I woke, you two were missing. So I came up here to have a look. I'm just glad neither of you fell overboard."

"Overboard?" I grinned. "I think we can handle ourselves, Dally. But thank you for the concern ... Are you holding up?"

Dally had sweat running from the top of his forehead to the bottom of his chin. He wiped it away, smiling, "Just a nightmare, nothing special ... Did I interrupt something?"

"No, no! As if. We were just discussing our plans for Drewmora!" I explained.

Olivia stretched her arms. "To be honest, I'm all planned out! Dally's right. I need some sleep before the sun comes up. You two be safe now, you hear!" She walked towards the cabins. "Especially you, Dalton! If I have to jump into the swamp water because of you, I'm going to tell everyone that little tale you used to brag about to Simone and me. You know the one."

Dally's face turned white. "I was six, Liv! I didn't know what I was saying back then."

He looked back at me as Olivia descended into the rear of the ferry, and raised a brow, "I guess I'm not gonna be jumping into the water anytime soon!"

"Some things never change, huh?" I mumbled.

Dally leaned his arms on the railing beside me, inhaling the warm air. "What do you mean by that?"

"Just us. Olivia making fun of you for something, me laughing about it, you complaining. She's the only person I know who you complain to … Actually, Odd too."

"Odd!" Dally argued. "Well, it's his fault we're in this mess … Huh, I guess you're right. Maybe there's something about people whose names start with an O. Olivia had some hot friends back in the day." He fell silent. It was like the swamp knew he had something on his conscience.

His thick brown eyes watched me as his jawline flinched at the flies that buzzed around us. "Thank you," he said quietly. "Thanks for healing the cut."

I glanced at his shirt. "Oh, yes, your cut! How is it?"

He lifted his black shirt so that the left side of his belly was showing. His stomach heaved in and out; above it was a cut, still red and swollen, but shut tight. "The train's window didn't go too deep, thankfully." He pulled his shirt back down. "You didn't need to, but I should thank you."

"If I hadn't, you would have bled out on this ferry! We would never have made it to Drewmora."

He leaned away from me, eyeing the back of the boat. "You're probably right, but I … I don't deserve things like that. Kindness."

"What d'you mean, Dally? You're one of the bravest guys I know," I grabbed his shoulder. "You'd knock down the walls of any kingdom just to have Perry's back, or Bailey's, even mine. Of course you deserve kindness."

He avoided my eyes. "No, I don't Faith! I don't deserve nice things, okay."

"Why are you saying that?" He didn't respond. "Tell me, Dally! Why? Is it because of Perry? Ada?"

His face shrivelled in pain when I said her name. He shrugged, "I don't know, Faith! It's how I think. Perry deserves all the nice things in the world. It's why he has you. I just—for now, I don't deserve nice things. Not right now, but maybe later."

"Why later?"

"Because the world is full of terrible people. I've seen it! And if I can be nice to someone, or make another smile, or defend a friend, then I'd rather do that. I'd rather sacrifice what makes me happy so that other people around me can be happier for a moment."

He spat a thick ball of snot and phlegm into the pitch-black water. I watched it, the sound of splashing echoing below us. A small quiver of fog covered the canopies.

"That's dumb!" I said. Dally's brows shot up like I had just slapped him. "You need to be happy too. Weren't you happy with Ada? What happened to her, Dally?"

He put his head down and leaned in close. His eyes shone in the growing fog. I could have sworn he was about to cry. The world around us was gone, covered in a wall of grey. There was no duckweed, no green moss, no oaks, no Oogali Swamp.

Dally's voice was gentle, weary from the truth that hid behind his words. "I'm not a good person, Faith!" His eyes looked through me; he was ashamed to even watch the water. He spoke again. "Before Davis and Merkie, before meeting you all in the Forest of Farbe, I was with Ada every day. We were like a ... a piece of paper and a pen. You couldn't have one without the other if you were to read our tales. And we had many, but the ... the beacon got in the way ... She ———"

Dally's hand pushed me in the chest. Before I had time to react, I was already skidding halfway down the ferry. A girl, similar height to Zia with curly black hair and blue eyes, lunged at Dally. She pushed him back with a wet bow. As I recovered on the floor, another attacker appeared from the swamp water. He climbed over the metal bannister with a knife in his mouth. He had very little hair and a burnt scalp like the sun had bullied him in school. He prepared to jump.

I yelled Dally's name. He turned, raising a hand to the balding attacker. Instead of falling, the man and his knife flew upwards, as though an invisible fist had knocked him off balance. He bounced away from Dally.

The girl faced me. Her yellow crest began to calm, radiating light onto her bow. Her feet were perfectly paced; her back arched upwards and, when the sound of crashing wobbled the Bucketteer, she smiled at me. Like Dally, this girl raised her hand and stared at me. I could see my reflection in her eyes. The bald man lifted himself, his head was now lumpy and redder. As he did this, he noticed the girl's pose. He fumbled through his pockets as Dally approached him. Quickly, he tossed a small stone arrowhead.

Dally and he were head to head, white crest against black, as the arrowhead flew towards the girl. Clumps of the timber flooring began to disappear as though they had never been there. It was like the arrowhead was sucking them up. An arrow with an orange body landed in the girl's hand. She aimed her bow, loaded her arrow and angled her head to get the perfect shot. I threw my right hand before my chest, and the arrow hit.

My fingers were shaking. I could taste the stone of the arrowhead through my palm. My hand was like a brick wall. The pinch of the stone made me squirm as I covered my face. When I looked back at the girl, I saw bubbles. Her face fell.

"How could you ..." She turned to the man. "Murray, I need more arrows. Where are the others? This chick just turned my shot into bubbles!"

Murray dodged Dally's fist. "*Bubbles?* Kinda busy here, Georgia."

Some moaning came from below. The missing timber panels let moonlight into the cabins.

"What the hell's going on up there?" An older Fledding asked.

Suddenly, a rush of footsteps echoed above where the captain was driving. I could smell oil. The steps came closer—one figure leapt

Chapter 30: The Oogali Swamp

overhead. A white light, then a red light, an orange light and a green light. I rushed over to the bridge of the boat.

"Hey! Where do you think you're going?" Georgia yelled.

My legs took me to the stairs, which led to the front of the boat. The green light glimmered to the left of my eye. *SNAP!* An arrow landed in front of my face.

I pulled myself back and faced Georgia. "I don't want to hurt you!"

She stopped, pointing another arrow at me. "What is up with people saying that line? I'll be honest, I've never seen anyone turn my arrows into bubbles, but ——"

The Bucketteer's horn screamed. I thought my ears were going to pop. It settled and Georgia raised her bow at my forehead. "As I was say——"

The captain honked the horn again; it was louder this time. Georgia waited, licking her perfect lips.

It was silent again as banging echoed to my left. Georgia raised her chin. "So! Do you wanna make thi——"

The horn shook the swamp. Georgia pulled her bow down, biting her lip, and pointed to the bridge's window above my head. "If he does that again, I'm gonna get really grumpy and shoot something I shouldn't shoot." She waited for the horn to go off. It was silent—not even a grasshopper chirped.

I tried walking towards the spot where I had last seen the green light. "Please stop moving," Georgia pleaded. "I can't let you go down there!"

The fog around us began to sway. I stopped, eyeing the back of the boat. Dally groaned behind one of the metal walls.

"Okay." I put my hands in the air. "You don't have to be scared. I'm not that dangerous."

Georgia examined my arm. "You're a Kelt! Must know your plants then."

She lowered her bow, approaching me.

"Somewhat," I admitted. "My parents were into bee farming. You're a Bellcurve. It must be hard …"

Georgia's face was now a few metres from mine. She smelt of roses. "Oh, I'm too young to remember anything from the war … My friends just need one thing and we'll leave. I don't want to hurt anyone if I ——"

A ruckus of people bombarding the top deck forced the ferry up and down. Georgia turned back to where Dally and Murray were brawling. As she turned, I flicked her arrow and ran. Bubbles floated above her bow where the arrow had been.

Bolting ahead, the warm wind stuck to my face. Georgia called out, "Oh, now you're just being annoying!"

Footsteps echoed behind me. I ran and turned towards the ferry's engine room. The sound of arrows and gunshots rang behind the steel shelter. *I hope Dally's okay.* Something flew past my ear. Another arrow slapped the Bucketteer's barricade. I reached another grey wall. You could taste the nails that held it together as Georgia slowed her pace.

She raised her bow at me. "Don't go any further! I'm getting really sick of chasing you." Another scream of revolt echoed on the other side of the ferry. She raised her ear. "By the sounds of things, the others have arrived."

"You know I can just turn your arrows into whatever I want," I said.

Georgia grinned. "Sure. Bubbles." She laughed with wide eyes. "You can't be that powerful!"

"I am. Why haven't you shot me down yet? Are you afraid?"

Georgia shook her head. "Not afraid. Just don't want something bad on my conscience."

The fog grew thicker once more. A blue light appeared, flashing between Georgia and me. When my eyes readjusted, Olivia stood between us. Blue ash fell around her, burning the orange floor panels. Olivia raised her arms. "Settle, now. I really don't want an arrow in m——"

Georgia let go of her bowstring and an arrow flew through Olivia's shoulder. Just like Perry, Olivia's body was like water. The arrow flew through her transparent skin and bounced off the engine room's door.

Chapter 30: The Oogali Swamp

I ducked. Olivia rolled her eyes. "Yuck, that feels so gross. I don't have time for bandits. I've got other issues to deal with." A banging sound caught me off guard. Smoke sprayed from where Dally was as more men and women roared their battle cries. Murray appeared behind us, attempting to throw another arrowhead. The stone triangle floated in the air, heading closer and closer to Georgia. However, before it reached her hand, Dally leapt from the far side of the ferry and caught it mid-throw.

Landing back on his feet, Dally grinned like he'd just won the grand final in football. He pegged the arrowhead over the ferry's barricade and laughed, "Oh, did you need that?"

A metallic scrape rustled behind me. Dally yelled my name and, before my heart could jump, I was ducking under a swinging chain. A darker-skinned man came from the engine room, swinging a bike chain like it was a lasso. He called in a deep voice. "Blondie, hurry with that piece! We're gonna need more fog, pronto, Ever!"

Georgia groaned. "Great! Ravesh is here! Hey, bubbles, if I were you, I'd switch with the blond ghost-girl, here! He can be a little much in comparison to the other two."

I turned back to Dally. "You wanna switch?"

Dally shook his head. "I'm okay, Faith! This guy's cool. He's fun to throw around." Dally ran headfirst into Murray, swiping his hand to the left. Murray's body drifted down the ferry like gravity had been turned sideways.

Georgia raised her eyebrows. "Fine by me. Councillor!" She threw her bow towards Olivia. I was surprised how well-trained Olivia was. Her posture, her patience, how she swayed out of the way without a single sweat.

Ravesh cracked his neck. His dark eyes cooled my insides. I could smell herbs on his skin and soil. He groaned, "Unlucky!" The chain flew from the heavens, back to the ferry's top deck, crushing the timber slates below us. I tumbled out of the way, moving away from the engine room.

His arms tensed and the chain flew back into the air. His red crest was glowing like a pulsating vein. The chain flew towards me as I backed away to the Captain's Bridge. Beyond the fog, I could see the vines. I called for them as the canopies above dropped down to my aid. Three vines, like three fingers, curled around several metal links that created the chain, holding it still. Ravesh tensed his arm, his red crest sparkling. The chain vibrated with a pulse of energy.

The dark oak willow held up the chain like a spider brawling a python. However, the python fought back. After the chain surged, the smell of smoke made me cough. The chain's furthest link—the one at its end—opened up like it had a mouth and began to eat the vines I had summoned. Behind Ravesh, a blond girl climbed from the engine room and onto the barricade. I would have guessed it was Felicia, but I didn't see her face. She shimmied to the back of the boat, her long hair tickling her waist. The chain broke free. I felt the parts of the swamp water, what made it tick, and called for it. The thick sludge rushed up the side of the ferry and helped the vines. I waved my arm upwards and the water that flew into the air formed itself into a hand. This hand grabbed the chain, stopping it from eating the vines. I powered towards Ravesh.

As I charged, something caught my eye—a person I hadn't seen in a long, long time. Complete with curly black hair under a blue hat, brown human eyes, pale Ever skin and a full set of clothes, Bailey stumbled out of the engine room. *No, it can't be him. He just looks like Bailey. Right?* He followed the blond girl, barely noticing me as I stood frozen, mouth hanging open in shock.

Before I had time to recover, I heard a splash from above. Rain drizzled above my head; the water drops grew cold as the hand dispersed. I looked up to see the chain falling towards me, covered in mangled vines, beneath a thick-fogged sky. My heart softened, my eyes slowed the world, and I couldn't smell, taste or hear anything. I just watched, feeling the inner workings of the chain—each link, how they were melded together, the heat of the fire, the anger in its complicated master. *Ravesh*. His soul was three in one. I clicked my thumb and asked his other personalities to stop. "*Freeze!*" The chain froze above my temple like a silhouette of its former self. Ravesh was taking large breaths, frozen in a whipping position. He was stuck in time, except his eyes could still move, his lungs could still breath, and his face could still sweat.

I approached the dark-skinned Fledding and spoke to all three of them. "Ritesh," I called. Ravesh's eyes locked onto me. "I need you to leave. Before anyone else gets hurt." I couldn't explain the next few words or why I said them. "Just get everyone on that zeppelin." I clicked my thumb. "Unfreeze."

The chain hit another floor panel. Ritesh relaxed and admired the Oogali Swamp. "How did you ..." He turned to me with red cheeks. His voice was lighter, as though he'd swallowed a small amount of helium.

"Good luck!" He grinned at me and pulled his chain to his chest. The metal links twirled around his arm and he ran to the bannister. He climbed above it and followed in the blond girl's footsteps.

The sound of splashing shook the swamp. It was like several bodies had leapt into the swamp to escape the horrors of the Bucketeer. I ran to the bannister where Dally and I had talked earlier. Past the Captain's Bridge, where the captain himself had resurfaced to examine the damage, the fog had begun to evaporate. The world returned. The sound of crickets resumed, the scent of duckweed tickled my nose, and I could see a raft.

It was flat, made of dark oak, floating down the swamp. Ritesh stood there, braiding the blond girl's hair. Georgia and Murray sat, their crests cooling under the moonlight. Standing at the end of the raft was Bailey. *The old Bailey.* He stared at me, his green panda crest glowing in the shadows of the swamp. It was him; I could see it in his eyes as he realised what he had done. He tightened his fist as another voice rang behind me.

"Is that ... *Bailey?*"

I looked back at Dally. "Whoever it is, they've taken something from the engine room."

Olivia joined us. There was a commotion behind her. "There's been an emergency. The captain is docking in Penmond."

"How far away is that from Drewmora?" I asked.

Olivia turned to see the ferry swaying to the left side of the swamp. "Seven days' walk. Give or take."

Seven more days and we'd reach the others. *Just seven more days!*

Chapter 31

The Sixth Day
Bailey

We docked the raft by the spring that swept through the cave. It was chilly inside. The humidity from the swamp wore off the moment we trickled down the Bluway Creek. The timber of the raft knocked against the edge of the limestone.

Felicia sighed, "What a night!"

A familiar voice erupted from where the trees were. "They're back!" a young'un cheered. The little girl with light-brown hair with hints of blond and a braid on one side pushed through the grass fields. Assonance was on her tail. The girl, no older than eleven, jogged past me, smellin' of roses.

"You guys made it! Did you get it? *Did you get it?*" she asked, jumpin' up an' down.

Georgia pushed her playfully, steppin' off the raft. "Of course we got it, Mia."

Mia stopped. She wore suspenders, one undone an' tugged on the right, pushin' down on her feet. "So that means we're safe, right?"

There was a moment of silence in the cave. Milky shoved past Georgia. "It means we can fix Winnie! Flying her is another story." His voice was strong, but the cave felt chillier now. Mia's blue eyes dropped like she'd been told bad news in a hospital.

"Oh," she mumbled, turnin' back to the forest.

Georgia put out her arm, but by the time she reached out, Mia had already trudged back through the brown timber. "Mia! He doesn't …" Georgia huffed at Milky. "Why'd you go and say that, Yuri! Gah!" She ran off behind Mia, explainin' that things were gonna be okay. *That their group were days away from freedom an' safety.*

Assonance approached us. She brushed past me an' hugged Felicia. "I'm so glad you're okay!" Their hug was rather long an' tight. She hugged Milky. "We were so worried." Finally, she hugged me. "What happened out there?"

"An earful! I don't reckon we did de right thing, Assonance. It didn't feel right," I admitted.

"It was strange," Felicia said. "But these people, they need our help. Just like the Gieas and just like anyone else who camped under the Bywoe trees. I hope those who took passage on that ferry are okay."

"They'll be fine!" Milky chirped. "Ritesh and I have been scouting that swamp for some time now. We attacked only a few nautical miles from Penmond. It's a small fishing village that is quite underdeveloped. They would have heard the commotion of them silk'n horns the captain was honking. There's no way this little detour is going to cause much commotion."

Ritesh tapped Felicia's shoulder. "How's she holding?" he asked.

Felicia felt her crest. "Fine. It's late and I'm going to need my sleep if I am to fix this engine of yours."

Ritesh put his hands together. "Yes, yes! It is quite late. We shall rest and figure out what to do with Win Dixie in the morning."

We all wandered towards our tent-lets. Like our own Town of Tents, the people here were dandy enough to give Felicia, Assonance an' I a tent-let to share. As we stumbled behind the laughs of Assonance and Milky, I pulled on Felicia's arm. "I reckon we did somethin' real nutty!"

"What do you mean? Milky said ——"

"Milky could say anythin'!" I whispered. "I reckon Faith was on dat ferry!"

Felicia raised her left brow at me. "Out of all the ferries that journey through the Oogali Swamp, you think of all the possible passengers, Faith was one of them? Statistically, that ratio is far lower than you'd think!"

"It's not 'bout de numbers, Felicia!" I argued. "I know what my own eyes saw. She looked right at me when I couldn't hold the fog any longer."

Felicia took a moment. She sighed, "Well, even if it was possible that Faith was on that ferry, she'll be fine. You should take it as good news. She's heading to Drewmora, just like us!"

"I guess ya right. But what if ——"

"There are no what-ifs, Bailey!" Felicia stared at Assonance an' grinned. "If something is bound to happen, it will. And whether or not those things make us happy, it's not up to us to decide. We have no decision in this movement. We can only dance along the path and hope we don't fall." Our eyes met. "I promise you, Faith's a brave girl. Braver than me. No matter what the world puts in front of her, she'll make her own path to Drewmora."

I nodded as we reached the tent-let. It had a grey roof, a deer's skin for a rug an' two sacks for sleepin'. As we entered, Milky stayed at the front. "I'm going to check on the others. It's late and I haven't prayed to the Mother Light! I'll get Mia to fetch you all in the morning." He saluted us an' left.

I sat on one sack, while the other two cushioned up on the other across from me. Their voices were light as the scent of deer hide tickled my nostril.

"It's a good thing you didn't get hurt!" Assonance laughed.

"I knew this was important to you and your brother. And I didn't want to ..." They continued in hushed tones as I slouched back in the sack, restin' my noggin on the back of my forearm. I turned to watch 'em, exhaling all the stress from tonight's robbery. The two girls got closer again, their legs touchin'. Felicia's hand rubbed Assonance's knee.

"Are you okay?" Felicia asked.

Assonance jolted, "Oh, sorry! It's just ... I was just looking at your eyes." Assonance's eyes widened as her cheeks turned red. She looked away from Felicia, gulping and laughing away the comment. Stuttering, the bird girl calmly added, "Tell me more about what hap——"

I groaned, "Okay. Imma head out an' get some fresh air. I'll

Chapter 31: The Sixth Day

check on what we're doin' tomorra ... if anyone else is up." I trekked out of our tent-let. "Ye should get some sleep, Felicia. Tomorra's gonna be a bonkers leap!"

The girls began their gossip as soon as I left.

It was a strange joint to be in if I'm entirely frank. My noggin felt hot, my face was sticky, and my heart was poundin' so fast I thought I was gonna suffocate. I wandered alone through the fire-lit walls, the sandy dirt beneath my feet. A little giggle sounded ahead. Under a woollen blanket, layin' 'bove another's belly, Mia pointed to the cave's ceilin'. I stopped, hearin' a raw excitement in her voice as though the celebration season had neva' ended.

"So, how'd you get away?" she asked.

Georgia laid there, her belly likely warm from Mia's noggin. "Oh, we were lucky, all right. It was that Ever we found the other day."

"The one with the green crest? Bailey?" Mia asked.

"Yep! He made an ocean of fog as thick as ice, and before anyone could do anything, we were all safely back on the raft heading down the swamp." Georgia paused a moment an' chuckled to herself. It was a soothin' laugh, free from any worry. "You should have seen the whack jobs I had to distract!"

"Whack jobs? What kind?" Mia insisted.

"There was this funny-looking one! When Murray and I got outta the water, he was standing there, his mug all goofy looking and his crappy patchy beard. I smacked his head so hard he almost fell head over heels." The two laughed, the melodies echoing throughout the cave.

"Reminds me of Gerard!" Mia said excitedly.

Georgia rubbed her sister's hair. "Hey! I'm sure he's okay, Mia! Him and Sam, they're smart boys."

"They didn't have to be kicked out!"

"They chose to leave," Georgia's voice was stern. "And if they hadn't, we would never have been able to hide Win Dixie down here."

"It's not fair!" Mia cried, raisin' her noggin from Georgia's belly.

"Why'd they have to leave? We could have help——"

"Mia, *enough!*" Georgia urged. "You know the militia would have hurt us ... Come on, it's late. Let's get some rest!"

I could hear Georgia wincin' as she lifted herself. I turned 'round, hands in my cold pockets. Footsteps approached me from behind.

"Bailey? What are you doing out here at this time?" Georgia asked.

I faced her as if I had no clue what was happenin'. Their yellow crests glimmered gently. "Georgia! Is di——"

"Her sister?" Mia mused. "Sadly so. We were about to go to bed."

"I didn't know Bellcurves were so prone to staying up so late!"

Georgia crossed her arms, "I would be sleeping, but someone decided to have a ——"

"Boring time staying here, while you lot robbed a ferry!" Mia crossed her arms. "I just wanted to know what happened ... *What?* I did!"

Mia an' Georgia bickered just like how Perry an' Teala used to. Finally, Georgia patted Mia's braids. "Go to bed, Mia. I'll be with you in a moment."

Mia rolled her eyes an' reluctantly skipped away.

"Cute young'un!" I grinned.

Georgia rubbed her own knotty hair. "I should thank you, panda. I'm glad we caught the other two idiots in the net when we did. Otherwise, we would never have been able to get that last piece."

"Ye asked. I simply followed. No need to thank me ... How are ya feelin' 'bout tomorra?"

"With what? The engine?"

I nodded.

"Good!" Georgia began to walk. I scampered behind her.

"How long do you think it'll take for Felicia to fix it?"

"She mentioned six leaps of de moon to Ritesh an' I when we reached de Bluway Creek. So one week."

Chapter 31: The Sixth Day

Georgia admired the cave's walls, orange light dancin' against the limestone's stalagmites. "Wow! One more week and we'll be the kings of the sky," she cheered. "Free and safe and ..." She watched my eyes. I could see myself reflected in her iris, taste the rose on her neck, an' feel her relief. "What are your plans after this? How'd you even end up in the Driwood?"

I opened my mouth. Before the first word could slip out, Georgia butted in.

"Don't rush yourself. We only have six days for you to tell me the story!"

She laughed an' I told her everything, from Kelton Whide to Everbreen, to Central City to being with her. I didn't get a wink of sleep that night, but that was the first of many long, happy nights with such dilly fellas. I never knew so many things could happen in six days, but those six days went like fireworks. They popped with such nummy colours, I was freaked to see myself smile.

The first day, Felicia downloaded all the pieces for the engine an' became drowsy the moment everything lost its texture an' disappeared. From then on, although she could still trek an' talk, she would often lose her train of thought or stutter. She could barely figure out where we were sleepin' half the time. She napped twice as much an' would sometimes collapse if she trekked for too long. Assonance stayed by her side, an' would lay with her when the world rotated too fast. I was by her side too, fulfillin' my duty to get her anythin' she needed. That was 'til the afternoon when Milky asked me to go huntin'.

We got out into the Kuni Plateau. The eucalyptus swayed in the wind under the Driwood Forest. It was a harsh leap for huntin', but I was down for the challenge. I was rinky-dink on my two legs—we only caught three rabbits. Milky was more interested in understandin' who Felicia was an' how she met Assonance. I told him the story an' he said the most applesauce.

"I think she likes Felicia," he said. "Like, she's told me she's cute, but I mean ... Felicia's not really her type."

My heart tugged as a cold sensation spread through my belly like an ice cube had exploded inside my stomach. I gulped, discoverin' a whole history between the Milk siblings.

Milky wasn't the only fella I had some one-on-one time with. Murray loved to go fishin', so most days I'd chuck a few lines out with him an' he'd tell me this long an' complicated past between him an' Georgia. There was another tale 'bout how him an' Ritesh met back before the beacons lighted the skies in the Ptak Isles—his home.

The way the runaways here ran their community, it was so different. Ritesh would take Assonance an' I 'round while Felicia slept, showin' us their ways. The cave was full of several different-coloured crests. Fleddings—their red crest guided the runaways. Bellcurves—their yellow crests enlightened the runaways. Centrillians—their orange crests protected the runaways. Islanders—their black crests sheltered the runaways. There were even a few Drewans, an older Kelt who escaped Araidian's Tyranny an' three Evers. The Evers had turned into squirrels after the Great Transformation; two had brown fur an' another with black.

On the third day, they raced up the side of the zeppelin to help Ravesh, Milky an' I ready the balloon. *An' yes, I said Ravesh.* He was the stronger of the three personalities. Pullin' that mopey rope made my forearms flare, my arms burn an' my legs steady. But the pain was worth it 'cause seein' that balloon rise an' conk the top of the limestone was unlike anything I had eva' experienced. A few of the other fellas, hunters an' gatherers, ran on Murray's command an' pulled the balloon up. When the ceiling started to crumble, the smell of plastic covered the makeshift village, an' the sound of cheerin' made me chuckle.

Georgia was my favourite. She was fun to be 'round, loved to dance an' was someone I could just talk to endlessly. I was with her most nights, sittin' somewhere, listening to the little murmurs of the cave an' laughin'. I told her the tales from the Town of Tents, the cult where I had met Milky all those rotations ago, an' my time as a Kelton slave. She was eager to learn 'bout my life as a panda. How it felt. What it was like. When it had happened. To be frank, I couldn't remember a time when I wasn't a panda.

On day five, Milky an' Ritesh gave me a new jacket made from

CHAPTER 31: THE SIXTH DAY

sage-green nylon. It had large pockets with a zipper for my hands an' navy stripes down its sides. Ritesh winked at me an' said it suited the hat—the one Teala had bought me.

Before long, it was the sixth day an' Felicia's nose had begun to run red. Bleedin' during her sleep, she began vomiting in the wee hours of the mornin'. I leapt to her aid, shovin' whatever was soft under her nose. Assonance soldiered out to find help. When the tent-let's cover swayed from Assonance's quick steps, red covered Felicia's hands. She spat an awful amount of green phlegm onto the padded floor. I could smell the vomit, the bitterness to its bumpy ooze.

She grabbed my arm, "Bailey, this engine's killing me! I need it out, now ... Please."

I nodded, placing her arm 'round my neck. Like a tree trunk, she bruised my shoulder as I wobbled our bodies out of the tent-let.

My jacket's sleeve began to feel wet from a thick goo. The bitter smell returned as I carried Felicia forward. I tripped over stalagmites, shovin' myself towards Win Dixie an' the aroma of plastic. Hearin' the firelight crackle behind me, we reached the water. The oak canopies covered our noggins as red dripped, coverin' the grass with each step I took. The sound of Felicia's breath became heavy, as though she was tryin' her hardest to keep her lungs from suffocating. My arm gave way. Felicia dove to the grass, sludge pourin' from her mouth. It was raw on her throat—she had only stomach acid erupting from her belly.

She peered at me with tears in her eyes. "I can't!" she groaned.

I leaned down. "Don't say dat! Ye can, all right! Just a bit further an' whatever is doing dis to ya, it'll be dust."

Felicia curled into a ball, heavin'. She pushed an' pushed, groaning each time. "It's not ready!" she cried. I took a step back an' my face turned red. "Who cares! If it's killin' ya, don't put yourself through the pain. Ya don't have to do what other fellas tell ya to."

She tried liftin' herself from the grass. "But these people, they need our help!"

"An' I need you alive!"

I paused, realising that whatever I said, it wouldn't matter. I pulled her to my side. Her body fell into me as I managed to balance both of us. "What 'bout Assonance? She ... She really likes you, y'know dat?" Felicia looked away. I continued, "*She does!* Milky knows, he's told me 'bout whatever's goin' on between ya two. If ya not gonna live for me, Drewmora, the others, at least do it for her! Please."

Felicia pushed me away. Instead of fallin', her legs took her toward the balloon's shadow. She dropped a few feet from the cockpit an' her body vanished under the dark side. *Even the firelight was scared to dance there.* Assonance screamed as she reached us, Milky, Georgia, Ritesh an' Murray at her side. I was the first to see that Felicia's heartbeat had stopped. The others approached, kneelin' in shock.

Assonance was in tears the moment her knees conked the limestone. As I watched 'em, my noggin was overwhelmed with heat an' my vision was blurrin' from the tears. Three squirrels joined us. Mia, the other Bellcurves, Islanders, Fleddings, Centrillians—all the different-coloured fellas mourned as one. But Felicia's crest was still alight with bright white. Its panther shape never faded. That's when white flower petals began to fall above our noggins like raindrops, as though the cave had a sky. The petals appeared out of nowhere, cryin' with us.

There were thousands upon thousands of 'em, as though autumn had struck where we stood. I could smell the intensity of each petal's pollen, taste the sweetness to their stems. As more an' more glided downward from the stalactites, a white light blinded our eyes. Inside the main cockpit of the zeppelin, these numbers appeared as though the world was just a digital simulation.

When the light vanished, the numbers, each white an' random, popped like bubbles. I trekked closer to Felicia. Assonance's noggin covered her chest, staining her windbreaker with tears. But when I reached the balloon's shadow, a cough emerged from beneath Assonance's face. Everyone pulled back. Felicia sat upward, coughin' away the white flowers.

The petals stopped their descent as the runaways stopped their

Chapter 31: The Sixth Day

mourning. Felicia rubbed her sticky cheeks, moaning at the bitter smell an' the awful taste inside her mouth. "I'm okay. I'm okay!" Her white crest began to bleed, red drippin' beside Assonance's boots.

Milky offered her his hand. "You scared us there, Felicia. The silk happened?"

Felicia grasped his open palm. "I fixed your engine, that's what happened." Assonance pulled her close—she almost knocked her back down. Mia was wrapped 'round Georgia's arm.

Remesh came out, "Oh, my! By the fragile snow beneath my feet, I thought you ... you ..."

"Don't do that ever again, Felicia!" Assonance begged.

Remesh seconded the request an' that was the last time most of these fellas slept inside this cave. Celebration erupted moments later.

I nudged Felicia, "Told ya you could do it!"

"I did it for myself. Not for them." She watched Assonance cheer an' hug her brother. "But you were right. It's nice to know someone actually cares about me. That I'm not just being used."

I stood at her side, watching everyone dance and hug one another as Ritesh announced that Win Dixie was ready to fly. "Look how happy all dese fellas are! You did dis, Felicia!"

"*We* did this!" My hat's brim dropped down from her fingertips. Her eyes watched mine. "Bailey. Thank you."

Ritesh whistled an' the cheers of the many went silent. Droplets fell from the limestone as Ritesh took a deep breath; an onion stench on his tongue. "Everyone! It is time. We will rest, while Murray and I prepare Win Dixie. By midday tomorrow, I vow to you all that we will be free from those who are after us. We will be kings and queens of the sky, leaders of our own path ... We'll be free." His voice became monotone. "So please, collect all of your belongings, bring down your tent-lets and be ready when the sun hits the volcano's point."

Georgia told me that meant midday in Fledding.

I helped her take down her blue ten-let. Felicia sat with

Assonance, their knees close together as Assonance rubbed Felicia's blond locks. Georgia admired 'em.

"She was pretty amazing today!" She gestured to Felicia.

I joined her gaze. "She was." After all this time, I had one last question. "If she can do dat," I said. "An' if Assonance an' Milky can turn into ravens. An' if Ritesh has a spiritual connection with a bike chain. An' if Murray can create any object when he tosses one material over another … What's your gift? What does dat yellow light do?"

Georgia waited for the tent-let to deflate. She pointed at her turtle crest. "This thing? Nothing special." She went red, movin' her eyes away from me.

"Tell me!" I laughed. "I'm not gonna judge."

"You'll think it's silly!"

"Nah, I won't. I make fog. Can't be worse dan dat!"

Georgia giggled, "Fine … I can … I can grant any wish or desire for fifty-two minutes."

My feet went light an' I almost fell back. "Dat's incredible, Georgia! It's a strange time limit, but it's still amazing! Why fifty-two minutes?"

Georgia began foldin' the blue sheet that laid on the ground between us. "'Cause that's how long it took the darkness to cover all of Bellow's Curve. It's how long it took for my people to lose their home … If a flower wants to grow, I can make it grow as large as it wants. But once those fifty-two minutes are up, they're up!"

That was our last night together. The sun emerged along the water that rippled inside the cave. Ye could smell the remaining ash as the firelight walls lost their orange. The limestone returned to its plain self as I sat with Felicia, Georgia an' Assonance. We watched Win Dixie, an' midday came with a bang.

The ground rumbled like when the giant, Aeithalis, in Everbreen had awoken. The Kelt, who was a part of the runaways an' the black squirrel, raised their arms an' made a few of the stalactites fall, crashing into the oak trees. The sound of crashin' leaves, water splashing an' rubble fallin' vibrated the room. *Then, sunlight!*

Chapter 31: The Sixth Day

It gleamed so brightly, I thought my eyes were gonna pop. The ground above our noggins separated as the Kelt an' Ever moved the world around us away from Win Dixie's balloon. A eucalyptus tree dropped from the emerging light. The cave was split into two, one side movin' left, the other side movin' right, 'til there was a large enough gap for us to ascend into the air. We were not in a cave anymore. We had created a ravine where the roots of the eucalyptus trees could be seen. Where the oak tree forest was simply a layer hidin' from the Kuni Plateau. Where Win Dixie ascended into the sky an' flew towards Drewmora. We were finally headin' there. *We were going to reach it.*

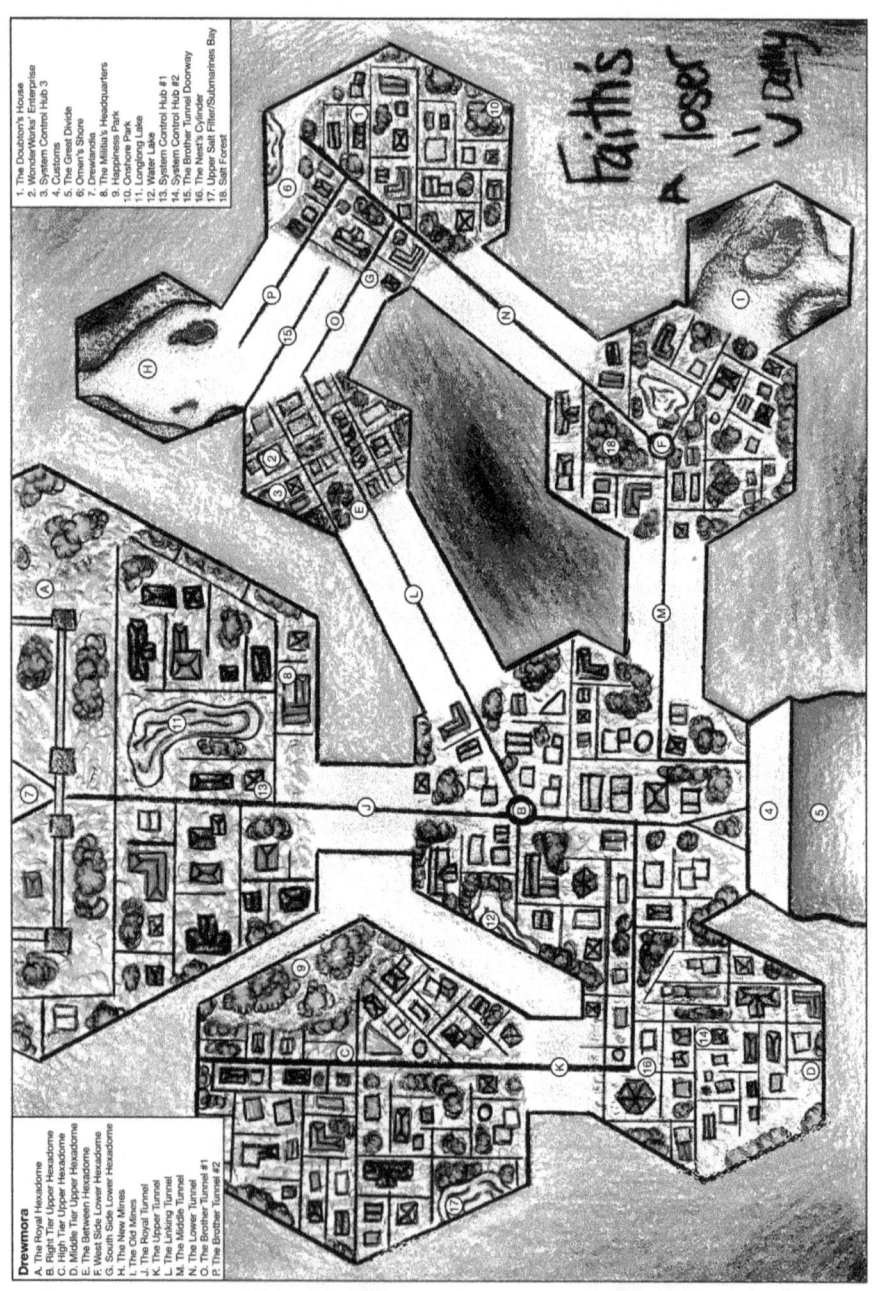

Chapter 32

The Place Where the Water Splits

Perry

It'd been five days since Kyle had been taken. Mr Doubtson had told me over and over that this was the fastest way to Drewmora, that we couldn't go any faster. But I had to get there. I needed to get to Drewmora. *I needed to defeat Papercut. I needed to beat Juice* …

It was night once more along the Bluway Creek. The land was drier here, the grass yellow as the scent of saltwater took over from the Full Sea. We'd have travelled further, but Mr Doubtson insisted that we rest. I sat, watching the water with Zia. Holdie was clasped so tight in my gloved hand, Zia thought I'd break him.

"Taylah told me that we're almost there," the princess said. "She says we'll most likely arrive tomorrow."

I focused on an owl chirping on the other side of the river. "Good. We can find Kyle, your father, the others! I can finally stop Juice!"

I heard a slap and my head swayed to the left. "You're not alone in this, Pear! Like you said, we'll find the others, we'll find Kyle. I get you're worried, but ———"

"It's my fault, Zi!" I looked her in the eye. She adjusted her position, so she was sitting opposite me. "If I was stronger, if I was wiser. If I just knew. Kyle would have never been hurt. He would have never been taken. Senator Hartway would never have died!"

Zia raised her voice, "Hey! Do *not* blame yourself for the senator's death! None of us could have done anything, not even Odd or Othello.

No one! Not even Juice. From what I remember at home—of who he was, his family's animal, their crests—they were good people. His own blood helped design the Castle of Glass. They helped create the borders for the Floral. And Juice was a good friend. You knew him more than me. This Papercut is not him!"

"But it is!" I mumbled. "I saw it, his eyes. They burned with anger. I'd never seen him like that before."

"What was he like?" Zia asked. "I didn't spend much time outside the castles' walls. You, Kyle, Faith … Everyone has spoken highly of him!"

I chuckled, "Of course, it was Juice! He didn't shut up … but everything he said, it was meaningful. A joker. You would have liked him. Could make the grumpiest Dally smile. He and Kyle were close. Lot closer than me. He was no Papercut. I just hope Sam and Gerard stay safe until we return."

"If what they say is true," Zia leaned back. "It may be harder for us to enter Drewmora. We should find that fellow your sister had arrangements with."

"Giuseppe? Sure but … What about the Kelton spy? Are you not worried anymore?"

"I don't know." She shrugged, "If there is one, they'll either be on my tail or Titan's. Can you still feel them?"

I nodded, "Yeah. I can feel Olivia a little more, but Teala's there too. You?"

"Every day since the accident! You miss Faith, don't you?"

"*So much!* I just wish she'd tell me that things are going to be ——"

The sand behind us shuffled. "Sorry to barge in unannounced. Father said it'd be best to change your bandages. May I?" Harry kneeled next to us. An excited Taylah skipped around, sand flicking from her boots. She had a doll in her hands.

I glanced up, "It's fine, Harry! The blood hasn't seeped through yet and I haven't felt any pain since I got sliced."

Harry's eyebrows shot up. "You can't feel anything in general."

"He's right, Pear. Just change them over. There's no harm," Zia insisted.

Chapter 32: The Place Where the Water Splitse

Harry leant closer and I shoved the bandages away. "Keep them, Harry! I'm happy with the ones already wrapped around me. Bandages like those are expensive. No need to put any more of my blood on them."

Harry was lost for words.

Taylah stood in front of me, watching the water's ripples, the moonlight glistening as though we were standing in front of a mirror. I tickled the back of her knee, "Apparently, this little one said we'll be reaching Drewmora tomorrow. Is this true, Harry?" Taylah giggled at me, sitting on the shoreline.

Harry wrapped the cotton from the bandage roll around his right hand. "We sure are! It's going to be a big day. The militia have gotten strict as of late with passports and immigration. New rules from General Ko. Taylah's probably just excited to learn how to swim."

Taylah stuck her tongue out at her brother. "No! I don't want to swim. I just miss my bed." She played with the doll, its vinyl legs and red dress getting sandy from the damp waterbeds.

Zia stood up, "Is that Kyle's doll Taylah?" she asked.

Taylah examined us, her gaze hesitant. "Uh … Yep! He gave it to me on the second night you were with us. Said it'd protect me from the scaries that lurk under bridges and in the water. He said Maggie will protect me from scary monsters like trolls!"

I grinned, "Sounds like Kyle! So what do we do when we get there?"

I turned to Harry, who had a handful of instructions. One of them even made Zia go red in disgust. But before she could protest, I calmed her down. We weren't walking into Drewmora tomorrow. No, Mr Doubtson had something dumber in mind. But first, we have to reach the place where the water splits.

The morning came early—it had since Everbreen. The sun in the east rose faster than in the west. I felt like I'd lost many hours of sleep since the train crashed; each hour lost, each moment where I could leap closer to Drewmora, burned my heart. We'd been walking quite a while until the dirt and grass turned to sand. The sound of crashing waves, the smell of salt, and the northerly winds all came at once. As I pulled the wagon with Harry, I realised we'd reached the Full Sea. I'd never seen such blue water, such clear waves, such white sand.

"So, this is Camel Hump Shore!" Zia exclaimed.

"Aye! She's a pretty sight for my fish-dry eyes!" Mr Doubtson said happily. He led, his footprints marking the sand. It was smooth sailing. The sand was heavy, and it was hard to pull a cart through, but once we managed to adjust to our sinking feet, Harry and I made some distance. His face was covered in a coat of sweat. *Was mine?* We pulled and pulled. I was worried about my jacket—its white suede was rather tender from Juice's katanas. Harry was an excellent sewer, putting the right sleeve back together with a blue stitching line. It gave him an excuse to teach Taylah some tricks too. As we pulled, and I could have sworn the blue stitches were tearing, Zia took her boots off. Taylah and her frolicked on the shoreline, their bare feet sinking into the moist sand.

Halfway through, Mr Doubtson ordered Leo and James to take over. They groaned and sighed, but before long, my hands were free, and my boots were wet. Taylah laughed at me for not taking them off but, to be fair, just hearing the water rise and fall back into itself was enough to calm my troubled mind.

"What does the water feel like?" I asked.

Zia scampered in front of me, smiling. "It's nice. Not too warm, not too cold. The sand is soft like, ah … Bailey's fur after you wash it." That got me laughing.

"The water is calm today!" Harry called. "Been rumours of anger inside its waves."

"Come now, don't put fear in the Kelts' blood. There's no proof of the Full Sea being angry. She be as beautiful as the day I first lay my eyes on her. Even her heart still beats purity," Mr Doubtson said, pointing to the blue beacon. I was so accustomed to them being just coloured lines in the sky. I forgot how radiant the beacon was. The Drewan beacon, as blue as the sea, burst upwards so bright, I was shocked that we had managed to get lost searching for it.

However, the closer we drew to Drewmora, the more the beach changed.

A metallic box glistened ahead of us. It was rather large in shape and there was an aluminium fence around it. Its panels crisscrossed with one another, tied together to stop us from travelling any further.

Chapter 32: The Place Where the Water Splitse

The wind started to howl, pinching past my ear like a wolf in the night. Mr Doubtson raised his arm.

"We best head upward off the shoreline."

"Why's that?" Zia asked. Her toes were covered in sand as were Taylah's and Harry's. Harry was the first to leave the sandbanks.

"Father's right. We best head up. It'll be dark before long and we still need to go through customs."

"What's going on?" Zia demanded.

Mr Doubtson pointed to the fence ahead. "It be simple, Yer Majesty. We won't make it down the shoreline—too many campers."

"Campers?" I wondered aloud.

"Aye. Campers, homestealers, refugees—people who do not belong here. They be camping on the shoreline just ahead."

"That be their fence," Harry explained. "We won't be able to go that way; the militia's blocked it off." Harry put his boots back on.

Leo and James stood still. The wagon fell back, smacking the sand.

"Are you referring to those who come from other shores?" Zia asked. "Are these beaches, these lands, these shores not Drewan? Why is there a fence? Are they keeping us from the shoreline?" Zia shuffled along the beach, her feet burning from the sun's heat. She licked her dry lips and stood next to Harry.

"No, we can walk along the shoreline as much as we desire, Yer Majesty. That fence is for our protection, yer see," Mr Doubtson explained.

"What do you mean *protection?*" I said, moving away from the water as the waves crashed more sharply. "What's wrong with camping on the shoreline?"

When no one answered, Zia and I shrugged at one another and followed the others. Leo and James continued pulling until we reached a sandy grass field. The fence was now closer.

"Would ya have a look at that!" Leo remarked. "There be more of them now, Dad!"

"No, no, you're seeing waterworks, Leo! There's no way the militia would keep piling up the shore like this!"

As we continued, the blue beacon became more powerful. I

started to hear the crashing tunes of the water. It was as though the largest waterfall was right in front of us, but there was no falling lake, no rivers that descended, just the smooth waves of the Full Sea.

You could smell the alloys of the fence, its freshly made panels wrapped around the shoreline like a cage. Behind the fence, people of all different colours sat, walked, played, cooked and slept. Tent-lets of all sizes were scattered up and down against the second heap along the Camel Hump Shoreline. But this, so far from Drewmora, was merely the beginning. Zia watched, her grey eyes focused on the fence.

"These people shouldn't be living like this. They should be sheltered in proper housing, have proper clean clothes—not these rags they decorate themselves with," she cried. "Do the senators know? The King's Hand? Senator Carvanah would never allow this!"

"My apologies, Yer Majesty. But these fences here may have been placed by us Drewans. The order was from Central City back before the beacons started to shine. They just announced more infrastructure down the Camel's Shoreline to keep these imposters from entering our home. General Ko argued to find another way, but the Regime does not argue, even with the general." Mr Doubtson looked away from the fence. All the Doubtsons did.

The louder the crashing water echoed, the more crazed the people behind the fence became. I saw coloured crests I never knew existed. Purple, crimson, onyx, tangerine and grey. These people were from different continents. *How'd they get here?* A clawing rattled the fence. "Let us out!" someone howled. Their indigo crest of a hyena sparkled behind the fence. Dozens of fingers wrapped themselves around each alloy panel. These people were captives, trapped in an asylum with nowhere else to go. Zia looked away as more metallic banging rattled near our ears.

There were hundreds upon hundreds of tent-lets, small fires, and groups of men and women of all ages; it was a hundred times the size of our Town of Tents and a hundred times more dangerous. Their woven jumpers, their linen shirts, canvas pants and poplin skirts were torn and ragged, smudged with salty smears of dirt and ash. Many had bruises covering their bare skin. The more steps we took, the more insane they seemed. It was like walking through an outdoor jail;

CHAPTER 32: THE PLACE WHERE THE WATER SPLITSE

there was no end to its madness. Thousands of people, all wanting a home. Wanting safety. Wanting happiness. Yet, each was lost, held captive under the rule of Central City. Under the law of my own people. And there was nothing I could do to help them.

I could hear the breeze begin to anger. Behind the fence of immigrants, there was a split in the sea, as though a god had pushed the water apart, splitting the Full Sea in two, and leaving a massive crater for Drewans to walk through. At the end of the divide, where the water returned to its usual full self, there was a gigantic dome submerged within the ocean. It was a valley as long as a football field with two walls of water surrounding its sides. Hundreds of Drewans with carts, horses, cars, trucks, sheep and travel bags walked and drove towards the dome. The ground beneath their feet was orange and moist. A road went from one side of the valley to the end where the hill we stood on emerged. In the far distance, above the water, there was a brown line, straight and dense. *The train tracks!*

I took a step forward towards the slope and the valley. Mr Doubtson raised his voice, "Er, what're yer doing, Perry?"

I turned back. "Walking to Drewmora … That is the way to Drewmora, is it not?"

Mr Doubtson shook his head. "No, no, no! That is the Great Divide. The front entrance for all Drewans. And only Drewans. They won't let any Kelts in."

"What about a princess?" Zia mused.

"I'm afraid not, Yer Majesty … It's time now that we hide you in our wagon."

Zia's face went red.

I was trapped, laying under a blue tarpaulin sheet next to a groaning princess. The wagon smelt worse on the inside. It reminded me of Calvin the Ever, a donkey obsessed with mushrooms. Laying there, I could see the blue walls of the ocean's divide and the occasional timber box. Zia somehow knew what she was writing in her journal as we wobbled in the darkness for what felt like an hour. I could hear cars drive past, their exhausts hot and ready; trucks pulled their horns throughout our slow, rugged gallop, masking the muffled voices of other Drewans eager to return home.

Harry's head bobbed under the tarpaulin from time to time to check on us. Then a demanding male's voice in front of Mr Doubtson, ordered, "Slow down." Several men in blue uniforms, similar to those who protected Parliament House, stood tall in their metal and blue bicorne hats with orange feathers. The wobbling stopped and my body slipped down the wagon.

"What business do yer have here?" one of the guardsmen said.

"It just be a few materials for the miners. I got a warrant. And receipt. From up in Central City and a few from Kattagow." Mr Doubtson fiddled with his pockets.

"Quite a trip then, eh? Yer lot must be more tired than a seasnapper. What kinda materials?" the guardsman asked.

"Hey, now! Just a lot of new pickaxes, some bronze for smelting, gunpowder and such."

"That be for the old mine. The one that got blocked up by rubble. You miners clearing it up?"

"Aye! The dynamite here will help with that!"

Dynamite. By the Light! Why didn't he tell us that before we got cooped up inside the wagon! Zia's eyes widened; I could see myself in their grey reflection. Now that he mentioned it, I could taste the bloody gunpowder. *That knobhead!* I fidgeted, putting my finger on Zia's lips as soon as her mouth opened. We had dragged this thing all the way from Kattagow and now he tells us there's dynamite in it. *We're sitting on a bloody bomb!*

As my heart clenched and we began wobbling, laughter sounded. "By the salts under my own saggy chin, that be Harry Doubtson?" a younger male voice cheered.

"That's not a mirage of any kind I've ever seen. That's Harry!"

"The salt are you doing so close to the borders of the city? You're not be pretending to work for us again, are you?" a more feminine voice asked. From what I could see, we'd reached a giant metal frame; behind it was a row of circular doors that looked like a cut-up pizza. The guardsmen and woman laughed. They each had a khopesh sheathed on their back.

Harry's head dropped. "Hiya, there, Pip. Chloe ... Jericho. Mind letting us through?" he asked. "I've been gone an awful long time. Would love nothing more than a home-cooked meal and my ol' bed."

Chapter 32: The Place Where the Water Splitse

The younger male voice spoke again. "Aye, by all means. We don't want to keep your family waiting. Whereabouts are you from again, Mr Doubtson?"

"Lower Hexadome, Officer. The South Side Dome." Mr Doubtson's voice was quite confident. Harry sighed.

The group of cadets giggled as Harry's head straightened. "Aye, you knew that Jericho! Now can you let us through? We have our passes, all the paperwork for the items we're bringing under the hexadomes. The whole lot."

"Well now, it's not as simple nowadays. Of all people, I'd have thought you would know that. Seeing how many times you've wanted to join the militia," Jericho mocked.

"Don't be so harsh on the fishlegs. He's trying his hardest. What? He only failed the physical twice last year." Girly laughter reached my side. Presumably, Chloe was strutting around, investigating the wagon.

"Hey, Harry's gonna make it this year! He just needs one more go; he'll be a better guard than you hosers!" James roared.

More laughter bounced off the tarpaulin. Taylah crept next to Harry and grabbed his hand.

"Yer not gonna try again, Harry? Are you?" This voice was softer—maybe it was Pip. He sounded a little farther away, as though he was stationed next to the metal frame.

Harry stood strong, "Aye! I'm gonna try, and I'm gonna make it this time, I swear."

Jericho, a tanned, blue-eyed Drewan answered this time. "Is that right? Well, whatever makes you happy!" He grinned and Mr Doubtson raised his voice.

"That's enough now, Jericho. I don't need to have a word with your commanding officer, do I? It seems you'd rather ridicule the citizen you've pledged an oath to protect rather than letting us be on our way. My son's aspirations are surely none of your concern and seeing how ..." Mr Doubtson stood away from the wagon. He put his arms into the air. "Yes! Commander Malvitch! We have a situation involving these fine young men and women under your battalion."

The commanding officer approached us. *I recognised the name, but where?* His footsteps were proud and did not sway. A familiar voice groaned, "Jericho if it's about the salty wagon, you've heard the orders from the general. Apologies, sir ... Mr Doubtson! I'm glad you've returned safely. What may be the problem?"

How did he ...

Giuseppe appeared in front of me, a khopesh sheathed at his waist. Jericho propped himself as straight as he could, his long arms to his side as though they'd been glued there.

"It's no trouble. I might be overreacting. We're just having issues going through the underway. May we proceed, please?" Mr Doubtson put five papers into Giuseppe's chest.

Giuseppe paused, analysing the papers, each with an image of one of the Doubtsons. "Harry! Good to see you're well. Looking forward to your latest attempt in the trials this year." Giuseppe handed the five slips back to Mr Doubtson. "I understand the confusion, Mr Doubtson. Yer see, after the dangerous incidents in Central City, we've stapled down on security."

"How so, Commander?"

"We're gonna have to have a look at yer wagon. Won't take a moment, but we're going to have to remove that sheet yer have there."

Mr Doubtson backed away and Harry turned around. His eyes met mine and

I could hear my own breath as I shuffled to Zia's side. Her clear skin under the tarpaulin glistened black as her lips moved without sound.

"*Oh, crud!*" she mouthed. We rustled and twisted, avoiding everything between us—the boxes, the gunpowder and the sand beneath us. Outside, Mr Doubtson voice was dumbfounded. "Certainly I, of all Drewans, have a right to cover my possessions under a tarpaulin. I've been gathering materials from Kattagow and other simpleton villages since the end of the Echo Wars. Long before your time as a commander."

"Look, Matthew. Can I call you Matt?" Giuseppe asked.

"You may not! I do not wish to take part in Drewmora's downfall ..."

Chapter 32:   The Place Where the Water Splitse

"Sir!" Giuseppe's voice was firm. "I apologise for the inconvenience, but these are direct orders from General Ko. I cannot disobey them; you know what the penalty is for myself, my lieutenants and my cadets."

Shadowed figures gathered around the wagon, staining the blue tarpaulin with dark shadows. I lent Zia my gloved hand, but she slapped it away. Tilting my head, I lowered my eyebrows and flared my nose.

Harry's voice erupted, "I don't think ——"

"You don't think what, Harry?" Giuseppe demanded, becoming angry.

"I ... I don't think checking what's beneath the tarpaulin is the best course of action. We ... we've seen a fair lot out there along the Bluway Creek. Maybe yer should check under the wagon. We coulda ... I coulda accidentally dragged something along."

Zia waved her arms at me, shrugging, clueless to my intentions. I sighed, and her face went red—she slapped my side.

"What?" she whispered.

"Grab my hand!"

"*Yer hear that?* Was that a voice? Mr Doubtson, you don't have any unwanted guests in your wagon here, do you?"

"You accuse me of acts that'd hurt our city and its people. You think me a terrorist, Commander?" Mr Doubtson demanded.

"Take the sheet off. NOW!"

The shadows surrounded us like an ocean of black, their fingers pinching at the tarpaulin. Zia grabbed my hand. WHOOSH!

The sheet was removed, pulled to the left side of the wagon. As it flowed down to Chloe and Leo's legs, Harry and Taylah smiled. The wagon was empty of any stragglers. No unwanted guests in sight. It carried only resources for the miners, such as dark oak boxes of dynamite, some alloys for welding pickaxes, and a layer of sand.

Jericho dropped to the ground and shuffled himself under the wagon's belly. He knocked his left knuckle against the wagon's lower skeleton. I crept over his legs, the moist sandstone beneath my feet squishing under the pressure of my boots. Zia followed, her right hand wrapped around mine like a glove. Her body shook as the world around us turned blue. And no, I'm not talking about the ginormous walls of water that flowed up as though gravity had been spun inside out. Giuseppe's, Jericho's, Harry's and Mr Dotubson's voices became more muffled than before.

My heartbeat jolted inside my ears as I made my way around the wagon. Everyone was oblivious to our footprints in the sand. In her left hand, Zia held her journal, her eyes doing most of the talking. *I didn't think it'd work. I had never tried this before.* But as we walked towards Drewmora, the tarpaulin was placed over the wagon once more by Jericho, Chloe and Harry.

Zia's eyes met mine. I put my trigger finger on my lips, and she gulped. *Guess she wasn't used to being invisible.* I held her hand like it was a tether, keeping us both safe. *If I let go, who knows who'd see her!* Behind us, a hallway for the gods lingered like a tunnel, its walls of water high, the hill before the shoreline an echo in the distance, its crowded buoyancy thick with more Drewans, militia, trucks and cars. Zia looked away as we continued backing away from the Doubtsons.

The great large frame shook with the wind. It arched hexagonally like the dome behind it. The dome had lights glowing radiantly with buildings as tall and as complex as those from Central City. There was a whole ecosystem with trees, charcoal roads, towering skyscrapers, sidewalks and streetlights behind each hexagonal brick of glass. We scampered to the circular doors.

Pip was tall; he had a sharp jawline and snot under his nose. He scratched at his blond curly locks as we passed under the frame and moved his fingers onto a metallic pad that was as thin as paper. The light from the pad reflected on his face with a red glow. When we gained some traction, the red light vanished, and he examined the frame. He picked at the chunk of sleep near his blue eyes and licked his lips. Back and forth, he analysed the pad, scratching his head in confusion.

There was a row of frames all different sizes for individuals, wagons, cars, trucks, smaller and larger vehicles. Zia's breathing tensed. She recovered after the grey frame was behind us. *What the heck did she feel?*

Chapter 33: Above and Below the Full Sea

We approached the circular doors. Each door spun open with a metal crunch. You could smell a brush of cool air erode from inside as they opened. Like the sort of smell cars give off when their air-conditioning is warming up. We approached the one closest to us and the six triangles rotated open. *Ahead of us was Drewmora!* We took a step inside and watched the underwater city come alive. The circular door shut. *We made it!* Drewmora!

Chapter 33
Above and Below the Full Sea
Faith

Olivia had a confidence in her voice as she explained how the trees that surrounded us were not merely oak. "Redmers. They have a similar shade to oaks, but their bark has been tainted red from the constant flow of sap."

"And you know this, why?" Dally asked. His hair was thick, flowing back to reveal its dark brown hues. The salty scent of the Full Sea was close. Yet in front of us, behind us and in between were the Redmer bush.

"I learnt about it in the Ptak Isles when I was studying," Olivia mused. "They're an eerie red, aren't they? They're more common in colder parts of Euphoria. Think near Fleddington and the alps that cover the far-off land in the north."

I saw a glimmer of metal in the distance. It sparkled for a moment then faded under the pear-coloured leaves that covered the ground. "Then why are there so many around these parts? We wouldn't be far off the Jackson-Lee Desert."

"There's not that many once you open your eyes." Olivia turned to her left; we had reached the end of the bushland.

It was like the trees were afraid of growing any closer to the water. Dirt bundled behind sandhills and the waves remained quite still. We had reached an inlet. Beyond the leaves of the Redmer, there was a grey metal line that slithered across the ground. Black stones held the metal rod atop the dunes.

"How ironic! More train tracks," Dally observed.

Chapter 33: Above and Below the Full Sea

I laughed, "Oh? Do we go up or down the ——"

Olivia pushed me behind to the rising hills of sand. My heart shook; the sand felt sticky between my fingers and boots. Four people, crests covered with bands, wore half black and half white masks similar to the one Dally carried in his bag. Olivia was the most silent, lost in thought. I could taste the bland crumbs of sand as I reached the top of the dune.

"Are those the ones who attacked you and Perry in the Cabana?" I asked.

Their masks were made of a maché, half corroded by what seemed to be a powerful source of heat. Each figure had a blue uniform similar to the one Giuseppe wore in Central City. They crowded an empty dock that would hold a few smaller boats no bigger than a car.

Dally was almost out of breath. "Similar. The ones from the club didn't have masks as detailed as those."

You could hear one walk across the rotting timber, the dock creaking under his leather boots as he carried a burlap sack. He handed it to the second, who sliced it open with a knife. White powder like flour exploded from inside. The third figure took it, and with the fourth poured the powder into the Full Sea.

A bitter scent like rancid sweat came from the dock. "What the hell are they doing?" Dally muttered.

"Whatever it is, it doesn't look good. We should stop them!"

Dally's crest began to glow; however, before either of us could stand and charge, Olivia put an arm out to hold me back. Her arm was stationed at my breasts, firm as she watched the four. "Patience. There's a cat!"

Dally and I propped our heads up. *She was right!* There was an orange cat.

It was a Scottish Fold the size of my arm's length. Its blue eyes examined the four masks as it climbed a timber hut beside the dock. The one who carried the sacks jolted at the first sight of the hairy feline. He staggered back and yielded. The cat tilted its head to the left—Perry would say *that was a very similar move to what I normally do*, but the cat cocked its head so far, I thought it was going to snap its neck. Under the man's wristband, a blue light shimmered. A flare of bubbles sprayed from his hand and the largest one, so reflective and round, caught the cat. The cat floated and floated, trapped within the bubble's thin liquid walls.

The three other masked ones rose. The woman cutting the sacks slapped the back of bubble boy's head. "The hell'd you do that for? It's just a cat."

The cat continued to watch them. "Yer heard of bad omens. Cats are one of 'em. Don't trust the salt ——"

A more mature voice sounded from the dock's end. "Can you get another salty sack? Stop whinging about the cat. Ain't no omens out in these parts."

A flash of grey knocked us to the side. There was a stench of burnt coal. The flurry of passing metal was so fast and close to my face, I slipped down the dune. A train had arrived. The cat meowed as sparks shot out from under the train's two carriages. Olivia stood as I picked myself up, rubbing the sand from my leggings.

Dally asked, "Why would a ——"

"It's an omen!" Olivia walked to the head of the train.

I kept behind her. "An omen?"

"Yes, Faith! It's what the Drewans call their gods. Omens from above the sea. The water in the sky."

"And the cat? You're going to explain that, right?" I slid on the sand, reaching the cloud of black smoke from the train's engine.

Dally was gone.

Behind the layers of burning iron, I heard a scream. "I've been looking for that cat for a very, very long time and *you* put her in a bubble." A familiar voice yelled. He paused, relaxing his tone. "Oh, Hebi! Of course you would. Getting poor folk to do your bidding. You men and women have heard of bad omens, correct? I am only half an omen, but that's my cat. Be gone or ——"

Dally suddenly joined in, screaming. His voice was muffled behind the train. Olivia and I bolted around its front, sand flicking up as we reached the dock. Martin, the demigod who protected the train stations, the one who helped us in Everbreen and Central City, stood beside Dally. The four masked people lined up behind one another.

Chapter 33: Above and Below the Full Sea

A black sludge festered beneath the timber slats of the dock. It dripped over the dock's mould and cracks and caught the masked ones' legs. Olivia walked towards them, the sludge infecting the shoreline. It was as though the dark mud had a will of its own.

Martin stood tall. "Stay back! The darkness does not offer a safe return. Even you, Councillor, would be lost if you were to touch it."

The line of masked ones was soon covered in black goo. It was like a wave of darkness had engulfed them, one at a time, from the back of the dock to the front. The one who could create bubbles laughed. The black sludge grew over his head and consumed him. All that remained was his mask, floating in the Full Sea.

The sludge had vanished, taking the dock and the masked ones with it. Dally trotted forward into the ocean. "Where did they go?" His boots were covered in water. "The dock—it was … it was right here?"

Martin stared forward. He placed his finger along the shoreline. "It is not the right time, ripe and strong. These are preparations for later."

"Hebi? She was controlling them, wasn't she?" Olivia wondered.

"Yes, Hebi could be the culprit. And if she seeks to hurt the Full Sea, I must be ready at the Drewmora Station."

Martin picked up a handful of sand and wandered back to his train.

"Hurt the Full Sea? Hold on, we're heading to Drewmora. Mind if we tag along?" I pleaded.

"I second that!" Olivia hurrahed. "If these lackies wish to vandalise the Full Sea on Drewan land, the militia will need to know. I can arrange a meeting with General Ko as soon as we get to WonderWorks!"

Martin eyed us down. "Now, I can't let ya do that! No, no—this is of higher business than you simple folk."

"Hey, we're not simpletons!" Dally pointed to the cat, still purring inside its bubble. "We can get your cat! How'd you lose it again?"

It took me a few goes; my crest was burning like a furnace, but I eventually popped the bubble. The cat descended gently as though there was an invisible escalator beneath its paws. Dally's hand was raised in the air, shaking to his crest's glowing white light. Martin was overjoyed. You could smell the sap of the Redmer, a sweet smell behind the cat's orange fur.

He grinned. "Well now! I don't really know how to thank you all. I've been looking for this one for over a century."

"Odd told us the story," I said. "I'm sorry things got so complicated between you two. No wonder you didn't want to grant us passage to Central City."

"Oh, don't be ridiculous. I was always going to give you that extra carriage. There are rules that forbid me from sayin' anymore. What I can tell you is that there was a Good Spirit who told me of this here track." He kicked the track behind his feet where his train awaited. "Where that dock would disappear from the past and where that bubble you so kindly popped would have floated and floated all the way to a place unknown to man. No train tracks lead there, and I am bound to the tracks, you see." He swung himself onto the front carriage. "Now, get on! We have a city that needs helping, fiends that need stopping, and a mastermind that needs finding. ALL ABOARD!"

The train screeched against the metal tracks, wobbling Dally and me from side to side. Olivia held on, her wrists strained as she gripped a handle on the carriage's ceiling. She stared at the forest that covered our right side. The Redmer trees soon vanished, replaced by smaller and lighter shrubs. Then the bushes became plains of yellow grass similar to the fields in Jinkie's Gap. Dally and I watched the Full Sea to our left. Its waves appeared larger and more vicious the closer we got to Drewmora. The water crashed against rocks as black as charcoal, and I tasted raw salt as we sped past the shoreline like a bullet.

The wind pulled my hair; it swayed, like the waves flowing back into the ocean. Time felt almost untouched. Below the water, beneath the clear blue purity of the sea, there was a glass dome glowing like a candle in a pitch-black cave. Beside it were smaller domes, all light blue with pillars and specks floating amongst their inner workings. It was as though the gods themselves had dropped a snow globe the size of a mountain into the deep, dark blue depths of the Full Sea.

Chapter 33: Above and Below the Full Sea

Dally grinned, pointing to the dome.

"There she is! Drewmora! They're not kidding when they say it's a blue city!"

Beyond the sea, there was a blue light shimmering in the sky. *The beacon!* Its power raged above the water like a waterfall that could break the Earth in two. It was darker than the light hues within the sky but brighter than the navy within the ocean. My heart tugged when the light caught my eye. Its blue ferocity beckoned me like a lighthouse, yet I felt a pain in my gut. I turned to Olivia, and the train swerved to the left. Gone was the dried grass and sand. Martin's train headed towards the shoreline.

The Full Sea surrounded us. Below were grey rails, sharp and burnt from years of use. Beneath these rails hid the pitch-black of the ocean. *We weren't on land anymore!* The train's alloys churned as saltwater sprinkled onto my nose. It felt cold, refreshing to my heated forehead. I smiled at Olivia as Martin pulled a rope above his head. The train's horn made the water ripple.

We had reached the mighty dome beneath the water and, upon its summit, there was a glass platform. The rails squealed and the train stopped with a black ball of steam above our heads. Olivia stepped off the metal carriage first, stretching when her feet hit the glass. I joined her. There were no more rails for the train and no more platforms for people to stand on. Only a shack and a glass cylinder the size of an elevator. After the track ended, the beacon emerged from the water. It was maybe a little doggie-paddle away—half a swim. You could hear it pulsate, like a heart beating a sapphire echo into the sky.

"Strange looking station," Olivia remarked.

"This is not the station, I'm afraid. We have reached The Nest! 'Tis where the man of old folk would go to look for any lost ships, unnatural dark phenomena or simply the tide!" Martin explained.

"Like a crow's nest on a boat!" I said.

Martin grinned, "Something like that. Come, come. We still have a ways to go." Martin pushed his right hand into his pocket, the sound of metal brushing against his fingers. He pulled out a bundle of keys, each clasped together by a single orange string that looped into a lanyard. He fiddled with the many different-shaped keys, some long and shiny, others skinny and round, and a few small and fragile.

The glass cylinder stood beside the shack like a rock and on its left was a grey knob. Martin placed one of the many keys into the knob and the cylinder opened. Half of its front rotated away from us.

He ushered us in. "Quickly, now!" Olivia waltzed in first, then Dally and myself. We all stood, the glass surrounding us like a jail cell. Martin stayed where he was and locked the door behind us. The cylinder closed. Martin's voice became muffled.

"Tell Odd he owes Peaches and me catnip!"

Dally's arm swung onto the glass. Like plastic, it glimmered differently each time his fist came into contact with the cylinder.

"Hey, what are you ———" Dally yelled.

From the moment we were closed off, I could smell an uncanny amount of sanitiser. Olivia grabbed Dally's arm. "It's okay, Dally! He's not coming with us."

Martin nodded on the other side. "I wish you luck, but I have others to warn. If you can, find Othello The Wise." The churn of a metal gear turned and the glass beneath our feet became less stable. I clasped onto the cylinder's sides as Martin saluted us farewell.

"But what about the general? The king?" Olivia mumbled.

"I'm sorry, king?" I wondered.

"Don't worry. I think it'd be best if we find the princess first!" Olivia sighed.

We descended down and down until the sky, the train and the shack had disappeared completely. Martin's figure was a black dot and his cat, Peaches, a distant memory. The world became blue.

Water surrounded us from one side of the cylinder to the other. We had been completely submerged as the cylinder steadily descended like a pulley. Smog clouded the glass walls. *It was warm, yet were we meant to be cold?* The water afar was pitch-black, yet below, there were so many shades of blue. Clownfish swam past my eye. There was a swarm of tuna to my left, a couple of turtles near Olivia's rear and a shark, keen for blood, behind Dally. There were hundreds and hundreds of fish.

Coral and seaweed swayed to the tune of the ocean. Below us was the giant dome, lighting the sea with its sharp hexagons. We reached the third largest of the seven, each dome made from thousands of hexagonal glass fragments, moulding to accumulate into a single semicircle. Each dome was alight, turquoise from the water's touch. Inside them, there were buildings as tall as the complexes from Central City and as diverse as the treehouses from Everbreen—as homely as those from Kelton Whide. The water soon vanished as we entered one of the glass hexagons. It got sucked up like a toilet bowl once the cylinder touched the hexadome. *And then, surrounding us was Drewmora!*

There were skyscrapers as tall as the ancient trees of yesteryear. Hovercars and bikes glided through the hexadomes at insane speeds, almost like the fish from before, and many Drewans roamed like ants. Some had mud smeared on their faces—I can only imagine how bad they smelt. Giant metal gears and wheels rotated from an overabundance of chimneys and large orange brick buildings. Their plaster was old, their gears rusty as they span, crunching the many minerals inside their workshops. The water surrounded each piece of the hexadome; however, the blue was rather light, like an artificial sky.

Across the hexadome there were randomly placed dreamcatchers, similar to Teala's, hanging from its glass. Tradesman drilled their web-like Redmer branches into the hexagonal glass as though they were preparing for something.

"Those are some big dreamcatchers!" Dally remarked.

They were large, almost the size of a Giza Rock, some hanging from the top of the dome, others sticking to the side like a spiderweb.

"Freaky. Teala would love this place," I mused.

"She would!" Olivia said. "Giuseppe told me that they go up once a year in celebration of the Drewan's dreams!"

"Mardi Mimpi? The celebration of sweet dreams. Isn't that a Tinket tradition?" I asked.

Olivia shook her head. "No, it's celebrated here too. The Drewans live the furthest from their omens. Dreams are a powerful thing in the traditional world!"

The further we descended, the more the city engulfed us. By far, this was the most futuristic, particularly in comparison to the rubble roads and trees of Everbreen, and the boring concrete blocks and waterways of Central City. The cylinder stopped and the ground became more stable. I thought I had sea legs when the glass cylinder opened again.

The air smelt fresh yet artificial. There were small trees, their leaves a dark emerald and their bark a lighter brown. There were thousands of roads and, around their black lanes, many vehicles glided past us. I couldn't stop looking up. We were so deep underwater, so far away from the mainland. *What if the glass were to break? Why is nobody scared?*

There was a whole ecosystem. Each building had steam coming from its many gears, which turned like one well-oiled machine. On the side of the glass, near where the hexadome reached the seafloor, there were dark grey pipes and vents. Below, on the street, although there were parks and schools and people, I could see we had reached an industrialised row of factories so large and tall, I thought that something was amiss.

"Here we are!" Olivia cheered, exiting the cylinder. "Let's hurry to WonderWorks. The quicker we get there, the quicker we can find the princess and Perry and Teala!"

No, this was it! We really had made it. The world before me felt almost unreal. Yet, I hadn't the slightest idea of the danger that lurked in this steampunk utopia. We were trapped!

Chapter 34

The Third Way to Drewmora
Bailey

The wind on my face was soothin' as if it were a warm fire in the middle of winter. The air up here was so fresh, untouched by sea salt. Surprisingly, Win Dixie was somewhat open. Georgia an' I held onto the zeppelin's raw ropes, careful not to move too quickly and burn our palms. It was a dandy view though, the Full Sea. Unlike anything I had eva' seen.

We joined the others inside the cockpit. A flurry of wind pieced at the airlock door. Its weight pinched my arms. Everyone's eyes latched onto us as Georgia entered. I closed the door; its bronze steel sealed itself an' the wind stopped. It was quiet.

Ritesh approached me. "How were the waters?" he asked.

"Swell! Still ... Dere's a lot of tent-lets on dat shoreline!" I said.

Georgia put her arm on my shoulder. "That means we're close, huh? Spotted one of the hexadomes just ahead."

"In a sense. It means our friends will be departing soon!" Ritesh's eyes dropped to the metal floor. I put my arms into the air.

"Dat's dandy! We can find our herd, make sure they're dilly. After, I reckon Perry, Dally, Faith—*everyone*, in fact—would be happy for ye fellas to join our Town of Tents."

"From what I've heard, it does sound like a nice place to escape," Georgia added.

Ritesh searched her smile an' grinned at me. "Maybe we'll park Win Dixie there and say hello."

Felicia had her arm on Murray's shoulder. "You'll want to slow the engine down in about eight minutes. Good flying, Captain!"

Murray laughed to himself, blushing red. "Captain? You think? Me?"

"It suits you. Keep me posted." She tapped him an' wandered to us. "We'll be arriving soon."

"How deep do ya reckon it is? The Full Sea?" I asked.

Felicia inhaled, "Very deep! The exact amount I can't quite calculate, but I can estimate. It's similar to the sun, but I can't see where the sea's floor is!"

"An' what about fifty-two minutes?" I crossed my arms. "Seeing dat we're so close, ye think that's 'nough time?"

Mia was beside me, her smile as wide as eva'. "When I see you next, can you tell me what the water feels like?"

I raised an eyebrow. "I beg ya pardon?"

"Okay, so I'm a Bellcurve, and I've never touched saltwater. I was born after the war! I'm only curious. It can be a *white promise*."

"An' dat is?" I asked.

"At home, it means if you accept it, we'll see each other again!"

"Dandy! I'll be honoured to tell ye about de water."

"That's if you make it there," Georgia interjected. "Then return to us safely!"

I glanced at her. "Bett! We'll be safe, ain't dat right, Fel——"

Felicia was gone. Ritesh was beside Murray, watchin' the Full Sea pass under us. The others, like the squirrels an' Kelt, sat 'round or watched the sea outside the cockpit. Georgia an' I joined 'em, while Mia stayed inside playin' with another Fledding.

Georgia asked, "You nervous?"

"If dis is about swimmin' down an' reaching de salt filter in fifty-two minutes, then I'm clammed up." Georgia sat, danglin' her legs down to the void of navy. I sat beside her. "It's been so long since we last saw everyone."

"Now isn't that the truth?" Georgia sighed. "There used to be a lot more of us back inside the cave."

Chapter 34: The Third Way to Drewmora

"How'd you end up dere? Together? You're all from different cities with different crests an' beacons."

Georgia's eyes lingered on the water. "We were experiments, most of us. Taken in the middle of the night by warmongers and ... Look, we ... we all have a past here. I'm surprised Ritesh even said yes to your ridiculous ploy!"

"Ploy?" I retorted. "Georgia, we need to get to Drewmora. Dere are fellas in danger!"

Georgia's face went red. "Yes, well, there are people there that can hurt you! They did tests on us—hurt Teshi so bad, they pretty much gave him two other personalities. They scarred and brainwashed Juice! They created M——"

She paused an' looked away from me.

"I'm sorry." I leaned closer to her. "But I ain't runnin' away. I can't let others boss me 'round! Not anymore. I wanna save my mates, okay! Dat's what I want to do, an' if I die along the way, at least I'll die happy! How long since ye last ..."

"We left two years ago!" Georgia uttered. "Ritesh and I. Found the rest along the way! We had to leave others behind. You're a good person, Bailey! A leader. I hope you and your friends, whoever they are, all live happy lives."

I don't know what got into me, but I grabbed her hands an' smiled—it hurt my jaw! I watched her blue eyes an' admired the hexadome deep within the water. "We'll all live happily. Together. 'Cause you're gonna meet 'em. You, Ritesh, Milky—you're comin' with us. An' Mia an' Murray. Everyone!"

"Is that right?" Milky's voice was pricklier than the others. I turned, lettin' go of Georgia's hand. Next to him was Assonance, a grin on her face as though she'd seen a video of a puppy.

"Naw! You two are too much!"

Georgia scrunched her face. "Speak for yourself! Have you seen you and Felicia? I'm going to have to build a cement wall between you two if we don't get off this flying hunk of junk soon!"

Assonance pointed at her chest. "Me and Felicia? We haven't even ... No, we're just close, that's all. Bailey, you know that, right?"

"I don't think Felicia does! Wait, are ya ——"

Suddenly, Win Dixie's horn exploded before me. Georgia's face lit up as I lost my train of thought.

"Huh! So that's what that's like. Kinda funny," Georgia mused.

What? I searched 'round the outer deck on the zeppelin an' suddenly the burst of wind softened. This heat glistened on my face an' the salt of the Full Sea reeked. Milky examined the sun, the Drewan beacon tinting it blue.

"We've arrived!" He propped himself near the edge of Win Dixie, his left hand wrapped 'round a rope and his right blockin' the sun's gaze. "Drewmora! Looks smaller than I'd imagined!" He turned to us.

Georgia snarled, "Well, it's big enough to get trapped inside!"

A slitherin' sound emerged behind us. Ritesh an' Murray exited the cockpit with Mia an' a few of the others. It seemed the whole group was here as Win Dixie floated above one of the larger hexadomes within the Full Sea. Milky's eyes dropped the moment he saw Ritesh's face. "It's time, isn't it?"

"Aye! We can't stay here for long. I don't want to end up trapped down there. Not again!" Ritesh crossed his arms.

Murray's arm swung, colliding with my shoulder. "Imma miss you, panda!" He grinned an' looked at Assonance. "You too, little dove! You be safe, ye hear?"

Before Assonance had time to speak, Milky cracked a smile. "We ain't doves, Muz! We're ravens—orange ravens. The most stubborn, hot-headed and resilient members of Central City!"

Assonance's eyebrows dropped an' her lips quivered. "You're not coming, are you?"

Milky wrapped his arms 'round his sister. "You have your friends, I have mine. And although I'd love to join you, these people need me; you know, the Mother Light, the whole baggage I bring." He lifted her chin. "Hey! No matter how far you are, no matter how deep underwater, what colour the city's beacon is, whether on this continent or the next, I'll be able to feel you!" He rubbed her crest. "*Here!*" He tapped her chest where her heart would be. "*And here!* And if I never see you again, just feeling you under the orange light in my crest will make me happy! It'll make me want to keep moving, to keep pushing forward until I am able to see your face again! D'you understand?"

Assonance pulled him close, tears formin' in her eyes. She sniffled, closing her eyes an' takin' the deepest breath.

I felt another jab at my right shoulder. Georgia's fist moved away from my side. "It's not gonna be the same without you, Ever! You better not die on us, okay?"

"I still have to tell Mia 'bout de water ... I guess I'd like to introduce ya to everyone too. Especially Faith. You'd like Faith!" I laughed an' turned to the small crowd aboard the zeppelin. "An' dat goes for all of ya! You're all welcome to come live with us in our Town of Tents. It's just east of Everbreen. Shouldn't be too long on ol' Win Dixie 'ere! Just have to get to Drewmora first!"

"And in fifty-two minutes! You think it's possible?" Murray asked.

Assonance let go of Milky. "Flying may be my preference, but we have to make it! Odd and the princess need us!"

"It'll be chaos down there!" Ritesh murmured.

"It already is, Teshi!" Georgia said. "But if these three can help us the way they did with Win Dixie, I'm sure Drewmora's in safe hands!"

"Speaking of *three*, where's Felicia?" Milky wondered.

"Here!" Felicia called at the back end of the zeppelin. "I'm calculating—dividing litres into metres and those metres into minutes. But the sea, it's so dark! Like ..."

"The nothingness. It only lingers near the yellow beacon. No need to fear, Felicia!" Georgia mused. Her voice was stern, proud.

"Are you okay, Felicia?" Assonance asked.

Felicia stood on Win Dixie's outer deck, her feet flat, her eyes focused on the sea below; her jaw was tense. She paused, still in thought, an' her head tilted up to watch us. "Fifty-two minutes. We can make it! We have plenty of time!"

"Are ye sure?" Murray asked.

"Got it calculated, Captain!" Felicia winked.

Assonance, Felicia an' I stood at the edge of Win Dixie's outer deck, lined up like a row of scuba divers. The zeppelin shook back an' forth as Murray lowered her into the Full Sea. The water was flat like a rug, and the smell of the sea salt was now nauseating. My heart was warm, burnin' at my chest as I started to breathe real funny. Then the deck stopped fidgeting. We were metres above the water. It'd be like fallin' backwards off a diving board at the local pools in Everbreen.

Georgia approached Felicia. Assonance was between us, her eyes eager for this nightmare to be over. The sea was warm, yet my body was freezin'.

"Once I touch you, the fifty-two minutes begins! Do you understand?" Georgia explained.

Felicia nodded, "So once you touch me, I better rush to the water, huh?"

"Do you remember where to go?" Ritesh insisted.

Felicia nodded, "Yep! Your diagram was very detailed. Straight down to the bottom rim of the hexadome. Once there, we should be able to find the salt filter and submarine bay."

"And behind all that is the trash disposal. That's the safest way for you all to reach the Upper Hex!" Ritesh recited.

All three of us nodded.

Georgia took a deep breath, her yellow turtle crest blossoming under my eyes. She raised her hand to Felicia's sweaty forehead. "Wait!" Felicia ordered. "Just in case my math is wrong and we … we don't make it! I …" She leaned in an' kissed Assonance. It didn't last long, but they both grinned.

Felicia looked Georgia in the eye. "I'm ready!"

Georgia's crest reflected on Felicia's cheeks. They closed their eyes, their foreheads wrinkling. Georgia's fingers tapped gently. Before I knew it, Felicia had jumped, splashing so loudly, I almost had a heart attack.

Assonance exhaled, stuttering under her breath. She stared at Milky, who had a grim look on his face.

"We will see each other again. And we'll visit Mum and Dad, okay? You be safe down there," he cheered. "I love you."

"I love you too!" She leapt into the water.

Georgia stood in front of me, the whole group behind her. Milky,

Chapter 34: The Third Way to Drewmora

Murray, Ritesh an' Mia smiled. "Goodbye, Bailey. I wish you luck on your endeavour. You'll need it," Georgia said.

"You too. Don't let anyone boss ye 'round, all right! Omehwai!"

"And what does that mean?"

"I see you, I hear you. We'll meet again."

Georgia grinned an' I could feel the tip of her hand on my noggin. My feet lost their sense of place an' the wind pinched at my hat. Georgia took hold of it, its blue polyester fallin' further an' further from my view. Win Dixie was above me; I felt the cold taste of salt.

At first, it was dark. I felt like I was suffocating. A bitter liquid drenched my lungs, an' the inner sides of my mouth were freezin', full of saltwater. When I thought it had all entered my throat, when my stomach became too overwhelmed, it stopped. Bubbles protruded from my mouth as I coughed all the salt away. My eyes were dim, yet the water did not sting 'em. The more I blinked, the more bubbles passed my view, headin' up to the sea's surface.

My arms reached out, swayin' back an' forth as my legs kicked gently at the water below me. A black line passed my eye. I jolted back, before realising it was only a stingray. Its fins glided through the blue like a plane. Below me, there was an ensemble of colours— red, green, yellow, white an' grey—coverin' the ocean's seaweed an' rainbow corals. The fish were like the spirits from home, so vast in size an' width an' shape. Their pectoral fins were so strong an' agile, their patterned scales all varied in the water's reflection, their dorsals sharp an' tails quick.

Sage seaweed wrapped its way up the waves of the water like an upside-down vine. I swam toward their sticky flow, unable to smell the depths of the occan. Zippin' through like a paper plane in a classroom, I searched for Assonance an' Felicia. I stopped my swim. The hexagonal pieces to the hexadome trickled upward, glowing 'round the fishes an' above the layers of sand. A tickle ran down my shoulder.

I turned an' Assonance swam next to me, her brown hair swayin' behind her as though gravity had lost its touch. She pointed down, bubbles formin' from her nose. Felicia, her silky blond locks like a web of light, floated near my left shoe. She gestured for us to follow.

We swam under the vines. Red an' yellow corals like rocks sat beneath us. Their rough edges had little crabs an' sea cucumbers dancin' beside a cluster of purple reefs that swayed back an' forth. The hexadome's glass walls grew in size as our bodies pushed forward like rockets. A few clownfish popped their noggins up to investigate the commotion. The seaweed eventually lost its tether in the sand as we reached the high tier of the Upper Hexadomes. Above a series of concrete walls, the glass of the hexadome began. We had reached the city's walls—the place where the water stopped so that the Drewans could live. Felicia stopped. Her hair flared around her as we watched the grey rim. Large circular vents were implanted, each releasing bubbles as black steam drooled into the ocean. My face grew warm just lookin' at the steam. I nudged Felicia, pointin' upwards. She nodded.

I swam, pushin' my light body up an' up 'til the concrete was gone, replaced by several hexagonal pieces of glass. Behind the glass lingered a city like Everbreen. Except, instead of cottages made from timber an' trees, these factories were made from iron an' bronze. They towered like the many blocks in Central City, an' glimmered behind the hexadome with wheels an' gears spinnin' at an endless clog.

At the centre was a clocktower so tall I thought it'd reach the surface of the sea. Behind it, the beacon's light burst like a firework. I read the time. We'd been down 'ere for thirty-five minutes! I swam back down to the girls, but when I reached the concrete rim, Assonance was gone. Felicia was rubbin' the vents. I tried speaking, but each time my mouth opened the water made me cough. Felicia gawked. I tapped the top of my wrist as if I had a watch an' her eyes grew large.

We swam past a whole wasteland of dead coral an' reefs. Below me, there was a shadow of a shark. *Wait! No, that was two sharks!* I searched up as a small hammerhead an' requiem shark circled schools of fish. They were unfazed by our bubbles as Felicia charged down the side of the hexadome. I kept my pace behind her 'til a pair of hands grabbed her left leg. They came from within the concrete rim. We both pushed away, arms in front, ready to swing on with anythin' in our way.

Assonance covered her face, the sound of the water swayin' 'round

Chapter 34: The Third Way to Drewmora

her body. My heart stopped beatin' so fast an' Felicia's arms dropped to her side. Assonance was inside a small openin', large enough for a car. She waved us over. We had no choice but to follow. *If this didn't lead inside to fresh air, we were bound to drown.*

We had entered a tunnel of complete darkness. I scurried behind the girls, watchin' our backs like it was a nutty habit. I could only see Felicia's boots in front of me an' hear the bubbles comin' from my nose. A sharp scrape rang ahead. It sounded as though something was openin' an' closing over an' over again. *Open, shut, open, shut, open, shut!*

Blue lights glimmered at the wall's roof skirtings like fireflies, forming a runway with one exit. Assonance slowed her pace. Her legs dangled above the harsh concrete below us. The blue beams put a spotlight on the garbage filter. It was a circular door with two sharp semicircles at the top an' bottom. One, two, three, *shut*. One, two, three, *open*. Three seconds. The girls both looked at me, then each other. Our eyes had now adjusted to the sea life, however, time was runnin' short. This filter had to be the way in Ritesh had described.

Assonance pointed at herself. Felicia's eyes grew large as she held her hand back. One, two, three, *shut*. One, two, three, *open*. Assonance pulled away. We'd all have to go through this filter unless we swam back. But we were down deep in this tunnel. There was no turnin' back! *Open ... Shut.* Assonance's orange crest glistened in the water. *Open ... Shut.* She looked back at us an' than focused on the door. Her hair floated in the water, her hands swayed in the dark blue light an'—*open ... shut* she was gone.

Felicia's eyes met mine. She took my hand an' grinned. I nodded an' she swam for the door. She waited, my gut clenching. I could taste the salt. My nose quivered. *Open ... Shut.* Felicia vanished. More water entered my mouth. I tried spittin' it back out, but this time it kept coming. I held my breath. The fifty-two minutes were up.

Open ... Shut! I launched myself at the door, my lungs straining each second I swam. *Open ... Shut.* I didn't want to stuff this up. Too soon I could get squashed, too late an' I could get squashed. The iron filter squealed open an' darkness laid ahead. I pushed my feet against nothin'. *Open...*

I tried to adjust my eyes, holdin' my breath just a little longer. I could hear water fallin' an' my insides strugglin'. *I can't do this!* It was too much. I swam an' swam 'til my body lost traction. I got swept into what seemed to be a tube. Rushin' water pulled me forward as crashin' waves bounced all 'round. A small fraction of light lingered ahead. *No, that's not light, that's ...*

I spat the water from my mouth. My chest heaved as my lungs tried to gather more air. I groaned, landin' on rough solid concrete. I'd neva' been so grateful for breathing. *I neva' wanna stop breathing eva' again. I neva' wanna swim eva' again!*

My eyes burned from the artificial light beneath the hexadome. *We did it! Drewmora!* I glanced 'round, seeing Felicia leanin' her noggin against a bronze wall. Her chest rose an' fell quickly. Assonance was out cold on top of her legs. My hair dripped down my forehead. The crashin' water vibrated beside my boots as I placed my arms beneath my heated chest. I pushed an' pushed but it was like liftin' weights with spaghetti. *Impossible.* A shady figure approached the alley.

I couldn't make out their face or their clothes, but they had a smile as large as Mia's.

"What are you doing here?" Felicia groaned.

"Waiting for you, dear Gah Ma!"

I heard a slap of flesh. My body shivered. I pushed an' pushed an' reached my feet. My body swayed, but before I could fight or skedaddle, a hand snatched my crest arm. His finger trapped the green panda an' his eyes caught mine.

"Hmm. Now, aren't you curious!" the figure laughed.

My forehead stung an' the world went black.

F.W.. .R..4.3. ..21.

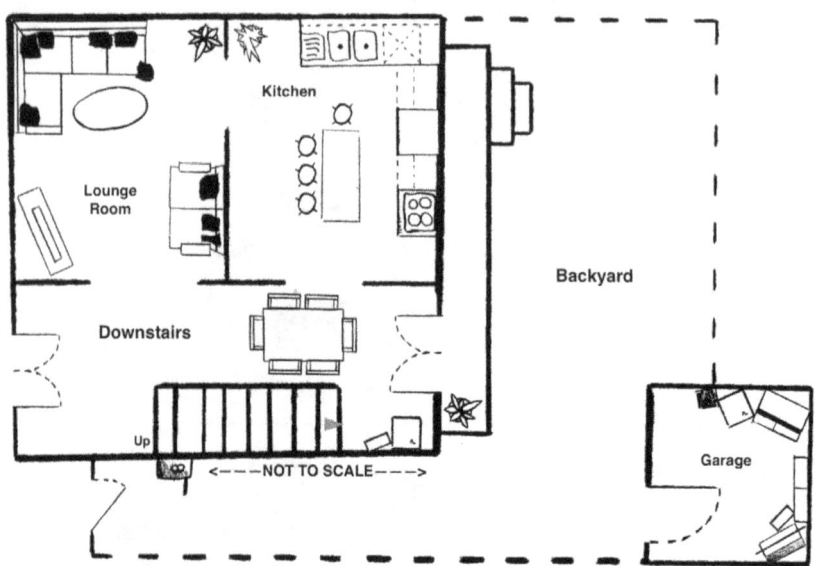

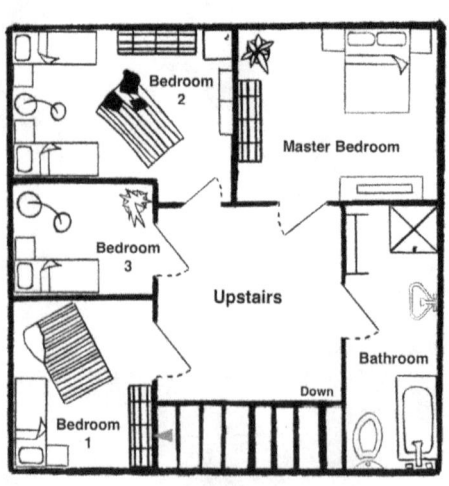

South Side Lower Hexadome

Residents: 5

Property of Drewmora

Chapter 35

What we Know

Perry

"You can let go now, Perry!" Zia cried.

Her hand was still attached to mine like a postcode on a postcard.

"I'm not letting go, Zi! Not after that mess in the Great Divide. If they're that tight on security, I don't think us Kelts are very welcome here!" We'd given up on the silent act as crowds of people rushed around us. A few were confused.

Leo stepped back from the wagon just ahead of us. I stopped, Zia tugging on my invisible arm. "Why are you stopping?" she demanded. "And what do you mean we're not welcome? A Drewan is a Kelt's brother in arms. We've fought both the Echo Wars and the Battle of the Major Lands side by side."

"Before the beacons were put back on! Zia, things change, especially when half the continent are now animals."

"Okay, okay. We can hold hands. It's just … it's getting sweaty down there, and it's gross. You can't feel it, so why bother … Hey, can people hear us when we're … y'know, invisible?"

I nodded, "Yep! Don't worry, we should be fine. There's a lot more Drewans than I thought. I've never seen such crowded streets—well, except for Central City."

"Oh, you didn't visit Assonance's parents. The whole city was twice as crowded."

Harry patted Leo's head and grabbed the wagon with James.

They pulled, and I shoved Zia forward. We followed them past long rows of brass towers made with screws and gothic arches so pointy I thought my fingertips were going to bleed. Zia muttered to herself.

Fake grass and lamps made from corals and framed in copper surrounded the left side of the road. A fog of black smoke tickled my eyes as grey and black flying bikes swam through the sky. They looked like metal fish, with sharp fins pointing obtusely towards the ground, small cockpits for one rider, and tails that would move depending on their direction. In front of the tail, there was a fan made from paper and brass, spinning like a boat's rotor.

After the buildings—some tall, others framed with timber and the remainders connected with bridges and hallways—we reached a glass tube the size of a tunnel you'd find at a highway. The Doubtsons stopped to have their blue crests scanned by the militia stationed at the tunnel. Once Taylah's blue dolphin was assessed by the lady and her cadets, they passed under another grey frame and continued through the glass tunnel. Holding my breath, I nudged Zia, who had run out of complaints and was wide-eyed and silent.

We wandered under the frame, fleeing into the tunnel. Above the glass, the sun gleamed behind a layer of ocean life and dark blue water. It reflected in the many waves that wobbled above our heads. The sweet scent of sanitiser covered the glass bricks that surrounded us. Sharks, tuna, goldfish, crabs, whales—*you name it*. The sea animals slipped past the glass tunnel like ants in a nest. The taste of the air was off, heavier than usual. Zia believed this was because it was most likely artificial. *Explains the over-saturation of cleaners.* Each glass brick we passed, each road or clump of grass, had a gardener, janitor or groomsman at work.

Out of the tunnel, the buildings became more like cottages. Similar to the Sporangia Sector, these homes were clumped together, each overlapping one another like Old Man Jinkie's house. Each home had orange clay bricks made from the sands within the Full Sea, thick tempered glass as hard as the stone common in Mrs Fishburne's house, dark-grey roof slates and small terraces with lush green ferns no higher than my waist. This was the Lower Hex. The further we walked, the more lost I felt.

We traversed under another tunnel and through too many patchy

Chapter 35: What We Know

roads. There were potholes aplenty and rough, unpolished sidewalks as though the cement had never been smoothed over. Finally, we reached a house at the end of the South Side Lower Hexadome. Behind it, there was a concrete rim the size of Kattagow's eucalyptus that had several circular vents.

Mr Doubtson calmed his arms. There was a metal clank as the wagon came to a halt. Harry nudged James' shoulder, gesturing for him to go inside. Mr Doubtson picked up a set of keys, approached his door and stood there aimlessly next to Taylah. He searched his front terrace, gulped, took a deep breath and opened the door. The family hustled inside as Harry wrapped his arm around a dry oak fence gate. A clip unlocked and he pulled the wagon through to the back garage. It was like Bailey's barn. *Miss that fluffy oaf!*

I pulled Zia along, waiting for Harry. "Now what? Actually, why don't you let go of my hand, and we can go talk to Matthew inside, huh?"

I grabbed her hand tighter. "I wanna try something first."

"Try something? Perry, I swear to the Light of Hope, if I end up on my arse, I will stab your groin!"

I skipped. "Geez! That's a little harsh, don't you ———"

"It's been a long day and I'm hungry! Plus, your hand isn't the nicest to hold."

I pulled her to the fence. "Can I *please* test this out? I didn't even think holding your hand was going to turn you invisible. Like, I knew I could turn myself invisible, but somebody else, well …"

"Oh, my … If my hands weren't full, I swear to the Mother Light, I'd ———"

I rolled my eyes and walked through the dry oak. My body faded through. Then my hand got stuck and Zia groaned. "Perry! That hurt! Why'd you ———"

As she complained, I let go of her hand, rushed to the fence gate and shoved it open.

I pulled a red-handed, grey-eyed spitting Zia through the gate and locked everything as fast as I could. Her eyes sparkled and she searched the backyard.

"Perry, where are you?" she roared.

I can see her, how come she can't ... Oh, wait, my bad! I calmed my crest and its light faded. Zia's face dropped the moment the world lost its blue tint. There was a loud crash to my left as Harry dropped a box of gunpowder.

"Hey, Harry!"

"Perry! Zia! I thought you two had vanished—lost inside the city, or even outside, in the Great Divide! How'd you ... How are you?"

I raised my hands. "It's a long story."

"You two will have to be careful around here. Heck! Without a travel pass, if the militia catch you ... I don't think Dad and I would be able to help much."

"Militia?" Zia queried.

"Aye. The boys in blue."

"The ones who were rude to you in the Great Divide?" Zia's throat was raw.

Harry dropped his head. He couldn't say the next words without stuttering. "They're not that bad. They're just being honest. I'm going to make it this year, they know it! They're just hosers!"

I approached his side. "Well, they weren't nice to you, Harry. And you don't deserve that—no one does. At least you know you're better than them."

"That's not the right advice, Perry!" Zia urged. "Harry, you need to stand up for yourself, otherwise they're going to treat you like ———"

"Rotten sand beneath their boots!" Harry mumbled. "I already heard that one." He stared at his house. "Don't worry, guys. Trust me, you wait. Next administration and I'll be one of the best the Drewan militia has ever seen."

A door hinge creaked behind me. There was laughing, along with footsteps. Mr Doubtson walked in, arms crossed, Taylah smiling by his side. "Well, looky here," Mr Doubtson cheered. "Seems like we be having ourselves some guests!"

Night covered the hexadome. It was chilly here. Not the temperature, but the mood. The whole glass ceiling was covered by a dim moonlight that swayed to the waves above our heads. My fingers were tense as I sat

Chapter 35: What We Know

on a timber chair. Zia complained about how uncomfortable they were, but she kept her voice quiet—she didn't want to hurt Mr Doubtson's feelings after his kind hospitality. Leo and James argued over who had the controller for the game box under the lounge room's orb. The orb had blue clouded images and the time of seven-thirty. I could hear the dinging of Mr Doubtson's wok and stove.

Taylah was loud next to my ear. "And what happened next?" she begged.

Zia smacked her hand on the mahogany table. "That's when he stabbed her. Right then and there! Obsidian wielded the knife of the White Light, the blood of Hope along its sharp Pristious metal, the metal of the gods. Hope shielded her wound, fresh from her lover, her hands filling with blood. They cried together that night as she bled in his arms. By morning, Hope had died in the middle of a white plain. The rock where her body lay soon glimmered with the markings of the spirits. That's where the beacon is today, guarded and protected within Whide's Cathedral. Beneath the statue of Hope."

"Why was the field white? Did it snow?" Taylah asked.

Zia shook her head. "No! No, when Hope's blood was drawn, white flowers fell around Jinkie's Gap for the next seven days. They came from the heavens as though it were raining."

"And what happened to Obsidian? Did he get banished to another world? Like Malegtah, the omen of ... of ..."

"Of corals!" Harry finished.

Zia smiled at him. "No, he was not banished. After he murdered his long-lost lover, he went berserk! One of the first with human blood to do so. He's been an outcast from the heavens ever since!"

Taylah was stumped. "Berserk? He could have killed himself or ——"

"Lost his crest," Harry muttered. "And yer say he's still out there, running away from what he did?"

Zia nodded, tight lipped. "Yes. And good riddance. He killed a good god! And a better woman. Better than any other prince or princess that ever ruled Kelton Whide."

I grabbed her fist with my gloved hand. "Hey, don't say that! You and Titan are doing the best you can!"

"In a Town of Tents, Perry! I can't even find my father!"

"We've been here for less than a day! We'll find him. And Kyle, Faith and everyone."

She pulled her hand away and leaned back on her chair. "And where do we even start?" She dumped her journal on the table, flipping through each page. "I've written page, after page, after page and I've got nothing. I don't know where to look or how we could even find the others. What if they never made it?"

This time, I slammed my fist on the table. "*Don't say that!* You can feel Titan. I can feel Teala and Olivia, and if they're all right, Faith and Dally and Bailey and everyone else are okay, and that includes Kyle! They're not dead until I see a body ... All right? We start with what we know! That's what we do, that's what Odd would do! That's what he always does!"

"And what's that? Feel the hexadome's glass to see if I can feel my father?"

Zia's eyes were red. I bit my lip and calmed my bursting chest. "We ... We visit the militia!"

Harry stood from his chair. "You wanna *what*? Perry, did yer not hear me today? The militia will throw you out if they catch you without a travel pass." Taylah looked like her heart was going to explode.

Mr Doubtson yelled from the kitchen. "Harry! Tone it down in there, will yer?"

Harry leaned on the circle table, his arms long and strong. "Perry, what are yer thinking?"

"I'm not!" I admitted. "I'm just using what I know. Giuseppe's here and he was on our train. The train that crashed and separated everyone. He ought to know something, at least something we can use to find Olivia and maybe the others. Hell, even Mr Kingsleigh!"

Harry sat back down. "Okay, then! Giuseppe, it is!"

Chapter 36
Visiting The Militia
Perry

I awoke to the loud arguing of Leo and James. Their voices were still ripe with puberty, cracking every third word as they battled for the remainder of the good cereal. I picked myself up, and it smelt like coffee beans. Next to me was a leather lounge that sank more and more the longer you sat on it. Zia's face was scrunched up under a blanket, her black hair frizzy above a thick white pillow. I cracked my knuckles, a habit I barely noticed now and reached for my gloves.

"Morning!" Taylah cheered.

She skipped inside the living room with a smile as big as Teala's.

Zia moaned, turning over in her bed. I continued tightening a glove around my left hand. "Morning! Happy to be back home?"

"Aye! It's the best, having your own bed. Hey, why do yer wear gloves?"

I pulled my right glove over my hand. "It's hard for me to grab things. I wear gloves so I can hold my staff properly."

"Well, that's quirky!" She tilted her head to the left, making me grin.

"Quirky indeed. You're a funny kid, you know that?"

"Why do you say that?" Taylah asked.

I laughed, "You ask questions. I like people who ask questions."

She held her hands behind her back. "Well, I like princesses and knights."

I stood. "Oh, I'm no knight. But thank you. When this is all over,

I'd be happy to teach you how to swim."

"That'd be great, but I'll have to let Dad know."

I patted her head and we walked into the kitchen.

James had the last bowl of Milky Loops. Leo rolled his eyes, climbing the kitchen bench to reach another bowl.

"Where's Harry?" I asked.

"Probably at the lagoon!"

"He likes to go for morning swims," Leo explained. He jumped from the bench, bowl in hand.

Those two should hang with Gerard and Sam. I'm sure they'd get along.

After waking Zia, Taylah asked her father if she could fetch Harry. Behind the house, about a two-minute walk past a grey fern and some spinning gears that smelt of rusted iron, there was a lagoon. It was no longer than a freeway and as wide as a public swimming pool, reaching the outer rim of the Lower Hex. Two arms jumped from the water, splashing their way towards us. Taylah, without a second thought, called for her brother. The arms continued pushing through the water. Taylah screamed louder, and the arms stopped. Harry's head popped up from the silver water, his hair drenched.

"Hiya there!" He reached us, climbing out of the water. "Sorry! Shoulda mentioned my morning swims to yer last night."

"It's fine, Harry. You ready to head off?" I asked.

Harry rubbed his head with his towel. "Aye, about that! I've been thinking and ..."

"Don't you start with me, Drewan!" Zia exploded. "I don't care if you're being bullied. If you can't face the people you're scared of, or if you just want to make up another excuse for those stale corns who make fun of you, that's fine, but we're going now! And you can either join us or stay hiding in your shell until the next ... what? Administration?"

I fanned her with my left hand. "I think what she's trying to say, is that you should come with us. Your choice, Harry. But it'd be better and safer if you did join us. We'd be happier if you did!"

Harry was quite tall for his age. A few months older than me, he was a few hairs taller than Dally, but then again, twice as skinny. His

CHAPTER 36: VISITING THE MILITIA

strut was unlike most from the Town of Tents. Similar to Gabe, he strolled with an eager gaze and a robust kick in his step that made my slouch more noticeable. We had to enter more of those glass tunnels, going down the back streets. Through the Lower Hex, we reached a fork. Harry continued down the left side of the tunnel.

"The glass here, it feels sad!" Zia murmured.

Harry kept his pace, leading us. "What d'you mean? Can yer feel the glass, like it's alive?" he wondered.

"No, the glass isn't alive, it's simply stuck in a moment of time. Once a panel for a window is made—or a wall, or even, say, one of the hexagonal bricks for your hexadomes—the essence of the glass freezes. Through my crest, I can feel that essence," Zia explained.

"She can also become a part of the essence if she wants to," I mumbled.

"So what was the glass like at my house?" Harry asked.

Zia examined a yellow starfish clinging onto the tunnel's outer walls. "Proud. But here, it's as though this dome was never meant to be."

Harry grinned, "Aye, we're heading to the Royal Hex—the largest of the hexadomes. It's where most politicians, royals and the militia sleep."

"And what about WonderWorks?" I asked.

"That's in The Between, just up ahead. Why? Do you wanna go there?"

I watched Zia, her eyes still firm on the glass around us.

"Yeah," I said. "Maybe we should visit it after we ask Giuseppe everything we need to know!"

Out of a second tunnel, the metal steampunk lost its hold. The wheels and gears were nowhere to be found, and there was greenery. Every street, every complex of mansions, every gothic arch had an abundance of ferns, trees and grass. *How do they manage to grow so many in the dark depths of the ocean?*

The militia's main headquarters was to the right of the connecting tunnel. We followed Harry until he became weary. He started to tiptoe as we travelled down a fence with thick layers of cement between the crisscrosses of orange bricks. I could smell the burning of bark, almost like someone had burnt paperwork. There was an opening. Harry's lip quivered the moment he saw what was behind the fence.

"There ... There are no guards. Where are the men? They should ... There are usually men stationed here. Where'd they go?"

There was an empty carpark with one large beige truck. I pulled my hood over my head and crept to the fence with Harry.

"Well, if no one's here to complain, they can only get angry at us later. That's if there is anyone to see!" I mused. "So which way to the entrance?"

Inside, the burning smell of paper was worse. It'd make you cough if you were there long enough. The front desk was empty, and the office chair was vacant with a smidge of dust. I could hear Zia's footsteps behind Harry's and mine. She tugged on her blue glass shard, her white glove tight around her right hand. "Is it normally this empty?" she asked.

Harry shook his head. His forehead was sweaty, his face white.

"I was hoping for a party. This is a little disappointing. Maybe they're all using the bathroom?" I suggested.

Zia rolled their eyes. "How many militia are in Drewmora, Harry? Just to clarify things with Perry's ... theory!"

"Ninety-three. Not including fourteen of the latest cadets."

Zia nudged me, "So you think ninety ... What's that—a hundred and seven people are using the restroom at the same time?"

I put my hands in front of me. "It can happen! I don't know the dietary needs of each Drewan. Maybe there's been a robbery or some sort of hit and run?"

"Aye, could be!" said Harry. "But for them to leave HQ defenceless ... I've never seen that before."

"Let's hope someone's home! Do you know where the commanding officer's rooms are?"

The elevator was squishy. A blue light flashed with each floor the box climbed; we all grimaced, avoiding one another's eyes. The elevator shook with the effort of carrying all three of us. After a while, I caught the scent of blood. The shaking came to a halt, the

Chapter 36: Visiting the Militia

doors pulled apart, and a river of red covered the carpet. I gulped as my staff extended before my heart had time to react. Zia crept next to me. Just outside the box, there was a dead body covered in the blue uniform of the militia. He was a few years older than us, brown hair like mine with an uneven smile, tanned skin and wide, frightened blue eyes. Something had pierced through his chest where his medals of honour hung. Blood was sprinkled all over the floor.

"Geez!" Harry gagged.

Above the red-stained floor, the lights flickered on and off. After the first body we stumbled across, there were many more. At least twelve or thirteen. I was afraid to count.

"So much for a hit and run!" I joked. I heard a splatter. Turning, Harry was white-eyed, wiping vomit from the side of his mouth. "You can stay in the elevator if you'd like. Go back downstairs!" I told him.

He shook his head. "I'm okay, Perry! Onwards. We needa make sure Giuseppe's okay, right?"

"Right!" Zia's glove was tense. She clung to her shard as if it were keeping her alive. "Who could have done this? Murder so many in cold blood?" she thought aloud.

"I have an idea. They each have wounds in their abdomens. This was not a spontaneous attack."

"You're right, it was planned. These aren't bullet wounds—this was art!" Zia said.

"Art? No, this was a massacre, princess," Harry insisted. "Look at these innocent men and women. They didn't deserve this. They were just working. They were protecting the city!"

I kneeled next to a deceased woman in her mid-thirties. Her curly blond locks were knotty from blood. I examined her neck—it had been sliced open with a sword. The wound was still fresh, blood flowing from the slit. "Well, whatever it was, the murderer may still be here."

A squeak echoed in an office cubicle to my right. Zia called my name as she bolted towards the sound. Harry chased after us. I ran through the first wall on my right. The other side was a lot brighter with open windows and a blur of computer screens. Behind the monitors lurked a shadow. *Papercut! It has to be.* One of Zia's shards ricocheted off a timber desk. I closed my eyes and vanished.

When I reappeared near the shattered shard, white ash fell around my body. A hooded figure swung their arm towards my face. I clipped the punch to my left cheek and rolled my eyes. *Why'd he have to go and punch my bloody head?* The oak of my staff collided with his next punch. Before I could stop myself, I had my gloved hand around the back of his neck, his two punchy hands gripped tightly behind him, and a realisation that I had nothing to slam his face with. "Ah, wait a tic! This isn't how you …"

I teleported to the closest wall, a column between two windows covered with staggered blinds. I slammed the shadow's head into the wall, and he moaned, "Get your arms off me, Kelt!"

I pulled off his hood.

This isn't Papercut!

The shadow continued complaining. "Last person who teleported me somewhere ——"

"Was probably my sister! Or am I mistaken, Giuseppe?" I pushed back on his neck, exhaling. Another shard of glass exploded by our faces in a flash of white light. "Zia! My head!" I yelled.

She peeked behind me, Harry on her tail. "Oh, you got him. My bad … Hey, you'd be able to just fade through it anyways." She sighed, wandering closer. "Oh, would you look at that. Just who we were planning to visit!"

Giuseppe calmed as his arse dropped onto one of the many blood-drenched seats. He seemed exhausted like something had tried to take the light from his crest. He had a fresh wound on his left cheek and red smeared on his hands and neck. His blond hair was sticky and thick on his forehead. With his right hand, he rubbed the back of his scalp, moaning. "The hell's the meaning of this, Harry? Why'd yer bring outsiders here, of all days? Why now?"

Harry opened his mouth. I pointed at Giuseppe. "Don't blame Harry. He hasn't done anything wrong. And certainly nothing as vile as this." I gestured to the room, a river of blood still so fresh you could taste the bitterness. "The heck happened here, Sep?"

Giuseppe stopped rubbing. He licked his lips and gawked at Zia and me. "How are you two even here? You should be dead."

Zia raised her hand, and her shard melted like a waterfall, dripping from her hand. The next moment, beneath her white glove, she revealed a glass sword. Its sharp end dropped to the carpet, slicing the chequered bumps in half. I latched my arm around her shoulder just before she did anything we might regret. Giuseppe remained unamused. "What'd you say!" Zia demanded. She took a step forward. "Do you understand what we've been through? I could have your head!"

"In Kelton Whide!" Giuseppe smiled.

Zia's face went red. She raised the sword, aiming its sharp end at Giuseppe. I placed my hand around her arm, which pulsated as her body shook. She took her eyes off Giuseppe and shrugged my hand off her arm. The sword shrunk until the shard was clasped inside her glove.

"How'd you get here? You were on the train. You were on our carriage! We didn't even see you at the river!" I asked.

"I have my ways. The militia sent a few shuttles for myself and my cadets after the attack." Giuseppe leaned back. I opened my mouth, but this time his voice was twice as harsh. "I searched for your sister! Delayed the shuttles a whole day to search that salty Driwood Forest. And she ——"

"She's fine! Thanks for asking," I remarked.

"You know where she is? I need to ——"

"Need to what?" I raised an eyebrow. "What would you have done? Saved her? Doesn't seem like you've done anything! She's still out there!"

"I would have ..."

I raised my voice. "Would have what, Giuseppe? People died that day! We were lucky to get out able to walk. And you what? Got picked up in a shuttle!"

He leaned forward, his arms tense on the table. "I had my orders!"

"And what were they?" Zia demanded.

Giuseppe looked Zia in the eyes and said three words that made my jaw so tense I thought it'd break. "To kill you! For what you saw in the House of Senates. General's direct orders. For me and me alone!"

Harry stuttered, making excuses in the background. *The Militia would never do this! Not General Ko!*

Zia eyed down Giuseppe. "You burnt down the inn!" She watched the ground, then the bloodied bodies. She gulped, walking to the desk, towering over Giuseppe. "I'm still alive, which means you failed. So why are you here?"

Giuseppe smiled, his teeth as perfect as the day I met him.

"Don't act like you knew I'd come ... Why are you here?"

Giuseppe didn't say a word; he just laughed. "TELL ME!" I heard the desk slide against the carpet before Giuseppe screamed.

After I separated the two, I discovered a glass shard embedded in Giuseppe's hand. "Geez, Zia!" I shoved her off, then turned to Giuseppe. "Why didn't you just answer her?"

Giuseppe reached for the shard with his free hand. I caught it as his face went red. The scent of his blood lingered under my nose. "Okay, okay! I don't know! Just my orders. It's funny." He cried, smiling.

I shoved his free hand away. "*Funny?* What do you mean? The heck happened here? Why are all these people dead? And why are you ——"

Giuseppe pulled the shard from his hand and threw it over the desk. "It was the EXPERIMENT, okay! He came in here and sliced them all open, and if they continued screaming, he'd ... he'd just cut 'em again!"

"The experiment?" Harry queried.

"Then why aren't you dead?" Zia insisted.

Giuseppe raised his hands. His left was dripping red. "'Cause I don't go near them. Not the salty experiments! I don't touch 'em! I just ... I try and help. Give 'em food. And I'm a commander, I got paperwork to do. These pricks down here probably deserved what they got. Well, some more than others. The general has his orders."

I sat down, lowering my voice. "So these members were, what—rude to the experiment?"

Chapter 36: Visiting the Militia

Giuseppe wiped blood from his forehead. "They probably treated the paper kid like crap! He had this anger on his face like I'd never seen before."

"Paper kid? Papercut! You know ... Where'd he go? Tell me!" I ordered.

Giuseppe watched the closest window. "He's gone. Was pretty wounded when he turned into that plane of his and flew outta here!"

"And what does General Ko want with Papercut, experiments, dead militia?" Zia asked.

"I don't think he wants dead militia! He just ... I don't know. From what I gathered, it's got something to do with Othello the Wise."

A wheel screeched behind the window. Someone had parked outside. A few voices were muted behind the walls of the HQ, laughing.

"Othello the Wise? What's he got to do with all of this?" I asked.

Giuseppe searched the tight blinds. "I just take orders, kid! You have to get out of here. All I know is that they're going to use the beacon and tomorrow's Mardi Mimpi! Our celebration for sweet dreams!" He shoved me to the side. "You need to get out of here! And make sure your sister's safe. And the princess! You too, Harry!"

"This coming from a man who wanted to murder us a week ago!" I argued.

"What about you?" Harry asked.

"Just go, Perry! Get to the beacon. I'll do what I must. What I'm asked to. Your answers should be at the blue light. If not, then let's hope the omen of the waves can save us all."

I had never seen his face so white before. After stumbling over more dead bodies, Giuseppe left us in a stairwell. The elevator opened on the floor of red when we had reached the exit.

Where the beacon shined, he said, but only darkness prevailed.

CHAPTER 37

THE SECRETS INSIDE WONDERWORKS
Faith

The WonderWorks main enterprise was a colossal machine of iron and gears spinning its proud produce of tent-lets, phones and Mr Kingsleigh's wealth. Its dark bronze walls were so sterile in comparison to the natural complexities of the WonderWorks' tree in Everbreen. Towering like a staircase to the surface of the water, the large blue logo imprinted across its front coloured my face in a dark navy. Pipes crisscrossed around its walls; steam guzzled from their vents and the visible screws that attached each wall panel to the tower's scaffolding glimmered with a sour taste of freshly handled metal bars. A drill squealed as though it was digging behind the tower. But alas, there was no drill in sight.

We walked past a crowd of miners, their faces stained with mud, their gloves coated in dust and their shoulders tight from the many pickaxes they had carried over the years. Beneath the hexadome hung hundreds of dreamcatchers; the air conditioning was freezing. The tiles were loud against Olivia's boots as she marched forward, confident in her knowledge of the tower's layout. She turned left past a gigantic enclosure of trees, frogs and birds, the size of a four-storey building that opened into a large atrium. Dally gawked at the ceiling. I could barely see the lights, it was so high!

Crowds of Drewans covered the balconies of the third and fourth floors; many cubicles and glass walls were on the fifth and sixth. Olivia walked to a row of chest-high marble desks hiding beneath the dim orange light of the second floor's balcony.

"Hi!" Olivia said. "I'm here to see Mr Kingsleigh. I understand he's very busy, but I'm not really in the mood to argue with you. Can you please call his secretary and let him know that his parliamentary advisor from Central City has arrived, healthy and able."

She turned away from the dark-skinned Tinket, whose pink crest glistened above her keyboard. "Oh!" Olivia smiled and turned back to the receptionist. "And let him know that the train service was more than excellent! Thank you."

We followed her to a line of elevators, each opening and closing like an organ's pipes. Olivia wandered into one of the blue cylinders and pressed the button for floor twenty-five. As we stood, I could hear Olivia take a deep breath.

"This place is fancy!" Dally mused. "Lotta steam!"

Olivia focused on the sealed doors before us. "It's from the machines downstairs."

"Where does it go? The steam?" I asked. "Aren't we closed off inside a dome?"

"Yes," Olivia nodded. "The steam flows to the outer rim of each hexadome and gets filtered into the Full Sea."

"Isn't that bad for the ocean life?" I argued.

Olivia shrugged, "I don't know. I just want to talk to Charles and find the princess before it's too late."

Dally muttered, "Too late? What do you ———"

"Are you a broken seed?" Olivia asked. "Ever since the explosion on the train, there's been something building up in the background. Seeing those lunatics filling the Full Sea with whatever was in those bags just made things worse."

Dally crossed his arms. "Right. I'm sure Martin will deal with those knobheads. Olivia, don't stress. I'm sure everything's gonna get sorted, especially once Martin warns whoever he plans to warn!"

"Did the attacks on Kelton Whide blow over?"

We all kept quiet. Dally huffed, his face reddening. "Well, you don't have to put all this pressure on yourself! You're exactly like your brother, you know that? Every time we find out something bad's going to happen, he acts like it's his mission and his mission alone. Like he's the only one who can save the day! Pisses me off!"

The elevator doors opened to an enclosed office. Olivia whirled around, staring Dally in the eye. "Why do you have a constant desire to argue? I put pressure on myself because people are in danger. And it'd make me very happy if I could make sure that they weren't any longer." She stormed out of the elevator. "Now, wait here! I have a meeting with the devil, and I seem to have misplaced my good shoes!"

Dally was left speechless as Olivia marched towards a Drewan receptionist. I tiptoed to a cluster of blue chairs with large cushions covering their backrests—they smelt of fresh linen.

"I don't argue that much!" Dally mumbled, sitting beside me. He had his arms crossed again. "I'm just opinionated. I like to state my thoughts, that's all." He turned. "What's up with her? She's changed since Kelton Whide. Like, she's bossy all of a sudden, and what's with the slight obsession with Zia? I don't even love Zia that much!"

I squinted. "You love Zia?"

"That's not the point! What's gotten into Olivia? Ever since the accident at the Jakoo River, she's had a weird aura about her!"

I watched his face gauge mine, anticipating agreement.

I looked ahead, "Well, we've all ... You know, Liv's an adult now, Dally. She knows what she wants, what makes her happy and I think she's prepared to do whatever it takes to achieve that! And I got to admit, I admire that!"

Dally slapped his hands against his knees. "Great! So you like the change? Fantastic! If you admire it—and this is some advice from myself—just don't end up like her. Think of Perry! The poor stale corn. He'd ... well, by the Light, if you ended up being anything like Olivia, he'd probably ..." Dally closed his lips. "I'm not going to finish that! I know what's good for me."

I gave him a glare so intense I thought my eyes might fall out. "Good. Are you scared of me?"

He looked like he thought I was joking. "What? Yeah, sure. A little. But not as scared as I am of Zia. But you're both nothing compared to an angry Ada."

Chapter 37: The Secrets Inside WonderWorks

That got me smiling. "Do you miss her?"

"Every day! She's a hard one to forget. Are you missing Pear?"

"Every minute," I laughed. "But knowing he hasn't got himself killed is a relief. You think they made it?"

"Here?" Dally scratched his forehead, "Maybe."

Olivia returned, looking unamused but proud. She gave me a small smile. "Good news. Charles is ready to meet. The bad news is that you two can't come. I'll be back soon. Try and stay out of trouble ... Oh, and they said a Mr Odd is expected for a meeting this afternoon. Sounds like someone we might know." She winked at me.

"Mrs Caduca?" The secretary called, "Sir Kingsleigh is ready for you."

Olivia disappeared behind the door to Mr Kingsleigh's office.

Dally sighed as he stood, "Great! Odd's here." He stomped off to the stairwell. I heard the door creak open and chased his invisible footprints.

Inside the untidy grey cemented walls of the emergency stairs, I yelled, "You're *leaving*? What if Odd's here?"

"What if? What, so he can tell me I smell funny and give you some random nonsensical compliment. The guy hates me. Why would I willingly walk into that?"

I followed him down a few steps. "He doesn't hate you! If he hated you, he wouldn't even speak to you. Plus, he's one of those people who would say that he hates you to your face."

"Oh, don't give me that, Faith. You know he hasn't liked me since day one. He was going to kick Davis and me out the first time I met him."

Dally stopped at an opening, his back to the lights marking the twenty-fourth floor. I waltzed around, placing my foot between him and the exit. I crossed my arms with a frown. "If he hated you, why would he ever let you go and get files for him? Why would he trust you enough to go with him to the Cabana? Why would he trust you to do anything with Perry?"

He was baffled. "Well ... 'Cause of Perry! He trusts him, not me. He just knows that Perry would be a lot happier if I was forced to go along rather than you, or Zia, or Gabe!"

Two Drewan militia guards stormed up the orange hallway behind the opening. I kept my eye on them. They were adorned in blue uniforms, each with three small medals pinned to the left side of their chests. A white hazmat suit marched behind them, emitting a hazy breathing from its oxygen mask.

"How could one of the experiments escape? We check their vitals every hour. And for one to go from one side of Drewmora to another and simply kill a room full of you, militia, is ludicrous." They were heading for us.

Dally continued to argue; his ranting the loudest thing on the otherwise silent floor. I pushed him back into the concrete wall, feeling his warm breath against my right palm. His eyes twitched as I put a finger to my lips. The hazmat suit stopped at a metal door. Beside it was a set of buttons like a phone. The lady behind the rubber dialled a code and the door turned green with a gurgling sound. I pulled my hand from Dally's mouth as his breathing relaxed.

"Well one of them escaped, and from what Commander Malvitch said, we have reason to believe one of your wairiths are involved," the right cadet said.

"Thirteen of us have been murdered! We're not leaving 'til we see the salty lot of 'em," the second guard insisted. Dally peeked behind the opening. He watched them enter the metal door and raised his hand, his crest igniting. The door swayed and began to close behind the second guard. It froze, instead of closing.

"D'you wanna investigate some experiments?" Dally asked. I had already leapt over and held the frozen door for him. It was so light!

"One step ahead of you!" I said with a grin.

Dally loosened his fingers and a sudden weight pushed into my shoulder.

Behind the metal door, the floor's orange lights vanished. The smell of burning steel, skin and paper caught my nose, making me gag.

"So this is how we're staying out of trouble," Dally whispered.

I focused on the darkness ahead, goosebumps spreading up my arms. We had reached a barren grey hallway, empty except for several long rectangular windows and white metal doors. Behind the windows were Bunsen burners, equations on whiteboards, test tubes, flasks and white tiled walls stained with a thick hardened red goo. I could taste the overabundance of sterilised stainless steel.

Dally tiptoed in behind me. "What do you think they're doing with wairiths? Ain't that the two-headed dog Daegon had?"

"Not sure," I shrugged. "This took a quick turn. A moment ago we were arguing about Odd. Now, I think Odd's gonna be jealous. We might find out something he doesn't know." I smirked to myself.

"Well, when a lady in a hazmat suit says the words *experiments* and *kill* in a tower filled with workers, it doesn't suggest the presence of safety precautions. Let's just not get killed here, okay?"

"Agreed!"

It was quiet as if no one but us were inside this part of the building. Dally threw open the first door he could find. I stomped my foot the moment I heard the loud screech of the hinges. Dally shrugged at me, confused. A metallic bang echoed as though someone had knocked a coin against a bar. Then the three voices echoed.

"You see, they're all there. I told you!" Her voice was more muffled; it was most likely the one in the hazmat suit. I leapt behind the door, and Dally ducked under the glass as the three wandered past us. I could still hear their sombre voices through the thick walls.

"And what about the Kelt? Where is he? Not with the others?" the second soldier demanded.

"He's in his quarters. I'll take you there now."

"The freak has his own quarters? By the salts beneath your chin, why would you give a sea cucumber like him such privileges? He deserves to be thrown into the ocean to feed the sharks of Omen Legar!"

"Because without the *sea cucumber*, the monkey from Everbreen and many more would not be locked in those cages. He's our best chance to productively gather a varied sample group. We must ..." Their voices faded behind the exit.

Dally's head bobbed up from behind the glass. The metal bars dinged again. "A Kelt?" He asked, staring at me as if I had an answer. "Should we follow them? Maybe save the guy ——"

"And then what?" I searched the laboratory. "I'm all for saving a Kelt, but if they're keeping a watch on him, what good could we do? We know he's here and we know where *here* is. Let's have a look around and see if we can get some information. When we find the others, we can rescue the Kelt."

Dally leaned back against the wall. "You got a brain on ya, don't you?" He examined the red goo. "If we find something new, I'm telling Odd!"

He touched the red. I could hear his finger stick to it a moment. "This is blood, Faith!"

"Do you think they're doing experiments on hu———"

The metal ding echoed even louder. *It was coming from this laboratory!*

This time Dally placed his finger over his lips. I nodded, sidestepping to the only other door besides the entrance. I walked past a test tube filled with a light beige goo that smelt of burnt flesh and bubbled when I got close. The storage door's handle was reflective. My distorted hand was firm as I absorbed its cold alloy. I threw the door to the right, and both Dally and I raised our arms, our crests so bright we could be stars. The bitter, metallic tang of blood reeked inside. Red covered the room from top to bottom; dusty shelves had containers, rundown machines, weapons similar to those Quentin stored under my house and one worn paper katana. In the centre, leaning on the wall opposite from us was Papercut.

He was kneeling, half-naked; his paper cloak had gashes and slices throughout, blood oozing from his knees and arms. There were fresh bullet holes in his shoulder and shrapnel covering the once sterile floor. His right hand was shaking, and a large stapler was pressing down into his left bicep. His blue eyes watched mine. Tears drenched his cheeks.

Dally pushed himself in front of me. "Get back, Faith!"

I pushed him. "Oh, don't bother. Look at him! He's injured, Dally. What could he ———"

Papercut moved his left hand towards Dally's leg. Dally tensed his hand, the katana moving as though the wind had picked it up. It was swept from the shelf and landed in Dally's grip. He readied it. Papercut threw up a cue card with ink as dark as the night's sky. Dally and I both froze. I snatched the card like it was a gift. The ink read,

Chapter 37: The Secrets Inside WonderWorks

Please, don't hurt me! How did he ...

Dally groaned, rushing forward. His crest lost its light and Papercut's back slapped the back wall. The stapler dropped to the floor. Dally's hands were wrapped around his sliced-up paper cloak, pushing his chest against the iron wall. "How do you know our names? Who are you?" Dally demanded. "WHO ARE YOU?"

I pushed myself between the two. "Enough, Dally. Can't you see he's hurt! Let go of him."

Dally stared me down. "Let go of him! What are you thinking?"

I pushed the cue card in his face again. "I'm thinking he communicates with these. So stop being a stale corn and let the man speak."

Dally took a step back and Papercut dropped to the floor like a lucky coin in a fountain. He was breathing heavily as more blood poured from his shoulder. Tears were ripe under his eyes as he offered me his free hand. He flicked out two fingers with another card between them. I took the card. *Dally's still got a tough push in him!* it read.

He retracted his hand and began unwrapping his bandana. It was amazing how different he looked with it on. This whole time, merely with a hood and a bandana, Juice was almost unrecognisable. *But it was him.* Although now more bruised and tired, he grinned at us.

With his bony white fingers, he offered another card.

I read it aloud. "Miss me?" I smirked to myself as Dally's face went white.

"What happened to you, Juice? Who did this to you?" Dally asked.

The next card said in detail that he'd been trapped in Drewmora since Araidian's Tyranny. He'd been a key component to an experiment on souls. *The Drewan militia did this to him. They turned him into this mess. They turned him into Papercut!*

I lowered myself, our eyes on the same level. "Why won't you speak? You can talk to us, Juice. We're your friends!" I pleaded.

He chuckled silently. He couldn't speak. He'd lost his voice box when the white beacon hit the sky. I reached out to him. He knocked my hand away. "I can help you!" I cried.

"You look like a mess, pal. Faith's the best help you could have asked for!" Dally cheered.

Juice shook his head. His next card just said *I killed them!*

"Who'd you kill?" I asked.

It was hard to read his explanation. I gave the card to Dally the moment I finished it. It was too much! He'd been hurt by all these guards, tortured by scientists, ridiculed by the public and tormented by the ones who gave him orders. They had injected him with a silver liquid that made his crest rage for days. Before he knew it, he was more paper than he was flesh. He was fed up. Today was the day he went rogue, killing all the guards—whoever hurt him. But there were more, many more, and he was just getting started.

"Who's been giving you orders?" I asked. "Who told you to kill Mr Kingsleigh! And why didn't you stop? Why'd you kill Senator Hartway?"

He handed me another card. *Mr Kingsleigh? I never tried to kill Charles Kingsleigh. I only pretended. The senator was always my target. With him out of the picture, the Masked Ones can begin to mine in Tinkette Valley, and with the Lupo from the mine, they can start a new era.*

"Who are the Masked Ones? Is Charles one of them?" Dally asked.

"And what is this new era?" I added.

There are many masked ones. Many names, many faces. Othello, the prophet. He wants an era of darkness more than anyone. An era where we are not bound by our crests, our cities, our religion or our colour! Complete equality.

"Othello? What's he got to do with this?" Dally demanded. Juice was having trouble breathing; his stomach heaved in and out laboriously. I offered my hand, yet he pushed it away again.

Dally turned for the exit. "Just leave him, Faith. He's got his staples!"

"Dally!" I yelled. "Staples shouldn't be used for cuts. That's inhumane. He's our friend."

Dally came back, licking his lips. "We need to find Othello! I mean

Chapter 37: The Secrets Inside WonderWorks

..." It sounded as though that came from deep down. A thought not meant to be said. Dally sighed, "You're right. Man up, Juice, and let her help you." He rolled his eyes at me. "Okay, let's man-handle him!"

After a struggle, Dally managed to get Juice in a headlock. I placed my hand on his cloak and felt the pain that resided beneath it. I felt the many tears and screams, the constant fear of death in the back of his mind and a dark void. *Desolation.* Juice struggled left and right as his warm, tender skin burnt my crest. I closed my eyes, hearing the constant drip of blood from his knee.

Visions appeared. A grey hand with skin to the bone handed Juice papers—targets! One, a monkey alive, captured in Everbreen. The second, Senator Hartway, killed in Central City. A third and final in Drewmora ... *Oh my, that can't be! As if he would ...*

Tap, tap, tap! Suddenly, Juice's breathing slowed. The visions stopped. He relaxed his sway and his legs began to shake. His eyes widened and his mouth dropped open. His wounds were now gone, but I could still feel that darkness hidden beneath his ice-cold skin. I pulled my hand away as he gulped.

Dally let go. He smacked Juice's shoulder playfully—like two friends in the days before the beacon's light.

"See I told ya! She's one heck of a catch, huh?" Dally cheered.

Juice frowned, pushing past him. He snatched his katana from the door and stared at us, sighing.

"Juice, what are you doing?" I asked.

He dropped two cue cards and took a step back into the laboratory. Dally rushed to the entrance yelling his name. Then darkness.

I could hear Dally's shoulder collide with the metal. He huffed and puffed as my crest's light shone on the two cards. The first said, **Thank you, but I'm Papercut!** Dally snatched the second one from me and read it aloud. "Follow the carpet! *The hell does that mean?*" He groaned. "By the Light, when I get my hands on him. I'm going to smash that katana to pieces and ..."

I heard a metal ding. The same from before. It wasn't a coin, I realised—it was a bell.

"Dally! Do you hear that?"

"Hear what?" He glanced around the dark storage room, breathing in the dust. Another fidget erupted. It was like someone was knocking on a door, trying to escape but Dally and I were side by side, and there was no one else in the room.

I shone my crest on the shelf to our right; there was a see-through plastic box you'd find in most attics. Perry's mum used to keep his toys in one like this when we were younger. Dally had the same feeling of nostalgia. But this box wasn't like Leila's. No, this one was haunted. It was possessed, fidgeting back and forth as though a demon was trying to escape from the inside.

"What on earth?" Dally uttered.

"Should we ... open it?" I wondered.

"It could be anything ... Ah, stuff it. On three." Dally clasped his hand on the right yellow handle. I followed. "One. Two. Three!"

We both shielded ourselves as a familiar green carpet burst from the box. Othello's flying carpet, Gregory, looked back and forth. Without a second thought, Gregory flew to the door, gliding under the small gap between it and the floor. He slid under swiftly, like a spider catching its prey. A bell rang. The flowing tunes of the carpet float away as the bell dropped to the ground. I picked it up.

Dally grinned, "Ah! Follow the carpet! Now I get it. Faith, help me with the door. We got a carpet to chase!" Our crests burned and the door flew open. I couldn't decide whether it was me or Dally who broke the lock and pushed the door open, but the green wool of Gregory flew out of the laboratory and down the hall. We chased the patterned rug all over WonderWorks until we were in the atrium. No one seemed to notice Gregory's many holes and tears. Dally and I ran like maniacs into the main Drewmora streets.

Flying cars and hoverbikes drifted in the air like birds on a highway. All of a sudden, Gregory burst into the crowd of flying vehicles.

Dally waved his hands about, "Well, great! Now what? Can you fly?"

I rolled my eyes and searched the WonderWorks carpark. "No, I can't fly. Not yet. Just give me a moment!"

Gregory was still in my sight. Beneath him and behind a dark fern, two hoverbikes had the bodies of a stingray. Without a word, I bolted to the closest one.

Chapter 37: The Secrets Inside WonderWorks

Its cold steel cooled my thighs as I felt the inner working of its motor. "What are you thinking? We can't—that's stealing, Faith!"

"Like you've never stolen anything before. We'll return them! I promise."

There was a flare under one of the cylinders. I could start the ignition by changing some of the interior's atoms.

"So much for not causing trouble!" Dally scoffed, leaping onto the one beside me. His face was white in comparison to the spray-painted black aluminium. "Do you even know how to work one of these things?" he asked. "Hell, how are we even gonna turn it ..."

My crest was alight, and my motor roared.

Dally's face sagged. I tapped the front of his bike and it began to purr too. I revved the right handle and pushed my foot down on the pedal. When I looked down, the car park was a few metres below me. *I was flying!* Gregory was a prick in the distance, entering a tunnel. Dally's white face joined mine. We were two floating learners as the traffic diverged around us.

"Faith, are you sure about this?" Dally insisted. "You're not exactly the best at driving Odd's van, and I ——"

I pushed my left hand into his face. "Don't wanna hear it! Follow the carpet, right?"

I leaned, ducking my head, and pushed as hard as I could on the metal beneath my right boot. Luckily my hair was tied back rather than blowing in my face. Strong winds rushed towards me, reeking of smog from the other flying chariots. I found it hard to keep my eyes open. Slowing and getting faster was easy; avoiding others was the hard part. Gregory was an expert flyer, weaving in and out of tunnels, between buses, alleyways and through to another hexadome. We flew through red lights; I could hear honking, a rush of air and Dally's engine roaring behind mine.

I don't know how far we flew, but when I pulled my head up and saw what was ahead, a cold hand took hold of my heart. *The blue beacon!*

Chapter 38

The Blue Beacon
Bailey

My noggin was so hot. *The sky!* It was gone. So much blue in my eyes; I could taste a smoulder of dirt across my tongue an' behind some of my teeth. Liftin' my right cheek, my stomach gave in as a giant statue of a lady beckoned in front of me. She was made from limestone, etched perfectly as though still alive today. Her eyes were carved from lapis-lazuli gemstones, which reflected the magnificent beam behind my noggin. I could feel it radiating beneath me.

I swung my face an' admired the beacon with my own eyes. It flared up with so much strength, breaking through the tunnels of shafts, carts, tracks, dirt an' whatever else protected the earth's core. My left leg was heavy. I turned, seein' Assonance out cold, using my shin as a pillow.

I nudged her, "Oi, wake up! Ona!"

There was a moan behind me. Felicia had mud smeared throughout her damp hair. She examined the cave, her cheeks as red as fire. Placing her palm on her forehead, she asked, "Are you okay?"

I shuffled over to her side, draggin' Assonance with me. Before I could open my cakehole, an older voice chuckled beside the statue.

"Here lies Happiness! A gift that cannot be opened with mere force, anger, nor any form of love, gratification, entertainment or any satisfying impulse of human destiny. She is wielded by few, held by less and indulged by only a certain couple. The rest ... well, they've only been fooled. Satisfied by pleasure, enjoyment in succeeding. Love! But what if I told you that here, in this cave, where this blue

Chapter 38: The Blue Beacon

light shines, where this soil is most ripe, where Drewans believe the centre of the earth hides—here, happiness was once felt."

Othello ran his finger along the statue. He paused, rubbin' the dust from the limestone between his fingers. His eyes were white—he had no iris of sage green like before. Just white, as though he had 'em rolled back.

Felicia was stern. "What do you wish upon ——"

"SILENCE!" He approached us, towerin' above with a blue light shimmerin' along his face. Ye could see it through his pale white eyes. "The beacon is speaking to me." He stopped, inhaling as though it hurt. "The world is an unhappy place, you see. I understand that. That we seek contentment through others. A simplistic gratification offering both materialistic and internal amusement."

I pushed myself back. "Why are ya tellin' us this?"

He eyed me down. His voice was so different from before; it was pure evil. "Are you not happy being a human again, panda? Or are you simply gratified by the realisation that you've always been human, you've just had other ways of communicating said knowledge without your appearance. *Are you really happy, panda?* Or is it an illusion of misguided relief?"

"I am happy! I've always been happy!" I argued.

He pointed at me. "Even as a slave under the white light?"

I examined the ground. Felicia snapped, "Oh, stop talking in riddles, prophet. What is your point? Why try and manipulate his emotions?"

Othello touched her chest. "Because you know a secret. And you knew it the day I visited Serenity. You knew it years ago. And I am so close to figuring out why the world is unhappy and how I can make everything equal."

"De world isn't unequal. It's not unhappy!" I uttered. "That's your perception, from how you've been raised, your environment, ya age! I spent three years of my life a slave to fellas with a different coloured crest!" I gulped, holdin' back tears. "Equality is not de answer to whatever ya seek. Dere is no such thing 'cause we're too complicated. But understanding difference by appreciating' our unique gifts ... Jus' look at us. A Centrillian, an' Ever an' a Kelt, together in front of ya.

As friends an' maybe even more! So once ya understand dat we are all unequally equal, maybe then you'll be able to open the gift of happiness ya seek, Othello! So stop with the riddles, ya manipulation, an' tell us why we're 'ere! *What do ya want?*"

Othello was taken aback—so was Felicia. He licked his lips an' raised his hands. It was then that I noticed a sparkle of green from his right wrist. "Very well, panda!"

I heard a groan—the smack of flesh. Felicia shivered, her right cheek gleamin' almost orange. Othello pulled back his fist. "Where is Ada?" he demanded. Before Felicia swore, I threw my body before hers. "You will never find her! She is gone from this world!" Felicia screamed.

Othello bit his lip as Assonance moaned beneath my boot. For an oldie, he sure had some ripe knuckles. "I may be old, but this information is ageless, girl! Tell me. You may make me a grateful prophet!"

My side was shoved across the mineshaft. Felicia leapt to her feet, her crest glowin' so bright I could barely see the beacon. But her strategy was amiss. Othello clicked his fingers. I could have sworn the beacon grew in size as though it were angry. A white flower blossomed beside Felicia's foot. Then a tree root. They were like bubble-wrap, poppin' on the dirt floor. A red rose here, another dark oak root there. But the ones that surrounded Felicia covered her approaching feet. She was just over an arm's length away from Othello when she began to fidget. Her legs were welded shut by the many roots. My hand felt this sharp pressure. When I searched it, a green root infected with thorns wrapped itself 'round my open palm. It pinched! I could smell the pollen as I tugged, restrained.

Othello stood his ground, smiling. "Nature's pure, is it not? More perfect than you and I. It smells sensational, provides not only oxygen but food and other necessities. And you think, I, the Master of Spirits, the lord and brother to Mother Nature herself, could be attacked by a dumb blond upon the light of the blue beacon. You couldn't reach me even if you gave it everything you've got!"

Felicia grinned, "Thank you for noticing my hair colour. But trust me. I'm not trying to reach you. Unless I miscalculated!"

Chapter 38: The Blue Beacon

Her panther crest glimmered. White numbers appeared above their noggins. Behind the numbers, a brown line formed as though it was comin' from a digital portal. It was bulky at first, 'til suddenly, Felicia's staff fell from where the numbers appeared, dropping between herself an' the prophet. She caught it an' the numbers popped like balloons. Timber slapped skin, and Othello's body swayed towards me. At the end of Felicia's Bywoe staff, blood dripped red.

Felicia clawed at the roots clinging at her ankles. Othello tried to balance himself, turnin' his red face towards me. His whole left cheek was covered in blood. He growled. "Where's the girl! Where is Ada? The simpleton turned Kelt, the eaten soul, the one you sheltered all those years ago? Where did she go?"

I pulled an' tugged, yet the root had torn my skin. Groaning, I heard the Bywoe timber echo. All I could see was the dirt beneath my bruised chin. I lifted my neck. Othello had overpowered Felicia; her staff had fallen an' her blond hair was swayin' from the beacon's light.

"Get off me!" Felicia ordered.

"Tell me so I can leave this hole before it is doomed!" Othello spat, drool drippin' on Felicia's forehead.

I roared, retaliating against the burnin' under my hand. My crest stung so much I thought it was goin' to bleed. A ball of black smoke drifted towards Othello, growin' darker an' darker. I ignored the pain and closed my eyes, feeling the air. It was like the sharks from the Full Sea, so intense an' powerful, gliding 'til it made contact with Othello's chest.

Grey fog covered the cave's walls. The moans from Othello echoed from within. His temple was warm with blood. I lifted myself, placin' my teeth 'round the root, an' pulled. When my noggin flicked back, the thorns an' stems ricocheted into the air. I could taste my blood an' the greenery Othello had trapped me under. My right hand was boiling hot; there were three holes, runnin' red. I needed to be quick. *I need to find Felicia an' Assonance!*

I tumbled through the fog, hearing more groans. Ye could barely see the beacon's light. Felicia screamed. I ran towards her voice, toward the shimmer of blue.

"You will not be able to find her prophet!" Felicia mocked. "She remains hidden by forces neither you nor I have the power to outwit!"

I couldn't find her! An' where was Assonance? I was probably makin' things worse! I relaxed my hand, my green crest calming as the fog dispersed. When the grey vanished, I saw that Othello had Felicia in a headlock. His fingers were tangled in her hair as his plain white eyes searched me. She groaned. *Assonance was gone!*

I stood tall, raisin' my hands. The prophet spoke. "Powers, you say. Hidden forces ... Well, thank you for your sacrifice! You are just the first for what I hear is planned in Drewmora. Hebi thinks she's won! That she's stolen this land from me—this world beneath the ocean." He tensed his arm an' another thorny vine came from the dirt hole the beacon had erupted from. It wrapped itself 'round Felicia's neck. Her face went purple as she gasped for air. I clenched my own hands, green light blinding Othello's prideful grin.

I screamed, "Stop! Get dat thing off her or I'll ... I'll ..."

"You'll what, panda? Blind me with fog?"

I roared, but instead of fog hitting Othello, a brown raven no larger than a rabbit flew through the blue beacon, squawking at the prophet. She flew beak first, into his eye. Othello squealed, coverin' his right eye as blood dripped between the gaps of his hand.

I ran to Felicia, ripping at the vine. Its thorns splintered my fingers. Each time I pulled, it wouldn't budge. She was chokin' and I couldn't do anything.

Assonance sliced Othello's wrinkly forehead. I pulled again as Felicia's eyes teared up; they looked like they were gonna pop. I screamed, forcin' all my muscles to cramp, yet nothing. Then a spark glistened beside my left eye. The vine had been severed in half! A glass shard in the shape of a dagger lodged itself within the dirt beside the beacon. *I know these knives!*

I caught Felicia as she gasped for the cave's muddied air. She coughed violently. A white light flashed beside the raven. When it vanished, Perry dropped from the sky, staff in hand. I heard his staff bounce off the prophet's skin. Once, twice an' a third time that made the wise ol' man tumble back. Zia strolled out of the mine, holdin' a

Chapter 38: The Blue Beacon

glass bow an' arrow, just like Georgia's. She ignored me, lips tight as she pointed her arrow at Othello.

"From rich fools, to paper wearing assassins, to dirty soldiers, and now malicious prophets," Zia said. "We just can't catch a break, can we Perry?"

Perry adjusted his stance. "It wouldn't be fun if ... All right, I'm vibing with this, but I'm too tired to think of something witty. Sorry, Zi!"

Suddenly, a cloud of dirt whipped my face. It was like some fella had slid along it to reach me. Actually, some fella did slide along the dirt. His hair was as blond as the Camel Hump Shores, his eyes as blue as the Full Sea. He had large lips an' a perfect smile.

"Lift her up, eh? We can carry her out while the others distract the crazy old guy!" he suggested.

The raven moulded itself as its wing transformed into arms. Assonance landed beside Perry. "'Bout time you two rocked up!" she quipped.

Zia grinned, "Now that's what I'm talking about! Ona, is this prophet bothering you?"

"Oh, he's been a nuisance since we arrived!" The blond boy shoved Felicia's arm 'round his neck as I supported her left side.

Othello began to chuckle, "The old fool was right. You are a peculiar group, aren't you?"

"Which old fool?" Perry demanded.

I could hear Felicia's feet drag across the dirt as we reached the start of the mineshaft. Another familiar scream came from within the darkness.

Wait, that's Dally! His thick brown mane zoomed past us in a blur. It scurried 'round the beacon as though it were a boat searching for the safety of a lighthouse. Dally held the end of Othello's flyin' carpet, his legs dangling in the air like a rag doll. He screamed as the carpet wiggled itself up an' down like a wave, whackin' into as many limestone walls as it could. A thud eventually stopped everyone from fighting. Dally's crown an' back were against the cave's back wall. He groaned, "Son of a—*argh!*"

"DALLY! *As if you just* ... I told you not to jump on it until I gave the word!" Faith was aghast. She couldn't care less about the beacon. Instead, she eyed me down. "Bailey?" she wondered.

"Faith?" Perry called.

I raised my eyes an' turned to him. "Perry?" Before any of us had time to explain ourselves, Greg, the carpet, floated down to his master. Othello grinned, blood drippin' from his torn red eye. He placed one leg on the flyin' mat.

"Othello, Perry!" the prophet mused. "He was right! You are all going to die unhappy. Unchanged from the day you were born!"

Zia readied her bow. "You're Othello ... Aren't you?"

"Looks can be deceiving, girl. You of all should know that, dealing with spies especially!"

Faith eyed me down. She pulled out a metal bell so shiny I caught my disfigured self within its reflection. It had a tear mark with green stitching a similar shade to Greg's.

Before he flew away, Othello pointed at Perry, eyeing all of us with his plain white gaze. "Let me give you all one last word of advice before Drewmora is no longer needed. As I said to the Gah Ma and the panda, the world is an unhappy place, burdened with inequality, disease, the strong, the weak and the delirious immobilisers like yourselves. And once you've seen how it has become worse for wear, like I have, once you see that the irrational insecurities of the few do not outweigh the many, then you may smile."

Perry licked his lips. "You are worse than Odd with that mumbo jumbo malarkey. What are you trying to tell us?"

Othello raised his voice. Faith took a few steps an' he paused. He stared at her an' it looked as though he had gotten a chill. She held the bell an' glared at him. The metal ringing was calmin'; It took the heat from my crest. Othello placed his palm against the cave's limestone. "No, no! You cannot hold me back or I will ... I will ... Argh!"

His screams of fear eventually turned to screams of pain. His left eye rolled back an' his green irises returned. He spat out the blood from his mouth an' dropped to his knees, shivering. I had never seen someone's eyes so frightened an' scared before. They were just pulsating at our ankles. "Wha' ... What is the meaning of this? Who

CHAPTER 38: THE BLUE BEACON

... Why ..." He rubbed at his bloodied eye an' began to cry. "My eye! What have you done to my eye!"

Bloodied tears moistened the dirt. He searched our faces as though this was the first time he'd seen us since the Parliament House. "Tell me! What has happened under these limestone walls? What led to my bloodied eye and disfigured face?"

Zia lowered her bow, pointin' at Felicia. "You tried to kill her! By the Light, if Perry and I hadn't made it in time, you'd probably have her soul haunting you right now!"

The prophet, white-faced an' bewildered, examined the blond boy an' myself, holdin' Felicia's unconscious body aloft. He mumbled a name. Was it *Ada* again?

He gulped an' stood, wiping his tears. "I apologise. Only the unfortunate should go through what you few have endured." He observed the beacon's light, offering his right palm to Faith. "The bell, please."

Faith tiptoed to his side. Ye could hear it ring as the cold metal cooled the prophet's hand. He smiled, "Thank you, dragon!" He clasped the metal an' stared at the beacon. "You all must leave now! Drewmora is not safe." He reached out to grab Perry's shoulder. Perry stood back. Othello's eyes were wide now, as though he had seen what was to come.

He looked at me. "Do you not heed my warnings? You must depart from this forgotten land ... Before it's too late!"

"We've spent the last few days trying to get here, and you want us to leave?" Perry raised an eyebrow. "Why?"

"I warn you, he has plans to move on... You have 'til morning to leave the city!" He leaned back on Greg. "I have errands to attend to. That was not myself you collided with. I am deeply sorry you had to see that, young ones. Leave the city before it's too late!"

Greg began to float higher an' higher, gliding 'round the beacon. Othello yelled, "Begone from this dome, from the sea of change. Time is of the essence. 'Til morning, I tell you."

Perry gawked at him. "What do you mean? What just happened?"

"Wait! Do I apologise?" Assonance wondered.

Zia absorbed her glass bow an' arrow. It faded away, becoming a shard within her white glove. "Othello! You cannot run away from us. What is the meaning of this? Explain yourself!" she ordered.

The carpet sprinted to the exit. "I have errands to run, Your Majesty. We shall discuss this at a later date, I'm afraid. Leave this city; rid yourselves of the blue beacon before it's too late! *I beg you all!* Farewell and good luck. I have a demigod that needs a stern talking to!"

Does he mean Odd?

Greg vanished in a blur of green an' with him, the prophet was gone. When I looked at the others, they were all admirin' the stalactites prickling from the ceiling. Assonance scurried to Felicia's aid, yellin' her name as though it would heal her swollen throat.

Felicia grinned, liftin' her noggin. "You can put me down. I'm okay," she mumbled. The blond boy searched my eyes. I nodded an' together we placed Felicia down like she was a panel of glass. Assonance dropped to her knees, tears formin' as she caressed Felicia's blond locks on her lap. I took a deep breath an' approached the others.

Faith an' Perry seemed to be having a starin' contest. Their eyes were stuck on one another and their footsteps were heavy. The moment they became one, Perry lifted Faith so high I thought her noggin was gonna conk the roof. His arms were so firm 'round her waist, her hair so elegant as they danced joyfully before the blue light. It was dandy enough just hearing 'em laugh! Even Zia smiled, leanin' her arm on the blond fella's shoulder. His face turned red like he'd eaten somethin' spicy.

"Faith, right?" he asked.

"Oh, yeah! That's Faith, all right!" Zia grinned.

When Faith's feet met the ground, her eyes strayed from Perry's hood. "Oh my! Dally's out cold! I told him not to ——"

Perry spun 'round. "I got it!" He vanished.

A white light appeared. Perry nudged Dally's shoulder. "Wakey, wakey, sleepy. The big bad confusing prophet's alter ego has gone, and you're not allowed to sleep when ... *Man*, I am out of it today! Dally ... Wake up. Dally! Woohoo ... Dally?"

Chapter 38: The Blue Beacon

As Perry smacked Dally's cheeks, Zia's brows dropped, analysing my black hairs. "Who are you?" She pointed at me like I was an imposter.

I musta gone all white, 'cause Faith came to the rescue. "That's Bailey, Zia! Wait, how are you …? What happened to you? When did any of you get here? We were in WonderWorks with Olivia and we ran into …"

Her voice trailed off as the blond boy eyed me down with the same confusion as Zia. "Isn't Bailey meant to be a panda?" he asked.

"That's what I thought! I never really knew him before the attacks." She pointed at me again. "If you're Bailey, how are you walking on two feet with skin and hands? Why aren't you a panda?"

I raised my hands. "One question at a time." I pulled up my sleeve an' my green panda crest glistened. Zia's mouth dropped open. "It's a long tale … Were you at WonderWorks with Olivia?" I asked.

"Olivia?" Perry uttered. He held Dally, teleportin' back to us. When the white ashes dropped 'round the two, Dally fell to the ground. "You're here with Olivia? Wait, is Teala with you? And if Olivia's at WonderWorks, does that mea———" His eyes met mine. "*Bailey?* Why are you a person and is that stubble under your chin? And why haven't you hugged me yet?"

His arms surrounded me. "You dandy or what?" he asked, tightening his grip 'round my back.

I hugged him back. "As dandy as one can be, seeing dat we had to swim 'ere!"

Perry pulled away. "Well, at least you're here!"

"Yes, we're together again!" Faith cheered. "We're just missing a few, but I'm sure you two can both feel that Teala and Titan survived the accident. Right?"

Perry an' Zia nodded. The princess seemed preoccupied with the commotion behind me. "Those two seem to have become rather close," she whispered.

I turned to see Felicia laying on Assonance. The Centrillian held her so snug, I thought they'd kiss again. I faced the pack again. "Very close. They've been like dat since I've been back on my two feet."

Faith smiled, "How sweet! I'm happy for them."

"Geez, Felicia has changed, hasn't she? Whatever goes. I rate it!" Zia mused.

Perry was stunned. His eyes shot up, still baffled by the two girls. "Wait. You're telling me that Felicia Moore, the girl that had every boy wrapped 'round her little finger in school ... The one who would get what she wanted when she wanted it, who lost her virginity at like thirteen ... that she's a ... a ... les——"

"Don't you finish that sentence, Perry!" Faith demanded. "Not if you know what's good for you ... People change, learn new things about themselves."

"Whoa!" Perry raised his hands. "I wasn't gonna debate it. Just *did not* see that coming, not one bit. Talk about a plot twist, geez!" He pointed at Dally's legs. "And he's gonna be just as curious. Maybe worse when he finds out!"

"Good!" Zia giggled. "Now my question is, why is Bailey a person? I thought Evers couldn't change back to their human forms?"

"I didn't do dis." I rubbed at my bloody palm. The wound was still burning. "It was dis man on a boat. He took me in when I was runnin' from dese fellas an' next thing I know, I woke up on the Jakoo River with no fur, no tail, jus' the skin on my back an' a softer heartbeat!"

"The man on the boat! You saw him?" Faith grabbed my arm so tight I forgot 'bout the pain in my palm.

"Yeah! With a straw hat an' all dese gifts in his boat!" My eyes widened. "Wait, was he de one who saved ya in Farbe de day before my Ma visited?"

I was sure Faith was 'bout to say *yes*, but the blond fella spoke first.

"The old guy," the boy said. "He said Drewmora was lost, that we be doomed! In the morning, that's Mardi Mimpi. What does he mean *doomed*? Mardi Mimpi is a sacred time. Who was he? Why was he trying to kill that girl there, and then all of a sudden, begging for us to explain ourselves like he'd been possessed?"

Perry opened his mouth. "Look, Harry! This is pretty complicated. We're not exactly a simple group. And that old fool was delirious— you saw him take off!"

Chapter 38: The Blue Beacon

"But after what Giuseppe said!" Harry, the blond boy, snapped. "Look, I don't care how confusing this all is or what past you all have. I just want to save my home! I have family here and friends and ——"

Zia put her arm on Harry's shoulder. "We understand! Trust me, you have no idea! I'm not sure about the others, but I have some ideas about this doom intended for Drewmora."

"Me too!" Perry added. "And I say we stick to what we came for. To stop the assassination of Charles Kingsleigh, to end Papercut and to find Lord Kelton!"

Zia's smile was bright, as though she'd almost forgotten her father.

I pledged, "An' any more unnecessary deaths! De blue light still shines in dis cave! Dat means we still have time, mate! We'll figure things out."

Faith stood beside Perry, "Harry, right?"

Harry nodded.

"I may not know much about the Drewan culture, but I know the people that surround you. And I can only promise that we'll try our best. I myself don't want any more homes lost. And that includes yours!"

Harry nodded. He walked towards Assonance an' pointed at Felicia. "If the stories from Perry and Zia be as true as they say, then I believe in you and the not-so-furry panda. Now hurry! Let's pick these two up and get them somewhere safe. If the militia returned to their headquarters, they'll be here to check on the beacon ... Now, we have to be quick! Are you with me?"

Chapter 39

Pulling Strings

Perry

Shoving Dally's body through the front of Mr Doubtson's was more of a nuisance than a headache. My arms shook under his weight, but I couldn't feel the pain in my muscles or the churn in my veins. Bailey held his legs as we flung him onto the lounge. Felicia was carried in like an angel, lavishly propped on some cushions, her hair resting on a fluffy pillow on the main lounge. Leo came from the kitchen. An aluminium packet rattled. I turned around as Dally groaned. Leo had two chips in one hand and one in his mouth—the rest were on the floor. His lips quivered when he realised how many people were inside his house.

James emerged, his face furious. "Leo, you took the good ... Wow! They've managed to ———"

They said the next word together. "*Multiply!*"

I pointed at Dally's legs. "Mind if he has the lounge for a bit? We had a rough morning!"

Leo nodded, "Harry, yer want us to get Father?"

Harry's eyes widened. "No! No, don't ... He can find out when he finds out. Until then, make yourselves useful, and get these two some water and blankets."

There was so much noise, I had to take a moment. I made sure Bailey kept an eye on Dally and left for the backyard.

Behind the timber fence, a few streets away, there was a giant lift. It scaled the hexadome with two Drewans inside. *Were these window*

CHAPTER 39: PULLING STRINGS

cleaners for the dome? Like a fire truck, the lift eventually reached its limit; when it stopped, the first of the long-haired blonds inside began drilling web-shaped sticks into the hexagonal glass frames. I could hear the drill bit rattle. The second stretched her arm and pulled a giant dreamcatcher. She grabbed its timber side and secured it on the dome. There were hundreds here in the Lower Hex, all different shapes, with feathers each representing a different colour from the eight major cities.

I rubbed my eyes, hoping for that soothing feeling you get when you're hot-headed and stressed. But no luck—I did find some gunk in my eyebrow. I took a deep breath. Although the air smelt thick, it was calming to breathe. Harry had a small backyard. Almost half the size of the barn Bailey used to sleep in. *Lucky Bailey's not a panda, we'd have nowhere to put him.* I enjoyed the temporary silence, knowing that tougher times were ahead.

A wisp of paper touched something soft. It's a hard noise to describe, but we all know it. Like when a piece of paper is swept by a subtle breeze. I looked at my feet. On the sage ferns, there was a paper card. I picked it up, and it had that familiar ink. **Let's end this, White Wolf! Tomorrow. Come find me at WonderWorks. Lvl 24!** I flinched, staring at the metal slates that covered the roof. There was no sign of the paper assassin. Not even a footprint.

"*Boo!*" I turned to the pitched sound. Taylah was behind a pale shrub in the middle of the yard. Her arms were in the air and her fingers were out like claws. I grinned and waved my arms at her.

"*Whoa! You got me* ... What are you doing out here?"

Taylah leaned in behind the shrub. She picked up Holdie and the wooden vinyl doll, its red dress a little worse for wear after all these years. "I'm teaching Maggie how to play catch!" she giggled.

"Maggie?"

"My doll, silly. The one Kyle gave me."

"Oh ..." I inhaled and clapped my hands together. "All right then. Show us what you got!" I dropped to my knees and awaited her throw. Taylah prepped her feet and threw the metal sphere. Its shine bounced off my gloves and we both smiled. I examined Holdie; he was still in a reasonable condition. I raised my eyebrows at the little

Drewan. "You didn't go through my bag, did you?" She rolled her eyes, avoiding my gaze.

"Maybe."

I opened the back door for Taylah. "Come on, grab Maggie. We're going in now."

Entering, I could hear Dally. "Look at you, party animal! Come here."

I turned the corner, Taylah hiding behind my hood. Dally had his knuckles on Bailey's crown, rubbing his fist along his scalp. Bailey laughed, trying to get off the ground. "Oh, and Ona! Gee, Faith, you found the whole group while I was out." He peeped at Faith, restricted under a white blanket. "Is that the princess?" He paused, putting his arms out. "Why am I not getting any hugs?" Zia succumbed to his exhausted excitement. Assonance also wrapped her arms around him, and that's when his face sagged. He stared at Felicia. "Oh, I see!" Her throat was still purple.

I crept inside, not making a single noise, and wrapped my left arm around Faith. "Faith, we should check on Olivia," Dally said. "Her meeting is bound to be over, and you promised we'd return those ——"

He turned his gaze to me. I'd never seen him so thrilled. "COME HERE, you sack of stale corn!" I brought Holdie with me, wrapping my arms around the idiot.

"By the Light," I laughed. "You smell like a week-old hay bale!" I pulled away as he spotted Holdie. I bit my lip. "I'll explain myself."

Zia nodded, "We should. Then we'll visit Olivia! Won't take a moment, Harry."

After telling the story of the WoodWood Brothers, Assonance volunteered to stay behind and care for Dally and Felicia. Although Dally was persistent, he hadn't adjusted to Zia's stern demands yet. He hid under his bedsheets as the princess' face turned red. Taylah was excited to stay behind with Assonance as Leo and James were scolded by Harry—Bailey winked at them and told the twins that this was a job for soldiers, that if anything happened, if Mr Doubtson returned from the mines, they'd need to call Harry immediately. They eventually nodded, and we left for the Between, the hexadome that sheltered WonderWorks' Drewan enterprise.

Chapter 39: Pulling Strings

As we marched, more dreamcatchers were being drilled into the domes. It was refreshing to see all the sharks, the fish and the seahorses without the endless maze of Redmer branches. The Between was a smaller hexadome that connected the Lower Hex with the Upper Hex. Harry strolled under the highway of hovering traffic. Metal vehicles coloured like the fish glided only a few metres above our heads, honking their horns and stopping at several sets of lights. I walked with Bailey at the end of the pack. It was nice to hear Zia and Faith laugh together as Harry led us through the metal towers.

"What's the point of roads and sidewalks if everything hovers?" I whinged.

"Hmm," Bailey shrugged. "Order, I guess. To maintain de old an' to figure out de new."

I couldn't help but smile. "I miss that kind of advice." I nudged his shoulder. "How's the human side of life treating you?"

He admired me with those brown eyes, still so cat-like. "Refreshin'! Kinda dandy to have my hands free, but I'm not as front-heavy as I used to be." He paused. "To be frank, I kinda miss it. De way I could tell who someone was jus' by their scent, how I was always warm an' snug no matter if it were de hotter seasons or de colder. Even trekkin' is all clammed up."

"So, you do miss it?" I asked.

He shook his head, "Somethin' like dat! I reckon it's still 'ere," he rubbed his crest. "Somewhere!"

A blue sign caught my eye. Like the beacon above us, in this glorious state, the WonderWorks logo was towered above us. We trudged along until its bronze metal walls surrounded us, and we entered the main atrium.

Zia sighed, "It's so cold in here! Have they even heard of a heater?" Harry and Faith both had an idea of where to go and we all crammed ourselves into an obnoxious blue glass elevator. An old Drewan lady behind me was squished, while Faith pressed the twenty-sixth button.

Harry scrunched his face. "We'll be needing to go higher than that if we're to see Mr Kingsleigh!" he said.

Faith raised her eyebrows. "But that's where I last saw Olivia. She said she had a meeting with him on that floor."

"Twenty-six!" Harry gawked. "That's the waiting room level. She would have been invited to his private waiting room if she were invited in. But my dad told me that as soon as he's ready, he takes you from floor twenty-six and does the actual meeting on floor fifty-two where his office is."

"He has a whole floor just for waiting?" I mused.

"Why did your dad have a meeting with Mr Kingsleigh?" Zia asked.

Harry smiled, "He and the miners were having trouble with the new conveyors WonderWorks provided. Dad thought it'd be more beneficial if he met the big guy himself!"

Through the glass cylinder, you could see each level pass. There were labs; Drewans in coats with clear plastic goggles tapping on grey pads and orange sparks; cubicles with Drewans in suits typing numbers and answering phones; and glass rooms with large sleek desks, countless chairs, whiteboards, and stands with diagrams and pie-charts. Then the elevator stopped, and the doors opened.

Bailey ducked out first as I followed with Harry. The walls of this level were a cold grey with blue and red carpet. The scent of a man's aftershave carried us to two dark oak doors with golden knobs. As we approached them, they automatically revealed the receptionist. The room was refined and well furnished, with lavender lounges, a crackling fireplace made of steel, a row of bookshelves that loomed so high I thought my neck would snap and a peculiar mix of metallic statues which stood in each corner of the room.

Mr Kingsleigh was shaking Olivia's hand in the centre of the room. "I'm so glad you've brought this to my attention. And again, apologies for the train. We searched up and down the Pilum Bridge and down the Jakoo River but only managed to find a handful of survivors. I'm glad you managed to arrive safely and in a timely fashion. I'd be lost without you, Councillor." His head tilted up as we stormed in. *Well, I did most of the storming, but Zia had a clear tenseness to her step.*

Mr Kingsleigh smiled. "Ah, the children." He looked to Olivia, a dimple creasing in his smile. "Your brother and his friends have managed to get here safely as well. Are they with you?"

Olivia's eyebrows sparkled. She turned to me and said something a

Chapter 39: Pulling Strings

little unsettling. "*Your Majesty!* Thank the Light you're okay …"

I crossed my arms. "Hold on a second. It's been weeks sin——"

Olivia bit her lip and raised an eyebrow. I looked away, grinning at Mr Kingsleigh, and spread my arms apart. "Since we've been in the company of Mr Kingsleigh!" I continued. "How's the business going, sir?"

"Yes! How are the latest *experiments* for the new tent-lets? We're a big fan, aren't we, Perry?" Faith added.

I nodded, "Oh, the biggest!"

He had a blue woollen suit with a crisp threaded tail and a fluffy white collar like he was wearing a wolf's fur around his neck. He placed his bony hands together, bruises tight around his knuckles and three rings. One on his right, a red pearl, and two on his left, a wedding ring and a thick silver band with the letter W.

He took a deep breath and pointed at us. "You must be Faith! Olivia's told me many tales about you. Good things, I promise." He paused and glanced at Harry and Bailey. "I'm glad you enjoy our products. We've worked around the clock to provide the best goods we can offer. But, please, for my sake, do not dismiss our essential services as *experiments*. Especially the many prototypes we seem to go through. Isn't that right, Olivia?"

He and Olivia laughed. It sounded forced. "My Alice would have liked this group. You Kelts are good comrades to have." He adjusted his blazer. "I shall leave you. I believe the Doubtson here knows the whereabouts of the exits. He may escort you, Councillor. Thank you, Harry! I'll see you next week! Simpalo." He smiled and left for the two doors behind him.

Exiting the elevator again in the atrium, Olivia hugged me. She smelt of trimmed grass. Baffled at Bailey being back to normal, she went through what we had at the beacon's light. Afterwards, she and Harry went to the front row of receptionists to investigate any *out-of-the-ordinary* purchases from the company.

Faith was unusually quiet. "What's wrong with you?" I asked.

She said one word that made my heart burn. "Juice! They ——"

"He's Papercut, Faith. Juice is Papercut! He's the one who killed Hartway, who's going to try and kill Mr Kingsleigh." I searched my surroundings. "Well, he won't. I'm going to stop him!"

She tilted her head to the left. "You're not going to do anything! Perry, I know Juice is Papercut. Dally and I bumped into him. He's a slave here, an experiment within these walls." She searched our surroundings. "And I think Mr Kingsleigh instructed him to kill the senator!"

"Faith, what are you …"

"Did you not feel it in there, Perry?" Zia asked. "Kingsleigh's office? He's got his hands in something. And whether he was the one who pulled the strings for Hartway's death, I don't trust the man."

"And he's got power in the militia!" Bailey took a step forward. "They've been a problem, have they not? You remember how he treated the poor general—scolded him for listening to other commands!"

Faith nodded, "Bailey's right! When Dally and I found Juice, he was bloodied, hiding from two militia members. He said that they had been treating him terribly. Like he was just a tool!"

"He was covered in blood!" I argued. "Faith, you didn't see what he did! He murdered thirteen of the militia this morning!" I calmed my voice. "Is he dead?" I asked.

Faith shook her head. "No, I … I healed him!"

"Why would you …"

"*'Cause he's our friend.* Just like Zia. Felicia … Kyle!" She crossed her arms.

Olivia returned. "I'm glad you found yourselves a local," she smiled. "Harry's agreed to escort us to a final destination. A little errand I'd like to run before my work here becomes a little more of a preoccupation. Shall we?"

Chapter 40

A Prideful Spy

Perry

We journeyed through the Between, past the South Side and into the Lower Tunnel. Like the rest of the Lower Hex, the West Side hexadome had small buildings with bronze roof slates and smaller steel shacks with giant rotating wheels. There was a decline in traffic. Only one or two hovercrafts glided past our heads.

"You really think Mr Kingsleigh's behind this? Behind Papercut? Behind all the murders? The train even?" I asked.

"It seems like a dandy conclusion," Bailey shrugged. "But, he could jus' be part of de show. Remember, Araidian had both Odd an' Irene behind his crooked schemes. Maybe Mr Kingsleigh's jus' playin' his part."

"He's right. There could be someone else," Zia suggested. "Where the heck are we going?"

Olivia turned to the princess. "Somewhere to calm your senseless theories. Now, I understand that Charles may look like a menacing hunk of stale corn, but he's had it tough since his daughter's death! Come—we're going to see someone who might have some answers."

Harry slowed his step as the glimmer of the sunset above the ocean shimmered into the hexadome's glass. We had reached an extra cluster of houses, each with walls of thick laminated bamboo pillars. His shoes knocked hard against the rubble path and he took out his phone. With two fingers, Harry pinched at the black screen.

"This should be it," he said. "Are yer sure you told me the right address? I think there be another Ando Road in the Upper Hex!"

Olivia tapped his shoulder. "No. You've been a great escort, Harry! This is as I imagined. Who knew? Follow!"

Olivia turned into a narrow driveway. A bridge arched over our heads; little droplets of water dribbled onto the moulding timber below our feet. The bridge was made of vines, each a diluted blue, purple or red. We all crept lightly as Harry's face became pale. "Yikes, I don't like these vines."

"Why are dey so colourful?" Bailey asked.

"They're the result of when coral adapts to an unpredictable environment. An evolution, I suppose," Harry explained. "But the council usually cuts them down. They grow fast. Wouldn't want them to cover the hexadome's glass."

I turned to see that Faith had latched onto my right hand. She smiled and pulled away. "Sorry! Old habit."

I took her hand and smiled. "That's fine! Just let me know if my hold's too tight!" She smirked and Olivia stopped. We'd reached the end. A grey garage door shone in front of us.

Olivia put her right knuckles against the door. She knocked three times and chanted, "White tears, white heart, white knife. I, the Kelt of the wolf, come bearing gifts." Nothing happened. She turned to us and her eyes drooped. "Well, that didn't work! Guess he's not answering. Let's go!"

Zia stormed to the door. "You take us an hour out to the middle of nowhere just to turn back and go home? If this so-called someone has a theory about Drewmora's destruction, I wanna hear it!" Zia knocked on the door. *Damn, even my insides get nervous when she lashes out like that. I swear, if Odd's inside, I'm gonna kill him!* "White that, white this," Zia chanted. "Let's get over the Kelton procession and just open the door! Do you hear me?"

Harry nudged Bailey. "She always this demanding?"

"Always! But something usually triggers her." Bailey said.

The door opened. You could hear the wheels spinning as a chain lifted the metal sleet from the ground, rotating it under the ceiling. Behind stood a man with a brown beard with grey patches as white as

Chapter 40: A Prideful Spy

the heaviest snow, emerald green eyes, torn clothes, two bruised bare feet and a glimmering white koala crest. Without a crown, without a row of Kelton Guards, without any glass—Lord Kelton hid behind the sleet. I joined Bailey and Harry.

"That explains the trigger."

Olivia lowered herself to her knee. If it wasn't for Faith's hand, I don't think I would have dropped so fast. By the time my right knee aligned with my chest, the only people standing were Zia and Harry. I had never seen Zia so still, so focused on what was in front of her. She tightened her fierce grip around her white glove.

"So this is where you've been!" She scanned him from top to bottom. "Unshaved—no shoes, simple rags."

"Zia." The king said calmly.

"Why didn't you come home? Mother's been worried sick. I thought you were dead. By the Light, I'd be better off if you were! Look at you. *Pathetic.* Why are you here, hiding from your people? We've been wounded, killed, attacked, and you hide under the glass of Drewmora's domes!"

The king's voice was brusque. "I have my reasons. The world is not always as simple as you dream it to be! I cannot return without triumph, not after I've failed my people … And from what Olivia has told me, you've done no better, meandering in the Forest of Farbe while your mother maintains the peace between the Kelts and the other major cities. To say I'm disappointed would be a mere cry to how I really feel! You've ———"

"I was held captive for over a year!" Zia yelled. She approached her father. "Titan lost his stomach. He cried for you, night after night, in pain. And all you can say is that you're *disappointed?* I am your daughter!" She looked away from him and lowered her voice. "I've been raised expecting protection, royalty, perseverance … Hope! Yet when it came time to be rescued, it was not the Kelton Guard who saved me."

The king pointed at me. I looked away. They were like any other father and daughter arguing, but their royal blood deemed me unworthy of watching. "And has Perry not been rewarded by being sworn into the Kelton Guard? Those were my direct orders to Roofus.

My direct orders—so that a trusted member of my alliance could lead you *here*, safely!" He sighed, standing proudly in front of Zia. "Are you not before me? Is what I see an illusion? Have I not managed to rid you of Araidian's tyranny so that you may stand here? I understand this is not the Royal Hall of Glass but does my face before yours not illustrate the lengths I have gone for you to be here?"

Zia was speechless for once. She looked away, muttering to herself. She looked at Olivia. "You were the spy this whole time? But …"

"Why do you stutter, young one?"

Zia had tears under her eyes. "Because I can't think! I have no thoughts and you would know that if you'd been there the day they vanished. The day the beacon took them from me. The beacon you pledge by blood to protect …" She burst into tears.

The king leaned down. He wiped away Zia's tears and rubbed her cheek. "Come now, my little koala. The world is too dark to hold your tears of light. I tried my ——"

"Exactly, you tried! And you still have no idea of what I lost. You're not my father. My father died the day Kelton Whide fell!"

Zia stormed off under the rainbow vines. Harry dodged out of her way and called her name. He gulped, seeing the king's gaze, and jogged after her. *Geez, if I were him, I would have run too.*

Lord Kelton gestured for us to stand. His face was still grim, but he seemed almost relieved. "Please, take rest. We have many things to discuss. Drewmora is in grave danger."

Faith took a step forward. "Your Highness, if I may?"

He nodded.

"What do you know about this danger? Same goes for you, Olivia. Does it have something to do with those masked soldiers infecting the Full Sea with the bags of dust?"

"I'm afraid so. But it is much more complicated then dust and sea salt." The king and I locked eyes. "What is on your mind, Perry?"

"My Liege, I am not the same boy who would visit the Castle of Glass with my father during the winter months. I am grateful for your decision to make myself, Faith and even Bailey a part of your guard, but why are you here? Maybe Her Royal Majesty has taken a toll on me, but why have you not returned home, and why do you wish to save another town that is not your own?"

He smiled, "You've answered your own question, wolf! The day Araidian attacked, he attacked my men, my castle, my brothers and I. Your mother foresaw his betrayal, but I did not believe her. It was the first time in my life I felt utterly vulnerable. I was a failure that day and I've been a failure ever since. They held me captive at the Statue of Hope and shined the beacon's light right before my eyes. Failures do not deserve to bear the crest of white light, especially that of the royal koala! So I cannot return, not until I have redeemed myself."

I turned to Olivia. "And you've known! This whole time, you knew where he was, what he was doing, and you never thought once to tell Zia!"

"I had my orders!" Olivia said. "There were moments, especially before the train, when I wanted to tell her, but simply convincing her to go to Drewmora on her own accord was hard enough."

I believe my cheeks must have turned white. "Well, aren't you and Giuseppe just made for each other. Orders this, orders that!"

"Orders are good, Perry. Trust me, I'd know!" Bailey whispered. He bowed. "Your Highness. I may be an Ever, but I lived under your _____"

"I know who you are. Bailey Giggles," the king grinned. "I did sign your papers the day we gave you to the Caduca household. And from what I understand, if you had not led Perry and Faith to Everbreen, my daughter would still be held captive by that miserable tyrant, Araidian!"

Bailey nodded.

"Enough with the debating!" Lord Kelton sighed, "There is an infection that surrounds us as we speak. I believe this dome is at risk of an outbreak."

"What kind of outbreak? Like a virus?" Faith asked.

The king shook his head. "Much worse, I'm afraid! Insanity ... Someone wishes to kill all the Drewans in the Lower Hex." Lord Kelton took a moment of silence. I wanted to ask so many questions, but a conversation with the king was no conversation to be had.

Weirdly, Faith was calm. "How?" she wondered. "That's more

than a third of the Drewan population. Your Highness, who wishes to cause such chaos? Why?"

The king pulled up his right sleeve, its end muddied. "That I do not know. Mr Kingsleigh has invested a lot of time and money into the Tinkette celebration of dreams. He's even had some of General Ko's militia up in skylifts, drilling the Redmer timber of those dreamcatchers into the hexadomes. Tenses my skin just mentioning them. I believe these ... *dreamcatchers* are a part of this destruction."

The king stumbled out from his hidden concrete hole. "From what Martosia has informed me, they will be using illusion."

"Illusion?" Olivia questioned.

The king rubbed his crest, its light dim. "Yes. You've heard me correctly. *Illusion*. My son can vouch for me. Perry, you've experienced this illusion."

The king and I locked eyes again. I know why Father enjoyed his company—I felt wanted. "The Cabana!"

"From what I've heard, Charles was using the club and Oddington as a test for his real plans."

"You know Odd?" My voice was loud, as though the king were beneath me. I stuttered, "My Liege, what are you insinuating? How do you know Odd?"

Surprisingly, Lord Kelton smiled at me. "You saw masked lunatics, correct?"

I nodded.

"You were poisoned by a very powerful hallucinogenic designed for demigods. The masked people were never there! The Cabana was only open that one night ... Tell me, Perry, did you have something to drink that night?"

I was taken aback. "Yeah, Dally bought the first round. We both drank Tinkette Club."

Faith grinned with nostalgia as Bailey gawked. "An' I got conked in de face with a bucket-load de moment I stuck my noggin into de shindig! Straight after dose masked fellas were after us an' we had to skedaddle. Even Odd was shook!"

Lord Kelton clicked his fingers. "Exactly. You all had some sort

Chapter 40: A Prideful Spy

of interaction with liquid inside the club. As a result, you were chased by those masked ones."

"And now we're surrounded!" Faith muttered.

Olivia stood next to the king. "So they're going to try and saturate us all in water, make us go insane and wait 'til we all kill each other."

"But I jus' swam in dat water dis morning! I swear to de spirits, I did! Felicia an' Assonance too." Bailey watched the driveway and murmured an unfamiliar name. "*Georgia!* She wished for our safety!"

"And what was this Georgia's gift?" Lord Kelton asked.

"She could grant any wish for fifty-two minutes," Bailey said.

I picked at the dirt under my nail, "You can buy a lot of things in fifty-two minutes."

"That is not how a Bellcurve's gift works, wolf!" The king turned to me. "The Ever's theory may be correct. It could have been that the prophet intended for his arrival this morning or the mere fact that the water isn't poisonous yet. Which means they're waiting!"

"Waiting for what?" Faith asked.

"An opening ..." The king examined the hexadome's glass.

He seemed as though his eyes were stuck to the sky. "A celebration. Just like Kelton Whide. Just like our Tomorrow Festival."

"Another tyranny?" Olivia asked.

Lord Kelton shook his head. "Unfortunately, no. Not a tyranny, a complete renewal. Only a small handful, mainly the people here in this conversation know this." The king strolled into his garage. "Olivia and I will need time to plan, to organise, to spread the word as far as we can. Us five right here are the most crucial to Drewmora's survival. We are their only hope! Otherwise, I will never be able to return home!" He waved his right palm at us like we were servants. "Leave us!" he ordered. "We will inform you of our plan tomorrow. Meet us here, midday. By then, the attack will have occurred, and we will have the best opportunity to save everyone."

I tried arguing, and so did Faith, but the king was determined to get on with his plans.

He closed his garage door. Olivia stood in front of it with a white face. "You heard the king. Here, tomorrow." She approached me and wrapped her arms around my hood. "Stay safe. I will feel you." She rubbed at her crest.

I poked mine. "I'll feel you too. Omehwai, right?"

She rubbed my hair—I wished I could feel it. "Omehwai! Now go, Perry! We are closer than ever." She grinned at Faith. "You protect him. Okay? I know you'll do good. *Midday!* This will all be over. Tell the princess I'm sorry." Olivia hugged Bailey. He was as shocked as me. "And you, keep them all safe!"

Bailey grinned, "I will!"

"I know." Olivia looked into his brown eyes. "You are as much a Kelt as you are an Ever. You deserve to know that."

We ventured under the rainbow vines. Zia's laugh echoed down the street. We had no idea what was awaiting us tomorrow. Olivia called out, "Remember! Midday, tomorrow. All of you!" All I could think about was Juice. I was going to beat him tomorrow. I was going to stop his madness and end him for good. *I was going to win!*

Chapter 41

Promises

Faith

We returned to Harry's in a void of silence. Dally leaned against a grey wall, his head stiff beneath a painting of a boat in the waterways of Central City, laughing as Felicia laid on Assonance's lap. Taylah had plopped herself in the centre, her legs spread on the carpet.

"And Mrs Nixon pointed at Perry and was like, *I beg your pardon, Mr Caduca!*" Dally smirked, twirling his fingers. "Perry pointed at the glad-wrap between his fingers and just said, *Oh, don't you want the sandwich?* She turned red the minute he stopped speaking and screamed about how *this was a maths class, not food technology.* I just stood up, snatched the damn bread and shoved it in my mouth. We both ended up in detention for two lunches." He cracked himself up.

Felicia smiled, "I remember that. You had to sit two doors away from each other."

Dally pointed at the blond Kelt. "Yeah. You came up to ask Gawthorne about cheer. Couldn't stop laughing at us."

"You did cheerleading?" Assonance asked.

"For sport." Felicia's eyes leapt to Zia. The princess was crestfallen; her eyes lingered on the beige carpet.

"Oh, there you are!" Felicia's face dropped as Zia continued to ignore everyone, not saying a word. "What happened to her?"

Perry sighed, "We found the king!"

"What? Lord Kelton?" Dally asked. "The old knobhead who used to make my mum pay taxes after kicking Dad out?"

Perry couldn't bring himself to respond.

"Yes, that *knobhead*, Dally!" I affirmed. "He's been hiding here ———"

Harry took charge. "And he's spreading the word on what the prophet told us. He be making a plan and is going to save us! I hope he tells Mayor Pythalone and General Ko. That'll save us. We'd better start packing some things. Best we be safe if Mr Kingsleigh plans to kill everyone in the Lower Hex. Heck, we're right in the middle!" He stumbled forward, raising his voice, "Leo, James! Is Father home? We need to get a move on. Boys?"

James emerged from the kitchen. "Hiya, Dally! Think we found some games yer might like. I got *Psychonauts*, the new *Call of Gears* or … Leo, what was the other one?"

Leo popped his head from the corner. "*Manhunter*. It looks kinda whacko!"

Dally took the cases from James. "Thanks!" He put them beside him on the couch. "But I think it'd be best if we played them later."

James frowned, "That's okay." Perry caught his eye. "That reminds me. These two kids about a year younger than us came and knocked on the door. Said they were looking for you, Perry, and your girlfriend and the Ever!"

"What kids?" Perry asked.

Leo stepped forward. "A boy with light-blond hair and lots of freckles and a real nice-looking girl. She was tanned with browny-yellow hair."

James nodded, "Aye, nice on the eyes!"

Zia stormed up to them. "You saw Titan and Teala!" James and Leo gulped. Had they seen Zia's wrath before? "How long ago? Do you know where they went?"

The two Drewans shook their heads. "Not too sure," Leo mumbled.

"But they said they'd be back later. Even promised."

Zia threw her hands in the air. "By the Light, why is everyone useless today? We'd be better off if we all just died on that stupid train!"

The princess stormed into the kitchen. Harry rolled his eyes. "I just spent all afternoon making her happy just for you two to muck

Chapter 41: Promises

it up!" He followed her. I could hear their raised voices in the next room. Perry was speechless, staring at the front window. The moon had set its beam upon the Full Sea; its glistening white light bobbed with the waves.

"Ah!" Felicia said. "Seems like Lord Kelton and our princess still get along. Just like old times!"

I giggled at the remark. It *was* just like old times.

Assonance asked for more details, and Bailey joined them, discussing what the king had told us.

The twins were more tanned than me, with the smoothest skin, pale, fair hair and blue eyes that matched their crests. They stood tall when I approached. "You two shouldn't worry about the princess, she's ———"

"Moody?" James guessed.

I smiled, "Something like that ... Thank you for telling us. And thank you for caring for our friends."

"What about me?" a little voice said. It was higher than Teala's, almost like the days from before Araidian's Tyranny. I turned to Taylah. She had Kyle's doll between her legs.

I leaned to her side. She looked identical to her three brothers but with dark scarlet hair. "Why, you've been the greatest help of them all. You cared for Perry, Kyle, Zia and Maggie here." I pointed at the doll and she grinned.

"And how do yer know that?"

"Because Perry told me. And ———"

The doorbell rang.

Its metallic rattle was louder than most. The whole house went silent, even Zia and Harry closed their mouths. Bailey pulled open the door. The streetlights from outside bathed his face as he said, "Doubtson residence. How may I help you?" On the other side, I heard laughter.

"Now that's a phrase I thought I'd never hear again!" a girl's voice chirped.

Before Bailey had time to reveal their names, we all crowded the doorway. On the concrete porch, standing with dirty shoes above a

Welcome straw mat, Teala and Titan waited for us. Both of their faces seemed thinner and more mature. I felt tears building behind my eyes.

"Well, can we come in?" the prince asked.

After we all hugged and reunited, we gathered in the dining room. Teala had something important to tell us. Harry bumped into me, putting his phone to his ear. "Hiya ... Dad? What's up?" He wandered into the lounge room. The blue orb shone against his jumper. A mothball stench caught my nose as he rested his hand on his hip. "And what do you expect me to cook for Perry and Her Majesty? They can't live on frozen fish fingers and pizza ... So you're not coming home. Are yer sure? ... Aye, but we need you more! Okay, okay! Stay safe. And please, for me, try and get home as early as yer can. I have a bad feeling about tomorrow ... No, that not be the omens talking. No, there's no salt under my chin, I jus' ... I love you. I'll let the others know. Okay, bye!"

His eyes met mine and he frowned, "My father."

I moved away from the wall. "Sounds like you really care about him!"

"Aye!" Harry nodded, putting his phone away. "He's had it tough, especially when Mum passed away. Let's go see what the two newbies want, eh?"

I followed him, hearing Teala's voice. "The train was no accident! Someone sabotaged the Tinkette enchantment Senator Hartway blessed my dreamcatcher with, which absorbed a certain darkness across the Pilum Bridge. I should apolo——"

"Hold on, hold on!" Perry instructed. "How on earth did you and Titan manage to get here? And how'd you know to look here once you managed to get into the city?"

Titan laughed, "Well, Odd snatched the stupid dreamcatcher outta my hands, and it blew up. Next thing I know, the dummy jumps on Teala and me and the whole train was a wreck. After that, we got off in a little town near the swamp. What was it called?"

"Penmond!" Teala said. "We rested in Penmond for a day."

"The train still worked for you?" Zia asked.

"By the time Teala awoke from the explosion, it was nightfall. Odd held me back. I would have jumped off ——"

CHAPTER 41: PROMISES

"And broken your leg? Or worse!" Zia argued.

"No! To go back and look for you, but Odd said we'd be better off reaching Drewmora."

Teala nodded, "He said he knew you'd all make it here soon enough and, well, here you are."

"Why'd you get off if the train's destination was here?" Felicia wondered.

"Why do you think?" Titan exclaimed. "The corny demigod got nervous once the bottom half of the train blew up. And after all his warnings, we were off the next day. So much for ———"

"Odd grew suspicious of the militia!" Teala explained, cutting him off. "He said that to be safe, we'd best depart at Penmond. He had been meaning to collect something from an old friend or something along those lines."

"Oh, the cat!" Titan muttered. "Yeah, we ended up looking after this orange cat for a few days but lost the dang thing! We did a whole lotta stuff, but that's not important. We don't have much time!"

Their story was honest, but one thing was missing; and by the way Dally had crossed his arms, I supposed he'd noticed it too.

"And why isn't Odd telling us this?" I asked.

"Agreed. Why isn't he here to order us around? Where is he?" Dally added.

Titan and Teala shrugged in unison.

"He said he had a meeting. Wandered off somewhere and gave us an address," Teala said.

Harry urged, "Was it for my house? How'd he …"

Teala shook her head, "No! No, we saw ———"

"My dad! The king, we saw him!" Titan blurted, "And I told him the story of Irene's Family, Everbreen, the Town of Tents, Central City, Parliament House and the train. He told us about Mr Doubtson, whoever that is, and said we should give him and his children a visit."

"What are you trying to tell us?" I asked.

Teala stepped forward, "Well, if my dreamcatcher caused this much trouble, if it had the power to tear us apart and destroy three train carriages—imagine the power one of those hanging on the hexadomes would have!"

Bailey mumbled, "Ease up. Are ya sayin' …"

Titan couldn't stay quiet. "They're all going to blow! Every single one of those dreamcatchers is made out of the same redmer timber as Teala's. Odd even said they had similar Tinket engravings."

Leo raised his hand, "That's 'cause Mayor Pythalone has a lot of respect for the pink city!"

"Aye!" James pushed Leo from his spotlight. "Every year we hang 'em 'round, but not all of them are made from redmer. Only the little ones. The big ones are a sort of plastic, I think."

"Dat's right! From what Lord Kelton said, Mr Kingsleigh doesn't wanna drown us. He wants to jus' wet us enough so we all go nutty from de poison," Bailey added.

"Poison? We swam in that water this morning!" Assonance argued.

"And even if these … *explosive dreamcatchers* manage to pierce through the hexadome's glass, Drewmora has emergency shielding," Harry rubbed his chin. "A protective layer of metal should surround each glass hexagon in a matter of minutes."

"A matter of minutes is long enough to saturate half the dome in knee-deep water," Felicia pointed out.

"But once there's a breach, Father says the vents should kick in twice as strong and suck all the water into the Full Sea!" Harry explained.

"Is dere a way to turn dese emergency systems on?" Bailey asked.

Harry searched us all. Perry was a shadow, deep in thought. "The only ones who can turn on such important protocol are the mayor, the senator and General Ko!"

Perry turned his head to Harry. "So we find the general and we stop this whole thing. Once those protective protocols kick in like Harry said, the shielding layer of metal will close any holes from the explosive dreamcatchers, and the water will get sucked into the ocean."

"And we can tell the general Mr Kingsleigh's plans and he can help us round up the infected before things get outta control," Dally added.

Zia's grey eyes widened. "*No!* We can't trust the general!"

Dally waved his arms in the air. "Why not? You got a better idea?"

"No, I would have said my idea out loud if I had one! The general, he ... he let Papercut into the House of Senates."

"What do you mean, he let him in? Did he just open the door for the poor senator?" Dally asked.

"He pushed open the back vent. I saw him! It was the same vent Papercut flew through to enter," Zia's throat was raw.

"No, no, no! General Ko would never stoop down to that paper guy's level," Harry uttered. "He's an honourable man. I'm sorry, Yer Majesty, but that can't be true!" His face was a creamy white, as though he was scared of his own words.

Dally crossed his arms. "I'm with Harry! The general is the best and most efficient way for us to save Drewmora. I'm not letting something you might have seen change that!"

Zia moved to Felicia. "Do you believe me?"

Felicia avoided her eyes. "It's plausible. But I agree with Dally. We do not have much time, and if it is only your eyes, unfortunately, that is not enough evidence to fully calculate a conclusion."

Zia waved her arms at Assonance. "Come on, Ona! You love politics. Can't you see how I'm telling the truth?"

Assonance stuttered, turning red the second the princess laid eyes on her. Titan said he didn't care if she was telling the truth. Teala merely suggested that Odd might have seen the same thing. Bailey kicked at his feet.

"I'm sorry, Zia! But dere's no other way outta dis!" he said. "It's either we find de general or let de whole Lower Hex drown in insanity!"

I had never seen tears like these, so clear and bubbly, drip down Zia's cheeks. She tugged on Perry's hood. "You have to believe me, Perry! We can't trust that stale corn! He tried to kill us—you, me and Kyle—at the inn. You remember. You know!"

Perry frowned at her. He stared at the ground and, without a single word, walked to the backyard. Zia called for his name, but still no answer.

"You know I'm telling the truth." She looked at me. "You believe me, right?"

I grinned. It was cold at the edges of my cheeks, but I tried my hardest to keep my mouth tense. "Of course I do, Zia! But you only saw the moment when he opened the vent for Juice to sneak in. Odd and Perry told me that Juice had three targets. Maybe the general was the third." The general wasn't the third target; that poor soul was standing in this room. I wanted to agree with Zia, I really did! But General Ko was the only plausible way for us to help Drewmora. She pushed past Dally and Bailey. Harry reached out for her, "Zia, we can still think of a new way to approach the general. Especially if yer don't ——"

She slapped his hand away, her eyes swollen from tears. "Don't talk to me, Drewan! You're worse than my father!" She pulled her journal from her jacket and slammed the front door.

I felt this stinging in my belly—it made my stomach heave. Titan walked to the front of the house. "I'll go talk to her." he grinned, "*Please*, don't wish me luck. This is only the scariest thing I've done since stealing Teala's stupid dreamcatcher!" Titan left.

Teala rolled her eyes. It was nice to see her little face again, those green eyes. She smiled at me. "I'd go talk to Perry, but I don't think now's the time. You saw his face. I don't know what's going on, but can you?"

"Of course, Tea! No need to ask me. I'm glad you're safe and well. You should talk to Bailey. I think he missed you the most." I headed for the back door, "Oh, and when I return, we're spilling the tea over all the new plants you've found for the collection!"

Teala laughed, skipping to Bailey, Assonance and James.

Outside, the subtle breeze was freezing. Steam drifted from my warm breath as the stars twinkled above the Full Sea. Just like how Odd had described it all those years ago. It truly was *a city under a constant moving painting*. The clarity soothed my mind, the fresh air an eye-opener to the details in Harry's tiny backyard.

Perry had taken refuge against a dark oak pillar that held the square terrace a few centimetres off the ground. I lightened my steps, the timber creaks becoming distant. Perry was too preoccupied to notice.

CHAPTER 41: PROMISES

Clenched in his black glove was a cue card. I read Juice's words and said, "Tell me you're not thinking about fighting him!"

He turned around, his green eyes sticking to me like I'd caught him dealing drugs. He stuttered, "I don't know! You heard Zia. We can't trust the general. Heck, we can't even trust Odd! So maybe I do want to fight him. Just so I can be alone! So I don't have to tell Taylah that she might die tomorrow." He sighed. "I just ... I want to go back home. I don't want this pressure of saving kingdoms, saving all these people who have nothing to do with me or my crest."

"But we can't!" I said.

"Exactly, Faith. And the day we left, I told everyone in the Town of Tents that we'd return with Kyle. That we'd have a new member in our family!"

"And we will." I rubbed my fingers along Perry's cheek. "We'll find Kyle, we'll save Harry and Taylah, we'll go back and sleep in our tent-let, and things will go back to how they were."

Perry clasped my hand. "No, they won't! We just argued with Zia because we know we have one shot at saving this city. And maybe that shot needs me to run off and fight Papercut!"

"You mean Juice!" I pulled my hand away. "He's still our friend, Perry! He's still the same Kelt we went to school with."

"I need to stop him!" Perry raised his voice. "I'm the only one who can! Not Dally, not Bailey or Zia. Me!"

"Why?" I begged. "Ever since you saw him in Everbreen, you've had this vendetta! Why do you need this? Tell me."

A tear drizzled down his cheek. "Because he could hurt you! If any of you are there, he will hurt you! I can't let that happen again. I'm the one who needs to get hurt. Not them!"

All of a sudden, my palm had collided with his pale cheek.

He frowned, "Why'd you slap me?"

I raised my palm again. His head bent to the side—it was like a raging fire.

He continued to stutter. I slapped him a second and then a third time.

When I lifted my hand again, he caught my wrist, holding my

dragon's white light under his glove. "Stop! Geez, what's gotten into you?" I tried to break free. Perry's voice was high-pitched, "Calm down, Faith! I'm sorry. By the Light, if you don't want me to go, I ——"

"Did you feel it?" I demanded.

"Feel what?"

"The slap! Did you feel it?"

He looked away, rubbing his cheek. "No, no I didn't!"

I snatched my hand from his grip. "But your cheek's red. So you might not be able to feel it, but your skin still turns red if it's hit. Your flesh still bleeds if it's cut. You still die if that light on your wrist turns off! Just like me, Bailey, Zia, Ona and everyone else in that house. Now, it's been a long day, and the last thing I want to do is slap you again." I took hold of his gloved hands. "We're a team, you and I. Those people in that house are family—you just admitted that!" I pulled him close, his chest warm. "Promise me you won't go! Promise me you won't fight Juice, or Papercut, or whatever he is. Friend or foe! There will be another way to help him. There has to be. Please. Promise me you won't go."

He held onto me like a shield. "I promise!"

Chapter 42

Uninvited Interruptions
Faith

I felt a gentle shove, so sudden, it woke me from my slumber. When my eyes remembered the world, Harry's tanned Drewan hands were shaking my shoulder.

"Oh, crud! Gee, sorry 'bout that. You're not Zia. Back to bed you go. All good there, Faith!" He smiled and leapt over me. I picked myself up, rubbing my eyes. The thin blanket wrapped around my legs reeked of dog.

Titan yelped. "What the? Who did that?" He sat up, his blanket slipping to reveal half a sock on his right foot. His face was blank as he scratched his hair, "Was that you? Wait, this isn't where I fell asleep." He stood and took a few steps forward. "I was next to Bailey and—Whoa!" He toppled over.

"Argh, Titan!" Assonance sat up abruptly, her hair covering her face. Her shoulders dropped as she saw my tired self. "Morning, Faith! Did our royal highness wake you too?"

Before I could answer, Zia stormed into the lounge room. The beige carpet was covered by an array of green woven blankets, thin blue and red fleece sheets, and a few thicker covers made from white cotton. Zia stood on top of them, unamused. "After the argument you caused, Mr Doubtson, I don't think so!"

Harry rushed behind her. "How many times do I have to apologise? I just wanna cheer yer up. It won't take long."

"No! I'm not going. Especially not alone!" the princess argued.

Titan stood, "And why is my beloved sister already angry so early in the morning?"

Zia pointed at Harry. "This stale corn wants to show me his gift! Like I care. After the hassle you caused with your little comment on the general ——"

"Don't blame that whole debate on me," Harry bickered.

I looked at Assonance, then at the brawling couple. "I'll come!" I said. "Who knows? Harry might have that special gift we need to defeat Mr Kingsleigh and save the Lower Hex!"

Zia looked at me, surprised.

I was more surprised by Titan. "I want to come too. Can't let Zia have all the fun!"

When I stood, Perry, Bailey and Teala were missing. Zia said she had seen them upstairs with Taylah and the twins. I wanted to check on Perry, but we didn't have time. Harry said his father would be home soon. Assonance agreed to come, having felt cabin fever yesterday, she wanted to see a little more of Drewmora before the Lower Hex was covered in knee-deep water. Dally and Felicia were in good enough hands with Bailey.

We journeyed down Harry's street. The road was like home, black and rough with refined concrete kerbs. There were so many Drewans—kids playing hockey on the street, the elderly washing their plants or waving to their neighbours and a little one who looked fresh out of the womb. At the end, near the cul-de-sac, a small hidden pathway was covered in those colourful vines from yesterday.

Assonance had a smile on her face. "It's nice here!" she mused. "Maybe after all of this, we should come back for a holiday. Heck, I know Felicia would like that!" She laughed to herself. "And I know, Faith, the Town of Tents is on the other side of the continent, but I can ask Yuri!"

"Yuri? Your brother?" I wondered.

"You remember!" She looked at me as though I were a ghost.

"Of course I remember, Ona! He was important to you. What's Yuri got to do with us coming here?"

Chapter 42: Uninvited Interruptions

Assonance looked away, still grinning. "He's got himself a silkin' zeppelin, just like the ones from home. He and his friends gave us a ride on it. We could be back to the town in a matter of hours. Actually, ask Felicia, she's better at that kinda math."

I couldn't help but ask, "So you and her are pretty serious? Like, are you a couple or ..."

She laughed, "I don't know. Like, we messed around, and she kissed me first, but I ... I'm not sure."

"Well, would you like to be in a relationship with her?" I asked.

"Of course! It's just ——"

"Take my advice. Felicia's a pretty girl! Snatch her up while you can, especially if you think it's right. You don't want to regret anything, you know. Before it becomes too late!"

"And you gotta wait for the right moment," Titan blurted. "'Cause girls can be moody. Like, Zia's a nutbag one minute, then the next she's crying, and after that, I'm scared for my life. Then she's a nutbag again!"

I stared at the little prince. "And what do you know about relationships?"

"HEY! I HEARD THAT, TITAN!" Zia yelled.

"Me? Oh, this and that! I'm no scientist, but I was stuck with Teala for over a week. Maybe I don't get relationships, but I do get something about women."

"And what's that, prince?" Assonance asked with a grin.

"It's that I don't have a clue as to what goes on in your heads. You're like ... what's something Odd would say—women are like rivers, while men are like waterfalls. We're one and the same, but we men make rapids and fall just to land in your laps or something along those lines. Gee, ask Odd next time you see him. He'll ——"

Titan covered his ears with his hands and flinched. He groaned as if his ears just popped. I went to his aid, but Zia's scream was a lot louder. Harry held her, the two flinching. After a moment, Titan's face went back to normal, his eyes blinking rapidly.

"Tye, are you okay?" I asked.

He cracked his neck. "Yeah! I just ——"

"Felt something!" Zia said. Harry held her side and she looked at him. "How much further?"

He searched ahead. "We're almost there. This way!"

Little sunflowers sprouted near my boots. We had entered a patch of dark-green sage. The scent of pollen was strong between the light red and orange canopies. Trees of dark oak with bloody sap were scattered around a lush field with a sandstone path. Harry glanced around, making sure the empty park was extra empty. I was surprised no Drewans were here.

"Just like Hilly Park in Kelton, huh?" Zia cheered, grinning at Titan and me. She slapped Harry's bottom. "Well, Bluey. What've you got?"

Harry exhaled and turned to face us. Assonance sat on the closest bench, her knees cracking when she adjusted herself.

"Take your time, Harry!" I said.

He took another breath and his blue crest ignited like a fire. "Alrighty! Gee, I don't know guys. Yer sure?"

Zia licked her lips, "It was your idea!"

"Beggars can't be ... whatever that saying is!" Titan added.

"No judgement here, Harry! It's not like you're going to turn into a raven ... Right?" Assonance joked. Harry nodded, his lips tightly pressed together. He chuckled, "Aye, no raven here!"

He pulled out his left hand as though he were holding a tray. He wiggled his fingers. They stopped, his bones tensing as a dark grey cloud loomed over us. The wind picked up, blowing my hair as Harry held onto the invisible energy in his hand. Titan bit at his nails, Assonance clasped onto her bench and Zia crossed her arms. I waited for the lightning to strike. Harry closed his eyes, took a deep breath and let go. His arms dropped to his side, his eyes opened, and his shoulders relaxed. Zia and I looked at each other. *There was nothing.* Harry didn't do anything.

The clouds separated as the sun shined behind the Full Sea.

Zia widened her eyes, "I'm sorry, but was I meant to be amazed by that? It was a cute performance—very dramatic—but what was it you exactly did?"

CHAPTER 42: UNINVITED INTERRUPTIONS

Harry's brows dropped. He pointed at the ground. "My shadow! It's not ... Titan's talking to my shadow!" The black silhouette that had once rested under Harry was now shaking Titan's hand. Titan stood back as the dark figure danced in and out from three dimensions back into two. The shadow waved at Zia and me.

It looked at the ground and leapt into it like it was paint at the end of a brush. Being one with the grass, it approached our shadows, their elongated figures swaying in the sage.

"I call him Hairy," Harry noted. Titan and Assonance grinned.

Zia was unamused once again. "Well, no wonder you couldn't make it into the militia! He's not very menacing, is he?"

The dark reflection of Harry leapt from the grass and, like a statue forming itself before us, it stood face to face with Zia. Hairy, the shadowy figure, didn't have many words, only exaggerated body movements. He crossed his arms and looked away from Zia.

"Zia!" I scoffed. "Don't say things like that! Who knows, maybe Hairy's really good at brawling!"

"I agree!" Assonance cheered. "And if it were sunset and Harry made him at a good angle, Hairy could be twice, maybe three times your size. Think about it, Zi!"

"It definitely feels real!" Titan walked to his sister's side. He shivered, "Man, is it me or did it just get really cold here?"

I searched both Assonance's and Harry's eyes. It wasn't cold at all and they both knew it. "Hairy, don't mind the princess," Harry said. "Do that thing that makes Taylah laugh."

Hairy leapt back into the painting and did a handstand. As his body flipped up and his legs reached for the trees to our left, the black figure dropped to the ground. Titan and Assonance found themselves laughing. Harry smirked and so did I. When we both glanced at Zia, a little smile lingered on her face. She tried to hide it from the Drewan.

Suddenly, her eyes bulged, and her whole body began to shake. Titan covered his ears again. The prince and princess protected their heads; tears rushed down Zia's cheeks. They screamed and screamed. Assonance, Harry and I asked what was wrong and tried our best to help. *But what could we do?* They just howled as though their brains were bound to explode.

Titan's face was red. He pushed his eyes closed, "NO, NO, NO!" He fell backwards, biting his tongue, causing blood to drip down his chin. I held him in my lap.

Harry tried to wrap himself around Zia and hold her steady. She pushed him away, crying, "The glass. Something's wrong with the glass!"

An explosion ignited inside the dome, its echo making the glass hexagons shiver. It was loud like a house demolition. Fire sizzled as people began to scream. Another explosion roared. Harry turned his whole body towards the loud vibrations. Then there was another! And another! And another! There was an explosion after an explosion, and we were in the centre of it! *Insanity! It has begun!*

Chapter 43

Insanity Begins
Bailey

Teala rushed downstairs with an eager smile on her face. I rubbed the sleep from my eyes. Leo an' James wrestled each other for the new toothpaste tube. "On Mother Nature's sphere, where could Perry have gone? Did ye see 'im leave?" I asked.

"Like I said, Bailey, he was talking to me the moment I fell asleep, and after my dream, when I realised how important Ori was, he wasn't there anymore."

I stopped with three carpeted steps remaining. "Ori—what now? So ye didn't see 'im leave then?"

Teala turned to me. "Nope. Just hope he's not doing anything stupid … Looks like he's not the only one who's left!"

I wandered into the living room to find the leftovers.

Dally yawned, peekin' at me. "'Bout time someone rocked up. Where are the others?" he asked.

Teala shrugged, "We were going to ask you the same thing. Need anything?"

"Some water would be nice!"

Teala rushed to the kitchen. Felicia rolled her eyes. "You can get the water yourself, Dally! You should be more than well after your slight tumble."

"How would you know? You were half-unconscious when it happened." Dally sat up, raisin' his eyebrows.

Felicia smiled, "I'm just saying. You took harder blows back when you played football."

"Aye, de star athlete from Kelton Grammar—I heard them stories," I chuckled. "Heck, Perry was like a proud mum the day ye team won de game against Fleddington Private College!"

Dally raised his hands, "I'm not much of a star player anymore."

Teala rushed in with two glasses of water. Dally took hold of one. She handed the second to Felicia. "Thank you, Teala. How's that dream of yours?"

Teala stared into Felicia's eyes. "Funny you asked," she mused. "You're actually in it now. You have a new name though."

"A new name?"

"Yes! You're all in it. And Dally's … Well, it's hard to say what Dally is! But Bailey's a panda, twice as strong and twice as scary."

"You think you'll ever turn back?" Dally asked me.

I stared at them an' shrugged. "Couldn't tell ya! Some leaps I hope others I prefer to stay as I am."

Suddenly Taylah rushed into the lounge room. She wore a blue bucket hat, holding Kyle's doll in her arms like a baby an' grinned at us. "Hiya! Hope yer had a good sleep. You wouldn't know where Harry is? I need help with my swimming … Actually, is Perry here? He said he'd give me a lesson."

Teala an' I hid our faces. Taylah got the idea an' frowned. She skipped 'round me. "That's …"

Teala offered her hand to Taylah. "It's okay! I could teach you if you'd like. I'm sure if we go now ——"

"No, no. Perry can give me a lesson another time. Like yer said, it's bad in the Lower Hex!"

Teala pulled her hand away. "You're right!"

Taylah turned 'round, smiling at me. "I'm sure Harry went for his morning swim. I'll go check for him at the lake. I'll be back soon."

"Wait, Taylah!" Dally called.

Taylah turned. "I'll go there and back and won't stop to talk to anyone. Promise. Bye!"

Chapter 43: Insanity Begins

I searched the pack as the front door slammed after her. "Someone should go after her! De water, it ... it might not be safe!"

"Already on it!" Teala cheered. A red light blinded my eyes. Teala had vanished; red ash fell, staining a white doona cover.

Dally leaned back, rubbing his eyes. "Was little Teala as *on-the-go* as little Doubtson? She almost gave me a heart attack."

I chuckled, "They're very similar."

I took a seat between the two. "So what were ye two talkin' before Teala an' I stumbled in?"

"Well," Felicia said. "We were just reminiscing. On the good old times!"

"So ye two have a past?" I asked.

"We do. Felicia and I were in the same class in year seven, and when I started going out with Ada, we went on a few too many double dates with some random Felicia was sleeping with!" Dally said.

"I didn't sleep with all of them!" Felicia argued. "Just some ..."

"Yeah, you don't even like guys anymore! How'd that happen? What went where and why?" Dally asked.

I raised my voice. "Dally, don't ask dat! That's a very ———"

"It's fine, Bailey!" Felicia played with her fingernails. "I think I've always preferred girls. Even when I was at school with Ada and Faith, it was there. But Faith had the perfect *'they're bound to be together'* relationship with Perry. And then you and Ada started dating. I just stuck to what I knew, not what I felt! So I could fit in." She placed her cup of water onto the floor above an orange blanket. "I'll go more into it when this is over." She groaned, "It's about time we search———"

Suddenly the whole house swayed like it were part of the Full Sea. Even Leo an' James' bickerin' stopped. All I could hear was my own breath and ringin' like the aftermath of an explosion. A chill climbed down my arms as Felicia ducked. Dally covered his head as I leapt for the window. Outside, amongst the hilly roads of the Lower Hex, smoke as black as midnight billowed into the air. Drewans ran back an' forth like when ya step on an ants' nest. A nasty scream made my toes curl.

"It's happening!" Dally said. I looked back, but before I could open my mouth, another explosion burst my eardrum. It came from the right side of the house. Sneakin' down the last step, James kept his noggin low.

"Are these the explosions?" he asked.

I was almost out of breath. Felicia picked herself up. "I believe so!" Another bang howled—this one was further away. Dally approached the front door. "We need to find the others! Now!"

Leo was stuck halfway up the stairs. "But what if we get wet?" Another explosion rang, the vibration of the ground givin' me nausea. The ringin' in my ear continued as I followed Dally.

"Best bet we have is to not let de water near ya," I admitted.

James was stunned, "'That's impossible!"

"If the water gets sucked out, we won't have to worry about that!" Felicia urged. "And besides, only one of us is likely to get wet if we stick together. So keep close!"

James an' Leo questioned Felicia's logic as Dally heaved the door open. The screams an' cries of the Drewans scarred my ears. Some agonised, others fearful, an' behind 'em, there were screams from deep down—they were crazed. Water gushed down the glass, but thankfully there was barely any on the road. We jumped collectively as another explosion shook the ground, its growl twice as furious as the ones before. Made my chest quiver. Clouds of smoke covered the air like a charcoal-scented fog. I took a step forward. A Drewan man who had his daughter in his arms bumped into me and kept on running. She was barely outta her ma's belly! He turned his head, apologising quickly as he marched towards the closest exit. *The tunnel that led to the Between.* There were rushed footsteps echoin' all around.

"Where do we start?" I asked.

Dally an' Felicia examined the chaos.

Ahead, behind layers of dreamcatchers, a hole pierced one of the hexagonal glass panels. It was like when ye crack a windscreen. Water gushed from its centre. James raised his hand, "We should ..." His eyes grew big, he shivered, turned white an' gulped. He didn't look at me, Dally or Felicia, just somewhere in the distance. Tears gathered under his eyes. When I went to ask Leo what was wrong, he had the same expression.

It was like the two had had their hearts squashed. Their dolphin crests shone, blurrin' my vision. They turned 'round an' began to skedaddle, calling for their sister.

"TAYLAH! Tay! No, no, no!"

"What happened to them?" Felicia asked.

My heart stung like poison had dripped inside it. I searched Dally. He stared at the black in the road before chasing after the twins.

Felicia followed him, "We'd best make sure they don't touch the water!"

We bolted through what seemed to be half of the Lower Hex. Ripples of the Full Sea covered more of the streets. Ye could hear how tired the twins were, their wheezes raspy as we approached a sort of lagoon. Our footsteps weren't the only ones in the muddied brown sand. The water was completely still, a perfect reflection of all the destruction. Leo an' James called for Taylah, pacin' back an' forth against the shore. They contemplated jumpin' in the water, arguing about how dangerous it was.

In the sand, on her knees, Teala was crying. Her noggin faced the water, her chin down as she wept.

"Teala!" Dally called.

I kneeled beside her. "Hey, why are ya crying, little one?"

Leo an' James' calls drifted away in the background.

"I couldn't save her!" Teala cried. "I tried, but ... but she just pushed me away. She ... She did this, Bailey! I tried. Tell me I did the best I could! 'Cause I did, I promise I did!"

"What do ya mean, Tea?"

Teala pointed ahead. Drifting in the water was Taylah. Her face was submerged, and her hair spread out like a dreamcatcher. Her body was still; there was not a single ripple to break the reflection. Next to her body, the vinyl doll was gradually sinking into the still water.

Leo an' James ran to the waterbeds. "Taylah! No, Taylah!" Leo screamed.

James took off his shirt, preparing to jump. "I'll get her!" He stormed ahead, his left foot seconds from the water. Dally ran towards him and their bodies collided. James coughed from the impact in the sand as Dally lay on top of him, holdin' him down. Leo looked at his brother, then his sister. He had so many tears in his eyes. He took a step forward.

"Don't you touch that water, Leo!" Dally ordered.

Leo pointed at Taylah's body. "But … But someone has to get her! We can't let her …" He held back, afraid to finish.

Felicia tiptoed to him. "It's okay! I can get her for you, but you need to step away from the water. If you touch ——"

"I'll go mad! I know, but my sister's out there!" Leo yelled.

Felicia offered her hand. "It's okay!" Leo took it an' Felicia held him close. Her jacket was soon wet with tears. Rubbing his back, she said, "She's with the omens now! She'll be safe. I promise you, we'll get her."

"TAYLAH!" Harry ran onto the sand. His eyes were red. Zia, Titan, Assonance an' Faith stumbled behind him. Titan looked like he was about to pass out. Harry slowed his sprint. His eyes lingered on Taylah's body as he began to wail, droppin' to his knees, "No! Not Tay, not Tay! She can't … that's not her! It can't be!" He noticed James pullin' away from Dally's hold, Leo in Felicia's arms an' Teala shaking. He stood, havin' trouble breathing, and took a step forward.

"Don't go in that water, Harry!" Dally yelled.

Harry took another step.

"*What are you doing?* It's poisonous. You saw those poor people!" Assonance called. Harry's eyes were on one goal an' one goal only. *Taylah!*

Faith called out, so did I, but he kept on goin'.

"Enough!" he screamed. He pointed at her corpse a few steps from the water. "She's my sister and she deserves better than this!" He gulped, wiping away his tears. "No one deserves this! No one!" He turned away from us an' took another step.

"Harry, don't!" Zia ordered. "If you get in that water, Taylah will not be the only one your brothers lose. Do not abandon them. Do not abandon us!"

Chapter 43: Insanity Begins

Teala began whispering under her breath. *I tried, I tried, I tried!* I hugged her. Dally glanced at Faith, holdin' James down. Harry waved his arms, confused—he was a step from the lake. "Well, someone has to get her! And if it's me, then it's me. Maybe this is my gift. I'm sorry!" He sniffled an' took one last step into the water.

Faith clapped her hands together an' slammed the sand with her two palms. She called for Dally, who let go of James an' tensed his fingers out like a fan. Their crests shone white an' blue as the sand began to move. Ricocheting off Faith's palms, the sand wobbled up an' down like a wave. Ye could hear it fall an' rise like raindrops as the sand melded 'round Harry.

As his left shoe lowered above the lagoon, an invisible force pulled Harry back. Dally levitated him into the air. Harry dropped to the ground an' the sand opened an' caught him like a monstrous mouth. Then the cries of a sandstorm whistled. The hole began to rise. When the sand was level again, Harry laid in the centre where the hole had been. Faith lifted her palms from the ground, sweat drippin' from her forehead.

As Harry lay, half-unconscious, James sprinted for the water. Dally an' Faith were too tired to respond. Assonance had barely turned into a bird by the time he reached the shore. Zia cried an' Titan sighed. Felicia tightened her grip 'round Leo an' I fell, my chin hitting the ground with a thud. *Teala was gone!* I picked myself up. As James leapt into the lagoon, a red light appeared above him. There was no splash; only red ash.

Another flare of red burnt my face. Reappearing beside me, Teala an' James sat on the sand. James looked like his belly was turned inside-out.

"What'd yer ... What'd yer just do?" he asked, dazed.

"I teleported you here." Teala watched Taylah. "I can at least save one of you, can't I?"

Zia an' Faith leaned over Harry. He groaned, "Why'd you ... *Why?*"

Faith smiled, "Because you were being a doofus! Zia and I specialise in the art of the doofus!"

"We'll find a way to get Taylah back, but right now we need to get out of here!" Zia said.

Harry lifted himself, spittin', "Not without her!"

Dally approached the three. "So you're going to tell your brothers to stay down?"

Harry glanced at him, "Not a chance!" He curled his hand into a fist and his crest howled blue. A black figure that looked exactly like him appeared an' swung at Dally. Dally's left cheek went red. Shocked, Zia pushed Harry.

"Tell Hairy to stop!"

Hairy? What? Harry's silhouette swung at Dally again. The Kelt ducked, baring his teeth. Assonance flew to his rescue—she glided next to the figure's ear.

"Stop, Hairy! Stop, it's okay!"

The figure eyed her down. Her wings spread, dodging its punches.

Zia readied her shard. "Tell him to stop!" she demanded.

Harry stood. "I don't take orders from you! I'm not a Kelt! I'm a Drewan, born to swim, born to build, born to fight! So get out of my way princess, before I make you move!"

Faith tried to calm 'em both as Titan ran over to protect his sister. I stood an' this rage took over me. I growled like a bear. *Like a panda!* It caught everyone's attention as my teeth shone. "You touch her, Drewan, an' ye'll have to deal with me!"

He laughed, "*You!* Don't fool yourself, Ever! You're nothing to them! They're whites, superior to you and me! You're not one of them!"

"It doesn't matter what colour ya crest is!" I took a step closer. "We're all equally unequal. So stand down before ya do somethin' ye'll regret!"

Harry's blue eyes towered over me. "And what?" he asked. "Will I release the panda?"

"ENOUGH!" An older voice roared louder than me. An older fella strolled towards us. "Harry, get away from the Ever and tell yer shadow to stop attacking the Centrillian and Kelt! Leo, stand tall, and James, put a shirt on! This is not how I've raised my boys!"

Harry turned to Mr Doubtson, "But Father!"

"I know!" He had tears drippin' from his cheeks. "By the salts on

Chapter 43: Insanity Begins

the omen's chin, I know! I felt her life drain itself from the beacon's light! I felt her drown, just like you."

Harry urged, "So you know that ———"

"Yes! But am I behaving like you? Like your brothers? These people around you—whether green, orange or white—want to help you! Do not take that kindness for granted!" He put his hand on Harry's shoulder and sniffled, "You are my blood. My salty good-for-nothing blood. And you are young!"

Leo an' James approached their father. Mr Doubtson hugged 'em as though they were one. "Jameson, Leonardo and Harriet! You are my sons, your mother's kin! I've been raised under these glass walls—I've barely been anywhere past Kattagow to the capital. Will you explore the world for me?"

Harry stuttered, "What do you mean? What are you saying, Father?"

Mr Doubtson took a deep breath, rolled up his sleeves an' approached the shore. "I have made my decision. I have lived a good life, raised good boys. Now the omens above the sea call for your sister and I!"

Leo an' James begged their father.

"You are to not to go in there!" Harry screamed.

Mr Doubtson smiled, tears fresh under his eyes. "Your mother gave me angels, Harry. And I raised you below the seas." He laughed. "How foolish. Fly for her—*for me!* Maybe we'll see each other again! But when I hold my little ..." He held in the last of his words. Tightenin' his grip on the boys, Mr Doubtson looked at us all. "When I hold my little girl in my arms, you need to go. The city is not safe! I will take Taylah's body as far as I can, but it is up to you to make her grave."

"No, Dad!"

"We are Drewans, son! You remember that! We are the heart of the sea, the shoulder of the world, the greatest colour of them all. You hold that proudly. And I will hold Taylah! Just one last time."

Not a single step was taken from anyone. Only Mr Doubtson. The greyin' hairs on his arms shivered as his left boot dropped into the water. It sounded cold. His breathing calmed as he pushed through the perfect reflection of the lagoon. Harry took a step forward. Zia, with tears in her eyes, held him. Mr Doubtson sank deeper an' deeper the further he went. When he reached Taylah, half his body was consumed by the water. He turned her body 'round so her face could see the Full Sea. *Their home*. He pulled her close an' the two swayed in the water. For a moment, he held her so tightly I thought the world had stopped. Then the entire hexadome turned red.

A siren shrieked all 'round. The dome's glass looked as though it had been stained with blood. A rush of water exploded past us an' my hair blew to the side. I could feel the cold hums of the wind. Goosebumps crawled along my arms as Titan an' I searched the streets behind us. A wave leapt onto the road; the emergency lights coloured it a poisonous red. It splashed from house to house.

Titan took a step back. "What now?"

"I think it's safe to call dat a tsunami! We gotta get outta here before de water touches us!" I ordered.

Zia pulled Harry. "We have to go! It's not safe here!" she pleaded.

Harry watched his father an' gulped. "To the Between!" he cried. He took the first step away from the sand.

Leo an' James followed their brother.

"What is that noise?" Assonance asked.

"Most likely the emergency siren for when the Hexadomes have been damaged!" Felicia guessed.

"Then why'd it take so long for it to turn on? It's been at least fifteen minutes since the first explosion!" Faith noted.

Harry's voice broke free, "It's the start of protocol. The main system control will be in the Between. 'Bout a block away from WonderWorks."

"Do you think my father warned the general?" Titan asked.

Harry nodded. "If he is as perceptive as they say, then yes. I'd say it's likely he could have warned General Ko."

"So we're not escaping?" Teala asked.

Leo shook his noggin, "*We can't!* The only way out is the Great Divide, and even if we managed to get to the Upper Hex, the water from the sides of the Divide could still splash and hit your skin!"

Chapter 43: Insanity Begins

"Well, it's either that or we can go swimming!" James stared at the hexadome's ceiling.

The waves of the Full Sea were large an' aggressive, as though they could feel the pain of the blue beacon. I took in my orders.

"Understood!" I marched with Harry. "We can't escape so the safest option is to take shelter in de joint where dey control de metal shields for de hexadomes. Will the general be able to help us?"

"I hope so!" Harry uttered. Zia's face was grim. *But this was it.* The walls 'round us were cavin' in. All that surrounded us was death! Litres an' litres of pure insanity.

Chapter 44

A Poet's Duel

Perry

The glass doors to WonderWorks split open for me. *He knew I was coming.* Inside, the iron machine that built Mr Kingsleigh's enterprise was motionless. It was empty. My solitary footsteps echoed as I entered the atrium. There was no one—no receptionist, no businessmen and women, no friends. Just me and my hood! The echoes of my breath sang as I read Papercut's card. *Level twenty-four, huh?* I scrunched it in my glove, and it fell to the sterile white and blue chequered porcelain tiles. Holding the metallic alloys of Holdie close, I examined the atrium. *So many floors for what? Alice?* As my eyes took in the towering rows of glass rails, there was silence.

The creak to the fire escape's door was harrowing. It croaked so loudly I thought a thousand security guards would be after me. The mundane concrete grey of the steps made me rethink my plans. Juice may be a nutcase, but he must have known that this number of stairs was going to kill me first. *Well, no time like the present, right?* I heaved up one and another, passing floor three, floor eight, fourteen, twenty-five ... *Oh! I've gone too far!* Backtracking down a flight, I peeked behind an opening. The orange lights flickered down the hallway. All the doors were closed, except one.

I shouldered past the steel door, the smell of burnt flesh clawing at my nose. My feet crept through the dark walls of another hallway, this one with rectangular windows and tiled white laboratories behind them. Each lab was closed off. An orange haze danced off the hall's back wall. At the end of the dark abyss, Papercut rested his knees

Chapter 44: A Poet's Duel

on the harsh concrete floor, a test tube and a burning white candle in front of him. His eyes were closed, his paper cloak tight around his face. You could see the paper, how it swayed perfectly around his body like a layer of skin.

I took another step. He opened his eyes, black bags beneath his calm gaze. First, he admired the floor, a sad evil inside of him like he'd seen how the world would end. Then those blue eyes, as clear as the Full Sea, caught me. I put my hand to my staff. *Tap, tap, tap ...*

Papercut picked up the test tube and watched me. His two katanas were sheathed behind his back. He looked at the beige ooze within the glass cage. It bubbled, boiling as he examined it.

"Give him back, Juice!" I pleaded. I held out Holdie, my fingers prepped on his stimulate button. Juice smiled behind his bandana. He placed the test tube Kyle was trapped inside against his paper belt. The belt's paper unwrapped itself like a vine and took hold of the tube. *Is it alive?* He raised his arms into the air and yanked on the two katanas. Their paper-thin blades were so sharp they sounded like metal swords. I moved my finger away from Holdie and shoved him into my pocket. Then, I unsheathed my staff.

Papercut and I stared at each other, awaiting the other's attack. Around and around, we walked—both experienced in the dance—our arms firm and our eyes focused. I thought of nothing else but him. He raised his right sword and pointed it at me. I adjusted my father's staff behind my head and prepared.

Paper hit timber like steel against steel. He was faster than me. *Much faster.* He clipped my shoulder and stabbed right through my stomach. I fazed through and hit his head. No matter which end of my staff it was, Papercut was one step ahead, blocking one move after the next. The window to the laboratory approached our right side. I jumped onto it, kicking off the glass. Juice guarded his face. I teleported to his exposed side, slicing down. Staggering back, his eyes were now more intent. Silently, he snarled. One sharp end after the next sliced at my arms, my legs and my face. My staff got tangled between his katanas. I smiled, relieved. He was far from impressed.

My head flew back as his forehead knocked against mine. I didn't feel anything; it just shook my insides. He kicked my knee until my body fell in front of him. Then this sting crawled down my shoulder. I looked, blood rushing down my sleeve as his right sword planted itself into my collar. I gripped my staff and my crest ignited. I tackled his body. Transpiring though his paper cloak and legs, I reached the back of the hallway where the candle flared—its orange dance brought a chill to my spine.

I picked myself up and grinned. "I get why you call yourself Papercut now! Cute." I swung my staff. Left, right, left, right, left ... *Right!* I had never swung so hard in my life. I had the advantage of space. The white light of my teleportations surprised his left side, his back, his right side. I didn't stop. White ash dropped to the floor like rain. I had trouble breathing; my last swing made Juice's face drip red. His left katana flew, knocking the candle back. His paper bandana became soggy as his nose dripped a stream of red. He ripped it off, tasting the blood as if it were a treat. His face was still the same from school. Even bloodied, it was him! *I can't let that stop me!*

He grinned, wielding his right katana like a knight's sword. Before I knew it, I had been launched through the door. The orange light of floor twenty-four coloured our fighting silhouettes. He jumped, I parried. I swung, he countered.

Like a never-ending moving painting, we managed to dance up the stairs. His skin turned white as he bled more and more. However, the more he bled, the faster he threw his katana. His gloved left hand wrapped itself around my neck. My head dangled forty floors above the bottom of the fire escape. I gulped, knowing that the sway of my neck carried all my weight. I bit my lip so hard that the taste of blood sprinkled down my throat. I tugged onto my staff as if it were a railing holding me steady. When my eyes closed, I was two flights away. Papercut steadied himself. We continued our tango until we ran out of steps to climb.

If he shoved me against one wall, I'd knock him down a flight. *Heck, if I'm lucky, his tumbles might break Kyle's test tube, and I can turn on Holdie.* Then we could both take him down. Unfortunately, we reached Mr Kingsleigh's waiting room and Kyle was still locked away. I spat out blood, putting in as many swings as I could muster. He was as white and tired as I was. Both of us were half dead, waiting for the other to collapse. I shoved my shoulder into his

Chapter 44: A Poet's Duel

side. He stumbled back, knocking one of the strange statues in the corner of the room. Juice stabilised his footing and gritted his teeth.

There was only one way of winning and it was going to burn! I clenched my teeth. I knew his jab was coming from the left side, but instead of blocking, I let the paper slice the side of my stomach. It skimmed me enough to make tears boil and drip. My knees gave way.

I groaned, kneeling in front of him. We were both so exhausted, our huffs and puffs were almost like wheezes. I shivered from the nauseating sting. Juice lowered his weapons and watched me, a frown under his bloodied nose. I could hear a whimper. *Tears?* Juice cried. A cue card landed in front of my face. In black ink, it read, *You are the first person to ever get blood on my paper ... An honourable opponent. Goodbye, old friend!* He raised his hand for one last swing.

I heaved the left end of my staff into his stomach. Flinching, the katana fell. I caught the paper, its surprising weight pulling my fragile arm down. Juice's eyes widened. He swung. I fazed through his left fist, jumped away from him and vanished. Reappearing with both my staff and his katana, I knocked his head back and forth until we tumbled over to the other side of the room. Juice's back collided with the bookshelf. Thousands of books of all colours fell around us as I screamed once more. I pushed the katana at his belly. He gasped like a ghost had scared him. When he looked down, his blood covered my hand. I had pierced the right side of his abdomen.

I left the sword where it was. He smiled at me. Eventually, the smile became a grim silent laugh. I shoved my hand into his belt and yanked the test tube from its hold. Kyle was mine. I had won! I took a step back as Juice remained plastered against the wall.

"WHAT IS THE MEANING OF ... Oh, by the salt on the omens'!" Mr Kingsleigh stepped out from his office. His arms fell back from the two massive doors, their golden frames showing two bloodied soldiers.

I shoved my red glove at his face. "So this is where you're going to detonate those dreamcatchers, huh? From your own office. Even Alice wasn't that scummy!"

His brows dropped, "Caduca! How dare you say my daughter's

name in vain! What is the meaning of this? Who is this man you've stapled to my Bywoe book cabinet?"

I gestured to Juice, whose bloodied smile vanished. "You know damn right who this is! You sent him to kill Senator Hartway! He works for you—don't lie to me."

"*Senator Hartway?*" His voice lost its stubborn tone. "I've never seen this boy in my life!"

I laughed, "Well, if you don't know who this is, why are you here alone? Where is everyone, huh?"

"It's Mardi Mimpi, a public holiday, Perry! I'm here because this is my company. Unfortunately, I do not get the pleasure of holidays … That does not make this vile situation any more acceptable." He turned to his receptionist's desk. "You have some explaining to do, young man. I … I need to call the militia and have them take you both in!"

He put the phone to his ear. A spark of white made his hand dance. The phone fell to the ground. I turned to Juice, who held a paper throwing-knife in between his fingers. He shook his head at Mr Kingsleigh. *Are they not partners? Was Senator Hartway's death really an accident?* I took a step forward, and Holdie fell from my pocket. Its metal clunk echoed under my voice.

"Where's the detonator, Charles?" I demanded. "We can stop this before it even begins. You just have to tell me where it is."

Mr Kingsleigh shimmied backwards, "*Detonator?* What salty seas do you live under boy? I have no need for detonators, especially here in my office."

I swung Kyle's tube like a wand. "The detonator for the dreamcatchers. You've been infecting the water. Lord Kelton said it himself. You've been poisoning the water and you want to kill everyone inside the Lower Hex! You want to detonate the redmer dreamcatchers, I swear on Hope's Light, you do!"

As though Kyle's tube was a gun, Mr Kingsleigh raised his hands in the air. "Dreamcatchers? Detonator? How dare you accuse me of such atrocities! The Lower Hex is where I was born—why would I want to destroy my home, my people, my own past?"

"Yes. Why indeed!" A more crisp and patient voice said.

Chapter 44: A Poet's Duel

Mr Kingsleigh lowered his guard. "General! Thank the omen's shores you've arrived. These two hooligans have made a right mess of the place. I was on my way to call you and your men."

"Is that so, Charles?" General Ko emerged from the shadows with a weird grey device clenched under his thumb. Etched on the device's grip were the markings of alchemy. "I've never known you to be a man of orders. Who are these ... hooligans?"

Kingsleigh gulped, "What is that in your hand, Ko?"

The general admired his tensed thumb, "This?" he smiled. "Renewal! For lack of a better word. It's the key to restoration, an overhaul to rebuild our world!" He had blood across his blue uniform. Seven medals of honour sparkled like fireflies; his knuckles had been peeled purple, throbbing at the bone. "Are you scared, Charles?"

Mr Kingsleigh lowered his hands and stood next to me. "Who are you?"

Such a weird question, yet the general found it amusing. "Me?" He smacked the centre of his chest with the detonator, his thumb still stubbornly tense. "I'm the General of Drewmora's finest. The militia of the sea ... Aren't I?" Before Charles could answer, General Ko sighed. "I ... I have a wife, Loretta. We met when I was fourteen down in the Lower Hex. There was a fair, and we put our feet in the water in this little lagoon, hearing the celebrations of the first Mardi Mimpi. That's when I was eager to dream. *I was young!* Still eager the day my first son was born and my second. And when Liana, my daughter, learnt to walk, I was sent to war! To fight a battle we'd already lost ... The only thing keeping most men sane back in the Echo Wars were their dreams of loved ones. I killed beasts during that war and other men with different coloured crests. That was I, Charles. As I am now."

Charles placed his arm in front of me. "Your voice is cold, General. Your light is ..."

I glanced at his crest and it was colourless. My heart started to flutter as the cold sting lost its hold.

General Ko examined his right wrist. "Off? How peculiar." He stared at me. "What's your name, boy?"

"Perry," I said.

He shook his head and stumbled past Papercut and the bookshelf before entering Mr Kingsleigh's office. We watched him as the doors swayed and stayed open.

Behind them, there was a magnificent window towering over the Between. It would make Zia drool, it was so finely melded. General Ko placed his hands behind his back, the detonator tight behind his waist. He stared at the Full Sea and the city beneath it. *Drewmora.*

"Perry, do yer know why Charles has invested in caging those immigrants on the shore? Yer saw them, yes?" he asked, a plea in his throat.

"To keep them safe until we have enough housing for them. Until we can register them as citizens. Until they're able to work in our economy," I guessed.

A grin spread across the general's cheeks. "A very studious answer. *Enough* is the key word I enjoyed. Here, we've barely built past the Royal Hex. Heck, the newest hexadomes are the New Mines and the Between. But this old dome was built even before my time. So tell me, why build when you can redevelop what has already worked in the past?"

"What are you saying, General?" Charles asked.

The general turned to us. He showcased the detonator like it was a toy. "I'm saying, once my thumb leaves this small, fragile device, you will have witnessed a renewal. We will eliminate those poor miners and useless hosers on government payments and use the cheap land and resources to house those waiting ashore. It'll be a dream come true!"

"You ... You'd kill our own kind just so other coloured crests could move in and destroy us from the inside? Are you mad?" Mr Kingsleigh yelled.

"No!" The general's cheeks turned red. "By ridding ourselves of the weaklings, the lazy scum who live on welfare and the disposable everyday workers who barely achieve as much as you and me, we can make the blue beacon the most powerful in all of Euphoria! Think about it. We could have a thousand innovators like yourself in a decade; there'll be less crime and we can get those desperate on Camel Hump Shore to work for their survival. Drewmora will be

Chapter 44: A Poet's Duel

a sanctuary! And we salty Drewans will be the most advanced and powerful colour since the omens walked the planet!"

"Ko, this is not you! You would never kill innocents! So, tell me again. Who are you?" Charles ordered.

I crept around Mr Kingsleigh's office. The general groaned. Beneath his anger, a sharp metallic slice whispered.

"I told you already Charles," General Ko affirmed. "I am I as I was myself yesterday. However, for the life of me, today has felt rather lifeless. I haven't dreamed in a long time, you see." He raised his hand, his thumb itching from its hold. He saw my concerned eyes. "Are you weary of my hold, Perry?"

I nodded, "A little! If you let go of that button, the dreamcatchers explode, won't they?"

He smiled, "Another studious answer. You could make yourself an academic, yet you stand here bloodied with a test tube and a ... I know that staff. You're Quentin's boy!"

I stopped. *He knew my father!*

"He would have loved this innovation!" the general muttered. Every word made my stomach swirl. "To rid Kelton Whide of its weak and poor. Rest his poor salty soul. He is with the omens now ... Tell me, white wolf, why should I keep hold of this ... detonator? I'm curious about your answer."

"Because it's wrong," I said. "Even my father wasn't as cruel as you! From what I've heard, you both came from the Lower Hex. Which means Drewmora needs kids born and raised in those poor households and those families on welfare because those kids can grow up to be something amazing! No matter how hard life can be, those who fight through it like Mr Kingsleigh here, they can build enterprises and inspire others. Not by playing the games of your gods. You are not one of them, no Light of Hope, no Master of the Seas, no Good Spirit. Like you said, you are you as you were yourself yesterday. And tomorrow's a new day. Anything can happen!"

Mr Kingsleigh nodded at me. The general pouted, abandoning his smile. "An academic in the making! Unfortunately, this is not my decision. A little blond girl told me to do this, you see. And my thumb is getting—Argh!"

A white paper katana pierced through General Ko's uniform. I watched his eyes as he gasped the echo of death. Papercut held the katana's end, pulling it out from his back. The detonator fell from the general's grip and hit the floor as if it were made from a landmine. A howl sounded outside, wobbling the WonderWorks tower. Behind the window, smoke swayed, and a hole pierced the Between's hexadome. Water poured through it like a tap in a sink and Drewans cried as if the world was ending.

I yelled at Juice. "No! Juice, you … you …" The walls of Mr Kingsleigh's office tinted blue. The noises of fear and death were lost. The general's body was frozen in time, stuck falling to the ground. Papercut's blade was still fresh with blood, motionless after its murder. Mr Kingsleigh's face remained wrinkled in revolt. Behind him, past the door, Odd lifted a blue book from the floor. The fire to his right stopped its dance, afraid to move without the demigod's permission. I turned to him, the only moving piece within the destructive picture.

Odd sighed, "Renewal. What a … What was it he called you? Ah! What a *studious* word." He laughed to himself, strutting past me. Glaring at the general's corpse, he placed the book behind his coat and admired the hole in the hexadome where the water was frozen. "I saw Othello yesterday. He was missing an eye. I always did like that bird girl … Seems you've gotten yourself in quite a mess. Foolishly alone, aren't you?" He faced me.

His eyes had bags as black as smog, his skin was oily and thick hairs pinched at his cheeks. "Why have you …? Can you turn back time? You can stop this from ever happening, right?" I pleaded.

Odd raised an eyebrow. "Do I look like a magician? I can't simply turn back time on something like this. 'Twas meant to happen. And there are rules. I cannot change the nature of the world, nor can I erase tragedy. Trust me, I've tried."

He leaned down and took hold of the general's wrist. Odd frowned. "Seems the general's crest has been tampered with."

"What, his code?" I asked.

"Yes. His lifeline has been re-sewn now, dating his death for this moment in time." Odd licked his lips and tilted his head to the left. "It reads: *in a blink of an eye, a sword woven from paper and blood will plunge*

Chapter 44: A Poet's Duel

through the heart of the Blue Killer Whale. His heart shall stop beating before four people and a fifth trapped in glass." He looked at me. "I see you've had some troubles getting here. As did I." Odd stood. He admired the window once more. "Seems insanity has infected this major city. All because a man had the aspirations to strengthen his people."

"By killing the weak!" I argued. "That isn't strengthening anything, that's ———"

"A different perspective," Odd said. "Is it not? You and I, we each have a different view on the matter. And in all honesty, it's not a terrible plan."

Odd approached me, the blue city behind him, lighting his sides as though he were a saviour. He pointed at the tinted blue walls—the walls of time. "Yet, even Araidian would have a certain mercy on this matter. He'd want to partake in the murder, not just join it. Do you know what this is? What we are standing in?"

I shrugged, "Frozen time? A space between the seconds ticking and ... I don't know, space?"

Odd grinned, "Of sorts. An in-between. When I learnt how to freeze time, an old friend called it a *blink*. It's like holding your eyes open long enough to see the reality of things."

He placed the book on Charles' bywoe lacquered desk, its dark-grey timber glistening with the embroiled markings of the old Drewan tongue.

"So we've lost?" I cried.

Odd shook his head. "Not necessarily. But the alchemic reaction from his finger leaving the detonator has caused the redmer dreamcatchers to explode. Ergo, we stand frozen, moments before the underwater city becomes almost overwhelmed by fear and primal disgust."

"Thank you for recap, genius! You said his crest had been tempered with. Who'd be able to do something like that?" I asked.

Odd nodded, "Now that's a good question. What exactly is fate if ours can simply be rewritten through the knowledge of a dead language? Do we even have the ability to choose?"

"I can choose," I argued. "I chose to come here and I ... I chose to lie to Faith! 'Cause I didn't want her to worry or get hurt by him."

My finger lingered on Juice's murderous eyes.

Odd turned back towards the receptionist's desk. The tapping of his boots stopped the moment a metal glare caught his attention. He leaned down and picked up Holdie. "Or is it the illusion of choice?" he wondered. "I'm going to tell you what's going to happen. I'm going to click my thumb, you're going to act shocked, and Juiceton is going to flee for his life. I'm going to run out of the elevator once that happens and, when it does, you're going to turn on this studious device Daegon made. Am I clear, Perry?"

I nodded, "Since when do you give such specific orders?"

"Since Othello's Good Spirit told him to tell me to tell you! A rollercoaster of mouths and ears, but this game of whispers has come to an end." He threw the metal pseudosphere. When it reached my red gloves, he groaned, "'Tis going to be a long day … Do talk to Teala when we find her. She's missed you. Heck, so have I!"

When General Ko's falling body hit the ground, the room lost its blue-tinted skeleton, and a gasp roared from Mr Kingsleigh's mouth. Papercut raised his blade. He took a few steps back until his Achilles' tendon rubbed against the glass window. His blood-soaked paper boots squeaked against the refined panel. Another explosion echoed, this one further away. Behind Juice, there was a grey cloud in the Full Sea, its centre yellow and its smoke flowing up to the shore like an oil spill. I heard the hard thud of bones. Mr Kingsleigh was on his knees, his hands held high above his colourless face.

"Please don't kill me! I have a daughter and a wife. I donate to several charities, I swear. I promise, I'll donate to more. I'll ——"

Papercut shoved his back into the glass. The shatter of the window made my ear almost bleed. His cloak, sword and crest fell down the tower. My legs were already standing on the window's shards. When the wind caught hold of my hood, knocking it aside, there was no dead body at the bottom of the tower where the sidewalk was. Just a few white papers floating down weightlessly, as though the city was not drowning itself.

I jolted. Another explosion burst from the dome. My heart raced

Chapter 44: A Poet's Duel

so fast I thought I was next to fall from the window. "CHARLES? CHARLES! We need to ..." Odd stormed in, his face neutral. He helped Mr Kingsleigh to his feet. "Are you okay, Charles?"

Kingsleigh stuttered.

Odd looked at me. "Perry, what are you doing here?" Before I could speak, he squealed, "Is that the general? What on Light's arse happened here?" The tower shook. The lights inside the office blinked and my grip on Holdie tightened.

"I think it'd be best for us to leave the building. We can regroup and gather ourselves inside the militia's System Control Hub for the Between," Mr Kingsleigh noted. He pushed away from Odd, glanced at General Ko's corpse and left for the fire escape.

Odd crossed his arms at me. "And you're here because ..."

I scratched my head, "Uh ... I was here to figh———"

Odd shook his head.

"To ..." I saw Holdie in my grip. "To help a friend."

Odd nodded, picking up the book he had previously left on Kingsleigh's desk. "A friend, huh? Well, you can tell me on the way. How far is the MSC Hub?" Odd asked.

We walked to the receptionist's waiting room. Mr Kingsleigh ignored him. I pegged the test tube at the ground and Charles turned to us. "Why have you ..."

His eyes caught the boiling bubbles of the skin-coloured sludge. The scent of burning flesh made the rich man gag. I clicked Holdie, its white lights turning on and off; you could hear his little engine roar. He span faster and faster until he flew from my hand. The device glided to the sludge, floating higher and higher as the skin colour started to mutate. Gasping, Kyle's old self from the WoodWood cabin dropped to his knees. His face was covered in sweat as he shook next to the fireplace.

"Gah, now you let me out!" he cried. "Why didn't you do that the moment you grabbed me from Juice's belt? The next time I see that knobhead, Imma punch him so hard, I-I'll turn into a troll again!"

I offered him my hand. "Well, at least you're still conscious when you're that gooey stuff!" I said.

His windbreaker with brown stripes and second-hand boots were still wrapped around his body. He took my hand. "That's right! And I never ever want to be trapped inside a t-test tube ever again. Gah, talk about starving to death. Lucky that form doesn't eat itself like the human body."

When Kyle was on his feet, Mr Kingsleigh flicked his tongue up and down the rim of his mouth. He waved his hands, "Another one! By the salty omen's chin, I never want to see another one of your tagalongs ever again, Odd! Now, can we please evacuate to the Hub. I should have clearance. If not, I've nicked the general's card. Shouldn't take any longer than a few minutes to get there."

"No worries, boss! We're right behind you," Odd said.

I took another step with Kyle, and this cold burn climbed along my stomach, pinching my chest. I dropped to my knees and my hands pushed against the slice from Papercut. Kyle leaned down, catching my side.

"Perry, what's wrong?"

I gritted my teeth, not wanting to admit it. "I ... I don't think I can walk! It hurts. It hurts too much! Argh!" We were stuck until I could find my footing. But the screams outside were getting louder. My crest burned. I could feel a sadness had overwhelmed Teala. I needed to find her. I needed my friends!

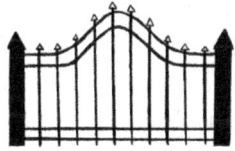

Chapter 45

Open The Gate
Faith

The militia's System Control Hub was a grey metal dome. It looked like a giant tank, glowing red under the dying hexadome. You could smell the salt of the Full Sea; the vapours of smoke stung our eyes as we tumbled behind Harry. He was the most tired, red-eyed with rosy cheeks. He gulped, peeking behind a towering complex's corner, and waved his hand, ordering a halt. We huddled behind him, the metal of the complex's wall cold against my jacket.

"The system control should be just ahead," Harry muttered.

"Well, why don't we go then?" Zia demanded.

Dally made a move for it. Harry's dark shadow blocked his path. Dally swung his arms. "If this thing touches me again, I swear on Hope's Light, the sun won't ever shine a shadow on you, Harry! Why are you stopping? Do you not hear all the cries and the water?"

Harry gave Dally no attention. He had other concerns.

Beyond the complex, there was a whimper. I rubbed Dally's back, his voice relaxing. "Settle, Dally. I'm sure he has his reasons. Remember, he just lost …"

My voice drifted as I noticed what had made Harry stop. A girl in a blue uniform maybe two or three years older than us cried. She wore the militia's colours, a yellow strap wrapped diagonally around her shoulders and torso. She sat behind a black steel fence with sharp spikes at its head.

Leaning on a timber crate, she whimpered, "They're gone, Jeri! What the salt do we do now!"

A second figure walked past her in a similar uniform. He was holding a crate in his arms. In his scabbard, his khopesh shone, and his bicorne hat was tight around his head. "We do what we're told. Especially now that Commander Malvitch's run off with those Kelts inside. We're the highest-ranking officers at this Hub's gate and we're going to keep it that way!"

"And what about the people outside? Do you not hear them screaming? The hexadomes are leaking. And we're in the centre of it!" the girl argued.

"We stand guard, Chloe! That's what we've been told and that's what I intend to do! Now, where did Pip run off to? And wipe 'em tears before the salt on Giuseppe's chin gets any dustier."

An older man in rags and his orange-haired daughter approached the fence. We all waited quietly. The father crashed his thick blackened arms against the metal bars of the fence. The rattle grabbed the cadets' attention.

"Let us in. Please! They're going insane out here. My daughter, she ——"

A crack of flesh echoed. The father pushed away from the fence and gripped at his nose. Blood poured through his hand. As tears smudged his eyes, a third soldier wielded his khopesh. The boy with blond curly hair growled at the two, "Get away from the militia's property. You're not welcome here!"

The father latched onto the fence. "Please. Yer don't have to take me, but at least take my daughter! They've gone mad, all of them! People are ripping at each other—murder, I say. By the omen's shores, please let her in. Please!"

Harry sighed. The blond soldier readied his blade. He had an eager thrill in his ocean blue eyes. "Touch the fence again sir, and I'll have to cut that hand of yers off!"

The tanned soldier at the back ran to his side. "Enough, Pip!"

Pip, the blond boy, took a step back.

The tanned cadet glanced at the girl and gulped, "I'm sorry sir, we ... we don't have any clearance from our commander. General

Chapter 45: Open the Gate

Ko has not deemed it safe to let pedestrians in. Without that, we cannot open the gate for you. I ... I'm sorry!"

Zia leaned on Harry's shoulder. "Those are the cadets that teased you in the Great Divide!"

"They didn't ... Just let me think. We can't enter either, not without clearance."

The father dropped to his knees, begging the two cadets. "Please. May the omens have mercy on my own salty soul. If she stays out here, I don't know how much longer I can protect her."

"Sir, we can't!" the tanned cadet insisted.

Pip raised his khopesh, "Stand and leave us! We are the law of the sea, and if yer disobey us, we have no choice but to punish you!"

Harry growled. Dally raised his eyebrow at me as Leo grabbed his brother's arm. "Harry, don't! They'll just hurt yer again."

James approached them, "We can find somewhere else that's safe. Yer know they won't let us ———"

Harry pushed away from the twins.

Bailey chased after him. "What on de spirits are ya flippin' doin'?" he asked.

We all cried out his name as Hairy vanished.

The father's cries became sorrowful as he stood. His head fell.

"Please, sir. Leave. We will offer yer safety when General Ko orders it!" the tanned cadet said.

"LET HIM IN, JERICHO!" Harry demanded.

Bailey turned around and saw that no one else had followed. He continued his pace with the Drewan as Jericho grinned. "Well, well, well! If it isn't Harry! Come again to try yer luck?"

Harry shook his head. "No! I've come to save this man's life and his daughter's. Something I thought yer pledged an oath to?" Harry stopped at the foot of the fence. Jericho and Pip laughed.

"We did pledge that!" Jericho said, "And that means we follow orders. This man and his daughter don't have access to this facility. And neither do you or this Ever freak."

Bailey crossed his arms. "Ease up, I didn't mean to offend ya.

What does dat yellow strap mean 'round ya fancy uniform? You a cadet?" he asked.

Jericho's khopesh sliced the air. He pointed it at Bailey. "It doesn't mean anything to you. Now get away from the fence before I come over there and ——"

"What?" Harry asked. "What are you going to do, Jeri?"

The moment Harry raised his voice, Leo and James launched themselves down the street. Racing behind them, we all gathered behind Harry. Jericho and Pip found this all the more amusing.

"Ah, even more Doubtsons. Where's daddy, boys?" Pip chuckled.

Jericho snarled, "Look, Harry, we're going to stay right here, and you're going to stay out there. Yer heard the man. The Drewans have gone mad! And you were always the runt in the pack, huh?" Jericho searched all of us. "I'm sorry, everyone. But without our general's permission, the best I can offer is the Linking Tunnel towards the Upper Hex. Shouldn't be any longer than a thirty-minute walk."

His eyes latched onto Zia's grey irises.

She grinned, "No, you're going to let us in!"

Jericho smiled, "And why's that, Kelt?"

Zia took a step closer to the fence. "Because I said so. Do I have to repeat myself?"

Pip raised his brows. "If you want to make my ears bleed? What, are you a princess or something?" He laughed with Jericho. The third solider joined her brothers. She was as red as Harry, smiling at Teala and the little orange-headed girl. I approached her.

"You look sensible," I said. "Is there anything we can do to get in?"

"I've always dreamt about this place, can we please come in?" Teala begged.

Chloe raised her hands, her freckly cheeks leaking tears. "I'm sorry. I wish we could, but … we can't!" she cried.

Titan tapped Dally, "You think his sword's fake?"

Dally grinned, "Yeah. Looks like their general gave them pretend swords so they didn't accidentally stab out their eyes or something stupid." Dally slapped the fence. It shook from his palm.

Chapter 45: Open the Gate

Pip's eyes flared. "What'd yer just say. You're going to regret that, Kelt!"

Dally smiled, "Good! Now we're talking."

Felicia pulled him back, "Stop being so thick-headed, Dalton! Stirring the snot-nosed imbeciles won't help our cause. We'd have more luck breaking down the fence. I even calcu——"

Jericho pointed at her, "Yer break down this fence, yer break Drewan law. And you're not even a part of the blue beacon's shine, so the punishment would be worse than death!"

"Death!" Assonance gawked. She stood in front of Felicia. "Well, may I be more rational. Could I fly over and negotiate with you three in a more civilised environment?"

"Centrillian, I'd be happy to, but without orders, we cannot let yer in!" Chloe said, wiping her tears.

"Well, we're not leaving until you open this gate!" Zia yelled.

Pip leaned down to her height and grinned. "Sorry, love. But you're standing too close to the fence!" He raised his hand, the handle of his khopesh tight in his grip. He threw the blunt side at Zia's nose. Before the black grip collided with her forehead, a black figure grabbed Pip's arm. He jolted as Hairy pulled his wrist back.

"Get this thing off me, Doubtson!" Pip yelled, stuck in Hairy's grip.

Jericho ran to the edge of the black metal bars. "Harry, I order yer to let him go! You are not only breaking the law, you're also ruining yer chances of ever being one of us."

With a quick lunge, Harry pulled Jericho's uniform into the steel bars. The side of his head and chest made a sudden ding. Breathing steadily, Jericho dropped his khopesh. His crest was a blue clownfish. Harry was face to face with him, the fence no longer an obstacle. There was anger in Harry's throat.

"My sister died today!" he began to cry. "So I don't care about your salty rules or being a part of this terrible military. I just want to keep my family and friends safe. And if I can save anyone else along the way, yer won't be able to stop me! Now let us in. None of us are safe. Not you, not Pip, not Commander Malvitch, not even General Ko! Drewmora is dying. There is no order. Do you understand? Do yer?"

Jericho bit his lip. He pulled away, stuttering, "Chloe, open the gate." Pip argued, but Jericho insisted, *"Open the gate!"*

When we entered, Jericho told Pip and Chloe to let anyone else in who asked or begged. "I'll take you to Commander Malvitch and explain the situation," he told us. The loud call of the sirens faded as the red of the emergency lights vanished. We left the Drewan father and his orange-haired girl in the lobby. It was freezing inside like they had left the air-conditioning on overnight. Iron bars covered the windows. Titan was mesmerised by the high metallic ceiling as blue lights flickered to the thunderous screams overhead.

The further we walked, the darker the hall became. You could smell sweat and rust as our boots tapped against the marble floor.

"It's certainly a lot bigger on the inside," Assonance mumbled.

Felicia held her close, their hands intertwined like beads wrapped around a rosary. Felicia admired the architecture, "Clever designers, you Drewans. Always prepared for the worst situations. You've placed beams every metre and drilled their feet into the marble."

"Tightly too! I've never seen anythin' like dis joint before. Even ya WonderWorks wasn't as steady!" Bailey added.

Felicia was right—every meter, a large rectangular beam made from brass launched up and arched over our heads. Each arch crisscrossed with the next beam closest to it until their paths stopped at a large stainless-steel door. It was the size of the gate outside with dark-blue carvings etched down its centre and corners. Jericho stopped.

Harry crossed his arms, "Why's the Central Control closed?"

"Coulda been that king's orders," Jericho muttered, sighing. They stood still as Leo and James took a seat on the cold reflective floor.

"Well, are you going to open it?" Zia demanded.

Jericho smiled, "You need to teach your new girlfriend some manners, Haz!"

Both Harry and Zia turned a yellowy-white. "Please don't call me Haz!" Harry cried.

Zia was harsher. "And do not assume things, cadet. I am no one's girlfriend."

Harry's scrunched his face for a moment. "Yah!" he mumbled.

CHAPTER 45: OPEN THE GATE

"We're not ... She's not my girlfriend, that's right!"

Dally laughed.

Jericho had a similar mischievous grin. "Aye, if you're going to play her, yer can at least inform her of our particular militia delicacies. Yer know them as much as I do."

Zia was ready to argue. Harry sighed and faced her, "He's right! This is a *D door*."

Behind them hid the system controls for the hexadomes and weapon units for the militia. "Cadets, unfortunately, don't have access, so normally they stay open. This is the first time I've ever seen one closed."

"That's the same for me," Jericho said. He took a step forward. "Aye, we've already broken one of the rules. And if this goes over my head, I'm blaming the whole thing on you, Doubtson!" Jericho felt the panel to the D door's left. It was black with a keyboard wedged inside its polished steel.

"And why would yer do that, Jericho? I was simply doing your job!" Harry argued.

"You were being foolish. General Ko has given no word to any of the commanders—we were not allowed to open that gate!"

"Please repeat that sentence one more time," Dally cried. "I didn't hear you the last seventeen times. Pal, we don't care if your general gave the order or not. All we know is that you don't want to touch that water you got dripping in your stupid domes. Oh, and who builds their city underwater?"

"DALLY!" Zia screamed. "Enough." She clapped her hands and pulled me towards the D door. "Well, on you go!"

"And that means?" I asked.

She waved her hands around. "Do your thing. Turn the door into sand or steam or anything. Just not water, heavens forbid."

Jericho and Harry roared, "*NO! Not the D door.*"

"Why not?" Zia demanded.

"They'd have our heads if we destroyed a D door. Gah, that's worse than opening the gate for you lot," Jericho said.

I rolled my eyes, "You militia sure have a lot of rules, huh?"

"An' a lotta punishment for failin' to abide!" Bailey chuckled. "Worse dan what I had in Kelton Whide!"

"Well, we gotta get inside somehow! Any ideas?" Teala asked.

Harry dropped his head, "They have codes."

"Yes, clearance codes," Jericho sighed. "We're all trapped out here until the commander or the two other Kelts open it from the inside."

Titan ran head-first into the door. He laughed, "Then why don't we just get their attention?"

It felt like we'd been knocking for an hour, but no one had heeded our call. Dally was the last to give up, his veins sticking out along his arm. He snarled, "Stupid door! What is wrong with your military, Harry? Why can't you all just have equal authority?"

Jericho grinned, "And have cadets in places where commanders negotiate and strategize? We'd be a dead city within a week! We've built every wall, every metal wheel, every mine underwater to protect our secrets from those on land. And we're certainly not going to start giving them up all because a handful of Kelts, a Centrillian, an Ever and a backstabbing family decided it'd be best if we hid inside the Hub!"

Dally pointed at Jericho's bicorne hat, "I'm starting to see why Harry has a grudge against you!"

"I don't have a grudge against him!" Harry argued.

Their voices carried through the MSC Hub like fingers on a chalkboard. I rested with Teala and Assonance, our backs against the left wall, its cold slates soothing to my overworked head.

"I don't think we're ever going to get inside!" Assonance sighed.

I watched the right wall with her. "Well, it's not too bad out here. We could be worse off. Like outside."

A palm slapped against the metal door. Zia was furious. "We're never going to get in at this rate!" she cried.

"Not so fast, princess!" a familiar voice laughed. It was reassuring, hearing it again after so long. It made my heart slow down.

With his arm wrapped around a white hood, Odd stumbled through the Hub with Mr Kingsleigh and Kyle. My smile grew so large I thought my cheeks were going to split. I never thought I'd be so glad to see that metal device floating above Kyle's head.

Chapter 45: Open the Gate

Mr Kingsleigh waved a blue card. "I believe I have clearance." He nodded to Jericho and Harry. "Cadet. Doubtson!"

My smile fell as I realised who was underneath the hood. Perry's face was as white as the grim reaper's, his eyes bloodshot.

"PERRY!" I screamed.

Odd waved feebly. "Yes, yes, let's all worry for Perry after we open the D door."

Perry was surprisingly light. It was as though he hadn't eaten in days. He offered me a smile, trying to hide his immense pain. "Hey, Faith!"

The realisation dawned on me—I knew who had done this. A warm rage coursed through me. "You went, didn't you? You went to fight him! You promised!"

"Fight who?" Dally cried.

Teala latched herself onto Perry's side. His eyes ignited like she had cut him herself. I had never seen him in so much pain before.

He whispered, "I'm sorry."

Dally didn't leave time to answer. He pulled Perry off his feet and supported his other side.

There was a sharp scrape behind me. Odd winked at the princess. "Please, thank me later. Oh, and when we get back to the Town of Tents, I want to have a gander inside that journal of yours. I'm curious as to what kind of adventure you had without me."

She grinned, shaking her head.

Odd put out his hand, and Titan slapped it as hard as he could. "Nice going, jackass! Took your time. Where have you been the last day and a half?"

Odd gestured to Mr Kingsleigh. "With my boss. Apologies. I was meant to visit yesterday, but the business industry sleeps for no one, and that includes me."

Bailey rushed over to us. He clapped his hands. "I got 'im. Ye rest now, Kyle, take de load off ya shoulders!" They switched places and we all huddled through the D door.

Chapter 46
Escape Plan
Faith

On the other side of the D door, there was a narrow hall that was circular in shape. It was like walking into a spacecraft. White lights bloomed on the other side; chirps and beeps from monitors and rushed footsteps brushed past my ears.

"I'm trying, my Lord, but nothing is working. I'm sorry, but I don't have clearance for that. Only General Ko is allowed to begin the shutdown!" a familiar voice argued.

"Giuseppe, your people are dying, if you do not begin the sequence, they will all perish in the water of insanity! You must!" a woman said.

We burst through the tunnel. Three figures turned to us. The first thing we heard was, "PERRY!"

Olivia's blond hair fell over her brother's forehead. Dally and Bailey placed him on a table. The tunnel came out to two staircases—one that went right and another that went to the left. Down past the black railing and around the stairs there was a conference table of lacquered oak, blue sheets, haphazard paperwork and several pens. Perry's blood oozed over the sheets.

I clasped his head in my arms, hugging him, hoping the bleeding would stop. Lord Kelton and Giuseppe stood at either end of the room. There were a thousand monitors, all displaying something different; computers the size of cars were plastered behind me in my brass chair. Giuseppe had a bloody bandage wrapped around his left hand, which clasped a rifle.

Chapter 46: Escape Plan

"Put in the digits, Commander. As king, I order you to!" Lord Kelton pointed a glass sword at Giuseppe. The Drewan commander leaned his free hand on a black monitor—its keyboard was dusty.

He shivered, "I can't, My Lord!" His eyes latched onto Jericho. "What is the meaning of this, Cadet? Why have yer let these stragglers inside?"

Before Jericho could answer, Lord Kelton raised his voice. "Commander Malvitch, I order you under the white light of Kelton White, under the glass of the western hexadomes, for the protection of all Drewans—*put in the code!* You cannot disobey one of the eight leaders of Oberon!"

Giuseppe dropped to the floor, bits of paper falling with him. He cried, "I don't know the code! I swear to you, My Lord! Only General Ko knows the numbers to initiate the shutdown protocol. I ... I have failed you!"

Olivia took her eyes off Perry for a moment. "Don't say that, Sep! We can work this out. Where is the general? Can you call for him?"

Odd and Mr Kingsleigh searched each other. Guiseppe shook his head, "It's possible. But I don't know how long it will take for him to reach this section of Drewmora."

"Call him and I will speak to him directly!" Lord Kelton instructed.

Odd mumbled, "Apologies, My Liege! But I don't think that will be of any value to you. There have been some unfortunate ... *complications* since the Lower Hex was attacked."

Lord Kelton gave Odd an arrogant eye. "Oh, the prophet-in-training. What is it? I am in no mood to tolerate riddles and philosophy."

Odd sighed, "Well ..."

"The general's dead!" Perry cried. "I saw him die ... He ... He's gone!" Perry tossed and turned, pleading for the pain to stop. I clasped him close as Olivia and Teala joined me.

Giuseppe's face lost all hope. "Dead? What do yer mean dead?"

"He means the general's soul has been taken by the omens, Commander. You and your squad are some of the last militia in the Lower Hex," Mr Kingsleigh said.

Jericho took a step back. "No! Not the general. He can't be dead! Say they're lying, Commander. This cannot be true!"

Giuseppe lifted his hand. "Odd, what were yer going to say? What were yer going to tell Lord Kelton?"

Odd frowned, "Perry speaks the truth. General Ko has reached the heavens. I myself witnessed his body go cold."

Giuseppe dropped further down. "Then we're doomed!" He slapped his hand against the marble. "Without General Ko, we cannot turn the shield layer on. The glass has lost its protection. The water will continue to flow. There is no saving us now!"

Lord Kelton clenched his see-through sword. "By Hope's Light, there is always a way!" He turned away from Giuseppe, his greying beard bristling under his hard-worked fingers. "But we must act quickly." He placed his arm on Odd's shoulder, "I am placing my daughter and son's life in your hands, Oddington. As well as you, Drewan. Kingsleigh, correct?"

Mr Kingsleigh nodded, kneeling down to Lord Kelton. "Anything for you, My Lord. We may bear different colours, but inside us all hides the same warm blood."

"Good! Councillor Caduca and Commander Giuseppe shall escort you all to safety."

"And what are you going to do, Father?" Zia chirped. Her voice was like a bark compared to the lord's ferocious howl. He raised the glass between his fingers. "I will hold the glass together before it breaks and drowns the Drewans under the blue beacon's shine!"

"You can't!" Zia squealed.

"It's my duty, Zia. I am king, not just in Kelton Whide, but to any who need my help." He caressed her cheek. "Your eyes have turned grey. Like the glass—the glass that protects, that holds life. We are the masters of glass, little bear. I've failed my people. But I can still save Drewmora!" Titan and Zia hugged their father. Before long, Lord Kelton abandoned us for the domes that surrounded the Lower Hex. His crest's light, the white koala of peace and justice, vanished.

Jericho leaned on the railing, nudging Harry. "So yer really are a salty princess. Looks like you've outdone yerself, Haz!"

"Can yer stop calling me ———"

Chapter 46: Escape Plan

"You need to watch your mouth, Drewan!" Dally yelled, pointing his fingers at the cadet.

Jericho smiled, "This again! Yer like to argue, don't you, Kelt?"

"Jericho, stand down!" Giuseppe picked himself up. "The princess' father just left to save us. Not for his own Kelts, but us Drewans. Yer speak when you are told to. Understand? Olivia, what's the plan?"

"We wait here. Bring anyone else inside the Hub until we can get the attention of Mayor Pythalone."

"The mayor won't have anything to do with this, this is militia business, not council!" Harry said.

"He's right! Only General Ko knows the codes." Giuseppe rested on the black monitor. "By the time the mayor finds out, it'll be too late. He'll need to do a whole system reboot and that could take days. After that, we're going to have to get assessed. If the water is as deadly as yer say it is, he'll know, or someone in his party will, and they'll put us in detention centres for months on end."

"Well, staying here is our safest option. Perry's already injured, and if anyone else gets infected by the water, we're all doomed!" Olivia sighed.

"Why don't we try an' escape?" Bailey uttered. "Get outta de Lower Hex, run for a hexadome dat's safe?"

"Bailey's right!" Felicia cheered. "If what the commander says is true, we will have to scour for food, and we'll be much worse off in a detention centre. If we can make it to one of the connecting glass tunnels that surround the Between, we should be twice as safe. Especially if we stick close together. We might all make it to the Upper Hex in one piece!"

Harry, Jericho, Leo, James and Giuseppe glanced at one another with fear. Giuseppe clenched his fist. "With the emergency sirens, it means the tunnels have been cut off. We're trapped in the Between."

"But the Between is connected to the New Mines, is it not?" Odd asked. His face was eager, and his finger was tight around a blue book. He wandered towards Perry, Teala and I.

"What are you suggesting, Odd?" Zia asked.

He watched us all. "There are many ways into Drewmora. Through the Great Divide, like many, through the Nest or simply by swimming and hoping you won't run out of breath. What if I told you there was a fourth way in?"

"It's true," Teala said. "There is another way under Drewmora!"

Harry scratched at his elbow. "Aye, each hexadome is linked to one connecting tunnel. The Between and the New Mines do share a brother tunnel."

"Which means it's possible to reach the New Mines," Giuseppe cheered.

"Which means we can escape!" Odd placed the book beside Perry.

Perry squirmed so much that the book began to shuffle closer to the table's edge. "Well, that settles it," Odd said. "And if we stay here, Titan will get hungry within the hour, and from my past experience with a hungry Titan, that is never a joyous occasion. Remember, it is Mardi Mimpi! We will all dream tonight!" The book slipped from the table. I braced myself for the noise as a blue crest ignited. Jericho flinched—his hand flared out like a fan towards Perry and me. He huffed and puffed as a bubble consumed the falling book. Mid-fall, the bubble bounced into the air, floating higher and higher. The book was trapped. Odd raised an eyebrow, slashing at Jericho's work. *Pop!* The book dropped into his hands. Dally eyed me down. Even Olivia was taken aback. *Was Jericho one of the strange masked ones from the dock?*

"Does the cadet have any siblings?" Olivia asked Giuseppe.

"Ah ... Yes, a brother and sister, I believe. Jericho?"

Jericho nodded, "Aye, m'lady. A half-brother and younger sister. They'll be safe in the Upper Hex, I can assure yer."

"Good for them!" Dally muttered. "No time to waste, right? Faith, you look after him, okay?" He waved at Bailey and Kyle. "You two wanna come and check the streets with me? We'll scout ahead and make sure there's a safe passage for us to follow."

Bailey nodded, "Swell idea. Cadet, can ya come with us? Could use ya Drewan knowhow!"

"Hey, it's not a boys-only club, is it?" Felicia asked. "You're going to need my brain to figure out which way's best. Remember, I always have things ——"

CHAPTER 46: ESCAPE PLAN

"Calculated!" Bailey laughed, wrapping his arm around Felicia.

Kyle jogged behind them, Holdie racing after his head. "Wait, so what's up with the water?"

The five left.

Odd examined his book, "How curious."

He walked over to the commander. Mr Kingsleigh joined them.

"Try and contact the mayor from here. If not, one of his councillors. Heck, even the senator will do," Odd said.

"I'll try my contacts and see if I can't get someone to warn the Royal Hex!" Mr Kingsleigh took his phone from his pocket, clicking away.

Perry cried out in pain; I could smell his blood. Holding him still, Teala asked, "Can't you do something, Faith? Can you stop the pain?"

My crest had been burning this whole time. I hugged Perry tighter. "I'm trying, Tea, but he's fighting it!"

Teala's face scrunched, "Fighting? Why would he ——"

"Perry, you let this girl help you or so help me Hope! I'll kill you myself!" Olivia screamed.

I closed my eyes and pushed. My muscles began to heave, my hands began to cramp, and I had never felt my crest burn so furiously. It felt like someone had ignited a fire on my wrist. When I opened my eyes, Perry had tears in his eyes; his body shook, and my crest had blood dripping from under its white light.

Assonance reached my side with Harry and Zia. She saw the blood on my arm and, instead of arguing with Perry's half-conscious body, offered her left hand. "Hold my hand." She gave Teala her right, "You too, Tea." She waved to Titan, "Come. Join us!"

"What are you doing?" I asked.

Assonance grinned, "Helping. In Central City, holding hands is a bond of love. My parents used to tell my brother and me that when two people hold hands, they become one. They are linked from that moment onwards. If he's fighting back, then you should hit twice as hard!"

"Oh, I'd kiss you, bird girl!" I cheered as we surrounded Perry.

Odd raised his brows. "Disappointing orgy!"

Titan mumbled, "What's an orgy?"

"You don't need to know, prince," Olivia said. "Are you going to help or not, Mr Odd?"

Odd gave her his hand. "Of course, Councillor. Let's all hold hands and chant something, huh? The human touch can sometimes be the most powerful cure of them all."

"Odd, shut up!" Teala instructed. She closed her eyes and took Assonance's and Olivia's hands. We stood in a circle, surrounding Perry. A blue and orange light emerged among the cluster of white. The mumbles of Giuseppe and Mr Kingsleigh disappeared. I gripped Perry's hand tightly. Our crests became one, and I closed my eyes.

When I opened them, I was in a white abyss. My heart pounded so loud I thought the world was pounding with it. I could hear voices. *Spirits.*

You see, he sees.

The darkness grows.

The dead soul prevails.

Perry laid in a ball just ahead. His white hood was almost transparent in the abyss. Falling from the sky was a sea of colour. All the colours of the world, like paint, had come from the heavens to cleanse Perry. His hood was soon covered in reds, blues, greens, yellows, blacks, pinks, oranges and whites. His face remained clear from the many shades, and his eyes opened. I could smell the grassy scent his family always had, and the incense Leila suffocated their house with. And I could see Perry, young and innocent.

The abyss vanished. I was in Kelton Whide. We sat upon Hilly Park, admiring Whide's Cathedral. Everyone was with us. Juice tackled Kyle as he pushed half a rice cake in his mouth. Dally danced with Ada, hugging her so tightly I was surprised she didn't laugh. Bailey told Teala and Titan stories of the fantastical Everbreen, so far away and magical. Felicia clasped Assonance's hand as they watched the clouds go by. Giuseppe handed Olivia a white rose. And Zia told Harry about the wonders of her kingdom, all the little things a royal should know.

I turned my head. Next to me was Perry. He leaned against a light oak tree. "What?" he asked. "Faith, what's wrong?"

CHAPTER 46: ESCAPE PLAN

I could still feel Drewmora under my tongue. "You're holding back. Why?"

He lost his smile. "Because I lied to you. Because I needed you and you weren't there, and it was my fault." He looked to the others. "Look at them. They're all so happy. It's just like before we left. Before everything!"

"Is this what you see? Why you're fighting back?"

"Fighting back?" he asked. "Why would I fight back? Faith, I'm dying. You can heal wounds, but death. *It's too late ...*"

When his mouth closed, I felt as though I was falling. The oak faded and the happiness in the world vanished. I closed my eyes, preparing for the impact of whatever waited beneath me. I gulped, not feeling a thing. When my eyes opened, I was in the Town of Tents. *Is this my tent-let?* Outside, the grass of Farbe was empty. I was alone. The town had been torn through. Blood covered the crops, tent-lets had gashes through their delicate fabrics, and bodies were aplenty. Perry's staff was in the centre of it all.

"'Bout time you showed up!"

I turned to see Teala. Her arms were crossed.

"He's going to kill me!"

"Who?" I asked her. Her face was more mature, her skin smoother, her hair longer; she was taller. "Who else, Faith? I'm sixteen tomorrow. Isn't that exciting? You're finally in my dream."

"Dream? I'm trying to save Perry!"

"And you will. Like Assonance said. Just hit twice as hard." She offered me Perry's staff. "Look after him. When I'm gone. Bailey too. And Olivia. Should get going though, my brother is dying!" She grinned and poked my forehead. I yielded and my eyes went foggy.

When my vision cleared, I could hear metal against flesh. Perry and Juice sliced at each other until Perry lost his balance. He took a step away from Juice and shivered, blood dripping from his side. Juice raised his paper katana and I screamed. Both of them turned as I wielded the staff. With all my might, I leapt in front of Perry and swung. However, when the timber reached Juice's katana, he vanished.

A chill breeze tickled my neck. *Where did Perry go?* I was outside the

Hub. The emergency lights had been turned off. Dally, Felicia, Kyle, Jericho, Pip and Bailey wandered outside the gate. Chloe stood guard.

Bailey glanced at me. "Hey, Imma check over dere!" he said.

He ran to me. "Bailey, it's me! Can you …" He ran right past. When I turned to see where he went, he was gone.

"Hey, Felicia, have you seen Bailey?" Kyle asked.

Felicia shook her head. "He was just over there a minute ago." They called the Ever's name, but there was no response. Then I heard a troubled breath. A gasp.

"Bailey?" Dally asked, approaching me.

Bailey stood by my side, his face white. "Don't come near me, Dally!"

"What happened, pal?"

Bailey began to cry, "I've been conked. De water, it's … it's touched me. Please, don't come near me!"

I stumbled and fell. When my face smacked the road, I saw Perry. I was back in the System Control. Perry's and Assonance's hands were in mine. Perry was still, breathing slowly. I lifted my head, my crest losing its bright light. Teala and I both yelled, *"Bailey!"*

Did she see what I saw?

I let go of Assonance, "Bailey, we need to check on him. I think he's been infected!" Before I had finished, Titan, Zia, Assonance and Harry bolted for the exit. I watched Teala, her forehead dripping sweat. "Did you …"

She nodded, "It's like that every time I close my eyes."

Perry smiled, "I can't feel anything. Doctor, please take me to bed. I think I'm still dying!" I rolled my eyes as he laughed, lifting himself. Olivia and Teala hugged him.

"You're okay!" Olivia cheered.

Perry nodded, "No thanks to Faith. Pretty much brought me back from the dead."

"I didn't know you could do that!" Odd said. He had a worried gaze.

"Neither did I." All of a sudden, I could taste Perry's dry lips. He pulled away. "I love you so much! I knew I should have listened to you." He leapt from the table and put his hood on. "Now, let's find Bailey."

Chapter 47
Closing Eyes
Bailey

The cold sting made my hands clench. The stain left goosebumps along my arm an' my heart almost gave way. My feet froze as the ground covered my shoes in dust. My fingers were shakin' as Dally called my name. "Bailey! What happened, pal?"

My chest quivered as his footsteps came closer. A growl lingered under my breath. "Don't! I've been hit. Don't come near me, I swear by the spirits, if ye do I'll ..." A wolf's howl burned my brain. I thought my eyes were gonna fall out, they pushed so hard against my skull.

I heaved as Dally came closer. I had to protect him. I needed 'em to get away. I roared, "GET AWAY!" A bear-like sigh came afterwards. My teeth were sharp along my lips. They almost pierced at my flesh as Dally took a step back. They needed to get to the New Mines. *I needed to get as far away as I could.*

Kyle and Holdie joined Dally, "There there, Bailey ... No need to yell. We can get through this. We'll just need to take our time."

"NO!" I lunged at 'em. I couldn't explain why, but when I stopped, Felicia gathered herself behind the fellas.

The cadets were not far behind. They all needed to leave me. *Now!*

"What's gotten into you, Bailey?" she demanded.

"The water got him! He's ——"

I was gonna see those masked freaks again an' kill any of 'em that came near. My crest burned as another howl shook my bones. I dropped, slappin' my hands against the charcoal road. I could feel my face turn red, smell the metal of the Hub, taste the sweat from my skin. It hurt so much as if the wolf was drilling a hole into my noggin. My chest heaved in an' out. I wanted to vomit.

A grey smog now covered the far streets of the Lower Hex. Felicia ignored it an' leaned down. "It's going to be okay."

"No, it's not! Leave me. Now, Felicia. Get 'em an' leave me 'ere."

Dally stomped his feet. "We're not leaving you, Bailey."

"I SAID LEAVE!" I had never shouted so loud before. They stumbled back in astonishment.

"BAILEY?" Assonance called.

Zia an' Titan yelled my name too, runnin' past Chloe at the gate. Ye could barely see 'em past the fog.

"Bailey, you knob, where'd he ..." Zia gasped, seeing the fur along my arms.

"What the salt is happening to him?" Pip demanded, pointin' his khopesh at my stomach.

"Cadet, get 'em away from me please!" The whole group surrounded me. "Ye need to leave me. I'm done for! Go! To de mines, leave. Now!"

No one moved. Kyle an' Jericho searched behind me for any water or waves. I gripped my nails along the rough asphalt, my skin rippin', blood smudging along the black.

Thick black hairs covered my arms an' hands. My fingers were the only skin I had left. *Was my face covered too?* My pants looked tighter 'round my knees. Assonance looked down at me.

"No, Bailey! We can't!"

"Great, now the water makes you hairy!" Harry sighed. "Come, Bailey, we just gotta sprint down a few blocks. You'll be chipper!"

"Harry, take de princess an' prince as far away from me as possible. Please. Felicia, protect Assonance ... I ... I don't know how much longer I can—*Argh!*"

The howl of the wolf called. But this time there was a tiger an' a dragon. It roared again, with more critters joining the wolf's call. Each time my eyes would water more an' more. I could smell their filthy fur; the panther's spit, the raven's feathers, the armadillo's armour,

Chapter 47: Closing Eyes

the dolphin's laugh, the koala's silence ... Faith an' Teala tumbled onto the pavement. They turned to me, Olivia escorting 'em past Chloe. You could hear 'em in the thick grey fog. Sprinting as fast as he could out of the grey, Perry slowed, approaching my half-human, half-panda form.

"PERRY!" I begged, "Get 'em away from me. Please."

He kneeled in front of me. "It's fine. You know I can't do that ... But I can wait for you. I'll wait for you until you feel better." He stood.

I closed my eyes, feelin' the fog I had created. It was moist along my bloody hairy fingers. I could smell the cologne on Harry's neck, the berry perfume on Olivia's wrists, the salt of the Full Sea drowning the Lower Hex an' Perry's fresh blood. I could hear their heartbeats, a melody as magical as the burnin' silent hums of their crests. I admired my shaking hand: six fingers, distorted an' shameful.

Picking myself up, I looked at Perry. "I'm not askin'!" He turned to me with a frown. "Ye all need to leave me! I'm serious."

"Bailey, this isn't the Town of Tents. We're not going to wake up if you close your eyes one last time!" Faith said.

I stared at her. "Exactly. I've accepted my fate. Now leave me!" This anger took over my insides. I snarled, my lip quiverin'. With a roar, I demanded, "LEAVE! NOW! Or I'll kill de lot of ya ..."

Another howl. I could hear all the critters of the forest. My bones ached, my knees shook an' my heart stopped. Perry's voice echoed, "BAILEY! Where are you?" After, Faith called for me and so did Zia, Teala, Dally, Felicia and Assonance. Heck, even the cadets called my name. I laid still, unable to feel my face. I rolled back an' forth, tryin' to feel the end of my paws. The fog drifted. I forgot how heavy I used to be. My tail rubbed against the road, then it stung. *Someone's foot just ...*

I growled, somersaulting onto my four paws. My noggin had to readjust to being so hunched over. But it all came back so naturally.

"Oh, gee, I'm sorry, Bailey! Please don't eat me." The fog faded. We both stopped. Kyle caught his breath and smiled, "You're a panda again." He laughed; I could hear raindrops splashing around us. One the size of a small coin fell so hard it made Kyle scream. The water oozed down his temple as the fog vanished.

"No, no, no, no, no!" he screamed. "I've been hit! I-I've been hit! By the Light of Hope, I've been hit! Why?" He glanced 'round, blinking. Holdie continued to float. "Okay, nothing's happened. What was I meant to see? I'm not going to turn into an armadillo, am I?" he asked as Assonance pulled him away from another falling droplet.

"You gotta be joking!" Dally mumbled.

"It's raining? Underwater?" Titan mused.

"That's not rain!" Olivia stared at the ocean from around the Between. "That's the Full Sea."

There were long cracks along the hexagonal pieces; smaller fractures spread out from each one. The Full Sea dripped through the cracks, watering us like a garden in a forest.

"Take cover!"

Perry tackled Faith, Olivia pulled Dally an' Felicia, an' Teala yanked Assonance out of the way. A white, red an' blue light covered their bodies. When the lights vanished, they were gone. Ash fell onto the road as the water drenched Kyle, the cadets an' myself. However, one person remained.

Zia pushed her arms into the air. She held 'em out screaming, her white crest burning. Harry had ducked out of the way with Chloe. He was mesmerised by the princess' beauty as she cried in pain. Her hands shook at the hexadome. I glanced up. The cracks were slippin' away. It was like watching a time-lapse of someone fixing a windscreen. The sharp white lines an' cracks grew smaller an' smaller 'til the hexadome covering the Between returned to its previous self before the dreamcatchers had blown.

A white figure appeared behind Zia. She dropped to her knees as the smell of ash drifted off Perry's hood. He had water droplets covering his shoulders. Something slapped the road. Zia, Perry an' I turned. Titan lay on the road, his eyes closed an' his crest bleeding from under its white light.

Zia crawled to her brother, screaming his name. She held him in her arms as he lay, drained from repairing the hexadome. Olivia appeared under a blue light, sighin'—she was wet as well. *Everyone was wet!* A clappin' sound echoed behind 'em. Odd brushed past Harry an' Chloe with a frown.

Chapter 47: Closing Eyes

"So much for staying dry, huh?" He rolled his eyes an' examined me. "That's curious!" He admired Zia an' Titan's work an' whistled, "And that's pretty spectacular." A droplet hit his forehead. He jolted, dryin' himself. "Oh, come on. Really!"

Perry grinned, "Well, now we're all infected."

"Yeah, but I don't see any masked lunatics yet!" Kyle said.

He's right! I hadn't seen any an' I was the first to fall victim.

I crawled to Perry. "I haven't seen any either." I caught my breath. "Are we all infected?"

Perry nodded, pattin' the top of my noggin and between my ears. Not as satisfying when I coulda done it myself moments before. "Teala could have teleported earlier, but I was too late. By the time Faith and I reached the Hub, we were already wet."

A red light appeared, Assonance topplin' from its centre. Red ash fell 'round her an' Teala. Assonance hugged her stomach. "Oh, my! That was disorientating." She shook her noggin as the others gathered 'round us.

Jericho an' Pip took their time behind a large motel. When they reached my furry side; a line of Drewans accompanied 'em. We were surrounded by fifty, maybe sixty fellas. Dally kneeled beside Zia an' rubbed her back. Felicia an' Assonance held hands again an' Harry escorted an elderly lady with Chloe. "Nuts! Yer guys got all wet, shoot!" Leo cried.

"What? Did it rain or something? How'd yer manage this?" James asked.

Harry guided 'em to us as Commander Malvitch, Mr Kingsleigh an' Chloe collected the remaining survivors from both the Hub an' the Between's saturated streets. *I hadn't realised how many had joined us.*

"Is that everyone?" Faith asked.

Leo an' James eyed each other curiously.

"There's a lot more than what I last counted!" Felicia said.

Mr Kingsleigh was distraught. "By the omen's salty chins, how are you all as wet as the Full Sea herself?"

"It rained," Teala mumbled.

Giuseppe lowered his rifle, "How? It's not forecast to rain in the Between until next week."

"What she means, Sep is that the Full Sea leaked," Olivia said.

Giuseppe raised his weapon, its metal shimmering in the wind. "So you're all infected!" he gasped.

The crowd was speechless.

Perry pushed the rifle from his sister's face. "Hey, watch where you point that thing!" he demanded.

"You watch yer tongue. You're infected, Caduca!"

"Calm down, Giuseppe!" Olivia cried. "Can't you see that your people surround you? This is no way for a commander to act, especially in front of all these Drewans!"

Giuseppe's brows creased. He took a step back from us. "What Drewans? The only ones I see are my cadets, Mr Kingsleigh and the Doubtson boys."

We all examined the crowd. Now a hundred blue-crested civilians surrounded us, barricaded us, trapped us. Dally picked up Titan, his weight tight on the white tiger's muscles.

Odd sighed, steppin' back to back with Perry, "Oh, no, here we go!"

"Harry, where'd you find that lady?" Perry asked.

Harry held her wrinkly fingers. She smelt of vanilla cream. "Just by the gate. She asked me if I could ..." The elderly Drewan let go of his hand. Her eyes had no irises; she stared at him, a ghost of what she was before.

"What on the seas are you talking about?" Mr Kingsleigh demanded.

"And you, cadets. Where did you find these stragglers?" Odd asked.

Jericho shrugged, "Like Harry said, they asked for our help, and we gave it to 'em. We were going to bring 'em back to the Hub."

"Do not lie, Jericho! There is no one behind you or Pip!" Giuseppe said.

"Yes, there is! Look, Commander." Pip pointed behind him. The crowd was now twice as large.

A small warm body leaned into my fur. I turned to see Teala, her chest racing. She gulped, *"They're here!"* A thud like the bangin' of two

Chapter 47: Closing Eyes

metal plates echoed. Behind the glass of the Between's hexadome swam a ginormous dark-blue shadow. Everyone's eyes, including Giuseppe's an' Mr Kingsleigh's, watched it. However, the growing crowd remained more concerned with us. It was an elongated figure with a sharp upper fin, a tail as large as WonderWorks' tower an' a bumpy sword-like nose. It sent chills down my spine as the metal bang jolted the ground. Further down in the Between, the artificial daylight began to dissipate. Darkness came for us. Each of the dome's hexagonal glass pieces turned red, one by one. With each thud, another turned the shade of blood 'til the whole hexadome was covered in an ocean of black. The hexadome had closed its eyes.

When it was hard to see, when ye could only feel the person's breath beside ya, when our crests were the brightest lights in the Between, the many fellas that gathered 'round us changed. The moment the lights turned off, they each wore a half-black, half-white mask, staring towards our herd. All ye could hear was Holdie spinnin' above Kyle's crown.

"RUN!" Odd yelled.

Like creatures without souls, the masked Drewans crawled on top of one another, pinched at each other's skin, pounded their own flesh in an attempt to claw out our eyes. Kyle's fist smacked one of the masks into the road, and another hit the end of Perry's staff. I followed Felicia an' Faith as Zia pegged a glass knife into the black half of a Drewan's mask. Although their skin was broken, they did not bleed, they did not scream, they did not stop!

They chased us past the Hub's gate. Chloe joined our sprint as loud horrendous squeals beckoned behind us. At a confused jog, Leo an' James followed their brother's white face.

"Odd, where do we go?" Zia asked, turnin' down the following avenue.

"We need to reach the Brother Tunnel. Once there, we can find the mines. However, I'm not too familiar with Drewmora!"

Dally heaved his shoulder into a masked one's neck. "Harry, lead!"

"If he's leading, I'm going with him!" Jericho zoomed ahead as we passed metallic clogs an' wheels. They were frozen, stuck as the masked ones caught up to our heels.

Assonance pulled Felicia along, "Just don't look back!"

"Honey, not in a million years!" Felicia laughed.

Harry an' Jericho turned another corner. Awaiting us was another army of masked ones, their lifeless eyes still and motionless.

"Let's look back, let's look back!" Assonance yelled.

Harry trotted back, and his blue crest ignited. Hairy left the ground as the colours of the world returned. The dark red abyss left the dome as Hairy's dark, shadowy-self cracked his knuckles. Pip readied his khopesh. Chloe unsheathed hers.

"Cadets, lower yer khopeshes!" Giuseppe ordered.

"Hey, Harry yer know the shortcut, right?" Jericho asked.

"What do yer mean?"

Jericho pulled Chloe's arm. "Take her! Not all of us shall die down here. Stand down, Hairy!"

The shadowy figure waved Jericho away. "What are you talking about?" Harry asked.

"You are not militia! Yer don't need to sacrifice yerself for Drewmora. But we do!"

Jericho swung. Harry braced, catching Chloe's side. "Go down Eloise Parade! You'll reach the tunnel faster that way. We'll hold 'em off!" Before Harry could answer, he pulled Chloe back.

Jericho and Pip roared, "FOR DREWMORA!"

They vanished amongst the lunatics. The crowd of masked ones tore through the two cadets like wrappin' paper durin' the celebration season. We could only hear the khopeshes as one of the distant masked ones floated into the air within a blue bubble.

The masked ones were still on our tails, an' now a handful blocked our path. Harry pulled Chloe towards a skinny alleyway with rainbow vines covering its path. Hairy's dark figure leapt, tearing through the rainbow. We migrated through, but the masked ones were inbound. My paws took off and ye could hear their weight against the asphalt. I turned my body, my side slappin' five or six of the masked one's stomachs, as a white light appeared in front of me. Perry's staff took down two. Faith's crest was like a fire—she slapped the road. The asphalt beneath my feet peeled away as a wave of black grew next to

Chapter 47: Closing Eyes

me. A wall made from the road grew up an' up as Faith ran out of breath. It stopped growin' the moment she lifted her arm.

The squeals continued behind us as Olivia called our names. We ran while Odd guarded the group's back end. The sea of masked ones tried to overwhelm him. He snapped his fingers, clapped his hands an' spread 'em out like he'd performed a magic trick. The swarm stopped their squeals. They were frozen still as Odd lowered his hands. His white rabbit crest didn't glow at all. *Was he even using his gift?*

"Mr Odd, come!" Olivia ordered.

Odd an' Mr Kingsleigh brushed past my fur.

"By all means, Miss Olivia!" he laughed.

Only one of us remained. The commander lowered his rifle. His lips were dry. Olivia called for him. He looked at the asphalt wall Faith had created. Ye could hear the cries of Pip an' Jericho behind it.

"We need to go, Sep!" Olivia pleaded.

"But ... They were my responsibility. And I can't even see what they were running towards. What are yer fighting?"

The frozen masked ones behind him began to twitch. One moved an arm.

"Giuseppe, please. I can't lose you too!" Olivia cried.

"LOSE ME TO WHAT? Olivia, what is chasing you?" he pleaded. He tossed his rifle to the floor, his blond hairs dangling down his temple. You could taste the confused stress under his eyes.

"The dead Drewans from the past. The ones that succumbed to the darkness years before your militia began. We are running from a past we cannot escape. It may be history, but the world has not forgotten!" Odd said. He picked at the muck under his nail. "Now, commander, I recommend you follow us, otherwise, when you inevitably get saturated by the oncoming flows of the Full Sea, you will be alone to fight your ancestor's mistakes. Plus, Miss Olivia here will continue to whine, and I think I'd rather a bullet from that rifle. Do I make myself clear?"

Giuseppe approached us. "But the cadets ———"

"Are fighting enemies you cannot see," Odd finished. "Like you said, what are they fighting? Is it even real?"

Giuseppe watched the black wall, and Olivia gulped. I jogged 'round the commander, who was baffled by my size. Before I could think, the top of my noggin pushed at his shoulder blades. He galloped, takin' his rifle as I pushed him towards Olivia. She yanked his arm through the vines an' the swarm began their chase once more. Even Odd sprinted as fast as he could. He an' Mister Kingsleigh were well in shape for this kinda workout. The swarm of masks fumbled over one another like a crashin' wave of insanity. They cantered, grasping at my tail.

Ahead of Faith an' I, Zia yelled, "Which way, Harry?"

"Straight for now! I don't know," he cried.

"It should be to our left, kinda," Chloe said. Ye could hear the shrieks from the masked ones, their horrible disfigured bodies becoming more rotten the further we ran.

"What does the tunnel look like?" Assonance asked.

"It's got a grey frame around it which detects people's crests and has South Hexadome imprinted above it," Harry explained.

I could feel fingers tingle against my tail. I pushed forward, clippin' Perry's boots.

Felicia pulled Assonance. "No, you can't!"

Assonance's orange crest ignited. "I won't be long. I'm just going to scout ahead. I promise you, my hand and yours will be together again! I'll be fine." Her fingers let go of Felicia's an' began to shrivel an' snap. They melded together into brown an' orange wings that fluttered above Dally's noggin. The raven took flight, "I'll find where it is!"

Before long, Assonance was gone. Felicia kept her pace as we exited the alleyway. We hit another large two-lane road that smelt of burnt hairs from the dreamcatcher holes beyond the Between. Harry jolted back an' forth before turnin' left.

More masked ones gathered outside the alleyway; they appeared from thin air. Each street around this one was covered in a herd of 'em. Hairy kicked the side of one as Chloe sliced another with her khopesh. The metal chimed as one of the masked lunatics reached for Kyle. He tripped over his feet, catching Holdie in his hands. When the metal device slapped his skin, a strange bubbly noise echoed. Holdie

Chapter 47: Closing Eyes

stopped spinning. The masked one jumped towards Kyle. Midway through, the stuttering Kelt dissolved into a ghastly smellin' ooze. It made Leo an' James gag. The masked one tumbled as Holdie boiled in the sludge's crisp coating. It began to bubble 'round the metal alloy. Holdie span once more, awakening from his slumber. Pushing up an' up, it grabbed Kyle's noggin an' reformed his human body. Leo an' James cheered him on.

We continued running. More metal buildings an' frozen gears covered our path. It seemed this metallic maze never ended, no matter which way Harry turned. "Turn right here, Doubtson!" Mr Kingsleigh ordered.

Unsure, Harry nodded, "Yep, good idea."

"Yes! Then left Harry, you're almost there!" Assonance called. She was a few metres above, flappin' her wings like an angel. We followed her calls, passin' a familiar sign in blue: *Eddy's*.

Perry's brows dropped, "I didn't know Eddy had a shop in Drewmora!"

"Huh, would you look at that!" Odd laughed. "He must be expanding!"

With a final turn down Eloise Parade an' one last corner, our hearts began to warm. The tunnel's entrance was down this last street. With the screamin' behind me, our boots, shoes an' paws tumbled into the glass tunnel. I turned with Faith to see that we'd skedaddled faster than we had thought. The swarm huddled fifteen metres behind us. Harry an' Chloe fell to the ground, Zia an' Dally caught their breath, Perry cheered with Kyle, an' Teala guided Leo an' James inside. The swarm were gaining traction.

Assonance flew down. Her wings grew outwards into long arms; the feathers above her noggin dripped down into a luscious coat of honey hair, her beak shrunk into a small button nose an' her claws flattened out to become feet. She smiled at all of us, "I knew we could make it!"

Assonance was the only one outside of the tunnel. You could hear her arms rub against her windbreaker. Felicia shoved past my fur an' reached for the bird girl. Assonance took hold of her hand—their fingers touched but did not connect.

I had never seen anyone's eyes light up so quickly with so much fear. You could see the life fade from Assonance's face as her fingers began to fall.

"Assonance?" Felicia asked.

Her face had turned white; her chest stopped moving. A tear fell from Assonance's brown Centrillian eyes.

"Hold me!" she begged.

I could feel a flurry of wind push against my snout's hairs. My heart began to race again as the sound of water pounded against the metal buildings. It sounded like the wolf's growl.

Faith and I turned. Behind the swarm of masked ones, there was a tidal wave the size of the giant from Everbreen. It crushed all the buildings in its path as we all reached out for Assonance. A crowd of hands pulled, yet she took hold of none. A black arm, burnt from a scorching fire, wrapped itself from behind Assonance, gripping her chest. Its black, nail-less fingers clasped at her chin an' cheeks. Her scream stopped, smothered by the hand. Behind the frightened bird girl, a half-black, half-white mask pulled her into the swarm. Felicia ran towards her. I pushed ahead, Perry vanished into a white light, Giuseppe loaded his rifle, an' Faith slapped the glass, all tryin' to reach her.

Perry got the furthest, appearing above the swarm. His hood fell over his noggin as his staff extended to crush anything below him. Before his feet reached the ground, a panel of glass flew towards him. It knocked him back into the tunnel, flyin' past my side an' crashing next to Zia. The princess stood an' gulped. Another panel of glass pushed back Faith, Felicia, Giuseppe an' me. Assonance disappeared under the masked ones as the glass panel covered the tunnel's exit.

Felicia screamed her lover's name, but the words became fragile behind the layer of glass melding itself around the tunnel's entrance. The grey frame was soon covered in a thick layer of sharp, white Kelton glass. Zia ran her fingers along the glass, her crest alight like a torch. She yelled, but the glass would not bend to her will. It was stuck. Behind the swarm, Lord Kelton stood in the distance. He watched us, melding the glass in front of us. Silently, he lifted his hand at his daughter to say *stop*. He smiled.

Chapter 47: Closing Eyes

The tidal wave crashed past more buildings.

Assonance screamed. I yelled her name.

"Tell him to let us through, Zia!" I begged.

Zia smacked her forehead onto the Kelton glass. "He won't. He's protecting us!"

"But not Assonance!" Felicia screamed. "She's out there, she needs us! Please, Zia, do something, *anything!* Break the glass, I beg you! They're killing her!"

Zia clapped her hands together an' her cheeks turned red. She screamed at the layer of glass that held us within the tunnel. She screamed an' screamed; her blood-soaked koala crest burned. Her knees hit the ground.

"Why, why, why? Just let me through! You bastard. I hate you. I hate you!" she cried.

Felicia put her hand against the glass. The water from the tidal wave covered the swarm, covering the metal buildings, the clogs an' wheels, the WonderWorks tower, an' everything else. Lord Kelton closed his eyes as the water made him vanish. He was gone … *Assonance was gone.*

My paws felt sore. I could see my own blue reflection within the Kelton glass. Chunks of dirt, rubbish an' leaves floated along the deep-blue water. It was like the entrance to the tunnel had become an exhibit in an aquarium. Water swayed back an' forth, corpses floated like jellyfish. The Between was gone. Cold tears dripped down my furry cheeks. Another thud echoed inside the tunnel. Felicia dropped beside Zia. She cried, "She's gone! She didn't deserve to …"

Zia wrapped her arms 'round her friend, the Full Sea a glass wall away from us.

We had nowhere else to go but the New Mines. I rested my snout on Felicia's left shoulder. Assonance was lost! She was right. Not all of us were going to make it. I just wished it was me, not her! *It should have been me.*

Chapter 48
How Did We Get Here?
Perry

By the time my eyes remembered the world, the tunnel was covered in a shade of blue. *Had Odd frozen time?* Assonance was right there; I was so close, until ... *Lord Kelton*. He shoved me back. He was the one who did this. He ... My eyes adjusted, and there was a sound of tears. A wall made from Kelton glass shielded us from litres and litres of deep seawater. Smog drifted from my shocked breath as I shuffled to my feet. *Assonance was right there! I was right there!*

I glanced at Dally, who had placed Titan against the tunnel's glass wall, far away from the mourning crowd. He rubbed the prince's head.

"What happened?" I asked.

Dally turned to me, hiding the obvious tears that burnt his eyes. His lip quivered. "We were too late!" He looked away, concentrating on Titan to suffocate his grief.

I watched the water pass overhead. A broken metal *W* from the WonderWorks Enterprise floated behind the layer of navy. Zia and Felicia hugged each other. Silence filled the tunnel. Giuseppe had Olivia in his arms, Odd had retreated to the opposite wall, and Faith's head had dropped—she held Teala's hand. *This can't be true! Lord Kelton would never ...*

"No! I tried to reach her. I was right there." I ran to the glass wall, hoping the water would vanish the moment I touched it. "She was right there! Why would ..." My heated glove left a ghostly handprint against the glass. I pulled it away and turned to the others. Faith's arm

Chapter 48: How Did We Get Here?

left my shoulder as I pointed at Odd. "It's an illusion, right? This isn't real. She isn't ..." I gulped, afraid of the word.

Odd picked himself from the ground. "It is an illusion, yes."

"Well, let's go and get her then. I'm sure Ona's just scratching at the glass wondering why we're all messing with her!" I said desperately.

Odd dropped his head, "Perry, it's not that simple. Mr Kingsleigh, do you care to explain?"

My chest sank. Mr Kingsleigh approached me. "The water before you is not an illusion, young wolf. Lord Kelton and the Centrillian are in the hands of the omens now."

No, this can't be. "They could have swum up to the shore. Bailey and Felicia arrived here that way. I'm positive Assonance would have swum back up, if she swam all the way down."

Bailey lifted his head. "Perry, we swam down 'ere under a spell. We held our breaths for fifty-two minutes, an' even after all dat time, we barely survived."

"But ——"

Zia stood. "JUST DROP IT! *They're gone!* Both of them. You can't change that, and neither can I!"

Zia was always bossy, always in the right even when she was wrong—always a firm authority to wage your bet with—but I had never seen her like this before. Tears dripped down her cheeks like droplets down a waterfall; her eyes were swollen from a sheet of moisture and her lips quivered like we'd reached the snowy alps in Fleddington. I tightened my mouth. I could barely hear myself think. They were really gone.

I turned to Odd, "No, Odd. You promised her parents that you'd bring her back! You told them—you said it to their faces. We can't leave until we find her. We can't!"

Odd crossed his arms, "What do you want me to do, Perry? Jump into the Full Sea and swim after her? You've been out for half an hour; even if I managed to find her body under all the debris, I don't think her parents would appreciate holding hands with whatever is left over!"

My fist tightened. "You take that back! She's not ——"

My whole body slapped the wall to my right. My crown hit the glass as the smell of Dally's breath covered my face.

"Enough! She's dead, Perry! She's gone, and so is the king." His arms were firm on my shoulders. "No one could have survived that, you know that! So stop talking about her. Can you not see what you're doing? Just look at the girls … Just stop!"

When he let go, my shoulders sagged. I turned to see Felicia in tears. She stuck to the Kelton glass like glue as Bailey rested his snout against her side. Zia wet her journal like a raincloud, writing vigorously. There was no hope, no victory. *No Assonance.*

Faith was by my side when Dally returned to Titan. Her eyes were as wet as the others'. I pulled out my arms as she covered me with that coconut and strawberry scent. Holding her tightly, I closed my eyes. At that moment, tears escaped me, yet I never felt them. Faith grinned and wiped them from my cheeks. I was glad she had made it—I was glad we had all made it, but …

I let go of Faith. Teala still had a fragile smile. Patting her head, I ruffled her moist hair. She giggled, watching the water. "Just like my dream."

"You knew?" I asked.

She frowned. "No! I didn't see this, not Ona! But I saw you and me watching the water." Our eyes met. "Today is not a good day, Perry. It's the start of something much worse than this."

Before I could ask what she meant, a voice echoed down the tunnel. "*Whodi who!*" I turned to see Leo waving his arms. You could barely see the shine from his Drewan crest. "We found it! The door, we found it, Commander."

"It's just down here. A five-minute walk!" James cheered. He was the only one who had a sign of relief in his voice.

"Door?" I asked.

Mr Kingsleigh turned to me. "The door to the second brother tunnel."

"Which will lead us to the New Mines and out of Drewmora," Odd said.

Harry raised his hand at his brothers. "Good eyes, boys. Wait there, we'll come when we're ready to cross."

CHAPTER 48: HOW DID WE GET HERE?

He nudged Chloe, her khopesh still clenched tightly in her hand. "I'm ———"

"Don't talk about Pip and Jeri!" she whispered. "They were not the nicest of Drewans, but they did not deserve to die in there."

Harry nodded, "Okay. Do yer want to look after those two? I'll gather the princess, make sure she's feeling up to it."

"Of course. I'll keep an eye out for those masked ones. If there were that many in the Between, I can't imagine what the rest of the Lower Hex looks like. Yer have my sword." Chloe winked at him.

"And you, my salt!"

They laughed.

He skipped around Odd and me before slowing as he approached Zia. He offered the princess his hand. "It's only my hand, not my shadow's," he mumbled.

Zia continued to write. His fingers caught her eye.

She stopped, "Must be nice knowing what you can and can't control."

Harry leaned down, "And what does that mean, princess?"

"You wouldn't understand." She watched the Kelton glass her father had created to protect us from the incoming water—it mocked her. She gave Harry her hand. Once on her feet, she moved away from the glass, and a crack stained white. I observed it, curious. As she walked away, the mark of Kelton Whide stained the tunnel's glass for all to see.

Dally picked up Titan, Olivia gathered herself, and Giuseppe checked on Chloe and the twins. Felicia was the last one to move. Bailey begged her to come, but she waited. She waited for Assonance to fly down with a smile as large as the day before the weekend. To tell us that we were going to be all right. *She waited for her hand to hold hers.*

"I will not leave ye 'ere!" Bailey cried.

Felicia did not reply. He pushed at her elbow with his snout, bit the back of her windbreaker's collar, but no matter what, she just watched the water.

I patted his belly. "It's fine, Bailey. You go along with Faith. We'll be with you in a moment." Faith ushered him along as the two continued down the tunnel with the rest of the gang.

I crossed my legs next to Felicia, watching the water sway back and forth. It was like a never-ending painting, always moving one way or another. It was quiet, a nice quiet. Not like someone had died, but as though the memories of those who were no longer with us were warm and fresh inside our minds. "Do you think I'm dumb?" I asked.

Felicia finally stopped looking at the water. "What kind of ——"

"Just wondering ... You have the best opinion, always calculating ahead of time. Everyone respects the Gah Ma Fel, Felicia." Tears fell from my eyes. "I don't even remember how we got here, you know! It's like a nightmare." I looked into her blue eyes. "I was right there. A moment from her hand. And then *this* ... I've known you a long time, Felicia. And I'm sorry. I'm sorry I didn't reach her in time." I stood and faced away from the Between. "Things will be better when we wake up!"

"Do you mean it?" she asked.

"You're Felicia Moore. Trust me, I would know." I left her.

When I joined the others, they smiled. Not at me, but at the person who followed. Felicia, with her knotty blond hair, pale red cheeks and panther crest, sighed, "When this is over, can we make her a tia e'mona?"

"And what's dat?" Bailey asked.

"It means *a home for the soul.*"

Faith stood next to her, "Of course. I think I know a perfect spot for it!"

We journeyed down the tunnel, the ocean black as the sea life seemed scarce. There were no sharks, no seahorses, no fish. *Nothing!*

A grey wall covered the right side of the tunnel. It looked weird between the layers of glass. It had a silver railing that smelt of sweat as Giuseppe lifted himself onto a platform. Above the platform, there was a small door no larger than my bedroom back in Kelton Whide. It had a grey knob and thick, peeling paint. Next to it was a pad. Giuseppe waved his hand in front of the pad and it ignited with blue numbers. He clicked in a code and a grinding sound jolted the tunnel. You could hear a suction noise as Giuseppe pulled the

Chapter 48: How Did We Get Here?

door open. He leaned against it, his head missing for a bit. Then he appeared again and waved us over. "All clear!"

Odd laughed, "How can it be all clear when you haven't even gotten wet?"

He approached the door and Giuseppe froze. "On second thoughts, maybe not clear." The commander sighed.

Kyle and I peeked behind them to see that the brother tunnel was an identical tunnel that led to the South Hex one way and the New Mines the opposite way. However, through Holdie's light, it was clear that this tunnel was covered in a thick layer of black water. You could hear it sway like an enclosed swimming pool. It must have been knee-deep, maybe more. There was no way to tell unless someone …

Odd jumped in and water sprayed against my shoes.

"Watch where yer goin'!" Giuseppe ducked out of the way.

Odd's pants were soaked to his ankles. He shivered, "Wow, that is colder than it looks!" A cold smog drifted from his old breath. I rubbed along the side of the door frame as Odd kicked the water and chuckled to himself.

"I'll teleport Bailey to this side. There's no way he can fit through this." I turned back down the railing and steps. "You all go through. We're almost there!"

Kyle jumped into the brother tunnel, then Zia, Harry and so on.

Bailey waited for me. "What's on de other side?"

"A tunnel like this," I latched onto his fur. "Just prepare to get a bit more cold and wet!"

"Wet?"

We vanished.

Bailey jumped up and down. "Oh, cold, cold, cold!"

Another splash came from behind. Teala had jumped from the door. Faith came afterwards, then Felicia. The only ones that remained were Giuseppe, the twins, and Mr Kingsleigh.

"Well, hurry up!" Dally said.

"We can't!" James cried. His heels were firm on the concrete beneath his shoes.

"We'll get infected if we touch the water," Giuseppe explained.

Odd crossed his arms. "Well, this is the only way out. If you stay there, you'll eventually get infected anyway. Isn't that right, Felicia?"

Felicia nodded, holding her hands together. "With the amount of water from the Between and, furthermore, within the Lower Hex, you'll be covered in water within the hour."

Harry pushed through the stream. "It's all right, James. If yer see one of those masked freaks yer hit them first, eh!" He looked at Leo. "Father would have wanted us to go this way! And yer both have each other's back. Do it for Taylah!" A splash shocked the Drewan, and he wiped droplets from his eyebrow.

Giuseppe held onto the doorframe like a sloth fresh from its slumber. Olivia offered him her hand. "There's no need to be afraid, Sep!"

He smiled, "I am not afraid. It's just ... To protect you, someone should remain sober from this vile infection!"

"Someone like you?" She rolled her eyes. "You're too busy thinking like a commander. That's not the Giuseppe I know."

"Yer can do it, Sir!" Chloe cheered.

"It's just water. You're not scared of water, are you?" Olivia asked.

Another splash echoed down the brother tunnel.

Giuseppe playfully shoved Olivia's hand away. "We can agree on that! You're much scarier than this stuff. Much colder too."

She gasped, slapping his shoulder.

Mr Kingsleigh was the last one in the doorframe. "It's not worth it. I believe this is where I leave you all!" he noted.

Odd shrugged and started to walk off. "Suit yourself, Charles. I'm sure Alice will be happy to see you. But we're wasting time." You could hear his legs push through the black. "This way, everyone."

I looked at the rich man. "Are you sure you don't want to come with us? You heard Felicia."

He leaned down, "Perry, you're an honourable man. Keep them safe. I still have some errands to run. I'm sure I can find my way safely to the Upper Hex."

I tried arguing.

CHAPTER 48: HOW DID WE GET HERE?

He continued, "This is my home, after all. Good luck. And tell the commander to cherish that sister of yours. She's a good soul!" He winked at me and turned back to the tunnel. Giuseppe chased after him, but after a few arguments from Harry and Dally, the commander calmed himself and followed Odd into the New Mines.

"So this is the last ever hexadome to be built in Drewmora?" Faith asked.

"Aye! It finished construction almost sixty years ago," Giuseppe said.

"Mmm, Dad says it's rather small," Harry added. "It's mainly for the minerals found within the quarry. They've been a real game-changer for people like Mr Kingsleigh and the factories in Bungonia."

The tunnel expanded outwards, creating another smaller hexadome of a similar size to the Between. Instead of roads and blocks of land, it had metallic rails with minecarts. A few metres from the tunnel's exit there was a steel tower that zigzagged up. The tower held a massive platform that had different machines on each side. One was a crane and another a thick rope with many large bins attached to it. It smelt of gunpowder and that dry scent freshly ploughed dirt has. We wandered a moment around the giant tower to see layer upon layer of dirt mounds. Each swayed like the Full Sea's waves against the Camel Hump Shore. Inside one large hill the size of a two-storey house, a large opening was blocked by a mine-cart.

"So where exactly is this exit, Odd?" Dally asked, unimpressed.

Odd ploughed through more water. "Down a mineshaft. Should take us roughly three hours to reach the exit upon Epping Hill. But once we're out, we'll be overlooking the Full Sea, and feeling the real wind on our faces."

Odd's feet stopped. His head glanced at the smaller hexagonal glass pieces that surrounded us. This hexadome had no dreamcatchers, no redmer timber, no cracks or holes; just plain, thick, transparent glass.

"Well, which way?" Dally argued.

"Dally, relax. Let the demigod think!" Faith scowled.

Odd was frozen. He gulped as I approached his side.

"What are you looking at?" I asked.

"An old friend!" He pointed towards the end of the New Mine's glass. Like in the Between, a towering dark figure swam past the glass. It was the largest thing I had ever seen—even larger than Aeithalis— and we slept on his back for over a year. Its fins brushed against the hexadome. *Was it watching us? Watching Odd?* No one made a sound. It was the master of the ocean, piercing through the sea with its sword-like nose.

"What is that thing?" I whispered, half astonished, half frightened.

"A marraboo," Odd muttered. "Or an omen. She is warning us!"

"Warning?" Harry asked. The water around our feet started to wobble. There were ripples. *Something was coming.*

Chapter 49

The Fourth Way
Perry

A loud ruckus of repulsive groans and screams gathered within the rear of the brother tunnel. Giuseppe and Faith turned to see a wall of darkness. The cries of pain became louder and louder, as though an army was gushing towards us through the ankle-deep water. I readied my staff as Zia tightened her grip around her shard of glass. Giuseppe checked his rifle's ammunition before backing up into Olivia.

The hideous shouts made the water shake like we were onshore. Bailey joined my side, watching the tunnel.

"What *is* that?" Leo asked, bracing himself next to James.

"Nothing good!" his brother replied.

Felicia's crest ignited. Kyle readjusted Holdie above his head, the metal device slowing its spin. Harry's black silhouette, Hairy, joined us—so did Leo's shadow and James'. My staff extended out into its longer form. The grotesque army was inbound.

Out from the shadows came at least a hundred masked ones, each missing limbs, skin rotten and burnt, eyes gouged out behind their drilled-on masks. They clawed at us with their shredded clothes, frostbitten fingers and sharp, dirty fingernails. In the centre, a masked one stumbled to the ground, a glass arrow lodged within its chest.

"That's an ugly sight!" Giuseppe cried. The crack of his rifle deafened my ears. I appeared above the insane flock of decomposed Drewans. Their skin reeked of mould as I plunged my staff into the face of one of the masks.

"Odd, where's the exit?" Faith demanded, placing her hand onto the flooded ground. The water started to bubble around the masked hoard. You could hear the bubbles pop as they tried to escape the water. Was it getting warmer? Faith dug deeper into the fluid. A handful of masked ones were soon overwhelmed by several large clouded bubbles. When the bubbles popped, the handful was gone. Faith grinned—I guess whatever she did had worked.

"Or freeze time!" Dally uttered, kicking a masked one's knee. It stumbled next to him and he continued to stomp on its arm and head.

"Time is not that simple, Dalton! Gah, now I understand why Perry likes you so much. You're both so ———"

"ODD!" Bailey screamed. You could hear the bear inside his deep voice.

"What?" Odd asked.

"De exit. *Now!*" Bailey barged through a pack of masked ones; a ball of fog as thick as a thundercloud followed his tail, knocking everything either side of him to the ground.

Odd slumped and sighed. He mumbled to himself, strolling through the dirt mounds. Clicking and clapping his fingers, he froze three masked ones that tried to tackle him. "This way, you bossy lot!"

We followed Odd's voice, knocking away anything that tried to intervene. There were so many. Harry's shadow pummelled a masked one over and over again until the white side of its mask crumbled. His brother's shadows were behind holding back the hoard as Kyle put his own hands into the water like Faith. He tugged on the moistened soil and closed his eyes. When he opened them, a boulder made from dirt flew from the ankle-deep water. It was so large and magnificent, drifting higher and higher until it started to plummet. It squashed another group of masked ones.

Kyle raised his hands in excitement. Faith slapped his left palm and laughed, sending a wave to knock down another handful. Although we'd knocked or squashed them, they continued to swarm. Odd pushed at the cart lodged in the mineshaft's entrance. He rattled his arms, yet it wouldn't budge.

"A little help, Dalton!"

Teala grabbed Dally and Titan. They vanished in a cloud of red.

Chapter 49: The Fourth Way

When they reappeared next to Odd and the mineshaft, red ash fell and burnt the soil.

I turned to see Bailey leap. His furry chest phased through my neck. I gulped as the fog behind his tail pushed down more masked ones. The twins became overwhelmed as their shadows lost their strength. Olivia grabbed them, vanishing in a blue light. Retreating, they appeared near Teala and Dally.

Another shout came from Giuseppe. Chloe sliced through the herd, standing side by side with her commander. They were the most organised in comparison to the rest of us, throwing things and hoping for the best. Zia had swapped her glass bow and arrow for a ball-and-chain and was throwing it into the heads of the many. Harry stumbled away from her as she got all her anger out. My arms lunged, and I slipped, rearing my staff at Faith's back. A mask ran into its end. She smiled at me, her hand dripping with water.

Dally closed his eyes and spread his hands out at the minecart. It started to shake, the water swaying to the motion. Kyle danced with Holdie, dodging back and forth. A masked one crept behind him. I could have stopped it, but I was too far. Teleporting wouldn't work. It was now or never.

I yelled, "Zia, shard!"

She threw a glass dagger at my forehead. I launched myself into the air, and the end of my staff hit the incoming shard's side. It bounced, ricocheting towards Kyle. The masked one dropped from the impact. Before I could celebrate, a body pushed down onto my back. I swayed, trying to maintain my balance. I could hear Faith scream. Then Kyle. The gnawing of the masked knobhead above me burnt my brain. He was crushing me!

Suddenly, the water jolted. Felicia took a step forward and yelled. Her crest was so white I thought I had reached heaven. As she approached the hoard, white flower petals started to fall into the ankle-deep water. They made gentle ripples as though the water was pure and healthy. Each petal was no bigger than a pinkie finger, curled up and dropping like rain.

Felicia took another step forward. She put her hands together as my feet caught themselves. The blond Kelt kneeled in the water, tears rushing down her face. She clenched her hands into fists and tightened her whole body into a ball. I had never heard her yell with so much power before. Not even Zia had a roar like that. I looked down and the ankle-deep water was gone. It was just dirt! Above it, white numbers floated, like ants crawling in search of food. One at a time, the numbers popped like the bubbles Jericho could make.

I turned back to Felicia, who held her bywoe staff with a flare in her eyes. She threw the staff at my back and a blur of water sprayed the unbearable weight off. I heard a heavy crash against the rough ground. Her stick was like a gurney; a tsunami of water flew from the head of the timber as if a hose was hidden inside of it. As the water escaped the bywoe, it pushed the masked ones off us like soap on skin. They drifted away, leaves flowing down her serene creak. She swung the staff, knocking another masked one's head to the moistened dirt. Her steps were precise as she hit one after the other. The water was fast, her bywoe staff was harsh and, when she freed Kyle and Faith, the masked ones started to retreat.

It was weird not being bound by the abundant water from before. The ground squished against our boots as we shuffled to the others. *Dally'd better have that minecart out of the way!* Felicia hosed down each of the masked ones, and although her rage kept us afloat, there were far too many for even her to handle. Dally's hands started to shake, glistening with the glow of his tiger crest. The cart's steel and black wheels floated in the air as though held by wires. It wobbled above the twins' heads, swaying to the motion of Dally's arm. He lowered his strain and the cart plunged into the dirt behind Giuseppe's heels. The commander jolted, feeling the hot breeze. Inside the cart, there were piles of stone and steel. It must have weighed tons.

Odd tossed Titan into Dally's arms. "Spectacular. You still stink though. This way, everyone!"

Dally's arms dropped—his face was red with anger. "Did you really just say that after I ——"

Zia barged into his back. "Oh, enough talk. Get a move on!"

They raced behind Odd into the darkness of the mine. You could smell the residue of gunpowder, strong under the fumes of metal pickaxes and sweat. Bailey turned to Felicia, who straightened her bywoe staff. "Felicia, we need to go!"

Chapter 49: The Fourth Way

She turned, the water still spraying. "If I move, they'll keep chasing us!" she argued.

Giuseppe retreated, firing one last round before following Olivia into the mineshaft. Bailey pushed back the remaining mask ones with Hairy.

"Felicia, please, we need to go now! It's now or never. We're not leaving you!" Faith yelled.

Felicia focused on the hoard, the water from her staff bouncing off her face.

Teala and the twins rushed inside. I backed myself against the entrance, my staff slapping the oak of its left post. Pebbles tumbled down the dirt mounds as Faith stood next to me.

"Harry, get Chloe out of here!" I ordered. Harry snatched Chloe's hand, so suddenly, she dropped her khopesh. It banged the wet dirt as they shimmied into the mine.

"Felicia!" I yelled. She wouldn't budge. "You will not kill yourself in here. Not here!"

Before I braced my crest to ignite and teleport to her side, Holdie appeared next to Felicia. Its metal spin slowed, lowering itself into Kyle's grimy hands. He offered the device to Felicia.

"Go!" he uttered. "Hold him for me, will ya? I'll hold off the hoard."

Felicia gawked, "You'll be worse off than me. Kyle, leave—I'll be right behind you."

"No, you won't! You'll die. I can't lose another friend. Not after Juice. Not after Maggie." He offered Holdie again, hovering his left thumb over the power button.

"Kyle, what are you doing?" I screamed.

Bailey covered his face—he heeded to Faith and me. We all screamed their names, but, before our words could make a difference, Holdie lost his spin. Felicia held the device in her hands, and Kyle was no longer. The beige sludge returned and bubbled as the odour of burnt flesh repulsed Felicia. The hoard of masked ones were three hundred and growing, clustering within the tunnel like termites in a timber cottage. The sludge started to sizzle. Felicia tightened her grip on her staff, then ...

Something spectacular happened.

A giant fist made of dirt and brown rock materialised from within the sludge. It jumped out, smacking the New Mines' soot with a heroic might—it was twice the size of Felicia. With the shoulder came a familiar head; however, instead of being made of cobblestone and vines, it was made of dirt, rock and limestone. The troll from the Cobblestone Bridge towered above the hoard. It made my heart race, seeing such a vulgar beast. Yet, something was different about its physique. Instead of pounding my back over and over again, it swung its strong rocky arms into the hoard, bulldozing the masked ones like bowling pins.

Felicia reached us. She dropped her staff as the water stopped. The roars of the troll continued. It grabbed a masked one with its arms and tossed it from side to side. You could hear the crunching of bones as the troll wrapped another hand around the masked one's torso. The masked one split in two as the troll pulled its hands apart. Its arms swiped left and right as the hoard tried to climb its rocky knees and arms. Covered by a crowd of masks, the troll looked at us and screamed, "RUN!"

The hoard came from every angle.

I waved my arms at the entrance. "Go, now! We'll be right behind you!" Faith ran into the darkness first, then Felicia. Bailey's fog dissipated as he stumbled into the mine. Kyle ran on all fours towards me and the mine. *It was him, it had to be.* He barged into the metal tower and its steel shook. I turned to the entrance. On top of the minecart's rails, the troll blocked the light from the Full Sea with his legs. The groans and cries from the masked ones echoed behind stone as the troll roared, "FRI!" A pounding blow vibrated the rails. "END!" he screamed.

I took a few steps back, and a furry body trapped my hood. "Did ye know he could do dat?" Bailey asked.

"I don't think *he* knew he could do that!" I turned to the panda. The troll's battle cries were behind us. "Where are the others?"

Bailey and I wandered a few metres until we caught Dally's voice. "I didn't drop the kid, Zia! I think I would have remembered something like that," he scowled.

CHAPTER 49: THE FOURTH WAY

"We all know how daft you can be. Maybe you just don't remember. Don't think I didn't see you and Odd tossing him back and forth like a football," Zia complained.

We turned a corner of dark limestone to see the gang illuminated by candlelight that danced over their backs and heads. Their shadows were like waves. Harry, Leo and James' crests were restful as were their shadows. We joined the dance. Titan groaned at the blur of light.

He rubbed his eyes. "Why's everyone looking at me? I swear, I didn't do anything. Where are we?"

I smiled at the little prince, but the moment was cut short. An irritated growl roared behind Bailey and me. A single masked one had gotten past the troll. It stood, its head tilted to the left as it strolled towards us, drool dripping from its mask. It rushed towards me. The firelight swayed, frightened by the mask. Teala yelled my name as I tried to swing my staff. But I was too late.

Its claws ripped at my shoulder as Bailey ran towards me with sharp teeth. A shot from Giuseppe's rifle made the room white. A ringing noise overcame my ears as the masked one fell from my red shoulder. A cold sting consumed my arm. I held it, rushing warm pain flaring up and down. The masked one ran towards Faith. Her crest glistened, but something shielded her.

I glanced up to see Odd's rabbit crest light the room. He flung the masked one back—once, twice—then wrapped both its arms around its spine. Holding its restrained hands, Odd frowned. A white light shone. When it vanished, Odd's hands held the air. The only thing that remained was a gust of steam where the masked one stood and its half-black, half-white mask, which fell from the air—it lodged itself into the dirt. Odd lowered his guard and walked away. Not a word was said until Titan cracked up.

"What just happened? Where'd that mask come from?"

Olivia helped me to my feet. I leaned on her side.

Dally took the mask from the ground, "Wha'? This thing?"

Titan nodded, "Yes, that thing. Perry fell to the ground, then he was bleeding, and then Odd danced around, and the mask appeared."

"You couldn't see it, could you?" Felicia queried.

"See what?" Titan laughed.

Odd clapped his hands. "Sleeping! That's it! How didn't I see it earlier? That's how we escape the hoard, we sleep!"

"Sleep? What are you talking about?" Zia asked.

"And are you going to explain what you just did to that thing?" Dally insisted.

Odd shook his head. "I don't need to explain myself. Isn't it obvious? Titan's been asleep since the Between. There's not a chance he'd react like that if he saw what I just did. Trust me, I spent the last week and a half looking after the little prince."

"So we sleep, and when our eyes open the masked ones will be gone?" Olivia asked.

"Those are my favourite words from this whole ordeal. Correct, Councillor. You win nothing. So, heads down. Bedtime!" Odd laughed.

Giuseppe placed a bandage around my shoulder. Dally knocked it as hard as he could when the commander was finished. I could smell the aloe vera from the medikit Chloe carried on her utility belt. It was fortunate she had it. We all cosied up against Bailey's fur. Teala said it was warm and asked about the roars outside. I smiled, "That's Kyle! He's going to keep us safe. He's the barricade keeping those monsters away from us."

I could hear Faith's voice. She was talking to Felicia and Bailey. "I hope I dream about Assonance. Maybe we'll fly in the sky together. Watch the world go by," she said.

Felicia grinned, "That sounds like a lovely dream. I'll see you all when my eyes open!" Bailey giggled; Teala's head rose to his laughter. I closed my eyes and the world went black.

When I opened them, it felt like only a few minutes had passed. Harry slept next to Zia—I hope he dreamed of Taylah. Where was she anyway? I hoped she was safe with her father. Olivia slept under Giuseppe's arm, his rifle close by. I stepped over them, the deep breaths of Bailey pushing the twins' unconscious heads up and down. The troll's cries were gone. So were the masked ones. The mine's entrance was alight with the artificial daylight of Drewmora.

Odd sat by the entrance, his eyes open, bags as black as the night sky. "You're a fast sleeper!" he said, picking himself up.

Chapter 49: The Fourth Way

"It was only thirty-seven minutes," Felicia mused. I turned to see Holdie in her hands.

"And what are you doing up?" I asked.

"No one left behind! No Kelt, no Drewan, no Ever ... No Centrillian. No one!" She raised Holdie, deep in its slumber.

The light from the New Mines hurt my brain. Under the mounds of dirt, there was a beige-coloured sludge and nothing else. No water, no masked ones, no insanity—just a brave melted boy. Felicia turned Holdie on. It started to spin, launching from her hands. The device floated above the sludge and, like freezing water, Holdie refrigerated the sludge until it became Kyle once again. He was sweaty; he reeked of mud and ash, dropping to the floor with several fresh bruises and cuts. He was out cold! I lifted him. Felicia looked at me as I adjusted my arms under Kyle's legs and back.

"What now?" she asked.

I walked into the darkness. Kyle was safely in my grasp. "We wait. Let the others sleep ... It's time to go home. *Together.*"

Chapter 50
Paper Snow
Faith

The light of Epping Hill lingered in the distance. You could smell the fresh air of Oberon, the shore of the Full Sea and the grass, healthy and green. The soothing breeze drifted past as I took a step from the darkness and saw the world above the ocean. Epping Hill overlooked the dark navy smoke under the Full Sea, rising from the luminescent hexadomes that seemed tiny.

The pollen and leaves brushed by with the wind. The trees swayed left and right, a relaxed serenity above the waters of Euphoria. Redmer trees grew down to our left as we stood at the foot of a stone mountain—its top seemed almost too far to see. Behind it was the Bluway Creek and the Forest of Gyr. Here, by the shore, the sand was a golden hue, climbing high before transforming into the seaside grass of Epping Hill.

Titan launched himself into the grass. It made an outline of his body as he rubbed his head into the green. "I never want to leave this ground ever again!" he cheered. The hill jolted. I turned to see Bailey, sitting with his legs crossed next to a cluster of sunflowers. He admired the view as the sounds of wind and water tickled his fluffy ears. He grinned at me.

Dally came next, a gloomy stare on his face. I think Assonance's death had taken a harsh toll on him, but he would never admit it. Hell, it had taken a toll on all of us. Kyle and Holdie zipped past. The former smelt the world, closing his eyes, groaning at the black marks along his arm. Felicia stood beside the panda, her right

CHAPTER 50: PAPER SNOW

hand caressing his fur as they admired the domes that had once trapped us.

Olivia's laugh took me by surprise. "I always told Dad that Drewmora was a terrible school holiday getaway."

"I still think it would have been better than Tinkette Falls," Perry mused.

"No!" Teala said. "You know Mum has a sensitive stomach. She would have been sick the first night under those domes! Then she and Dad would have argued, and it would have been a nightmare."

Olivia smiled, putting her hand on Teala's shoulder. "Exactly. Dad may have been big and scary to some, but he would never mess with Mum."

"He was always a softy when it came to her, huh?" Perry chuckled.

Giuseppe tapped his hood with his rifle. "I agree with Perry. Drewmora is much better than those salty waterfalls up in Tinkette Valley!"

Olivia and Teala stared at Giuseppe.

Perry raised his brows and tapped the commander's shoulder. "You don't want to enter the argument, especially with these two nutcases. Together, they're worse than Faith. Didn't you hear? Their mother's a prophet!"

Hold on, did he just say what I think he just said?

"Oh my gosh! Really Perry?"

He giggled with Giuseppe.

Harry, Chloe and the twins took in the view. They stood, eyeing the relaxed water ahead. You would never be able to see all of the pain and destruction by looking at the blue city from up here. Down on the shore, there was a metal fence. Its crisscrossing steel protected empty tent-lets and a herd of immigrants. From afar, you could tell that those colours did not belong on this land, yet they were here, incarcerated like prisoners.

The hole we travelled through was dark—it crumbled as we passed through.

"It's going to be a long walk back to the Town of Tents!" Dally urged, stretching his back.

"You mean Kelton Whide?" Olivia asked.

"We're not going back to Kelton, Olivia!" Zia argued.

"And aren't we going back to Central City?" Giuseppe put a hand on his hip, staring at Olivia.

"You're going back to Central City?" Teala asked Olivia.

"I have to. There's much to report and, with Giuseppe, we can explain what happened to the …" She avoided Zia's eyes. "King. You all should go back home!"

"We can't!" Harry said. "And we don't have money to survive in Central City. Where do we go?"

"With us!" Bailey uttered. "To the west, to the Town!"

"But what about the prince and princess?" Olivia wondered, turning to Perry and Teala. "What about Mum? She waits for your return every day."

Perry and Teala searched for ants until Odd spoke.

"I believe that is a good sign, especially coming from a prophet. It means that they will return, does it not? I myself live in Everbreen. And as a final service to Lord Kelton, I promised I would take care of his daughter and son. If they choose, they may go back to the Town of Tents with Dalton and Bailey. And that goes for all them. They are not children anymore. And I'll keep an eye out to make sure they live peacefully."

Suddenly, a roar of engines and gears squealed above our heads. A dark shadow covered us. However, instead of readying themselves for battle, Bailey and Felicia cheered.

"Georgia! Ritesh!" Bailey called.

"Captain Murray! … *Yuri!*" Felicia gasped.

A bronze zeppelin blew back my hair; its balloon was the size of a double-decker bus. Felicia waved her hands in the air.

"You know them?" Zia asked.

"Yes!" Bailey cheered. "They helped us get to Drewmora!"

Felicia slowed her wave. "I think they saw us. The captain's finding somewhere to land."

The zeppelin hovered above the shoreline. *He can't be, can he?*

Chapter 50: Paper Snow

"He's not naïve enough to land on the shoreline?" I asked.

"Sounds like Murray," Bailey said, heading down Epping Hill.

Perry followed. "Well, it's better than walking!"

A metallic clonk echoed as we pushed through the redmer trees, their red-drenched sap staining my hands. The sand blinded us as we emerged in front of the Full Sea. Camel Hump Shore had never looked so beautiful.

A crowd of different coloured crests covered the shoreline next to a bronze glass box and a deflated balloon. Our footsteps marked the sand, and the group turned as we approached them. Bailey and Felicia ran ahead.

"Hey, Ritesh, Captain! It's us!" Felicia called.

From the forest, they looked like most sheltered in the Town of Tents, but as they got closer to Felicia, it hit me. *I know those names. I know those faces! These are the people who robbed the ferry!*

Felicia and the group collided. They hugged as Bailey slowed his pace.

Murray beamed. "Ah, so you're a panda again?"

Bailey nodded, "Yep. Seems I jus' can't keep my human form, aye! Where's Milky an' Georgia?"

Ritesh, the dark-skinned Fledding, gestured to the sleeping zeppelin. "Inside, making sure Win Dixie's down and secure. Gah, you really did get outta there!"

Murray waved his finger in the air. "We've been flying back and forth for you. Are these your fr——"

"FELICIA! Get away from them!" Dally screamed, his eyes latched onto Murray.

Murray broadened his shoulders. "Oh, round two, huh, Kelt!"

"I say we pick up where we left off!"

"Dally, ease up! Dese are our mates!" Bailey yelled.

Dally's finger lingered on Murray. "But he attacked us on the ferry. In the swamp, they tried to ——"

"I'd shut that mouth of yours, muscles!" a familiar face said. Wearing a blue hat, Georgia pointed her arrow's head at my chest; her bow was firm as she grinned at me. "Otherwise bubbles over here is going to lose that hand of hers!"

Before I could say something, Zia's crest ignited. Her glass shard turned into a bow and arrow of its own. She pointed it at Georgia's head. "You shoot her, and you can say goodbye to that eye of yours!" Zia affirmed.

Georgia moved her aim from me to Zia. "I'm starting to like this group!"

A blue light glimmered next to Zia.

Olivia appeared, dropping onto the sand with blue ash falling around her. Perry readied his staff as Hairy left Harry's shadow, its black form staring at the other group.

"Whoa, whoa, whoa! I go away for two minutes and this is what I return to? By the Light of the Hopeful Mother, why is everyone at each other's throats?" A boy took a step closer and gawked, "Felicia? What are you ...? Where's Assonance?" The words made Felicia tear up. She couldn't face him.

It was him—he was Yuri!

My own heart burned—he had no idea. He reached out to Felicia as a confused frown reshaped his Centrillian lips. "Felicia, what happened down there? Where is she?" he asked.

Bailey took a step forward. "She's ——" He couldn't finish.

Yuri looked him in the eyes. "Bailey, is that you? Why's she ...? Where's Ona? Tell me!"

Before Bailey could answer, Perry lowered his staff. "She didn't make it. She's gone. I'm sorry! It's my fault."

Yuri lunged at Perry—he charged towards him and his hood. I ran to them with Zia and Olivia; Yuri was already pushing Perry. "What do you mean she's *gone?* I can still feel her in my crest's light. She's still there!"

"She couldn't have survived what happened! I'm sorry, your crest is wrong, she's gone!"

Yuri hammered his chest. "No, no, no! She can't be gone. My crest still burns like she's still here. I would have felt it." He cried, falling into Perry. The two dropped together into the sand. His tears dropped onto Perry's white hood. "She can't be dead, she can't!"

CHAPTER 50: PAPER SNOW

Perry pulled him close, tears running down his face. "She is. I'm sorry, I couldn't reach her in time. She's dead."

Yuri slapped him again and again. His crest could still feel her, but why? If Mr Kingsleigh and Giuseppe could see the water, she would have drowned with the king.

We listened to his cries, Felicia's echoing in the background. The sea crashed beside us and the zeppelin, a cruel reminder of Assonance's fate. Georgia lowered her bow, a tear falling down her cheek. I tapped her on the shoulder, and she nodded at me. "I'm sorry I tried to shoot you. A friend of Ona is a friend of mine. Is she really ..."

"We really did try to save her, but ..." I sighed.

"You don't need to explain it to me. She had a good soul, a kind heart. Yuri hasn't stopped talking about their reunion since the day she, Bailey and Felicia jumped into the Full Sea."

The blue beacon gleamed in the distance as we watched the waves settle. There was a rare peaceful silence among the group—it was the silence of grief. There was no room for clustered thoughts, heated arguments or diabolic city-ending conundrums. Just silence for the sake of silence.

Then something pinched the metal of the zeppelin. It sounded like a monster growling; a white shine reflected off Win Dixie's bridge. Kyle dodged out of the way. He groaned, landing on his bruises. Perry picked himself and Yuri up as Felicia dried her tears. A frightening figure mounted the deflated balloon, blood splattered across his paper cloak, a katana firm in his right hand. He gazed at us furiously.

"*Juice!*" Georgia choked. She knew his name? How?

Perry readied his staff as Ritesh swung his metal chain. Papercut launched himself off the zeppelin, joining us on the sand. The little ones travelling with the runaways scurried faster than fleas on a dog. Of course, Dally was the first to collide with his katana. They danced around one another for a moment, hands and arms splintering by.

"Juice, you don't need to fight us. It's over!" Dally took hold of Papercut's hands. "Calm down. You don't ——"

He was cut short, flung violently against the side of Win Dixie's bronze steel. The clash of metal echoed. Papercut continued his duel with Ritesh. His chain flew past the ninja with ferocity; you could smell the sweat along the metallic loops.

"You should be dead, Juice!" Ravesh cried in his deeper tone.

He tossed the chain again; it peeled past Juice's shoulder like an awful breeze. With his katana, Juice threw the Fledding's body forward. There was a pain in his footsteps; the more he moved, the more aggressive his demeanour became. He threw his arm into the air.

Ravesh flew back with so much force that a wave of sand hit Georgia and me. She raised her bow as Hairy took the next swing. The black shadow caught Juice off guard. Before long, the dance became more dangerous. Papercut grabbed the figure by the throat. Lifting it into the air, Harry began to shake. As his shadow choked, his knees tore through the sand, and his eyes bulged from his skull.

Zia gasped, shooting her arrow. The glass landed inside the paper cloak's elbow—blood ran red. Papercut dropped the dark figure. Hairy faded away, returning to Harry's kneeling body. Papercut had eyes only for Zia. Perry and Yuri ran towards us.

I need to stop Perry before he gets himself killed again. But Zia's in trouble! *I can't save them all, can I?*

Papercut swung his sword at Zia's arms. The clang of glass echoed all around us. Titan clasped a stained-glass sword. His hand bled under its handle as he used Zia's shard against the paper warrior. However, Juice was almost twice the boy's age. He tore through his tight defence, clashing his katana into the sand.

Behind them, Kyle helped Dally to his feet. Bailey ran towards Papercut with all his might. His eyes were focused; his paws took him like a bullet. Juice lifted his katana and leapt, kicking Harry's head. The impact from the kick launched his body into the air, and he floated like a falling piece of paper above Bailey's powerful stride. Bailey pushed his claws into the sand and came to a stop.

Juice plummeted down, smashing Bailey's chest into the shore. Sand covered the poor panda's fur.

Kyle waved his arms, "Juice! Stop. You don't have to do this. This isn't you!"

The words made Papercut stop. He pointed his katana's end at Kyle and Holdie.

Chapter 50: Paper Snow

"Go on!" Kyle stood his ground. "You've already kept me in a cage. Killing me isn't going to change a thing!"

Juice went for the attack. Giuseppe's rifle rumbled so loudly I thought another dreamcatcher had exploded. Papercut sliced the bullets in half.

"You killed my men!" Giuseppe yelled.

As Papercut dealt with the commander, Yuri and Murray diverged around his paper cloak. One came from the left, the other from the right. Murray launched onto his legs, while Yuri took down his arms. In one motion, the dance continued. Murray's face clashed with Papercut's boots as blood ran red along Yuri's white, frightened face. He gulped, cheeks still swollen from his tears as his hand dropped from his wrist. Blood decorated Murray's chin with a spurt of red. Yuri quivered eyeing the tender meat where his hand had once been. His body fell.

Papercut raised his katana for the finishing blow. However, when he lowered his sword, Felicia slid beside Yuri, blocking the sharp side with her crest hand. White numbers appeared around the sword as Juice's eyes grew wide. The katana began to lose its paper-like texture. When he finished his attack, the katana had disappeared under the warm light of Felicia's crest.

Georgia let go of her arrow and her bow's string ached. Papercut swayed away from its aim, and it hit the sand. Perry vanished in a hue of white. He was going to attack! But where? How? What was Perry thinking?

Another groan came from Dally, "Now you've done it!"

They tossed back and forth on the shore, sand spraying from their kerfuffle. The sound of a blade cutting through flesh made my stomach clench. Dally's cheek was as red as a warm fire. He fell to the sand as Papercut rose to his feet.

Murray threw sand into the warrior's eyes. Papercut wiped the yellow pebbles from his face as Murray sprinted out of his way.

Odd stood beside me. His voice was grim. "He needs to die."

"No, he doesn't. He can still see reason! Juice can ——"

"Juice is gone, Faith! Perry's known that since the first day he saw him in that paper cloak. Look at him."

"Then why don't you do something about it?" I pleaded.

"Because this is not my fight. I had no idea it could ever be this bad ... Time has tortured the boy. He has lost everything!" Odd put his arms around my shoulder. He grinned at me. I felt his hands slam into the top of my chest. It burned as Juice's arms swung between us.

Odd dodged his attacks. "I don't even know who you are. Why are you fighting me?" he laughed. He took hold of Papercut's arms and spun him around. "Panda, batter up!"

He pushed Juice's paper into a ball of fog. The fog was so thick and dark; it tore through the paper, causing him to tumble into the sand mounds beside Georgia and me. However, the hit was not strong enough.

Papercut, the moment his head hit the mounds, snatched at Georgia's legs. A red light took her. She vanished, appearing with Teala next to Felicia. A soft hand grabbed mine so tightly I thought I would lose blood flow to my fingers. The world tinted blue. Juice's face, bloodied and bruised, was before mine, his eyes wide.

I turned to see Perry's bare hand around mine. His grip was as tense as his gaze. He watched Juice stand, scaring the children who hid behind Olivia. Perry's voice remained relaxed. "He needs to be stopped."

"We're not going to kill him!" I told him.

"We won't ... Just help me. Please. I can't do this without you!"

I watched Juice push Kyle, his bloody claws staining Holdie's spinning steel red. Perry pulled me along. *So this is what it feels like to be invisible. I didn't know he could do this.* Kyle dropped to the shore, spitting blood from his swollen lip. Papercut grasped Holdie as if it were a lucky coin. It was now or never.

Perry let go. The moment he did, it was like Juice could sense us. He searched for our invisible silhouettes along the dance floor of the shore, waiting for his sparring partner to return and attack. He lost his hold on Holdie, propping his feet out like a ballerina. Each step was conscious and calculated. Perry vanished from my side. Papercut's eyes—no, *Juice's eyes*—saw me for a second before white ash appeared behind him and his paper cloak.

Perry launched himself a few metres above the shore. He flew like

CHAPTER 50: PAPER SNOW

a raven, plunging the end of his staff into Juice's temple. Perry's body shook. Papercut's strong left hand latched onto his neck. Harry ran to our aid, as well as Giuseppe and Bailey. But I had to make the call. *Perry needs me. Juice needs me!*

I charged forward, hearing Perry's gasps for air. "Let go of him, Juice!" I ordered, pulling at his right arm. I yanked, feeling his white possum crest under his paper clothes. It did not shine, it did not glow; it was not proud of its colour. Juice's hold on Perry's throat remained strong as his furious eyes, bloodshot around the ocean-blue irises, stared into my soul. My crest erupted. This pain from Juice's frozen heart latched onto me. A silver substance trailed out of his crest, off his paper cloak and onto my hand. It was torturing him. I could hear his old voice scream in fear.

A glimpse of the Drewan WonderWorks' Labourites echoed inside my head. Juice, like what he was back in Kelton Whide, was plastered onto a wall. These people in lab coats held him down and injected him with a silver liquid. It dripped onto the shore as another image echoed. Georgia and Ritesh laughed with him. However, their laughing stopped. A door opened. A man with no face instructed soldiers to hold them down and tase them with a blue light of electricity. Crying. There was a shuttle made of glass that drifted through the Full Sea. Juice had hit the eject button; the man with no face hunted him down. Inside the shuttle, Georgia and Ritesh waited for him, but he never returned, lost to insanity.

Paper covered his hands as Juice's crest lost its light. He screamed as his skin turned from beige to a moonlike white. He couldn't scream anymore. He looked at himself in a shattered mirror. I was inside his head as we both looked at what he had become. With a paper cloak and bandana covering his mouth and nose, he was Papercut, not Juice.

He pulled away from me. The visions stopped as Perry's body smashed against the sand. Kyle went to him as Juice began to scamper. The silver liquid covered my redmer-stained fingers, dripping as though it were alive. Once in the sand, it dissolved and faded into the sea. Juice's eyes watched mine—he was bamboozled, shocked. His crest's light shone under his paper cloak. He held his shaking hands before the light and grinned. The others slowed their pace as Juice's pointing finger began to fade away. As it vanished, a small piece of paper-like confetti took the end of his finger into the blue sky. As more of his finger turned into the confetti, he watched us. Another finger faded, becoming another line of confetti within the sky. Like paper snow, his hand left the world, floating into the air. He reached out to us. Two cue cards dropped into the sand.

His shoulder began to vanish. Tears dripped from his eyes as his face glowed. Juice smiled at me. His cheeks vanished, then his blue eyes and brown hair. It was like he had accepted this; his whole body transformed into the confetti. The snow drifted into the heavens, flying towards the blue beacon. Juice was gone! Only the two cue cards were left.

The one on my right had my name. I clasped the card, its black calligraphy as neat as before. **Thank you for freeing me, Faith,** it read. When I looked down, Perry had taken hold of the second card. He and Kyle helped each other up.

"Well, what does it say?" Titan asked.

Perry grinned, holding the card above the shoreline. "Omehwai!"

The word turned the crashing waves into a peaceful melody as an arm wrapped itself around my waist. Perry's grasp was tight; his forehead rubbed against the side of my head.

"We did it!" he cried. "We finally won."

I hugged him back. "*You* did it!"

Chapter 51

Spreading Gifts
Bailey

Teala admired the shoreline with Odd. "Is he gone?" she asked.

"I believe that is a question for another day, Tea." The ol' demigod had a gloom in his gaze as they waited for the waves to settle. I joined 'em.

"De Full Sea's schmick from up 'ere! An' ye don't have to thank me, Odd. I wanted to *strike while de iron was hot* ... Is dat the sayin'?"

Odd smiled, "Close enough. No, I'm glad you got what *batter up* meant. Panda, you're one of the kindest men I have ever had the fortune of knowing ... And the hairiest too!"

We laughed awhile, 'til a screeching cry took us for simps.

"Somebody help!" Felicia cried.

Blood was smeared along her hands an' windbreaker as she wrapped the jacket 'round Milky's limp arm. His eyes looked like they were gonna fall outta his face. His body shook, but his gaze remained frozen. 'Bove the bumps of his dry lips, he watched his severed left hand, lifeless on the shore. The scent of blood an' burnin' paper bristled as I collided with Ritesh.

We reached 'em, the herd circling the two like it were some kind of ritual. Ritesh kneeled next to Felicia, his hands readying above Milky's cleaved wrist. He put pressure against the windbreaker. Milky did not jolt or cry; he simply watched his bodiless hand.

"It's going to be okay, bud. We're going to make it through this," Ritesh mumbled, swaying as the fresh blood began to clot against the nylon of Felicia's windbreaker.

Finally, Milky groaned. He kept his focus. "Ritesh? That isn't my hand, is it? That ... We can sew it back on, right? Make things better? Bring Ona back?"

Ritesh's face dropped. He pushed his short black hair back. "We'll try our hardest, I swear we will!"

A little girl gasped behind Olivia an' Teala. "Oh, no. Milky, are you o——"

Mia stepped from behind the two Kelts, her eyes lingering on the blood an' the hand.

Her face turned white as tears built up in her blue eyes. "Mia, stay back! You shouldn't be looking at this. Come with me." Georgia leapt in front of her sister, shielding her. She pulled Mia's right wrist, dragging the little Bellcurve's legs along the sand. She cried, askin' for answers. They shuffled past Murray. "Go help him, numbnuts! Find some bandages. Anything!" Georgia ordered.

As Murray searched the shore, Faith an' Perry joined us. Leo squirmed, seeing the blood, Zia held Kyle, and Holdie examined Papercut's butchery. Milky was losin' himself. His eyes drooped, and his tongue was out as he began to have trouble breathing. He heaved, almost half unconscious.

I turned to Faith. "Can ye do something for 'im, Faith? He'll ..."

Milky chuckled, "Die? Well, at least I'll be with Ona. She can't be ..." He spat a ball of bloody phlegm onto the sand. It popped, coatin' my front claws. Tears dripped from Milky's eyes. "I don't want to die. This isn't my time; the Hopeful Mother doesn't want my soul. Not now. *Not ever!* I ... I ..." He wept words I could barely understand.

"Please do something, Faith! You're the only one who can," Felicia begged holdin' Milky close.

Faith stuttered. Perry ushered her forward. "If you can help me, you can help him. We couldn't save Assonance, but we can save her brother. Spread your gift!"

Faith kneeled next to me—her crest was crisp. The waves crashed an' her voice sounded almost unreal like an angel. She pushed Milky's chin up with her dirty fingers. "So you're Yuri? Ona told me a lot about you. She really looked up to you, did you know that?"

Yuri's tears stopped. "Looked up to me? You knew Ona?"

CHAPTER 51: SPREADING GIFTS

"Sure did. I've known her for quite some time." Faith offered Milky her hand. "May I show you something?"

"Is it about Ona?"

"Of course. You can trust me." Milky was hesitant, but eventually, he fell for the sweetness of her voice. Their hands became one.

Faith smiled as her crest ignited like starlight. "Yuri, you'll need to close your eyes. I promise we'll keep you safe. We'll keep you and Ona safe!"

The Centrillian closed his eyes.

Odd tiptoed to Ritesh's side. "Bailey, I think Faith's performance would be much smoother if there was a little more grey in the air. Something creamy!"

I looked at Faith for confirmation.

"If you'd be so kind!" she said.

Focusing on my crest, its green light shined against my black fur. Its light glistened along Harry's face; the twins squinted as Chloe blocked the gleam of the sun. It was soon engulfed by a clouded grey that covered the redmer trees, the crashin' waves an' the tiny yellow pebbles that shifted beneath us. I shared my gift to hide Odd. He picked up the severed hand an' watched the blood drift off the shore. He smiled at me an' vanished behind a thick wall of my own fog.

Behind the grey, all the colours of the world radiated like fireworks. Perry's white wolf crest was as clear as daylight; other colours surrounded his silhouette. 'Twas a rainbow of blues, greens, reds, blacks, whites, yellows and oranges. It had been a minute, but that minute felt like an hour. I calmed my crest's glow as the fog began to dissipate.

When the shoreline returned, Odd was gone an' so was the hand. I was not the only person to notice. Ritesh, Felicia an' Perry gave me a curious eye as I devoted my attention to Milky an' Faith. Milky was smilin' as Faith helped him to his feet.

He held her hand tightly. "Thank you."

Faith let go. "No need. I did it for Assonance."

Milky lost his grin. He pulled the windbreaker from his arm— it peeled off like a table-cover, revealing a clean wrist. Although he was still missin' his left hand, the arm looked as though it had been surgically removed an' stitched back with great precision and care.

Milky glanced at his people and bit his lip. "Well. What are you looking at?" He took a step forward. "Let's make sure there's no more funny business. Murray, stop running about and check on Win Dixie's engine; Pleffin, check down the shoreline and make sure no one followed that lunatic; Spice, you check down there." He turned back to Ritesh. "Teshi. Any other ideas?"

Ritesh stood, "Little ones, stay near the zeppelin. I want everyone to be on high alert." He pointed at Dally, still slumped in the sand. "And can someone see if that guy's okay. He got the crap knocked out of his head."

Chloe saluted the runaway. "Understood. I will check on him, Sir!"

She skedaddled to Dally's side, pushin' his unconscious body 'round so his face took in the sunlight.

"*Sir?*" Ritesh gawked.

"I think she's taken you for a commander," Perry laughed. "Name's Perry ... I hear you helped my friends on their journey to Drewmora." They shook hands. "Thank you."

Ritesh raised his brows. "Bailey holds you in high regard. You do not disappoint." He put his arm 'round Perry's hood. "We must discuss this Town of Tents and how you all plan to get home. Come, this way."

"Can someone give me a hand?" Chloe yelled from afar.

Titan skedaddled towards her. "I'd rephrase that if I were you. Might be a little too soon, if you know what I mean. Oh, let me jump on Dally, please, please, please!"

For some reason, when my bottom hit the ground, my paws burned from the weight of my body. I watched Harry help Felicia to her feet. He asked if she was cold, prepared to take his jacket off.

Felicia giggled, "You're too kind, dolphin. I shall wash my windbreaker in the sea. Would you like to keep me company?" Milky returned the windbreaker. It was soaked with stale blood, yet Felicia continued to giggle. She kneeled on the shoreline, Harry an' Hairy beside her, swishing the jacket against the Full Sea's bubbles.

Chapter 51: Spreading Gifts

Kyle nudged my side. "I don't think we've ever really talked!" he chirped.

I smiled, "Our lives have been ratha too busy for small talk. What would ye like to know?"

"This and that! You did carry me from Everbreen to Central City. I think it'd be best to first say thank you," Kyle said.

"Thank me? Please. You're de one who almost killed himself to protect us in de New Mines. I should be thankin' you ... Oi, now dat I have ya, did ya know ye could turn into ———"

"Into a troll?" he mused. "To be honest, I just did what made me happy. I've hurt a lot of people during my time as the Troll from Under the Cobblestone Bridge. I just ..."

"Ye did dandy! No need to put more pressure on yourself. Trust me, you'd end up like Perry."

I told Kyle about the Town of Tents. How we ran it. How everyone did their chores. How once a week Gabe would fly down to the pizza place in Everbreen an' bring back thirty pizzas with Assonance an' a few other flyin' Evers. How on the second week of a full blue moon we'd all gather in the town's centre an' sing an' play music an' just enjoy the night's sky. And how I had made the system for chores so that it was equal for everyone. *I missed it.* Afterwards, he said something quirky.

"What? Are you the mayor of the town?"

"Me?" I asked. "By de spirits, never. I jus' understand de importance of keepin' everyone happy!"

Suddenly, Odd returned. He joined Olivia, Giuseppe an' Zia as they discussed something about Central City. Teala rolled her eyes an' left, joining Kyle an' me.

"What are dey on about?" I asked.

"The end!" Teala admitted. "And what to do next."

I gazed at Win Dixie. Murray flicked the switches in the cockpit.

"Well, I'm sure Murray, Milky an' de rest would be happy to give us a lift back to de town ... That's if I fit on de damn thing. I wasn't dis heavy before." I looked at Win Dixie, spotting a familiar grin. Georgia leaned down.

"You good in there, Muz?" she called.

Murray shoved his thumb at her, "Right as rain."

She turned an' our eyes met. "Howdy, stranger," she said. "Been a while since I last saw you like this. You've gotten a little fat there, Bailey!"

Teala giggled, "I like this one. Who's your friend?"

Mia ran an' shook Teala's hand. "I'm Mia. This is my sister, Georgia, but she can be a nightmare sometimes. Just don't make jokes about cakes and you should be okay." She caught sight of me. "Jeepers, is that a panda?"

"That's Bailey, you silly," Georgia muttered.

"Bailey ... This is what you used to look like? Wow!" She examined me from noggin to toe.

"Hi, Mia!" She scratched my fur. "Oh, gentle. Dat spot's real sensitive."

Mia jumped, "So what does the water feel like in the Full Sea?"

I grinned—*I'd almost forgotten. It was only a few days ago—but so much has happened since.* "Refreshin'!" I watched the shoreline. "Why don't ya take ye shoes off an' have a feel for yourself?"

Mia asked Georgia a hundred times before she rolled her eyes an' said yes. Georgia laughed. They walked away, Georgia's eyes still firm on mine. "Glad you made it out safely," she said. "I would ask you to come with us, but no one bosses big ol' Bailey around, remember!"

Her an' Mia left.

"Did you really say that, Bailey?" Perry wondered.

"He sure did!" Ritesh laughed.

I faced 'em, "Say what?"

"Well, I don't rule the town, Ritesh! No one does. If you want to know if you can stay the night, we'd be happy to have you, but Bailey's the one you got to ask. He practically runs the place!"

"Told you," Kyle muttered with a smirk.

I frowned, "No, I don't. I jus' maintain things like de chores."

"And the peace," Faith said.

"Wait, Bailey did you allow them passage into the town?" Odd

Chapter 51: Spreading Gifts

demanded. He approached us. "Well, if they're sleeping there, we'd better be getting a lift in that zeppelin. What is that thing? Vintage Centrillian? I haven't seen one like that with bronze steel and a circular balloon in almost a hundred years. Very traditional, I must say!"

"A hundred years? You all right in the head, pal?" Milky asked.

Faith laughed, nudgin' Odd's shoulder. "Just an old Kelton phrase. I also agree, very traditional."

Ritesh waved his hands. "Yes, yes, you can all come with us. Might be hard with Bailey being so large, but he and Felicia practically fixed the damn beaut!"

A cough of smog left the back of the cockpit. Murray raised his arms. "Ah-ha! Purrs like a baby. I told you it'd be safe to land her 'ere, Ritesh!"

Ritesh rolled his eyes. "Well, keep her steady. Last thing we need is for her engine to give out again." He looked out to the shore. "Poor old Juice. He didn't deserve that!"

"He seemed happy when bubbles here did what she did!" Georgia said.

Faith frowned with regret. It was going to take time before she came to terms with what she chose to do. Mia was behind her, playing in the water with Harry. He watched her like how he'd watch Taylah— gentle eyes on a gentle soul. Felicia was ringin' out her windbreaker, admiring the Full Sea.

"You knew Juice?" Kyle asked.

"That we did. Spent months with him trapped under those domes down there." Ritesh pointed to the Upper Hex; black smoke still lingered behind its hexagonal glass pieces. "He helped us when times were tough. Us and his brothers."

"Then he became that monster ... Hunted down Sam and Gerard," Georgia scoffed with a grim voice

"The WoodWood brothers?" Teala asked.

"That's right. They used to travel with us, but things changed; the little ones were in danger. They chose to leave us." Milky's voice was dry.

Perry laughed, "Well, don't worry. We'll pick them up on the way home."

"You know where they are?" Ritesh gawked.

"Nowhere special, but yes. I think we might know!" Kyle crossed his arms.

"Speaking of home, where exactly can that thing take us?" Odd asked.

The rest of the group gathered. The paths down the shoreline, behind the redmer trees an' beyond, were safe from any stragglers or strange unknowns. Harry guided Mia back to Georgia. He joined his brothers, awaitin' the future.

Olivia took the first step. "We'll be needing a lift to Central City or at least somewhere near the Flatlands."

"Market Vilé will do. I can get us safely to the capital from there," Giuseppe said, his rifle still close by his side.

"And what do you plan to do there? Olivia, you should come with us," Perry begged, approaching his sister.

Olivia hung her head. "I'm sorry, Pear, but there is far too much at stake. With what happened down in those hexadomes, Giuseppe and I cannot abandon the Regime. Someone needs to tell them the truth. And Mr ... *Odd* has given me his address in Everbreen. I'll visit you when I can. When things are cleared up and we know that Lord Kelton's sacrifice has not gone unacknowledged."

"So we can go back to the town? You don't want us to go back to Kelton Whide anymore?" Teala asked.

Olivia rubbed her sister's cheek. "Of course I want you to return home where it's safe. Like Odd said, Mum is still expecting you. But I know you'll be safe. You've survived this long, and with Bailey keeping the peace and Odd's wisdom, I'm sure you'll be in safe hands. But I want a feast the day I visit! It'll be mainly for you and the town, but nonetheless, I'll eat what I can."

Georgia looked at me. "I didn't know you were the leader of the town."

"I'm not. But like ye said, no one bosses me 'round," I laughed.

Kyle slapped my side. "You better order a big ol' feast then."

"Yes, we'll have the biggest feast we can manage!" Faith cheered. She looked at the princess. "And what about you, Zia? Do you plan

Chapter 51: Spreading Gifts

to come with us?" Zia looked pensive, but before she could answer, a groan sounded behind me.

"My bloody head. Where is he? I'll ..." Dally, with a bandage on his right cheek, was on his feet, furious.

Teala shivered—I think she was going to miss Olivia. Although years apart, in the days they had been together, Teala was a different soul.

Dally huffed as Titan leapt on him. "He's alive! Everyone, he's okay."

Dally held the prince. "I swear, Titan, I don't have any food. Get off!"

After they settled, Chloe led 'em to us. "Just a hot head, a little cut and a minor concussion. He should be better with a good night's rest and something cold to stop the swelling," she said.

Dally had puppy-dog eyes. "Oh, did you finish him off while I was out? Damn. Wait, is he ..."

Kyle laughed, "We don't know, Dally. We're all as clueless as you. But we're going home, that's for sure!"

"*Home,*" Dally whispered longingly.

Zia nodded, "Yes, home!" She pushed her feet into the sand. "I've been thinking about what Olivia said. I've written a page and a half, and there's no easy way to read what I've written." She took her journal out. "Someone needs to return to Kelton Whide."

"But Zia," Perry cried. "If you go, you won't be able to return to the town. You know that. Your mother will not let you outside the city, let alone outside the Castle of Glass."

Titan grinned, "She will, Perry! 'Cause we're both going home. Someone needs to tell her about Father. It's not about what we want; it's about our friends, our people, our family!"

"He's right," Zia said. "But with this ... what was it? Win Dixie? We'll be back before you know it. And besides," Zia looked at her journal, "We're royals. Father would have wanted this. It's not the easiest way, but it's the right one."

"You'll come back to de town, won't ya?"

Titan hugged my side. "Of course we'll come back. I'll fight off Roofus myself if he tries to stop us."

Zia's fingers brushed down my snout. "And we'll be in a castle made from glass. *Glass*. Not much can trap us if we're surrounded by glass."

"Except an overwhelming amount of water." Kyle froze. He bowed to Zia. "I'm sorry. I didn't m-mean it like ——"

A small grin coursed along her cheek. "Rise, Sir Matthews of the White Armadillo. If it weren't for you, we'd still be trapped."

Kyle went red. Odd rolled his eyes. "Okay, okay, okay! Wonderful work team, but my word, we've been on this shore for an awfully long time. I'm ageing with each page we turn. The captain of the zeppelin has the engine warm and ready. But, before we board, I have a final request for you ... Runaways!"

Ritesh, Milky, Mia, Murray an' Georgia looked at the demigod. "Go ahead," Milky said.

"You and I, Yuri, are going to Central City with the councillor and the commander. I know a couple that is in need of an apology and a few tissues for tears. I believe your one-handed self will do wonders for their spirit." Odd put his arm on Milky's shoulder. "This is not a request."

Milky nodded, "I understand. You're right. I'll go with you to see them, but I will not stay in the capital. I belong here, with these people. With my brothers and sisters!"

Mia an' Ritesh took us to the zeppelin. There were subtle murmurs all around. Felicia was with Faith, excitement in her voice.

"Can we line her tia e'mona with rows of white and orange flowers?" Felicia asked.

They were talkin' about where Assonance's shrine was to be placed.

"I'm sure we can find something. We can put one down for Taylah as well? And Lord Kelton? Maybe beside Davis' grave on Spirit Hill. What do you think, Dally? Harry?"

Harry held back tears. "It's a great idea. I'll let the twins know. They'll think of something nice for it. Thank you, Faith. Felicia."

He hugged his brothers.

Dally ran his hand through his mane. "I'll need to clean it up, but it sounds sweet. I think Davis will enjoy the company."

Chapter 51: Spreading Gifts

Teala an' I were the last to join 'em on Win Dixie. Georgia gave Perry a hand into the cockpit. Dally an' him soon laughed at something. Olivia said a peculiar word, which made the two light up an' giggle. Faith began to defend her.

Teala was lost, admiring thee crashin' waves. My fur felt the flow of the ocean's wind. Together we watched the blue beacon. "Still looks schmick, don't ye reckon?"

"Like nothing else in this world," she said, a croak to her voice. She had goosebumps along her arms. I lowered my noggin next to her. "Teala, are you okay? Ye not worried 'bout ——"

"No! I'm not worried." She looked at me, her green eyes firm an' determined. "Something has been awoken, Bailey. Today is not a good day. We did not win anything along this shore."

"What do ye mean? Teala what have ya seen? Was it your dream?"

Her nod was stiff. "Something changed when we slept in that mine. I did not have my usual dream."

"What dream did ye have?"

She looked back to the shore. "Something is closing in. Something much worse than Araidian and Papercut. I dreamt of the darkness, Bailey. I dreamt of my death. Perry's hood. A dying soul."

"Your death? Perry's ... Tea, what are ya sayin'?"

Perry's voice interrupted us. "You two coming or what? The captain's gotta weigh you in, Bailey. We'll leave without you, y'know!"

An arm pulled him back—his noggin vanished behind Win Dixie's bronze walls. Olivia stuck her noggin out.

"Oh, ignore him. Take your time. The faster we depart, the faster I leave you. And I'd rather take my time, especially with you two."

"Three!" Perry urged. "Us *three*."

Teala leaned down an' picked something up—one red rose wet an' dying from the salt of the sea. It wilted as she handled it. "For the collection. I'm sure with some sunlight and water, she'll be happy and healthy."

She skipped away from me.

"Tea! Are you gonna finish what ye were just sayin'?"

She stopped an' her body slouched. I became aware that she

suddenly looked much older. "For another time." She smiled, "Are you going to join us?"

I took a final step along the Camel Hump Shore, the blue beacon behind me as the sounds of the Full Sea howled along the inflating balloon that held Win Dixie together. The metal zeppelin took flight like a great eagle, proud an' fierce. Ahead was the future, our Town of Tents. *Home!*

Teala played with her rose surrounded by the others. We were a giant family; even Odd managed a smile. He rubbed her hair as Dally put Kyle in a headlock. Faith an' Zia laughed as Giuseppe showed Leo an' James how his rifle worked. Chloe had a look at Perry's bandaged shoulder an' Felicia helped Titan figure out this riddle Senator Carvanah had told him. In the commotion, Olivia patted my noggin.

"Thank you for keeping them safe, Bailey!" she said.

I laughed an' admired my family. Her arms wrap 'round my fur. It was unequally equal. My happiness. *Something almost remarkable!*

Come Join Us
and Let's Grow Together
The Colours of Humanity Continues

/oliver.smuhar/

Other book by Oliver Smuhar

FireWorks

A novel inspired by true events.

Come gather, come gather, for Illuka, the koala, is ready to explain how he and his friends survived the 2019-20 Australian bushfires.

Yes, yes, he is, he is! All of the animals in the bush have come together to uncover the truth behind Alinta, the flame, and her dancing orange lights.

Please, join us, join us! Open this classic adventure, and follow Illuka and Bouddi, the sugar glider, as they explore the Blue Mountains and face the black sky.

Quickly now. The family herd is waiting!

Cold hands.

A novel inspired by true events.

Tyler McBaker is trying his best!

He tries to look after his delusional mother, but she's too drunk to care. He tries to save his best friend, but he's stuck inside an illegal rabbit hole. Most of all, he tries to keep moving forward. Yet, each day passes, and Tyler becomes more sick; he's sick of the melancholy and wants to die.

After a failed attempt at his life, Tyler meets Amberley.

Amberley is trying her worst!

She tries to move away from her friends only to miss them once they're gone. She tries to be positive around her parents, but the doctors are stuck inside a medical rabbit hole. Most of all, she tries to stop moving forward. Yet, each day passes, and Amberley becomes more sick; she's sick with sepsis, and she's going to die.

In search of happiness, or maybe a cure, Tyler and Amberley learn the true virtues of what it means to be alive.

But which one's the culprit—the one with cold hands?

GLOSSARY

The events that take place during The Gifts of Happiness are of the *Light Age Era* (1856 - 2125 ags), in the year 2119. This era began after the *Conquest of Darkness* in *Admire, Bellows Curve*. It was a time where the beacons were forcefully turned off by the humans after the Gods and Spirits declared sanctity for all after their disputes during the *Grieving Era* (1595 - 1855 ags). Through the reconciliation of Gods and Spirits, the humans were given one day to celebrate their ancestor's achievement in attaining complete harmony, which was placed on the *Tinket* Calendar of Span 12. This was the beginning of the tradition known as *Ascension Day*. After the destruction and evacuation of *Bellows Curve* in 2090 and the rise of the *Echo Wars*, *Kelton Whide* and the remaining six cities of *Oberon* increased their militaries, only accepting *converted colour*ed citizens and families born from *original colour* to live within their walls. At the end of the *Echo Wars* in 2101, the people of *Kelton Whide* grew wearisome. Thus, *Lord Kelton* declared a new protection strategy, *The Floral*, in celebration of his daughter's birth. The seven remaining Major Cities of *Oberon* began to drift, only meeting to negotiate in *Central City*, for political, ethical, global and environmental issues. A few days before The Birth of the Trees, the prophet-in-training, Odd, plans to steal files from his new WonderWorks' partner, Gwyneth Patroli; however, he's going to need Perry, Dally and Zia's help if he is to succeed. This is where our journey begins. Because words in this world are different to our own, this glossary is here to explain what some places, cultures, languages and specific terms mean as they may not have a description within the story itself.

Araidian's Tyranny: Beginning with the attacks in Kelton Whide, Araidian's Tyranny was the event that led to the reignition of the eight beacons in Oberon. The tyranny ended when Araidian was found by

Everbreen Police unconscious inside WonderWorks' basement.

Ascension Day: This is a day of celebration where the people of Euphoria celebrate peace, the achievement of harmony for humans, Gods and Spirits, and the beginning of the Light Age Era.

A.W.: Stands for "*Araidian's Warriors.*"

Beacon: The heartbeats of the Gods. Their beacons protect and sustain the citizens of each major city. These powerful lights burst from special Giza Rocks and are coloured by their internal nature. Most beacons reside in major cities.

Bellcurve: The title for those who have been blessed with a yellow crest. Although Bellows Curve was lost to the Darkness during the Echo Wars, many BellCurves still roam Oberon and Bungonia displaced but not forgotten.

Bellows Curve: The city of the Yellow Beacon. It was once home to the yellow coloured families of Euphoria, however, due to the rise of the Darkness during the Echo Wars, the citizens were evacuated, leaving their city in chaos. In its prime, it was Oberon's largest harbour, intaking majority of resources, tourists and immigrants.

Birth of the Trees: The yearly Everbreen tradition that celebrates that day the first tree was planted by the Spirits on Aeithalis' back

Bungonia: The smallest continent of Euphoria. It is home to the Grey, Turquoise, Magenta, Tangerine and Purple nations, families and royals.

Central City: The city of the Orange Beacon. It is home to both the orange coloured families and the majority of the politicians and governors of Oberon. Known initially as Sporangia, the city is in the centre of the continent. It is the land where regulations and laws are agreed upon by each major city and a common meeting ground for national disputes and arrangements.

Centrillian: The natives of the orange city, Central City. Centrillian slang is derived from the traditional Kimerian language of the old age.

Crest: The insignia burnt onto every individual's wrist who is declared a citizen of Euphoria. Believed to be magically engraved onto an embryo, eight weeks after conception. A person's crest showcases their city of origin, family blood, spirit animal, soul, class and primarily their identification within society.

Drewan: The title for those who inhabit Drewmora and are blessed with a blue crest. It should be noted that they're not cold-blooded and they don't have gills—that's only in the fantasy stories.

Drewan Militia: The military which is trained to protect Drewmora. Under the command of General Covidious Ko, the militia have been an integral part to the Echo Wars and the Conquest of Darkness. Their most recent guard was in Central City where they protected Parliament House for several seasons after Araidian's Tyranny.

Drewmora: The city of the Blue Beacon. It is home to the blue coloured families of Euphoria, *Drewans*. Instead of being on land, it is under the summit of the ocean. Being submerged within the Full Sea in the east, the Drewans follow closely to the laws of Central City, being one of the most advanced and post-industrialised producers for Oberon.

Echo Wars: A plethora of small wars between the major cities of Oberon. The main fight was against the people of Bellows Curve and Fleddington. The war ended after the notorious *"Battle of Fields"*.

Ever: The word used for a follower of the Spirits and/or a citizen of Everbreen.

Everbreen: The city of the Green Beacon. It is home to the green coloured families of Euphoria and follows the regime of Central City; however, the citizens do tend to place the Rules of The Spirits higher than the laws of the government. This city is one with Mother Nature, and the residents live alongside the Spirits, placing the land before themselves.

Euphoria: A planet in the Guitra Galaxy. Home to many continents and islands, such as Oberon, Bungonia and Kimeria.

Farbe: In Tinket, Farbe stands for dead. It is the name given to the largest forest in all of Oberon, which covers most of the westside, spreading towards Bellows Curve.

Fledding: The title given to those blessed with a red crest. Rumour has it that a Fledding cannot feel the cold and that they're tongues are blue.

Fleddington: The city of the Red Beacon. It is home to the red coloured families of Euphoria, placed in a volcano that has gone extinct aeons ago. Located in the snowy alps towards the north of Oberon, Fleddington is home to the banks and wealthiest citizens of Euphoria. It is protected from the cold by the volcano's everlasting warmth.

Floral: An invisible blue forcefield that protects Kelton Whide from attacks outside their city walls. It is held up by the random *Pillars* that surround Kelton Whide's farmland.

Flower Carrier: Only after the age of nine, the youngest member of the family is summoned to carry their family's bouquet onto the walkways of Whide's Cathedral. This is to show the citizens of Kelton Whide their family's power and strength to endure the celebration of their ancestors.

Gods: The rulers and creators of Oberon. The Gods watch the colours of people from the heavens above and are still worshipped by many.

Good Spirit: Half Spirit, half God, Good Spirits often hide within the land and nurture the beings who live on it. Being abandoned by the righteous Gods, Good Spirits are forced to live their days with the insignificant and lesser, humans and their coloured crests. Each of the eight known Good Spirits are linked to a single prophet. However, there may be more that are yet to be found.

Giea: A small round creature, which some believe resemble an egg. The highest a Giea grows is to a person's hip, and tales say that if scared, they can turn humans into stone. Orange furred Gieas live on the outskirt of Tinkette Valley, while other brown-furred Gieas have been spotted in the Cyrillic Forest, north of Central City.

Giza Rock: Enchanted rocks, initially powered by the Spirits to connected with the Gods that hide in the clouds. They subtly glow ancient scriptures that are unreadable to the eyes of any human except Tinkets.

Hebi: The daughter of Ankh, the first evil Spirit to ever live in the lands of Euphoria. Cursed by the Darkness, which she spread through the lands to avenge the suffering of the innocent, beginning the War of Flowers.

Hex: The abbreviation for Hexadome, often used by Drewans and the many locations of the blue city, such as the LowerHex, UpperHex and RoyalHex.

Hexadome: The hexagonal domes that surround and keep Drewmora, the blue city, safe from the seawater that engulfs it. Rumours say that Drewans used to be born with gills, and because of this, they preferred the sea more than the land. As a result, the blue city is deep within the Full Sea, safely shielded under the hexagonal glass bricks which create its many hexadomes.

Hope: A goddess who sacrificed herself to begin the White Beacon in Kelton Whide and the formation of the white crests that are engraved onto its population.

House of Representatives: The lower house in the Parliament of Oberon, consisting of 146 members from varying political parties including the Liberal Party, the Alliance and the Socialist of the Old.

Irene's Family: The name for Irene and Kygo's human trafficking industry.

Islander: The title given to those who are blessed with black crests. Most islanders prefer the skies rather than the land.

Kelton: Being the abbreviation for Kelton Whide, Kelton also refers to the royal family who rule over the farmlands throughout Jinkie's Gap and past the Hydu Mountains.

Kelton Guard: The protectors who guard Kelton Whide against any disputes and wars from national or international cities.

Kelton Whide: The city of the White Beacon. It is home to the white coloured families of Euphoria and produces the largest amount of resources for the globalisation between Oberon and the two other major continents. Worshippers of the Mother Light, Kelton Whide is run through the monarch of its Royals, and it is known as one of the safest cities in all the lands.

Lady Kelton: The title given to the Queen of Kelton Whide and is obtained to only original white coloured females, born and raised under the Floral. The current Lady Kelton is Lady Vivian Kelton.

Lord Kelton: The title given to the King of Kelton Whide. They must have the royal blood of Hope herself or be a part of the royal family. The current Lord Kelton is Lord Lafayette Kelton.

Mardi Mimpi: The Tinkette Valley celebration for dreams. Although celebrated nationally in Drewmora, the celebration of dreams is to acknowledge the connection the natives of Oberon have with the land, their ancestors and their dreams.

Marraboo: Ancient Spirits who have not yet accepted death and have instead taken the form of mystical beasts that are a part of nature. Commonly found in the Forest of Farbe.

Marraboo Berries: Berries that grow and drop from the magical Marraboo's horns, roots and petals. Most commonly found in the Forest of Farbe and cause hallucinogenic intoxication.

Moonlight Markets: The yearly celebration in Central City where different political members set up stalls and adverts to explain why they should be voted and elected as a member of the House of Representatives.

Oberon: The second-largest continent of Euphoria. It is home to the White, Green, Blue, Black, Red, Pink, Yellow and Orange nations, families and royals.

Prophet: A person of pure peace, who advocates through the communication of Gods, Spirits and humans. There is one Prophet in each major city, and they are humble towards the new governance of Central City. They must have a strong connection with a Good Spirit to achieve the title of Prophet.

Ptak Isles: The city of the Black Beacon. It is home to the black coloured families of Euphoria and is where the most highly skilled academics go to study. Being a floating city, untouched by the ground, the city's isles hover high in the sky, offering the newest innovations in their research. It is home to the headquarters of not only WonderWorks but many other large companies.

Senate of the Royal Eight: The upper house in the Parliament of Oberon, which consists of eight senators from each major city. Rarely meeting, the Royal Eight often gather to discuss indigenous affairs, national crisis and international debate.

Spirits: The protectors of both Mother Nature and humans. Spirits are of the land and were originally formed through the old essence of the Gods. Some are souls of the dead, and others are the aura of the envious.

The Alliance: With 36 members in the House of Representatives, the Alliance favours left-wing politics over social hierarchy. Gaining popularity during the 22nd centenary, the left-wing party advocate for social equality and egalitarianism.

The Great Transformation: An occurrence initiated by the summoning of the Green Beacon, as many—but not all Evers—were turned and shape-shifted into animals, forever stuck in the form of beasts.

The Liberal Party: With 47 members is the House of Representatives, the Liberal Party enforce liberal conservatism. This party focuses on social, economic and ethical issues, where individuals should be free to participate in the market with minimal government intervention.

The Light: The symbol that represents the Goddess Hope as she is believed to be seen in the present as a pure white light.

The Runaways: A smaller group of refugees who escaped the secret laboratories from inside Drewmora's WonderWorks' Enterprise. The group consist of several people with different coloured crests including, Yuri Milk, Ritesh Acharya, Georgia Anderson, Mia Anderson, Murray Wilson, Sam Lovermyer and Gerard Lovemyer.

The Socialists of the Old: With 38 members in the House of Representatives, the Socialists support the traditional Kimerian worship of the Gods and the categorization of individuals based on socioeconomic factors like wealth, crest colour, bloodline, spirit animal, race, gender and occupation.

The Strings of Reality: A display made from strings. Used by Othello in his studies on how different types of alternate realities vary in comparison to his own.

Tinket: The word used for the natives of Oberon, who reside in Tinkette Valley.

Tinkette Falls: A popular tourist destination where floating islands produce natural springs and waterfalls. The closest location for outsiders to enter Tinkette Valley.

Tinkette Valley: The city of the Pink Beacon. It is home to the pink coloured families of Euphoria, Tinkets, and is described by historians and journalists as a place where fairy-tales come true. Even with the outskirts of this city being a tourist destination, the city itself is hidden to any who do not wield the pink crest as it is so old and sacred. Trespasses may find it almost hypnotising.

Tomorrow Festival: A celebration by the citizens of Kelton Whide, where everything is 80% off, as they sell all types of goods and services to begin a new financial year with a clean slate.

Troll: A beastly type of Marraboo that takes the form of a small giant, commonly hiding under bridges, beanstalks and beds.

War of Flowers: An ancient war between the Evil Spirits lead by Hebi, the Demon, and the Nourishing Spirits who protected humankind from extinction.

Wairith: The result of when a spirit is resurrected and intertwined with its alive soul. Most commonly found with two heads, wairiths were common in Sporangia and Bellows Curve.

Whide's Cathedral: The centre building of Kelton Whide. This is a church of worship and the site where Hope, the Goddess of Light, was killed by her lover, Obsidian.

Win Dixie: The Runaway's zeppelin that Bailey, Felicia and Assonance help to rebuild after they split from their group heading towards Drewmora.

WonderWorks: The largest robotics industry in Euphoria, owned by Charles Kingsleigh. WonderWorks produces and manufactures tent-lets, phones, orbs, fishtanks and holograms.

Ever Slang

Applesauce: Nonsense
Balled Up: Confused
Bett: Okay
Blues: Depression
Blue Moon: Month
Bonkers: Big
Boocoo: Much/A Lot/Very
Bull: Nonsense
Buzz Off: Leave
Clam Up: Refuse to Speak
Chirpy: Happy
Conk: Hit
Crackhouse: A Lot/Most
Crackpot: A Crazy Person
Crickey: God Damn
Critters: Animals
Crumb: A Mean Person
Curtains: The End
Cushy: Easy/Simple
Dandy: Great/Fine/Okay
Differ: Change
Dilly: Excellent
Doohickey: A Device
Drifted: Left
Earful: Excessive
Ease Up: Wait
Fancy: Like
Fellas: People
Fetch: Get
Frank: Honest

Firewater: Alcohol
Full Quarter: One Week
Gas: Joke
Gatho: Gathering/Party
Gander: Look
Gussy: Dressed Up
Head: Go
Hoosegow: Jail/Prison
Igniter: Lighter
Jeepers: Wow
Jerky: Meat
Joshin': Kidding
Meathooks: Hands
Mellow: Relaxed
Misses: Girlfriend
Mopey: Sad
Noggin: Head
Nummy: Good
Nutty: Bad
On 'De Spirits: Seriously
Pinch: Grab
Pissy: Angry
Poophole: Trouble
Rank: Gross
Righto: Fine
Rinky-Dink: Run Down/Old Fashioned
Rotation: Year
Schmick: ...Nice or exceedingly well.

Schmooked: .... Beaten	**Tic:** .... Bit
Scratch: .... Money	**The Sack:** .... Bed
Shook: .... Afraid	**Trek:** .... Walk
Simp: .... A Stupid Person	**Well:** .... Better
Skedaddle: .... Run	**Whacked:** .... Tired
Spruce Off: .... Avoiding Duty	**Whipper:** .... Heck
Spunk: .... Good Person	**Whoopee:** .... A Good Time
Steamed Up: .... Excite	**Yesternight:** .... Last Night
Strewth: .... True	**Yifan:** .... Marijuana
Swell: .... Good	**Zozzled:** .... Drunk

Giea Translation

Bevosa: Sleeps
Faw: Down
Felti: Free
Gah Ma Fel: Wise One
Gek: These
Gelhi: They're
Gelti: There
Gep: Them
Gi: The
Gumo: Now
Lamalayo: Everyone
Layi'demo: Yourselves
Li: We
Lo: Go
Ma Ankhalo: One Mother
Nah: To
Nokala: Friends
Ohi: Are
Pardo: Others
Peporious: Prepare
Quelto: Quickly
Ra: And
Tiki: Time
Timin: Stand
Tlihi: Seek
Toi: Our

THE ART IN
THE GIFTS OF HAPPINESS

THE GIFTS OF HAPPINESS uses certain artworks to add depth within the world of Euphoria. These artworks include the fifty-three hand drawn chapter images, the five maps, the two floorplans and the fourteen painted character crests. Some of the artworks have been inspired by other artists' creations and royalty-free images. Oliver Smuhar has reimagined, recreated and adapted each of the artworks within this book through water paints and pencils. The artists and companies The Gifts of Happiness would like to acknowledge, include MrDrawToon (YouTube), VectoryOne (VectorStock), Trainspotter90 (DeviantArt), Tattoolcon (Etsy), Tattoo Daze, Tattoos Time, Focus no.5 (Shutterstock), Only Tribal, Rikley Stock (Shutterstock), Tattooic, Michelle Parker (ClipArt), FotoLog, Adam (Draw Central), Joanna Rosado (Dreamstime), Anton Shcerbakov (iStock) and Esther Vis (Pinterest).

CPSIA information can be obtained
at www.ICGtesting.com
Printed in the USA
BVHW070857180321
602885BV00001B/15